the Devil's Fire

MARIAM EL-HAFI

The Devil's Fire

MARIAM EL-HAFI

Copyright © 2021 Mariam El-Hafi

All rights reserved.

First published in 2021

Revised Edition 2024

This is a work of fiction. Names, characters, places, and incidents are the product of the author's imagination or are used fictitiously. Any resemblance to actual events, locales, or persons, living or dead, is coincidental.
No part of this book may be reproduced, stored in a retrieval system, or transmitted, in any form or by any means, electronic, mechanical, photocopying, recording, or otherwise, without prior written permission from the copyright owner.

ISBN: 9798879198515

Cover design by Miblart

Interior layout and design by Mariam El-Hafi

Edited by Melissa McCarthy

For permission requests, please contact:

authormariam@outlook.com

To learn more about the author and their other works, please visit

Ko-Fi: Author Mariam (bonus chapters can be found here)

Facebook: Author Mariam

Author's Note

The Devil's Fire primarily follows the perspective of Althaia,
serving as an introduction to the world and its characters for future stories set in the same universe.
This means that the story is centered around Althaia's experiences and viewpoint,
allowing readers to become familiar with the world and its inhabitants through her narrative.

The Devil's Fire includes explicit sexual content, graphic violence, profanity, and discusses sensitive topics that may not be suitable for all readers.
It is advisable for readers to exercise caution and discretion when considering whether or not to engage with this book,
as it may contain content that could be offensive or disturbing to some individuals.

"Tonight, the world will burn for you, my Althaia."

Prologue
DAMIANO

Blood splattered on my face faster than I could even process what was happening. The sound of gurgling had me slowly widening my eyes when I saw who was hit. I dropped to my knees, pressing my hand onto her neck where blood kept sputtering out.

"You'll be okay... you'll be okay." The words came out of my mouth hastily, but she was choking on her own blood, watching me with fear in her eyes as tears filled them. I gritted my teeth, trying to stop the bleeding, but deep down inside, I knew I couldn't.

"Find them! Find who did this!" I shouted to my men, my chest heaving uncontrollably in fury.

"Don't close your eyes." I pleaded. Her eyes drooped, but they never fully closed. She placed her hand on my cheek, giving me a silent plea before I watched her eyes become lifeless and her hand dropped to her side.

I cradled her body into my arms.

"Open your eyes. Open your eyes!" I shouted, but she remained unresponsive.

"Why, Damiano?"

I stilled and stared into her eyes, which were open but glazed over with no spark of life.

My eyes narrowed in confusion. Something was not right. Her eyes were cold and lifeless, yet her mouth was moving, screaming at me.

"Why did you let me die, Damiano? Why? Why? Why?!"

I snapped my eyes open.

I let out a breath as I stared at the ceiling before sitting on the edge of the bed, my head dipping between my shoulders as I rested my elbows on my thighs.

Once again, she was tormenting me in my dreams, giving me another sleepless night. I've been having this dream for four years, and the anger from it is still deeply engraved within me. If I had put her first instead of being absorbed in building my empire, maybe she would still be alive instead of haunting me.

Knowing I wouldn't be able to sleep, I took a shower and got dressed to do what I do best; handle my businesses and make sure they all went smoothly. It was the only distraction I could give myself before she tormented me again for failing to protect her.

I was in one meeting after another, killing one fuckhead after another. The slightest things set me off; looking at me the wrong way, breathing too loud, wearing too much cologne, anything to let my trigger finger work overtime.

Must be the lack of sleep.

My brother, Lorenzo, and my right-hand man, Antonio, loved to remind me how I was a pain in the ass when I was sleep deprived. They were probably the only ones who could get away with saying that and not end up with a bullet between their eyes.

I went back to the manor to take another shower to wash off the blood. Some piece of shit thought he could steal from me as if I wouldn't notice. I liked to deal with them directly. I loved to make them into my personal punching bag, except that my gloves were made of knives. It was messy but satisfying.

Freshly showered and dressed in slacks and a dress shirt, I went to the Volante mansion to attend my brother's engagement party. Arriving, I took a quick glance around the decorated backyard as I sipped my whiskey. I had my men stay vigilant in case Gaetano Volante tried something funny.

I pulled out a cigarette and took in a deep drag as Lorenzo and his fiancée, Cara, made an appearance and mingled with the other guests.

"That shitface, Michael, isn't here. Find out where he is." I ordered Luca.

"He's coming right there." Giovanni informed me before Luca could get to it.

I inhaled deeply from my cigarette and blew out the smoke as my eyes narrowed on the woman Michael was with. I observed her closely as they exchanged some words before Michael walked away.

"... She's hot." One of the men nearby let out a low whistle at the sight of her.

"... Gorgeous." Another one commented. I couldn't blame them; she was a fucking beauty.

My gaze slid down, drinking in every inch of her body. She had long, brown curly hair flowing down to her waist. The dress she was wearing hugged her body deliciously, and the generous amount of her cleavage on display left little to the imagination.

My gaze went up to her face and our eyes clashed. I almost let out a smirk when I caught her checking me out since she wasn't being discreet about it either.

Fucking hell, she had the most striking green eyes I had ever seen, and I found myself becoming lured into them. I tilted my head slightly to the side as I continued to look at her. She looked oddly familiar.

Then I finally realized who she was.

Michael moved in front of her, obscuring our view of each other before I could signal for her to come over.

"No one is to go near her." I told my men firmly, and I received grumbled responses in return.

"That's Althaia Volante." I informed them, and everyone looked back at her in surprise.

I let out a low laugh, rubbing my jaw as my eyes never once left her.

Now, how the fuck was she alive and well, when the file clearly stated she died?

ONE

ALTHAIA

I looked in the mirror and nodded in approval at my appearance. I was wearing a long black silk dress with a backless design, thin straps, and a deep V-plunge neckline that revealed quite a bit of my cleavage.

The dress was fitted at the top and gradually loosened at the hips, with a long slit on the right side, which stopped at mid-thigh. To complete the look, I wore open-toe black stilettos with gold ankle straps.

I did a simple brown smokey eye which complimented my green eyes and had them look a bit cat-like. I let my long, curly, and thick brown hair fall as it was but accessorized it with a sparkly hair clip to lift some of the hair away from my face on the right side.

"Get it together. What's the worst that can happen?" I continued to fiddle with my hands before forcing them to remain still as I took a deep breath, building up the courage to leave my hotel room.

The worst that could happen was my father being angry at me for showing up and throwing me out.... My eyes widened and my face paled. I hadn't thought that was a possibility until now.

I quickly shoved that thought away. I was here for Cara, not him, and there was no way I would let that stop me from attending her engagement party.

Cara and I have always been close since we grew up together in the same household, as our fathers were running a business together. Long story short, I found out that my father and uncle were involved in organized crime, and since they would always be busy, Cara spent time with me and my mother.

Sadly, Cara's mother died in childbirth, and my own mother raised Cara as if she were her own daughter. Aside from that, we were a happy family.

At least, that was what we thought.

There was stuff you didn't notice because you were busy being a kid, right? So, as usual, Cara and I were nosy and tried to eavesdrop on my parents when it sounded like they were fighting one night. We had crept down the steps to get a closer look and listen to what was going on, but we couldn't hear anything.

But what happened next shocked us both and had our jaws dropping to the floor.

My mother, Jacinta, slapped the fuck out of my father that night. We remained silent, stunned by what had just happened, before we ran back to our shared room and pretended to be asleep so we wouldn't be caught snooping.

The next day, my mother had our bags packed, and we left. I remember crying so hard because Cara wasn't coming with us. My mother tried to take her with us, but my uncle refused to let her go. It pained my mother to leave Cara behind, and I was sure she had her reasons why we had to leave.

The reason for that was still unknown though.

My father and I didn't stay in touch after that, even though I tried to call him because I missed him, but he never once called me back. He then changed his number. Message received.

We moved to Florida while my father stayed in California. I met up with Cara whenever it was possible. However, it became more difficult for her to leave the house the older she was because her father turned *insane*, to put it mildly. He was always intoxicated with drugs and alcohol, and he turned into an abusive monster.

I wanted to get Cara out of there, to get her some kind of help, but she begged me not to do anything or to tell anyone what was happening. I couldn't understand and became frustrated with her, but then my blood ran cold when she admitted her father wouldn't hesitate to kill her if she tried to run away.

In fear of her life, I was forced to stay put and not to tell a soul about it.

So, to say that I was nervous to be around them all for the first time in forever was an understatement.

"... Don't get sick." I whispered to myself as I took a deep breath. I felt nauseous.

"Let's go." I sighed, finally working up the courage to get going, and I made my way down to the lobby.

Cara sent a car to my hotel to escort me to the mansion, my former home. My heart beat a little faster at the thought of going there after so long. So much has happened since the slap.

My father found himself a new wife not long after we left. He even has a stepson, Carlos, from his wife's previous marriage whom he treated like his own flesh and blood. I would be lying if I said it didn't bother the shit out of me to hear he was treating someone else more like his own child than me.

Cara instantly spilled the tea, said my father had totally downgraded, and I was prepared to give the stink eye to the woman my father ended up marrying.

On the elevator ride down to the lobby, I felt myself getting more nervous, and my hands fidgeted around the little gift box I had with me. It felt like my stomach was in a thousand knots.

"Get it together, Althaia... It's just family." I breathed out, trying to calm my nerves.

I took a final deep breath as the elevator doors opened to the lobby and clutched the small engagement gift in my hands. It wasn't anything grand, just two champagne glasses saying, 'Mr. Right' with a mustache, and the other 'Mrs. Always Right' with red kissy lips. It immediately made me think of Cara because she had the impression she was always right. Even in situations where she wasn't, she still was, according to herself. She could be a little cocky sometimes.

Nearing the middle of the lobby, I stopped in my tracks when I spotted the tall, blonde-haired man in a gray suit that hugged his body to perfection.

"Michael?" I asked in shock. He spun around and grinned when he saw me.

"Althaia! Long time, no see." He smiled at me, showing off his pearly whites. It has been so long since I last saw him. My first crush ever. Damn, now I remembered why I was obsessed with him.

Michael had the most beautiful blue eyes I have ever seen, a sharp jawline, and a clean-shaven face. The way he styled his dirty blonde hair gave the 'I didn't bother to try' look, which made him look quite hot.

We actually dated when we were younger. He just didn't know.

I just stared at him, my mouth ajar, as I couldn't believe my own two eyes.

"Damn, Althaia, just take a picture if you're just going to stare at me like that." He chuckled, and I felt my cheeks heat. He still had an effect on me.

"Don't flatter yourself, Michael. I was just surprised to see you here." I laughed, hoping he didn't notice my flushed cheeks.

"Yeah, well, I kind of overheard Cara saying that you were coming, and she was going to send someone over to come and get you. I couldn't believe that *the* Althaia was coming, so I said I would come and fetch ya." Michael smiled and tucked his hands into the pockets of his slacks.

His eyes slowly scanned me, trailing down my body, and then up again to meet my eyes, giving me a lazy smirk.

"Can't say I regret the decision. You look stunning as ever, Althaia." His blue eyes darkened, and my heart raced when he gave me a look.

"And you look handsome as ever, Michael." I returned with a smile as he sauntered up to me with a sexy grin on his face.

Two

ALTHAIA

"No way! You got yourself that car?!" I gaped at the gleaming black Aston Martin as he escorted me outside.

"Sure did! Worked my ass off to get it." He looked at his car pridefully.

When we were younger, he would always talk about wanting an Aston Martin. We used to love talking about cars when we were kids and became so excited when we saw those luxury cars in movies. I was a sucker for those cars.

Michael opened the door for me, and I immediately glanced around as I climbed inside, almost afraid to move in case I would ruin something. It was one sexy car, and just sitting in an Aston Martin felt surreal. And he was looking so fine driving it.

A sexy man deserved a sexy car.

"So, how come you're attending the engagement party?" I asked. Sure, we all knew each other, and we were close growing up, but he was always talking about traveling the world, so I didn't think he would have stuck around.

Michael glanced at me quickly before refocusing on the road.

"Ah, I forgot you don't know." He smiled, and I gave him a confused look.

"Don't know what?"

"I work for your father now."

Oh.

"So, does that mean you're a part of the ... *family* business as well?" I didn't know how to word it exactly. It all sounded so strange on my tongue and made me slightly uncomfortable. Even though I didn't know much about it, the word *Mafia* should be enough to know that it was definitely *not* a safe career.

"Family business, you say?" Michael chuckled. "Is that what you call it?" He continued to tease.

"Well, how else would I say it?" I chuckled, and he shrugged.

"Dunno, Mafia? Family business sounds so ... boring." He said as if it wasn't a big deal.

"Mafia..." I said out loud, like it was a strange word. "You're saying it like it's a normal nine-to-five job you have. What happened to the 'I want to travel the world' dream of yours?" I slightly faced him with a brow raised.

"Who said I don't get to travel the world, bellissima? I get to travel around, and I get to make a shitload of money. That's a win-win situation for me." He laughed, and I felt a small tingle erupt in my stomach at him calling me beautiful.

"Wait, do you speak Italian now, or is it just that one word to hit on women?" I asked in a teasing tone.

"You don't really have a choice but to speak the language when the Italian mob guys are around. Gotta defend myself if someone is out there planning to shoot my white ass." Michael was cracking up, like he just told the funniest joke ever.

"I guess you're right." I couldn't help but laugh along with him.

"What about you? Still speak the language, or is it long forgotten?" He wondered.

"Not really, it's mostly forgotten." I told him. I was not as fluent as I once was, but I wasn't about to tell him that. I didn't want anyone to find out I still knew the language because I wanted to hear if anyone was trying to talk shit about me.

"I still know a few words here and there. It's just my mom and me, so there really isn't any need to speak Italian." I bit down on my lip, hoping he didn't catch on to my lie.

My father was Italian, and my mother was Greek, so naturally, I grew up speaking both languages. My mother was fluent in Italian since she was married to my father for so long. Since we no longer lived with my father, there was no reason for my mother and I to speak Italian.

Michael faced me and gave me another one of his beautiful smiles. He was one handsome man with ocean-blue eyes that you could easily get lost in. I averted my gaze, so I wouldn't be caught staring for too long. His handsomeness made me a little nervous.

"Yeah, I get that. No need to worry, I'll be your personal translator during your stay." He tilted his chin upwards like a soldier ready for duty. I let out a small chuckle. He looked so proud.

"Funny how the tables have turned, huh? It used to be me who translated stuff for you." I teased. His lips curved up as he drove through the huge gates of my father's mansion. Anxiety was building up as we approached the entrance.

"We're here!" Michael sang as he parked in front of the stairs to the house. "Hold on a second." He stopped me when I was about to open the door. Michael quickly stepped out and made his way to my side and opened the door for me as he gave me his hand.

"Thanks." I smiled, holding his hand while attempting to exit the car gracefully, without flashing him too much leg with the long slit.

Stepping out with my right foot first was a mistake as the slit rode higher up, giving him a full view of my tanned thigh. Michael's eyes dropped to my bare skin, and I hurriedly placed my other leg out and stood up. My cheeks got all hot when I saw Michael smirking.

Clearing my throat, I looked down to make sure my dress was still in place, and I wasn't accidentally flashing anyone. If people were going to talk about me, I certainly didn't want them to talk about how they could see my thong.

"Still wearing the necklace, I see." Michael's eyes followed my fingers as I adjusted the necklace between my breasts. He gave a small smile as he touched the gem.

"Of course! Nonno gave it to me. This way, he's always with me. I never take it off unless I get wet." He let his hand fall to his side and gave a full-on smirk.

"Yeah?" He inched closer to me. "How often are you wet, then?" Michael whispered while looking deep into my eyes, and my breath caught in my throat.

I was pretty sure my face was as red as it could be, and my heart beat a little faster at our closeness. I gave his arm a light smack as I sidestepped him. I felt like I couldn't breathe when he was so damn close to me.

"Shut up, you know what I mean. Let's go. I don't want to be too late for the party." I said hurrying him along.

I heard him laugh as he shut the car door and walked up next to me. He took the small gift from me and put his hand on my back.

"Ready?" He asked, and I gave a brief nod. I took a deep breath, mentally preparing myself and hoping everything would turn out okay.

Together, we made our way upstairs and into the mansion I once called home.

Three

ALTHAIA

As soon as we entered the mansion, a wave of nostalgia hit me as I looked around. I made so many memories in this house, and even though most of the interior had been changed, there was still a sense of familiarity.

The staircase had been remodeled into a glossy beige that led to two small separate staircases on either side to get to the top floor. A sparkling crystal chandelier was suspended from the center of the staircase and small spotlights lit up the rest of the ceiling, giving it a nice, elegant look.

I guess my father was too busy with the mansion to phone me back.

I mentally scoffed but forced myself to think of the good times. The twelve years that I stayed here were amazing because I had Cara and Michael.

As we walked towards the back of the mansion, we could hear music and people talking. We passed through the French doors to the garden outside and followed a stony path that twisted around the corner to the house's right side.

I enjoyed the view of the gorgeous flowers and plants of different colors on either side of the path. I had to admit that the gardener did one heck of a job, because it felt like I was walking through a meadow of many beautiful colors.

Since we were still out of sight from the other party guests, I halted in my steps just before we rounded the corner to join the party.

"Just take a deep breath, Thaia. You will be fine, I promise."

I glanced at Michael, and he gave me a comforting smile while giving my hand a gentle squeeze. I tightened my grip on his hand, relieved he was here.

"I know, it's just nerves getting to me. It's been a long time since I've been here, and there are just so many memories." I gave him a brief smile back. He pulled me closer to him, which I welcomed as we turned the corner.

"Wow." I breathed out as I took in the sight in front of me.

A big open space with massive trees dressed up with strings of lights from one tree to another created a ceiling of light above our heads. The garden was decorated with round tables with linen tablecloths, and vases with gold engravings, holding white and soft pink camellia flowers in them.

If this was just the engagement party, I couldn't imagine how grand the wedding would be. And it definitely would be grand just by looking at the glamorous people present here.

"Yeah, I agree." Michael spoke, taking in the backyard. "I'll put this on the gift table. Can I get you something to drink?" He motioned his head to the far-right side, where the bar was with a bartender.

"Anything without alcohol would be great, thanks. I want to stay as sober as possible." I let him know. A few glasses of champagne were usually not a problem, but I was still nervous as hell, and I would probably just down one drink after another.

I couldn't risk it.

"Sure thing! I will be right back." I watched him as he went on his way to the gift table.

Shit, now I'm alone. I didn't think this through.

I searched the crowd to see if I could locate Cara. What I didn't notice was that half of the people were already staring at me while I was in my own little miserable bubble. I moved my feet slightly as I felt uneasy with everyone's eyes on me.

I suddenly felt underdressed because it was like the backyard had been filled with models from *Italian Vogue*. I have never seen so many beautiful people gathered in one place. Women had on long, gorgeous gowns, and men wore suits that made them appear as if they didn't come from this violent world.

It was intimidating.

It was easy to see that I didn't belong here, and I wouldn't mind being rescued right now, as I gave some awkward smiles to the people who looked at me.

Where the hell was Cara?

I kept looking around to see if I could spot her somewhere, but there were too many people.

Someone caught my attention as my gaze fell on him. My breath caught in my throat, and I couldn't take my eyes off him.

He's gorgeous. Breathtaking, actually.

His black dress pants showed off his strong legs, and a black dress shirt that clung to his body. He was mouthwatering. The dress shirt, slightly unbuttoned, exposed a hint of his chest, while his sleeves were rolled up to his elbows, revealing heavily tattooed arms. His dark hair, styled with a shorter length on the sides and longer on top, added to his overall perfection.

This man was the embodiment of perfection.

My gaze traveled from his feet to his face, tracing his body along the way. His presence enthralled me so much that I couldn't help but keep my gaze on him for a moment longer. Towering in his tall frame, he stood there smoking a cigarette. Even from a distance, I could feel the immense power radiating from him.

I was intrigued.

He cocked his head to the side as he studied me. He pinned me with his gaze, and his face remained completely emotionless. His eyes were intensely focused on me, and I felt like I was in a trance, unable to look away as we remained locked in a stare from afar.

"Don't look at him like that." Michael abruptly appeared in front of me, taking me by surprise, and obstructing my view of the man. "He has killed people for staring at him the wrong way." He stated as he handed me a drink.

"Huh?" I breathed out and blinked at him, confused. "I was just looking around. How am I supposed to find the person I'm looking for if I'm not allowed to look?" I gave a soft chuckle at his exaggeration and raised a brow at him.

"The way you looked at him can get your ass shot." Michael gave me a stern look, making it clear that this was not a joke. I looked at him with wide eyes, suddenly feeling scared that the man would shoot me because I took my time to look at him.

"Wait, really? Oh, shit! What should I do? Do I apologize?" I spoke in a hurry. I didn't mean it in a bad way; he was truly too beautiful not to look at.

Michael let out a small snort.

"No, just don't look at him. I don't know if you have heard of this, Althaia, but you have a mean resting bitch face. You looked like you were ready to fight him or something." He spoke under his breath.

I choked on my drink, making a fool out of myself as I laughed.

"Thaia!" I heard Cara call out as she suddenly showed up and headed towards me with a wide smile on her face.

"Cara!" I squealed, matching her excitement as I quickly handed my drink back to Michael, not caring that it spilled a bit.

I walked as fast as I could in my heels and embraced her with a tight hug. It had been so long since I last saw her, which truly sucked because we were like two inseparable sisters.

"Oh my God, I have missed you so much. It really is not the same without you." She hugged me tighter into her tiny frame.

"I know." I chuckled. "I've missed you too!" I stepped back, holding her hands as I looked her over.

"Cara, you look amazing!" I stared in awe at her gorgeous dress. A gorgeous, long flowy rose-colored strapless gown with a corset-like top with silver detailing that cinched her waist, making her already full breasts even bigger. Her raven hair was tied up with a few pieces framing her face, and her makeup was flawless, making her hazel eyes pop.

She looked absolutely breathtaking.

"Mom really outdid herself with this dress. It's more than I could ever imagine." She winked slyly, and I dropped my jaw.

"I didn't know you asked mom to make you a dress!" I squinted my eyes at her.

My mother was a designer and made drop-dead gorgeous gowns. When we moved, she opened her own little shop, and it blew up in no time. Eventually, we had to expand and now it was a well-known high-end boutique.

"Yeah, well, I didn't want you to know because I wanted the dress to be a surprise, and -" Cara put her hand over her heart and held my hand. "I love you so much, but you fucking suck at keeping something like that a secret." She said, smiling innocently.

I was about to say something, but she was right, so I shut my mouth. I was the type of person who would get you a gift and within the next few minutes I would send a text saying, 'guess what I just got you!' Case in point, she already knew what I had picked out for her engagement. I literally took a picture of the champagne glasses and sent her a text message that said, 'OMG, these are so cute! I'm getting them for you' and sent her the picture.

"Fair enough." I muttered.

"But damn, look at you! That dress is so hot on you. Who are you getting your titties out for, huh?" Cara put her hands on her hips and wiggled her brows at me. Typical of Cara, always has something dirty on her mind.

"No one." I rolled my eyes. "My tits are more covered up than yours." I pointed out.

"True, but I have a man now that I need to impress, so he knows what awaits him, if you know what I mean." She winked, making me laugh.

"Speaking of man..." I muttered while glancing around to make sure no one was within earshot. "Are you absolutely sure you want to do this, Cara? You can always, I don't know, run away? You know I'll come with you." I said in all seriousness. If she wanted to leave the country, I would drop everything and go with her. She means the world to me. I would do whatever I could to keep her safe.

"You know I can't do that. He will hunt me down and definitely kill me if I ever think about running away." She gave me a sad smile. "Besides, anything will be better than living with my father. I just have to get away. I need to *breathe*." She sighed. As much as I hated to admit it, it was true.

Her father was an absolute abusive maniac. One time he came back home, intoxicated from both alcohol and cocaine, and almost beat her to death. Somehow, he gained a tiny bit of his senses back and stopped before it was too late.

I hope one day someone will give him the same treatment.

Amen.

"This is my way out of here." Cara reassured me.

"As long as you're happy, I'm happy." I gave a small smile and pulled her into another hug.

"Are you done catching up? I'm feeling all lonely here by myself." Michael wrapped an arm around my shoulder and pouted his lips. "Isn't this awesome? The trio has finally reunited at last!" He beamed with excitement, and I just shook my head at him in amusement and removed his arm from my shoulders. I did not spend that much time getting ready for him to get my hair into a tangled mess.

"Come, let me introduce you to my soon-to-be husband." Cara gestured at a group of men puffing cigars and drinking whatever their choice of poison was. But what caught me off guard was that they were already staring at us.

Definitely nothing intimidating about that.

Not at all.

"Have fun with that." Michael mumbled, eyeing the men with a blank stare.

"Are you not coming with us? Didn't you just say that you were lonely standing by yourself?" I gave him a teasing look.

"Yeah, but I'm not that lonely. See ya!" He took off before we could say anything else.

"Let's go." Cara held my hand and together we made our way toward the group of men who were observing our every move.

For some reason it felt dangerous, and I wondered why.

FOUR

ALTHAIA

As we neared the group of men, I tried not to stare at anyone longer than a second in case they would take it the wrong way. They were huge and intimidating and kept watching us as we approached them, but Cara was unfazed.

She led me over to the two men at the center of the group; the two most terrifying-looking men. And one of them was the man Michael told me not to stare at, and holy shit, that man was even finer up close.

I couldn't take my eyes off him.

I was nervous to approach him as his eyes followed me, and his stare made my heart race. He didn't even try to hide it as he shamelessly checked me out, which gave me mixed feelings. I was not sure I was supposed to like his attention on me.

"Althaia, meet my fiancé, Lorenzo." Cara introduced. I looked at the man next to him and wanted to drop my jaw. He was about the size of a tank! He was so muscular and tall that I had to tilt my head up a little just to meet his gaze.

Her vagina is going to be so wrecked.

I shared a quick look with Cara, a smug grin on her lips saying, 'I know' like she read my thoughts, which made me crack a smile.

Tank Man was quite handsome with his closely shaved head, dark brown eyes, and a strong jawline with light stubble.

"It's nice to meet you." I smiled and stuck my hand out for a handshake. He looked down at my hand with a bored expression, letting it hang there before shaking it.

Well, that was lovely.

"And this is his older brother, Damiano." She gestured to the one I had looked at for too long.

They were about the same height, though Tank Man was more broad-shouldered than Damiano. Tank Man was, well, like a tank, but

Damiano was way more intimidating, his golden-brown eyes so cold and deadly when he stared at me.

I almost wanted to gulp.

"Pleasure to meet you." I smiled nervously at him and went for a handshake. He didn't just stare at my hand as Lorenzo did; thankfully, he shook it immediately.

"Althaia." Damiano said my name, as if he was seeing how it sounded on his tongue. "Pleasure's all mine."

A shiver ran through me at how deep his voice was, and it elicited an inappropriate response in my body. I felt my face flush.

This man was seriously *otherworldly*.

Damiano glanced at Tank Man, also known as Lorenzo, and it was almost like they were having a silent conversation. Whatever it was, it had Lorenzo grab Cara around the waist, and they walked off.

Cara looked over her shoulder and gave me a confused expression. I looked around and realized that the rest of the group had disappeared too.

"Uh..." I trailed in confusion.

"Althaia."

I shivered again as I faced Damiano, who already had his eyes set on me. He reached into his pocket and took out a pack of cigarettes, offering me one.

"Oh, no, thank you."

"Good choice." He gave me a small smirk and held the packet up to his mouth, took a cigarette between his lips, all while looking into my eyes. There was something about the way he did it that was incredibly hot.

"So, Althaia." Damiano spoke while he lit up his cigarette and took a long drag from it. "You look awfully well for a dead person." He spoke, blowing out smoke.

"I'm sorry, what?" I shook my head like I didn't hear him right.

"Your file says you're dead." He continued as if it was the most normal thing to say and blew the smoke right into my face.

I waved the smoke away and frowned at him.

"What are you talking about? I think you have me confused with someone else." I chuckled awkwardly.

"Althaia Volante, twenty-four years old, born on November seventh because her parents fucked on Valentine's Day. You died instantly in a car accident on New Year's Eve three years ago." He said, inhaling from his cigarette as my expression fell.

"Usually, dead people don't look this good." Damiano gave me another look-over.

"I don't know what you are talking about. Besides, my name is not Volante. It's Celano. Big difference. You must have me confused with someone else because I'm pretty sure I'm not dead. Obviously." I gestured to myself as I was literally standing in front of him in the flesh.

"Obviously." He finished his cigarette, and my eyes followed the bud as he flicked it away. I glanced back at him, seeing his eyes lingering on my necklace between my breasts.

Damiano reached out to touch my necklace, and I reflexively stepped back. His eyes locked onto mine, giving me a warning look, like he was telling me to stay still.

"However, you are wearing the Volante heirloom around your neck." He stepped closer to me and my heart beat faster when his hand trailed up and held my chin. I swallowed hard as he tilted my head slightly upward so I could meet his eyes.

His face was getting closer to me, like he was going to kiss me, and my eyes went wide. But Damiano moved his head at the last second, his bearded cheek brushed against mine as he stopped by my ear.

"Makes me wonder why your father is hiding you from me." He whispered, and it sent a chill down my spine.

Damiano slightly stepped back and dropped his hand to his side. He shot a look over my shoulder and my stomach dropped in fear when I saw his expression.

So deadly and fucking feral.

I had to get away from him.

I spun around to leave, but halted in my steps as I came face-to-face with my father.

"Papá." I breathed out in shock. It was strange seeing him in front of me after so long, and though we hadn't kept in touch, my heart still missed him.

"What are you doing here?" My father snapped at me, absolutely livid.

My heart squeezed. I guess the feelings were not mutual.

"What, you don't want to see your daughter? Don't worry, I'm not here for you." I frowned back.

Everybody stopped and stared at us. Wasn't that just fucking lovely? They were all witnessing a shitty father and daughter reunion. He clearly didn't want me here, and it made me feel like shit.

Great, so the worst that could happen, happened.

THE DEVIL'S FIRE

I crossed my arms, shoving my feelings away as I was about to leave, but stopped when Michael's tense form moved forward to stand behind my father, posing as a bodyguard.

Someone grabbed me around the waist and pushed me into their side. I let out a noise of surprise at the sudden action and saw it was Damiano who held me firmly.

"Gaetano, such a beautiful gem you've been hiding." He taunted in Italian.

My father clenched his fists as he looked at Damiano, but Damiano just cocked his head to the side with a devilish smirk.

"Michael, take Althaia away from here." My father ordered firmly.

"Holy shit!" I shouted when Damiano whipped out a gun and pointed it at Michael. I tried to break free, but Damiano held me tight.

"Don't even think about it." He snarled at Michael while he crushed me to his side to prevent me from leaving. My legs would have given out in fear if he hadn't had such a strong grip on me.

Michael tried to grab me again, but before he could even take a step, the sound of a gunshot rang out in the air, making me cover my ears as a scream escaped me.

"I won't fucking miss your head if you move one more time." Damiano stated in a deadly low tone.

I could feel my knees weakening with each passing second. Michael's jaw clenched when he saw the fear on my face. I glanced at my father for help, and it looked like he was having an inner battle as he assessed the situation.

Now I knew why the fuck it felt dangerous to approach Damiano. He was crazy!

"Keep her out of this." My father hissed.

"And why should I when you're the one hiding her, Gaetano?" Damiano bared his teeth in a sinister smile.

"She has nothing to do with anything!" My father yelled at him.

"Now, now." Damiano chuckled, not fazed at all. "I'll be the judge of that." He pulled me in front of him, and it felt like I was facing the Devil himself.

Damiano loomed over me, his eyes narrowing with a menacing intensity that sent shivers down my spine. I swallowed hard, a paralyzing terror gripping me, as I dreaded what he might do to me.

"We'll have a little chat together soon." He said with a wicked smirk as he ran a thumb along my jaw.

I couldn't talk.

I couldn't even breathe.

I just stared at him, my eyes wide, while my heart felt like it was about to jump out of my chest. What was I supposed to say, anyway? Tea or coffee? I was pretty sure he preferred blood.

And I could only hope it was not mine he was after.

He leaned back, gave me a wink, and walked off. I exhaled and my legs buckled, making me stumble. But a pair of arms caught me mid fall before I hit the ground. I was spun around and saw Michael had grabbed me.

"Are you okay? Are you hurt somewhere?" He frantically asked as he looked around at my face. I couldn't answer him as my eyes went to Damiano's retreating form.

He was walking away as if he had no care in the world with his hands tucked into the pockets of his slacks.

FIVE

ALTHAIA

"Althaia!" Michael called my name sharply.

"I'm okay." I tried to reassure him, even though my voice was barely audible.

"Michael, take Althaia to my office." My father snapped, his face twisted with anger. Michael didn't need to be told twice and practically carried me inside the mansion.

"You can let me walk now. I'm okay." I reassured him again. He loosened his grip on me, but he was still holding me close as we entered my father's office.

I plopped down on the couch and started massaging my temples as I felt a headache coming on. My mind was all over the place. One moment we were shaking hands, and the next, people were trying to shoot each other. It was a not-so-friendly reminder of what kind of people they were.

Michael sat on the coffee table in front of me and handed me a bottle of water.

"Thanks." I gave him a small smile and took a big sip.

"You good?" He asked, leaning forward as he rested his arms on his thighs.

"Yeah, just so confused right now." I sighed and sank back onto the couch.

Before Michael could reply, the door swung open, and my father stalked in. Michael and I both rose, watching him walk up to his desk. He leaned against it, fixing me with a stern glare.

"Do you have any idea of what kind of trouble you have put yourself into coming here?" He snapped, and my mouth dropped open.

"How the hell have I caused any trouble just by showing up?" I exclaimed.

"Watch your language." He said firmly, and I scowled.

"I should be the one asking questions because that man, *Damiano*, said some really crazy stuff about me out there." I crossed my arms and eyed him suspiciously.

Even though he was wrong about the last name and car accident, everything else was correct. As much as I would like to think it was coincidental, I knew it wasn't.

"Why did he call me Volante, hmm? And why in the world did he say that I died three years ago?" My eyes narrowed.

My father closed his eyes and pinched the bridge of his nose.

"I was trying to protect you, figlia. But I'm afraid I have done more harm than good." He sighed and looked at me again.

"Protect me from what?" I uncrossed my arms as worry crept in.

Fuck, should I fear for my life now? Move to a different country and change my name to Fifo? But I don't look like a Fifo.

"I don't want you to get involved in this mess, but since he already knows you're alive, there's no point in hiding this from you." He went to the minibar, filled up a glass, and chugged it in one gulp.

I waited for him to elaborate. My dad pointed at the couch for me to sit, and he settled on the one opposite me. Michael went and stood to the side and listened.

"I'm only going to tell you what you need to hear. When we started going into business with la Famiglia Bellavia, things were going great. Then it took a turn, and a war almost broke out. The last thing I wanted was for them to find you to use you against me. So, I faked your death." He shrugged.

"What the actual fuck?" I shrieked, and my father shot me a warning look. I was supposed to be dead?

"But he said Althaia Volante, I'm a Celano." I pointed out.

"Celano is a name your mother and I both decided for you to have so people wouldn't be able to track you down easily." He explained. "I never gave you my family name because I want to protect the only daughter I have."

So, that was what he meant when he said I was causing trouble. It made sense now. In all fairness, how was I supposed to know that? No one told me I was supposed to play fucking dead.

"I couldn't take the chance of you going around and introducing yourself as Volante. Word would get out, and he would track you down fast to get what he wants." He sighed, and it left me stunned once again.

"So..." I trailed off. "Does that mean I'm in any kind of danger now? Should I be worried?" I asked, probably looking like a lost child.

If my father had faked my death, then that meant Damiano was more dangerous than I realized. I knew he was too gorgeous to be a sane man.

My father's eyes softened.

"You don't have to worry about anything. This is why Cara is getting married into their family. It's for assurances for both families."

"What?!" I rose from my seat as I erupted in disbelief. They were just giving Cara off as if she were some kind of peace offering? "You are sending your own niece into the arms of psychopaths!"

"She knows what she's getting into, and she happily agreed." My father retorted, getting to his feet.

No shit. Her father was a complete maniac. Of course, she would do anything to get away from him, even if it meant being with another psycho. Anyone was better than her own father.

"Well, does that mean you trust them now since Cara is being married into their family?"

"No, I don't trust them one bit. Especially Damiano. He's the Devil." He spat out, and I just gaped at him.

"Then what's the point of her getting married to one of them?" I asked. "If he's the so-called Devil, then why do you send Cara into their arms, huh?"

"Sometimes you have to sacrifice for the greater good." He said calmly.

"What greater good? Don't you even care that they could kill her?" I shot back.

My father just sighed and shook his head.

"Listen, there are things you don't need to know. This conversation ends here." He said, leaving no room for discussion.

I wanted to shout at him, to make him realize how ridiculous all of this sounds. Instead, I exhaled slowly as I knew it would fall on deaf ears.

My father approached me, gently resting his hand on my cheek.

"I don't want to involve you even more in this mess. Just leave it to me and trust me when I say it's for the best for everyone."

"You still have some explaining to do." I said, and he cracked a slight smile as he looked over my face.

"You've really become a beautiful young lady. La mia bellissima figlia." He spoke softly.

I couldn't help the warmth that filled my heart at his words. I wrapped my arms around him and held him tightly without thinking about it.

No matter how much I wanted to be mad at him for not even trying to be around, the little girl in me who wanted her father didn't care right now. What mattered was that he wasn't rejecting me as I had feared.

My father chuckled softly when he hugged me and kissed the top of my head. I decided that everything else could wait and just enjoy this small moment with him.

"Awh, look at that. A father-daughter reunion." Michael said in an almost cute voice.

"Oh shoot, I forgot you were still here." I laughed as I unwrapped my arms from my father, and Michael just pouted at me.

"I should find Cara and apologize for ruining her party." I just hoped she wasn't too mad at me. "Will you give me a ride back to the hotel? I'm assuming there isn't much of a party going on right now." I asked Michael.

"Sure thing!"

"You should spend the night here and not in a hotel." My father chimed in.

"Thanks, but maybe some other time? I feel like my head is about to explode, and I need a little time to myself to process everything." I admitted. He looked disappointed but was understanding.

I said my goodbyes to my father, and Michael and I made our way out of the office in search of Cara. But I couldn't help that my mind wandered to a certain golden-brown eyed Devil, going by the name of Damiano, and his promise that we would have a chat soon.

A deadly man that somehow still had me curious about him.

"What a grand entrance you made tonight." Michael playfully bumped his shoulder into mine.

"Tell me about it." I chuckled. Michael walked me to my hotel room to ensure my safety, which I was grateful for.

I swiped my keycard and held the door for Michael to enter as well.

"Not bad, Thaia. You got yourself a luxury suite." He whistled in awe as he looked around.

"Well, I thought I would take advantage of this opportunity and treat myself a bit." I grinned. I had asked for the biggest suite in the hotel because I wanted it to feel like a real vacation.

The suite was split into two large rooms; a lounge area with soft couches that would swallow you and a huge flat-screen TV, and the other with a king-sized bed. It had to be a king-sized bed because I had this irrational fear that if my arm or leg hung off the bed, some kind of nasty creature would definitely grab me.

I slumped down in the armchair and unstrapped my stilettos, sending them flying in different directions with a kick, then leaned back and closed my eyes. I moaned in relief as I curled my toes, making sure the blood was flowing down to them.

"Wow, that could not sound any more sexual." Michael said with a smug tone. I opened one eye to catch a glimpse of him smirking as he settled into the couch across from me. In response, I flipped him off, which only made him laugh. "Why do you even wear those? They look so painful."

"Because they are hot as fuck." I stated, as if it was the most obvious thing. "Not everyone has been blessed with height like yours. I need the additional height, so I don't disappear in the crowd of all you tall people." I explained while struggling to unclasp my necklace.

"There is nothing wrong with your height. It's cute and suits you. You're obviously blessed in other areas." He wiggled his brows and gestured to my breasts. My dress was actually quite revealing at the top, which gave him a great view of my cleavage.

"Creep." I teased and tried not to blush under his gaze. "Can you help me take off my necklace? I think the lock is stuck or something." I asked to distract myself from the intensity in his eyes.

"Sure."

I rose to my feet, and lifted my hair so he could get better access.

"Thank you." I said once he slid off the necklace and gave it to me.

My brows shot up when Michael trailed his hands down my back and rested them on my hips. I stilled when he pulled me in close until I was against his chest. A small sound came out of him when I felt his lips touch my neck.

My breath caught in my throat, and tingles erupted in my stomach when he wrapped his arms around me with his hands resting on my stomach.

"You look absolutely gorgeous tonight." He whispered in my ear. I opened my mouth to say something, but nothing came out. "Goodnight, Althaia." He gave me a small peck on my shoulder and walked out of my hotel room.

I remained right where I was, looking at the door he just walked out in surprise.

Still in a daze, I went to the bathroom. I needed a cold shower to help me figure out if any of it was real, or if it was my imagination playing with me.

I turned on the cold shower for just five seconds before switching to the soothing warmth. A sigh of relief escaped me, and my tense muscles finally relaxed. Though, I couldn't fully let go of my racing thoughts, especially those about Michael and the way his hands had sensually traced down my body.

Just thinking about it made me blush.

I had a major thing for him when we were kids, and maybe he felt the same way about me? I let out a frustrated groan as these thoughts overwhelmed me. I was a total mess after meeting the Devil, and now Michael just had to add to that pile of confusion.

To get my mind off things, I gave a full-blown concert performance in the shower, using the shampoo bottle as my microphone as I sang 'Butter' by BTS at the top of my lungs.

My singing came to a stop when I heard the hotel door open and close. Room service must have arrived, and I hurried to dry myself off.

I threw on the big, fluffy bathrobe and slippers, then headed out to the lounge area to devour the delicious food I knew was waiting for me.

I was *so* ready to stuff my face.

My heart stopped beating, and I froze when I spotted someone on the couch. A hand extended towards the lamp resting on the end table beside the couch and switched it on.

It was the Devil himself.

Damiano.

"Good evening, Althaia."

Six

DAMIANO

I entered the lobby of one of the fanciest hotels in Los Angeles and went straight to the reception desk.

"Mr. Bellavia, so great to see you again! Are you here for a meeting?" The receptionist greeted me with a wide smile and quickly checked her computer.

"No, I'm here for pleasure." I told her.

"Oh, excellent! But I'm afraid all our master suites have been booked. If you would give me a minute, I will have something figured out for you right away."

"No need to." I stopped her before she could make any calls. "I already have a room. It should be under the name of Althaia Celano."

"Just a second, and I will find it for you." Her red nails tapped on the keyboard as she searched the database.

"Bill her stay on my card. I will only be here for a few hours. Order everything you have on the menu, plus a bottle of your best champagne, and send it up." I slid my card towards her and checked my watch to signal my impatience.

"Certainly, sir! I can see that room service has already been ordered."

"Then add to it." I snapped.

"Of course, my apologies." She tapped her red nails on the keyboard again before handing me my card back, and a keycard. "Master suite 7173. Anything else I can do for you, Mr. Bellavia?"

"That will be all." I grabbed my things and tipped her for her time before heading for the elevator. I stopped and turned around to face the receptionist again. "Ensure the neighbors that if they hear screaming, there is nothing to worry about. I play rough." I smirked, watching her face slightly blush.

"Absolutely. I will make sure you have nothing to worry about." I gave a brief nod and went to the elevator.

I fished out my phone from my pocket and turned my back to one of the elevator doors when I saw Michael stepping out. That shitface had a smug smile on his lips, looking satisfied as he exited the hotel. The sight of him alone made me almost sneer and empty my gun into his face.

Soon.

I reminded myself. Soon they would all have a bullet between their brows, and the Volante family would be no more.

I swiped the keycard and cracked the door open just enough so she wouldn't be able to notice. I listened for any movements, but it was quiet. I slipped into the dark room and quietly closed the door behind me. Stepping further inside, I heard the shower running; she was singing.

It was safe to say she didn't know how to.

I searched the entire hotel room for anything that would give her away. This could be Gaetano trying to play dirty; claiming her death was for her security while secretly training her to be a spy or an assassin. He wouldn't be the first to resort to such tactics, and I was determined to get ahead of him to ruin his plans.

More like putting a bullet in his plans.

I checked through her luggage, checked her phone on the nightstand, and even checked under the bed but found nothing that showed she was anything other than a normal civilian. Despite that, I had to keep my eye on her in case something showed up later.

I planted spy cameras in places where she wouldn't notice them. This way, I would get to see her every move. Now, I waited for her to get out of the shower.

Fucking hell.

Her singing was dreadful, and it took all my self-control not to yank her out of the shower just to make it stop.

The water stopped running, and I waited once again for her to get out. Frowning, I went to the hotel door, opened it, and slammed it shut to hurry her the fuck up.

I took a seat on the couch, and she *finally* came out of the bathroom. She was humming as she stepped in my direction before stopping in her tracks, her eyes narrowing unsurely at me.

It was dark and the only light came from the bathroom, but it was not enough for her to see me. I reached for the lamp next to me and flicked it on.

"Good evening, Althaia."

She blinked once.

Then a sound that I wouldn't even describe as a scream escaped her mouth. I watched her turn around clumsily, tumbling down to the ground, before she quickly leapt up again and ran back to the bathroom. I let out a slight chuckle at the amusing sight before I heard her locking the door.

Entertained, I walked up to the door and knocked, hearing a yelp from the other side.

"That was quite dramatic of you, Althaia." I said with a hint of amusement in my tone. I heard her gasp as if she was almost offended by my words. I crossed my arms and rested my shoulder against the door. "It will take me nothing to kick this door down if you don't come out."

"I would like to stay in here…"

"Get. Out. Now." I ordered her. I had already wasted too much of my time waiting for her to get out of the shower.

"… How do I know you won't shoot me the minute I come out, huh?" She questioned, attempting to sound brave, but her voice was shaking. I went completely silent to mess with her. "Are you fucking serious?!" She yelled and banged on the door.

I bit back a smirk.

"If I wanted to shoot you." I said calmly. "You wouldn't even have made it to the bathroom. This door wouldn't have stopped me from shooting you, either. I can simply put a bullet in you through the door." I stated. I could have put a bullet between her brows the second she stepped out of the bathroom.

But I didn't.

"Come out. I don't have all night."

"Why? Because you have other people to kill?" She asked cockily, and this time, I let out a wicked smile.

"You have five seconds to get out here before I kick this door down and drag you out. And trust me…" I trailed off, my voice going low. "You don't want me to drag you out."

I could almost hear her gulp, and I was enjoying her fear.

Finally, I heard the door slowly unlocking, but she didn't open it. I stepped back, knowing she would make a run for it. She flung the door open as she attempted to run past me. My arm shot out, and I immediately grabbed her.

"Let me go!" She shouted with her nails digging into my arm, but it wasn't doing anything. I just sighed, unimpressed, and plopped her down on the couch. I shot her a warning glance to stay in place when she moved to run away again.

"Good girl." I praised when she stayed still. Althaia looked completely taken aback by my words, and a blush slowly crept to her cheeks.

Ah, she has a praise kink.

It tempted me to let out a wicked grin but refrained when a knock sounded on the door followed by 'room service'. The server strolled in with the serving cart and placed different plates on the table.

"Is this to your liking, Mr. Bellavia?" I looked at the bottle and gave a short, expressionless nod. The server poured champagne into two flutes and put the bottle back in the ice bucket. "Anything else I can get for you?"

"That will be all." I tipped him and he went on his way.

I handed a glass of champagne to Althaia, clinking my glass to hers, and took a seat across from her. I took a sip as I eyed her, but she just looked at me with wide eyes in confusion.

"Are we celebrating something?" She asked.

"Yes." I replied, watching her eyes narrow.

"What?"

"You coming back from the dead." I smirked.

"Ha ha, so fucking funny I forgot to laugh." I cocked a brow when she rolled her eyes at me.

"Eat." I ordered, leaving my face blank as I nodded towards the food.

"No, thank you. I'm not hungry." She crossed her arms and glared at me.

My eyes swiftly darted down to her breasts when they were pushed together. Her robe had come undone a bit, giving me a glimpse of her ample cleavage. And frankly, it made my cock twitch at the sight.

Her stomach then let out a big rumble. Althaia's eyes widened, and her face instantly flushed.

"Okay, so maybe I'm a little hungry…" She muttered, embarrassed. "But how do I know you won't shoot me while I eat? Because that would be seriously fucked up! Making me feel you're fattening me up, ready for slaughter like a pig." She kept on rambling. I just raised a brow while sipping my champagne.

"You curse a lot. A lady shouldn't curse. It's not befitting." I smirked when she gaped at me.

"Good thing I'm no lady then! And they're called sentence enhancers; they help get the message across." She huffed, obviously offended.

"Eat." I ordered her again. I fucking hated repeating myself. It gave me a strong urge to bend her over and spank her pretty ass for not listening.

"But how –"

"I won't shoot you. Now shut up and eat." I snapped.

"Rude! You shouldn't tell a lady to shut up." She snapped back.

Oh, she's a fiery one.

"I thought you clarified that you were not a lady, no?" I tilted my head slightly to the side, giving a rather devilish grin. She frowned.

"... Whatever."

"I'm not a patient man. Eat." She still hesitated and looked back and forth between the food on the table and me. "What is it now?" I gritted out in annoyance.

"I'll eat, I promise!" She assured me quickly. "It's just that... It feels weird to eat if you're not eating... Like, are you just going to watch me?" I stared at her blankly, seeing her become uncomfortable and squirming in her seat as she looked at me with her big emerald eyes.

Fucking hell. Her eyes are so fucking green and so fucking innocent-looking.

I gave her a long look before I grabbed a plate of pasta and ate. I watched her shoulders sag with relief before she focused on the food. I simply watched her as she ate, observing her body language and waiting for her to make a surprise move.

But she never did.

Instead, she ate her food in such a way that had me hiding a smile behind my hand as I leaned back in my seat. Her eyes closed, and she completely forgot I was present.

I pulled out my gun and aimed it right at her head when she grabbed a knife to cut her food. This woman had zero awareness as she simply continued to eat, unaware, in pure bliss.

Not a threat.

I tucked away my gun, finished my food, and leaned back to watch her again. She let out a satisfied sigh when she was done, and her eyes were slowly drooping.

"Impressive." I said as I rubbed my jaw, biting back a smile when she jumped in startlement. She could definitely eat, and, for some reason, it filled me with contentment to see her like this.

"Okay, listen. Let me just say this and save you some time; I know nothing. I don't know why this or how that. Nada. I hadn't talked to my father in twelve years before tonight, so you're really not going to get anything out of me." Althaia said tiredly.

"I know." I gave her a smug grin, and she raised her brows in surprise.

"Then why are you here?" Her eyes sparked with curiosity.

"That's for me to know and you to wonder about." I could tell my answer displeased her. She was like a damn open book; so easy to read.

I leaned in, resting my arms on my thighs, and took my time looking at her. She looked at me almost as if I was a fascinating piece of art.

"You are an interesting, pretty little thing. You have my attention." I smirked and watched her swallow hard.

"I'm not sure I want it." She said in a breathless whisper, and my cock fucking twitched again.

I stood up and went to the door before my dick got visibly hard. I rested my hand on the handle, glancing at her over my shoulder as she stared at me with those big, green innocent eyes that instantly made me hard.

"Goodnight, Althaia. It was a pleasure." I winked and left.

SEVEN

ALTHAIA

"Thaia, get your ass up!" I heard Cara shout while constantly banging on the door.

I let out an annoyed groan.

I couldn't sleep all night, tossing and turning with my mind racing about all that had happened. And that Devil named Damiano did nothing to ease my mind.

When he said we would have a chat soon, I thought it was just to scare the shit out of me, which worked. And then he freaking showed up out of the blue like the Devil he was.

I know I have complained about how my life was getting a little too boring, and said I desperately needed some excitement in my life. Don't get me wrong, I was grateful for everything in my life and what my mother has provided for me. Because of her, I was living a comfortable life.

But that didn't mean to land me directly into the arms of a Mafia Boss! I should pack my bags, run, and never look back. I really should. But I hate running.

Oh, and that wink he gave me last night? I am ashamed to admit that it made me hot.

"Thaia!" The constant banging on the door didn't stop. Not even once. It just kept going with Cara on the other side as she continued to yell at me to open the door. I let out a big, frustrated groan as I rolled out of the bed.

"My God, Cara!" I snapped and swung the door open with my eyes half-open.

"Finally!" She exclaimed. I ignored her and returned to my bed, getting under the blanket and pulling it over my head, intending to fall asleep. I was too tired to deal with her right now.

"What are you doing? Get up!" The blanket was suddenly pulled from my body, and I was going to rip her head off.

"Cara!" I snapped again, and I sat up and searched for the blanket. "Let me sleep, it's early!" I complained. I gave up on finding the blanket and plopped down on the bed again.

Whatever, I was tired enough to sleep like this.

"Early? It's one in the afternoon! Let's go get lunch." She scoffed. "And close your legs. We can see your vajayjay."

"Don't fucking look then." I hissed in annoyance.

Wait.

"We?" I asked, confused. "Who's 'we'?" I raised my head to look, and to my horror, Michael was present, resting his shoulder against the doorframe.

"Mornin' to you too, Thaia." He just stood there and smiled all innocently at me. I closed my legs and screamed.

"Turn around!" I clumsily tried to get out of bed. Cara was definitely not helping as she stood at the end of the bed, laughing so hard that tears were visible in her eyes.

I ran to the bathroom and slammed the door shut, hoping the ground would just open and swallow me.

"Your dad wants you to join a small dinner party a week from now." Cara said, before taking a bite of her sandwich.

We were at a café, sitting outside and having a bite to eat while we enjoyed the scorching sun that was currently baking us.

"Why?" I asked, taking a sip of my second dose of iced coffee. I desperately needed caffeine today.

"There is no point in hiding you anymore, so you might as well come to the different occasions." Michael explained.

"So, he's just going to forget the fact that he never bothered to reach out to me all these years and expects me to be, I don't know, okay with it?" I questioned. Even though we hugged, his lack of effort to reach out still hurt me. I longed for my dad all those years, and he clearly didn't care.

"You have to understand where he is coming from. If he called you or showed up at your place, you might as well be dead now." Michael shrugged as he casually explained.

"People are ruthless, Thaia. They will do anything to get what they want. The things I have witnessed." Cara shuddered and Michael nodded in agreement, looking less bothered than Cara.

I let their words sink in as I thought about it. If all of it were true, would I have been abducted and tortured? Would they have mercilessly cut into my skin to retaliate against my father? Cut off my limbs and deliver them to his residence?

The thought of that made me sick. I didn't know what these people were capable of.

"Are you coming then?" Cara asked with a hopeful tone.

"I can't. I only took this week off." I gave her an apologetic smile and received a bored look.

"You work for your mother. I'm pretty sure she can let your ass off for a few more days."

"And because she is my mother, she is hard on me." I pointed out. My mother took pride in her boutique and her work, and I suppose I inherited her skills as well.

I have always had a passion for drawing, and art has always fascinated me. I went to college to pursue it, but it wasn't fulfilling in the way I wanted it to be. So, I dropped out and worked with my mother, and we turned our skills into a family-owned business.

"One time I messed up an order, and she was a second away from pulling out the wooden spoon to whoop my ass." I scoffed at the memory. My mother was the type of person who would whoop your ass in a heartbeat with her beloved wooden spoon.

"Not the wooden spoon!" Cara and Michael said, and we all burst out laughing. Whoever misbehaved, my mother would whip out the wooden spoon, regardless of who they were. And since we grew up together, Michael received his fair share of whooping as we had the habit of making trouble.

"I'll talk to her; she never says no to me." Cara bragged, and I rolled my eyes at her.

"Sucks to be an only child, and not even be the favorite." I joked and let out a dramatic sigh. "What's the dinner party about, anyway?" I asked.

"They say it's for making up about the engagement party, but it's most likely to do damage control. It's nothing major, only Lorenzo and Damiano are coming." Cara explained. I tried not to show a reaction at the mention of Damiano. I knew I shouldn't, but the temptation to see him one more time clouded any rational thought.

"Again, I'm so sorry about that." I apologized, but Cara simply waved me off, not bothered about it.

"Bah, you guys are so boring!" Michael complained and threw his head back. "I thought we would do something fun." He sulked.

"I told you we were just going out to eat and do some shopping. Nobody asked you to come. You just dragged your ass with me." Cara rolled her eyes at him.

"I was bored, and there wasn't much to do, anyway. Besides, wouldn't you rather have me around instead of... what's his name?" Michael snapped his fingers as he tried to remember. "Oh, Maso!" He exclaimed.

"Maso is a great guy. He just takes his job way too seriously and basically breathes down my neck, but still a great guy." Cara chuckled. Her father wouldn't allow her to leave the house without an escort, and Maso was assigned to be with her wherever she went. He was a very serious guy and not a type that would smile. At all.

"Yeah, yeah, whatever. Let's just go. My ass is getting numb." Michael rose from his seat and stretched out his arms. The white t-shirt he was wearing rode up and revealed some of his toned stomach.

I gazed for a little longer than I should have. He was nowhere near the build of Damiano, but his physique was quite nice, actually. My eyes roamed his body till they met his eyes, seeing he was already looking at me with a smirk on his face.

"Like what you see, gorgeous?" He winked. I felt my face flush with embarrassment that he had caught me openly eyeing him. He didn't seem to mind, though.

"Stop flirting and let's go." Cara hurried us, rolling her eyes in a playful manner.

Michael put his arm around my shoulder as we made our way to the boutiques. Feeling his stare, I peeked up at him and he had a playful grin.

"I definitely liked what I saw earlier." He whispered in my ear.

"Shut up." I smacked his chest, my cheeks heating, and he just let out a chuckle.

EIGHT

ALTHAIA

Mother wasn't happy.

In fact, my mother was mad.

She became so enraged that she stumbled over the English words and had to switch to Greek. That was how you knew she was mad when she had to switch languages.

She wasn't that angry about me not coming back; she was furious that Cara had 'forgotten' to mention that she was marrying into la Famiglia Bellavia. It was apparently a big deal because she started yelling and cursing Cara's father, then she cursed my father for allowing this to happen.

I, on the other hand, knew nothing about *la Famiglia Bellavia*. So, I did some digging with a Google search. It turned out they were rich and powerful as fuck. Like *next level* shit.

They owned all sorts of businesses, including hotels, nightclubs, and casinos. Mind you, that was the legal part of their businesses. The other part? Well, they *controlled* everything from the street-corner drug trade to the highest levels of government. Obviously, there was no concrete evidence to back up the claims made by journalists who were trying to do some digging on them as well.

But I believed it.

Damiano's powerful presence, how he carried himself and the way he radiated *deadly*, made me believe all of it. It was incredibly fascinating. I also wondered if he owned the hotel I was currently staying in. Would make sense given how he suddenly had access to my room.

Or he simply broke in.

Who was going to stop him? Absolutely no one when he had this much power in his hands.

I haven't told Cara or Michael about Damiano showing up. Why? I wasn't too sure myself.

Since I had time to kill before the dinner party tonight, I did some more digging on la Famiglia Bellavia. I read articles on how law enforcement had tried to detain Damiano, but since they had no evidence against him, he was *untouchable.* Of course he was if he had the highest levels of government in his pocket.

I let out a small whistle as I continued to read the article, completely impressed. This was taking the word powerful to a whole different level, only poking my curiosity even more in this mysterious Devil going by the name of Damiano.

A knock on the door jolted me out of my current Google search. I closed my laptop and headed for the door, knowing it was Michael on the other side, ready to take me to my father's mansion.

"Wow, hey there." Michael looked stunned as he gazed at my dress. "That dress is... hot."

"Thank you." I grinned. It was a tight red wine-colored dress, and it hugged my figure nicely. And of course, I had to finish it with a pair of red bottom stilettos to complete the look.

"My lady." Michael did a dramatic bow and offered me his arm. I chuckled and linked my arm with his as we made our way out to his dreamy Aston Martin.

"Can I drive your car?" I asked. Michael laughed as if I told the funniest joke.

"That was a good one, Thaia." He chuckled as he opened the passenger door for me.

"I meant it." I said, and he looked at me for a long time, trying to see if I was serious or not.

"Ha, nope!" He erupted and ushered me inside as I gaped at him.

"I'm an excellent driver!"

"And I don't care!"

"I promise I will drive like a granny."

"No can do. This is my baby." He caressed the steering wheel gently, and I let out a scoff at him for being so dramatic. "You can be the DJ. I never let anyone be the DJ."

"Wow, what a privilege." I let out a sarcastic smile. "I don't want to be the DJ. I want to be the driver." I was hoping he would get tired of me nagging and would give in.

"I want to be the driver!" He mimicked in a high-pitched voice, and I gave him a blank stare.

"I don't sound like that." I frowned, then sighed in defeat. Michael just grinned and switched the music on.

"This is my favorite song!" Michael yelled and cranked up the volume. I looked at him in shock as he started singing to BlackPink. How was this man, a member of a Mafia, singing at the top of his lungs to BlackPink? When he noticed my surprise, he dimmed the volume.

"What?"

"What do you mean 'what'? You sang every single word in Korean without missing a single syllable!" I exclaimed.

"That's because I kind of speak Korean now." Michael said proudly. "I was exploring one day, and I stumbled upon Koreatown. I ended up eating a shit ton of food, and I kept going back so much that they just know who I am now. I made a few friends and learned the language."

"Aw, look at you being such a foodie." I teased, making him chuckle. "Hey, now we can talk shit about people without them knowing!"

"Wait, you speak it too?" It was his turn to be surprised.

"Why are you surprised? I'm the one who listens to K-pop and watches K-dramas. I'm just not allowed to listen to or watch anything Korean-related around Cara. She's a killjoy when it comes to that." I snickered.

I had a phase where I only listened to Korean music and only watched K-dramas. And I may have talked non-stop about the dramas until she became fed up with me and banned me from ever talking about it near her.

"Typical Cara, so uncultured." He shook his head in amusement, and I seconded.

We came to a stop in front of the mansion, and as usual, a few of my father's men were outside on duty. Michael helped me out of the car at the same time a sudden loud screeching and revving sound of a car rang out in the air.

The car was racing fast towards us, and my eyes slowly widened when I thought it would hit us. But it made a harsh stop before it could.

"Are you fucking kidding me?" Michael mumbled as we both stared at the car.

"Holy shit!" I looked in awe. It wasn't just any car. "Tell me my eyes are deceiving me, Michael. But is that a Bugatti La Voiture Noire in front of us?" Fuck Michael's car. This one was a sexy beast. This car was probably the closest thing to a real-life Batmobile. All black, shiny, and *so sexy*.

The car door opened and who emerged from the driver's seat?

The Devil.

Of course, he would own that car! I moved closer to get a better view, wanting to check out every single inch of that sexy beast. But Michael wrapped his arm around my waist and tried to lead me to the mansion.

Annoyed, I removed his arm and rushed over to get a closer look at the car. I was stunned as I circled the car, taking in every detail from the unique front fascia to the rear fascia with its six exhaust pipes. The details were insane!

"Wow!" I whispered to myself. I was so focused that I hadn't noticed people staring at me as I studied the car. Even Damiano's intense gaze was focused on me as he watched me trying to get a peek inside. Feeling shy by the sudden attention, I let out an awkward chuckle.

"Sorry, it's a beautiful car. Can I have a look inside?" I asked. Damiano didn't say anything and just opened the door so I could look.

I slightly leaned forward, trying to contain my excitement as I took it all in. It was gorgeous!

I drew in a sharp breath when I felt someone extremely close behind me. Almost brushing against my ass. I straightened up and almost let out a yelp when I saw how close Damiano was to me.

"Let's go, Althaia." Michael walked towards me, but Damiano sent him one sharp look. That was enough for Michael to halt in his steps as he glared at him, looking pissed.

"Do you want to drive it?" I whipped my head to Damiano.

"Are you asking me?" Pointing to myself in surprise.

"Who else?" He tilted his head slightly to the side, looking amused.

"Are you being serious?" I squinted my eyes as I questioned him. I would rather not get in the car, only for him to say, 'just kidding' and drag me out.

"Very." Damiano said, gesturing with his head for me to get in. I let out a big grin in pure excitement. I was about to get in when I glanced at Michael, his face full of rage as he glared at Damiano.

"Oh, uh, thanks, but maybe another time?" I gave a faint smile, trying not to show how disappointed I was turning down this once-in-a-lifetime opportunity.

I sighed as I walked past him, but I feared Michael was about to do something stupid. Michael wasted no time wrapping his arm around me, roughly shoving me into him, and hurrying up the stairs, almost making me trip as he practically dragged me with him.

What the hell was his problem now?

"Michael, relax. You're hurting me." I winced when his fingers dug into my side.

He finally snapped out of it and immediately let me go. I started massaging my side gently to ease the pain. This was definitely going to bruise.

His eyes followed my actions, and instant regret showed on his face.

"Shit, Thaia, I'm so sorry." He ran a hand through his hair.

"Are you okay?" I asked. Michael usually kept his cool, but this time I feared he would do something stupid and get hurt. It wouldn't take a genius to figure out who would win the fight.

"I'm the one who should ask if you're okay." He sighed and gave a small smile. "Don't worry about me... he just pisses me off every time I see his stupid face."

"Or is it because he drives a sexier car than you?" I teased and bumped my shoulder into his.

"You're such a gold digger, Thaia! One minute you're begging me to let you drive my car, and then you see his stupid car and forget all about mine." I burst out laughing. Michael looked like a kid who had been denied candy.

"Well, what can I say? I'm a sucker for cars I will never be able to afford on my own." I continued to tease him. Michael didn't even bother replying and kept giving me a sour look as we made our way inside.

"There she is!" My father was beaming when he saw me and held out his arm for a hug. A smile crossed my face as I embraced him.

Our relationship had grown in such a short time since I decided to stay in town for an extra week. I was happy that he was making an effort to get to know me, and we would meet up for breakfast and lunch.

He wanted me to stay at the mansion, but I was still hesitant about that. I didn't want to rush and risk ruining our relationship. It was better that we just took it one step at a time.

I also made sure he fixed the whole 'Althaia Volante is dead' situation. People now knew I was alive, so there was no need to continue the lie. My father even changed my name from Celano to Volante. It was time for me to claim my rightful name, as he had said.

"Figlia, do you remember your uncle? He has just returned from a business trip." He gestured to the man in front of me. Of course, I remembered him. I would never forget the only person I have ever truly wanted to kill with my bare hands.

I forced a tight smile as I looked at him with no intention of stepping closer to him. He looked unrecognizable with his greasy, shoulder-length hair, looking like he aged fifty years since the last time I saw him. His skin had a grayish tint, and his face was all wrinkled. He looked like he had been brought back from the dead.

"Althaia, look how you've grown. You've turned into such a beautiful woman." My uncle said, his eyes glancing at my body and stopping for way too long on my breasts.

Fucking creep. I hope you die, you sicko.

Luckily, he tore his eyes away when Damiano and Lorenzo made an appearance, and my heart beat just a little faster.

He was even more breathtaking today. I bit my lip as I shamelessly checked him out; the way his muscular body looked in that dress shirt sent a steady pulse between my legs.

Then our gazes locked, and his eyes slowly traced a path down as I licked my lip. His intense stare quickly returned to mine, radiating a mesmerizing allure. I felt as if I were drowning in the captivating depths of his gaze.

"Gentlemen." My father greeted them, and it took everything in me to look away.

Lorenzo gave a curt nod, and Damiano shook my father's outstretched hand, keeping his face blank. I have come to learn that Lorenzo wasn't much of a talker, but he was one of the most feared men, and I could see why. His huge build and the mysterious silence around him screamed like a deadly assassin to me.

"Dinner is almost ready. In the meantime, let's head to my office and talk business." My father led the way to his office.

Since they were going to talk business, I might as well make my way upstairs to Cara's room. Before I had the chance to take a step, a hand squeezed my ass. I gasped and turned around to see who would dare to do such a thing. Shockingly, I was faced with my uncle. He winked at me before he quickly followed the rest of the men.

Nausea overwhelmed me.

I walked away as fast as I could with the need to sanitize my entire body. I rounded the corner towards the stairs when the most annoying high-pitched voice stopped me.

"Althaia, darling!" I winced at the voice. I spun around and saw Morella, my father's wife, heading my way.

We haven't officially met because, well, the engagement party didn't exactly go as planned, and my father and I would meet up at neutral places like restaurants or coffee shops. I have been trying to avoid meeting her, but it looks like I couldn't get out of this one now.

I wanted to like Morella, but I just couldn't. One reason was because I had a hard time accepting she was with my father when I still wished my parents would find their way to each other.

The other reason was because of what I found out from Cara. Morella supported uncle in beating the crap out of Cara to instill discipline. I was not a violent person, but for that reason alone, I wanted to punch her in the face.

"Hello, Morella." I put on a smile. She caught me off guard when she suddenly grabbed my shoulders and kissed both of my cheeks with big kissy noises.

"Darling, how are you? Oh, darling, look at you in that dress!"

I tried not to flinch as her voice went an octave higher for every word that came out of her mouth. Who uses the word darling so many times?

"I'm good, thank you." I said, my eyes landing on her lips that had way too much filler in them. They were coated in a red lipstick, making it look like a giant butthole that was about to explode.

I snickered in my mind.

"Darling, have you had the chance to meet my son, Carlos?" Her lips stretched out in a big smile. I tried to keep my face neutral and not flinch at her voice. How was it possible to talk so high-pitched?

"Oh no, I haven't seen him around so..." I tried to walk away, but she put her hand on my shoulder to stop me.

"Your father is always keeping him busy, darling. Even I barely get to see him nowadays." Morella sighed.

"Oh well, gotta keep the business going, right?" I tried to leave again, but she kept talking, and I forced on a smile as I listened to her. I was sure I was going to suffer from tinnitus.

I glanced over Morella's shoulder while she babbled on about something I couldn't care less about and saw Cara. I had to stifle a laugh when Cara started making gag motions with her finger before she approached us. The sound of her heels clicking made Morella snap out of her rambling and face her.

"Cara, darling! Don't you just look gorgeous!" She complimented. Cara did look stunning in her dress. The way it hugged into her waist and was tight around her hips, giving her the shape of an hourglass.

"Thank you, Morella." She smiled as if she hadn't just made gagging motions behind her back. "Is dinner ready yet?" Cara asked before Morella started her rambling again.

"Oh yes, I was about to get the boys. Be a darling and tell them dinner is ready." She told us before heading back to the kitchen.

"Thank God she's gone. I was about to break my own neck if you hadn't come in time." I said in relief and linked my arm with hers.

"Oh, you're so welcome, darling." She mimicked Morella, and we both burst out laughing.

Everyone chatted away as we waited for the appetizers, but all I could think of was this was not the original seating arrangement.

My father was sitting at the head of the table. To his left sat Lorenzo while to his right was Morella, next to her sat my uncle, and in front of me was Cara.

That meant Damiano was sitting right next to me.

This was either going to be a blessing or a curse. I haven't decided yet.

Unfortunately, Michael couldn't stay due to 'duty calls,' as he had mentioned before leaving.

I found myself sitting so close to Damiano that it made me a little nervous. I tried to distract myself by quietly talking to Cara and tried to ignore how close I was to him.

Appetizers were served, and I stared blankly down at my plate. It was some kind of green liquid in front of me, and I wasn't even sure it could be classified as soup.

There was no way I was eating it.

I then accidentally made eye contact with Morella, who gave me a big smile and an encouraging nod to try the green stuff in the bowl. I picked up the spoon to pretend I would eat and waited until she stopped looking at me. And of course she waited for me to try it.

I scooped up a bit of the green liquid in my spoon and tasted it. I held my breath as soon as it touched my tongue. A very pungent taste of something I couldn't even describe covered my entire mouth. I forced it down as I looked at Morella, who was giving me a Cheshire smile, waiting for my response. I gave her a tight smile and an awkward thumbs-up. She nodded in approval, returning to her conversation with my father.

I grabbed the glass of water and chugged half of it. Glancing at Cara, seeing her trying to pinch her nose discreetly as she ate. The sight of her made me snort out loud, but I quickly tried to disguise it as a cough. Cara squinted her eyes at me as I tried to hide my smile behind my hand. She quickly checked around and flipped me off.

Oh no, she didn't.

I stretched my legs as far as I could and kicked her leg. Her eyes narrowed, and she tried to kick me, but I was quicker and moved my legs away.

And crashed them right into Damiano's leg.

My eyes widened and my face went hot when he faced me with that expressionless look on his face.

"Sorry." I whispered with an apologetic smile. His lips curled up ever so slightly, making me look at him in surprise. If I had blinked, I would have missed it.

I looked away and saw Cara with a smirk. I was going to make her pay for that. I was about to move when he put his hand on my thigh and stopped me. So, now I was supposed to sit through dinner with his hand on my thigh, and my legs pressed against him. That wasn't nerve-wracking *at all*.

I reached for the wine and took a big sip to calm down my racing heart.

My breath halted when Damiano caressed my thigh excruciatingly slowly. It made my body tingle like crazy and made me almost violently shiver. I gulped down more wine. If I kept going like this, I was going to get drunk in no time.

Another plate of food was served, and this time, it looked promising. Steak with roasted potatoes and glazed vegetables. I almost moaned out loud when the very tender and juicy piece of meat melted on my tongue.

I stopped chewing for a second when I felt Damiano's hand going up even further on the inside of my thigh. I shifted my gaze to him, but he was facing my uncle and listened to whatever he was saying.

I went back to eating my food, ignoring the way his hand was making me feel. But it was getting dangerously close to my private area. I could move my leg away to stop him, but I didn't want to, it felt so... *nice*.

Maybe a bit too nice.

My cheeks were getting warm, and I couldn't decide whether it was because of the wine or because of him.

His hand continued moving up, and I bit down on my lip when his fingers brushed *right there*. I couldn't suppress the shiver that rippled through my body. Damiano gave me a quick look before refocusing on Cara's father, his hand tightening on my thigh.

My legs parted, thinking about how his fingers would feel inside of me.... I was up on my feet in a flash, excused myself to the restroom, and hurried out of the dining room.

I rested my hands on the sink and looked at my reflection in the mirror. My face was flushed, a hue of red on my cheeks as if I had been out in the sun for a while.

I turned on the faucet, getting my hands under the running cold water for a bit, and then pressed my hands on my neck and chest to cool myself down.

I shouldn't be attracted to someone like him. He was dangerous, and not someone I should mess around with. But I couldn't help it. His touch elicited a faster reaction from my body than ever before.

I took a deep breath to compose myself and opened the door to return to the dining room.

I stopped dead in my tracks as Damiano stood in front of me, and the pool of heat returned between my legs with intensified force, making my clit throb almost painfully.

Damiano stepped in, making me take a few steps back until I was against the counter. He shut the door and locked it, never taking his eyes off me, and my heart was pounding inside my chest.

Nine
DAMIANO

Fucking hell.

I pushed my chair back, keeping my face blank as I stalked off in the direction she went, not caring how the chatter paused.

I stopped right in front of the bathroom door, and when it opened, a small gasp escaped her plump lips. I gritted my teeth at the sound as my dick pressed painfully against my slacks.

I walked towards her. One slow agonizing step at a time, until her ass hit the sink behind her. I let out a satisfied grunt as my eyes trailed down her curves. I rested my hands on the sink, caging her between my arms as I leaned in closer to her, hearing her breath hitch.

"Do you have any idea what you have done?" I asked, my voice low and gruff. I watched her nervously gulp as she stared at me with those bright green eyes of hers.

"No." She whispered. My hands tightened around the sink.

"You have no business showing up in your little, *tight* dress." When my fingers brushed against her bare pussy, I almost fucking lost it. I cocked my head to the side. "Tell me, Althaia, what were you hoping to achieve wearing no underwear?"

"No panty lines." She replied in the same breathy whisper. I briefly closed my eyes, my cock twitching at the sound of her breathy voice.

"No. Panty. Lines." I slowly repeated.

I leaned in closer until my lips brushed the shell of her ear as I whispered, feeling her shiver as I did so.

"And when you bent over, letting every single one of those hungry men out there look at your ass?" I asked.

Her chest heaved and her hardened nipples brushed against my chest. My knuckles whitened as my grip on the sink tightened even more.

"Hoping I gave them a nice view."

"It was a *pleasant* view. So much that I wanted to stab every single one of them in the eyes for even glancing at you."

"Oh..." She breathed out. Her response caused me to smirk.

I looked at her angel-like face as she gazed at me with a swirl of excitement and curiosity in her eyes.

So open, like a damn book.

"You're curious about the wrong things, Althaia. I'm not a good man. You should run." I warned her.

"No, thank you." I raised a brow at her reply, watching her as she studied my face, a smile threatening to break free on her lips. "I don't run."

"I will make you run."

"Not going to happen. I would rather fight you than run."

"Really?" I asked, amused.

"Yes." She answered confidently.

A wicked smile appeared on my lips as I swiftly wrapped my hand around her throat. Her chest rose and fell when I slightly squeezed. A flash of fear appeared in her eyes, but excitement overpowered her so easily.

Silly woman. You should run.

"You're five foot nothing, Althaia. You can't harm me." I let out a taunting chuckle.

"Five foot *two*. Those two inches are important." She scowled, clearly offended that I had failed to include her precious two inches of height.

I almost laughed. She was amusing.

"They won't make a difference here, *piccola*."

Althaia's eyes narrowed at the pet name.

"We'll see."

Althaia raised her leg to knee me, but I was faster and blocked her terrible attempt at an attack.

"Would have hurt if you succeeded. Want to know why?" I asked, and she cocked her head to the side curiously.

I gripped onto her thigh, hiking it up to my hip. I stepped in between her legs and pressed my lower body into her. Her eyes widened when she felt my hard cock against her pussy.

"You don't know how hard it is to hold myself back." I grunted in a low voice as I slowly rocked my hips into her. A low moan escaped her lips.

Fuck it.

I lifted her on top of the counter and pressed my lips to hers in a bruising kiss. She responded immediately and moved her incredibly soft lips against mine.

My hand tightened slightly more around her throat as I bit down on her lip and shoved my tongue inside, wanting to taste every single bit of her.

"Spread your legs for me." I growled out, and she complied without hesitation.

Good girl.

My hand on her thigh found its way to her pussy, and I groaned against her mouth when I felt just how wet she was for me.

I stroked teasingly but never fully penetrated her.

"Are you going to do something, or do I have to find someone else to do the job?" Althaia exhaled sharply in annoyance.

"Fucking brave of you to say that with my hand around your throat." I snarled and increased the pressure of my grip on her throat.

She gasped and wrapped her fingers around my wrist. Her mouth parted just as I shoved two fingers inside her pussy; domineering and unforgiving, leaving no question of who was in control.

Althaia bit down on her lip, trying not to make a sound but failed so miserably as sweet moans escaped her plump lips while I finger-fucked her.

"Let's see how hard you come with my fingers only." I snarled. Her hand dove into my hair, curling tightly as I devoured her lips.

Her tongue slid against mine, making me let out a satisfied grunt. I slid out my fingers before driving back inside. Each time I pulled out and thrust back in, her pussy rewarded me with slicker arousal. And all I could think of was how good she would feel squeezed around my cock.

I groaned.

Althaia took in a sharp breath when I released her throat and exhaled a moan as I played with her clit with my thumb.

"Oh, fuck…" She whimpered.

"Your voice is so pretty when you moan for me." My voice was deep and husky as I continued to rub circles on her clit.

I was aching. I needed a release so fucking badly, and that dress was not helping. I wanted to tear it off, look at her beautiful body, and taste every single inch of it before fucking her tight pussy with my cock.

Her eyes drooped in pleasure and her head kicked back. My lips descended to her exposed throat feeling the softness of her skin, as I grazed my teeth along her neck before gently sucking on her skin.

"Oh, God..." Althaia shuddered, and her legs trembled. She was close.

"Come for me, Althaia. Let me have it."

I pumped my fingers deeper and faster, curling my fingers inside of her as I stroked her clit. I felt her clenching around my fingers, and I grabbed the back of her neck as my mouth covered hers once again, swallowing her cries of pleasure with a low growl.

Her body quivered as she rode out her orgasm, dropping her head on my shoulder while panting heavily.

"Good girl." I murmured and kissed her shoulder before slowly pulling out my fingers.

She faced me with her hooded eyes in time to see me licking her juices off my fingers. Her eyes were entranced by my movements.

"You taste heavenly." My mouth turned up in a smirk when a blush crept across her face.

I was tempted to clean her sweet pussy with my tongue, and it took everything in me to refrain myself from doing so, knowing I would have to fuck her if my tongue tasted her pussy.

I helped her down from the counter, holding onto her waist to steady her when her legs wobbled. I cupped her chin to make her look at me.

"Believe me when I say those fucking bastards will never be able to make you come. Because I will cut off their hands before they could even try to touch you." I promised. Her brows raised in shock, and I shot her a sly wink before I left the restroom.

"Holy fuck..." I heard her mumble to herself before the faucet turned on.

I had to take a minute to calm down and adjust myself. Once I made sure my length wasn't about to burst free from my pants, I made my way back to the dining room ignoring Cara's teasing smirk and my brother's look as I passed them in the hall.

Ten

ALTHAIA

My thighs were still slick with my arousal, and I took my time cleaning myself up to gather my thoughts. I was left satisfied but also with a strange, conflicting feeling swirling around my body.

Have I lost my mind?

I could have stopped him. I *should* have stopped him from fucking me with his fingers. But I didn't want to, and I wasn't sure how to feel about it emotionally because my body betrayed me completely by reacting so quickly to his touch.

It must be the wine!

Yes. It was clearly the wine that prevented me from thinking rationally and had me spreading my legs for him like my life depended on it. I mean, for a split second, I thought it was over for me with how he was choking me.

I took in a deep breath and tried to fix myself, so it didn't look like I just came all over a man's fingers less than two minutes ago. A man who literally could snap my neck like it was nothing if he wanted to.

Yes, I have definitely lost my mind.

Taking a deep breath, I stepped back into the dining room, and my body fluttered as I met Damiano's piercing eyes. His arm was at the back of my chair as he took a slow sip of whiskey. His face was emotionless, not even a flicker of recognition that we had done something that we shouldn't have in the restroom.

"Darling, are you okay? You didn't finish your dinner." Morella asked and put her hand on my cheek. "Oh my, you're burning!"

My father stood up and gave me a concerned glance. He pressed the back of his hand to my forehead, and the creases of his frown deepened.

"Figlia, are you okay? Do you need to rest?"

"No, no, I'm fine." I said quickly and gave them a reassuring smile, but they didn't look convinced. "I just need a little fresh air and I'll be okay. I promise."

"Yes, go get some fresh air. Dessert will be out in a little while." Morella said, and luckily, they returned to their seats.

I gestured for Cara to follow me, my face flushing as I tried to avert my gaze from the piercing golden-brown eyes that were fixed on me.

As soon as we stepped out, the night breeze with its slight coolness touched my heated skin, and I briefly shut my eyes and breathed in the fresh air. My moment was interrupted when Cara grabbed my arm and dragged me away from the entrance. She stopped when we were hidden behind a large tree.

"Okay, spill it. What is going on between the two of you?" Cara raised her perfectly arched brow at me.

"Between whom?"

"Don't play dumb with me, Thaia." Her eyes were heavy with suspicion. "I saw the way he was looking at you."

"I don't know what you're talking about." I mumbled, looking away.

"I heard you."

I whipped my head back to her, seeing her grinning widely at me.

"You heard...?"

"Yup. So, did you fuck?"

"What? No!"

"Then what? Because whatever it was, you were enjoying it. Big time." Cara wiggled her brows at me with a teasing smirk.

"Ew, you were listening?" I wrinkled my nose and looked at her in disgust.

"I'm not a creep, you freak." She rolled her eyes. "When you left, Damiano got up and left as well. I thought I would check on you since you walked off like your ass caught fire. Turns out your vagina was on fire with need because I heard you enjoying yourself in there." Her laughter filled the backyard, and I felt my cheeks burn with embarrassment.

"You are *loud*, honey." She continued with a grin.

"Oh my God, just stop!" I hissed and walked away from her. The embarrassment was too much for me, and I wanted to sink into the ground.

"So, what *did* you do?" Cara fell in step with me, and I sighed, knowing she wouldn't let it go if I didn't tell her.

"Nothing... he just... touched me." I said, struggling to find the words.

"Ah, he finger-fucked, didn't he?" She asked with a chuckle, and I groaned at her choice of words.

"Something like that." I admitted.

"Does he know you're a virgin?"

I stopped to look at her when her voice turned serious, shooting her a confused look.

"I'm not?"

"You might as well be. When was the last time you got some? I heard that if you wait long enough, a new hymen will grow back." Cara burst out laughing at her own joke, and I gave her a blank stare.

"You're really not funny." I scowled while she continued to laugh.

"Oh, well, looks like your man came out to check on you." She responded with a playful smirk on her lips.

Damiano was standing in front of the entrance, smoking, while his eyes were fixed on me. Tank Man was next to him, his mouth moving as he said something to Damiano before Lorenzo's gaze was back on Cara.

"He's not my man." I muttered. "It's yours who came out to check on you."

"Mhmm." Cara winked, and I shot her a look to tell her to shut it as we walked toward them.

They moved aside, allowing us to enter, and Damiano flicked away his cigarette butt before trailing closely behind as we made our way back to the dining room.

We showed up just in time to hear the clatter of plates as dessert was being served. Damiano rested his arm on the back of my chair again, and I felt the warmth of his fingertips tracing the back of my shoulder.

I reached for my refilled glass of wine and took a large sip to calm my nerves.

"Slow down." Damiano spoke quietly, only for me to hear. I turned to face him, and his intense gaze bore into me.

It felt like he was unraveling my soul.

"Figlia, we were just talking about how both families should attend Sunday Service together sometime." The sound of my father's voice made me turn away from the Devil's eyes.

"Oh, I was actually planning on leaving at the end of this week, so..." I trailed off with an apologetic smile.

"Leaving? To where?" His brows furrowed in disapproval.

"I'm going home, papá. I wasn't supposed to stay this long, anyway."

"Nonsense! You're staying." He erupted strictly as if I was a child.

"I have to get back to mom. Plus, I have work." I tried to explain, but he wasn't having any of it.

"Is this what she's doing to you? Keeping you away from me all these years and making you work? No daughter of mine should work. You're staying. And no more hotels. This is your home." My father left no room for discussion.

I let out a quiet chuckle and shook my head, giving in, despite dreading the phone call I would have to make to my mother.

At least I would spend more time with Cara.

"Damiano, let's get back to my proposal. What do you say? With me in charge of your products, there will be far more distribution and more money!" My uncle's speech was slurred as he made his proposal with a cocky smirk on his face. He was already disgustingly drunk.

Damiano glanced at him with an unimpressed expression with one brow raised.

"If I do that, there will be no products left to sell. Your snorting ass will leave us out of business." Damiano spoke calmly, and my uncle's smile fell.

"Do you think I'm a crackhead?" He scoffed, his lips curling into a devious smile as his drunken slur continued to fill the room. "I heard that whore of a mother you have is a sniffing crackhead."

The room fell silent.

The atmosphere shifted abruptly as Damiano's eyes darkened, the golden-brown depths turning into an abyss of darkness. It was as if a storm had gathered within his gaze, brewing with an intensity that sent shivers through my entire being.

I stopped breathing, not daring to make a sound. *Fuck.* If a look could kill, this was it.

The dark intensity in Damiano's eyes was a lethal weapon that threatened to unleash its fury.

I blinked, and when I opened my eyes again, Damiano had grabbed my uncle's head. He violently slammed it down on the table, causing a sickening crack, before dragging him across it. The plates and glasses crashed to the floor, creating a cacophony of destruction.

I scrambled away from my seat, my heart pounding, terror gripping me as I watched the scene unfold before my eyes.

"I dare you to say that one more time." Damiano's voice was ominously low, making me shudder in fear.

Everyone in the room stood frozen, no one daring to interfere. He had Cara's father in a deadly grip, staring him down with his cold, lifeless eyes.

"Cara, take Althaia away from here." I heard my father say, but my legs remained frozen.

My father tried to reason with Damiano, but Lorenzo blocked him from getting closer. He looked like he was ready to kill my father if he dared to intervene.

"I said your whore of a mother -" My uncle didn't even finish his sentence as Damiano grabbed his jaw, his fingers digging in so hard it looked like he was about to break it.

He slightly turned his head to look at my terrified face. The look on his face had my knees weakening in absolute fear.

"Don't look."

That was all he said to me as he pulled out a knife. But I couldn't tear my eyes away from the Devil in action.

A scream of pain pierced my eardrums, as my uncle's tongue dropped to the floor. I followed the trail of blood, seeing my uncle's mouth sputtering blood out like a waterfall.

Cara's words were pleading as she tried to get me away, but my feet wouldn't budge as my eyes stayed glued on the blood.

I looked up when my view was suddenly blocked. Damiano was looking at me with a frown on his face.

"You're going to pass out if you don't breathe. Breathe, Althaia."

But I couldn't.

And everything went black.

Eleven

ALTHAIA

I let out a small groan, grabbing my head due to the pounding headache. I sat up and blinked a few times to adjust my eyes to the darkness in the room. It was Cara's room. Before I could get confused about why I was here, everything rushed back to me.

Blood. So much blood. And my uncle's detached tongue on the floor. I almost gagged at the image.

A beam of light filled the room as the door opened.

"You're awake." Cara stepped in and handed me a bottle of water. "Are you okay?" She sat next to me on the bed and looked at me with worry. I shrugged.

"He deserved it, Thaia. He's lucky he's still alive after talking like that." She scoffed, her voice laced with disgust and not at all bothered.

She was right. Her father deserved it, and more, particularly for how he has treated Cara over the years. But it was seeing the action unfold in front of me that had me black out.

He cut off his tongue like it was nothing. It was another not-so-friendly reminder of what kind of world I had stepped into and what these people were capable of.

"I need some painkillers. My head is killing me." I muttered and got up from the bed.

I slowed down as I walked down the staircase, watching how the entire place was packed with men.

"What's going on?" I wondered out loud. I saw Michael walking towards us, his face intense and alert.

"Althaia, are you okay?" He embraced me tightly in his arms.

"I'm fine." His shirt muffled the sound of my voice. "What's going on? Why are there so many men here?" I asked.

The entire floor was filled with men with their hands resting on their guns. I leaned into Michael, unsure of what was going to happen next.

"I'll explain later. Right now, I need to take you and Cara to your hotel for safety." He wasted no time and quickly ushered us outside.

Several cars were parked out front, with even more men standing outside. They were almost surrounding the mansion.

As Michael opened the car door for us, Damiano walked out with a group of men. They were standing close to him as if they were his personal bodyguards. What made me uneasy about him was that he looked so calm and composed, as if he hadn't just stuck a knife into someone's mouth.

He stepped down the stairs in a new shirt and jacket, and his eyes snapped to mine as if he could feel I was looking at him. He spoke a few words to his men, and I could feel the intensity of their stares as he walked toward me.

Michael moved quickly, standing in front of me to prevent Damiano from getting any closer.

"Don't even think about it." Michael said warningly, but Damiano's expression didn't change as he stepped closer.

"Move." Damiano's voice was sinisterly low.

"It's okay, Michael." I placed a hand on his shoulder to have him step back.

If Damiano could go as far as cutting off the tongue of someone in a higher position, then I didn't dare to imagine what he could do to Michael.

He ignored me and continued to glare at Damiano.

"Michael, please..." I tried to pull him away.

He finally listened and stepped back next to me, wrapping a protective arm around my waist. Damiano's expression hardened as he stared at his arm around me.

Oh, shit.

"Can you give us a minute, please? I'll be fine." I said to Michael as I quickly stepped out of his hold. He frowned, but I looked at him with pleading eyes. Michael didn't look pleased about it at all but stepped back and leaned against the car with his arms crossed, his gaze fixed on us.

I took a few steps to put some distance between us and the rest of the men to have a bit of privacy. I played with my necklace, looking anywhere but at the Devil.

"Are you okay?" Damiano broke the silence first.

I didn't know if I was okay. I wasn't really feeling anything, and I felt like my body was still in shock. So, I just shrugged.

"Look at me, Althaia."

I took in a breath before looking at him. He looked around my face carefully, searching for any signs of injury before his gaze met mine. My breath hitched when it did. How could I still find him hauntingly beautiful?

"I'm okay." I breathed out. He gave a slow nod before his brows furrowed.

"I told you to look away."

I blinked.

"I - Well, I'm sorry I couldn't quite comprehend what you were doing before you... *chopped it out.*" I swallowed hard, getting nauseous just even thinking about it.

"Don't think, do as you're told." He said sharply, letting me know how unhappy he was with me as his frown deepened.

"Noted..." I mumbled as I twisted my fingers around each other nervously under his intense gaze before finally finding the courage to ask him. "Why did you do it?"

Damiano tilted his head and cocked a brow at me.

"Not, uh, the tongue thing." I quickly elaborated. *That* was understandable. "The hotel, I mean. I received a refund." He looked at me for a while before answering.

"Because I wanted to."

"Are you keeping an eye on me?" I blurted out. I have been wondering about it ever since I learned he paid for my expenses.

"Yes." Damiano answered. My eyes widened. That was a response I was not prepared for.

"I already told you I'm not involved." I exclaimed.

"I know, Althaia." The way he said my name in his deep voice made my body tingle. So much that I rubbed my arms when goosebumps appeared.

Damiano stepped closer to me as he took off his jacket and wrapped it around my shoulders.

"But why?"

"Because I want to." His gaze was so intense, and my skin was tingling from our closeness.

"Is that a good thing?" My voice was barely more than a whisper.

"No."

"Oh..." His jaw slightly tightened at my response. "I would like to pay you back. For the hotel." I could almost swear he was about to smile.

"Goodnight, Althaia." Damiano lightly ran a thumb on my jaw before turning around to leave.

"Wait." I called after him. He slowly turned his head over his shoulder and looked at me. "Please, don't cut off Michael's hand. He means well." I pleaded.

I didn't get a reply. Instead, he let out a smirk and made his way to his car.

"Let's go, Thaia." I tore my eyes away from Damiano's retreating form and looked at Michael, seeing him glaring daggers at the jacket around my shoulders.

"Does it mean the wedding is off?" I asked after we arrived at my hotel room.

Cara was already lying down, her eyes half-closed, while Michael stood at the end of the bed with his hands in his pockets. He had been quiet the entire ride to the hotel.

"No, they have moved the wedding up." Cara explained.

"Really? I thought that since.... Well, *that* happened, they would break off the engagement and some kind of war would break out?" I tilted my head in confusion.

"It's strictly for business." Cara failed to keep her eyes open and dozed off. I looked at Michael for him to explain.

"Profit. Their products are the most sought after, and whether they like to admit it or not, we are the fastest in moving products with our connections. We can move twice as fast as they can, which means we make a shit ton of money. That's why there will be no war between the families."

"But why would my father still work with a man who just cut off the tongue of his brother?" I gaped in shock.

"Because there is more to it."

I waited for him to tell me, but he looked hesitant. He sighed and ran a hand through his hair.

"Look, I'm not supposed to say anything, but your father wants to gain access to their weaponry. They have currently taken over the biggest weapons trafficking operation. Every type of lethal weapon you can think of, they have it, and only them. And, with Cara marrying not just any man from the family, but Lorenzo, we hope to gain access sooner rather than later." Michael finished explaining, and my jaw dropped. When they claimed it was all business, they truly meant it.

"Shit… that's freaking awesome! I mean, it sucks for Cara, but still, it's like we're living in a movie!" I grinned in fascination.

A couple of weeks ago, I had lived an ordinary life. And now, I was getting a glimpse of such a dark world. It was terrifying, but so intriguing too. I couldn't help but be fascinated by it all. It made me feel alive in a whole different way.

I wanted to know more.

Michael's mouth curved into a shocked O, and then he erupted into laughter.

"God, Althaia. You surprise me in every way.

Twelve

Althaia

"You promised me, Althaia!" Cara scowled.

"I did no such thing!" I mirrored her expression.

I was in Cara's room, helping her pack her bags since she was going to stay with the Bellavia family to plan the wedding. Actually, she was packing while I was laying on her bed, flipping through a random magazine I found.

Since it was a good few hours between the residences, it was easier for her to stay at their place instead of constantly going back and forth to plan the wedding. And now she was trying to make me go with her.

"Yes, you did! Remember when we went out for brunch, and I told you I needed help planning the wedding? You told me you would be happy to help since you're staying here for a while and have nothing to do, anyway." She insisted.

I stopped flipping through the magazine as I tried to remember when I had said that.

"Are you actually trying to implant a fake memory into my mind?" I looked at her accusingly.

"No." She avoided looking at me.

"Yes, you are, you sneaky little bitch!" I threw a pillow at her face. She let out a huff.

"What are you going to do here alone, anyway?"

"I don't know. Eat and chill with Michael?" I shrugged.

I had been staying at the mansion for a couple of weeks now, and she actually had a point. I wouldn't have anything to do once she left. Unless I wanted to become best friends with Morella.

Yeah, no thank you.

I will probably go deaf if I have to listen to her speak one more time. I felt my skin crawling every time she called me 'darling.'

"You can eat over there. I'm sure they have everything you can wish for." Cara looked at me with hopeful eyes.

"Nah." I said, after pretending to think about it.

Normally, I would have found that to be convincing, but since I was trying to avoid the Devil, I was happy staying at my father's mansion.

"What if I make sure a chocolate cake is ready for you?" My brows raised at the mention of chocolate cake. "Besides, Michael will not be free all the time to hang out with you." She continued to argue, which was another good point made.

"I hate it when you're right." I sulked. Michael had been incredibly busy these days, and I had barely seen him around. "Why are you even planning the wedding? Just get someone else to do it for you."

"I am literally promised because of a business deal. The least they can do is let me plan my own wedding. And you have good taste, so you're helping me. I'm older than you; you have to do what I say." She let out a smirk.

"How lame of you to pull the 'I'm older than you' card. Which doesn't even work. But fine, I will go with you." I groaned as I rolled my eyes, and she squealed in excitement.

I resumed reading my magazine, trying to get some inspiration for my next design. Since I have once again extended my stay here, I have been working whenever my mother needed help, and I would email her my sketch ideas.

She has been surprisingly okay with me being here, which made me happy because I was enjoying the time with Cara and my father.

"I'm heading back to my room. I'm tired, and we have to wake up early for the Service tomorrow." I said as I rolled off the bed.

"Thanks for the help." Cara's voice dripped with sarcasm.

"You are *so* welcome." I snickered and closed the door behind me.

I lazily dragged my feet down the hallway when I caught the sight of Carlos coming out of his bedroom.

"Hi, Carlos." I gave a small smile. This was only my second time trying to talk to him. I had no clue what I had done to him, but he always seemed to be glaring at me.

"Bitch." He muttered under his breath as he walked past me.

I let out a shocked gasp, but anger quickly took over, and I grabbed his arm. "What the fuck is your problem?" I frowned.

Carlos ripped his arm out of my grasp and pushed me roughly against the door. Right into the doorknob. I cried out in pain when it dug into my back, and he quickly covered my mouth with his hand.

"You're my fucking problem!" He hissed at me. I raised my leg and kneed him right in the balls. He shrieked and cupped his precious balls in pain.

"Piss off!"

"You bitch!" He lunged at me again, and before I could even move, he slapped me with the back of his hand.

I fell to the ground and my head collided with the floor. A ringing sound appeared in my ears and my sight became blurry.

I blinked, trying to clear my vision, and watched Carlos walking away. I slowly stood up, groaning at the pain in my back, and held my cheek as it stung. I glared towards the stairs.

Wherever he was going, I hoped he would get shot.

I was in a bad mood as I walked down the stairs to meet Cara by the front door so we could get escorted to Church.

"What is that? What the hell happened to your face?" Cara looked shocked when she took a closer look at me.

"I had a little encounter with the cocksucker for ice cream." I frowned in anger. Now that I thought of it, he did look like a person who would suck a dick for some ice cream.

Cara's brows furrowed in confusion.

"Carlos." I elaborated, and her eyes widened.

"Carlos did this to you? Where the hell is that bitch?! I'm going to cut off his dick!"

"Be my guest." I couldn't care less about that scumbag.

The stinging I felt resulted in a freaking cut and left me with a nasty bruise. He was apparently wearing a ring, and it cut right into my cheekbone. I tried to cover it with makeup, but it was still visible. It didn't help that it was also a bit swollen. It still hurts too, and so does my back.

I hope he gets fucking shot.

When we arrived, a crowd of people were already present outside. I guess they took Sunday Services pretty seriously. Well, with the kind of business they were operating, I was sure they had a lot of sins to repent for.

I used to attend these services when I was younger, but since my mother and I moved away, we stopped going. She wasn't a big believer and only attended because of my father, who came from a Catholic family. I'm not entirely sure where I stand, but I do find comfort in the idea of a higher power existing in some form.

My father's face lit up as soon as he saw us and waved us over. A smile on my face broke out, and I forgot about that cocksucker for ice cream as I embraced my father.

"Figlia, let me introduce you. This is Dale, Fabian, and Andrea, great business partners and good friends of mine." He gestured to the three middle-aged men.

"Nice to meet you." I smiled at them and offered a small wave, which they returned with a small smile and a head nod.

"And you have met Damiano and Lorenzo."

"Sure have." I muttered, smiling sweetly at my father.

I was still avoiding looking at the Devil. He had occupied my mind ever since the dinner party. And once again, I was ashamed to admit that I have been fantasizing about his fingers.

Yup, I definitely need a holy bath to purify me from all the unclean thoughts I've been having... and acting on.

"Gentlemen, shall we head inside? The Service is about to begin." My father said as he and his business partners went inside.

I was about to take a step when I was suddenly being pulled backwards. I was met with the one person I was trying to avoid.

Damiano glanced at my face, and I felt my breath hitch. Tingles erupted, and my stomach fluttered when he softly cupped my chin as he examined the cut on my face. His features hardened the more he looked at the cut.

"Who did this to you?"

"Why?" I asked, interested to know why he cared.

"I don't like asking twice." His expression turned blank as he waited for my answer. "Althaia." Damiano said warningly, his patience wearing thin. But all I could think of was the sound of my name coming from his lips and the warmth it stirred in me.

"Carlos." I answered. He gave a brief nod and let go of me.

I quickly composed myself and hurried inside the church, finding my seat next to Cara. She gave me a teasing look, which I ignored, and focused on the priest.

Once the Service finished, we waited for my and Cara's things to be moved to a different car as Damiano assigned one of his men to escort us to their estate.

At first, I thought it was to spare my father's men the travel back and forth, but I quickly learned it was something about entering a different territory.

"Oh wait, I forgot my purse in the other car!" I said to Cara just when we slid inside.

I quickly went over to grab my purse. As I shut the door, the sound of screeching tires pierced the air. I looked to the main road and saw black SUV cars racing towards us.

"Get down!"

I froze in fear, my legs refusing to move when I saw guns pointing out of the windows. I squeezed my eyes shut at the sound of gunshots and felt the impact of being thrown to the ground.

I was prepared for some kind of pain and a hard landing. But it never came. Instead, I felt a pair of arms around me, protecting my head. I opened my eyes to see it was Damiano.

Protecting me with his body.

Thirteen

DAMIANO

I lit up a cigarette, the smoke filling my lungs as I inhaled deeply. The Service finished and everyone was slowly leaving the parking lot, but my eyes never once strayed away from her as they prepared to leave.

My eyes slid down her body, resting on that perfect, round ass of hers. Even dressed modestly, the dress still clung to her curves beautifully, making me fantasize about tearing the dress off her and bending her over the hood of the car.

I drew in a deep drag and released a thick cloud of smoke that lingered in the air. It was the only thing stopping me from succumbing to my lust.

I glanced to the side; Lorenzo was raising a brow at me as he caught me checking her out.

"In front of God's house?"

"Mind your own fucking business." I snapped, and he gave me a slightly amused look. An old lady gasped and gave me a disgusted look at my language as she walked by. I gave her a stare until she looked away and entered her car.

I scoffed, and it only amused Lorenzo some more.

I took one last drag of my cigarette before flicking it away. I had too much sexual frustration pent up, and it was all because of that green-eyed woman. She had me fucking my fist like a fifteen-year-old who just hit puberty.

"Let's go." I said and slid inside my car once my men had moved the girls' luggage.

I frowned when Althaia suddenly rushed out of the car, then my attention snapped to the main road. The sound of cars coming had me flinging the door almost off its hinges as my legs moved into a sprint towards her.

"Get down!" I shouted to her, but her body tensed up in fear at the sight of guns.

I gritted my teeth in anger as I reached out for her, wrapping my arms around her body and head, and I threw us behind the car for cover. I pulled her closer, shielding her with my body as glass shattered around us.

It blinded me with rage when her eyes opened. Filled with fear.

I'm going to fucking kill them.

"Hold on to me." I quickly glanced over her to make sure she was unharmed.

Althaia fisted her hands into my shirt, and I wrapped my arm around her waist to pull her tightly into me. I moved along the cars while my men were keeping them at bay so I could get her to safety. Lorenzo was keeping his fiancée safe, shooting after the cars and blowing up one of their tires.

"Keep your heads down." I told them both once she was safely inside. A flicker of worry reflected in her eyes as she looked at me. "Go!" I shouted to Dario and slammed the door shut for him to get them away from here.

More cars arrived, and the continuous sound of gunfire forced us to stay on the ground and take cover behind our own.

I reached for the machine gun stashed beneath the car. This wasn't my first time facing such a situation, and these fuckers firing at us either had a death wish or were sorely lacking in brain cells. Either way, they wouldn't stand a chance, and I was about to demonstrate just how swiftly I could bring their useless lives to an end.

"Antonio, Giovanni, to your right. Dom, Luca, to your left." They nodded in response and waited for my signal.

I moved along the car to reach the front with Lorenzo following my every move. I didn't have to tell him anything; we were one mind in two bodies.

We crouched down, waiting for the cars to approach. The idiots fired all at once, depleting their ammunition and forcing them to reload simultaneously.

I sighed.

"Go."

My men rose, dividing as they shot after the cars to create a distraction. Lorenzo and I stood up, back-to-back, and fired. The roaring blaze from the machine guns drowned out any other noises as the bullets went flying, taking them down one by one.

I aimed for the driver first, not giving him a chance to react as I made his face look like Swiss cheese. He slumped over the steering wheel and crashed right into a tree.

I walked over to the car, my grip tight on the machine gun in my hands. The car door opened with a loud bang, and someone scrambled out, trying to flee.

I sighed at his cowardice and shot him in the back until he fell to the ground face first. If he was going to turn his back on his comrades to save his own life, then he deserved to be shot in the back.

I opened the car door to see if there were any survivors. There was a man in the backseat with a gunshot wound to his chest, groaning in pain, and gasping for air. I raised my gun and shot him, his head flying back with a gaping hole in it.

The sudden, bright light of a phone screen caught my attention on the ground. I grabbed it when I saw an incoming call, shaking my head when I saw who it was. I turned to Lorenzo and held up the phone.

"Roberto." He sneered at the sight of his name, and I smirked.

"Wrap up and have someone clean this mess. We have someone we need to visit."

The sun was slowly sinking below the horizon, glinting off the sides of the container ships as we drove up to the warehouse.

I exited the car and quickly surveyed my surroundings as I approached the warehouse. Two men stood guard at the door, and I almost closed my eyes in annoyance when they aimed their weapons on us.

I looked at the approaching shape and heard Giannino's heavy footsteps as he made his way to us with two more men behind him.

"Bellavia!" He smiled with his arms half-raised in a welcome. "To what do I owe the honor for you to come all the way out here?" He stopped in front of me and clasped his hands behind his back.

"Where is Roberto?" I got straight to the point, my patience already worn thin. He glanced around and noticed my men were prepared if they tried to make a move.

"He's inside." He answered after having assessed the situation. I looked at Antonio and Luca and motioned for them to follow me and Lorenzo.

"Roberto!" Giannino called out.

Roberto came out from the stacks of pallets that almost filled the entire warehouse. He tried to remain stoic, but his slight gulp and trembling hands gave away his uneasiness.

"Roberto, tell me why you have troubled these gentlemen to come here?" His father asked suspiciously.

"I don't know what you're talking about." He tried to have a brave look on his face, but he kept shuffling his feet.

"There was a drive-by shooting just outside the Church earlier today. Someone knew our location and what time we would be there. Do you know anything about it?" I raised my brow at him, giving him a chance to explain himself.

His eyebrows pulled together in a frown as he shook his head. I glanced over at Antonio and Luca and gave them a quick nod. They drew out their guns and shot the two men Giannino had with him. I heard two more gunshots from the outside, and the men who stood by the entrance went to meet their creator.

"Damiano, I demand an explanation!" Giannino erupted.

"You don't demand shit here." I stated in a low tone, glaring at him. Then, I turned to Roberto, narrowing my eyes. "My patience is running low, Roberto. Tell me what you know about the episode."

Roberto glared at me, spat on the ground near my feet, and I glanced down at the spot before looking back at him.

"Wrong move." I said calmly.

Antonio and Luca grabbed Roberto's arms and forced them behind his back, straightening him up for Lorenzo to deliver a powerful punch to his stomach, followed by another to his ribs.

I pulled out my pack of cigarettes and lit one up. I took a long drag and looked at Roberto, who groaned in pain and tried to take a breath to compose himself.

"Roberto, one last time, and I'll spare your life."

"You don't spare anyone!" He coughed out, struggling to catch his breath.

"I am a man of my word." I promised him.

He looked hesitant before finally speaking.

"Look, I don't know who it is. I found a phone in my bag during my rounds. I received a phone call, but the static background noise made it impossible to identify the caller. Our orders weren't to shoot anyone; it was mainly meant to intimidate you. But if we landed a hit, we were promised rewards." Roberto quickly explained.

I stared at him for a while to see if he was telling the truth. He was.

"And where's the phone?"

"I dumped it in the water when I received the money."

"How much?"

"Twenty grand each." I pulled my gun out. "You gave me your word!" Roberto yelled.

"I did." I turned around and fired a bullet between Giannino's eyes.

"What the fuck man?" Roberto shouted.

"For raising a cunt." I said calmly as I walked over to him and crouched down to his level.

"I gave you my word that *I* would spare your life. But you see..." I nodded towards Lorenzo. "My brother's soon-to-be wife was there. I wonder what my dear brother has to say about that." I let out a wicked grin.

Lorenzo bared his teeth, pulled out his knife, and grabbed a fistful of Roberto's hair.

"My brother is into carving faces these days. I'm sure he will make you pretty." I smirked and gave his cheek a light pat.

"No–wait!" The sound of agony reached my ears as I walked away.

I stopped in my tracks and threw the bud away when I saw Carlos. I looked around and scoffed when Gaetano was nowhere to be seen. That bastard always took the easy way out and let his men do all the dirty work for him.

I changed my direction heading straight for Carlos, who was happily talking to his mates. I grabbed him by the collar of his shirt, as my fist went back and punched him repeatedly in the face.

I watched the blood smear out all over his face, but I didn't stop until I heard the satisfying crack when I broke his nose. No one tried to stop me. No one *dared* to stop me, knowing I would send any one of them six feet under.

I pushed him up against the car, gripped his jaw tightly, and pulled my knife out. The cries of pain sent pleasurable waves down my spine as I slowly cut deeply into his face.

"If you touch her one more time, I promise I will make sure you beg for your death." I tightened my hold on his jaw, and he quickly nodded.

I looked down at his hands, grabbed the one with the ring on it, and stabbed my knife right through it.

He choked out in pain as I pulled it out, wiping my knife on his shirt before letting him go.

I walked back to my car, now desperate to see the woman who had captivated me with her big, innocent, green eyes.

Fourteen

Althaia

"Do you think they are okay?" I asked our driver, Dario, for the hundredth time.

The poor guy was trapped in the car with me and Cara. I bombarded him with questions and couldn't stop talking. Surprisingly, he remained friendly and showed no signs of annoyance. He kept reassuring me that no one had been harmed, and everyone was safe. But his words failed to provide the comfort I had hoped for.

"Althaia, please shut up and leave Dario alone. He said they are okay, so hush!" Cara scolded and I clamped my mouth shut.

I kept checking my phone to see if I had gotten any messages. I texted Michael a while ago to see if he had heard from my father, but I still had no reply. I sighed and leaned back in the seat, staring out the window, hoping to distract my mind. Then my phone finally buzzed in my hand.

Michael: *I just talked to him,*
and he told me what happened.
Shit, Althaia, are you okay?

I breathed out a sigh of relief and texted him back.

Althaia: *Thank God!*
Yes, we're okay and safe.
We are on our way to the Bellavias'.

Michael: *Okay, stay safe.*

I smiled, my shoulders sagging in relief.

"See, we told you they are okay. Keep in mind, they know what they are doing. It's not the first time something like this has happened." Cara tried to reassure me while playing a game on her phone.

If there was one thing I admired about Cara, it was how quickly she could recover from literally anything. If you looked at her now, you wouldn't know that she had just been in the middle of a drive-by shooting.

"Well, sorry for worrying. It's not exactly an everyday thing for me." I said sarcastically.

"Right." She looked up from her phone with a teasing smile. "Or is it someone in particular you're worried about?" She wiggled her brows at me. I rolled my eyes, ignoring her, and looked out the window, feeling my cheeks heating slightly because she was right.

"Holy shit." Cara suddenly erupted, and I turned to see her fixated on something. I moved to the middle of the seat to see what had caught her eye, and my eyes widened at the sight in front of me.

At the very end of the road stood the biggest house I had ever seen—it might as well be a freaking castle! I glanced at Cara; her mouth was slightly ajar, and her eyes were wide with awe.

"I guess getting married is suddenly not so bad if it means I will stay in that." We burst out laughing at her comment, and I even saw Dario crack a little smile.

The car slowed down as we neared the enormous gates of the manor. As we drove into the grand, circular driveway, I looked in awe at the imperial sight of a large granite fountain with water cascading from the mouths of two towering lions.

I stepped out and was captivated by the vibrant colors of the scenery. The lawn and trees were a stunning shade of green, and the petals of the flowers were beautiful bright colors.

Cara and I looked at each other as our jaws dropped to the ground once more.

"If this is my new home, you're moving in with me." Cara said, completely stunned by the size of the manor.

"Deal." I agreed immediately.

"Or, you know, get married. I'm pretty sure my man has a single brother if you're interested." She grinned.

"I'm not." I scowled.

"Mhm, sure, babe." She replied with a cheeky wink, making my cheeks flush. "So, it's just the fingers you're interested in then?"

"Shut up." I gave her a quick whack on the arm to stop her from teasing me, just as we were approached by what appeared to be the housekeepers of the manor.

"Hello, and welcome! My name is Rosana, and this is my daughter, Sofia." Rosana welcomed us and gave us a warm smile, which we returned as we introduced ourselves.

Rosana was an older lady and kept a warm smile on her lips. Sofia didn't say much, but she was beautiful with her baby blue eyes.

"Let's get you two settled in, shall we? The men will bring your bags." Rosana said, and we followed her inside.

"Wow..." Cara and I said at the same time as we looked around.

The inside was even more majestic, with the two-way curved grand staircase with a black iron railing carved in a unique pattern. The biggest crystal chandelier I had ever seen in my life hung right in the middle, right above a black marbled round table in the foyer, decorated with a large black crystal vase with colorful flowers.

We headed upstairs and continued down one hallway until we came to a halt.

"This is where you will stay, Cara." Rosana opened the door, and we peeked in. The bedroom was ridiculously big and could easily be mistaken for an apartment.

"Althaia, you will stay just right down the other hallway."

"Oh, I thought we would stay in the same room?" I asked.

"Mr. Lorenzo ordered Cara to stay in this room. If you would please follow me, we will get to your room now."

I gave Cara a quick wave as I followed Rosana down to the other hallway.

My bedroom was just as large as Cara's. It even had its own lounge area with a gorgeous hand-carved fireplace. I whistled in my mind. How was I ever going to leave this place?

"Dinner will be ready in a few hours. I hope you'll have a comfortable stay." Rosana and Sofia smiled as my bags were placed inside the room.

"Thank you!"

Once the door closed, I couldn't resist doing a small spin to take in the room. A wide grin spread across my face as my eyes fell on the enormous bed. Unable to contain my excitement, I belly-flopped right onto the plush mattress.

"Feels like a cloud." I sighed in bliss. It practically sucked me in, and the silk sheets made it feel like heaven.

I closed my eyes, almost giving in to the urge to take a nap before I forced myself off the bed to explore the rest of the manor.

"How can one have this much money?" I murmured in awe when I opened the ensuite bathroom.

Everything was in a glossy beige marble design, with a bathtub and separate shower. There was even a mini chandelier hanging from the ceiling, and this time, I whistled out loudly.

I should ask if he's hiring.

I snickered at my own joke as I explored the rest of the bedroom and finally went to the double doors that led right out to a balcony to watch the sunset.

The view had me gasping.

There was a grand staircase that led right down to a swimming pool, with sprinklers shooting water high into the air. Beyond the pool, there stood a two-winged staircase, leading down to a beautiful garden filled with huge trees and flowers of all colors, creating a scene that belonged only in a fantasy world.

What left me even more in awe was how the two-winged staircase gracefully curved around a waterfall, its water glistening as the sun slowly set.

With such a breathtaking view, I was sure these people were secretly royals.

I reached for my satin nightgown and started the shower while tying my hair into a bun. A blissful sigh escaped me as the hot water slowly melted away the tension. Even though we escaped unharmed, I couldn't shake the anxiety of being shot at for the first time in my life.

It left me wondering how these people were so immune to it that they could go on with their lives like it was nothing.

With a sigh, I finished showering and untied my hair as I opened the door and turned off the lights, but immediately stilled when I saw a dark figure sitting in the armchair.

It was Damiano.

Damiano's intense eyes locked onto me, tracing my every step with an unwavering gaze, leaving me breathless in the magnetic pull of his captivating presence.

"You're okay." I said in relief. I didn't want to admit it to Cara, but I had been worried sick about Damiano.

He risked his life for me.

Damiano remained silent, his expression unreadable, as he extended his hand for me. Without giving it a single thought, I went to him and placed my hand in his. A small gasp escaped me when he deftly pulled me onto his lap, positioning me in a straddle. My hands instinctively found their place on his shoulders, steadying myself from the sudden move.

"How are you?" He asked, and my body tingled when he caressed me.

"I should be the one asking you. You're the one who acted like a bulletproof vest for me." I chuckled. He let out a genuine smile, and my breath quickly caught in my throat. It was a rare, beautiful sight that had my stomach fluttering uncontrollably.

My body acted on its own and I placed my hand on his cheek, caressing him with my thumb. I couldn't understand why I was feeling like this with him. He was a sinisterly dangerous man. I have witnessed that. It should be more than enough for me to leave and never return.

But the way he was making my heart beat faster whenever I thought of him, and the way he was making my entire body tingle just with his presence, gave me a hard time trying to think straight at all.

Damiano frowned when his eyes landed on the cut on my cheek.

"I'm okay. It doesn't hurt that much anymore." I reassured him. He cupped my face, his thumb softly traced over it.

"I should have put a bullet in his head." Damiano's eyes hardened, and his other hand tightened on my hip.

"Hmm, I did wish for him to get shot." I chuckled.

"Do you want me to?"

"Sure, why not?" I shrugged.

He moved to get up, and my eyes widened.

"Wait, no!" I quickly pushed him back into the chair. "I was only joking! Calm down, Mafia Boss."

He raised his brow at me, and I slightly blushed at the intensity of his stare.

"You can't shoot him." I told him.

"Why not?" A crease appeared between his brows. I looked at him in shock, trying to see if he was joking.

He wasn't.

"Because it's not... appropriate?" I trailed off, lacking a better word to use in this context.

He looked at me with a slightly amused expression. His hands were gentle as they went to my waist and he pulled me to him, melding my body to his.

"Tell me, Althaia..." He said slowly. My heart raced at how close our faces were, and the way his hands continued to caress my body. "What would be appropriate, then? Should I cut his face? Plunge a knife into the hand that touched you?"

"No!" I gaped. "Violence should not be the answer. Karma will get him eventually."

Damiano smiled and let out a small chuckle.

"You beautiful, purehearted woman." His eyes softened, and my breath hitched as I became completely hypnotized by him.

The way he smiled so beautifully and looked at me made me almost melt entirely into his body. It shouldn't feel this right to be in his arms. And I sure as hell shouldn't feel safe in his arms. But I did.

How was this man so deadly, yet so gentle with me?

I slowly wrapped my arms around his neck, playing with the back of his hair as we sat in a comfortable silence. Damiano closed his eyes for a brief second, relaxing under my touch as he caressed my bare thighs. They were slowly traveling up and down, each time going up higher and sending a steady pulse between my legs.

"It's late. You should sleep." He said after a while but didn't make a move to leave.

"I'm not tired." I wasn't ready to let him go. I wanted him to stay with me just a moment longer.

"Then let me help you get there." His voice went low as his hands slowly went under my nightgown. "Fuck, Althaia..." Damiano let out a small grunt and buried his face into my neck when he felt I wasn't wearing any underwear.

He plastered faint kisses on my neck, sending a shudder right through me as he slowly played with my pussy.

I moaned.

I wanted to be embarrassed by how wet I was when his finger slid inside of me, but I was feeling too good to care about it. I bit down on my lip to hold back my moans when he worked another finger inside of me and played with my clit with his thumb.

Damiano leaned back to look at me and pulled my lip from between my teeth.

"Let me hear you." His voice was husky, eyes locked on my lips as he fucked me with his fingers and circled his thumb on my clit faster. The waves of pleasure were too much for me to be quiet.

"Ah... Damiano..." I moaned as that tightening feeling of an orgasm was nearing.

"Fuck!" He suddenly stood up with my legs wrapped around him, his hands gripping my ass tightly until I was on my back on the bed.

Damiano's eyes lingered on me, slowly tracing the curves of my body with his hands as he pulled the straps of my nightgown down.

My chest rose and fell as my heart beat frantically as he admired my exposed breasts.

"Perfect..." He murmured, almost to himself.

I tried to calm down my breathing and placed my hands on his chest, slowly trailing down to his pants. They didn't get far as Damiano grabbed my wrists in one hand and pulled them above my head.

"It's already hard enough for me. If you touch me, I won't be able to hold back. I will lose control." He growled, but that only made my pussy pulse with need.

"Then lose control." My voice was barely a whisper.

"You don't know what you're asking for." His voice was strained, his hold tightening on my wrists as his eyes filled with lust.

"I do." I didn't, but fuck, I was desperate for any kind of relief.

"You don't." He said and trailed a finger from my collarbone and down to my breasts before pinching a nipple between his fingers. My back arched as I moaned at the feeling, a cocktail of pain and pleasure. "Because once my cock is inside of you, there is no going back for you."

"Fuck... Damiano!" I whimpered.

His words were not helping at all. The throbbing in my pussy was getting too much. I desperately tried to squeeze my legs together for some friction, but with him firmly wedged between them, I was completely blocked.

A dark, twisted smirk crossed his face in response to my actions.

"Oh, God!" I cried out when his fingers finally returned to my aching pussy, his thumb adding pressure to my throbbing clit.

"Damiano." He growled as he went faster, curling his fingers. "Only my name will leave your mouth." He grunted and sealed my lips with his, swallowing my cries as he sent me closer to the edge.

His lips trailed down from my lips to my breasts, taking my nipple into his mouth he sucked hungrily. An electric jolt surged through me, having my eyes rolling to the back of my head.

"Come. Give it to me." Damiano demanded as he sucked on my skin.

My back arched in pleasure, my breathing heavy, and my legs trembled as he fucked me faster with his fingers. He hit a spot that made me gasp before crying out in pleasure as my entire body shook at the powerful orgasm that rippled through me.

My eyes closed, unable to keep them open at the intense feeling that kept coursing through me. Damiano softly continued to kiss my neck, slowing down before pulling his fingers out as I tried to calm down my breathing.

I felt movement on the bed as my straps were put back in place before a blanket was pulled over me. His lips brushed against mine ever so softly, and I opened my eyes for just a moment to catch a glimpse of his face.

"Goodnight, Althaia." His voice was rough as he lightly caressed my cheek before walking out.

"My God, how much can you sleep? Wake up! We have stuff to do." Cara barged into my room.

Every single morning, she would barge into my room to wake me up at the crack of dawn. And every single morning I would imagine crushing her skull against the wall.

"Fuck off, Cara." I groaned in annoyance. I was not and will not ever be a morning person.

I felt the warmth of the sun as it hit my face, and I opened one eye to see Cara had opened the curtains. I groaned again and rolled over in my bed.

"You're such a child. Get up!" She ripped the blanket from my body. Another thing Cara liked to do to me.

"Give me a damn minute!" I huffed, and I sat up on the bed, rubbing my tired eyes.

Cara suddenly went silent, and I opened my eyes to see if she had magically died. She stood at the end of the bed, her eyes fixated on my breasts.

"What a fucking creep you are." I scoffed and her eyes snapped to mine.

"What the hell is on your neck and chest?"

"What do you mean?"

"You're covered in hickeys!"

My hand went up to my neck and my eyes widened. I quickly leapt out of my bed and made my way to the bathroom with Cara hot on my trail. I looked in the mirror and I gasped in horror.

Red marks were covering my neck and breasts.

"Oh, I wonder who gave you these marks." Cara started with a mischievous smirk.

"How am I supposed to cover all this?" I stared at her in shock.

"You're not."

"What do you mean I'm not?" I asked. The thought of walking around like this made me wish the ground would open up and swallow me whole.

"He's an Alpha male, Thaia. It's his way of showing that you are off-limits." She shrugged.

What the fuck? How is that even a thing?

"Yeah, no thank you. I'm covering this up." I grabbed my makeup bag and used *a lot* of foundation to cover the hickeys. It looked like a leech had attacked me!

"So, tell me, did you fuck this time?" Cara grinned, being nosy as ever.

"No." I muttered as I focused on covering my neck.

"Then what? Because damn! He obviously knew what he was doing." She laughed, and I just shook my head, not finding it funny at the moment. "Come on, don't be such a prude and tell me." She continued. I sighed.

"He just came to check on me." I mumbled, feeling my cheeks heat at the thought of how he touched me, and, well, *sucked* me.

"Oh, he checked up on you good. I bet he relieved some pleasant tension with his fingers." She snickered.

"Fuck off." I threw my makeup brush at her when she continued to tease me.

Fifteen

ALTHAIA

Planning a wedding was absolutely no joke. I had already spent enough hours looking at materials, colors, and flowers to leave me on the brink of insanity.

"You owe me big time after this." I told her as I looked at the color samples.

"Sure, babes, I will have Damiano ready with his fingers." She smirked.

Let me just say, I screamed in complete mortification, as we were not alone, and a few cleared their throats in awkwardness.

Two weeks has already gone by since we were welcomed into the manor, and it has also been two weeks since I last saw *him*. Not that I was counting the days, and especially not because I was thinking about him every damn minute.

Okay, so what if I was thinking about him? Not only did he save my life, but that man gave me some of the best orgasms with *just* his fingers. But seriously, who just comes to your room, pleasures you, and then disappears into thin air?

The Devil, obviously.

I scoffed.

I was apparently crazy enough to let him touch me without giving it a single thought. Now, he was nowhere to be found for a week, and I didn't know what that meant.

I let out a sigh as I walked down the stairs, but halted when I noticed a bunch of people rushing back and forth, carrying flowers, tablecloths, vases, and all kinds of decorative stuff.

"Rosana, what is all this fuss about?" I asked when I spotted her walking towards the stairs, carrying blankets in her arms.

"A party is being held tomorrow in the garden." She said cheerfully.

"A party? For what occasion?"

"For Mr. Lorenzo and Miss Cara."

Jesus, how many parties are they supposed to have?

"I guess I will need a dress, then." I sighed again. Now I had to think about that, too.

"It's mostly family and friends attending. I wouldn't worry too much about it." She smiled before walking off.

I continued my way into the kitchen to grab a bottle of water, already feeling exhausted at the thought of mingling with people I didn't know for hours. Was it really necessary to have yet another party? I mean, yes, I did ruin their engagement party, but how was I supposed to know that I was supposed to be dead, and not show up? And the dinner party was my uncle's fault. Hence, why he no longer has his tongue.

The thought of that made me smile.

"Ah, Dario! I was wondering if you could give me a ride. I need a dress for tomorrow's party." I asked with a bright smile when I spotted him. He was the only one I dared to ask, since the other men I have seen roaming around intimidated me too much. Besides, Dario seemed pretty chill.

"Sorry, no one is allowed outside the manor." He gave me a small, apologetic smile.

"Why is no one allowed outside?"

"Boss's order."

"Why?" I raised my brows in surprise.

"Can't say." He shot me a look, saying I should know not to ask.

"Well, this is an emergency. Would you rather have me walk around naked instead?" I was exaggerating, but if it got me out to a boutique, then I didn't mind pulling that trick.

Dario looked uncomfortable as he cleared his throat.

"I'm sorry, but an order is an order. I can't let anyone out. Especially you."

"What have I done to be grounded?" I asked, completely taken aback. Hell, I was twenty-four, no one *could* ground me.

Unless it was my mother and her wooden spoon. She would probably still use that on me even when I'm sixty.

"Miss, I can't tell you. I don't ask questions and just follow orders." Dario tried to explain to me once again.

"What a dickhead..." I muttered under my breath. Not low enough though, because Dario's eyes widened at the comment. "Then call your Boss."

"Miss, I really can't do that." He shook his head, having me cross my arms.

"It's Althaia." I corrected him.

"... Althaia, I can't do that."

"Why not?"

"He specifically gave orders not to interrupt him unless it's a life-or-death situation."

"Well, where is he?" I asked. Dario stared at me blankly, obviously done with this conversation. "Please?"

"He would really have my head if I told anyone."

I almost gave up, but then a genius idea popped into my head.

"Then give me his number and I will talk to him." Dario shook his head once again. "I won't leave you alone until you give me his number. And trust me, I can be even more annoying if I want to be." I gave him an 'it will be your hell,' look.

Dario sighed.

"Fine. But you didn't get this from me." He gave in, already wanting to get rid of me.

"Thank you, Dario!" I gave him a big hug, startling him with my actions. "I like you. You're a good one." I grinned.

"Don't say that. You will get me killed..." He muttered and hurried off.

I stared at his retreating form, confused for a split second, but then shrugged it off and made my way to my room.

I wasn't entirely sure what I was supposed to say to Damiano, but it was too late to back out anyway because I had already dialed the number and it was ringing.

I took a seat on the bed as it kept ringing. I let out a frustrated groan, about to hang up, when finally, he answered the call.

"Althaia."

I shivered at the sound of his voice. It really has been too long since I last heard his voice.

"How did you know it was me?"

"What's wrong?" Damiano asked firmly, almost concerned.

"Oh... erm, nothing. Well, I need to buy a dress for tomorrow, so I have to go out." It sounded more like a question than a statement.

"No." He replied immediately.

"What do you mean no?" I frowned.

"I said what I said. You're not leaving the manor."

"Why am I being locked in? I need a dress for tomorrow." I argued.

"I will have someone get you one."

"Thank you, but no. I want to go out and find one for myself."

"No, Althaia." He growled as a final order, and I let out a noise of frustration.

"Why the hell not?"

"Damiano, who are you talking to?"

I stilled when I heard a woman's voice in the background.

"No one." He replied.

I hung up and stared at my phone for a long time, just blinking at it.

Don't care about it. There wasn't anything between us anyway.

I kept telling myself that, but something in my heart tightened.

What a fucking dick!

Did he really think he could just come and touch me, and then go fuck someone else? My fist tightened around my phone as my blood boiled.

I took a deep breath to calm down and went to Cara's room. I barged in, but the only thing I saw was an empty bed. I heard the shower running and made my way there.

"Can you believe that bastard?!" I almost shouted. Cara let out a scream when I practically kicked the door open.

"Could you at least knock?! What if I was shaving?"

"Sorry. Back to my problem." I said dismissively, and she poked her head out of the shower to look at me. "I talked to the Devil."

"What Devil?"

"That Devil, Damiano."

"Ah. Why? Miss him?" She winked, but I only scowled.

"Fuck no. I wanted to go out to get a dress for the party, which you didn't tell me about." Now I was frowning at her for not even giving me a heads up.

"I told you about the party tomorrow, but you were zoning out. It's not my fault you decided not to listen." Cara rolled her eyes at me. "But what about Damiano?" She asked.

"I was on the phone with him, going back and forth about letting me go out. And then, I heard a woman's voice in the background." I explained.

Cara's mouth went slightly ajar at the information.

"What if it's the TV or something?"

"Nope. She said his name and asked who he was talking to. He said 'no one', and I hung up."

Cara sighed and looked at me sadly.

"Thaia, I hate to break it to you, but it's common for a man like him to have... affairs. Especially in his position, they usually have multiple women..." She trailed off.

I looked away as my heart clenched at her words. I couldn't look at her as I felt so fucking stupid at the moment. Of course, he would have several women. He was a Mafia Boss for crying out loud. Why did I even think he didn't just because he gave me a little attention?

"So, I'm just a side hoe then. Got it. Thanks." I jumped up and made my way out.

"Althaia, I'm sorry." She apologized, her voice laced with guilt.

"For what? I'm the one who's naïve and stupid." I gave her a forced smile and walked out.

I locked myself in my room for the rest of the day and cuddled my pillow in bed. I felt so stupid thinking that he might actually have cared for me a little. Maybe his actions toward me had me confused, or I was just delusional. It was not like I even knew him. I shouldn't care.

At some point, Cara came to get me for dinner, but I pretended to be asleep. She knew I wasn't but respected my wish to be alone.

I didn't sleep a wink at all, and it was now almost time for the party. My mind kept wandering to the golden-brown-eyed Devil, and then I felt even more stupid all over again when it hurt just thinking about him.

I huffed and dragged myself out of bed to take a shower, hoping it would help wake me up and refresh me a little. After finishing, I wrapped a robe around my body, and just in time, there was a knock on my door. I opened it, finding Rosana holding a gown bag.

"This was sent for you." She smiled as she walked past me and hung it up.

"Oh, I didn't ask for it..."

"Mr. Damiano wishes for you to wear it tonight."

A dress for the side hoe, how thoughtful of him.

"Thanks." I returned her smile. I wanted to say she could go ahead and burn it because I won't be wearing it, but it wasn't the poor woman's fault, and I shouldn't give her a hard time about it.

I ignored the dress and went through my clothes to see what I could pull together. After almost giving up, I found a dress that I had completely forgotten I had packed and was perfect for an outdoor party.

It was a black maxi dress with a halter neck. It had a twist in the middle that showcased my midriff, but the best part was the daringly high slit starting from the hip.

It was a revealing dress, and I had to be careful how I moved if I wanted to avoid flashing people. I had packed this one in case we decided to have a night out, but I guess a garden party would do.

I finished the look with my favorite pair of Louboutin.

Pleased with my makeup and outfit, I made my way out, but stopped when I saw the gown bag.

"He can wear that stupid dress."

And I kicked it.

Childish, but it made me smile.

I walked down the last steps to the garden and looked at the scenery in front of me. It was set up beautifully, but then again, this manor was out of this world, and I wouldn't have expected anything less.

The garden was filled with round tables, each adorned with colorful flowers and large candles that cast a gentle glow. The small torches on the ground created a mesmerizing pattern as their orange and yellow flames danced in the air. Servers walked around, smiling and offering chilled champagne to the arriving guests.

I grabbed a glass of champagne, giving a small smile to the guests, and went to find a secluded area in the back. I wanted to be a quiet presence and be there as moral support for Cara.

I felt an emptiness in my chest, along with a lingering sense of hurt. I wished Michael were here. I missed that goofy blue-eyed man terribly. He could always put me in a better mood.

"You're looking a little sour tonight, aren't you?"

I looked up and met a man with short, light brown hair and deep brown eyes. His jawline was sharply defined with a little stubble.

I was so lost in my thoughts that I didn't even hear the approaching footsteps. Surprisingly, he was rather cute.

"I'm not looking sour. I just suffer from resting bitch face syndrome."

He threw his head back and laughed at my answer.

"I see. I'm Raffaele." He extended his hand for a handshake. "But you, beautiful, can call me Daddy if you like." He said with a smug grin.

"Ew." I rolled my eyes at him but cracked a small smile.

"Your response pierces me." He brought his hand to his chest and feigned a pained expression before laughing. "And what is your name, beautiful?"

"Althaia." I smiled.

"So, you're the infamous Althaia." He raised his brows in realization.

"What do you mean?"

"Ah, word spread around like wildfire. Dead, but not dead." He said casually.

"Something like that..." I muttered. I guess I wasn't going to hear the end of that anytime soon.

The loud chatter of the party abruptly stopped as the people around us glanced up at the stairs. I followed their gaze and saw Cara and Lorenzo making their way downstairs. Lorenzo wore a sleek, all-black suit, while Cara was in a gorgeous, flowy light blue dress. She looked like a princess with the way the sequins on her dress caught the light and made her dress sparkle.

They were truly a sight to die for as they descended the stairs like a royal couple.

I made the mistake and looked to the other staircase, and my heart clenched at the sight. Damiano was walking down the step with a woman at his side, clinging to his arm. She was breathtaking, her caramel-hued hair flowing elegantly around her face, framing features that radiated pure beauty.

I shifted my eyes, not wanting to witness what I saw. Hell, even I would leave me for her. I quickly gulped down the last of my champagne, the bubbles tickling my throat before I made my way towards the bar.

I needed something stronger.

"Two shots of vodka, please." I requested the bartender. Maybe if I got drunk, I could turn in early and not have to see Damiano with someone else.

"Same for me!" Raffaele said cheerfully as he stood next to me.

I snatched a shot and quickly downed it. I looked over at Raffaele, and we both had a similar expression of revulsion on our faces.

"The first one is always the toughest." I laughed.

"Woo! It sure is." He shuddered in disgust.

"Ready?" I grabbed the next one. We grinned, clinking our shot glasses before we downed all the alcohol in one gulp.

"Now it's a party! What's next?" He rubbed his hands together.

"Maybe some water for now." I laughed at his excitement. It was still a bit too early for me to get shitfaced drunk.

"We'll do whatever you want, beautiful." He grinned, making me laugh at his flirtations.

Raffaele was fun to talk to as he continued to crack jokes. Most of them were inappropriate, but he was funny, and I was enjoying myself.

I looked over his shoulder, seeing Damiano talking to that woman. I wondered what she was to him, a wife or a fiancée. She must be someone important to him since people recognized her with no introduction. Men like him might have several affairs, but he wouldn't show up at his brother's party with a side piece. I knew that for a fact.

I glared daggers when she placed a hand on his shoulder, and he was listening to whatever she had to say. I never knew I was the jealous type, never had a reason to be. Until this moment.

Damiano suddenly spun his head and locked eyes with me. A bolt of electricity shot through me, and I quickly glanced away, trying to keep up the conversation with Raffaele with a smile on my face.

"We should find our seats. Dinner is being served." He held out his arm for me to take, and I wrapped my hand around it as he led the way.

We moved together towards the table where Cara, Lorenzo, Damiano, and that woman were seated. I looked around to find another table as I didn't want to be near him. But it was too late when Raffaele pulled out a chair for me to sit right next to... her.

Still, I thanked him with a smile as I sat, crossing my legs and leaving my entire bare leg exposed on top of the other. Raffaele was unabashed as he stared at my leg, taking his time and not making any effort to be subtle.

"That is... a *very* nice dress you're wearing." His eyes were still fixated on my leg as he scooted his chair closer to me. I usually tried to be more careful not to show too much, but tonight, I felt like being reckless.

"Thank you, Raffaele." I gave him a flirtatious smile and placed my hand on his bicep. "Oh wow, impressive." I complimented him. He flexed and winked at me, making me chuckle.

I glanced over to Cara, who had her eyes darting between me and Raffaele, sending me a silent message that Damiano was here too. I picked up a glass of champagne and smiled behind it before taking a sip.

I can play this game too.

"Woman, you need to eat before you get drunk." Raffaele chuckled.

"You don't need to worry about me. I know what I'm doing." I patted his thigh in reassurance. "Wow! You must really spend a lot of time working out." I said in awe as I lingered my hand on his leg.

"You bet I do, baby." He grinned. I giggled and continued to flirt with him as he gave me his undivided attention.

I ate my food while everyone else chatted around the table. I tried to act as though I didn't care, but I couldn't ignore the ache in my chest as Damiano and that woman talked. I felt more and more sulky about it.

I leaned back in my seat and glanced over at another table, feeling the weight of someone's eyes on me. Two women were whispering to each other while staring at me.

I flashed them a sweet smile, then dropped my expression as I flipped them off. They rolled their eyes before looking away. Seriously, what the hell was their problem? I was literally minding my own business.

My eyes grew in size when I noticed Lorenzo's intense gaze on me with a tilt to the side of his head. I slowly lowered my hand when I realized it looked like I was flipping *him* off, and not *them.*

That woman beside me erupted in laughter, and I could feel my face growing hot with embarrassment.

"I like her." She chuckled.

Well, I don't like you.

"She's a wild one, Arianna." Raffaele commented.

"Let's get another shot." I said to Raffaele as I stood up. I didn't want to be near her anymore.

"I don't think you should drink anymore." He quickly steadied me with an amused look when I wobbled on my feet.

"It's a party. I'm having fun!" I replied, then grinned when the music started to play loudly. "Let's dance!" I grabbed his hand and led him to a cleared area where we could dance.

Raffaele placed his hands on my hips and moved me into his pelvis until I felt the warmth of his body against my back as we danced. He twirled me to face him, and I wrapped my arms around his neck, our bodies intimately pressed against each other. And I hoped the Devil was watching.

Raffaele looked behind me with a sly smirk before grabbing my leg with the high slit up to his hip and dipped me low.

"Oh shit, that got me dizzy." I laughed when he pulled me up again. I let out a shocked noise when I was suddenly ripped out of Raffaele's arms.

Damiano grabbed him by the collar and punched him in the face and kept punching until he fell to the ground.

The music stopped, and shocked whispers filled the air.

"What the hell is wrong with you?" I yelled at Damiano and looked at a groaning Raffaele on the ground.

Damiano turned to face me, and a wave of nervousness washed over me as he gave me a look that said I should start praying for my life. His eyes were shaded with darkness, his jaw tightly clenched, and I couldn't help but feel like I was the next target on his kill list.

He stalked towards me and forcefully pulled me away from the party. I yanked myself out of his grip, but before I could even glance back to check on Raffaele, Damiano threw me over his shoulder.

"Are you insane? Put me down!" I banged my fists against his back.

Then a shocked yelp escaped my lips.

"Did you just slap my ass?!"

"Yes, and I will fucking do it again." He growled, and I felt another sharp sting on my ass.

He continued to ignore my yelling and walked at an inhuman speed as I tried to get him to put me down.

"I'm going to be sick..." I mumbled when I started to get dizzy.

Damiano kicked a door open and plopped me down on a desk. He rested both of his hands on the desk on either side of me, caging me in. I gulped as I looked at his furious expression.

"What the *fuck* is wrong with you?" He hissed lowly. I crossed my arms and faced away from him. It looked like we were in his office. "Look at me when I talk to you." He ordered firmly, but still gently cupped my chin to face him.

I glared at him.

"Me? I should be the one asking you!" My frustrations with him finally exploded.

"What are you talking about?" His eyes narrowed and his voice was still deadly low, but I didn't give a fuck anymore.

"You think you can just come into my room, mark my freaking body, and then just disappear for God knows how long? Not to mention showing up with another woman!"

"What woman?" He questioned. I clenched my jaw and shook my head at him for playing dumb.

"Just let me go." I tried to move away, but he kept me caged between his arms.

"What *woman*?" He pressed on again.

"That woman... *Arianna*." I spat out her name.

Damiano went silent and kept looking at me for a while. He then sighed and leaned back a bit.

"You're letting another man touch you because you think I'm with her?"

"I'm not fucking dumb." I crossed my arms.

"Don't *ever* let another man touch you." He snarled, leaning closer to me, warning me to not defy his order. I leaned in as well as I kept a fierce glare on him.

"Good thing I can do whatever I want. Just like *you*." I gave a sarcastic smile as I poked his chest with my finger.

Damiano clicked his tongue in annoyance as he kept looking at me.

"She's my sister."

I blinked.

Then I burst out in laughter.

"That's like the oldest excuse in the book." I wiped the tears from my eyes as I continued to chuckle. "You didn't strike me as the type of person with a sense of humor, but that joke was really good."

A crease formed between his brows as he looked at me, likely trying to figure out if I had lost my mind.

I probably had.

My laughter died down when I heard faint voices outside the office.

"... I told you not to do it." Arianna sighed as she opened the door with Raffaele behind her. He was rubbing his jaw with a scrunched-up face.

Damiano turned his attention towards them, and I quickly jumped down from the desk to create some space between us.

"I wanted to see how pissed I could get him. Yo, Damiano! Did you have to go for the face?!" Raffaele erupted.

I took a moment to really look at Arianna, and that was when I could see the resemblance between them. They had the same golden-brown eyes and the same nose. She even has some of Lorenzo's features; a literal mixture of them both, but I had been too caught up in my jealousy to see it.

Oh, fuck me already.

Sixteen

ALTHAIA

Arianna rolled her eyes in Raffaele's direction before casting a disapproving glance at Damiano.

"Damiano, did you really have to punch him in front of all those people?"

"He's lucky he's even alive." Damiano calmly replied.

"Is this how you welcome your cousin into your home?" Raffaele huffed out, and my eyes slowly widened.

"So... you're all... related...?" I pointed at each one of them.

"We sure are, gorgeous." Raffaele winked, which earned him a punch in the stomach from Damiano.

"Raffaele, shut up! And Damiano, stop hitting him." Arianna sighed in annoyance.

"Don't worry, I can take it." Raffaele wheezed out with his hands on his knees as he tried to compose himself.

"You're not together...?" I looked back and forth between the two of them, and the more I kept looking at them, the more I could see they were related.

"That would be incest, love." Raffaele straightened up. Arianna was quick and hit Raffaele in the head, sending his head flying forward before Damiano could get to him.

"I knew I shouldn't have let you come with us. Be quiet before I rip your tongue out." She threatened. Was this a thing with this family, ripping out someone's tongue?

"God, just let me die now." I groaned in pure embarrassment, hiding my face in my hands.

Arianna came up to me, her face lit up with a smile, and placed a friendly hand on my shoulder.

"I'm sorry. This was not how it was supposed to go. Damiano is just very private and doesn't share much. When he was on the phone, we heard a woman's voice, but he wouldn't tell us anything. Asshole over there, Raffaele, thought it would be a good idea to flirt with every woman present to see if he could get a reaction out of my brother."

"Totally worth it." Raffaele grinned.

"You're lucky he didn't kill you." Arianna shot back.

"Honestly, for a second there, I actually thought he would." He laughed, completely unbothered. Arianna shook her head and faced me again.

"I'm sorry for all this fuss. I'm Arianna, Damiano's and Lorenzo's younger sister."

"I can see that now... I'm Althaia." I gave her a small smile. My body was so hot from embarrassment.

"We'll have a chat later, I really want to get back to the party. Let's go, you idiot." She quickly walked over to Raffaele and dragged him by the arm out of the office while he complained about being abused today.

I glanced around the office, avoiding eye contact with Damiano. How could I ever face him after the way I had acted? I wish I could disappear into thin air.

"Come here." Damiano sat down on the couch, and the intensity of his gaze struck me as he looked at me with that blank expression of his.

I slowly walked up to him, my face still red from the embarrassment. He wrapped his arms around me when I was within reach and placed me on his lap.

His intense gaze felt like it was burning into me as he took a strand of my hair and twirled it around his finger. I had to take a deep breath before I could look him in the eyes.

"I - Well, you could have said she was your sister."

"You never asked."

"How was I supposed to ask if she's your sister or someone you're fucking?" I slightly frowned.

"Maybe if you weren't busy letting another man touch you." He shot back with a raised a brow.

"... Whatever." I mumbled.

"You didn't wear the dress I sent." His voice went low, and my body tingled when he faintly brushed his lips against my bare shoulder.

"I was mad..." I admitted quietly.

"I see." Damiano checked out my dress, his eyes stopping on my leg. "This is too much for other men to see." He frowned, placing a hand on my bare thigh.

"That's the point." I grinned and his eyes narrowed.

"You're playing a *dangerous* game with me, Althaia." He shifted me to straddle him and buried his face in my neck. "The only reason I'm holding back is because of you."

I didn't know what he meant by that, and I wasn't sure I wanted to know. Instead, I focused on how his lips faintly touched my skin, and it gave me that fluttering feeling in my stomach.

"Where were you?" I finally asked. Damiano leaned back to look at me.

"Italy."

"Oh, why?"

"Nothing you need to concern yourself with." His smirk was smug, and I responded with a dissatisfied look at his answer.

I wanted to know, but instead, I traced my fingers over the buttons of his dress shirt and noticed black ink behind his white dress shirt.

My curiosity got the best of me, and I couldn't help but unbutton the first ones to have a peek. I could only make out a bit of the top of the tattoo, so I slowly undid every button and opened his shirt.

A hooded skull wearing a crown sat in the middle of his chest, with large angel wings covering the rest of his chest. I trailed my fingers on his tattoo, completely fascinated by it. It was such a beautiful work of art, and the details on the skull and wings were incredible.

I glanced up at Damiano, who was watching me intently with his piercing gaze. I felt a rush of shyness wash over me, and I had to look away.

"We should get back to the others." I tried to get off his lap, suddenly remembering I had left Cara all alone out there. Well, almost. Tank Man was with her, and they seemed to get along well.

"Do you want to?" Damiano stopped me by holding me in place. I was about to answer but was distracted when his hands slowly slid under my dress and played with the string of my thong.

My heart beat faster, my whole body getting that electric feeling the more he touched me. And I was getting excited by it.

With a swift motion, he tore the string, causing a gasp to escape me. Just as quickly, his fingers found their way between my thighs, and slowly stroked the slit of my pussy in back-and-forth motions.

"Tell me, Althaia…" Damiano grunted as he slowly slid a finger inside of me. "Who are you wet for? Me or Raffaele?"

"Huh… what?" I asked, unable to focus as a small moan escaped me.

"Tell me." He demanded, shoving another finger inside of my pussy. I threw my head back when he curled them inside of me while his thumb played with my clit.

His fingers were *thick*, filling me up completely with just two fingers.

"You!" I moaned out, rocking my hips to feel more of him.

"Such a good girl." Damiano praised, his voice heavy with lust, and it sent waves of tingles in the pit of my stomach. "Do you like it when I praise you?"

"Yes... God, yes!" I panted. He wrapped his arm around my hair, yanking my head back.

"Didn't I tell you only my name will leave your mouth?" He sneered and pulled his fingers out.

"Damiano..." I whimpered, trying to grind against his hand to feel those pleasurable waves again.

"Atta girl." His fingers were back inside of me, and I moaned loudly. "Fuck, Althaia!" He growled, swallowing my moans and pumped his fingers faster while he tasted my tongue.

Damiano pulled my lip between his teeth, lightly biting and sucking down to the sensitive part of my throat. His fingers, his lips, and his tongue on my skin had me wanting more.

I wanted all of him, to *feel* all of him, and I think he felt the same when he looked displeased when my dress stopped him from getting to my breasts. Before I could even blink, Damiano grabbed a knife and cut the straps of my dress, watching it fall around my waist as my breasts were exposed to him.

"Really? You ruined my dress!"

"That's the fucking point." He hissed, the dress tearing as he ripped it down. His mouth was on my breast, sucking hard on my nipple before I could even complain about ruining my dress.

My back arched with the way his tongue circled on my nipple, his teeth grazing me before sucking on my nipple hard again. It had my eyes rolling to the back of my head.

Damiano laid me down on the couch, pulled away my thong that he already tore, and used it to tie my wrists together above my head. He hovered over me, studying me with those incredible eyes.

"Look how beautiful you are." He whispered, as if it was to himself while he trailed fingers from my throat, down to my breast as his thumb brushed my nipple in a soft caress.

Damiano straddled my hips, and my loud breathing filled the office as I watched him, wondering in excitement what he was going to do next.

His fingers closed around my neck, and I could hear his zipper being pulled down. I squeezed my thighs together, my pussy throbbing and in need of some kind of relief. Damiano knew what I was doing, and it earned me a devilish smirk.

"If only you knew how many times I've fucked my fist at the thought of you." He hissed between his teeth. It wasn't until then that I noticed his other arm moving. I strained my neck to catch a glimpse, but his hold only grew tighter, not allowing me to see.

"Fucking hell..." He grunted in pleasure. I squeezed my thighs, savoring the moment of watching him moan and hiss with pleasure. Even though I couldn't see, I was still dripping, knowing he was pleasuring himself on top of me.

His eyes went down to my breasts, groaning as he stroked himself to the sight of them. He was breathing heavily, his hand squeezing around my throat as he came with a grunt, and his warm release seeped into my dress.

Damiano gave me a lazy smirk as he tucked himself back, resuming his position between my legs, his fingers immediately sliding up and down my slit.

"Want to be a good girl and come all over my fingers?" He asked, his voice husky as he spoke.

"Yes." I replied eagerly, almost begging him to let me come.

I closed my eyes, shuddering in pleasure when I felt his warm mouth taking in my breast. His fingers slid inside my wet pussy with ease, curling them again while he massaged my clit with his thumb.

I was moaning loudly, clenching around him as my body trembled when I felt myself closing in on that explosive wave of pleasure.

"Damiano..." I panted as he edged me closer and closer with the skills of his fingers. I moved my hips against him, gasping as everything tightened.

I was almost there, ready for the incredible orgasm that I have been waiting for.

Then he stopped.

My eyes snapped open at the sight of Damiano pulling away. Standing at the end of the couch, he buttoned up his dress shirt and shot me a sly smirk.

"Why did you stop?!" I almost yelled in frustration. I was so close, and he left me hanging!

Damiano just tilted his head at me.

"Behave, and I might give you what you want." He spoke in a low tone. My mouth hung open as he headed towards the door.

As he rested his hand on the handle, he turned to look at me, his gaze traveling down to my dress while I struggled to free my wrists.

"Looks like you need to change." He winked and left. My eyes went wide when I realized what he had done.

I got punished by the Devil.

SEVENTEEN

ALTHAIA

I was still frustrated when I made my way back to the party after changing. Not only did I have to use my teeth to untie my wrists, but I also had to hold on to my dress and make a run for it to my room. I was lucky I didn't bump into anyone on my way.

Damiano *really* made sure to ruin my dress by not only cutting it but also cumming all over it. He also left me no choice but to wear the dress he sent. After seeing it, I did regret not taking a peek at it earlier because the dress was stunning; an off-shoulder emerald sequin dress with a sweetheart neckline. It was long and hugged my figure nicely, making it a much more appropriate choice to wear.

Oh, well, I got the reaction I wanted.

The party was in full swing again, and people were dancing, drinking, and chatting with each other, forgetting what had happened earlier.

"What a dress!" Cara checked me out when I reached her and Arianna. Since there had been a slight misunderstanding, there was no reason for me not to get to know her.

She was his sister, after all.

"That is gorgeous! But why did you change?" Arianna asked.

"It got ruined..." I frowned. Yes, I was mad that he ruined my dress, but I was *pissed* that he left me hanging when I was so close.

"How?"

"Your stupid brother cut it." My sour reply was met with laughter from them.

"Well, if you weren't too busy sulking, you might have noticed that every man was eyeing you hungrily, as if you were their next prey." Cara chuckled.

"He almost shot up the whole place." Arianna shook her head in amusement.

"Sorry, I don't know what came over me." I gave an apologetic smile.

"You like him." Cara teased and Arianna joined with a look.

"No." I mentally beat myself up for letting it come out too quickly.

"Tsk, you're not fooling anyone with your jealous ass." Cara raised a brow. I gave her a blank look before mirroring her teasing smile.

"At least I won't be the only one jealous here." I grabbed her shoulders and turned her around to face where Lorenzo was standing with Raffaele and Damiano. The two women I had flipped off earlier had gone up to the group of men; one of them being bold and flirting with Lorenzo.

"Oh, hell no." Cara placed her drink aside and marched right over to her man.

"I wanna see that!" Arianna was entertained by it all, and I chuckled as I followed them.

I let out a small smile when Lorenzo immediately noticed Cara. He wrapped his arm around her waist and pulled her into him. The woman finally received the message that he was a taken man, but looked annoyed as she took a step back.

It made me wonder how one gets the courage to approach Tank Man? One look from him and I would run for my life. Scratch that - *speed walk* as I don't run.

The other woman was happily chatting and flirting with both Raffaele and Damiano. She kept touching Damiano's arm, which triggered something in me. I glared at her hand, imagining I ripped it off and slapped her with it.

I blinked, shocked by my thoughts. When did I become so jealous?

"I see you have finally dressed up and joined the classy side. That dress was slutty, to say the least." She looked me up and down and laughed. I couldn't stand her snobby attitude, especially when she laughed like that, making me want to sneer at her.

"Please, I could walk around naked and still be classier than you." I rolled my eyes at her.

"Honey, don't mistake this for the street corner you work on." She had a smirk on her face as she flipped her hair back.

Did she just call me a prostitute?

"How would you know where I work? Oh, wait! Don't we work for the same pimp? I do recall seeing you on the streets last night..." I trailed off, pretending to think about it. "Ah, yes, it was you! I barely saw you as it was one car after the other you got in and out of. You must have made *a lot* of money that night." I looked impressed as I gestured to the Vera Wang dress she was wearing.

Her smirk disappeared, leaving Raffaele trying not to laugh and choking on his drink. I flashed an innocent smile as Damiano raised a brow and took a sip of his drink.

"Do you have any idea who I am?" She glared at me.

"No, which means you're irrelevant." I shrugged.

"You little –" She hissed and took a step closer to me. She halted when Arianna suddenly stepped in front of her.

"You better be careful with your next words, Zahra." Arianna's voice went low, and her entire demeanor changed into a menacing one. Her voice was so cold that it sent a shiver down my spine.

"She should be careful. She might accidentally get hurt." Zahra spat out.

"If she does, I won't hesitate to cut your throat open. You know better than to fuck with me." Arianna's voice was full of promise. Zahra was smart to keep quiet and took a step back.

I hid my amazement as I saw how Arianna dealt with her. For a split second, I forgot who these people truly were.

"We should go." The other woman, who had tried to flirt with Lorenzo, grabbed Zahra's arm to get away from us. Zahra huffed, but before she turned around to leave, she looked at Damiano with a seductive look.

"Damiano, we should get together soon. I will make our time memorable, like last time." She winked. Zahra shot me one last look, a smirk on her lips, before walking away.

"Who even invited her? I've always hated that bitch." Arianna frowned, still staring at their retreating forms.

"Was she always like that? She is not aging well." Raffaele commented with a slight shake of his head. The whole time, I remained silent and burned a hole in the back of Zahra's head with my glare. I really wanted to gorge her eyes out and force them down her throat.

"Let's go get you a drink to calm down before you do something stupid." Cara whispered to me, and I let her lead me to the bar.

"Why does this taste like water? Did you give me water?" I slammed down the shot glass and squinted my eyes at the bartender.

"Yes, I'm cutting you off. You've had enough."

"It's a party, I'm having fun!"

"I'm just doing my job. Listen, lady, I'm not about to get my head blown off because of you." He turned his back to me before I could even say anything.

Scowling, I spun on the bar stool and looked at the partying people. I was left by myself when Cara went to the bathroom, and I was not in the mood to make small talk with anyone.

Then my eyes landed on Lorenzo heading somewhere, and I hurriedly jumped off the bar stool, barely avoiding a fall.

"Lorenzooo." I giggled as I staggered over to him. My balance was a bit off after the shots I had earlier.

Lorenzo came to a halt when I called out to him, and I couldn't help but continue to giggle.

"Why do you always look so serious? Are you not having fun?" My vision blurred, and I stumbled, unable to hold my balance.

Lorenzo's firm hand steadied me as I stumbled, and I pouted when he didn't answer me.

"Want to know a secret?" I gave him a big smile, leaned into him, stepped on the tip of my toes, and put a hand to the side of my mouth to whisper to him. "In my mind, I call you Tank Man."

I laughed hard as soon as I told him.

"Tank Man, you get it? 'Cause you're all macho-macho." I stretched my arms out wide, trying to mimic his broad build.

"You should stop drinking." He said, not impressed with me.

"So, he speaks!" I gasped dramatically.

"What do you want?" He looked at me impatiently.

"Rude!" I scowled. "Whatever. I'm here to tell you, if you ever, *ever*, hurt my Cara, I. Will. Hunt. You. Down. Mister." I pushed my finger into his chest with every word.

"Really?" He crossed his arms while looking at me with a blank expression.

"Yes! Look at me, I am strong. I work out." I flexed my biceps to show him. I looked at my arms and grimaced when I saw my non-existent muscles.

"Okay, so maybe I don't work out. I mostly eat, but that should count as a workout, right? You know, I reach for the food to get it in my mouth. That's like going back and forth. I should be shredded by now."

"You talk a lot."

"You're so mean." I pouted before a genius idea popped into my mind. "You know what? We should be best friends because you're marrying my best friend. We should all be best friends together!" I couldn't contain my excitement and hugged him tightly with a big smile on my face.

"Althaia." The familiar voice of the Devil spoke, making me turn around to look at him.

"Oh, look who came over, Tank Man. It's il Diavolo." I giggled.

"You're drunk." Damiano pulled me away, and Tank Man left.

"Noo... you made my best friend leave." My voice dripped with sadness as I watched him leave.

"Come, let's get you to bed." Damiano held me gently and led me to the stairs.

"Are you going to do naughty things to me like before? Or are you saving that for Zahra?" I asked as I dragged out her name. Damiano ignored me and ended up carrying me as I kept tripping over my own two feet.

He opened the door to my room and seated me in the armchair, crouching to take off my heels.

"Oh, that feels so good. I think the blood has stopped flowing to my feet." I sighed and curled my toes.

I was ready to crash when Damiano gave me a hand up and unzipped my dress. He helped me out of my dress before leading me to bed. I flopped onto the mattress, closed my eyes, and snuggled into the pillows.

"Do you like her?" I mumbled to him.

"She's not my type." He answered quietly and felt him pull a blanket over my body.

"That's not... an answer." I slurred, tiredly.

"No."

"Who's.. your.. type then?" The room fell silent, and I thought he left. I was almost asleep when I felt fingers brush some of my hair away from my face.

"Goodnight, Althaia."

I woke up with the most pounding headache I have ever experienced in my life, and my mouth was drier than the Sahara.

I sprawled on the bed with my eyes barely open, the bright sunlight streaming through the windows making me regret the champagne and vodka from the night before. Why did anyone let me drink champagne *and* vodka? That combination is fucking deadly.

Yes, I refuse to take responsibility for my own actions when I was suffering this much.

With a groan, I forced myself to the bathroom for a quick shower. Although a bath sounded heavenly, I feared I might never get up again if I indulged.

After my shower, I made my way to the kitchen at a snail's pace, inhaling deeply as the smell of coffee reached me.

"Good morning!" Raffaele shouted in a singing voice, making me wince.

"For the love of God, stop." I groaned, covering my ears.

"Someone had quite a bit to drink yesterday." Arianna commented as she sipped her coffee.

"How are you all fine? I feel like shit." I said, placing my head on the cold surface of the island and sighing in bliss. The chilliness actually helped my headache.

"No shit. I'm surprised you're even alive. You kept taking shot after shot. You are one tiny human, but you sure can drink." Raffaele laughed.

"Ugh... why did I do that to myself?" I groaned.

"You don't remember what happened yesterday?" She gave me an amused look as he handed me a cup of coffee.

"Not really. As long as I didn't do anything too embarrassing, then I think I'm fine not remembering. You know what, even if I did, it's better that I don't remember anything at all."

"Mm-hmm, well, you did become best friends with Tank Man. Or at least tried to."

I had my mug midway, about to drink from it, when I looked at Raffaele.

"Wha- ho–how do you know? What?" I rapidly blinked, trying to figure out if I had heard him right.

"You were yelling at him, calling him Tank Man, and saying something about him being macho-macho." I looked at Arianna, mortified. Suddenly, the entire night came rushing back to me and my eyes widened.

"You've got to be kidding me." I put my head in my hands, trying to hide from the embarrassment. "I really made a fool out of myself last night, didn't I?"

"We had fun watching you. Actually, I think that was the best party I've ever been to in my life." Raffaele laughed.

"What a sad life you have had in your... mind sharing your age?" I asked.

"I'm thirty-five." He winked, and I gaped at him.

"I would have never guessed!"

"Ah, what can I say? I like to take care of myself." He wiggled his brows and flexed his biceps. I gave him a little shake of my head and turned to face Arianna.

"And you?"

"I'm twenty-six like Cara." She smiled.

"Does that make you the oldest of us all?" I looked back at Raffaele.

"Nah, Lorenzo and I are about the same age. Damiano is thirty-eight, though."

I spit out my coffee and coughed violently.

I let an old man touch me!

Arianna kept patting my back while I couldn't stop coughing. I finally calmed down and grabbed a bottle of water that I immediately downed.

"Jesus, calm down, woman. I was only kidding. He's actually forty-two." Raffaele continued with a smug grin.

"Raffaele, shut up. Are you trying to kill her? She just had a coughing fit." She smacked him on the head. He gave a pout and rubbed the back of it.

"Don't listen to him, he plays around too much. He's twenty-eight and so is Lorenzo. Damiano is thirty, not forty-two." She explained.

"Thank God." I let out a breath. I wasn't sure how to feel about it if Damiano was a whole eighteen years older than me.

Arianna let out a chuckle when she saw my relief.

"Is Cara not up yet? She's usually the first one up and loves to drag me out of bed." I asked when I noticed she still hadn't made an appearance.

"We're the only ones who came down for breakfast." Arianna shrugged.

"Payback is a bitch. I'm going to wake her." I smirked.

Every single morning, she would barge into my room and wake me up. Now, for the first time in forever, I had woken up before her and it was time to give her a taste of her own medicine.

I found a new surge of energy and I skipped down the hall to her bedroom, excited to finally disturb her peaceful sleep.

I did an evil snicker in my mind.

I stood in front of her door, and I quietly put my hand on the handle to make sure I wouldn't make any noise. I tried to contain my laugh when I carefully opened the door and tiptoed into her room.

My shoulders sagged in disappointment when I saw her bed was empty.

I heard the shower running, and I figured I might as well scare her a bit since I was already here.

I kicked the door open with a big smile.

"Boo, bitch–" I stopped in my tracks and stood frozen at the doorway.

In front of me was a freshly showered and a very *naked* Lorenzo.

I heard Cara squeal in the background and Lorenzo looked at me, completely unfazed that I had just barged in and continued to dry off.

I opened and closed my mouth like a fish, struggling to find any words as we looked at each other.

Cara said something and I snapped out of it.

"I am so sorry!" I yelled and turned around and ran out of there as fast as I could. By the time I reached the kitchen, I was out of breath, and three pairs of eyes snapped at me as Damiano joined the kitchen gang.

Great. Just great.

His brows furrowed as he took in my wide-eyed flushed expression.

"What's wrong?" Arianna looked behind me to see if someone was chasing me.

"I–Uh, nothing." I said and looked away from them.

"That did not look like nothing." Raffaele commented.

"It's nothing, trust me." I awkwardly laughed as I returned to my seat by the kitchen island.

"Althaia." Damiano gave me a stern look.

Oh well, here goes nothing.

"I saw Lorenzo naked." I blurted.

They said nothing, and I kept my head down, refusing to look at anyone. Then Raffaele burst out laughing. He was laughing so hard that he actually fell from the chair, clutching his stomach as he continued. Even Arianna failed to hide her laugh behind her hand.

"Were you spying on him?" Raffaele asked, still cracking up.

"Ew, no! He was in Cara's bathroom when I tried to scare her."

"They were probably doing it in the shower. Ah, maybe that's what the banging against the wall was in the middle of the night!" He grinned widely.

"Gross." Arianna grimaced in disgust.

"Lorenzo! Had a good time?" Raffaele looked behind me and wiggled his brows. Lorenzo ignored him and I kept my head down, suddenly very interested in the marble design.

"Anyway, I was thinking about spending the day by the pool. Do you want to join, Althaia?" Arianna broke the silence.

"I would love to, but I didn't bring a bathing suit with me."

"Oh, I have tons of new ones! Let's find you one." She said excitedly, and I followed her as she made her way out. I glanced over at Lorenzo, who was leaning against the counter, already studying me with a slightly amused expression.

"I'm really sorry… If it helps, I didn't see anything." I gave a reassuring smile. I wanted to make sure he didn't think of me as a creep who peeped.

Raffaele burst out laughing again.

"Damn, she just called you small!" He screamed with laughter.

My smile fell.

"No! That's not what I meant! I'm sure you're well equipped." My eyes widened in horror, and Raffaele was laughing so hard that he fell on the floor again.

Damiano's eyes slightly narrowed as he tilted his head at me, and Lorenzo just looked at me while sipping his coffee.

"I'm very sorry." And I sped out of there as fast as I could.

Eighteen

Damiano

"You're getting slow." I slammed Raffaele down on the training mat. He sprang to his feet and threw a sidekick towards my head. I blocked his kick, kept hold of his leg, and kicked his other leg as he fell to the floor.

"All right, I'm done." He groaned as he stayed down.

"Your reflexes are slowing down." I told him as I walked over to the bench and grabbed a towel to wipe the sweat off my neck.

Raffaele jumped to his feet, chugged down a bottle of water, and slumped down on the bench.

"I'm gonna blame the booze for losing this round."

"And your excuse last time? You're lazing around." I frowned. He might be my cousin, but he was still on my payroll, and I can't have any of my men slacking. It was not something I tolerated.

"Hey, I was definitely not lazing around with that blonde chick yesterday." He put his arms behind his head and let out a bragging smile.

"Don't fuck anyone important." I warned him.

The number of times I had to get his ass out of situations because he fucked the daughter of someone important to my business. He would play his charm on the ladies, making them think they had a chance with him when he was only after a onetime fuck. There were times when I was almost close to letting them kill him just so he would stop being a pain in my fucking ass.

"Speaking of fucking anyone important..." Raffaele started.

"Don't." I shot him a look, already knowing where he wanted to go with this.

"You don't even know what I was going to say!" He exclaimed, making me stare at him blankly in response.

"I do."

"I like her. Not like that, though." Raffaele said quickly when I sent him a deadly glare. "She's definitely something else."

I silently agreed. She was something else and nothing like the rest of the women who came from families who had the slightest bit of power.

"Who would have thought the daughter of Gaetano would have caught your eye? Or is she just a piece of the puzzle in the plan?" Raffaele's brows raised in curiosity, and I shook my head at him.

"No. She has nothing to do with it." I replied. Just as innocent as she looked, she was truly oblivious to what kind of world she had stepped into. If she had the slightest clue, she would have noticed me pointing a gun at her head in her hotel room.

"She could be faking it. It's always the innocent ones you have to keep an eye out for. Do we really believe she didn't know her own family name?" He questioned suspiciously.

"Her mother took her away when she was still a kid and had no idea what kind of business her father was running. If Stefano had done his job properly, he would have found her immediately." I explained.

"May his soul rest in peace." Raffaele sighed as he shook his head, and I gave him a smug look.

Stefano knew the consequences of not doing a job properly. I was not a patient man, and he fucked up when he didn't do a thorough search on Althaia.

"I have been keeping an eye on her ever since she showed up. She's no threat." I told him.

"Her mother?" Raffaele asked.

"She is a different story." I said, as we made our way out of the basement where the gym was.

"How so?"

"Since they arrived at the manor, the number of phone calls that couldn't be traced has increased." I told him. While Althaia didn't pose any kind of threat, her mother was someone I needed to figure out since she was an ex-wife of a mob boss. I needed to know why she left Gaetano, and why she was getting untraceable calls.

"Sounds like I need to look into that." Raffaele noted.

I nodded as we stepped outside by the pool. My eyes immediately found the green-eyed woman on the sunbed, laughing at something Arianna said.

My eyes trailed down her body, enjoying the red bikini she was wearing.

Red is a fucking good color on her.

My eyes rested on her chest when she adjusted the top that was a tad too small for her full breasts. It was definitely getting a reaction from me.

I quickly scanned around the area to make sure none of my men stood around looking at her. I know those bastards were checking her out the second she showed up at the engagement party, and I would fucking kill them if they were watching her dressed in a bikini.

"Cannonball!" Raffaele shouted, jumping into the pool, as water splashed right on Arianna and Althaia.

"You idiot!" Arianna yelled and angrily wiped the water off her face. He approached her with a mischievous grin and shook his head like a dog to mess with her. She tried to kick him, but he was quick and grabbed her ankle, pulling her off the sunbed.

Arianna's yelling died down when he threw her into the pool. She cursed at him when she returned to the surface and the idiot just stood at the edge, mocking her, not noticing Althaia coming up behind him. I watched her smiling as she sneaked up behind him and shoved him into the pool.

"You played dirty!" Raffaele whined, and she gave an innocent shrug.

"Whoops." She grinned. Her face was slightly scrunched up with her tongue in between her teeth. I was amused by the face she was making.

Althaia met my gaze briefly before quickly looking away when I came closer.

"I'm going to go get us something to drink." She muttered to Arianna, who was busy trying to drown Raffaele.

I followed her inside, well aware of what she was doing. Still, I couldn't help but stare at her round ass as she walked. I had to withhold a groan as I imagined all the things I would do to her. Including spanking her ass until it turned into a beautiful shade of red.

"You're avoiding me." I stated, trying to keep my mind elsewhere.

Althaia opened the fridge, still not looking at me.

"Don't know what you're talking about." She replied, pretending to be occupied by what kind of drink she wanted.

I watched the cold from the fridge making her to shiver slightly, and I immediately noticed her nipples hardening behind her top.

The image of the way she had arched her back for me to taste her breasts still freshly lingered in my mind, and the way she would moan. It awakened my cock even more, and I had to force myself to think of something else.

But that fucking red bikini wasn't helping.

"Look at me." I spoke with a gentle command.

"No, thank you." Althaia scoffed.

My mouth twitched seeing her grow more confident with me. I would never forget how scared she looked when she saw me at her hotel room and thought I was going to kill her. But I couldn't when she looked at me with those green eyes before she clumsily tried to run away.

The sight was too amusing, and definitely not something I had witnessed before. She really knew nothing about the world I lived in. If she had the slightest idea, she would have been more aware and looked for the cameras I had hidden in her hotel room.

"You should ask me." I stepped closer, knowing why she was avoiding me, but I wanted her to tell me.

"Why? It's none of my business."

"It isn't." I agreed.

"Great." Althaia's jaw clenched as she closed the fridge. She still didn't look at me and tried to leave.

I clicked my tongue, grabbed her, sat her on the counter, and stepped in between her legs. I noticed a hitch in her breath as I leaned into her. No detail about her body went unnoticed by me, from the way she would clench her jaw when angry to the way she would bite her on the inside of her cheek when lost in thought.

I knew her body too well.

"Althaia." My voice came out in a low tone as I looked at her. She shuddered when I said her name and I knew the effect I had on her. She had the same effect on me, too. Especially when she would moan my name.

Fuck.

The blood was rushing down, and my cock was painfully pressing against the shorts I was wearing. I wanted to rip the damn things off and take her right now, to bury myself so deep inside of her pussy that I have only touched with my fingers. For now.

"Use your words, Althaia. What's on your mind?"

I wrapped my arms around her waist and pulled her close, nuzzling my face into the crook of her neck. My lips barely touched her skin, and I could hear her breath quicken, making me crave the sound of her moaning my name.

"Zahra…" She breathed out.

"Hmm, what about her?" I asked against her neck, despite already knowing what she wanted to ask.

"You and her…?" She struggled when I lightly kissed her neck.

"No. Never." I replied. Zahra was an annoying type of woman and definitely not my type. I wouldn't even fuck her if I was desperate.

"But why did she–"

"To make you jealous. Which worked." I looked at her, and a blush crept up her cheeks. There was something endearing about it whenever she felt embarrassed, and I have come to like how her cheeks would get that flushed color.

"Oh..." She bit her lip and looked away, and I felt myself twitch down below at the sight. I gently pulled her lip and ran my thumb over her soft lips.

"Don't do that if you don't want me to bend you over and take you right now." I almost growled out.

I watched her bright green eyes and the way her pupils dilated. It made me think of all the wicked things I wanted to do just to make her scream in pleasure.

A small sound escaped her as she tried to squeeze her thighs together.

Fuck it.

I pulled her into me, our bodies pressed tightly together, and kissed her with an intense hunger that had been building inside me. Without hesitation, Althaia wrapped her legs around me and I pressed myself against her, causing her to emit a soft moan that I had been craving.

Her chest rose and fell with excitement as my lips traced a path from her jaw to her neck.

I pulled down her top, letting out a deep breath at how unbelievable her breasts are; round and so fucking perfect. I couldn't even stop myself before I dipped down and ran my tongue over her nipple. Althaia's hands went to my hair, and I could feel how fast her heart was beating as a soft moan escaped her plump lips.

My cock was hard as I thought about what it would feel like with her pussy clenched around me as I filled her up, and how she would clench so deliciously around my cock.

I heard the distant voices of Raffaele and Arianna coming closer. Annoyed, I pulled away and helped her down to her feet. Confusion flickered across her face for a moment, but then she heard their voices and quickly adjusted her bikini.

"Soon." I whispered to her, my voice heavy with lust. "I will claim your pussy soon." I gave her one last kiss before I turned to walk away.

I needed to fuck my fist before I lose control.

Nineteen

ALTHAIA

"I gave birth to you! I suffered for hours for you to come out of my vagina!"

"Mom–"

"My only child has forgotten about me!"

"Mo–"

"This is my fault. I let you go over there, and now look at you, not coming back to spend time with your poor mother."

"Mamá!" I said, frustrated, finally getting a word in. I was already in a bad mood since I was dealing with bad period cramps.

I was in bed, talking to my mother on the phone. Actually, she was doing most of the talking - I take that back; she was yelling at me because she has decided in her mind that I have forgotten about her.

"Mamá, I literally text you to let you know that I'm still alive, and nothing bad has happened to me. Besides, I did text you yesterday that I will be home soon to spend some time with you before the wedding." I sighed, finally able to explain myself.

"I'm your mother. I deserve more than text messages every other day! And you did not text me that." She continued to scold me, making me roll my eyes. It was a good thing she couldn't see me, or else she would have pulled out the wooden spoon.

"I have been busy helping Cara with her endless list of things that need to be done. And yes, I did. Check your messages." I let out a small groan and rubbed my back to ease the pain.

"Don't lie to me–oh, I see, you did text me. My bad, honey." My mother chuckled.

"Couldn't you have just checked before going all dramatic and screaming in my ear?" I sighed.

"No, sorry, honey. God created me this way, deal with it."

I shook my head and couldn't help but let out a chuckle with her.

"I promise I will be back soon. I love you."

"I love you too, honey. Feel better." A cramp hit me after I hung up, and I groaned loudly into my pillow.

This was fucking hell.

I had to stay in bed since I could barely move, which was probably for the best, considering I was giving people hell with my mood swings. Poor Raffaele—I even yelled at him for breathing too loudly. I haven't seen him since that episode; he's probably keeping his distance from me.

As if suffering wasn't enough, I also had cravings for greasy junk food, especially chocolate cake. My mouth was watering just by the thought of a chocolate lava cake with ice cream. The only problem was, I couldn't get out of bed and remained in a fetal position.

I picked up my phone and absentmindedly scrolled through social media for the hundredth time in the last five minutes. I was miserable and bored since everyone had plans.

I bit my lip, my finger hovering over a number I have been contemplating to call. I haven't seen him since our small moment in the kitchen, and something in me was craving to hear his voice.

He was like a sinful indulgence, and it left me imagining what more he would do to me other than his hands roaming my body with his hot breath against me.

I have been acting on the thoughts many times, and I kept fantasizing that it was his fingers pleasuring me instead of my own.

I squeezed my legs together.

Screw it. I'm calling him.

"Althaia." He answered right away. I bit down on my lips hard to stop a moan when his deep voice sent signals straight down to my pussy.

"Do you always pick up calls like that? It sounds so serious." I chuckled.

"It gets to the point."

"I guess. What are you doing?" I asked, not trying to hide that I just wanted to talk.

Damiano went quiet, and I was starting to think maybe he wanted to be left alone.

"Taking care of business." He finally responded.

"So, what does that exactly mean? Like killing people, torturing them, or just plain paperwork?" I wondered out loud, secretly hoping to get an answer.

"If I tell you, then I have to kill you." He sounded serious, but I could imagine him smirking as he said that.

"So, it's definitely something illegal." I stated, and he didn't deny it as he only let out a light chuckle.

"Are you feeling better?" Damiano's gentle tone made me smile.

"Not really. I feel like shit and I'm craving everything. How do you know?" I raised my brows in surprise. It was not like I had told him I was on my period.

"I may have gotten a complaint about you." He replied, amused.

"About me?"

"Yes."

"Why?"

"Raffaele said you were being a psychopath." He let out a deep, rich chuckle, and I dropped my jaw in shock.

"He what? Oh, that little ..." I sneered. "He should try to bleed for several days, along with cramps and back pains! It turns you into a psychopath." I huffed, and he just continued to chuckle at me.

"Watch it before you come on my 'who to beat up' list." My brows pinched in seriousness.

"Oh, really?" I could hear the amusement in his voice and pictured him leaning back in his big boss chair as he spoke.

"Yes. I'm strong. I could totally beat you up." I said cockily, even though we both knew it was the biggest lie. He could crush me with his pinky if he wanted to.

"You do realize I'm twice your size? You barely reach my chest."

"That won't stop me. I can just jump to get to you." I stated confidently.

"Hmm, I know exactly where you can *jump* on me." Damiano's voice lowered, sending a steady pulse between my legs and causing my entire body to flutter.

"I–I ..." I couldn't form a sentence and it was like my body was on fire.

"I believe it relieves cramps as well."

"I wouldn't know."

"You haven't tried it?" He questioned, and I could picture him with a tilted head and a raised brow.

"Not exactly that..." I trailed off. "But your shower head works wonders."

"Shower head, you say?"

"Yup. Love the water stream settings you've got there." I bit my lip to hold back a laugh.

"Hmm, I see." He said, entertained. "Tell me, Althaia, what do you think about when you're using *my* shower head to pleasure that sweet pussy of yours?"

My breath caught in my throat, and my pussy was begging for relief.

I opened my mouth, but no words were coming out. My cheeks heated just by the thought of admitting that I was always thinking of him.

"Piccola."

Fuck, I love it when he calls me that.

"Yes?" I answered breathlessly.

"I want to hear you."

"Hear me?"

"Get in the shower." Damiano ordered me, and a surge of excitement coursed through my veins. "Don't let me tell you twice." He growled.

My heart was racing.

"Okay." My voice was barely audible as I went to the bathroom.

"Such a good girl, piccola."

A moan slipped past my lips, and I clamped my hand over my mouth in shock. I could picture how that devilish smirk was on his lips right now.

"Undress and get in the shower."

I obeyed him like the good girl I am and got in the shower.

"Grab the shower head and get on your knees." Damiano kept instructing. "Are you on your knees?"

"Yes."

"Good. Now, place your phone in the corner and open the camera."

My eyes slightly widened by his request.

"But -"

"Don't make me repeat myself, Althaia." Damiano said impatiently. "Let me see you." He growled.

Without overthinking, I opened the camera.

Damiano entered the frame, his intense eyes darkening with hunger as he watched me. He was such a delicious sin as his gaze traced from my face, down to my breasts, before settling on my spread thighs.

"Fucking hell, piccola." Damiano groaned as he took me in. My chest was rising and falling rapidly to the rhythm of my heartbeat. "Show me, Althaia. Show me how you pleasure your sweet pussy."

I let out a small whimper, unable to resist the throbbing any longer. I turned on the shower, adjusting it to my preferred setting, and allowed the water to spray over me.

"Sweet hell, you're perfect." He murmured. I let out a shy smile as his eyes followed the shower head as I moved it between my thighs.

I sucked in a breath, biting down on my lip as the streams hit my clit.

"What did I tell you?" He snarled at me. "Don't do that. I want to hear you." Damiano demanded and I immediately let go of my lip, a moan escaping me as my body spasmed to the feeling.

I closed my eyes, lost in the sensation, as my other hand explored my body. I gripped my breast, squeezing and pinching my nipple. A jolt of pleasure ran through me, making me throw my head back as I savored the feeling.

Damiano's grunts made me look at him, and I watched as his eyes filled with a dark lust. My breathing grew louder when I noticed movement in his arm.

He was stroking himself.

It made my pussy clench as I watched him, sliding my hand down to my pussy and fingered myself to the view of him. I couldn't see more than just his face and chest, but God, it was enough as my entire body trembled.

I cried out as an intense wave of orgasm crashed over me. It was so overwhelming that I had to turn off the water to catch my breath.

"Fuck!" Damiano grunted, kicking his head back with a growl. I licked my lip, longing to see more of him.

He slowly raised his head and fixed me with a sated, dark look.

"Good girl. You look so pretty when you come for me." Damiano smirked devilishly, and his words had me almost breathless. "Next time, you'll be coming on my tongue."

It wasn't posed as a question; it was a promise.

My eyes fluttered open from a well-needed nap. I was knocked out the second my body hit the bed, well satisfied after my phone call with Damiano.

Just the thought of it brought a shy grin on my face.

I took a deep breath, my stomach growling at the scent of delicious food. I sat up, and my eyes widened at the amount of food that was placed on the coffee table.

My mouth watered as I stepped closer, spotting a pizza with extra cheese, just the way I liked it.

"To whoever brought me food; I wish you a long and good life." I said out loud and grabbed the still hot pizza. I was too hungry to care that someone had been in here while I slept. They obviously meant well because they brought me food.

As I was eating, I noticed a small black box placed in the center of all the food. I wiped my hands and reached for it.

"Wow..." I muttered in awe.

Inside the box, a pair of gold stud earrings gleamed brightly against the dark velvet lining. One large diamond was set in the center, surrounded by smaller diamonds.

A note was attached to it, and my heart pounded in my chest as I read the words written in neat, cursive handwriting. I couldn't help but smile.

For you, my Althaia
D.

"He can't be serious." I gasped. I grabbed my phone from the bed and sent him a text message.

Althaia: Thank you, but I can't accept them.

A few minutes went by, and my phone buzzed.

Damiano: *You don't like them?*

Althaia: Are you kidding me? They are gorgeous!

Damiano: *Keep them.*
They are yours.

I sighed and bit my lip as I looked at the earrings. Was it really okay for me to accept such an expensive gift? I ran my fingers over the earrings. They were so beautiful.

Damiano: *Try them on.*

I put them on, looked at them through my phone's camera, and fell even more in love with them. I snapped a picture with my hair pulled behind my ears to show the earrings and sent it to him.

Althaia: They're stunning. Thank you.

Damiano: *Beautiful.*

THE DEVIL'S FIRE

You're welcome.

His words had me blushing and smiling shyly at my phone.
The things he was doing to me.

Twenty

Althaia

"And why exactly can't Michael come and get me?" I asked again. Not only were his fingers thick, but apparently his head was too as I tried to knock some sense into him.

"I don't like him." Damiano gave a curt reply and resumed sifting through the scattered papers on his desk.

"Well, I do!" I said, and his eyes snapped to mine with a sharp look.

"Antonio will drive you."

"Why bother the poor man by going back and forth? I'm just going to my dad's house." I sighed as I kicked my legs back and forth.

I had made myself comfortable on his desk, watching as he went over a list of numbers. I hadn't wanted to disturb him, and I even considered leaving earlier, but he insisted that I stay. Besides, his hand rested on my thigh, and I couldn't find the will to move away.

"He will stay with you. For protection." Damiano replied, his eyes narrowing on something written on the paper.

"That's dumb. Protect me from what? My own father?" I wondered. He sighed and put the paper in his hand down to look at me.

"I have something I need to take care of and won't be there with you. With Antonio, it will give me one less thing to worry about." Damiano explained, making me feel bad when he put it like that.

"Okay." I gave in. "Where is he then?"

"Waiting for you. Come, I'll walk you out."

Antonio was already standing by the car when we walked out to the driveway. He actually looked like the type of man you would see on a fashion runway with his dark, dirty blonde hair, blue eyes, and short beard.

Antonio gave a firm nod when we approached him and opened the backseat door for me. Before I could even get in, an arm wrapped around me, and I was pushed flush against his chest.

Damiano cupped my cheeks and pressed his lips to mine in a long, sweet kiss that had me melting completely in his arms.

"Behave." He whispered when he pulled away.

"I always do." I grinned, but that just earned me a raised, unconvinced, brow.

"So, Antonio." I started. We had been driving for a while now and neither of us was talking. It made me feel slightly awkward sitting with him in complete silence.

I didn't really know what to say to him, but I thought maybe I could get to know him. All of them were dark and serious and never showed any emotion.

Antonio looked at me through the rearview mirror, and my mind went blank. All of a sudden, I didn't know how to make small talk.

"Uh, I'm sorry for troubling you like this. I'm sure you have other things to take care of." I gave him an apologetic smile.

"It's fine." He replied, cold and brief as I had feared he would. I sighed quietly to myself. I guess none of these men were really a fan of any type of conversation.

"How long have you been working for Damiano?" I tried again. I knew it was a long shot with this question, but I guessed I preferred awkward conversation instead of silence.

"Since day one. We grew up together." He answered.

It made sense then why he was one of Damiano's most trusted men. Well, I just assumed he was because wherever Damiano went, he was right there with him.

"That's nice." I smiled. "Do you have a family of your own?"

"Why the sudden interest?" His tone was sharp, and it left me startled.

"I'm just making conversation. They are fairly normal questions to ask when you want to get to know someone."

"Look, I'm just doing my job. I would rather not have you ask me questions." Antonio shut me down and refocused on the road.

Damn, what crawled up in his butt today?

I stayed silent. I would rather not piss him off. If anything dangerous actually were to happen, I wouldn't want him to just let me die because I annoyed him.

Yeah, I wasn't about to take that chance.

I was over the moon when we pulled into my dad's mansion driveway. It was one long ride, but it felt like decades after my failed attempt to make conversation.

I saw Michael by his car, chatting with one of my father's men. The second Antonio stopped the car, I jumped out in excitement.

"Michael!" I squealed as I ran up to him.

"Thaia!" His face brightened up when he saw me. I jumped up to him, my arms wrapping around his neck as he lifted me off the ground, spinning us both around as we laughed.

"Shit, did you get shorter?" He asked when he set me down and placed a hand on my head to measure.

"I'm wearing sneakers today, you jerk." I playfully smacked his hand away from me when he laughed at me.

"You're missed." Michael smiled. "It's boring without you guys here." He pulled me into a tight hug again.

"I've missed you too! At least we can spend some time together now. I'm going back to moms in a few days and thought we could hang out."

"Sure thing." Michael grinned. I followed his gaze when he stared at Antonio by his car, watching us. "What is he doing here?"

"Just making sure I get back and forth safely." I shrugged. "Where's my dad?"

"In his office. I'll go with you." He wrapped his arm around my waist and led me upstairs.

I gave Antonio a quick glance to see if he would be fine. He was already looking our way, and not once did he take them off us while he fished his phone out from his pocket.

"My beautiful figlia!" My father greeted me with open arms when we entered his office.

"Hi, papá." I gave him a kiss on his cheek and hugged him. My smile disappeared when I saw the dark circles under his eyes. "Are you not getting any sleep?" I frowned in worry.

"Don't worry about me. Just a lot of work lately." He gave me a dismissive wave and sat back behind his desk.

"Be careful, papá. Don't work too hard. You can have Michael do the hard work."

"Hey!" Michael protested, and I stuck my tongue out at him playfully.

"How are the wedding preparations?" My father asked.

"Good! It's going to be so beautiful. Cara has been killing me with all her demands, so it's nice to take a small break from it all." I chuckled.

"Good, good." He nodded and shared a quick look with Michael. Just as I was about to ask if everything was okay, the phone went off. I looked at Michael as my father took the call.

"I thought we could all go out somewhere. The weather's nice."

"As long as there is food, I'm down for whatever."

"Always." I chuckled. If there is one thing we both shared, it was our love of food.

I looked at my father when he hung up the phone and rose from his chair.

"Sorry, figlia. Something came up that needs my presence." He sighed.

"Oh...."

"I promise I will make it up to you when you come back, okay?" my father embraced me and kissed the top of my head before leaving.

"Looks like it's just the two of us, Michael. What do you want to do?"

Michael had an exaggerated thinking face with his index finger and thumb on his chin. Then he snapped his fingers as an idea popped into his head.

"I know exactly where to go! You will love it there." He rose to his feet and grabbed my hand.

"Oh, where?" I asked excitedly.

"It's a surprise." He snickered.

"I hate you." I groaned. I love surprises, but only if I didn't know about them. To tell me it was a surprise was something my curiosity couldn't handle.

And he knew that.

"You know, since I'm leaving in a few days..." I trailed off and Michael glanced at me. "Can I drive your car?"

"Ha! No." He scoffed.

"Come on, Michael! Let me just try it this once, and I promise I won't ever ask you again!" I put my hands together and gave him my best puppy eyes. "Please?"

He gave me a long look, with a small frown forming on his face.

"... Fine." He sighed, not happy about it. "But only this time!" He looked at me firmly to make it clear.

My eyes widened when my pleading actually worked.

"Oh my God, I love you!" I gave him one big, tight hug before I ran to the driver's seat, but stopped when Antonio made his way to me.

"Antonio, we are just going for a ride, and maybe grab something to eat." I smiled. Instead of saying anything, he looked back and forth between us before shaking his head.

"No. You're driving with me."

"You don't get it, I'm finally allowed to drive his car." I tried to explain to him how big of a deal this was.

"I don't care. You're driving with me."

"Don't tell her what to do." Michael got in his face. My heart started racing when I saw Antonio's face darken.

"And what are you going to do about it?" He stepped closer to Michael, daring him to challenge him.

"Michael, don't..." I grabbed his arm to pull him back. I feared they would try to kill each other. And how exactly do you stop a fight like that? Fucking beats me.

"Please, Antonio, can you just follow us in your car?" I asked with a soft smile. I had to separate these two quickly before things escalated.

Antonio gave Michael a long stare and then walked back to his car. My shoulders sagged in relief.

"Come on, let's have fun!" I tried to lighten the mood and skipped to the driver's seat.

As soon as I sat in the car, Michael started cracking up like crazy. He was laughing his head off, teasing me about my short legs and the fact that I had to move the seat all the way up to reach the pedals.

"Don't crash, the airbag will kill you." Michael continued with his lame jokes.

"Shut up before I kick your ass!"

"With what? With those short legs?" He screamed with laughter and slapped himself on the thigh.

"You're such a bully." I grumbled and started the car with a roar, and the sound filled me with exhilaration as I drove.

"Okay... easy now... watch out... Easy over there."

I rolled my eyes at Michael for being overly dramatic. It hasn't even been five minutes, and he was acting as if I was going to crash.

"I know how to drive."

"Tsk, you're a woman."

"What the hell do you mean by that?"

"I just mean that women suck at driving." He shrugged.

Oh no, he fucking didn't.

We were at a stoplight, and I got ready to give him a ride he will never forget. I pressed down on the accelerator a few times, making the car roar beautifully.

"Thaia, what are you doing?" He asked nervously. I smirked, waiting for the light to turn green while revving up the car. "Thaia–"

He didn't get to finish and instead screamed when I slammed my foot on the accelerator, going insanely fast. I was laughing like a maniac as I weaved through the cars — loving every second of it.

"Slo- slow down!" Michael finally yelled.

I slowed down and laughed as I looked at him. He was all the way back in his seat, his feet on the dashboard and arms to the side, trying to hold on to something while the color in his face was completely drained.

"That will teach your sexist ass!" I let out a satisfied smile.

"You're crazy!" Michael fumbled, and desperately tried to pull the seat belt over him.

I just laughed, speeding up and making him scream again in fear.

"Mmhh, this is so good!" I exclaimed as I stuffed pieces of meat in my mouth, savoring each bite. Michael's surprise was to take me to his favorite Korean restaurant, and we were having the best Korean barbecue I have ever had in my life.

"Damn, it's like listening to live porn with the sounds you're making." Michael flashed a cheeky smile.

"Why would you even say that?" I hissed at him. We were met with a look from the couple sitting next to us, and I gave them an awkward smile.

"It's hot though. Keep going." He grinned, completely unaware they heard him.

"Stop it." I gave him a death stare, and he just laughed while chowing down his food.

"You know what, let's get Soju Bombs." Michael said and quickly placed an order.

"Did you forget you're driving?" I asked. After that little stunt of mine, I wasn't allowed to drive his car anymore. Actually, he said he would never get in any car if I was the one driving.

Such a big baby.

"We're just getting one. Besides, we're not going back right away. I know another place to get dessert. You will love it." He smiled widely when Ji-Ho, a charming, petite older lady, placed the items for the Soju Bomb on the table.

I learned this restaurant was run by a family who adored Michael and treated him like one of their own.

"Thank you." She looked at me a bit startled when I expressed my gratitude in Korean.

"Oh, you speak Korean too?" She asked in Korean with surprise.

"I don't speak it that well. I'm still learning." I replied with a smile.

"Ah, what do you mean? You speak Korean so well!" Ji-Ho complimented and looked at Michael with a twinkle in her eyes. "Michael, such a pretty girlfriend, and she speaks Korean well! I approve." She winked with a thumbs-up and just walked away before either of us could say anything.

"Guess I'm your girlfriend for the day." I joked to Michael with a laugh.

"Does that mean I can take you home with me, too?" Michael wiggled his brows.

"Let us just do this." I rolled my eyes playfully as I reached for the glasses.

"Are you ready?" He asked, and I gave an excited nod.

"1...2...3...Soju Bomb!" We yelled together and slammed our hands down on the table on either side of the glass, making the shot drop into the beer, and we quickly downed it in one go.

"Hell yeah!" Michael yelled and slammed the glass down on the table.

"Why did we eat that much?" I groaned when we went for a walk. I was glad I was off my period so I wouldn't be extra bloated, but I still had to unbutton my jeans to make room for dessert.

"I say that to myself every time I eat there. But it's so worth it." He even patted his stomach as I agreed with him. My stomach hurt, but it was worth every bite.

We took a stroll through KoreaTown; laughing, joking, and losing track of time. It was only when I caught sight of the sunset that I reached for my phone to check the time.

And my heart dropped as I saw the eighteen missed calls.

From Damiano.

Shit! How the fuck did I miss his calls?

"Michael, it's getting late. We should get going now."

"Why? Do you have a curfew or something?" He joked.

"No, just getting tired." I lied and hurried him towards his car.

I bit down on my lip nervously when I realized that I totally forgot about Antonio. Damiano was most likely pissed. I didn't dare call him back now and thought I would just talk to him when I returned to the manor.

When we pulled into my father's driveway, I felt like my heart was about to explode at the sight of Damiano. He was inhaling deeply on a cigarette while his eyes never once left the car. I couldn't figure out if he was pissed or not because his face showed absolutely nothing. Next to him stood Antonio, and he didn't bother to mask his annoyance.

I gulped, not knowing what was awaiting me.

I exited the car at the same time my father walked down the stairs. He exchanged some words with Damiano before they shook hands. Damiano didn't say a word to me when I approached them, only gave me a glance over before making his way to his car and waited for me.

"Figlia, I'll see you when you come back for the wedding." My father hugged me.

"Take care of yourself." I smiled. "See ya, Michael. I had fun." He hugged me tightly and kissed my temple before letting me go.

As I walked to Damiano, his eyes stayed locked on me, making me even more nervous. I couldn't tell what he was thinking, and I was starting to hate when he wore his expressionless face.

He didn't say anything to me when I sat in the car, but the way he slammed my door let me know he was mad.

I sunk down in the seat, bracing myself for his anger.

The ride was painfully silent.

Antonio took off somewhere in his car, leaving the two of us alone, and it felt suffocating.

"That's not the way back... Where are we going?" I finally broke the silence and looked at Damiano. He straight up ignored me and didn't even glance my way. He had a tight hold on the steering wheel, making his knuckles turn white.

"If it's about Antonio, then I'm sorry." I apologized.

He let out a dark chuckle that sent a chill down my spine.

"You're sorry?" He sneered. "Imagine the fucking phone call I got from Antonio, saying that he lost you."

"I think you're overreacting. I was just hanging out with Mic –"

"I told you to behave." He growled out.

"I'm not a child! I can do whatever I want." I snapped. "I didn't lose Antonio on purpose, and I would have called him if I had his number."

Damiano fell silent once more. Then, he accelerated with such force that it pinned me back in my seat. He was driving insanely fast that everything around us blurred, and the other cars blared their horns as he maneuvered through traffic.

The fear of crashing made me nauseous, and I could feel my dinner rising in my throat.

"Please, slow down... I can't..." I squeezed my eyes shut and held onto the door.

"Cazzo!" He let out a string of curse words in Italian and slowed down.

As soon as he pulled over to the side of the road, I opened the door and took in deep breaths of fresh air, trying not to throw up. Damiano was quickly in front of me, crouching down, and placed his hands on my cheeks.

"Are you okay?" Damiano's brows pinched together. I nodded, feeling my body relax as I took another deep breath.

"Fuck, piccola. You're going to drive me crazy." He let out a heavy sigh before pulling me into his embrace.

His words caused a smile to spread across my face.

Twenty-One

ALTHAIA

"A hotel?" I asked when Damiano opened the car door for me.

"Yes." He pulled me to his side, providing me with some of his warmth as we made our way into the elevator. "I have an event to attend, and I want you to join me."

"Sounds nice." I replied with a smile as we exited the elevator onto the private floor. "What kind of event?" I asked as we stepped into the hotel room.

"Auction." Damiano replied as he grabbed a drink from the minibar. I gave a slight nod and went to the floor-to-ceiling window when some golden light caught my attention.

The golden light came from a large lake with sprinklers going high in the air, moving around to a soft rhythm with lights at the bottom.

"It's beautiful." I remarked, my voice filled with awe.

"Most beautiful." Damiano responded. I looked back at him, his intense gaze resting on me.

"You're not even looking." I chuckled.

"I am." His golden-brown eyes never left mine as he spoke. I quickly spun back to look out the window, trying to hide my blushing face.

My heart went wild when I heard him come closer and then felt him right behind me. An intense flutter rushed through me when his arms wrapped around my waist. I tried to control myself when I felt his breath close to my neck.

I couldn't focus on anything other than his hand that was slowly trailing down my stomach and stopped right at the button of my jeans. I looked down when he unbuttoned my pants.

"Keep your eyes up." His other hand wrapped around my throat, making me look straight ahead.

My back pressed against his chest as our eyes met in the window's reflection, and I inhaled sharply when his fingers found their way right between my legs.

I slowly exhaled when he took his time, teasing me while he kept his eyes on me. I relaxed completely against him, enjoying how he was slowly building my pleasure.

Damiano made a low sound with the back of his throat and flicked his tongue across a sensitive spot on my neck.

I let out a soft moan.

"That's it... let me hear you." Damiano spoke to me in this deep, husky voice. It almost made my knees buckle.

"Mnhm..." He let out a satisfied grunt, pleased with my reaction to his touch. My toes curled when he slid his fingers inside of me, slowly pumping in and out as he played with my clit.

"Be a good girl and open your eyes, Althaia." He whispered to me, and like the good girl I am, I opened them.

I watched how he fingered me in front of the window where people could see us. But I didn't give a damn about it when he was giving me slow waves of pleasure.

Our eyes stayed locked, and I bit down on my lip from the way he was looking at me. It edged me closer and closer to that explosive pleasure.

Then he pulled his hand away.

"Not yet." He said, before I could open my mouth and give him hell for leaving me hanging again. Damiano nuzzled his face into my neck, lips trailing until he reached my ear and whispered. "Tonight, you *will* come on my tongue."

He spun me around, grabbed the back of my thighs, and hoisted me up to wrap my legs around him. His lips were on mine, and he bit down on my lip as he kissed me with an intense hunger.

I pressed my lower half into him, feeling his already hard length and making him grunt in response when I moved against him.

We pulled away slightly as he undressed me, throwing my shirt somewhere behind him and my bra followed right after. All while I kept looking into his eyes that were darker than normal.

God, he is beautiful.

We were moving until my back hit the soft mattress of the bed. A slow, sweet kiss was placed on my lips, and I grabbed his shirt, unbuttoning each one until it slid off his body. My hands slid down his impressive, tattooed body and felt his hard, defined abs.

The rest of my clothes were tossed to the side, leaving me completely naked and laid out for him. Damiano leaned away and stood at the end of the bed, taking his time drinking in my body.

"Gorgeous." He admired, and there wasn't a single inch on my body he didn't look. I smiled shyly and watched him finally undress the lower part of his body; the part I often have been fantasizing about.

Damiano smirked lazily as he stood in all his naked glory. My eyes traced down his body, and my eyes widened before I quickly composed myself.

I knew he was big, but fuck, he was also *thick!*

Looks like my vagina is going to be wrecked, too.

He inched closer, his hands starting at my ankles and slowly sliding up to my knees. Damiano gently spread them apart, and I could barely control my breathing when he took his time with his gaze fixed on my naked pussy.

"Fuck, Althaia..." Damiano groaned as his eyes snapped to mine. He let out a subtle smirk before he lowered himself, his beard lightly grazing the inside of my thigh.

"Damiano..." I breathed out when I felt his warm tongue on me. My eyes rolled to the back of my head when his tongue slowly stroked my slit, and even more so when he sucked on my clit. I gripped the sheets, and my back arched when he slid a finger inside of me.

I raised my head to look at him, and his eyes were already set on me while I watched him eat my pussy. The sight of it alone made me moan, pushing me closer to the edge.

I was so close, and he knew it.

"Come on my tongue, Althaia." Damiano demanded with a growl. I fell back down on the bed, the explosive orgasm taking over my body, having me cry out in pleasure.

Damiano gripped my hips to keep me in place as he continued to suck on my clit bringing me beyond my orgasm.

It had my entire body trembling.

My eyes dropped when he slowed down and gave me a view of him licking his lips. And the dark look he was giving me let me know that this was barely a small taste of what he was going to do to me.

I couldn't tear my eyes away as he rolled on a condom on his impressive length. I had been with guys before, but nothing could compare to what he had.

The divine definition of a cock.

Our eyes met, and he had a slightly amused expression by how I was gawking.

"Like what you see?" Damiano tilted his head.

Yes.

"It's not too bad." I shrugged. I had to bite back a grin because he knew I was lying.

"Not too bad, you say?" A dark smile spread across his lips. "Let's see just how many times you'll be screaming my name tonight." He grabbed my ankles to pull me closer to him. A new rush of excitement built up in me when he hovered over me.

"Is that a promise?" I teased. Damiano's gaze snapped to my lips when I licked them.

"Always."

He rammed hard into my pussy in one go, stretching my walls with his thick cock.

"Damiano!" I screamed his name in a mixture of shock and gasp, my voice trembling by how he was filling me up.

"Fucking hell!" Damiano grunted as he slid out and then drove back inside me. I was so full of him it was overwhelming, but so good at the same time. And I moaned with each thrust.

He leaned back, placed each arm under my legs, and pressed my knees up to my chest.

"Fuck, piccola, your pretty pussy is taking me so good." He groaned as he watched how he went deeper, faster and harder into my pussy.

The tension in the pit of my stomach grew when his thumb found my clit.

"Let me have it. Come on my cock." Damiano demanded. My body listened to him, and all I could do was scream his name as I shattered in the throes of my orgasm.

Damiano slowed down before coming to a stop to let me catch my breath.

"Don't think it's over yet."

My eyes snapped open to look at him in shock.

"Wha - you didn't...?"

"I plan on fucking you all night." He gave me a smug smile and flipped me onto my stomach. I yelped when he slapped my ass so fucking hard that it stung. "Red is such a good color on you." Damiano kissed and caressed my ass to ease the pain.

Only for him to slap me again.

But this time a moan left me, loving that cocktail of pain and pleasure.

"Fuck, you like that, baby?"

"Yes." I whimpered as he slapped my ass again. It was making me drip all over the sheets, and it only seemed to please him when he slipped two fingers into my pussy, feeling just how wet I was.

"Perfect..." Damiano whispered and locked my arms behind my back before replacing his fingers with his cock in my pussy. His fingers trailed down the crevice of my ass, and my eyes slightly widened when he touched me right *there*.

Damiano pulled me against his chest with my arms still locked behind my back while his hand wrapped around my throat, and never once stopped fucking me.

"Tell me, Althaia, is your ass unclaimed?"

"Yes..." I panted, barely able to put a sentence together when I was so full of him.

A small, dark chuckle was all I heard before I felt his lips brush against my ear as he whispered.

"It won't be for long. I'm going to claim your ass just like I'm claiming your pussy."

"You won't fit!" I was barely able to take him like this; there was no way he would fit in my ass.

"Don't worry, we'll make it fit."

And he slammed me down on his cock while I screamed his name.

Twenty-Two

DAMIANO

I watched her sleep next to me, her plump lips were slightly parted as she let out a light snore.

It made me smile just watching how peaceful and so innocent she appeared, despite her looking thoroughly fucked.

Althaia was knocked out almost instantly, and just like I had fantasized, she let me do whatever I wanted with her.

She stirred and moved until her head rested on my chest with an arm across my torso.

I stilled.

It wasn't something I was used to, but I let her stay. She curled up entirely into my side and I made sure not to move, so I wouldn't disturb her while I watched her get comfortable.

Her lips went into a small pout, and I wanted to chuckle at how endearing it was but refrained myself. Instead, I brushed some hair out of her face and lightly caressed her cheek.

She let out a small sigh, snuggling her face into my neck, and continued to sleep soundly. I wrapped my arms around her and closed my eyes. For the past few years, my inability to sleep has plagued me and I knew tonight wouldn't be different, but the warmth of her body made me feel at peace.

When I opened my eyes again and looked at the time, it was already six in the morning. I had slept undisturbed for a couple of hours.

Althaia was still sleeping in my arms. I knew she wouldn't be waking up soon as it was too early for her. I wondered if she would yell at me like she did with Cara when she woke her up too early by banging on her hotel room door.

She was a funny little thing.

I slipped out of the bed and grabbed my phone when it rang.

"What do you want?" I spoke quietly into the phone, careful not to wake her up.

"Where are you? You left without even saying anything to me!" Raffaele whined.

"And why do I need to report to you about my whereabouts?" Even though he couldn't see me, I still raised a brow.

"I want to say it's because we're family, but you don't give a fuck about that, so I'm going to say because of security purposes. It's not a secret many want you dead." He cracked, and I let out a smug smile.

"Did you have anything important to say, or did you just want to be an annoying ass?" I asked him, but I already knew the answer.

"Why are you whispering? Wait! Are you with Althaia? Is that why she's not here?"

"Are you keeping an eye on her?" I frowned, not liking that he was keeping track of her. The bastard ignored me.

"You took her with you, and that's why you didn't pick up my calls." He stated, and I could hear his stupid grin through the phone. "You were balls deep inside of her, weren't you?"

"Fuck off." I hung up the phone. Before I could even make the next call, my phone buzzed with a text message.

Raffaele: *You so were, hahaha!*
That's my fucking boy!

I didn't bother responding and went back to return some phone calls I couldn't ignore if I didn't want anyone to fuck up my shipments.

I tossed my phone aside after making it clear to everyone I was not to be disturbed while I was away. Althaia would wake up soon now that it was almost eleven a.m.

I cleaned up the condoms and wrappers from the floor, knowing it would embarrass her if the maid came and cleaned it. I could picture it so perfectly how mortified she would be, and it tempted me to leave them on the floor just so I could watch her blush. My mind always went wicked with all the things I would do to her whenever I saw that adorable blush on her face.

Hell, even just thinking about last night was getting a reaction out of me. I was already getting hard, and I wanted to wake her up to relive a bit of last night. Somehow, I swallowed my greediness and went to take a shower to relieve myself.

A smug grin was on my lips when I saw my back in the mirror. Her nails left a lasting impression on my skin.

Red marks.

I liked it, and I knew this was her way of getting back on me for what I did to her. Too aroused by it, I stepped inside the shower, letting the water cascade down my body as I replayed every detail of the previous night in my mind.

I felt delicate fingertips tracing a slow path down my back. The feeling had me closing my eyes as I pictured her admiring the marks she left on me with a satisfied smile.

I pulled her in front of me; her long, curly hair framed her angelic face, and her bright green eyes looked at me with a soft glint that gave me a warm feeling inside my chest. It had me cupping her cheeks as I leaned down and kissed her incredibly soft lips.

"Good morning, beautiful." I greeted, making her smile shyly.

"Morning." Althaia sighed blissfully when I adjusted the water temperature to her liking. She preferred hot showers while I didn't, but I didn't mind enduring them as I admired her naked, wet body.

My cock twitched at the sight.

So fucking perfect.

The need to have her was too great and had me hoisting her up to have her legs wrapped around me.

"Are you trying to prevent me from being able to walk?" Althaia chuckled when she felt my hard length against her inner thigh.

"Hmm, maybe." I teased, burying my face into her neck, kissing her skin. "This way, I know you will stay put."

"Such a dick move." She breathed out when I played with her pussy, getting her ready for me.

"Absolutely, and I will show you just how much of a *dick move* it is." I promised. My hold around her thighs tightened when the tip of my cock felt the warmth of her.

I groaned.

"You feel so good around me..." I grunted, driving in deeper and picking up the pace, but still taking my time knowing she was sore.

Althaia's arms slid around my neck, and her gentle kisses on my jaw sent pleasurable shivers down my spine, along with her slow, breathy moans.

My thrusts were firm, driving in and out of her sweet and tight pussy that had me gritting my teeth as I was about to come in no time.

"*Fuck.*" I hissed, pulling out as I came. I grabbed her jaw and kissed her lazily before placing her on her feet with a small smirk on my face.

Then I kneeled.

"What are you doing?" Althaia asked in surprise.

"Taking care of you." I winked and dropped her leg over my shoulder. Her breath hitched in her throat when I latched onto her pussy while watching her face twist into pleasure.

"I feel like sleeping. But I'm also hungry." Althaia let out a small groan and plopped onto the bed with the freshly changed sheets.

"Hmm, we could stay in and do something else." I cocked a brow, gesturing to the bed.

"That look on your face tells me I'll be destroyed if we do, and I need a break." She laughed, making me chuckle along with her. "Wait, maybe we need to stay in since I didn't bring any clothes with me." She looked down at the robe she was wearing.

"It's in the closet. I had the hotel staff fill it up with whatever you might like." I said and slid the closet door open and grabbed clothes for myself.

"A dress would have been more than enough but thank you." She smiled as she looked through the clothes. "Are we staying here for long? When's the auction?"

"It's tomorrow. We'll stay for a few days." I said, watching her brows raise in surprise. "If you'd like." I added.

"Sounds fun." Althaia smiled, trying to hide her blushing face.

I refrained myself from smirking and grabbed a dress for her.

"Wear this one." I handed her the dress and watched as she let the robe fall to the floor before slipping into the dress. I tilted my head to the side when I noticed she wasn't planning on wearing any underwear.

"Things need to breathe. It's good for the body, you know." Althaia grinned.

"Hmm, easier access for me as well." I half-smirked, and she gaped at me.

"Have you not had enough?"

I grabbed her waist, pulling her closer to me as I leaned down to meet her face.

"No. I crave you endlessly." My voice lowered, and her breath caught in her throat at our closeness. Her bright green eyes gazed at me with an innocence that only made me hold her tighter. It ignited an uncontrollable urge to let loose.

"Should we get some food now?" Althaia asked, taking a step away with a shy smile. It was probably for the best. If she hadn't, I would have thrown her on the bed, and there was no guarantee I would go easy on her.

"Anything you want, piccola."

Twenty-Three

ALTHAIA

"So, why are we going to an auction?" I asked and sipped my latte. We found a cute, small restaurant, having a croissant sandwich for breakfast.

"Why do you think people go to auctions?" Damiano was entertained by my question, and I rolled my eyes at his response.

"I know why people go to auctions. I'm just curious why we are going." I elaborated. Damiano looked at me with a slight tilt of his head with a playful gleam in his eyes.

"See it as a get-together."

"Like with normal people, or…" I looked around to make sure no one could hear me. "With a bunch of Mafia people?" I whispered in complete seriousness. I watched Damiano sip his coffee, but it looked more like he was trying to hide a laugh.

"Businessmen. Let's say auctions are a way to show off your power and wealth." He explained.

"So, Mafia people." I corrected with a teasing smile. He shrugged but didn't deny it. "And why do you do that?"

"To make a statement that you have the power and all the means in the world to… get rid of anyone that dares to stand in the way." Damiano explained. "It's also another way of forming alliances between families and starting businesses. You would only want to have the most powerful and rich by your side."

"Really?" I said, intrigued, and he confirmed with a nod.

It made my heart beat just a little faster as I was reminded of what type of person Damiano really was. Yet, I wasn't scared of him. It was a dangerous world I had stepped into, but my fascination was sparked by the intrigue of what could unfold.

"But, uh… should I be worried about going with you?" I asked. One thing was to be around Damiano and his men, but a room filled with skilled killers who couldn't care less about me was a bit worrying.

Damiano gave me a serious stare, leaning forward and resting his arms on the table.

"They have a death wish if they dare to touch you." An involuntary shiver ran down my spine at the look on his face. His golden-brown eyes turned darker, and his voice was cold like ice. "You'll be safe." Damiano reassured me, and I believed him. He had already saved me once.

"Okay." I gave a small smile. "So, you'll have to, I don't know, carry weapons to such an event?" I asked. He leaned back in his chair, and the playful gleam in his eyes returned.

"You would be naïve if you didn't. I always carry *at least* one weapon anywhere I go."

"Even now?" I gasped in a whisper as my eyes went wide.

"Even now." He smirked.

"Where do you have it?" My eyes trailed down his body to see if I could spot anything.

"Why? Are you planning something?" Damiano cocked a brow, but the look he was giving me didn't help me figure out if he was serious or not.

"Of course! Oh, you didn't know that I have years of experience and I plan on taking you all down? I'm the next Queen, so be aware." I dramatically flipped my hair back and tilted my chin upward, exuding a confident flair.

Damiano looked at me to where he was actually smiling a bit. I wished he would smile more because that alone had my heart skip a beat.

"Who knows? You could be hiding your true identity while pretending you have no idea what's going on. Pretending to be innocent, but you're actually undercover."

"Oh, really?" I laughed. "That would have been badass! Sadly, I'm not that interesting, nor am I skilled in doing any of that. The only skill I have involves a pen and paper." I sighed. I was boring compared to him.

"That's something you should be proud of. You're very talented." His eyes looked intently into mine, almost making me blush by it.

"And how would you know?"

"I've seen your sketchbook. You have a very creative mind."

My expression fell.

"How much did you see?" I questioned, and a small, self-satisfied smirk crossed his face at my reaction.

"All of it."

I groaned in embarrassment as I remembered just how many full pages I have of him.

"Of course, you have..." I muttered and he gave me a wink.

We came to a stop in front of a tall building with massive double doors. Fancy writing in large gold cursive letters in French was on the glass doors.

"You're going shopping?" I turned to look at Damiano.

"It's for you. You need a dress for tomorrow." Damiano suddenly frowned and grabbed his phone from his pocket. "I need to take this. Go inside and see what you like." He picked up the phone and walked away to talk.

Shrugging, I went inside and stopped by the door to look around.

It was a boutique of sheer elegance, where gold and white intertwined to create an atmosphere of opulence. Gilded accents and mirrors caught the light, while crystal chandeliers twinkled above. Luxurious items were displayed in gleaming cases, and plush seating was waiting to swallow you whole.

"Excuse me, can I help you with something?" I was met with a pair of blue eyes of a fair skinned woman with bright red lips.

"I'm looking for an evening gown. Can you show me where you have them?" I smiled. It didn't go unnoticed that she was looking unimpressed by how I was dressed.

"Sure." With a forced smile, she guided me to the back of the boutique, where I saw rows of dresses hanging from racks. She stood to the side and raised a brow at me. I let out a small sigh and went to have a look when I realized she wasn't going to help me out.

A smile broke out on my face when I saw a familiar dress.

"I think that might be out of your price range." I looked over my shoulder, and she scrutinized me from head to toe.

"Why do you think that?" I slightly tilted my head with a smile, even though I wanted to roll my eyes.

I didn't like people like her; a type that will only help you if you screamed of money. Was she expecting me to come in a gown before she would be nice?

"That dress is a limited edition by Jacinta. Very few boutiques were fortunate to have her designs. Not that I would expect you to know who she is." The laugh that escaped her lips was a blend of amusement and superiority.

It made me frown.

"Oh, I'm familiar with her." I said and looked back at the dress. *Quite familiar, actually, since I came out of her vagina.* I wanted to say but held my tongue.

My mother's designs always made me proud whenever I saw them in boutiques, and this dress was even more special, which was why it was a limited edition. It was the first dress we worked on together that would be sold in other boutiques and not just our own.

When we worked on the dress, we explored hundreds of sketches, envisioning variations like a shorter style or a sweeping, trailing gown. In the end, we found a middle ground; the front of the dress tapered to mid-thigh in a graceful curve, while the rest cascaded into a sweeping train behind.

It was a stunning, elegant gown that I was proud of being apart.

"Look, I think we're both wasting our time here..." The sounds of footsteps made her suddenly stop talking. Damiano approached us with his usual stone-faced expression.

"Mr. Bellavia, it's so nice to see you again!" She beamed with an incredibly bright smile. I scowled when her entire attitude and posture changed. He ignored her, didn't even spare her a single glance, and I couldn't help but feel satisfied.

"What's wrong?" Damiano asked, and a frown creased his face when he saw the displeased look on mine.

"Nothing..." I muttered, but quickly found a smile and pulled the dress out to show it to him. "What do you think? I helped my mom make this dress. It even has my initials!"

I showed him the label on the dress, pointing to where it said A.C. just under my mother's name. "A.C. for Althaia Celano." I gave a small wink to the lady. Her face was quickly turning into a bright red shade that matched her lipstick.

"Your mother?" She asked, stunned.

"Where's Chloé?" Damiano snapped, clearly not wanting to waste any unnecessary time.

"Y-yes, I'll get her right away." She spun around and almost ran away.

"I'll get her fired if she made you unhappy."

"No, no." I said quickly. "But she could learn to be a bit nicer." I gave a small, reassuring smile. She was being a pain, but I didn't want to be the one responsible for her getting fired. My conscience would eat me alive.

"Damiano!" Another woman walked up to him with a big smile and greeted by kissing his cheeks. I felt my fingers twitch, as I didn't like how she greeted him and kept her hands on his shoulders while talking.

"... Althaia."

"Huh?" It was only when I snapped my eyes to Damiano that I realized he had been trying to talk to me. Chloé just gave a small laugh.

"I'm Chloé, the owner of this boutique." She introduced herself with a handshake.

"Oh, hi, I'm Althaia." I smiled and shook her hand.

"Damiano tells me you need a dress for tomorrow, yes?" Chloé said and had us follow her into a private room.

"Something fitting for an auction." He added.

"Of course! Let me just take your measurements." She asked me to step on the small stage while Damiano took a seat on the couch.

"I have a few dresses in mind for you to try. As you have a bigger bust, we might need to make a slight pinch at the waist to accentuate your curves. Is that okay?"

"Sure." I nodded, and she hurried off to grab some gowns for me to try.

I stepped down from the small stage and went to Damiano. He immediately wrapped an arm around me and sat me on his lap. He picked a strand of my hair, playing with it around his finger as his golden-brown eyes gazed at me. It gave me that fluttery feeling again that makes me want to scream into a pillow and kick my feet into the air.

"So jealous." He said, amused.

"I'm not." I denied immediately.

"You're also a lousy liar."

"Whatever." I retorted as my only comeback, but it only humored him some more. "Oh, wait, weren't you the one who beat up his own cousin for dancing with me?" I looked at him with a teasing grin.

"Mmhh. That will teach him not to touch what's mine." His words had my stomach tingle, even more when he kissed my shoulder and worked his way up to my neck.

"Chloé's back..." I whispered to him because that was all I could. I shuddered when he nibbled my ear before leaning away.

As we watched Chloé coming back with a rack of dresses, it suddenly hit me.

"I'm not wearing any underwear!" I whispered in a panic to Damiano.

"Hot." He replied, amused by it.

"Come, dear, let me help you." Chloé called me over as she hung the first dress in the fitting room.

"Oh, it's fine. No need to trouble yourself. I can manage on my own." I said and darted into the fitting room.

"Are you sure -"

"Yup! Don't worry." I quickly said and closed the curtains.

That Devil could have given me a heads up before we left the hotel.

I opened the curtain once I tried on the dress and stepped out to let Damiano see.

"No." He responded immediately.

"Why not?" I feigned confusion even though I already knew the answer. It was too sexy and too revealing.

"I said no. Try another one." Damiano was giving me a stern look, but I wanted to mess with him a bit.

"Well, I like it. It's making my tits look great. Don't you agree?" I grinned and looked in the mirror. My breasts looked like they were about to spill over at any minute.

The gown was of pristine white, and it caressed every curve as it cascaded to the ground. Its v-neckline was a tantalizing invitation, daringly halting right above my navel while the cups embraced my breasts with a provocative intensity.

This dress was so sexy.

"I really should get this one." I continued, and it took everything in me to not laugh.

"Absolutely not." Damiano approached me from behind. I turned to face him, and a fierce glare was present in his eyes. "Do you want men's hungry eyes on you?" It came out as a low growl from him, and it made me bite my lip at how sexy it sounded.

"Hmm, do you think they will like this dress on me?" I taunted him by seductively trailing my hands from my breasts and slowly down my body.

Damiano's eyes darkened, and I let out a shocked gasp when he suddenly grabbed my throat. He leaned in, our faces only a speck of dust apart.

"You don't know what kind of game you're playing with me, Althaia. Wear the dress and see how I create a bloodbath of any man whose eyes dare to linger on you." His expression was cold and ruthless, and I swallowed hard when I realized he meant every single word.

"Go. Change." Damiano gave a nod in the direction of the fitting room.

Without uttering a word, I went to change, completely astounded by what just had happened. Never had I been manhandled like that before. And fuck, it turned me on. More than it should have.

It had me biting my lip as I looked over my shoulder at him, seeing him with his arms and legs spread on the couch, his dark golden-brown eyes fixed on me with a head tilt. It made me want to pounce on him like a wild animal as my pussy pulsed at the sight.

Fortunately, Chloé was occupied with getting the rest of the dresses ready for me. That, or she just pretended to be. Either way, I was grateful she wasn't looking.

I tried on dress after dress and nothing impressed Damiano. It came to a point I didn't even step out of the fitting room. I would open the curtain for him to see, only for him to say no each time.

"What's wrong with this dress?" I asked in frustration. I couldn't count how many dresses I had already tried on, and this one seemed pretty safe; a long turquoise dress, neither sexy nor revealing, so what could be wrong?

"It's hideous." Damiano simply answered. I sighed and plopped down on the couch next to him. Chloé had a finger up to her mouth, thinking as she looked at the dresses I had tried on.

"Well, this was the last dress."

"I'll be right back." Chloé said and left.

"You're really impossible to please." I sulked.

"Is that so?" Damiano cocked a brow.

"Yes."

"If I remember correctly, and I do, you did a phenomenal job of pleasing me in bed." Damiano gave me a smug look. "And in the shower."

"Don't say that out loud!" I smacked his arm playfully, earning me a smirk.

"This dress will do!" Chloé returned, and I gave a look to Damiano to not say anything inappropriate.

I tried the dress, hoping it would be the last one and Damiano would approve of it. I really liked it; a floor-length wine-colored dress with its back gracefully exposed. It was adorned with delicate lace petals tracing the plunge of the v-neckline, revealing a hint of my cleavage. The bodice hugged me stunningly, while the skirt cascaded elegantly from my hips. It had a double high slit that revealed a glimpse of my legs beneath a sheer overlay of matching red fabric.

It was beautiful, but I dreaded Damiano's opinion.

Once more, I tugged the curtain aside. Damiano's gaze roved over me, taking in every detail, and my brows arched in surprise that his response wasn't an instant rejection. Stepping onto the circular stage, I did a small twirl for him to see the entire dress.

"We'll take this one." He nodded in approval.

"Finally!" I exclaimed in relief.

"I'll have it ready and send it to your hotel room as soon as possible." Chloé breathed in relief and smiled.

"I'm just going to use the restroom." I told Damiano once I was dressed in my own clothes. I needed to splash some cold water on my face to freshen up.

As I was patting my face dry, the door swung open unexpectedly. I turned around to find Damiano striding in. He drew me into his embrace, his lips crashing onto mine with an intensity that ignited the moment.

"Red is a fucking good color on you." He grunted, tugging on my lip with his teeth, adding an electrifying depth to the kiss that left me breathless. His hand lifted the hem of my dress, finding his way between my thighs.

"Here?" I moaned against his lips.

"I have no self-control when I'm with you. Turn around, baby."

Before I knew it, he had me bent over the sink with my dress hiked up above my ass.

Damiano had me sucking on his fingers, using my saliva to lubricate himself as he positioned behind me. His hand fisted in my hair, making me look at him in the mirror.

"Watch how I fuck you from behind."

And fuck me he did.

Twenty-Four

ALTHAIA

"You really don't know the meaning of a break, do you?" I playfully shook my head at him.

"It's your fault for being sexy." Damiano shot me a wink.

"Ah, right, blaming it on women when it's the men who can't control themselves." I retorted.

"I didn't hear you complain earlier. In fact, it sounded like you were *very much* enjoying it." A satisfied look crossed his face as his eyes roamed down my body.

"It wasn't too bad." I shrugged, pretending as if it didn't turn me on when I watched him take me from behind. "What's the plan for today?" I asked, hoping I wouldn't have to do more shopping after spending hours in a fitting room.

"Whatever your heart desires."

"Really?"

"I'm all yours." Damiano smiled, and I felt everything stop for a moment by how beautifully he smiled.

"You better not regret your words." I chuckled and started walking towards a nearby park. "Who were you talking to earlier on the phone?"

"Antonio." He answered curtly.

"Is everything okay?"

"You don't need to concern yourself with these things." Damiano kept staring right ahead, his hands in his pockets as he glared at people who dared to come too close to us.

The park was full of people enjoying the weather, and some even had picnics and were feeding the ducks. It was weird to be walking next to him as if we were a normal couple when, in fact, he was a big Mafia Boss.

"You always say that, yet you're going to drag me to an event full of dangerous people. Some info would be great, actually." I pointed out.

"It's not the same. The less you know, the better." Damiano gave me a look, warning me not to ask more questions. I pretended I didn't see it.

"Knowledge is power. You can't keep me in the dark forever."

He stopped walking, and his eyes locked onto mine as he tilted my chin upward with his fingers.

"You have a genuine innocence, Althaia, and this world is anything but. It fucks you up in unimaginable ways, so believe me when I say ignorance is a blessing for you. The less you know, the better." Damiano spoke with a firm tone.

I sensed the gravity of the situation when that crease appeared between his brows. Strangely enough, a jolt of excitement ran through me as he continued to look at me with his focused gaze.

"Am I not already a part of this world? Look at who my father is." I asked, wondering about the workings of it all.

"No." He let me go as he shook his head, and we started walking again, waiting for him to elaborate. "Your father might be a mob boss, but that doesn't mean you're a part of it just because you're his daughter. You have to take an oath."

"Omertá." I blurted, remembering I had read about it. It was a code of silence and a code of honor. Break it and you wouldn't live to see the next hour. "Honestly, I thought it was made up. Is it actually serious?"

"It's a blood oath; an unbreakable bond. Once it's taken, there's no going back. Only death releases you from it."

I nodded in awe, sucking in all the information he was giving.

"How do you take the blood oath?" He gave me a stern look, and I rolled my eyes in response. "Okay, then do you know anyone who has broken it?"

My question had him go silent.

"I do." Damiano answered after a while. I gave him a quick glance, noticing the blank expression on his face. Though my curiosity begged for more details, prying further was a line I couldn't cross in this matter.

"How many have you killed?" The question slipped out before I even had a chance to think about what I was asking.

"Don't even go there with me, Althaia." His warning came too late, as the next question had already escaped my lips.

"5, 10, 30, 100?"

"Althaia." Damiano gave me a harsh look, and I clamped my mouth shut.

"Sorry... I'm just curious, that's all." I sighed, but I knew I had overstepped.

"Your curiosity can get you killed." He retorted firmly. "No more questions." Damiano immediately said when I was about to say something.

"I want to understand your world better." I said quietly.

"Don't."

Damn

We walked in silence, as I didn't dare to utter another word. As we reached the end of the park, the air filled with the sounds of people screaming and laughing on roller coasters.

An immediate grin spread across my lips.

"No way, it's an amusement park!" I let out a squeal of excitement and grabbed Damiano's hand as I practically dragged him with me.

I couldn't contain my excitement as I looked around. I hadn't been to one in years.

I looked at Damiano and laughed. He seemed out of place, taking in the amusement park. He arched a brow in question when I continued to giggle.

"Don't be so serious here. It's a happy place! Brings back childhood memories, don't they?"

"Hmm, I see." He simply replied. I slightly frowned as I tilted my head.

"...You have been to an amusement park before, haven't you?" I asked.

"No." Damiano tucked his hands back into his pockets, his face remaining blank.

I looked at him in pure shock.

"What kind of childhood is that?"

"I was busy surviving and learning how to kill." He stated casually with a shrug of his shoulders.

A pang of sadness hit me as I pictured Damiano as a child, forced to live in a world in which he had no control over. A child robbed of his innocence, only to be taught how to be a cold-blooded murderer.

"Don't look at me like that." Damiano's eyes softened.

My arms went around him with no hesitation, and I held him tight. I had to blink a few times to stop the tears from showing.

"I can't give you your childhood back, but I can give you a great time in an amusement park." I linked my arm through his with a smile. "And the best food is here. I don't know why, but it's like food in these places tastes a hundred times better." I grinned at him. I caught a glimpse of adoration in his eyes, but it disappeared before I could be certain.

I didn't give it much thought as I looked for our first activity, determined to give him a good time.

"Damiano, look! A horror house. We have to go!" I tugged on his arm, leading the way.

And that was where I made my mistake.

"Damiano, you can't do that!" I gasped and quickly walked out of the horror house before any more people were hurt.

"He scared you." Damiano scowled.

"They are supposed to scare you. That's their job! Not the other way around." I sighed.

A poor guy, dressed up as Michael Myers, showed up out of nowhere in front of me with a big-ass knife and scared the shit out of me. Damiano took it way too seriously and slammed the guy to the floor, threatening him to the point he took off running, screaming for his life.

"I think you traumatized the poor guy." I looked back at the horror house, feeling guilty about it.

"Good." Damiano's reply had me burst out laughing.

"Try to loosen up a bit." I took his hand in mine as I looked around for our next activity. My smile widened as I led him to a particular stand. "Perhaps this is more your area of expertise." I bit my lip to hold back a snicker as I gestured to the target shooting game.

Damiano took a quick glance before meeting my eyes with a playful glint.

"You think you're funny?" A smile tugged at his lips.

"Oh, I know I'm funny." I winked and bought us a round. "Want to make it a competition?" I picked up the rifle confidently, staring at the shooting mark hanging on the wall.

"What's the winning prize?" Damiano crossed his arms, leaning against the counter, still humored that I was challenging him.

"Whatever the winner wishes."

"Whatever the winner wishes." He repeated with a smirk. "By all means, go right ahead."

I aimed at the small shooting mark, closed one eye to focus because that's what I had seen in movies. Once having a clear sight of the mark, I fired all of my shots.

And not a single one made it inside a circle.

I wasn't even close.

"Wow, that sucked." I scowled at the target paper. "How am I supposed to hit that little red dot when it's so far away?" I complained to no one in particular as I continued to scowl.

"Looks like we've found a loser." Damiano taunted, making me scoff at him.

"Don't be so sure. It's harder than what it looks like."

"We'll see." He winked, and I squinted my eyes, watching him pick up his rifle. He stood casually as he aimed and fired his shots. My eyes slowly widened when I saw him hit every single shot in the middle of the red dot.

Perfectly.

Silence followed right after as we both stared at his target paper; me with my jaw dropped, and him with a smug look on his face.

"You cheated!" I accused him.

"And how did I cheat?" Damiano raised a brow with a tilt of his head. I crossed my arms, my face still in a frown, as I couldn't think of how in the world he could have cheated.

"We have a winner! Pick your prize, sir." The guy behind the stand interrupted. Damiano scanned the selection above, picking a big, fluffy, white teddy bear with striking blue eyes, long lashes, and a pink bow tied around its neck.

"For you." His eyes softened as I smiled warmly, feeling my cheeks flush as he gave me the teddy bear.

"Thank you." I clutched the teddy bear in my chest.

He won that for me.

"Don't think you're off the hook just yet. I want to try one more, and I can feel victory this time." I told Damiano and handed him the teddy bear.

I bought another round and picked up the rifle once again. I had one eye open as I aimed for the tiny spot on the wall.

"You're holding it wrong. Let me help you." I felt a sudden rush of adrenaline as he stepped close behind me. He adjusted the rifle against my shoulder, and I could feel his breath on my neck as he helped with my aim.

"Both eyes open." Damiano's whisper sent shivers down my spine, and I held my breath as he pressed his body against mine. "Now, relax your shoulders and breathe."

I tried to concentrate as I followed his instructions. I relaxed my shoulders and let out a breath, focusing on my mark before firing. I lowered the rifle to have a look at my target paper.

"Oh my God, I did it!" I jumped up and down in excitement. It wasn't perfect like Damiano's, but at least they were all in the inner circle.

"That's my girl." He whispered softly before planting a gentle kiss on my temple. My body tingled, and even more so when his lips trailed down to my ear as he spoke. "For my prize, I want your ass."

"Uh, have you had a snow cone before?" I cleared my throat loudly, looking around to see if anyone heard him. Damiano chuckled at my embarrassment but went along with it.

"No. I don't have much of a sweet tooth."

"I can see that. There's not an ounce of fat on you." I poked at his stomach and felt his rock-hard abs.

"I'll undress for you later." He winked, and that was when I realized I had my hand flat on his stomach, feeling him up in the middle of the amusement park.

"I wouldn't mind." I mumbled, continuing to feel him up.

Damn, I'm no better than a man.

"Sit here. I'll be right back." I pushed him down on a bench. Correction, I *tried* to because he wouldn't budge, but sat down anyway.

I gave him the other teddy bear I had won and quickly went to get snow cones.

"Hi there, what can I do for ya?" The girl behind the stand smiled brightly.

"Can I have a blue snow cone, please? Oh, and one churro with sugar and cinnamon, thanks!" I smiled, but she just stood there, staring at me with an unreadable expression. The longer she looked at me, the more uncomfortable I became, and I shifted my weight from one foot to the other.

"Are you okay?" I asked, unsure of what was wrong with her. With a shake of her head, she snapped out of her trance.

"I'm so sorry! I didn't mean to stare like that. You have a very pretty face." She beamed.

"Oh, thank you." I chuckled, complementing her freckles in return.

"Let me just get you your order." She rushed to get me my snow cone and churro, her high ponytail of red hair swayed behind her. "Here you go! So sorry again. This one's on the house." She gave me an extra snow cone.

"Thank you so much. Take care."

I headed back to Damiano but had to pause for a second to get a better grip on the stuff I was holding. Out of nowhere, I had this creepy feeling like someone was watching me.

I glanced around, spotting the girl who just serviced me as she and another lady looked at me. She shot me a quick smile, and I gave her a tight smile back, and hurried back to Damiano.

I didn't like the way they were looking at me. I didn't know what it was, but it sure as hell gave me a strange feeling.

"You took too long." Damiano met me halfway with a frown on his face. I lightly chuckled at how funny he looked; a big, dangerous man like him was holding two teddy bears in his arms.

"It was only five minutes."

"Five minutes too long."

"So impatient." I shook my head. "Here, try this." I gave him a snow cone as we took a seat on a bench nearby. Damiano was holding it like it was some kind of foreign thing.

"It's not poison." I joked.

"I'm aware." He said but made no move to eat it.

"Come on, have some." I encouraged him and ate the shaved ice. I guess it was a long shot with the snow cone as he just ignored it and watched me eat mine, his eyes focusing on my tongue.

"Well, at least try the churro. It's covered in cinnamon and sugar." I held it out for him to try, but he just shook his head. "Your loss." I shrugged and took a big bite. I even did a dramatic 'mmhh' as I ate to tease him.

His sudden lean towards me caused me to stop chewing and lean back in response. I was left breathless as he slowly licked my lip, savoring the taste of the sugar that was left behind.

"Sweet, indeed."

Twenty-Five

Althaia

We spent the whole day at the amusement park, trying out different foods and playing games. I was a competitive person and would challenge Damiano at any chance.

"I don't lose, Althaia." He would say every time I lost to him, and it annoyed me to no end.

"I don't like you." I scowled and he would chuckle at me, but then he would soften the blow by winning me so many teddy bears that my arms were full. It had me smiling like crazy.

"My feet are hurting." I winced, staring at the flats I was wearing. They weren't exactly comfortable to wear after so many hours.

"Want to head back?" Damiano asked, and I nodded tiredly. All I could think about was getting off my feet and soaking in a hot bath.

We changed direction to get to the exit, and that was when I noticed a man changed his direction as well and followed us. The same man we have walked by a few times already.

My heart pumped faster. Something about it wasn't right. I tried to tell myself it was coincidental, but he had still been in the background wherever we were.

I squeezed the teddy bears closer to my chest and stepped closer to Damiano for a sense of protection. I wasn't sure what it was, but I had a feeling someone was watching us ever since that girl from the snow cone stand stared at me with that lady.

"Damiano..." I trailed off.

"I know." He said calmly, wrapping an arm around me and pulled me closer to him. "I was trying to distract you." He was speaking softly, but his expression was cold and serious.

"W-what's going on?" I couldn't help but stutter as fear filled me.

"I haven't seen them before." Damiano kept staring straight ahead, but his eyes were discreetly analyzing the crowd.

"Them?!" I shrieked in a panic. There was more than one?

"Don't look." He stopped me when I was about to. "So far, there are six of them. If you look around now, they'll know I've spotted them, and they might attack sooner than planned when we get out. They won't do anything now. There are too many people around."

My body tensed.

"Breathe, Althaia. I won't let them hurt you." I hadn't even noticed that I had stopped breathing until he pointed it out.

"O-okay." My voice wouldn't stop shaking and I could feel my knees giving up on me a little.

The music and laughter from the amusement park were fading as we made our way to the park we came from. It didn't help that the entire park was extremely dark, the few lamp posts were barely providing any light.

"Talk to me, piccola." Damiano's voice was still soft as he spoke to me, but I still felt my knees would buckle at any second.

"I'm scared." My voice was in a whisper, the fear I was feeling didn't allow me to talk louder.

"I know. It will be over soon." He promised.

Damiano led us down a shadowy path to a secluded area of the park. He suddenly stopped as he pulled me in front of him, pressing me up against a tree with his hands gripping my waist tightly.

"Listen to me, Althaia." His brows were slightly pinched as he met my gaze with a serious expression. "No matter what, you keep your eyes on me. You don't look anywhere else but at me." He ordered firmly.

I gave a small nod and stared at him wide-eyed.

"Do you trust me to keep you safe?" He asked.

I nodded.

"You'll hear gunshots, but they won't be too loud." Damiano leaned in closer, and I felt his hands moving around. Then I felt it.

His gun.

I looked down quickly and saw him twisting a silencer onto the muzzle of the gun. I gulped and looked back at him.

"They are close." Damiano's body was pressed against me, and his breath was hot against my lips. From the outside, we looked like a normal couple, having a romantic about-to-kiss moment up against a tree. But it was a matter of a life-or-death situation.

I fixated on Damiano's beautiful, golden-brown eyes that I have grown to care so much for.

In an instant, Damiano's gaze transformed, turning icy and resolute. His attention quickly shifted to behind me, and a sharp, involuntary jolt coursed through me as the crackle of gunfire erupted just inches from my left side. The pained moans echoed through the air, followed by the dull thud of bodies hitting the ground. I swallowed hard as the grim reality of the situation hit me.

With my body already tense, I could feel my muscles tighten even more when I saw two more muzzle flashes not that far from us. I was holding onto Damiano's shirt so tightly when I heard someone moving towards us.

I had to fight to keep my lip from trembling. Damiano looked back at me and gently placed his hand on my cheek, stroking it softly with his thumb.

"It's Antonio and Luca." He said quietly, but I still couldn't comprehend what he meant and squeezed my eyes shut when the sound of footsteps stopped right next to us.

"Breathe, Althaia. You're going to pass out." My eyes shot open, and I gasped for air, feeling as though I had been plunged into the depths of the ocean and was just now emerging for a breath.

Only then did I see Antonio and Luca were here.

"I–I can't feel my legs." I whispered to Damiano. My body was shaking, and my sight went blurry.

"I got you." Damiano wrapped his arm around my waist, effortlessly lifted me, and cradled me into him.

I wrapped my arms tightly around his neck, feeling the warmth of his skin against mine. The silence was only broken by the crunching of gravel beneath their feet.

I heard the sound of a car door opening and Damiano slid into the car with me on his lap. He still held me tightly, his hand caressing my back as the car drove off.

"Here, take small sips." A bottle was held to my lips, and the taste of fizz covered my tongue. I leaned back into him after a few sips, closing my eyes as I focused on his calm heartbeat.

We walked into the hotel room with Antonio and Luca following right behind us. Damiano sat me on the couch and wrapped a blanket around me before stepping away to talk to the others.

I pulled the blanket tighter around and pulled my knees to my chest. A bottle of water entered my view, and I looked up to see it was Antonio. They all seemed to wear this blank expression, allowing no one to see what they were thinking.

I thanked him with a small smile and held the bottle with my shaking hands, struggling to twist the cap open. Antonio took the bottle out of my hands and opened it for me before giving it back.

All three of them were by the window, talking in hushed voices so I wouldn't pick up what they were saying. I tried to listen if I could just make sense of some words but failed to do so as my own thoughts were all over the place. The combination of fear and confusion left me paralyzed, unable to move or think clearly.

I shifted my gaze towards them and noticed they were already focused on me. Damiano said something to Antonio and Luca before they left us alone.

"What's going on?" I asked. Damiano sat down next to me on the couch, and I felt his strong arms wrap around me as he pulled me onto his lap.

"How are you feeling?" He studied my face to see if I was okay, intentionally avoiding the topic.

"What's going on?" I tried again.

"You don't need to worry about it." He dismissed.

"You can't say that when I was in the middle of it." My heart was pumping violently. Were they after Damiano? ...Or was it me? The last thought had the color drained from my face.

Damiano cupped my face, his eyes narrowing on me.

"Please, tell me... I need to know." My anxiety grew as he hesitated, his gaze moving back and forth across my face.

"We don't know who they are. They weren't carrying anything to be identified with, which is a clue in itself."

"What?" I knew I wouldn't be able to rest until I had an answer, even if it was one I dreaded.

"Human traffickers." He answered. My heart stopped beating for a second and my eyes went wide in shock. "It's not unusual for them to be in such places."

"And they were after...?" I trailed off, already knowing the answer. Yet I couldn't get myself to finish the sentence.

"They were." He confirmed. My eyes drifted down to his shirt, and I absentmindedly toyed with the buttons. They were kidnapping people from the amusement park. It all made me sick.

"What about their bodies in the park?" I had to swallow hard at the thought of their dead bodies left in the park.

"They are being taken care of." Damiano spoke softly while I felt his gaze on me, but I continued to play with the buttons on his shirt.

"Okay." I said, relieved.

Damiano's touch was soft as he lifted my chin to meet his eyes.

"I won't let anything happen to you. You're safe." His eyes were full of promise. The warmth of his body enveloped me as he leaned in for a gentle kiss. "I promise you they will pay." He whispered against my lips, and I wasn't sure what he meant by that.

Twenty-Six

ALTHAIA

I sank into the bathtub, feeling the warmth of the water and the tickle of bubbles on my skin. The water enveloped me, and I let out a contented sigh, feeling the knots in my muscles start to loosen.

I made a mental note that I would never again wear flats to an amusement park.

I felt the weight of exhaustion settling over me, lulling me toward slumber. I hadn't slept. I couldn't when every time I shut my eyes, I would hear sounds of gunshots in my mind, and I would wake up, startled.

In the end, I gave up and spent the night tracing the curves and lines of Damiano's tattoos with my fingers, finding comfort in the steady rhythm of his breathing.

Damiano didn't sleep either, but I doubt he was awake for the same reasons. He was awake, comforting me by tracing soothing circles on my back. It was so calming that under normal circumstances, I would have been asleep in seconds.

What happened played repeatedly in my mind; the way I witnessed Damiano getting ready to kill. In an instant, his pupils contracted, his eyes adopting an icy, detached demeanor. I saw him transition into an eerie trance that took less than a heartbeat to enter.

It left me wondering about Damiano's upbringing and what could lead to such a detachment of his emotions, allowing him to kill without remorse.

My heart sank as I pictured a young Damiano with that same cold, distant expression I had seen; an innocent child with no other choice than to become a cold-blooded murderer. He was a Devil, and any person with a bit of common sense knew to stay hundreds of miles away from someone like him. Yet, I went to him for comfort and protection.

Did that make me naïve or just plain stupid? I haven't decided yet.

The water had turned cold, the bubbles vanished, and my fingers were shriveled when I opened my eyes. I had dozed off, managing to get only a brief hour of sleep.

I stepped out and wrapped myself in the incredibly soft bathrobe and exited the bathroom.

Damiano said he had to take care of something and took off after ordering room service for me. Normally, I would ask him where he was going, but I was too tired to interrogate him. Not that he would tell me, even if I asked.

"Oh shit, you scared me!" I put a hand up to my chest and let out a breath when I saw Luca on the couch. He was half asleep before I yelped and woke him up.

"Sorry, the couch sucked me in." He said as he sat up, running a hand through his jet-black hair. I had seen Luca around a few times before but never really talked to him. I liked that he was dressed casually in a white t-shirt and jeans. It made him seem normal.

"Yeah, it's really comfy." I chuckled a bit and went to the service cart. I grabbed the cup of coffee that was now cold, but took a sip anyway. I immediately grimaced and snatched a bottle of water instead.

"Where's Damiano?" I asked Luca and took a seat in the armchair.

"I don't know." He looked at me with his hazel eyes as he leaned back on the couch.

"Really?" I raised a brow, obviously not believing him.

"Yeah." He gave a half smirk, and I rolled my eyes. He wasn't going to tell me either.

"If you would like some really good coffee, there's a café just around the corner." I said with a hint of a smile.

"No." Luca immediately said, barely letting me finish my sentence.

"Why not?"

"Boss's orders. You're not leaving the room." He shrugged.

"You would be with me? And that's me assuming why you're here; to keep an eye on me." I pointed out.

"Ah, you see, they told me to be careful with you." He crossed his arms with a teasing look.

"With me? I haven't done anything." I said, a bit offended.

"Dario and Antonio said you have a way to get what you want."

"Ah..." I trailed off with a chuckle. He wasn't totally wrong. "It's literally around the corner. We'll be back right away." I promised.

"Nope." Luca shook his head.

"You look like you could use some coffee, too. They have great croissant sandwiches as well." I tried to lure him.

"Sorry, can't do."

"Fine, I'll just tell Damiano that you're letting me starve." It was a cheap shot, but I really wanted that coffee.

"You have food." He gestured to the service cart.

"It's cold."

"Good thing you have room service, then." He gave a half smug smile.

"Come on! It'll take the same time if we just went down to the café and get what we want. Thirty minutes tops!"

"No."

"I haven't slept all night. It'll be your hell." I challenged him.

"Good. It'll give me something to do." Luca grinned, and I gave up. I can see why Damiano left him to keep an eye on me. He wouldn't budge at all.

"So, we're just stuck here for how long?" I got comfortable and sat cross-legged in my seat.

"They should be back before we leave for the auction." Luca said. I looked at the time and saw that it was only ten a.m. There was still a long time since we had to leave around seven p.m.

I let out a small sigh as we fell in a comfortable silence while I zoned out, lost in my own thoughts.

"Are you okay?" Luca asked, and I looked at him. "About last night." He elaborated.

"I'm fine… Just shocked, I guess." The thought of being snatched if I was alone had my stomach churn with fear. "How did you guys just pop out?" I decided to ask, distracting myself from unpleasant thoughts.

"We're always around. We kept in the background to give you privacy."

"Oh." It was a bit creepy, but still impressive because not once did I suspect they were with us.

I took a long look at Luca and wondered how he ended up in this life. He looked too young, even with all the tattoos on his arms and neck.

"Can I ask how old you are?"

"I'm twenty-seven." He smiled. My eyes widened a bit.

"I'm curious how you ended up in this life at such a young age, but I guess that's not really any of my business." I said, and Luca gave me a look that said he agreed. "Are you in a relationship, then?" I asked. Maybe I could get to know him a bit better, since we were stuck for now.

"Sure am. We have been together for three years now." His expression softened at the mention of his partner. I couldn't help but smile at how happy he looked talking about it. And I also appreciated how he didn't seem bothered by my random questions.

"Does your partner know what you do?" That was something I was curious about. Were they allowed to know, or was it to be kept a secret?

"I expect her to know since she's related to Damiano." Luca laughed.

"She's Damiano's cousin? I did not see that coming." I lightly chuckled.

"He gave me hell for it when I made a comment about her in his presence. She's the most beautiful woman I've seen, and I blurted it out before I could stop myself. I didn't know they were cousins, and he was about to have my head." Luca's eyes sparked as he talked about her, and it made me feel warm to hear a man like him talk about his girlfriend like that.

"I couldn't keep away from her ever since."

"That is so cute! I'm happy for you." I beamed. The hopeless romantic in me couldn't help but almost want to kick my feet in the air at how adorable it sounded.

"Thank you." He smiled warmly.

"You know, you're different from the other men who usually are around Damiano. They are all so serious, it's terrifying. I tried to start a conversation with Antonio once, and he shut me down immediately. I think he hates me." I said and cringed at the awful attempt to make conversation with him in the car.

"He doesn't hate you." Luca was amused.

"You don't need to lie to me. It's fine. I know I can't be liked by everyone." I gave a small shrug, but he shook his head.

"You don't get it. He was just being careful. We all thought you would just be a one-time thing and we wouldn't see you again. Guess we were wrong."

"And who says this isn't a one-time thing?"

Luca raised a brow.

"You're not fooling anyone."

"It was a genuine question." I said, and he looked a bit surprised.

"You really don't know much, do you?" He leaned forward, resting his arms on his thighs. "We are all ordered to protect you with our lives if something were to happen. Which means you're not going anywhere."

My eyes widened at the information. We didn't have a label on whatever we were at the moment, but the thought of them having to sacrifice their lives just for someone like me did not settle well with me. At all.

"My life is not worth more than yours." I shook my head, displeased to know about it.

"But it is. That's how our society works."

"I don't like that." I frowned.

"You will get used to it." He shrugged, not caring that he was ordered to protect me with his life.

"Will I though? It all sounds so... extreme." I sighed. It was such a strange world; a world where only a scratch of the surface had been exposed to me. I never knew what to expect, and I kept telling myself I should expect the worst, but I didn't know what the definition of that was in their world.

Luca and I ended up chatting quite a bit before I decided to get my hair and makeup done early, so I wouldn't have to worry about it later. Since my dress was backless, I did my hair in an elegant, low updo with a few loose strands around my face.

I also ended up ordering room service since I was starving, and I had some much-needed coffee. Since we couldn't go out, I asked the receptionist if they had any card games. They didn't, but they were happy to get us something.

"UNO!" I shouted and smacked my card down on the table.

"No, you can't put a draw two on top of my draw four. So, you lose!" Luca threw his last card on the table with a smug grin.

"Yes, I can!" I insisted and removed his card.

"No, you can't. Look, these are the rules." He held up the packet and showed me the backside with the rules.

"Tsk, you're the last one to lecture me about rules." I teased, and he gave me a bored look. Luca was fun to hang out with and was a very competitive person. And so was I. Which meant hell broke out a few times. "Whatever, this game is boring anyway." I huffed and leaned back in my chair.

"Only because you lost all rounds. Sucker." He grinned, and I squinted my eyes at him.

"You so much cheated. Get up." I jumped up from my seat, certain that he was hiding cards behind him.

"Accept your defeat. You lost." Luca said, refusing to get up.

"Never!" I grabbed his arm with both hands, trying to get him up. I just didn't realize he would barely budge from his seat. Luca was staring at me with a brow raised as if saying, 'that's all you got?', which only made me more determined to get him up from the damn couch. Then he swiftly retracted his arm, making me lose my grip, and stumbled forward.

Right on top of him.

We both turned our heads quickly to the sound of the door opening and saw Damiano and Antonio entering the room.

Luca was the first one to react and sprang from the couch, taking me along with him. Damiano and Antonio's back-and-forth glances made me take a few steps back.

"He cheated!" I erupted in panic, only to realize my mistake as Damiano looked at the robe I was still wearing. "We were playing UNO, and he cheated." I quickly explained, pointing to the cards on the coffee table.

"And that's why you were on top of him." Damiano calmly stated, shoving his hands into his pockets.

"No, it's not like that -" I watched in horror as Antonio approached Luca, his fists clenched and his eyes blazing with a murderous rage that made my own eyes widen. I gasped in shock and moved quickly to shield Luca from harm, my arms spread wide to keep him safe.

"Let me just explain!" I yelled in pure fear. I couldn't understand why Luca said nothing when his ass was on the line.

"Antonio." Damiano called after him. He retreated and stood to the side as Damiano approached me. His eyes scanned me briefly before settling on Luca.

"Get. Out." Damiano hissed. Luca gave a quick nod and left with Antonio in tow.

"Don't hurt him." I said to Damiano with my heart still pounding at the close call.

"Why do you care?" He tilted his head.

"It's not what it looked like. I thought he was hiding cards behind him, so I tried to make him stand up and I lost my balance and fell." I explained, but Damiano didn't look convinced.

His eyes wandered over to the robe I had on. He tugged it to the side, his expression hardening when he saw I wasn't wearing anything underneath. He let out a scoff and turned around.

"Get dressed. We're leaving soon."

"Wait!" I followed him to the bedroom, but Damiano ignored me. He shut the bathroom door with a loud bang as he went inside. I stood still, gaping at the closed door, feeling my blood boil at his actions.

So, I kicked the door. Hard.

"Fuck!" I erupted in a whisper as pain shot up through my right foot.

Twenty-Seven

Althaia

I walked towards the elevator fast, or as fast as I could. My foot was still throbbing, and every step I took in my heels was agony. My anger towards Damiano was so intense that I couldn't bring myself to speak or even make eye contact with him. Since he wasn't trying to talk to me, it was an effortless task. But I could feel his gaze on me at times.

The only sound during the ride down to the underground parking was the hum of the elevator, making it feel like an eternity. Despite feeling Damiano's eyes burning into the side of my head, I refused to look away from the closed elevator doors, a frown still on my face.

The moment the doors opened, I stepped out towards the SUV where Antonio was. My eyes darted around frantically, searching for Luca, but he was nowhere to be seen. Just as I was about to turn around and confront Damiano about it, Luca stepped out of the driver's seat. A wave of relief washed over me, and I exhaled a long breath.

I ignored Antonio when he opened the car door for me and made my way around the car to Luca.

"You're not hurt, are you?" My eyes swept over him, searching for any visible wounds. Luca shook his head with a reassuring smile. "Did he rip your tongue out?!" I panicked when he didn't talk.

"My tongue is intact. Don't worry." His lips curved up, looking slightly amused by my reaction.

"Thank God." I let out another breath of relief before sliding into the car.

The car ride was silent. No one was making any conversation, and the only sounds were coming from the radio, playing softly in the background. I rested my head against the window, sighing as I looked out, and carefully tried to move my foot to ease the pain. It wasn't much of a help and only seemed to make it worse.

The silence was broken by the sound of a tinted window rolling up, dividing us from the front.

"What's wrong with your foot?" Damiano broke the silence. I ignored him and resumed looking out of the window. "Althaia."

"I don't know. Why don't you assume what's wrong?"

"Let me see."

"Nothing's wrong with it. It's fine." I snapped, and I was immediately hit with regret. I closed my eyes to keep my frustration from controlling me.

We went back to sitting in silence until I couldn't take it anymore.

"You don't trust me." I slowly stated. I didn't have to look at him to know his attention was already on me.

Five heartbeats later, he finally replied.

"I do."

"No, you don't." I faced him. I haven't laid eyes on him since he rudely shut the bathroom door in my face, and he looked irresistible in his black three-piece suit.

Damn him for looking this good.

"You sent him to our room to keep an eye on me, which means you trust him enough to do his job." I continued.

"It's not like that." Damiano's brows furrowed.

"Please, enlighten me then." I mocked a sweet smile.

"I don't like you close to other men."

I looked at him dumbfounded, waiting to see if he was joking, but he was serious.

"They work for you! Shouldn't I get to know them if I decide to stick around?" Now it was my turn to frown. "It's not my responsibility to fix your trust issues. Either you trust me, or you don't." I simply told him.

Damiano's amusement was clear in the way he arched an eyebrow.

"What's so funny?"

"You." He said.

My mouth fell open in disbelief.

"How am I being funny right now?"

"You're cute when you're mad." He smirked. He wrapped his arm around me, drawing me in close, until our faces were just inches apart. "You were so scared of me the first time we met... and now, you're sitting here, calling my ass insecure." His eyes lit up with entertainment, and I couldn't help but smile at it.

"The way you screamed in fear that day... Now, I'm making you scream for other reasons." Damiano's voice went low, and I felt a rush of excitement. The way he was looking at me made my cheeks flush with warmth. A steady pulse coursed through me, and I squeezed my thighs together. A smirk played across his lips, as it didn't go unnoticed by him.

"You owe me an apology." I whispered, leaning closer to his face, our lips almost touching.

"And how would you like your apology?" Damiano tugged on my lip with his teeth, and I almost let out a moan.

"I might have something in mind…" I breathed out. I pushed him back into the seat and straddled his lap. His hands reached for my hips, but I quickly grabbed his wrists and moved them away.

"No touching." I ordered him. He raised a single brow, conveying his curiosity, and I responded by giving him a flirtatious look.

Damiano's eyes snapped down to look when I wet my bottom lip. My hands explored his body, starting at his broad shoulders and tracing down to his sculpted chest. I continued further down until I felt the hard bulge in his pants. Moaning, I stroked him.

"Althaia, fuck…" Damiano tried to touch me again. I quickly shifted my position and sat on top of his hard cock.

"I said no touching." I moaned as I moved my hips slowly, grinding against him while he let out a groan of pleasure.

I moved slightly away and reached for his pants, unbuttoning them before taking hold of his length. With each stroke, he let out a low sound of pleasure, his eyes closing briefly before opening again.

"You better let me inside of you. Now." His voice was strained, grunting when I pumped his length faster. Then I slowed down with a grin. "You're going to be the death of me." He said through his gritted teeth.

"All in due time." I smirked. My fingers gently held his jaw, drawing him closer until our breaths mingled. He responded with a feral growl as my tongue met his lips, igniting a fire within us both.

"I want to make you feel good…" I whispered against his lips, stroking him faster as I watched him trying to restrain himself from touching me.

"Althaia…" Damiano moaned, his breathing getting heavy.

"Mhmm?" I replied, keeping my eyes trained on him as I closed the distance between us for a kiss.

Only to stop at the very last second.

"Oh, looks like we're here." With a swift movement, I rolled back to my side, opened the car door, and stepped out.

"Shit, fuck! Althaia!" Damiano called after me, sounding obviously *very* displeased, just as I shut the door in his face.

Heh.

"No need to, Antonio. He will be needing some time before coming out." I said to him before he could open the door for Damiano. He raised a brow in question. "He just got taught not to piss me off." I smirked proudly.

I looked toward the building where the auction was held. It was like standing in front of the White House. So elegant and extravagant. I inwardly groaned when I saw the enormous staircase, knowing it would be hell for my foot.

The car door swung open. With a glare, Damiano stepped out of the car, and I tried to look as innocent as possible. He stopped in front of me, and his eyes bore into mine with a fierce intensity. I had to slightly tilt my head up to meet his gaze. He towered over me, and even my heels couldn't make up the difference.

"You're going to pay for that." Damiano sneered, his voice husky as he spoke.

"I don't know what you're talking about." I smiled sweetly.

"You know exactly what you did." He sounded so displeased I had to bite back my laugh. I looked down at his crotch, seeing his bulge was still visible.

"If you behave, I might give you what you want." I retorted, using his own words against him.

I shot him a mischievous smirk and a flirty wink before turning on my heel.

The banquet hall was set up to be as extravagant as possible, with towering centerpieces and glittering chandeliers. The room was bustling with the sounds of chatter and laughter as the swarm of people, dressed in their finest clothing, mingled with one another.

I was taken aback by how many people were there, and I ended up playing a game with myself by guessing which ones were involved in a criminal organization, and which ones were... *normal*.

Antonio and Luca disappeared off somewhere to give us some privacy while we fell into a chat with too many people. Damiano was incredibly well-known, and the second we stepped foot inside, people practically rushed to have a word with him.

His presence attracted a crowd of people, all eager to share their business ideas and hoping for a partnership. He pulled me close and wrapped his arm around my waist, and I smiled politely while they talked.

"Is it always like this? Them trying to kiss your ass." I asked after we had excused ourselves from two men who wouldn't stop talking.

"Something like that."

"How boring."

"You've barely been here for an hour, and you're already bored?" He chuckled.

"I was hoping it would be more of a 'just sit and look pretty' kind of thing." I winced slightly and tried to lessen the pressure on my injured foot.

"Let's get you off your feet, then." Damiano was about to lead me away when another man called for him.

"Mr. Bellavia!" The man was with a woman linked to his arm as they approached us, and my shoulders slumped in disappointment.

"We don't have to talk to him." Damiano said, keeping a firm grip around my waist to help me a bit off my feet.

"No, it's okay. I can manage." I smiled at him.

"Mr. Roberts." Damiano greeted, and they shook hands.

"And who's the beautiful lady?" Mr. Roberts stuck his hand out to greet me.

"Althaia. It's a pleasure to meet you." I placed my hand in his, and he kissed the backside of my hand. I could feel Damiano's hand tightening around my waist, and I mentally rolled my eyes at him. I still leaned closer to him to ease him.

"Pleasure's all mine. This is my wife, Elena." He introduced, and we exchanged smiles. She was a beautiful woman with red hair, and her long silver dress was adorned with lots of jewelry.

Mr. Roberts wasted no time and went straight to business talk.

And he aimed his question right at me.

"Enlighten me, Miss Althaia. It appears that Mr. Bellavia's wine prices rise by the minute, making it one of the most expensive on the market. What distinguishes Mr. Bellavia's wine from the rest of the competitors at much lower prices?"

Well, shit.

He looked at me with scrutinizing eyes, waiting for my answer.

"Mr. Roberts, have you seen Mr. Bellavia's vineyards in Italy?"

Please say no.

"Unfortunately, I haven't been that lucky." He chuckled.

Bingo.

"They are without a doubt the greatest in Italy. You see, nearly all vineyards nowadays have abandoned traditional winemaking practices in favor of employing more technology than man. This, of course, reduces production time, but, if I may be honest with you and come with an opinion of my own, it also reduces wine quality." I said, but Mr. Roberts didn't look too convinced, so I continued.

"Not to mention that Mr. Bellavia is improving the economy by creating additional jobs in the community. It is not always about statistics, Mr. Roberts, it is also about a set of moral values that are beneficial to both people and society." I finished with a smile.

The silence that followed was nerve-wracking. I wasn't even aware that Damiano had a wine business, and I hoped what I said was at least somewhat true. I knew for sure Damiano was a hardworking man and took pride in his businesses.

Mr. Roberts kept staring at me for a while, not uttering a single word. Did I screw up?

"So, she's not just a pretty face." Mr. Roberts broke into a smile and looked back at Damiano. As I looked at Damiano, I noticed the way his eyes crinkled at the corners with a hint of a smile.

"She certainly isn't." Damiano agreed, and an overwhelming fluttery feeling hit me at his words.

"Let's talk numbers." Mr. Roberts told Damiano.

"Althaia, why don't you join me at the bar while the men talk? If I hear them talk about business anymore, I might just fall asleep." Elena laughed, and I gave an understanding nod. It could get tiring.

"Don't go anywhere where I can't see you." Damiano whispered in my ear and kissed my temple when I told him I wouldn't.

I followed Elena to the bar, and I sighed in relief when I sat down on the barstool, grateful to be off my feet.

"What's your choice of poison?" Elena asked while waving over to the bartender.

"Anything really. I'm not a picky drinker."

"I've got one for you!" She said excitedly. "Two liquid marijuanas, thank you."

A liquid what?

"So, Althaia, I haven't seen you around to these auctions before." Elena spoke before I had the chance to ask what drinks she ordered.

"It is my first time here. Actually, my first time coming to an auction, really." I smiled.

"Oh, you're not missing out on much. It's mostly the men going around, talking about their boring business and showing off who has the most money." She rolled her eyes, and I laughed because so far, it really was what they were doing.

"Two liquid marijuanas." The bartender gave us our drinks, and funnily enough, they were green.

I took a sip and was stunned by how fruity it was.

"It's good, right? I discovered this drink on my vacation in Cancún." Elena almost gulped down her drink as I gave her an approved nod. "Well, I have to say I'm surprised Damiano showed up with a date. He usually comes alone." She picked out a mirror from her clutch and retouched her lipstick.

"He comes alone?" I asked, surprised. Even though I didn't like to think of the women he had been with in the past, I did somehow expect he would show up to these kinds of things with a date.

"Oh no, sorry! He came with that woman… Oh, what was her name …" She tapped her nails against the glass of her drink. "Yes, Sienna was her name! He showed up with her a few times, but then suddenly came alone. Such a long time ago. I almost forgot about her." She said nonchalantly and finished her drink.

"Who was she?" I didn't bother to be discreet with my curiosity about the mystery woman.

"Hmm, I'm not too sure. I think they were engaged or something. She was wearing a remarkable ring on her finger, and I remember that because I was impressed with the piece of jewelry. As you can see, I'm a bit of a fan." Elena laughed, running a hand across her neck, and flicked her hair back to show her long earrings.

"It shows." I chuckled.

Elena excused herself to the lady's room, leaving me alone at the bar with my thoughts. Damiano has been engaged?

"Why is such a beautiful lady sitting alone?"

The sudden sound of someone speaking next to my ear made me jump. The man chuckled at my jumpiness and sat down on the barstool where Elena previously sat.

"I'm Alexei Vasiliev." He introduced with a faint Russian accent.

"I'm Althaia." I gave a tight smile. He didn't look scary, but I was wary of him since he had basically sneaked up on me.

"Just Althaia?" Alexei chuckled and took a sip of his drink.

"Why do you need more information? I don't know you." I said with a brow raised.

"Isn't that how you make new friends?"

"I don't need new friends." I retorted. Alexei threw his head back and let out a big laugh, attracting some attention to us.

"You know, you remind me a lot of a lady friend I had back in the day. Well, she was more of a lover than a friend." He chuckled, and I didn't know if I should be disgusted by this man telling me I looked like one of his lovers.

"Well, where's your lover now?"

"She got married." He shrugged.

"Huh, I see. That must have sucked."

"Ah, yes. She broke my heart and left me." Alexei clutched his chest and put on a dramatic expression to show how much it hurt him. "But she couldn't stay away from me, and we had some fun even though she was married." His blue eyes twinkled as he remembered back to those days.

"Why couldn't you just be together if you cared for each other that much?" I asked, now intrigued. It was like hearing about a sad romance movie.

"It's the things we love the most that destroy us. We were never meant to be." Alexei finished his drink. "We drove each other crazy, but she will always be my Solnishko."

"Althaia." My name was called, and I saw Damiano practically storming towards me with Antonio and Luca behind him.

"Bellavia! So good to see you again." Alexei stood up, but Damiano was not having it as he had a murderous glare on his face directed at the Russian in front of me. Damiano stopped in front of Alexei threateningly, and the few men behind Alexei shifted, now on guard.

Antonio's touch was gentle yet firm, as he positioned me between himself and Luca, a silent show of protection. Glancing at Damiano and Alexei, I hoped they wouldn't start pulling out their guns.

"I was just having a friendly chat with the lady. I did not know she was with you." Alexei chuckled and didn't seem to be fazed by Damiano's threatening demeanor. Alexei turned to leave but then stopped and looked back at me with a sincere expression. "You reminded me of good times, Althaia. Thank you." Then he left with his men following him.

Damiano was still looking at Alexei's retreating figure and when he was out of sight, he turned to me.

"Let's go to our seats. The auction is about to start." He held me by my waist and led me to a different hall.

"Is something wrong?" I asked Damiano. Alexei didn't do anything besides chatting with me, and he didn't seem to pose any threat.

"No." He replied calmly and walked us to our table. Damiano pulled out the chair for me, and I looked at him once he was also seated. Antonio and Luca joined our table as well.

"He was nice." I said quietly.

"He's not. Stay away from him." He slightly frowned and placed his arm on the backrest of my chair. The way Damiano had reacted and the men that were present had me thinking that Alexei Vasiliev might be a mob boss.

I was about to ask another question when the lights dimmed. A man in a burgundy tuxedo took to the stage, standing in front of the wooden podium with a microphone in hand.

"Ladies and gentlemen! Welcome to this year's auction. We are very pleased to see another year with a full house..." He carried on with his speech and did a recap from last year's auction. "Let us not wait any longer and have a look at our opening item."

The first thing that was auctioned was a Matisse painting. Art was my passion, but I struggled to grasp the artistic vision behind his paintings.

"... Do I hear a hundred thousand dollars?"

"For that painting?" I whispered in shock.

"Do you like it?" Damiano asked. I shook my head.

"And definitely not at that price." I muttered.

"Six hundred and fifty thousand dollars to the lady in the back. Going once... going twice... Sold!" A round of applause filled the banquet.

It all went fast. Each time an item was sold, another was immediately put up for sale and was sold in no time. The idea of bidding crossed my mind when I learned we were going to an auction, but the amount of money they were talking about had my eyes bulging. All I could afford was to leave.

"So, this is what you rich people do in your free time?" I asked. These people were throwing money on paintings like it was some mindless change.

"Yes. It's a nice way to remind people how much money and power you possess."

"Can't relate. Imagine how many chicken nuggets I could get for that money. Now, that's worth throwing money at." I said in all seriousness, and Damiano chuckled.

"We can get you some chicken nuggets after."

"I'm telling you; it's worth every penny." Damiano slightly shook his head, completely amused that I was discussing chicken nuggets with such seriousness.

"Ladies and gentlemen, it is with a great privilege that I stand before you today to introduce a true marvel of nature's artistry; the renowned Tiffany Yellow Diamond!" The entire banquet gasped by the incredible diamond necklace.

"This is one of the largest yellow diamonds that has ever been discovered in 1878 in South Africa. Expert craftsmen and lapidaries from the renowned house of Tiffany & Co. recognized its potential and undertook the delicate task of shaping it into a gem that would inspire awe for generations to come."

From the moment I laid eyes on the necklace, I was captivated by its beauty. The beauty of it was almost surreal. The necklace was a medium-length chain fashioned entirely from glistening diamonds. As my gaze descended along the chain, it left me awestruck.

An enormous yellow diamond.

"This awe-inspiring gem, cut into a cushion shape, is a treasure trove of 83 facets that form a mesmerizing dance of brilliance and fire. Among these facets, delicate needle-like projections extend outward from the culet facet, adding a touch of uniqueness to its splendor."

"Wow... That looks so majestic." I couldn't take my eyes off the necklace. "I can't wait to see who's going to bid on that." I said in awe and looked at Damiano. His gaze swiftly landed on my neck before lingering on the necklace.

"It's pretty." His simple statement made me laugh. The necklace was out of this world, and he thought it was only pretty.

"... Do I hear twenty million dollars?"

I choked on my own spit when I heard the starting price.

"Holy shit..." I muttered under my breath.

"Twenty-five!"

I heard the familiar voice and turned my head in its direction. It was Alexei Vasiliev.

"Twenty-five million dollars coming from Mr. Alexei Vasiliev!" The auctioneer said, delighted.

"Thirty." Damiano's calm demeanor was a sharp contrast to my own as I snapped my head back to look at him bidding on the necklace.

Is he insane?!

"Thirty-five!" Alexei happily bid, looking in our direction and grinning at Damiano.

"Thirty-five million dollars! Do I hear any more?" The auctioneer's eyes darted back and forth between them, waiting to see if Damiano was going to bid again.

"Going once... going twice..."

"Fifty million dollars." Damiano's bid had the entire banquet hall erupted in a flurry of shocked whispers. Damiano was completely unfazed, his eyes set on Alexei.

"Fifty million dollars from Mr. Damiano Bellavia!" The auctioneer let out a gleeful eruption. I glanced at Alexei, and he responded by raising his hands in surrender, a grin spreading across his face.

"Sold to Mr. Damiano Bellavia!"

The roar of applause faded away as I turned my attention to Damiano. I was lost for words. A freaking necklace had just cost him fifty million dollars, and he didn't bat an eye.

"You're insane." I breathed out in shock.

"Only for you, my Althaia." Damiano placed a gentle kiss on my bare shoulder before leaning in to whisper in my ear. His lips grazed my earlobe, sending shivers down my spine as I let out a small breath.

"I want you to wear it. And nothing else." He whispered, sending a pooling heat low in my stomach.

Twenty-Eight

ALTHAIA

"They must have a return policy." I kept telling Damiano as we made our way out of the banquet hall. The auction had finished after Damiano's bid, and then there was a long speech about how they were so grateful to see a full house.

After that, people came from all directions to congratulate Damiano on his bidding and to express their admiration for the exquisite necklace. Then there was a long process where Damiano had to sign what felt like a hundred papers and write a check. He wouldn't get the necklace immediately, as the one on the stage was a replica, and the real one would be sent to him with top security.

"That's not how it works." Damiano said, still completely unbothered.

"I don't think you understand how much money it is." I tried to explain.

"I do. I just spent it." He let out a smug smile. I stopped and placed my hands on my hips.

"I'm not accepting it."

"Too late." Damiano replied in an amused tone.

"You already gave me those earrings! Even *that* I think is too much." I expressed with a defeated sigh. "People are going to think you're my sugar daddy."

Luca let out a laugh, but quickly tried to cover it up by clearing his throat.

"Oh, you think it's funny, huh?" I squinted my eyes at him.

"I'll get the car running." Luca walked away while shaking his head, clearly laughing at me. I looked at Antonio, seeing him with a small smile on his lips, breaking the blank expression he always wore.

"Maybe you can knock some sense into that thick head of his?" I asked.

"I have tried for years. Unfortunately, he doesn't listen." He said, before following Luca to the car.

"Sugar daddy?" Damiano asked with a raised brow.

"Yes. But then again, do sugar daddies spend fifty million dollars on their sugar babies?" I now wondered about my own question.

"Only if the pussy is good." He winked.

"Damiano!" I gasped. "People can hear you!" I hissed at him and looked around to see if anyone had heard him. He drew me in close with a teasing glint in his eye, and kissed me deeply that it stole my breath away.

"Let them hear what they can't have. Your pussy belongs to me." He said against my lips, and my cheeks immediately flushed.

"My goodness..." With a gentle smack to his chest, I broke free from his hold and continued my way out to the car. His frank words left me feeling flustered.

When I reached the enormous staircase, I groaned.

"Why are there so many stairs?" My aching foot was a reminder that getting down would not be easy.

"Come. Let me carry you."

"No! People will look and they will definitely think I'm a spoiled sugar baby." I dismissed him and walked towards the stone railing for support.

"So stubborn..." Damiano sighed and before I knew it, he swept me off my feet and carried me in his arms.

"You're seriously too much." I muttered. I was full-on blushing now when I noticed people looking at us.

"Only the best service for my sugar baby." Damiano said loudly, and I wanted to scream in embarrassment.

"Put me down." I wiggled out of his arms, walked down the last steps, and hurried to the SUV. "He's crazy!" I exclaimed to Antonio and Luca and hurriedly slid into the car.

I stilled, a warm smile gracing my lips at the sound of Damiano's laugh. It was laughter untainted by pretense, a rare glimpse into his unguarded self.

And my heart warmed to the sound.

I winced in pain as I kicked off my heels in the car and tried to flex my foot. Examining it, I noticed some swelling and bruising. Damiano carefully lifted my foot onto his lap for a closer look.

"You kicked the door, didn't you?" He shook his head at me and gently massaged it.

"Maybe." I let out a sigh, feeling the tension melting away. "You know, if you're ever looking for a career change, being a masseuse is not too shabby." I laughed at my own joke as I imagined Damiano being a masseuse. His intimidating presence would only add more tension to the poor clients.

"Funny." He scoffed but cracked a smile.

"I wanted to ask, why did that man, uh, Mr. Roberts, ask me about your wine prices? Seemed a bit unusual for him to be asking me instead of going straight to you."

Damiano's eyes flickered with a knowing smile as he responded.

"Mr. Roberts has a distinctive approach to conversations. He likes to gather insights from unexpected sources, believing it provides a more comprehensive view of things."

"Smart." I chuckled. "Why the interest?"

"He owns a large chain of high-end restaurants. Each year, he attempts to persuade me to lower prices, and every year, I reject his idea without much explanation. The response you gave him intrigued him, offering a fresh perspective, and we settled a deal." Damiano explained, leaving me surprised.

"I guess I didn't screw up then. I didn't even know you have a business in wine." I must have overseen that part during my Google research about him.

"And yet you pulled out that answer to him." He said, almost seeming proud.

"I only told him the basics and added a twist to it. I don't even know if it's true." I made a small grimace, hoping it wouldn't cause him trouble.

"You were right. I do prefer traditional approaches. Mostly." He winked.

I snorted.

"You could never wait for marriage with a sex drive like yours."

"Likewise." He smirked, and I rolled my eyes at him.

"Keep your foot up to reduce the swelling." His hands traveled up the inside of my thigh, dangerously close to my intimate area. "Fortunately, your legs look amazing on my shoulders."

Before he could get to my underwear, I quickly moved and straddled him, wrapping my arms around his neck.

"They do. But that has to wait until we're back at the hotel." I brushed my lips against his, teasing him.

"Althaia." Damiano warned with a growl, his hands tightening on my waist.

"Yes?" I answered innocently. I gasped at the sudden grab of my throat, a thrill rushing through me.

"Don't be a tease." He sneered, clearly still upset from earlier.

"Still don't know what you mean." I grinned, loving the way he squeezed my throat at my reply.

Damiano's eyes narrowed, darkening as lust swirled in his eyes.

"Yeah?" He said, grabbing my wrists and forcing them behind my back. He kept them there with one hand while the other slipped under my dress, sliding my thong to the side. His touch sent shivers down my spine as his finger traced along my wet slit. "Look at you. So wet for me already."

I tried to grind against him, but he used his strength to hold me still. A finger slipped past my folds, and lightly circled my clit, barely putting any pressure.

"Damiano!" I called in frustration, trying to move to feel more friction.

"Yes?" He taunted with a cocky smirk. "What do you want, Althaia?"

I made a displeased sound when he would touch all the right places, only to move away when I enjoyed it too much.

"Stop it." I hissed at him, and a menacing smile spread across his face.

"Don't play games with me, Althaia. You won't win." Damiano shoved a finger inside of me, making me moan, only to quickly pull out again. "Understood?" He growled.

"Yes!" I gritted out.

"Good girl." He approved, and I threw my head back when he suddenly shoved two fingers inside of my pussy. It struck a wild sensation as I inhaled sharply.

"Wait!" I erupted, suddenly remembering Antonio and Luca on the other side of the tinted window.

"Soundproof." Damiano said, putting me at ease as he continued. His fingers stroked exactly where I needed them, and he never took his eyes off me, watching how pleasure danced across my face with satisfaction.

He pulled his fingers out of me, and just as I was about to express my displeasure, he swiped his fingers across my lips, coating them with my own arousal. I grinned, surprising him by sucking his fingers clean.

"Fucking hell!" Damiano grabbed the back of my neck, roughly pressing his mouth to mine. Our tongues danced, sparking a fire between us that only seemed to grow uncontrollably. I threaded my fingers into his hair while my hand wandered down to his length that was eager to be let out.

"Lift your hips, baby." He said, and I complied immediately, throbbing with a need to fill me up. I felt the tip of his cock sliding along my slit, both of us moaning as he sunk into me, filling me to the brim.

"You feel so fucking good." Damiano gripped my hips tightly as I moved back and forth, closing my eyes briefly at the pleasure. "You're making me behave like a starved man. I can't get enough of you." He softly moaned against my lips.

I smiled and tugged on his bottom lip with my teeth. His lips parted, letting me meet the stroke of his tongue, and demolished my mouth.

"Damiano..." I moaned against his lips, rocking my hips faster when my stomach slowly tightened.

"That's it." He growled, holding me tightly and roughly thrust inside of me. I let out a cry of pleasure, my hand on the window and the other gripping the headrest as he fucked me senseless.

I whimpered as his lips kissed the valley between my breasts, tugging my dress down with his teeth and teased my hardened nipple before taking it in his mouth. Our breathing became heavier as Damiano's hips moved quickly and relentlessly, making sure I could feel all of him.

"Come for me, Althaia. Let me have it." His finger stroked my clit as he panted with a grunt.

"Yes... yes..." My stomach was tightening, building my pleasure fast. My back arched, letting out a scream as pleasure crashed in like a blissful wave.

"Fuck!" Damiano growled, pumping inside of me until I felt the warmth of his seed.

I closed my eyes, resting my head against his as we caught our breath. Calming down, I looked at him with a smile, caressing his bearded cheek. Damiano gently held my chin, and the way he looked at me sent a rush of emotions through my body.

Our lips met in a soft, lingering kiss, and I was filled with a feeling I hadn't felt before.

Twenty-Nine

ALTHAIA

"Does my dress look all right?" I asked Damiano while I patted down my dress to make sure I wasn't flashing anyone before I stepped out of the car. He took a quick glance at my dress and gave a subtle nod before opening the door.

He offered his hand to help me out of the car, and I gratefully accepted as I held my heels. I refused to put them back on.

"Are you okay to walk?" Damiano looked at my foot.

"Yeah, I'm fine. Luckily, I don't have to take the stairs here." I said in relief.

"You know, there is a time and place for everything." Luca leaned against the car, looking at us with a playful grin. I blinked twice before turning to face Damiano with my face burning with embarrassment.

"I thought you said it was soundproof!"

"It is. We felt the car shake." Antonio commented, also with a teasing smile.

"Just great..." I muttered, walking away as I couldn't face them. I was more worried about them hearing us than thinking about shaking the car. Damiano was laughing, unbothered as always.

"Order some food. I'll be up soon." He smiled softly.

"Don't take too long."

"I won't." Damiano placed a kiss on my forehead, and my stomach flipped, making me let out a shy smile.

On the ride up, my stomach growled with the type of hunger that made me indecisive about what to order.

Fuck it. I'm going to order the entire menu.

I took my time walking down the hall to our room. My foot was still aching, but the way Damiano had massaged it made it feel a lot better.

"Seriously." I groaned under my breath when I realized he didn't give me the keycard.

I was about to turn around when a sudden noise made me freeze on the spot. My eyes almost popped out of their sockets when our room door opened.

A man dressed entirely in black, his face covered except for his eyes, stepped out of the room. My body refused to budge, even as my mind screamed at me to *run*.

I let out a shaky breath and swallowed hard, taking a step back. But a heel slipped out of my hand and dropped to the floor with a *thud*.

His head immediately snapped in my direction.

Our eyes met, and time seemed to stand still for a moment. Then he ran towards me. Fast.

I felt a knot form in my stomach before I finally let out a piercing scream. He didn't let it slow him down and instead picked up speed. My mind was in a state of panic, screaming at me to move, and my body finally responded with a jolt. I chucked the other heel at him, turned on my heels, and ran.

I ran as fast as I could towards the exit door, knowing the elevator doors wouldn't open in time. I grabbed the handle, throwing my weight against the door to force it open. I was almost out when a pair of rough hands grabbed me from behind, throwing me to the ground. The force of his throw was so strong that my head hit the floor, leaving my vision blurry.

I cried out in pain when he grabbed me by my hair and yanked me to my feet.

"Let me go!" I screamed. I thrashed around, trying to pull free from his iron grip, but I was no match for his strength and silenced me with a hand over my mouth.

Fear and panic consumed me entirely. His arms wrapped tightly around me from behind, trying to still me. My mind was racing with thoughts of escape, leaving me with only one thing I could do.

I threw my head back, hearing the sickening sound of my head colliding with his nose.

He loosened his grip on me with a grunt, enough for me to break free. I pushed him away, only to stumble and hit the ground face first.

My body was trembling as I tried to crawl away, tears forming in my eyes. Every time I tried to stand up, my dress would get caught under my feet, making me stumble and fall.

"No!" My nails dug into the floor when his hand clasped around my ankle, flipping me on my back.

I didn't have time to think, but my body knew what to do and kicked him hard in the face. He let out a low groan, stumbled backward, and the object he was holding slipped from his grasp, clattering to the ground.

The sharp, glinting blade of the knife made my heart stop.

Reacting quickly for once, I clumsily crawled to retrieve it. He immediately noticed and leaped for the knife. With the knife in my hand, I turned around, and my scream got stuck in my throat when he pounced on top of me.

Right into the knife.

A guttural sound escaped him as the knife plunged into his stomach. I stared at him in shock as his blood soaked through my hands.

"Oh, God…" My voice trembled as I saw him lose consciousness. With a gulp, I wiggled out from underneath his heavy weight.

I stumbled to my feet, my breaths coming in ragged gasps, and ran towards the elevator, stabbing at the button until the doors slid open. I kept my eye on him, making sure he wasn't making any sudden moves. As soon as the doors closed, I let out a sigh of relief and leaned back against the elevator wall.

My legs were weak, and I struggled to stand. I glanced at my trembling hands. They were drenched in blood. *His* blood. No matter how hard I tried to wipe it away, it only seemed to smear and spread across my arms.

It made me sick.

Shock and confusion overwhelmed me when the doors opened to the parking lot. My mind was blank, but my legs kept walking on their own. I felt a warm trickle down my face, and the metallic scent of blood filled my nose. I put my hand up to my face to wipe it away, only to see the deep red color of blood on my fingertips.

I stopped walking abruptly, my hand still trying to wipe away the blood that stubbornly kept trickling down my face.

"Althaia!"

I looked up just in time to see Damiano's stormy expression as he strode towards me. His eyes burned with anger as he took in my state. Luca and Antonio ran past me with their guns drawn, and Damiano pulled me towards him, his eyes blazing with fury as he held my face in his hands.

"Who did this?" He was trying to contain his anger as he spoke. I blinked, trying to shake off the confusion that had settled over me like a fog.

"I–He… There was someone… and I killed him…?" I raised my hands in front of me, the stickiness of blood still clinging to my skin. Tears welled up in my eyes, and I scratched my arms violently, desperate to remove the bloodstains. "Please… Get it off…Get it off, get it off!"

"Althaia, look at me. Look at me!" Damiano made me look at him as tears fell down my face. "What happened, baby? Tell me." His soft voice and gentle hands brought comfort as he wiped away the blood on my face.

"Someone... he came out of our room... he-he chased me and tried to kill me, but I..." I kept stumbling over the words, not able to form a single sentence that made sense.

"Shh, it's okay. I'll find out." Damiano's arms wrapped around me, providing a sense of safety and security as I continued to cry into his chest. He removed his jacket and wrapped it around me as the sound of footsteps grew louder, and I could feel my palms sweat as I turned to face Luca.

"No one's there."

"What? No, that's not right. He was there, on the floor. With a... knife in him." I swallowed hard, trying not to get sick at the image. But Luca only shook his head.

Did I imagine him lying on the floor?

"That means I didn't kill him, right? I–I didn't..." I looked up at Damiano. I recognized the expression he was wearing; the same one he had before he shot the men in the park. He held me close, his silence making me feel uneasy.

"What else?" Damiano asked. Luca looked at me, hesitating if he should speak in front of me.

"It's better you see for yourself." The seriousness in his voice had my heart drop.

"Althaia, get in the car. Luca, stay with her." Damiano moved away, but I held him tightly.

"Please, don't leave me here." I begged him. I knew Luca would do his best to keep me safe, but right now, I felt safest with Damiano.

He scrutinized my face for what seemed like an eternity, weighing the decision of whether or not to leave me here with Luca. He gave a small nod and pulled me closer to him.

"You don't go inside the room. You're staying outside with Luca." Damiano stated firmly to me when we stepped in the elevator.

The blood on the buttons caught his eye, and he held me tightly as we rode the elevator up in tense silence. I could feel myself trembling as I leaned closer to him, fearing that the man would appear out of nowhere and attack us.

As soon as we reached the floor, my eyes darted towards the exact spot where I had left him. He wasn't there. There was no trace of blood, not even a faint stain on the ground.

"I don't get it... He was right there." I pointed to where I saw him last. I stared at my hands, still stained with blood. I definitely didn't imagine it.

"Someone has covered his tracks. He wasn't alone." Damiano stated. The thought that there was more than one had my knees go weak.

We stopped in front of our room, and Antonio stepped out, his eyes immediately landing on me.

"Stay here." Damiano told me before slipping into the room, shutting the door behind him.

"Is it bad?" I finally dared to ask them. The silence was a dead giveaway that it was. I hugged the jacket closer to my body, trying to feel a sense of safety.

The sudden opening of the door startled me when it banged hard against the wall. Damiano's eyes blazed with fury as he stormed out of the room.

"I want the area completely searched and get Raffaele to check the security cameras. The fucker better be alive when I get a hold of him." Damiano spat out orders. They nodded and immediately went into action.

"What is it?" I asked nervously. The rage in Damiano's eyes was unmistakable as he snapped his head towards me.

"Let's get you out of here." He led me to the elevators again, and all I could do was glance back, wondering what was in there that had him reacting like this.

I pulled the jacket closer to my body, and my fingers brushed against something in the breast pocket. It was the keycard. Without a second thought, I slipped under Damiano's arm and sprinted towards the door.

"Althaia!" He shouted after me.

But it was too late.

The moment I pushed the door open, my hands went limp at the sight. The walls were covered in pictures.

Of me.

The pictures show me sipping on my iced coffee when I was out with Cara and Michael. Pictures of me when I was out with my father for brunch. And the most recent ones, pictures of me at the amusement park, holding snow cones in my hands. There were so many more. Whoever took the pictures was keeping track of me. There was no one else in the pictures. It was only me.

With a target mark on my face.

Thirty

DAMIANO

Althaia's eyes widened in horror as she looked around.

"What is this...?" It came out as a whisper, and her panicked gaze met mine. The sight of her shaking in fear flooded my body with a hunger to spill every drop of the fucker's blood.

"Enough. Let's go." I went to grab her to get her out of here when she suddenly gasped and put her hand up to her mouth and pointed behind me.

Cazzo. She saw it.

I blocked her view when she paled, her entire body trembling.

"Is that a heart?" She swallowed hard. "With my picture on?"

Althaia swayed unsteadily before her eyes rolled back. I caught her in my arms before she collapsed to the floor. I held her small frame tightly against my body. My eyes were fixated on the heart that was hung by a knife with her picture on it. Clenching my jaw, I walked out with her in my arms.

"Get Ellie to the manor." I instructed Antonio.

On the way down, I frowned as I looked at her busted brow that was still bleeding. I tried to think of who could have been after her already. I knew being with me was a major risk, but these pictures started before I showed my interest in her.

Whoever it was, the scumbag would have wished he died before I got my hands on him. For every scratch on her body, for every misplaced hair on her head, he was going to get a hole drilled into him.

And that's a fucking promise.

I parked the car in front of the manor, and Althaia groaned, slowly regaining consciousness beside me. I carried her inside the manor, and she winced at the bright lights overhead.

"Everything hurts..." She whimpered.

"I know, baby. I know." I whispered soothing words as I cradled her head into my chest. I was trying to hold her without squeezing too tightly as I watched her writhe in pain.

"What happened to her?" Arianna looked in shock at Althaia when I passed her.

I paid no attention to her and entered the room, gently laying Althaia down on the bed before heading to the bathroom. I filled the bathtub with water, rolled up my sleeves, and went back to her.

"You take her away for a couple of days, and she comes back like this? What happened?" Arianna sat next to her, taking in the sight of blood smeared across her face and hands.

"I don't know." I clenched my jaw, not liking my own answer.

"What do you mean, you don't know?" Arianna frowned.

"I'm looking into it. Get out and send Ellie up here when she arrives." Arianna knew better than to push me right now and silently left the room.

I removed Althaia's dress carefully and carried her to the tub. I grabbed a washcloth and wiped away the blood that covered her face and body.

"I feel dizzy..." She mumbled, leaning against me as I continued to wash her.

"It will go away soon." I assured her.

"Ellie's here." Arianna announced with a knock on the door.

"Who's Ellie?" Althaia tried to open her eyes, but the brightness of the lights caused her to squint and shut them once more.

"She's our doctor." I replied, almost smiling. Despite her agony and clouded mind, the mere mention of another woman fueled her jealousy.

I dressed her in one of my t-shirts and carried her to the bed again, placing her to sit against the headboard for Ellie to examine her.

"Okay, what do we have here?" Ellie placed her medical bag at the end of the bed and sat next to Althaia to look at her. "How are you feeling?"

"Not good... I have a banging headache, an annoying ringing in my ears, and my eyes can't really focus. It's making me dizzy." Althaia blinked a few times when Ellie turned off her penlight.

"It sounds like you have a mild concussion. I wouldn't worry too much about it as long as you rest. Avoid screen time and loud noises and you should be good." She carried on and examined her brow. "You'll need a few stitches for that, though." Ellie rummaged through her bag to get the things.

"I'm sorry, what?" Althaia frowned.

"I just need to stitch you up. It's nothing major and won't take long." Ellie gave a small smile while she cleaned the wound.

"Oh, hell no!" Althaia yelled and scrambled to get away from Ellie. She sprang up from the bed too quickly, making her sway and losing her balance.

"Althaia." I warned her sternly as I steadied her.

"A needle is not going near my face! Just put a band-aid on it and call it a night." She tried to dismiss it with a wave, inching away from Ellie.

"I need to close it to prevent a nasty infection." Ellie explained while she put on her gloves and prepped the needle and suture. "Now, sit."

Althaia's eyes widened and made a run for it.

Only to fall face-first to the floor when she supported all the weight on her injured foot.

"Oww..." She rolled on her back with a hand to her face as a fresh wave of blood trickled from her brow. I sighed in annoyance at her recklessness. I pulled her up and sat her down on the bed.

"Are you trying to fucking kill yourself?" I sneered out, giving her a firm look.

"Stop moving so she can fix you." Arianna told her, not impressed with how she injured herself more.

"No needles!" Althaia yelled.

"Don't be such a baby!" Arianna crossed her arms. "I won't hesitate to hold you down so you can get that nasty brow fixed."

"No, no, let us not do that." Ellie quickly said. "How about I give you something so you can relax? I'll have a look at your foot in the meantime and then come back to your brow, okay?" She suggested with a smile.

Althaia kept her eyes on the needle until Ellie packed it away. Only then did she relax and gave a nod.

"So, what happened to your foot?" She asked after giving her a pill and examined her.

"Uh, I kicked a door... And then someone tried to kill me, and I kicked him in the face."

Ellie felt around at the center of her foot, causing her to scrunch up her face in pain. Even though I didn't show it, I was surprised to hear that she had kicked him in the face.

"Can you tell us what happened?" Arianna asked. I watched Althaia closely as she became quiet. I didn't miss the way her hands trembled before she clasped them together on her lap with her eyes looking down at them.

"Not now, Arianna." I glared at her.

"It's okay." Althaia said, and I looked back at her. Twiddling her thumbs, she let out a deep breath and told us what had happened.

I could feel my anger rising, and the urge to leave and search for the fucker myself grew stronger. Instead, I clenched my jaw as she spoke while my fingers were twitching to get hold of the bastard to give him a painful death for what he had done to her. If she hadn't been fast enough to grab the knife, I would have found her dead.

Dead under my protection.

The mere thought of anyone taking her away from me made me see red. No one was going to take her away from me.

Not like how they took Sienna from me. I couldn't let it happen.

Not again.

Thirty-One

ALTHAIA

I blinked away the tears. I looked up to see Damiano staring at me with his hands in his pockets, his thoughts and feelings hidden, as usual.

"Okay, you're all set here." I looked down to see Ellie had bandaged my foot. "I don't believe it's not broken, but I would like you to come to the clinic to do a proper check-up. Until then, do not put weight on your foot, okay?"

I gave a small nod when she smiled and went back to grab a wipe and gently dabbed around on my brow.

"I really need to stitch you up now." Ellie said, and my nose scrunched up involuntarily as I imagined the pain of being sewn in the face.

"Fine." I murmured, feeling relaxed enough to agree. Whatever she had given me was working.

She pulled on a fresh pair of gloves, picked up the needle driver and tissue forceps, and moved closer to my face. Out of reflex, I smacked her hands away from me, almost making her drop the things in her hands.

"Try not to hurt my wife."

My eyes shifted towards the doorway where Antonio stood.

"She's your wife?!" I exclaimed in surprise and immediately looked at her hands to search for a ring.

"It's around my neck in a necklace. I can't always wear a ring as a doctor." Ellie explained when she noticed what I was looking for.

"How come I didn't know you were married?" I asked Antonio, looking at his hands and finding a ring I had failed to notice before.

"You didn't ask."

"I'm pretty sure I asked, and you were like, 'I would rather not have you ask me questions." I said, trying to imitate his voice.

"That sounds like Nino." Ellie laughed.

"Aww, she calls you Nino? That's so cute!" I beamed.

"You can't call me that." Antonio narrowed his eyes at me in a warning.

"Why not? It sure makes you less scary–Ow!" I yelled when I felt a painful pinch on my brow. Ellie took advantage of my distraction with Antonio to stitch me up.

"Don't move!" She tried to keep me still when I leaned away from her.

"That's it, I'm holding her!" Arianna sat behind me on the bed and held my head.

"Let me go!" I tried to get away, but Arianna was surprisingly strong as she had me in a headlock-like position.

"Careful, Arianna." Damiano told her firmly, and I sent him a glare that he was approving of this.

"You will get a scar if you keep moving. I'm almost done." Ellie scolded me and kept torturing me with her needle.

"Ow, shit! It hurts!" I winced and clenched my jaw when I felt another painful pinch.

"Stop being a baby!" Arianna hushed me.

"All done now." Ellie let out a breath and stepped back right when I thought of kicking her away from me.

"Already? Oh, that wasn't too bad." I said and Ellie gave me an 'I told you so' look.

"She's the most difficult patient I have ever had." Ellie chuckled to Damiano. "Come to the clinic tomorrow morning. Make sure she gets plenty of rest and doesn't move around too much. I have a feeling she's the type to defy orders."

"You have no idea." Damiano and Antonio said at the same time, and I gaped at them as Arianna let out a laugh.

"Funny." I gave them a blank look and lied down as exhaustion hit me.

Antonio's eyes followed Ellie's every move as she packed her bag and made her way towards him. He took her bag from her and kissed the top of her head before they both went on their way.

"So cute." I mumbled sleepily.

"That did not make me feel lonely at all." Arianna sighed and walked out of the room as well. A small chuckle escaped me as I got comfortable and let my eyes drift shut. The bed was like a fluffy cloud that embraced me and soothed my aching body.

A blanket pulled over me and my eyes fluttered open. Damiano's intense gaze was fixed on my freshly stitched-up brow.

"Get some sleep. You're safe." He spoke softly, his fingers gentle as they caressed my hair.

"Are you not getting in with me? You haven't slept at all." I asked with concern.

"You don't need to worry about me." He let out a small smile.

"A bit too late for that now." I said, and a gentle warmth showed in his eyes. Damiano leaned down and pressed a small kiss on my lips.

"Go to sleep. I'll send Arianna in to keep an eye on you."

"Okay." I sighed, disappointed that he was going to leave. Damiano caressed my face, and my mind eased, lulling me into a peaceful sleep.

I shifted around in bed when I heard faint voices in the hallway. It finally went quiet again, and I was on the verge of falling back asleep when the door suddenly burst open with a loud bang, making me jolt up with a scream.

"What the fuck happened to you?!" Cara's voice filled the room, and I blinked several times to understand where I was. An arm wrapped around me, startling me as I was pulled back, but relaxed when I saw it was Damiano, glaring at Cara.

"You can't just barge in like that." Arianna called after Cara, but she was ignored.

"What the hell happened to your face?" Cara sat in front of me, placing her hands on my cheeks to look at me with worry.

"You almost gave me a heart attack!" I scowled, but then a sharp throbbing in my brow made me wince.

"Don't touch it." Damiano stopped me when I was just about to.

"I feel like I have been hit by a truck." I groaned, resting my back on the headboard.

"You look like it too. Who did this?" Cara continued.

"Please, stop yelling. I can't handle loud noises right now." I sighed tiredly, too drained of energy and in too much pain to be interrogated.

"Keep your voice down. She needs to rest." Damiano said sharply, still glaring daggers at her, but she kept ignoring everyone. "Lorenzo, get your woman out of here." Damiano snapped. Cara was about to protest when Lorenzo came to get her out, but decided against it when she saw how exhausted I was.

"I will talk to you later." I gave her a smile to let her know I was okay despite probably looking the opposite. I saw her visibly relax before leaving quietly with Lorenzo.

I was enveloped in Damiano's embrace as he carefully pulled me in closer.

"Are you okay?" He asked softly.

"Yeah, just still tired." My lids were already drooping, barely able to keep me awake. "What time is it?"

"It's seven in the morning. Go back to sleep." Damiano laid me on the bed, his arms still around me, and my heart couldn't help but skip a beat at how warm and protected I felt with him.

"Cara seriously has nothing better to do in the morning than to wake me up." I sighed.

"Doesn't sound like a first time." He gave a small smile.

"If only you knew." I chuckled. "When did you come?" I asked.

"Not too long ago." His hand went under the t-shirt I was wearing, drawing soothing circles on my back. "Sleep, baby, I'm here."

My entire body felt stiff, and my face was hurting from kissing the floor too many times when I woke up. I looked over to where Damiano was sleeping, but his side of the bed was cold and empty.

How does that man even function? He barely sleeps.

I sat at the edge of the bed, trying to figure out how to get to the bathroom with my injured foot. I briefly considered hopping on one but immediately dismissed it as it would only make my body ache some more. So, with no other alternatives, I was forced to take the last option.

To crawl.

I tried my best to keep my injured foot elevated as I crawled on the floor, inching my way towards the bathroom like a fool. The room was literally the size of an apartment, and I was struggling. By the time I got there, I was out of breath, and I couldn't tell if it was because of the condition I was in or if I was just really out of shape. Probably a mixture of both.

After finishing, I reached out and gripped the edge of the sink to steady myself. I looked at myself in the mirror and gasped at the sight before me.

My hair was a *mess*, and it showed on my face that I had fallen one too many times, with three stitches visible just above my brow.

"I look like hell." I muttered. With a sigh, I began removing each hairpin from my tangled locks. I didn't have a brush, and I had to rely on my fingers to detangle my hair, which was a whole damn workout.

I went through the drawers in the bathroom and grabbed a spare toothbrush since there was an entire stack of them. I washed my face, dabbed it dry, and looked back in the mirror. I still looked like shit, but less.

I was about to limp to the door when it suddenly swung open.

"You can't just open the door like that. What if I was on the toilet?"

"So?" Damiano raised a brow and closed the distance between us.

"Well, I don't exactly want to pee in front of you." I remarked. His muscular arms trapped me as his face drew nearer.

"I have seen all of you. *Tasted* all of you." Damiano's hands moved down my back and grabbed my ass, hoisting me up. "There's nothing to be ashamed of."

"It's not the same." I said, amused, and wrapped my legs around him the best I could as he moved towards the bed. He took a seat with me still sitting on his lap.

"How are you feeling?" He asked softly and looked at my stitched brow.

"I'm sore, tired, and hungry. And this is itching." I pointed to my brow. "So, like shit, to put it in one word." I sighed and rested my head on his shoulder.

Even though I had just woken up, my body felt drained, but I knew it was because it was working hard to heal. Closing my eyes, I let myself sink into the sensation of his arms wrapped tightly around me and his steady breathing in my ear.

"We need to get you to the clinic." I felt his chest shake with a chuckle as I jumped on his lap when he suddenly spoke.

"Sorry." I said, a bit embarrassed that I was drifting off to sleep on him.

"Don't be. You can sleep when we come back."

"Like this again?" I joked.

"However you want." Damiano's lips curved into a small, soft smile as he gently kissed my lips before placing me on the bed. He brought some clothes for me to change into, but I only took the sweatpants, tucking the t-shirt into the waistband.

"You're never getting it back, just so you know." I warned him. I loved how it smelled like him.

"It's all yours, piccola." Damiano effortlessly lifted me into his arms and made his way towards the dining room. The closer we got, the louder Arianna and Raffaele's bickering became, having me chuckle as Arianna threatened to stab him if he didn't shut up.

"Look who made an appearance." Raffaele smiled from ear to ear when he saw us. "Oh, damn! When I said she won't be able to walk when she comes back, I didn't mean it like that." Raffaele erupted with a laugh just as Damiano sat me down on a chair.

I dropped my jaw at his comment, my face burning as he said that in front of everyone. Including Rosana and Sofia, who were in the middle of placing food on the table.

"Shut up, you idiot!" Arianna yelled at him, but it only made him grin.

"Did you fuck her that hard that she banged her head against the wall?" Raffaele continued with a laugh, and my face went completely red. The fact that Rosana and Sofia heard everything made it so much worse.

"Sofia!" Rosana's scolding filled the room after the loud sound of the plate clattering against the table caught everyone's attention on Sofia.

"Sorry, it slipped." Sofia muttered. She continued to place the plates on the table with force. Rosana apologized for her behavior as she followed Sofia out of the dining room.

"Are you okay? They told me what happened." Cara looked at me with concern.

"I'll be fine, don't worry." I gave her a reassuring smile.

"Is it really what happened, or is it just a cover-up story so we wouldn't know that you were fucking like animals?" Raffaele wiggled his brows at me with a teasing smile.

"Why would you think he did this to me?" I asked, picking up some fruit to add to my plate.

"Look at him, he's huge! And with all that pent up sexual frustration, I wouldn't be surprised if he finally let loose." He cracked up, and I considered throwing my fork after him. Damiano was doing an excellent job of ignoring Raffaele and just ate his food.

"Can we please talk about something else? I really don't want to hear about my brother's sex life." Arianna shivered in disgust.

"You're just jealous because you're not getting some." Raffaele gave her a smug look.

"Who says I'm not getting some?" She retorted and cocked a brow.

The second the words escaped her mouth, both Damiano and Lorenzo stopped eating and looked at Arianna. They both wore a look so menacing that I leaned back in my seat, not daring to make a sound. Even Cara had an 'oh shit' look on her face.

Arianna rolled her eyes, not fazed at all.

"Oh, so you can talk about how you all are getting some, but I can't?" She scoffed and crossed her arms.

"Who is he?" Lorenzo demanded with his eyes narrowing.

"Like I'm going to tell you."

"I just want a word with him."

"Does it involve a knife or a gun?" She asked, and a sinister smirk appeared on Lorenzo's face. "That's what I thought."

"Liar, you're not dating anyone." Raffaele gave a skeptical look.

"I'm not dating. I'm just having fun." She shrugged with no fear at all. Arianna did not give one fuck about the looks Damiano and Lorenzo were giving her, ready to kill whoever was 'having fun' with their sister.

"Go, Arianna! Is he hot?" I asked, shooting a sweet smile at Damiano. His eyes narrowed as he directed a fierce glare in my direction.

"I'm telling you; he is fine as fuck!" Cara suddenly erupted.

"You're done." In a split second, Lorenzo pulled Cara out of her chair, threw her over his shoulder, and walked out of the dining room with her, laughing.

Thirty-Two

ALTHAIA

"You don't have an infection, which is great. Remember to keep your stitches clean and dry." Ellie said and went to type into her computer once she was done examining me. "As for your foot, it's a mild sprain. Are you keeping yourself off your feet?"

"Damiano is carrying me everywhere and not letting me walk, so yes." I lightly chuckled.

"I've noticed. I'll get you crutches to use." She smiled.

"There is no need for them." Damiano dismissed.

"How am I supposed to move around, then?" I asked him.

"You're not supposed to. That way, I know you're staying put." He retorted with a raised brow.

"But I need to move around at some point."

"I'll carry you."

"...That can't be healthy for me."

"She has a point." Ellie backed me up.

"See! You can't argue with a doctor. She knows best." I grinned at him. His eyes slightly narrowed at Ellie before giving in.

"Tomorrow then. You'll rest today." He said as a final order, which I agreed to.

"Do you have any questions before you go?" Ellie asked.

"Just one. How long is this supposed to be like this?" I pointed to my stitched brow. It was tight on the skin, and I already wanted it off.

"Around five to seven days. Come back at the end of the week, and I'll have a look. Deal?"

"Sure." I smiled as I thanked her.

I let out a sigh when we were back in Damiano's car, thinking about my mother.

"I have to call my mom and tell her I won't be able to come home this week. I need to find an excuse." There was no way I was going to tell my mother that someone tried to kill me. She would have a heart attack.

"You'll get your phone later. I need to make sure nothing is wrong with it."

"What would be wrong with it?"

"A tracker, since you left your phone in the hotel room." He clarified.

"I don't know why I keep getting surprised by your answers." I mumbled as I thought back to last night. I nervously bit my lip while glancing at Damiano.

"Was that really a heart I saw on the wall?" I finally asked. I may not be familiar with his world, but I wasn't that clueless to not know what a heart with my face on it meant.

Damiano frowned at my question.

"A cow's heart."

"How do you know?"

"I just do." He replied curtly, and I dropped it. I was disgusted, but kind of relieved it wasn't a real human heart.

"What's going to happen if you find him?"

"*When*." Damiano stated as he parked the car in front of the manor. His expression hardened when he looked at my stitched brow. "I'm going to make sure he won't be able to lay a hand on you again." His promise sent a shiver down my spine, as if a gust of cold wind had passed through me.

I let out a small sigh, my stomach twisting in nervousness that I had become a target. Could it be people using me to retaliate against my father now that I wasn't dead on paper anymore?

A hand on my cheek brought me out of my thoughts.

"I'll keep you safe." Damiano's gaze held an intensity that sent a wave of fluttering butterflies through the pit of my stomach.

"I know." I gave a small smile as he caressed my cheek. Instead of feeling afraid or traumatized, his mere presence had a way of making me feel protected.

"Let's get you to bed."

"You're going to break your back if you keep carrying me." I chuckled as I wrapped my arms around his neck.

"As if you can hurt me. You're light as a feather." Damiano let out a playful smile.

"Liar, but I'll take the compliment."

"You're really tiny. Hm, most of you, that is."

I let out a squeal when he suddenly squeezed my ass.

"I'm not tiny! You're just huge." I said, feeling my cheeks getting warm.

"I know I'm huge." He winked.

"Tsk, don't flatter yourself. I've tried better *and* bigger." I bit my lip to stifle a laugh, and he scoffed loudly at my response.

"I've told you before, and I'll tell you again; you are one terrible liar. I always know when you're lying. Do I need to remind you who you're dealing with?" Damiano raised a quizzical brow at me as he stepped into his room, using his foot to close the door behind him.

"And how would you like to remind me?" I asked, a hint of flirtation in my voice. I shifted to straddle him when he sat on the bed, my lips hovered just a breath away from his.

"You need to rest." He replied yet remained unmoved.

"Hmm, you know what would really help me relax?" I whispered, watching his eyes darken.

"I know what you're trying to do." He grabbed my wrists to stop them when they traveled down his body.

"I'm just trying to help you out..." I looked down at his crotch that had a very visible and hard bulge that was so eager to be set free. "Looks painful. Don't you want me to help?" I began to grind my hips against his. In an instant, Damiano's hands shot out and firmly gripped my hips holding them still.

"Althaia." He warned, his voice husky from lust. It only made me more excited. I knew it would only be a matter of time before he would give in to me.

"Fine. I'm going to take a shower then." I gave an innocent smile as I pulled the t-shirt over my head, exposing my naked breasts to him. "Care to join? I'm going to be all wet and slippery." My voice dropped to a low, sultry tone as I trailed my hands from my stomach to my breasts. Playing with my nipples, a soft moan slipped from my lips as I kept my eyes locked on him.

Damiano's grip tightened around me. Suddenly, he had me pinned to the bed with him on top of me.

"You are one dangerous woman, and so damn irresistible." His lips pressed against mine with hunger, and I happily surrendered to him. I traced my hands down his body, ripping his dress shirt open, desperate to feel his muscular torso.

Damiano leaned back, tossing his shirt aside while his starved golden-brown eyes fixed on me. The way he looked at me sent a jolt through my body, and it made me want to squeeze my thighs together in response to the throbbing sensation.

Damiano pulled down my sweatpants, careful not to move my injured foot. He got off the bed, unzipped his pants, and slipped them down. My eyes were immediately drawn to his erect cock. I watched as he gripped his cock and slowly stroked himself. It had me soaked with arousal.

I sat up and wrapped my hand around his thick length. I ran my thumb over the tip of his cock, spreading the pre-cum along his shaft. Damiano's breathing changed, letting out a groan as I moved faster.

I was about to take him in my mouth, but he softly placed his hand on my chin, stopping me. Instead, he placed his two fingers in my mouth, watching with hooded eyes as I sucked on them.

"Atta girl..." He hissed as he shoved his fingers deeper into my mouth. He gently laid me on the bed, his fingertips tracing a path from my lips to the curves of my body, finally reaching the intimate ache between my legs.

"Damiano..." I softly moaned, his thumb lightly sliding along my slit before landing on my clit.

"Fuck, baby, you're dripping." He murmured.

I clenched my fists around the sheets on the bed because of how torturously slow he was going. I bucked my hips and made a dissatisfied sound. Damiano's intense gaze locked onto mine, a mischievous smirk playing on his lips, making me gasp as he shoved two fingers inside me.

"Look how pretty you are with my fingers deep inside your pussy." Damiano grunted.

"I want you..." I whispered, desperate for him to be inside me. His smirk widened as he hoisted my leg onto his shoulder. With a swift movement, his fingers left my pussy, and drove his cock deep inside with a single, rough thrust that made me whimper.

Damiano's relentless thrusts had me moaning, blending with his primal grunts that filled the room.

"La tua fica è il paradiso..." Damiano let out a soft moan, his thumb tracing gentle circles against my clit.

"Don't stop... keep going..." I panted, my entire core tightening around him when he spoke Italian to me. It was so fucking hot I almost came.

He slightly slowed down, hips moving against mine as he drove in deep, making me feel every inch of his thick cock that filled me up so perfectly.

"Vieni, piccola." Damiano gritted through his teeth. "Vieni per me." Damiano commanded. The overwhelming pleasure made my body tense up, my back arched, and my voice escaped in a cry of ecstasy as I orgasmed on his cock.

"That's it, baby." He groaned, tossing his head back as he picked up his pace, intensifying the pleasure that consumed me. His grip on me grew tighter as he grunted as my pussy clenched around his shaft, and soon, I felt his release inside of me.

Damiano collapsed on top of me, his heavy breathing mixing with mine. He gave me a lazy smile as he brushed his lips against mine in a soft kiss. I closed my eyes, savoring the moment with a rush of butterflies in my stomach.

"What did you do on your little getaway with Damiano?" Cara asked as she shoved her face with popcorn.

Arianna and Cara brought a bunch of snacks as we all lounged on Damiano's bed. I had planned on taking a nap after my shower, but since I wasn't tired at all, they came to keep me company since I wasn't allowed to move per Damiano's order.

"I don't want to hear details." Arianna said in a warning tone, and Cara let out a scoff.

"I do! I want to hear every single bit of it. Tell me, is he big?" Cara's grin was removed when Arianna smacked her face with a pillow.

"Don't be disgusting! He's your brother-in-law!"

"So? I want to know if big dicks run in the family." She replied and Arianna gagged, which only made Cara smirk. "I will even start by saying Lorenzo has what I call a monster cock. It felt like he ripped my vagina in two!"

I burst out laughing when Arianna put her in a headlock with her hand clamped against her mouth to make her stop talking about Lorenzo's 'package.'

"You're so disgusting! I don't wanna hear it!" She screamed at Cara.

"Okay, I'll stop!" Cara yelled behind Arianna's hand while she laughed. "Shit, you're freakishly strong! I thought my head was going to pop off."

"I thought she was going to snap my neck last night." I added, amazed by her strength.

"Look who I grew up with. They dragged me to work out with them and kicked my ass. One time I told them to chill the fuck out and go easy on me because I'm a girl. Damiano got so pissed and snapped. He said kill or get killed. No more complaining after that." Arianna chuckled.

"You learned all this as a kid?" I asked in shock.

"Hmm, I think I was around thirteen."

"You were just a child!" I exclaimed.

"It's normal for us, Althaia. Maybe if your parents didn't get divorced, you would have learned how to fight and use a gun like us." She shrugged.

"True." Cara commented. "I learned how to use a gun as well."

"What? Since when?! You've never told me that." I gaped.

"How am I supposed to bring it up? Like, 'oh, by the way, I know how to shoot people'?" She said, amused.

"Good point. Well, now I kind of feel left out..." I muttered. I had never even thought of owning a gun, but maybe I should?

Arianna studied me for a moment before a smile slowly formed on her lips.

"You know, you're tougher than you look. When I first saw you, I thought you would be more of a... timid person. But then I saw the way you fearlessly handled Damiano." She lightly laughed. "The innocence of your big, green eyes is deceiving."

"Trust me, I was scared of him. Especially when he showed up in my hotel room. I thought he was going to shoot my ass that night." I admitted.

"He was going to, but then saw you weren't a threat, so he didn't." Arianna said, popping an M&M in her mouth.

"...You're joking, right?"

"No. So, do you want me to teach you how to use a gun?"

"What the fuck?"

"Is that a yes or a no?" She asked, eating another M&M.

"You can't just say Damiano was going to shoot me that night, and then ask me a question like it's nothing." I exclaimed.

"I'm just joking! My brothers are not the type to hurt women." Arianna laughed when I gave her a blank look, not finding her joke funny. "Do you want to learn how to use a gun or not?"

"Can you really teach me?" My brows raised in surprise.

"Sure, why not? You need to learn how to defend yourself, so you don't end up with a face like that." She grimaced and pointed directly at my face. This time, I threw a bag of chips at her, which she caught with a laugh before it could hit her face.

"When can we start?" I asked, feeling a small rush of excitement at the thought.

"Depends. Do we have to wait for Damiano's approval, or do we just do it behind his back?" She raised a quizzical brow, and I could already imagine Damiano frowning with a stern no.

"What he doesn't know won't hurt him." I grinned.

"Exactly. We can start tomorrow." She winked.

"Okay, enough about that! Let's go back to what you were doing while being away from the rest of us." Cara wiggled her brows and Arianna groaned.

"Nothing, we just hung out." I shrugged.

"What are you, teenagers?" She was not impressed at all. "Give me the juicy parts! Did you finally fuck?"

"Please, don't -" Arianna started before I interrupted her.

"You really want to know? Fine. Yes, we fucked. We fucked so much I thought he was going to destroy me. I was so sore, but damn, that man can keep going like a fucking stallion. There was not a single place where he didn't fuck me. Happy?" I huffed out.

"Hell yeah!" Cara cheered, while Arianna looked mortified.

"Oh, and we also just fucked right there before you guys came." I pointed to where they were sitting. Arianna jumped off the bed, cursing us for being disgusting, which only made us laugh.

After some time, Arianna and Cara left the room when I struggled to keep my eyes open. Exhaustion finally hit me, and I fell asleep as soon as I heard the door close behind them.

Then suddenly, I couldn't breathe.

I tried gasping for air, but nothing filled my lungs. I couldn't even open my eyes, and my body felt heavier than before. So much I couldn't move. I tried to scream, but no sound was escaping me.

I was panicking, and my lungs were burning from lack of air.

I thrashed violently in bed, but it felt as if an invisible weight was pressing down on my chest. Using my legs as a last resort, I sharply rolled over and ended up crashing onto the floor.

I gasped, air finally filling my lungs. I tried to sit up, only to see Sofia lunging at me.

Her hands closed around my neck so quickly that I had no time to react. I could feel the tears stinging my eyes as she mercilessly pressed down on my windpipe, using her weight to her advantage.

"I'm so fucking tired of you thinking you deserve him! You don't!" She hissed at me. I tried to get her off me, but she refused to loosen her grip around my throat, even when I scratched her arms. I opened my mouth to speak, but all that came out were gagging sounds.

"I won't let you be with him! What do you have that I don't?!" Sofia yelled in my face. My sight went blurry, and I had to do something fast.

I pulled my arm back and punched her right in her nose. It was enough for her to loosen her grip as she cried out in pain.

I pushed her away, coughing as I struggled to breathe while stumbling to my feet to get away. But I didn't get far as Sofia quickly recovered and slammed me against the wall.

"So–Sofia, stop." My voice was hoarse and kept breaking when I tried to speak.

"What does he even see in you?" She looked at me with disgust as she kept me pinned against the wall. "You're not worthy of standing by his side, but I am." Her baby blue eyes blazed with anger as she yelled her true feelings, leaving me stunned.

"He's mine!" Sofia sneered.

"Then take him." I coughed out. Surprise showed in her eyes as she looked at me, and her grip on me loosened ever so slightly. That's when I grabbed her head and smashed her face right into my knee.

Sofia screamed as blood poured out of her nose, stumbling away from me and falling to the floor. I sprinted to the door, ignoring the pain shooting up my foot as I panted, desperately wanting to get away from her.

Swinging the door open, I glanced back to make sure she was still on the floor. The sight had my heart almost stopped beating when she aimed a gun at me with her trembling hands.

I let out a piercing scream as I threw myself to the floor at the same time the reverberating gunshot shattered the silence. With my body trembling, I tried to crawl away from the door, each breath becoming harder to take.

"H-help..." I croaked out. My throat felt like it was on fire, making me cough every time I tried to speak. I wanted to get up, but the weakness in my body overpowered me, leaving me on the floor.

"Althaia!" I heard several hurried footsteps echoing up the stairs, and a wave of relief washed over me as tears threatened to spill.

I flinched when suddenly a pair of arms grabbed me and pulled me up. Looking up, I realized it was Damiano who had pulled me close and held me tightly.

But he wasn't looking at me.

I followed his gaze and saw Sofia standing at the end of the hallway, her hands shaking as she aimed the gun at me. Her nose was still bleeding, but she paid no attention to it, her gaze fixed firmly on me.

"Sofia." Damiano's sneer twisted his face into a menacing expression as he pulled me protectively behind him.

"Move, Damiano. I don't want to hurt you." Her breathing was loud and harsh, her trembling hands struggled to take aim at me.

"Put the gun down. You don't want to do this." Damiano talked to her calmly. Her eyes darted behind us, and I instinctively turned to follow her line of sight. Antonio, Luca, and Lorenzo were observing her intently, their hands resting on their guns. Arianna and Cara were by the stairs, but out of Sofia's view.

"Look, I don't want to hurt anyone. I just want her!" Sofia hissed, looking back at me.

"Why?" Damiano spoke to her calmly, as if she wasn't waving a gun at us.

"She doesn't deserve you."

"That's not a good enough answer, Sofia." Slowly, he began to close the distance between them.

"No!" In a moment of panic, I reached out and grabbed the back of his shirt, afraid of what she might do.

"Don't fucking touch him!" Sofia screamed at the top of her lungs and shots were fired.

I froze and stopped breathing as I squeezed my eyes shut. When I didn't feel any pain, I slowly opened them and looked down at my body.

Suddenly a blood-curdling scream pierced through the ringing in my ears and made me snap my head towards the sound. Sofia was sprawled on the floor, her hands stained with blood, as she let out piercing screams of agony.

"What...?" I breathed out, looking at Damiano, only then noticing the gun in his hand.

Thirty-Three

DAMIANO

"Take her away. I'll deal with her later." I told Antonio and Luca, and they dragged her away as she sobbed.

I slid my gun into the waistband behind my back, focusing on Althaia as I gently cupped her cheeks to examine her. My anger flared at the sight of her bloodshot eyes, and her neck that was red.

"Don't talk." I said to Althaia when she winced as she tried to speak.

"How could something like this happen?" Cara pulled her away from me to look at her. Her eyes blazed with fury as she turned to glare at me. "Do you just let everyone have a gun in this house?"

"I don't."

"Good to know you're not keeping track of shit." She spat out, and I shot her a look, taking a step towards her.

"It would be wise of you to watch your mouth, woman." I warned her. Cara took a step back and looked away.

"S-stop it." Althaia's hoarse voice caught my attention.

"Try not to speak." I spoke softly to her when she placed her hand on her throat.

"Ellie is on her way." Arianna informed me, and I gave a quick nod.

Lorenzo stopped beside me; his hand extended to show me the gun Sofia had been holding moments ago. I shared a look with Lorenzo, and he nodded in agreement.

"Arianna, tell me how the fuck Sofia got a hold of your gun?" I snapped at her as I showed her the gun.

"I don't know." Her brows furrowed at the sight.

"You don't know?" I gritted my teeth as I walked up to her.

"I keep this one in my purse. I guess she must have snooped around and found it." Arianna sighed.

"You left your gun unattended? Then you better take care of her." I pushed the gun into her hands.

"Fine." She snapped and turned to walk down the stairs, but not before shooting me a look. "But I warned you, Damiano. I told you she would be a problem if you didn't get rid of her."

I rubbed my jaw in annoyance.

"Get Rosana to my office." I told Lorenzo as I turned to Althaia. When I reached for her, she stepped away from me, holding onto Cara.

"Can you help me?" She whispered to Cara as she refused to look at me.

"Don't be ridiculous, Althaia." I sighed. She continued to ignore me, limping to the stairs with Cara's help.

Frustrated, I clicked my tongue and motioned for Lorenzo to help her. I didn't like that he was carrying her, but I couldn't risk her slipping and breaking her fucking neck because she was refusing my help.

I closed my eyes and rolled my neck to get rid of the tension. My foolishness in the past was biting me in the fucking ass right now.

I entered my office to find Althaia already settled on the couch with Cara by her side. She was talking to Althaia softly, who kept her eyes down on her lap.

"My goodness, what happened?" Rosana gasped when she saw Althaia.

"Sofia did that. She tried to kill Althaia." I said, leaning against my desk. Rosana's eyes went wide, covering her mouth in shock.

"My Sofia? No, it can't be..." She shook her head, refusing to believe what she just heard.

"She stole Arianna's gun and tried to kill Althaia in front of all of us." My expression hardened. "I'm simply saying this out of respect for you. You have been good to the family, but you should prepare yourself." I stated calmly. I didn't need to clarify what I meant. She knew.

"No, please! Please don't!" Rosana cried out, grabbing my hands as she begged me to spare her daughter's life. "I'll do anything! Please, she's my only daughter."

"You know the consequences." I frowned.

"You can send her away. I promise to make sure she won't be any trouble. I'm begging you!" She sobbed, tears streaming down her face.

I was about to dismiss her when I looked at Althaia, her eyes soft and glistening with tears. In the traditional sense, she would have been the one to decide about what would happen to Sofia, given that she was the one who had been attacked. However, since she was not the type to dictate someone's death, I decided on her behalf.

Althaia looked at me as a tear escaped her eye. She gave a slight shake of her head before returning to look at Rosana with so much sadness.

I rubbed my jaw, not agreeing with her decision.

"Lorenzo, stop Arianna." I called out. Rosana's gaze locked with mine, filled with hope. "I'll send her away. But I won't spare her life if I see her again." I promised her. She cried tears of relief, her voice trembling as she promised she would ensure Sofia stayed far away from us.

Just as Lorenzo walked Rosana out, Ellie entered the room with her medical bag.

"Althaia, I only need a nod or a shake of your head to answer my questions, okay? I don't want you to talk until I know what the injuries are." Ellie said when she immediately noticed her neck.

I stepped closer when she examined Althaia, and I slowly felt relieved when she shook her head at most of Ellie's questions. She was going to be okay.

"Count yourself lucky." Ellie reassured with a smile. "Stick to a soft diet for now since swallowing is painful. Rest well, limit talking, elevate your foot to reduce swelling, and you'll be fine."

Althaia gave her a small smile and a nod as Ellie packed her bag and left.

"Leave us." I said to Cara. Irritation flooded through me as she turned her gaze towards Althaia, silently questioning if she was okay to be alone with me. Althaia had to reassure her she was going to be okay before she finally left us.

Taking a seat on the coffee table in front of her, I was met with a face twisted in a scowl.

"Did you date her?" She whispered, letting me know in her tone that she was pissed.

"No, we didn't date." I sighed. "But I did sleep with her. Once." I confessed. Disappointment filled her eyes as she shook her head.

She rose from the couch, but I stopped her from leaving.

"It was a long time ago. My mind wasn't... in the right place at that time, and she offered. I didn't turn her down. Then I left for months and came back in time for the engagement." I explained, which only made her frown.

"You fucked her, then you left, only to show up with another woman, whom you're now fucking?" Althaia scoffed.

"I never spared her another thought after that. I made it clear it was a one-time thing."

"Yet, you let her stay here."

"I know. I shouldn't have. Arianna warned me about it when she knew about you." I admitted.

Disappointment and anger welled up inside her, making her frown as she rose from the couch again. And I despised it with every fiber of my being.

"Piccola." I rose to my feet to help her. Her eyes flashed with hurt at the pet name I gave her before brushing my hands away.

"I don't feel like talking to you." Althaia limped to the door, using the furniture as support as she passed by.

"Let me help you." I sighed.

"I would rather not have you touch me right now." She didn't look at me, her voice cold as she tried to get away from me.

"I fucked up. It was a mistake." I called after her. Althaia stopped but didn't turn around to look at me.

"The problem is not who you've fucked, Damiano. It's the fact that you kept her around." I could hear the pain in her voice as she said those words, and I felt a sinking sensation in my chest as I watched her walk away.

Thirty-Four

Damiano

"Getting drunk now?" Arianna made herself comfortable on the couch in front of me.

"Shut up." I replied while pouring my third glass of whiskey and leaned back. I took a slow sip as I looked at her, noticing a few bloodstains on her clothes.

"What did you do?" I didn't care what she had done to Sofia, but I needed to know if she was well enough to get on a plane and get the fuck away from here.

"Just had a little fun with her. Might have smacked her around a bit, broke a few bones here and there. Her nose is broken, too. At least, it looks like it." She shrugged, checking her nails as she spoke. Lorenzo returned and settled down next to Arianna, pouring himself a drink.

"She'll be on a plane first thing tomorrow." He said and downed the drink in one go.

"Good. And Althaia?" I asked.

"Upstairs. Resting in Cara's room." I clicked my tongue at the information. She didn't even want to stay in my room.

"How pissed was she when you told her?" Arianna looked at me with a raised brow.

"You already know." I was in no mood to talk about it with her, and I definitely didn't want to hear her go on about how 'she told me so.'

She would always get that smug, satisfied expression on her face whenever she was right, and I hated it. If she had been my brother with that kind of attitude, I would have knocked it out of him in no time.

In a way, Arianna was a female mixture of both Lorenzo and me. She handled business the way we did, and one wouldn't think she would know how to defend herself by the looks of her, but she could easily take down a two hundred pound man.

"You know, Althaia has great survival instincts…" Arianna trailed off. I glared at her, not liking where she was heading with it. "Hear me out before you give me your death stare." She rolled her eyes.

"All I'm saying is if she can break Sofia's nose like that, imagine what she could do if she had proper fight training." She finished, and I tilted my head at the suggestion.

"Althaia broke Sofia's nose?" Lorenzo asked with a hint of amusement, not expecting to hear that.

"Oh, you thought I did it? Nope. I was about to, but then Sofia kept screaming about how her face was smashed into her knee and needed medical attention." Arianna laughed. The corner of my lips curled up, and a feeling of pride filled my chest.

"She's right, Damiano. We don't know who is targeting her. If we train her, she might actually stand a chance." Lorenzo added. I shook my head, not agreeing with them.

"No, I'll increase security around her."

"Because that worked so well for Si–"

"Don't you fucking say her name." I sneered in a warning tone, sending her a sharp look. A scowl formed on her face as she narrowed her eyes in frustration.

"Can't you see what you're doing?" Arianna continued. I rose to my feet and walked to my desk.

I didn't want to talk about *her*. I didn't even want to hear her name. The memory it brought back was so dark that I knew it would cause me to lose control. The urge to kill took over, and I spent months fighting to regain control of myself. A mere glance in my direction was enough to trigger a deadly response.

"You're making the same mistakes, Damiano!" Arianna said. I rubbed my jaw in frustration when she wouldn't drop it. "Althaia is different. She's strong enough, and she's not scared. If she was, she would run for the hills right now. Far away from you."

"You better stop right now." I spat out.

"I saw what you went through with Sienna, and it killed me to see you like that. If you're not careful, Althaia will taste the same fate as her."

"Don't you think I know that?! Fuck!" I smashed my fist onto the desk, shattering the glass in my hand. Her words made my blood boil with anger. Althaia was mine, and I wouldn't let anyone take her away from me. I would make sure of it. No matter what it takes, even if I had to burn the whole fucking world.

"Arianna, enough." Lorenzo snapped.

"Whether you like it or not, I'm going to teach her. It's for the best." Arianna finished and walked out of the office. The muscles in my neck tensed as I clenched my jaw, struggling to keep my anger in check.

The sound of my phone buzzing in my pocket broke the silence. My bloodied hand fished it out of my pocket to see it was Raffaele.

"What?" I snapped as I answered the call.

"We found him."

"I'm coming." I didn't wait for him to say anything else and hung up the phone. "Make sure Althaia doesn't move around." I told Lorenzo as I made my way out of the office, wrapping a handkerchief around my hand.

The sound of my footsteps echoed down the long corridor of the storage facility until I reached a specific steel roll-up door where Raffaele was waiting for me.

The door creaked as he pushed it up, revealing a narrow staircase that descended into darkness. It was built to be soundproof, deep beneath the earth's surface, so that even the loudest screams couldn't be heard.

We walked down the tunnel path until Raffaele broke the silence.

"I heard what happened. Who would have thought Sofia could go bat shit crazy?"

"Shut up before I shoot your ass." I kept staring ahead, not in the mood to talk about it.

"Right. So, another problem I want to take up with you. He won't talk." Raffaele said as we turned around a corner.

"I'll make him talk." I said, moving my neck from side to side. I couldn't wait to get my hands on him.

I was thirsty for blood, and my hands were twitching to beat the fuck out of him and let all of my anger out for what he had done to Althaia. I will make him wish he had never been born.

"You will see what I mean." He sighed and opened the door to the Chamber of Torture.

My eyes immediately landed on the blindfolded bastard. The room was silent except for his rapid breathing and the sound of the ropes creaking as he struggled against them. Giovanni and Dom were positioned in the back, keeping a close watch on him, not that he would be able to escape.

His face was bruised and swollen, and blood was seeping from the side of his head. I walked up to him and ripped the blindfold from his face. I tilted my head as I took a good look at him while he blinked a few times before he focused on me. He was of Asian descent.

Interesting.

"Talk." I ordered him. The bastard leaned his head back and gave me an arrogant grin before he opened his mouth. His tongue had been cut off.

My laughter was low and sinister as I clutched his jaw tightly. My hold tightened on his jaw, making him wince with pain as I leaned in closer.

"You're going to wish you had a tongue for what I'm about to do to you." I let a cold smile appear on my lips. "I will enjoy making you suffer for what you did. *No one* touches what's *mine*." I snarled in his ear before roughly grabbing a fistful of his hair.

The gratifying thud of my fist connecting with his jaw was the only sound in the room. I felt a rush of adrenaline as my fist connected with his face again, relishing in the feeling of power as he groaned in agony.

I kept going even when I heard the satisfying crack of his nose and blood gushing out from his face. I kept pounding my fist into his fucking face because all I saw right now was the image of Althaia, crying in fear.

I stopped and let go of him as I took in a breath. I didn't want to kill him just yet. With my sleeves rolled up, I strode towards the long table, my eyes scanning the weapons and tools, searching for the perfect one. I grabbed a hammer, feeling its weight in my hand, and a few nails. I pulled a chair over and sat down in front of him, his head hanging low already.

"You dared to touch her with your filthy hands?" I chuckled darkly. I gripped his arm tightly and held it down on the armrest. I could feel him tense up when I placed the nail on the back of his hand, and he started to shake his head, trying to signal for me to stop.

My lips curled into a malevolent smile as I raised the hammer and swung it down on the nail. The bastard screamed as it pierced through his hand as I nailed it to the armrest. He was still thrashing when I nailed his other hand.

But I was far from done.

I went back to the table and picked up a plier.

"It's a shame I won't hear you beg. I like to hear it." I sighed and sat back down in front of him. "But it's okay. I'll love it when you scream in agony, too." I chuckled and looked down at his fingers. He was already breathing hard, trying to squirm away from me, but it was all useless.

This was my playroom, and I was ready to fucking play.

I grabbed his fingers, and one by one, I slowly dragged each nail from its bed. I grabbed the drilling machine, its whirring sound filling the air as I tested it a few times before walking back to him. He was barely able to keep his eyes open as blood slowly dripped from his wounds. I was feeding off the sight. It only made me want to keep going, making him suffer as much as possible.

For Althaia.

I pressed the drill gun against his collarbone. The sound of his scream was music to my ears as I pressed the drill bit deeper into his flesh, feeling the satisfying resistance of his bone. The sound of screaming abruptly ended before I could penetrate all the way through.

"Weak fucker." I scoffed as I looked at him, passed out. I shook my head and grabbed a syringe, injecting him with a dose of adrenaline. He suddenly woke up, screaming and gasping for breath.

There it is. Music to my ears.

He kept shaking his head when I moved on to his kneecap.

"Already had enough? Too bad it's only the beginning." My laughter grew as I watched the point drilling into his kneecap, sinking into his flesh and bone. With each repetition, I could see the pain he was feeling, and it brought me so much satisfaction. The sight of him writhing in agony was like a feast for the hunger inside me.

I grabbed a knife and carved into his face and body, making him unrecognizable. I was completely covered in his blood, but I wasn't done just yet.

I lit up a cigarette, blood smearing on it as I inhaled deeply. With the same knife, I stabbed him repeatedly in the shoulder blades, twisting and turning to widen the gap.

I untied him, ripping out the nails stuck into his hands, and grabbed him by the shoulders. I dragged him to the stone wall, lifted him, and hung him right on the wall with his new holes in his back.

I stepped away as I pulled the cigarette from my lips, blowing out the smoke as I admired the work I had done. He was sobbing, head dangling and barely conscious.

"Now, that's what I call a fucking masterpiece." The sight of his flesh hanging made me let out a devilish grin.

If only I could present this to her.

"Feed him to the rats. While he's still alive." I ordered Dom and Giovanni and walked out.

Thirty-Five

ALTHAIA

Three days have passed since Sofia tried to kill me, and three days since I last spoke to Damiano. I have been staying in Cara's room as I didn't feel like seeing him.

Cara tried to talk to me about it, but I wasn't ready to talk loudly about how Damiano and Sofia had fucked. Oh, and how he somehow thought it was a brilliant idea to keep her under his roof while getting his dick wet by someone else.

I let out a loud groan and buried my face in the pillow, wanting to get him out of my head so I would stop thinking about him.

On the bright side, I was healing. My throat wasn't hurting anymore because I wasn't talking, and my foot was a lot less painful. I was still limping, but I could move it around.

"Get up! I'm tired of you being in that bed all the time." Arianna ripped the blanket away from me.

"Leave me alone." I grumbled and rolled in bed. This wasn't the first time she had tried to get me out of bed.

"Sorry, love, but you're getting out of bed today. Get dressed, we're leaving." Her words caught my attention. Curious, I sat up only for something to hit my face.

"Where are we going?" I asked, looking at the clothes she threw at me. A pair of training leggings, sports bra, and cropped t-shirt.

"Do you want to learn how to use a gun or not?" She looked at me with her hands on her hips.

"I do!" I said with a grin. "But just to be sure, does this training involve you making me run so you can shoot at me, and I have to dodge the bullets?"

"Is that what you think of me? A psycho who just shoots at people?" Arianna looked unimpressed.

"Yes." I shrugged my shoulders.

"You're not wrong about that." She laughed, and I stared at her in shock. "But no, I won't shoot at you, you idiot. You wouldn't be able to dodge them anyway if I did." She winked.

"That was not reassuring at all." I said, but she ignored me and continued to talk.

"Meet us outside. You have ten minutes to get ready before I drag your ass out." Arianna practically ordered before walking out.

I pulled my hair into a high ponytail after I was dressed and grabbed my crutches. I made it outside, where Arianna and Cara were waiting for me next to a sleek black car.

"Ready?" Cara asked with a bright smile.

"Sure." I mirrored her smile.

We drove for a while before coming to a stop behind the woods, where a massive building stood.

"This place is huge." I said in awe when I saw a large field transformed into an outdoor shooting range.

"We are one of the biggest families. We need to stay on top of our game. This is one of our places that we've recently expanded." Arianna explained as she led us inside.

"This is going to be fun!" Cara's voice brimmed with excitement, and I nodded along, feeling my spirits finally lift.

Descending through another door, we entered a vast open space with the sight of multiple shooting target papers hanging at the end. They were even human shaped with white markings.

"Okay, listen Althaia." I looked at Arianna standing next to a collection of guns, magazines, and knives that were on display.

"I'm going to tell you the basics and how to safely use a gun, so you don't accidentally shoot us. And Lorenzo would have your head if his dear Cara got hurt." She smirked.

"Yeah, I'm definitely shooting myself before he gets to me." I said in all seriousness. I didn't even want to imagine what Tank Man would do to me if I accidentally hurt Cara.

"Good idea." Arianna chuckled along with Cara. "Let's get started."

I placed my crutches aside and paid close attention to what Arianna was about to show me.

"When you pick up your gun, keep your index finger straight and position it right here on the ring guard. You're a newbie, so if you position your index finger on the trigger, you might accidentally put pressure on it and shoot." Arianna explained firmly.

"This button here is the magazine release button."

As she pressed the button, the magazine smoothly ejected from the grip of the handgun. It was empty, and she showed me how to fill it up with cartridges before pushing it back inside.

"... And here you just pull the slide all the way back until you can't pull anymore and let go. So, this is a semi-automatic gun, which means that every time you pull the trigger, the next bullet is ready to be fired without you having to slide it back. You're all set now." Arianna finished.

I slowly nodded, trying to take it all in.

"Are we not supposed to wear earmuffs and security glasses?" I asked, which earned me a blank look from her.

"Right, because you have time to put on earmuffs and security glasses when you're out on a real battlefield. You might as well get used to the sounds while you're learning."

"Oh, um, okay." I wasn't a big fan of the sounds, but I guess I just had to *get used to it*.

"If it gets too much for you, earmuffs are in the cabinet." Arianna smiled when she saw my distress.

"No, it's fine. I want to try without first." I decided.

"Great! Now, let's see how you do."

Following Arianna's instructions, I picked up the gun and positioned myself behind the line on the floor. With a determined grip, I pulled the slide all the way back, my eyes fixed on the target ahead. Despite feeling a little nervous, I could feel the rush of adrenaline coursing through my veins.

I fired a shot, and the powerful recoil made me stagger backwards. I let out a whistle. This was more powerful than I had imagined.

"Don't keep your feet in line. Place one leg slightly behind the other for support." Arianna helped me with my stance and had me fire again. This time, I barely moved and stayed in place, so I continued. It was fun, and I was actually enjoying it a lot more than I thought I would.

I lowered my gun to see how I did and scowled when I saw the result. I hit the paper, just not anywhere near the lines.

"This is harder than I thought." I muttered to myself. I watched Arianna and Cara when they started and huffed when I saw they hit the center perfectly.

"It's not that bad. You're doing better than most people for the first time." Cara tried to make me feel better while looking at my paper.

"Don't lie to me."

"Let me help." She chuckled.

They both helped and gave me advice on my stance and how high to hold the gun and where to aim. Every time I thought my aim was somewhat decent, my shots would miss by a long shot. It was a lot more difficult, but I wasn't giving up. The competitive side of me couldn't handle watching Arianna and Cara hitting the center. It made me feel like a loser.

"This sucks!" I groaned when I once again didn't hit the target mark.

"Relax. This is your first time. Did you expect to nail it the first time?" Arianna chuckled.

"I was hoping I had a secret talent or something." I sighed and placed the gun back on the table to take a break.

"Looks like we gathered an audience." Cara said, and I followed her gaze to where a wide window was at the top of the wall.

Damiano and Raffaele were watching us, and my heart skipped a beat as I looked at Damiano. His intense gaze was already on me, and my stupid body tingled. He wasn't wearing his typical dress shirt, but a black t-shirt that hugged tightly around his muscles.

I sucked my teeth in annoyance at how freaking hot he looked right now. But I was still annoyed with him, and I scowled to let him know his presence was still unwanted.

"How awesome would it be if I could shoot his dick from here?"

Damiano raised a brow at me, and Raffaele broke out in a laughing fit next to him. Out of the blue, Arianna stood in front of me, blocking my view of them.

"Listen, I know you're pissed, but joke or not, you're talking about shooting a mob boss. And that shit gets you killed." She said seriously, but her eyes twinkled with amusement.

"Oops, did I say that out loud?" I gave an awkward laugh and scratched the back of my head.

"You did. And they can hear you."

"Fuck me already." I mumbled in embarrassment.

At least Raffaele found it funny.

I leaned against the table and carefully moved my injured foot. I have been on my feet for a while now, and I was feeling a twinge of pain.

"Can we try out the knives?" I asked Arianna as I looked at the enormous collection of knives displayed next to the guns.

"Sure." She went to set up new target marks for the knives; these ones were different and made out of wood.

"Before you start–"

"What is there to know? Isn't it just throwing a knife and seeing if it hits?" I asked and shifted my body to the side, making sure my grip on the knife was secure before launching it towards the wooden mark.

"What the hell?" Cara gaped as we all stared at where my knife landed.

"Finally!" I shouted and punched the air in victory.

"Hmm, do it again." Arianna gestured for me to grab another knife.

"Probably just beginner's luck." I shrugged but grabbed a knife.

I stood with my feet shoulder-width apart, adjusting my grip on the knife and hurling it towards the target. It landed with precision; its blade aligned perfectly next to the other knife.

"Impressive!" Arianna's brows shot up in genuine shock. "Let me see how you hold the knife."

I showed her how I moved my wrist and threw a knife again. To everyone's surprise, it landed in the middle for the third time. A wide grin stretched across my face as I basked in the pride.

"You're even holding it with elegance. You draw a lot, don't you? Maybe the flexibility you gained from drawing has an influence on your throw."

"You think so?" I have spent hundreds of hours drawing, so my wrist isn't stiff as it was in the beginning. Unexpectedly, it turned out to be beneficial for my knife throwing abilities.

"It's possible. I can't even throw this well three times in a row."

"Hah, sucker." I teased, and she rolled her eyes at me.

I winced in pain as I stumbled, accidentally placing all my weight on my injured foot. I had totally overdone it now and needed painkillers.

"Wrap it up, she needs to rest." Damiano's voice echoed through the speakers. I looked up at the window and frowned.

"You don't know what I need. If I want to keep going, then I will." I was actually tired and needed to rest, but if he was going to tell me I needed to rest, then I would do the opposite. That was how petty I wanted to be.

Damiano's eyes narrowed at me before walking out of our sight.

"You two are going to drive each other crazy. I can feel it." Arianna laughed.

"Big time." Cara joined her.

The sound of the door opening had all of us turn our heads in unison. Damiano, with an angry expression on his face, was striding directly toward me. With his long strides, he was in front of me in no time. I placed my hands on my hips as I looked at him, ready to tell him off.

But then he swiftly grabbed me and carried me in his arms.

"Hey! Put me down." I tried to wiggle out of his arms as he walked us out, but he had a firm grip on me.

"Stop moving." He growled.

"Put me down!"

"No. You have overworked yourself. Now, stop being stubborn." He gave me a firm look.

I crossed my arms, turning my attention elsewhere, and trying to suppress the effect his touch was having on me. I had to resist the urge to lean closer to him and inhale his intoxicating scent.

My heart ached for him, yet my pride silenced my words of longing.

Thirty-Six

ALTHAIA

We drove back to the manor in silence. I sat as close as I could to the door to create as much distance between us as possible while facing away from him.

"How long are you going to be like this?" Damiano's deep voice broke the silence. I ignored him as I focused on the window, savoring the view of the stunning green fields.

"Althaia."

"You're the one who kept your *fuck buddy* around, so I'll stay like this however long I want to." I snapped, finally looking at him with a frown on my face.

"Fuck buddy? Is that what you're calling her now?" His hands clenched around the steering wheel.

"I'll call her something much worse..." I muttered under my breath, and Damiano rubbed his jaw.

"I already told you it was a mistake."

"Easy to say after you get caught." I swallowed hard, my emotions getting the best of me. "Did you sleep with her while being with me?" The thought made my heart clench, but I couldn't stop wondering about it.

"Don't be ridiculous." He growled when we came to a stop in front of the manor.

"That's not an answer, Damiano." A tense silence filled the air as we stared at each other, his brows knitting together. "Whatever. This whole thing was a mistake to begin with." Deep down, I knew I didn't mean it. It was the hurt part of me that spoke those words.

Tears welled up in my eyes, and I hurriedly opened the car door. Ignoring the pain in my foot, I rushed inside, consumed by an even greater agony in my chest.

I ignored Damiano as he called after me. I tried to pick up my speed, but his long strides caught up with me.

"Let go of me!" I yelled at him when he threw me over his shoulder. I felt the tears escape my eyes, my own body betraying me when it was at this point I didn't want to feel anything the most.

Damiano slammed the door shut to his room and dropped me on the bed. Without hesitation, I sprang to my feet and darted towards the door, but he held me once more. His grip felt like steel, forcing me to meet his gaze.

"You're going to listen to me." He said firmly. His hard expression slowly softened as he placed his hand on my cheek, and wiped away the tears that didn't seem to stop falling. "I may be many things, but a cheater isn't one of them."

I turned my head away from him, trying to hide the turmoil of emotions I was feeling. With a gentle touch, he lifted my chin to look at him.

"When will you get it inside of that stubborn beautiful head of yours that there is no one but you?"

"What else was I supposed to think when she was here all this time?" I asked, my voice heavy with sadness.

"I know, and I shouldn't have." Damiano's brows furrowed. "She never meant anything to me. I was willing to get rid of her, I still am, because that's how little I care about her. I gave an order but took it back because of you. I never take back an order. That's how much I care about you."

I looked into the sincere expression in his eyes, assuring me that he was telling the truth. I wasn't sure what to say.

Damiano gave me a soft look as he caressed my cheek.

"Are you going to stop torturing me now by not letting me see you?" He said with so much dissatisfaction that I let out a small, choked laugh.

"I would hardly call it torture." I playfully rolled my eyes, and he let out a soft smile as he cupped my cheeks.

"If only you knew..." He spoke quietly, and my heart went back to doing backflips. "You have no idea what I will do for you... *My Althaia.*"

A wave of intense emotion swept through me, causing my breath to catch and my stomach to dance with butterflies. I opened my mouth to say something but shut it quickly again as I looked at Damiano, surprised at what was about to leave my mouth.

Did I really feel like this toward him? I wasn't sure what this new feeling was. Ever since I laid eyes on this mesmerizing Devil, my entire life turned upside down, and now he was all I could think about.

Not trusting myself with words, I wrapped my arms around his neck as I slowly leaned in until our lips met in a soft kiss. Damiano pulled me flush against him with a hand behind my neck as he deepened the kiss.

"I've missed you." He whispered against my lips, and I let out a cheeky smile.

"Don't piss me off, and you won't have to suffer." I teased. He clicked his tongue, a smile playing on his lips.

"Mhm, beauty and danger. You're quite the lethal combination. So damn enticing." A low, guttural rumble escaped his throat as he grabbed the back of my thighs and lifted me.

I wrapped my legs around him, resting my head against his.

"I've missed you too." I whispered.

"Show me." Damiano smirked, walking until he sat on the edge of the bed with me on his lap.

My body heated with excitement as our lips met again. The relentless pressure of his mouth on mine was intoxicating, and I wanted nothing more than to feel all of him right now.

I grabbed the hem of his shirt and pulled it over his head, greedily feeling his muscular, tattooed body.

Damiano gripped my hips, pressing his hard length against me, and let out a low groan as I slowly rolled my hips. Piece by piece, our clothes were thrown aside. He let out a satisfied sound as he looked at my naked breasts, my nipples already hard.

With a devious smile, I pushed him onto his back, taking him by surprise, and straddled his hips.

"Fuck..." Damiano grunted when I took a hold of his hard cock, positioning myself so I was grinding my wetness along his length.

"I'll show you just how much." I held my breath as I slid down, taking all of him in as I exhaled a moan.

"That's it, baby. Take all of me." He moaned, slapping his hips against me.

"Damiano..." I bit my lip. The sensation of fullness had me rocking my hips faster. It was so intoxicating and so *fucking* amazing.

"Let me hear you, baby. I want you to scream my name." Damiano rubbed his thumb on my clit, helping me build up my pleasure faster.

Shockwaves scattered throughout my nerve endings as he held me tightly, quickening his pace as he fucked me wildly. I snapped my head back. The pleasure was blinding, his cock sliding in and out of me as he edged me closer to my orgasm.

"Come for me, Althaia. Come all over my cock." Damiano growled, his voice so hauntingly deep that it felt as if it was coming from the depths of hell. That was all it took for my orgasm to come crashing down, making me scream so loudly that my throat grew hoarse.

"Fuck, piccola. Fuck!" Damiano roared, baring his teeth as he spilled his cum inside of me.

Our heavy breathing filled the room, our bodies in a light coat of sweat. I sank onto his chest, and his arms instinctively found their place around my waist.

Thirty-Seven

ALTHAIA

"Do we have to do this now'?" I groaned to Arianna as she dragged me and Cara downstairs to their gym. Apparently, a new day meant a new activity, and today we were going to learn self-defense.

"You should be the last one to complain when it's you who's had near-death experiences." Arianna retorted as we entered the gym.

I grumbled but followed her anyway to a big mat for wrestling. Luckily, I would be more of an observer while Cara had to mock fight Arianna. I was already praying for Cara because she was going to get her ass kicked.

The look on her face showed just how much she didn't want to.

We were not the only ones in the gym. Raffaele, Damiano, Lorenzo, and another guy, whom I didn't know, were working out. I slightly bit down on my lip as I focused on Damiano.

He stood in nothing but shorts, beads of sweat glistening on his body as he relentlessly pounded the punching bag. I gawked at the way his muscles in the back looked intricately sculpted. I stared, captivated by his insanely defined back muscles.

God, he's delicious.

"Good Lord..." Cara muttered next to me as she shamelessly eyed Lorenzo. She was undressing him with her eyes while he lifted weights.

"Seriously? Eyes on me, bitches!" Arianna frowned at us with her hands on her hips.

"Yeah, yeah, chill." Cara and I snickered and took a place on the bench, facing Arianna as she stood in the middle of the wrestling mat.

"We will take it slow. Since you don't have any training, I will show you some basic, yet effective, defense moves." She started.

"I would say I'm doing pretty well for someone who doesn't know shit." I pointed out.

"True, but the goal is to teach you so you don't end up looking like that." She pointed to my stitched brow.

"As long as I get out alive, I can take a few punches." I joked, making Cara snicker. Thankfully, I was getting the stitches removed tomorrow before I left for home. My brow healed well and wouldn't be noticeable for my mother to ask questions.

My sprained foot was a different story, but I came up with a brilliant idea and said Cara accidentally pushed me down the stairs. Let's just say that if Cara lacked any sympathy for me, she would have attempted to permanently silence me for placing all the blame on her.

"Look who we have here. Whatcha doing?" Raffaele approached us with a big smile on his face. His constant smile or laughter was a refreshing contrast to the emotionless expressions worn by the other men.

"Arianna's teaching us self-defense." I told him and got comfortable on the bench.

"Oh, this is going to be fun! I'm up first." He eagerly declared and positioned himself directly in front of Arianna. She gave him a malicious glint in her eyes and smirked.

"Ready to get your ass kicked?"

"Tsk, as if you can take me dow -"

Before Raffaele could even finish speaking, Arianna sent a forceful kick in the center of his stomach, making him stagger backwards. She quickly grabbed his arm, pulling him to her as she wrapped her hand around his throat with such force that he made a gagging sound. She skillfully maneuvered her leg behind his and forcefully brought him down with a loud thud.

"Sorry, what did you say?" Arianna had a smug look on her face while Raffaele looked startled at her sudden moves.

"That doesn't count. I wasn't ready." He smacked her hands away and jumped to his feet.

"I would have said the same thing if I embarrassed myself like that." I teased with a laugh.

"Want to have a go at me?" Raffaele challenged me and smacked himself on the chest, trying to look intimidating.

"Can't." I pointed at my foot.

"Excuses, excuses. But then again, I don't have any hope for you. Cara might stand a chance, but you? You're so small and weak I can flick you away like a fly." He said with a smirk.

I got up, careful not to put too much pressure on my foot as I stood before him.

"Want to bet?" I challenged. Raffaele bent down and placed his hands on his knees, mocking my height.

"And what are you going to do, little girl?"

"Oh my God, what is that?" I gasped and pointed behind his shoulder. Raffaele turned to look, and that was when I quickly grabbed his shoulders to hold him in place.

And kneed him right in the balls.

I didn't go full force, but still enough to make his breath hitch in his throat. He cupped his balls and fell to the floor, groaning in pain.

"Fucking shit!" He yelled at me. I leaned forward as I grinned at him, now mocking him.

"That's what you get for underestimating me." I said and walked away.

A hand wrapped around my ankle, yanking me off balance, and having me fall to the floor. Now it was me groaning.

"That's what you get for being cocky." Raffaele's voice was still strained as he let go of my ankle.

"I'm going to kill you!" I shouted and got up on all fours. I grabbed my crutch and swung it towards Raffaele. He looked at me with wide eyes and quickly rolled away before the crutch could hit his head.

"You're a fucking psychopath!" He yelled as he got up to his feet. "Yo, your woman is crazy!" He yelled to Damiano, who was wiping the back of his neck with a towel while he made his way toward us with an amused look.

"Just how I like her." He said, helping me up and kissing my temple.

"It's true then. Psychos attract psychos." Raffaele huffed out.

"Quit whining, you crybaby. I barely touched you. In fact, I barely felt anything, so why are you making such a big deal out of it?" I gave a playful grin and sat down on the bench.

"Damn!" Cara burst out laughing.

"Barely you say?" Raffaele looked at me, offended. "You wouldn't be able to handle all of this junk." He grabbed himself outside of his shorts, and I scrunched my nose in disgust.

"Where? All I see is a pair of shorts that is *very* loose in that area."

"Goddamn, who hurt you, woman?!" He erupted, and it almost looked like he wanted to stomp his foot.

I couldn't hold it in anymore and burst out laughing. Even Damiano let out a chuckle, as he sat next to me. Raffaele was always after me with inappropriate comments, and it was finally time for some payback.

"Okay, enough, you two. We have stuff to do." Arianna sighed impatiently. "Are you ready?" She asked Raffaele.

"I am done dealing with you psychos. I'm gonna go somewhere I know I will be showered in love." He huffed in annoyance before striding away.

"Is that a nice way of saying a brothel?" Cara yelled after him.

"Fuck off!" Raffaele practically screamed on his way out, and another round of laughter erupted.

"Looks like you're up, Cara." Arianna said.

"Yeah, no thank you. I think I will just observe with Thaia here for now." Cara grinned, not wanting to end up like Raffaele. Arianna did not look happy about it and pinched the bridge of her nose in frustration.

"Hey, Dom, have you finished up?" She called after the guy I was unfamiliar with.

"Sure."

"Then get your ass over here."

As Dom walked up to her, she wasted no time and went straight to explain, using Dom to show vital points.

"... A blow to the bicep hurts like a bitch and causes temporary paralysis of the arm, which can loosen the attacker's grip on you." Arianna continued as we listened carefully. Even Damiano and Lorenzo stayed. Not that they needed to hear any of this, since they taught her everything.

Arianna instructed Dom to wrap his arms around her from behind, demonstrating how to escape if someone were to attack from behind. Witnessing Arianna in action like this was genuinely impressive, and it was shocking how she effortlessly brought down someone twice her size. They were going easy on each other, but there was no doubt she would be able to defend herself if something were to happen.

"Is something wrong?" I asked Damiano in a whisper when his eyes narrowed and tilted his head.

"Looks like I know who's messing around with my sister." He said quietly, and I turned to look at Arianna and Dom in surprise.

"How can you tell?"

"They are too comfortable holding each other. His hands keep lingering on her, and her cheeks get slightly flushed whenever he does." His eyes kept narrowing the more he told me.

"Don't you think you're reading a bit too much into it? They are running around and pinning each other down." I pointed out.

"Look carefully at their body language." Damiano instructed. I looked back at them again, trying to see what I had missed.

"Notice where he places his hands on her, and how she is slightly biting her lip to prevent from smiling." He explained, and this time it was obvious now that he had pointed it out.

Dom's hands were placed low, almost at her hips, as she explained another method of how to get out of a hold. A bit of the corner of her mouth would curl up whenever Dom held her. It was obvious to see he was holding her like he knew her body.

"I see it now!" I whispered with a grin. Arianna had refused to let anyone know who she was seeing, keeping her man a mystery.

"Aw, they're cute together, don't you think?" I smiled, feeling happy for Arianna.

Damiano turned to look at me with a blank face.

"No." He disagreed immediately.

"Don't be like that. At least it's someone you know." I tried to lighten his mood.

"Someone who works for me and didn't ask for my approval." He curled his lip in displeasure.

"Right, because it's so easy to talk to someone's big brother, who also just happens to be a Mafia Boss, and say they want to date their little sister." I raised a brow at him.

"Hey, you two! Stop talking and listen." Arianna scolded us.

"I was listening!" I said quickly and looked at her.

"Really? Care to show what I just did?"

Before I could come up with an excuse, Damiano swiftly rose from his seat and positioned himself at the opposite end of the mat, facing Dom.

"Let me have a go at it." Damiano said calmly and rolled his neck from side to side while keeping his eyes on Dom.

In an instant, Damiano swiftly ensnared Dom's arm, immobilizing it, and unleashed a rapid barrage of punches to his face. Dom tried to shield himself with his other arm, but Damiano deftly turned him around and executed a painful twist on Dom's arm, locking him in a merciless headlock.

Dom struggled vigorously to break free, but Damiano continued, intensifying the grip around Dom's neck. Not being able to hold his ground anymore, Dom tapped Damiano on the arm in surrender, only to find Damiano tightening his hold further.

Fuck, he's going to kill him.

"Damiano, enough! You're going to kill him if you don't let go!" I said in panic and tried to push him away, but his huge figure wasn't even budging as he kept tightening his hold. Dom was struggling and couldn't breathe anymore!

"Damiano!" I snapped, and he finally loosened his grip. Dom fell to the floor and gasped for air. I went to check on him to see if he was okay and let out a breath of relief when he was.

"Why did you do that?" I asked Damiano with a scowl on my face. He ignored me, his gaze focused on someone else. I turned around to see Arianna, her hands clenched tightly, casting a furious glare at Damiano.

Without a word, Arianna stormed out of the gym, the door slamming shut behind her.

"Do you think he will make it out alive?" Cara asked as we had our lunch in the garden.

"I hope so." I sighed, feeling sorry for Arianna and Dom.

I've tried to talk to Damiano about it, but he wasn't willing to listen. We went back and forth until he finally called Arianna and Dom into his office to talk to them. I was praying for Dom because Lorenzo was in there with them, and I just hoped they would try to have an open mind.

"Poor Dom. He really was about to die there." Cara said, also feeling sorry for him.

"I get they are protective of their baby sister, but to choke the man like that." I shook my head. "By the way, I haven't had the chance to ask you, but it seems like it's going well between you and Lorenzo?"

"It is." Cara smiled. "I do like him. A lot, actually. At first, he was just my way to get away from everything at home, but now I can see us being happy together." She said, her face lighting up with genuine happiness.

My heart warmed as I smiled, seeing how her eyes sparkled when she talked about him. She deserved to be surrounded by never-ending happiness.

"I'm so happy for you! And he better treat you right!"

"Oh, trust me, he is." Cara wiggled her brows at me, and I let out a small laugh.

"Good. Or else I will have to beat Lorenzo's ass! Which wouldn't even be fair to him because he wouldn't stand a chance against me." I snickered, and Cara hid her laugh behind her hand.

"I'm already fearing for my life." Lorenzo's voice came from behind me, immediately wiping away the smile on my lips.

I looked at Cara wide-eyed as I froze in my seat. She laughed, and I gave her a piercing glare for not giving me a heads up that he was near.

Lorenzo took the seat next to Cara, raising a brow at me.

"I... Uh... Haha, Lorenzo. Funny, you see, I was talking about someone else who just happens to have the same name." Embarrassment washed over me, my face turning hot, as I desperately tried to hide the fact that I hadn't just discussed beating him up.

"Who also happens to be with Cara?" He questioned.

"Please, don't kill me." I blurted.

"You better sleep with one eye open." Lorenzo's amused look met my eyes, but his comment about my life didn't bring a smile to my face.

"He's not going to kill you." Cara rolled her eyes at me.

"Who's going to kill you?"

I jumped in my seat when I suddenly heard Damiano next to me.

"How are you two built like that, but move around so silently?" I put a hand on my chest and let out a breath. He took a seat next to me, and Arianna joined too. Everything must have turned out okay since none of them seemed angry anymore.

"First you want to beat my ass, and now you're calling me fat? That just sealed your fate." Lorenzo continued, obviously now having fun joking about killing me. Was he even joking?

"I'm sorry, okay?! Have some mercy!" I exclaimed, and he actually chuckled.

"You want to beat Lorenzo's ass?" Damiano asked.

"I was just making a teeny tiny joke he wasn't supposed to hear, and now I have to die for it. It was nice knowing you, Damiano. I hope you live a great life."

"Is she always this dramatic?" Lorenzo asked, and Cara just nodded.

"Mhmm, pretty much."

"I'm not dramatic, you're just ... scary." I muttered.

"Please, you even think butterflies are scary." Cara exposed, making me gape at her.

"Really, Althaia? Butterflies?" Arianna scoffed, finding it absurd.

"No, I don't know what she's talking about." I frowned and crossed my arms.

"If you say so." Cara shrugged and got out of her seat.

"I'm really not. It's ridiculous to be afraid of butterflies." I rolled my eyes.

"Are you sure?" Cara suddenly said from behind me. I turned around, only to jerk back when I saw her holding a butterfly in her hand.

A huge one.

"Yup." My voice came out strained as I eyed the butterfly to make sure it didn't suddenly fly in my face. I hated butterflies. They were disgusting flying creatures.

"Is that why you're slowly leaning away from it?" Cara had an evil smirk on her lips.

"I'm not. I'm admiring it from afar." I said, trying to be discreet about it.

Out of nowhere, Cara brought the butterfly right up to my face, causing me to stand up from my seat and back away. I took a crutch and held it up, ready to swing at her if she came close again.

"I swear to God, Cara, I will hit you in the fucking head!" I yelled and kept backing away. The crutch got ripped out of my hands, and my arms got twisted behind my back in a firm hold.

"Put it on her face!" Arianna shouted in excitement while holding me in place.

"No! Okay, wait! I admit I'm scared of them. Happy? Now, let me go!" I tried to wiggle out of Arianna's grip, but she only tightened her hold.

"Too late!" Arianna laughed, and Cara was closing in on me with the freaking disgusting butterfly. I thrashed and yelled at Cara to stay away, but none of it worked, so I did the only thing I could think of.

I fainted.

Well, I pretended to faint and got limp against Arianna.

"Shit, did she just faint?" Arianna said in shock and laid me down on the ground.

"Oh my God, Althaia?" Cara tapped her hand lightly against my cheek, trying to wake me up.

The sound of a chair abruptly falling to the ground made me snap my eyes open, seeing Arianna and Cara hovering above me. I quickly sat up and pushed them away, causing them to fall on their backs at the sudden move. It gave me a clear exit, and I got to my feet, getting away from them.

"You're messing with the wrong bitch today!" I snickered, feeling like a genius with my plan.

Both Damiano and Lorenzo had stood up from their seats. Damiano was making his way towards me, only to pause when he realized I was fine.

"Don't do that again." He said with a frown, not pleased with the stunt I had pulled.

"I was not about to get a nasty butterfly on my face." I told him as he pulled me into him. Even Lorenzo was shaking his head at me, but he looked to be entertained.

"See, Damiano! I told you she has great survival instincts. That was fucking genius." Arianna erupted with surprise.

"Work smart, not hard." I said proudly and looked at them with a grin. Cara walked up to me and smacked my head.

"Hey!" I scowled, but she just glared at me.

"Don't pull shit like that again!" She gave me a warning look before going to her seat.

"How am I the bad guy here?" Before I could go after her and give her the same treatment, Damiano held me in place to look at him.

He leaned down, his lips trailing across my jaw before reaching my ear.

"You will be punished for it later." He whispered.

Thirty-Eight

ALTHAIA

I was dozing off in the car as Damiano was driving me to the clinic to get the stitches removed. It was too early for me to even be out of bed right now, but I had to make the most out of the day, since I had a lot of packing to do.

I looked at Damiano with my heavy eyelids. I needed at least five cups of coffee to get me going today.

"A little tired?" He gave me a half-smile, his hand caressing my thigh.

"It's your fault." I yawned.

When he said I would be punished, I didn't know what he meant by it. He stripped me, blindfolded me, and tied me to the bed. Since I couldn't see anything and only felt his touch, everything was heightened, which got me excited.

He painfully teased me as he kissed and sucked every inch of my body, while his hands roamed my most sensitive parts. And that was where his punishment began.

He wouldn't let me come.

"*Fuck, Damiano...*" *I writhed, unable to use my arms or even close my legs to feel some friction as he forced them to stay spread.*

"*Yes?*" *He taunted, feeling him smirk as he kissed the inside of my thigh, and having me hiss in frustration.*

"Quit playing around!"

"*Do you want to come?*" *He said as he trailed his lips to my pussy, his tongue stroking me, and deliberately avoided my clit.*

"Yes!" *I huffed. I felt him hovering above me, his lips now near my ear as he whispered.*

"*Then beg for it. Let me hear you begging for my cock.*" *Damiano's voice was deep with lust, his fingers teasing my pussy by gliding his finger along my slit.*

"Hell no." *I gritted my teeth. I wasn't about to beg for his cock.*

I'm not that desperate.

"Shame. Hearing you beg would sound... So. Fucking. Sweet." He moaned in my ear, replacing his fingers with his cock, but still not penetrating me. A soft moan escaped me when his mouth closed around my breast, his tongue playing and sucking my nipple.

The way he was gliding his cock along my slit still allowed my pleasure to build. I wiggled my hips to try to get the tip in. But he held himself back from penetrating my core. The way he sucked on my breasts and pinched my nipples sent waves of pleasure straight to my pussy. I moved my hips along with him, feeling my orgasm coming so close.

Then he fucking stopped again.

"Damiano!" I cried in frustration. I had no idea how long we had been going on like that, but it felt like an eternity. My body was hot and bothered as he kept torturing me.

"Yes, baby?"

"I... please..." I gave in, not being able to handle it anymore.

Guess I am that desperate.

"Please, what, Althaia? Use your words."

"Please, fuck me." My voice was heavy with desperation.

"Say it again." Damiano growled, sliding the tip of his cock along my entrance.

"Fuck me, please. I want you to fuck me." I begged. He let out a deep, throaty sound.

"As you wish, beautiful."

Then he slammed his cock inside of me, fucking me like he never had fucked me before. Damiano liked to be rough, and I loved it. I just didn't know he was holding back because this was a whole different kind of rough.

The perfect definition of fucking.

His balls were slapping up against my pussy until I came over and over again, and I screamed his name like my life depended on it. My whole body was trembling, and my eyes rolled to the back of my head in pure pleasure. I had never orgasmed that many times before, and it was mind-blowing.

It was incredible. I had experienced nothing like that before in my life. The pleasure, the pain... it was all so damn good. I was blindfolded, but he made me see stars.

And he didn't stop. That was the second part of my punishment; overstimulation.

I wasn't sure how many times I had come already, but I couldn't keep up anymore.

"Damiano..." I panted, exhausted.

"One more, baby. You can take it." He coaxed. He had flipped me onto my stomach, holding my ass as he fucked me from behind. My legs were shaking so badly that he was carrying most of my weight to keep me up.

"Look at you. You take me so fucking good." Damiano quickened his pace, feeling his body tense before he gripped my hips tightly, spilling his cum inside of me when I let out a silent cry as I orgasmed.

"Good girl. You took it so well." He praised me, and I collapsed on the bed, unable to keep my eyes open anymore.

"Are you feeling okay?" Damiano glanced at me, pulling me out of my thoughts about last night's pleasures.

"Why wouldn't I be?"

"You were struggling to walk for a bit. More than before." He gave a smug grin.

"You went quite...hard on me." I was incredibly sore to the point I needed to have my legs slightly spread, so it wouldn't be uncomfortable.

"Hmm, I tried to hold back, but watching you tied up like that, I couldn't help myself." He remarked. We came to a stop in front of the clinic, and he looked at me with hunger. I immediately recognized the look on his face when he ran a thumb over my lip.

"Oh, hell no! Don't give me that look. You broke my vagina. I need a break!" I scoffed.

Damiano let out a laugh, one I couldn't help but smile at as I enjoyed the rare sound. He looked so carefree right now, and the fluttery feeling in my stomach returned with a full force.

"Looks like it's too early for someone." Ellie chuckled when I struggled to keep my eyes open.

"I don't know how you people do it. I will never be a morning person. I value sleep too much." I tiredly leaned back in the chair so Ellie could examine me.

"It's not too bad if you go to bed early." She said, and I still disagreed. "Well, everything looks great!" She smiled.

She put on a pair of gloves and cleaned the wound before taking the tweezers and scissors in her hand to remove the stitches. Ellie had promised me this wouldn't hurt, so I was a lot more relaxed when I felt the cold scissors on my forehead.

I shuddered in disgust and felt a wave of nausea as I could feel the threads being pulled out.

"Are you okay?" Ellie stopped.

"Yeah, I'm fine. It's just weird to feel them coming out." I took a deep breath, trying to suppress my nausea. I directed my attention to Damiano's tattooed arms, focusing on the art. He had incredible taste, and each piece was executed with precision.

One of my favorites was the lion. The majestic creature bared its teeth in a menacing snarl; the sharp canines were on full display, poised for an imminent attack. Yet, what captured me most was the subtle detail; a chain delicately draped around its neck. I loved this one so much because I saw it as a beautiful representation of his name.

"All done." Ellie chirped.

"Already?" I asked in surprise.

"Yes. Everything looks wonderful, so you're good to go. Are you making sure you're resting and not putting pressure on your foot?"

"I'm making sure she's staying in bed and doesn't move around." Damiano commented, shooting me a wink that had me blushing.

"I'm getting plenty of rest." I smiled shyly.

I gave Ellie a big goodbye hug since I wouldn't be seeing her until Cara's wedding.

"What were you thinking about? You were smiling while she removed your stitches." Damiano asked as we drove back to the manor.

"Oh, I was looking at your tattoo, and how I think it somehow represents your name." I said, not knowing I had been smiling.

"Let me hear."

"Damiano means 'one who tames.' Lions are known for their ferocity and untamed nature and can easily overpower and pose a lethal threat. They are not creatures typically subjected to domestication. Yet, there's a contradiction in your tattoo since it has a massive chain wrapped around its neck. It's as if you've tamed the untamable, asserting your dominance as Damiano, the one who tames." I mused on his inked masterpiece.

Damiano responded with a knowing smile. He didn't say a word but instead took my hand to his lips, placing a gentle kiss on the back of it, all while his focus remained on the road.

"And your name?" He asked, keeping my hand in his.

"Althaia means 'one who heals and one who takes care.'"

"I like it. You are a pure soul, and your name suits you." He gave me a soft smile, making me return a shy one.

"You know, in Greek mythology, Althaia was the Queen of Calydon, and a woman of fierce passion. She is celebrated in an ancient story about the fate of her son, Meleager. When he was born, the Moirai, or the Fates in English, came to foretell his future, and they predicted he would die as soon as one of the sticks in the fireplace burned out completely. When Althaia heard that, she pulled the stick from the fire, put the fire out, and hid it in a safe place."

"Meleager turned out to be a very well-respected prince and one day, a large boar was sent to Calydon to ruin the land, and he was one of the warriors alongside Althaia's brothers and a famous huntress, Atalanta. Meleager killed the boar but gifted the skin to Atalanta because she had landed the first strike. But also, because he was in love with her, even though he was married to someone else."

"When his uncles heard of it, they were furious and insulted her, saying she was nothing but a mere woman and didn't deserve the gift. Meleager got pissed and killed both of his uncles for insulting the woman he loved. Althaia heard of it and became so enraged that her son killed her brothers. And then she burned the piece of wood that was supposedly keeping him alive. Once engulfed in fire, he died." I finished.

"I see. Interesting story. So, Althaia is a caring person until you cross her, to where she will even kill her son." Damiano summed it up.

"Yup, so you better be careful." I teased.

"Are you threatening me now?" Damiano looked at me playfully.

"Gotta keep you on your toes now and then, don't I?" I chuckled.

"I am trembling with fear." He mocked, and I jokingly smacked his arm. "Though I would have done the same as Meleager. Insult my woman, you're as good as dead." He winked.

"He killed his uncles. That's extreme." I laughed.

"When a man sets his sights on someone, he'll go to any length to ensure her protection, respect, and well-being. Whatever the sacrifice. He'll stand guard, making sure no one can take her away from him in any way." His eyes held mine, a gaze so intense, it wrapped me in warmth and a sense of... *love.*

That's what it is. I feel loved.

We had come to a stop at the manor, but neither of us made a move to get out as our eyes stayed locked.

"You sound like a supervillain." I said, trying to break the intense feeling before I said something I shouldn't. "They say a villain would sacrifice the world to save you. A hero would sacrifice you to save the world."

"I'm no hero then."

"No." I smiled. "You're my villain."

"Your villain." Damiano sounded pleased.

"You've got the car for it, anyway." I gestured to his Bugatti La Voiture Noire we were in. It was the sexiest car I had ever seen. "Oh! That reminds me, do you remember how you said I can try your car?"

Damiano leaned back and crossed his arms.

"I did."

"So... Can I?"

"No."

"What? Why not?" I said, completely offended.

"Because I said it purely to piss off that shit-face who works for your father."

The insult made me gasp.

"Don't call him that! What has he ever done to you?"

"Exist." Damiano said it so fast it had me cracking up.

"Then what would you have done if I had said yes on the spot at the time, huh?" I retorted.

"I would have enjoyed the view of the fucker's head exploding." He said with a satisfied smirk.

"His name is Michael." I told him but got a careless shrug in return. "At least I got to try his car. It's better than your stupid car, anyway." I bit my lip, so I wouldn't laugh out loud as I got out of the car.

Damiano approached me with an amused expression on his face.

"There is absolutely nothing he has that is better than what I have."

"Please, he has me, a badass friend. That beats everything you have." I said cockily.

Damiano towered over me, his hand slowly fisting around my hair, and gently yanked it to have me look at him. His lips were faintly brushing mine as he spoke.

"Yeah? I get to fuck you every night. He doesn't. I still win." His tone was low and deep. It had me shuddering and almost moaning at his words. My heart raced as I closed the little distance between us and kissed him, savoring the moment.

"Get a room before you fuck each other in front of us all." Raffaele's voice rang out, and I quickly pulled away in embarrassment.

Damiano released his grip on my hair, and we faced Raffaele. He stood by the entrance, hands on his hips, shaking his head disapprovingly at us. I had been too caught up in the moment that I hadn't noticed a few of Damiano's men were around too, amused by Raffaele's comment.

"You're such a creep!" I exclaimed with a scowl.

"How am I a creep when you're the ones about to do it in the driveway?" He shouted with a smug grin, making me gasp in shock.

"You're on my property. If I want to fuck her in my driveway, then I will. Whoever has a problem with it can get a bullet in the head." Damiano stated calmly, not taking his eyes off me.

"Oh my God, just stop..." I was full-on blushing now. I grabbed my crutches to get away from them.

"Damn! Pussy is that good, huh?" Raffaele kept going.

"Raffaele!" I screamed at him. A mischievous grin spread across his face, clearly enjoying himself. "Don't you have anything better to do?"

"Sadly, no." He pouted. "Unless... you're offering me something?" He wiggled his brows, blowing a kiss my way.

Raffaele's eyes met Damiano's for a split second before he bolted away as he laughed like a maniac. I looked at Damiano, only to see him in the process of tucking his gun away.

And they say I'm the dramatic one.

Thirty-Nine

ALTHAIA

"Tell me again why you're driving back home instead of flying. It will take like what? Five hours instead of forty?" Arianna asked while folding my clothes with Cara.

I had persuaded them to help me pack, saying it would go faster if I had extra hands helping me, and therefore, we could spend more time together. They agreed, but they just didn't realize they were doing all the packing for me, while I only pretended to pack so I wouldn't do a thing.

I truly am a genius.

"Because it's a metal coffin." I said, as if it was the most obvious thing.

"First butterflies, now planes?" She was not impressed at all.

"I'm not scared of flying. I just don't like to fly alone. Like, what if the plane suddenly crashes? I don't want to die alone." I tried to explain how it was a legit fear of mine.

"I guess that is a reasonable excuse. Better than the butterfly excuse." She teased.

"Just drop it already, okay? It's a freaking flying caterpillar. It shouldn't be flying in the first place!" I said defensively. While Cara laughed at our bickering, Arianna rolled her eyes and called me dramatic.

"So, you and Dom, huh?" Cara started and looked at Arianna with a grin.

"He is a hottie." I winked at her. Dom was an attractive man with a skin color of an umber, a dark-brown color, and with amazing blue eyes. I could definitely see why she would be attracted to him.

"Those eyes..." Cara sighed dreamily and then burst out laughing when Arianna sent her a glare.

"You two bitches are with my brothers. You better not talk about other men like that." Her eyes narrowed at us.

"Oh, chill. It's okay to look at the menu but not order." I joked.

"Hell yeah!" Cara seconded.

"Really? So, it's okay for Lorenzo to look at other women as long as he doesn't engage in anything with them?" Arianna raised a brow.

"I will pluck his eyes out if he even glances at one." Cara said with all seriousness.

"What did you talk about when Damiano called both of you to his office?" I asked.

"Just the standard talk. Either we drop what we have going, or we get married." She shrugged and kept on folding my clothes. Cara and I stared at her, dumbfounded.

"Seriously?" Cara gaped.

"He can't decide that!" I exclaimed.

"Then what?" Cara asked.

"I told him to shove his options up his ass." Arianna smirked proudly. "I'm not going to marry the guy. We're just having fun and enjoying each other."

"So, you're dropping him?" I asked.

"Hell no! The sex is too good. We're just going to keep away from each other for a few days, pretend it's over, and then just be more careful to not get caught."

"Damn... Dom got balls of steel to continue after almost being choked to death." I remarked.

"Can't blame him if the sex is so good." Cara commented. "Go get that dick, sis."

"I will." Arianna winked as we all chuckled.

We were almost done packing when Arianna had called me out after finding out I wasn't doing anything. I reminded her that Ellie told me to take it easy. Arianna and Cara shared a look and dropped everything from their hands and walked out.

"So much for helping a sister out!" I yelled at them, but Cara flipped me off.

I let out a sigh of relief when I was done packing and flopped on the bed. The softness of the bed cushioned my tired body and my eyes started to droop.

"Done packing?" I raised my head to see Damiano giving me a soft smile as he closed the door behind him.

"Yeah. I think I'm going to take a nap." I still had time to kill since I was leaving late in the afternoon, and a nap sounded so heavenly now.

Damiano sat down on the bed and handed me a small, velvet-lined black box. I sat up and saw the glimmer of the diamond earrings he had gifted me.

"I want you to wear these at all times. Don't take them out." He insisted sternly.

"Isn't it a bit too much for an everyday look?" I asked.

"No. I want you to always wear them. Put them on." Damiano urged.

"So bossy." I teased but put them on. "How do I look?" I put my hands on my face and dramatically fluttered my eyelashes at him.

"Beautiful." Damiano smiled softly, tucking some of my hair behind my ear as he looked at me. "One more thing; Luca and Giovanni will stay with you until you come back."

"Damiano, no." I immediately protested with a shake of my head.

"It's not up for discussion. They are staying with you." He frowned at my protest.

"My mom will freak out at the sight of them, and I'm not exactly planning on telling her why two men are with me, posing as bodyguards."

"They are going to stay out of sight. I need to make sure you're safe when I'm not with you." Damiano emphasized.

"And I will be. Didn't you say you caught the guy already?" I asked.

"Yes, but he wasn't working alone. Until I get my hands on the bastard that sent him, you're not going anywhere without security." He said, leaving no room for discussion. I sighed.

"You realize that I'm coming back a week before the wedding, which is eight weeks away. Are you really making Luca stay away from his girlfriend for seven weeks?" I tried one more time.

"I gave him time off to spend time with her. He just came back from Italy." He explained, not giving me any wiggle room to argue back.

"Oh, she lives in Italy?" I raised my brows in surprise, and he gave me a nod. I guess they were used to not seeing each other all the time then.

"Don't fight me on this, Althaia. I will not have it."

"Fine." I sighed. "But they better be invisible. I don't want them to scare my mom." I said, plopping down on the bed again.

"I'll make sure of it." Damiano promised.

"Thank you." I smiled and patted the pillow next to me. "Come, take a nap with me."

"I'm not tired." He stated, shaking his head and offering a faint smile.

"How? You barely get any sleep." I slightly frowned.

"I get the amount I need."

"No, you don't. Now, take off your shirt and get in." I ordered him. Damiano looked at me with a raised brow.

"And why do I need my shirt off?"

"Because I'm addicted to seeing you shirtless. Hurry, I don't have all day." I said impatiently.

"You're getting a little too comfortable bossing me around." He clicked his tongue, but still took off his shirt, leaving him in the delicious glory of his six-pack and tattoos.

"I've learned from the best." I winked, and he playfully scoffed.

Damiano went to lay beside me, and I sat up, straddling him to reach for my phone on the nightstand. I opened the camera and took a picture of him. I almost drooled at how irresistible he looked.

The way he positioned one arm behind his head, showcasing the definition of his muscles. It was pure porn. He looked at me with a slight head tilt as I grinned, snapping a few more pictures.

"You know what? I have an awesome idea for your next tattoo!" I said excitedly, putting my phone away.

"Let me hear."

"My name in big bold letters going down here." I trailed my finger down the side of his ribs and stopped at his waistband. "Or even better, on your butt 'cause that ass is mine." I burst out laughing at the idea of Damiano getting a tattoo on his ass.

"I'm not getting your name tattooed on my ass." He chuckled, pulling me down to lie on top of him.

"Shame. Your ass would have looked pretty with it." I gave a teasing wink.

"No one will touch my ass." He declared.

I let out a small smirk when my hand found its way down and squeezed his firm ass.

"I'm touching it right now."

"You can touch what's yours." Now it was him smirking when he saw the surprise on my face. Still, a smile found its way on my lips as I cuddled into his chest.

We lay in silence as he drew soothing circles on my back.

"I was wondering, how did you find the guy?" I asked. I have been dying to know ever since Arianna broke the news to me. I was mad at him at the time they found him, and she said if I wanted to know, I had to take it up with Damiano.

"Raffaele located him. He hacked into the security cameras, but as expected, the footage was wiped clean. However, what they hadn't considered were the surveillance cameras from nearby buildings, giving us clear footage of individuals entering and exiting the hotel." I raised my head, intrigued.

"He cross-referenced every person against the hotel's database to identify check-ins and check-outs, but still found nothing suspicious. Until someone walked out, his body language indicating he was hurt. Raffaele ran the database but found nothing that matched his face. He followed him and traced it back to a motel." Damiano explained.

"Raffaele is a hacker?" I asked in awe.

"That you find surprising?" Damiano chuckled.

"Well, sometimes he does come across a bit... stupid."

"I know. He can be smart when he wants to be."

"Apparently." I let out a light chuckle. "What happened to the guy?"

"You don't need to know." He furrowed his brows at me, not liking my question.

"But I want to know." I tried.

"Althaia." Damiano warned me to not ask about it anymore. I ignored him, leaning closer to his face.

"Did you torture him? Burn him? Drown him wearing cement shoes?" I listed.

Damiano studied me intently, his face remained expressionless. With a soft smile, I softly touched his cheek, silently letting him know I was okay to hear it.

"I made sure he had a painful death." He admitted.

"How?" I asked, running my fingers through his hair. I wasn't surprised. I knew he wouldn't make it out alive. Damiano went silent again, observing my face to see if I was okay to hear the answer.

"For every scratch, wound, and misplaced hair on you, I carved deep into his body and fed him to the rats when I was done." He said, his voice laced with caution as his eyes locked onto my face, searching for any signs of fear. But I wasn't scared anymore. I have come to learn what kind of man he was.

"How do you feed someone to rats?" I decided to ask.

"You place a cage that's opened on the bottom. Place it on their stomach, get a few rats and put them in the cage, then slowly heat the cage. It makes the rats desperate to get away from the heat and burrow through the flesh with their claws and teeth. They gnaw right into the bowel, causing excruciating pain." He explained.

"Yikes. I bet he regrets not staying in bed that day." I couldn't help but grimace a bit at the thought of rats gnawing into the flesh. "Poor rats."

"They made it out alive. He didn't."

"Thank goodness!" I said in relief.

Damiano let out a surprised smile and wrapped his arms tightly around me.

"My Althaia, what wouldn't I do for you." He whispered. A soft smile was on my lips as I rested my head on his chest. I closed my eyes as I listened to the sweet melody of his heartbeat.

Forty

ALTHAIA

"I'm going to miss you so much!" I hugged Cara tightly.

"Me too! It's going to suck without you."

"Ghee, thanks." Arianna faked an offended expression.

I couldn't help but let out a laugh as I turned to embrace her tightly. It was going to be so weird to be away from them for so long when we had spent so many days together.

"Now we can all get some sleep at night without you fucking like crazy every night." Raffaele started, and I gave him a blank look.

"Don't you ever get tired of your own stupid comments?"

"Never!" He grinned and gave me a bone-crushing hug that I returned. He was going to be missed. His comments, not so much.

I gave them one last goodbye and even shared an awkward goodbye with Lorenzo, where I patted his shoulder as a farewell. I didn't know why I still felt awkward around him, but I did. Probably because of the number of times I have humiliated myself in front of him. I guess he kind of felt the same about me too because he awkwardly patted my head as a goodbye.

"That... hurts to watch."

"So awkward..."

Arianna and Cara grimaced at us, making it all even more awkward.

"Don't make it worse." I mumbled as I looked at Damiano. The final farewell lingered, and he was the one I least wanted to let go.

The others discreetly walked away to give us privacy as I wrapped my arms around his neck, and his arms encircled my waist. With a tender lift, he hugged me close, burying his face into the crook of my neck, creating a moment I wished could stretch into forever.

I had to remind myself that I would see him again, but it was so damn hard to let him go right now.

"I will miss you *so* much." I whispered, and he met my gaze. He didn't want to let me go. It was written all over his face, his eyes expressing the unspoken words he didn't voice.

"I'm going to cry if you keep looking at me like that." I chuckled. I could feel my throat tighten as this got too emotional for me. Damiano gave me one of his beautiful smiles before he pulled me into a sweet kiss.

"I will miss you too, baby." He whispered against my lips. I placed my hands on either side of his face, caressing his cheeks as I drank in his golden-brown eyes, memorizing them.

How am I going to be away from this man for weeks?

It was going to be torture, but for now, I leaned in to kiss him one more time.

Damiano walked out to the car, where Luca and Giovanni were already waiting for me.

"Looks like you two are the lucky ones who get to spend so many amazing hours with me in the car! ... Okay, that sounded gross." I scrunched my nose when I heard it. "What I meant was, I give great concerts and you get to hear my amazing singing!" I beamed once again.

Luca just chuckled while Giovanni did not look like someone who was excited about what was about to unfold.

"I will need a raise." Giovanni looked at Damiano blankly.

"Hey! I have a great voice. Wait till you hear me sing in Korean!" I gave him a big smile. He blinked a few times before returning his gaze to Damiano.

"It better be six figures." He simply said and got in the car. I scoffed and called him a crybaby.

"Looks like you're going to torture my men." Damiano pulled me into him with a smile.

"Just a little." I grinned, and he shook his head in amusement. I wrapped my arms around his waist as he caressed my hair, his golden-brown eyes looked affectionately into mine.

"Stay safe, don't get hurt." He made me promise.

"You stay safe too. I'll be back before you know it." I said, mostly to remind myself that I would be back to see him again. Damiano placed a kiss on my forehead and held me tightly one more time.

We said our last goodbyes before I got in the car. My heart already felt heavy as we drove further and further away from him. Soon, he was out of my view, and I was left alone with Luca and Giovanni, heading home for the first time in two months.

"... When I make the bed shake!" I sang as I gave them my best performance to date of Ariana Grande's 34+35 song. Well, I thought it was great, Giovanni, not so much.

He threatened to throw me out of the car if I didn't shut up. He quickly realized he shouldn't have said that because it only made me sing louder, and I wasn't trying to make it pretty.

What a grumpy man.

"You should replace the bed with a car." Luca commented when I was done.

"Why's that?" I was in the backseat in the middle with my head popped in between their seats.

"That's what you did with Damiano. You had us thinking something was wrong with the tires." He laughed.

"Why would you even mention that?!" I exclaimed in horror. "And that's such an exaggeration!"

"It really isn't. I thought someone had shot the back tire. Besides, we weren't even far away from the hotel. You could have waited instead of shaking the car like that." Luca continued, having me scowl at him for opening his mouth about it.

"I'm for once happy that he's getting some. He's less up in our asses now that he's busy with you." Giovanni added.

"Oh, look at that! I'm making your life easier, yet you want to throw me out of the car." I scoffed. I have gotten to know some of Damiano's men; at least those who were closest to him, and it was often Antonio, Luca, and Giovanni who were around him the most.

"Whatever." He leaned back and closed his eyes. I just rolled my eyes at him.

"Anyway, I'm sorry to trouble you like this, Luca. I tried to talk Damiano out of it, but he wouldn't budge."

"Nah, don't worry about it. I'm happy to do it. I never got the chance to say thanks back then. This is me repaying you for saving my ass." He chuckled. I smiled and gave his shoulder a small squeeze.

"She saved your ass?" Giovanni opened his eyes, now interested in our conversation.

"It was stupid, really. We were playing UNO while Antonio and Damiano were gone. I lost all rounds and thought Luca was cheating. While I was trying to get him up from the couch, I fell on top of him. At the same time, they returned and saw us like that..." I grimaced as I explained to him.

Giovanni looked at Luca in surprise.

"Shit, and you got out of that one alive?"

"Barely. Antonio almost got my ass if she didn't step between us. Damiano made him back down when she did."

"You didn't even try to defend yourself! I know what it looked like from their point of view, but still, it was a misunderstanding." I frowned.

"But that's not how it works." I looked at Giovanni as he spoke. "If Damiano decides he wants to kill you, no excuse or explanation will save you. Luca was just accepting his fate. That's how it works."

"How does that even make sense? Honestly, the more I get to know about all of this, the more fucked up it gets." I sighed.

"Did you expect it to be all unicorns who shit rainbows?" Giovanni scoffed.

"No." I shot him a blank look. "I just get surprised by how dark and twisted it all can get."

"Oh, it can get dark and twisted. You should have seen what he did to the guy who attacked you." He smirked, and Luca turned to glare at him.

"Giovanni." Luca warned him not to tell anymore.

"Damiano told me already." I shrugged.

"He did?" Luca looked at me in the rearview mirror in surprise.

"Yeah. I asked, and he told me. Something about placing a cage with rats on him." I shuddered in disgust.

"That was nothing." Giovanni laughed. "The way Damiano nailed his hands to the chair and fucked up his hands for touching you. The best part was when he drilled holes into him and hung him up on the wall. He called it a fucking masterpiece. It was insane! And the guy kept passing out, which only pissed him off more." He continued to laugh, and I sat quietly while staring at him in shock.

A shiver ran down my spine as I imagined the scenario in my mind. Graphic pictures of a machine drilling furiously into the guy's bones had me feeling sick.

"He... what?" I blinked at him. Giovanni stilled and looked at me.

"... Didn't you say he told you?" He frowned at my reaction.

"The rat thing, yes... I didn't know he had left that much out of it."

"That's why you should have kept your mouth shut!" Luca gave an angry stare.

"Ah, for fuck's sake." Giovanni sighed in annoyance.

"It's fine. I shouldn't be shocked... I have, after all, witnessed him shoot people." I tried to reassure them, but I think I tried to reassure myself more with that statement.

"And you almost passed out when you did." Luca reminded me.

"Well, since then, my ass almost got killed twice. I would like to think I have gotten a thicker skin."

"Talk about having bad luck." Luca grinned, and I couldn't help but chuckle a bit.

We had been driving for six hours and I had to explain once again to Giovanni's grumpy ass why we were driving and not taking a flight back. Truth was, I was scared of flying. I would avoid it at all costs if possible.

I was lucky my friend, Jenny, was going on a road trip with a few friends, and since they were passing by, they could give me a ride so I could attend the engagement party. I didn't want to admit it to Arianna, she would only make more fun of me.

We pulled into a gas station so I could use the restroom and grab some snacks. When I was done, I filled my arms with whatever I could get my hands on; chips, candy, chocolates, and even grabbed a few drinks. Luca and Giovanni said they wanted nothing, but I still grabbed something for them, too. I grabbed enough to last us the entire ride.

As the cashier rang my massive pile of snacks and drinks, I opened my wallet but frowned when I didn't see my card in there. Instead, I saw a shiny black card in its place. I rummaged through my wallet to see if I had enough cash. I didn't. I sighed in annoyance when I didn't have any choice but to use the black card.

Quickly thanking the cashier, I stepped outside to make a phone call.

He picked up on the first ring.

"You took my card and replaced it with yours."

"I did."

"Why?"

"Because I wanted to."

"That's not an answer."

"I don't want you to spend your money."

"But that's the thing! I want to spend my own money, and not yours."

"Consider my money yours."

"Damiano..." I sighed.

"I miss you." He suddenly said.

"I miss you too." I smiled, forgetting why I was annoyed with him in the first place. I was already missing him like crazy, and it made me feel warm inside that he was missing me just as much.

I dropped my smile when I realized what he was doing.

"I know what you're trying to do." I said accusingly.

"And what am I trying to do?" He replied, and it was like I could hear his smug grin through the phone.

"You're distracting me by saying you miss me." I slightly narrowed my eyes even though he couldn't see me.

"Can't a man tell his woman he misses her?" He spoke softly, and my heart melted even more.

"As if this isn't hard enough, you have to say it like that?" I let out a light chuckle.

"I know. Call me when you get home, beautiful."

"I will. Don't get your ass shot." I sang out.

"Have you already forgotten who I am?" He scoffed.

"A man who drills holes into bones?" The words came out of my mouth before I could stop myself. I inwardly groaned at my stupidity.

It was silent. So silent I had to check if the call got disconnected, but it wasn't.

"Dami–"

"Who told you?" Damiano growled.

"It doesn't matter-"

"Who told you?" He demanded.

"Damiano, it's fine. I know you're worried about what I will think of it. What I will think of you... But I know who you are." I said softly.

He didn't say anything for a while. I knew he didn't want me to see that side of him. The much darker and more twisted side of him; to see what he was truly capable of. A man so dangerous and so deadly, yet he was gentle with me and allowed me to see the softer side of him he didn't allow others to see.

He was my villain, who would do anything for me.

"Damiano, I'm not going anywhere." I smiled as I imagined the frown on his face slowly disappearing.

"...You better come back to me." His tone was low and soft, having my heart flutter.

MARIAM EL-HAFI

"I will always come back. I promise."

Forty-One

ALTHAIA

It has been a week since I got home, and even though I miss the others terribly, it was good to be home and spend time with my mother. It has been crazy busy at the boutique, and I felt terrible seeing how exhausted my mother looked. I was happy to return to work next week, letting my foot rest so it could heal faster.

I was sitting on the couch in the living room as I watched the Seven Deadly Sins while eating a bagel with cream cheese for breakfast. Just as I took a big bite of my bagel, the doorbell rang. I let out a noise of annoyance, trying to chew faster as I made my way to the front door.

Who would be coming at this hour, anyway?

I brushed away any crumbs around my mouth and quickly made sure I looked decent enough to open the door.

"Delivery for Miss Althaia." The man said and handed me the biggest arrangement of red roses I had ever seen.

"From... who...?" My voice died down as he was already making his way back to his car.

I stared in awe at the huge flower arrangement as I walked back to the living room. I placed it on the coffee table, admiring the beautiful red roses. There were even a few white orchids on the side, making it look so beautiful.

A fancy crystal vase, adorned with a silk ribbon, held it all together. There was a small note peeking out from beneath the ribbon. I took the note, and a smile spread across my lips at the words.

With every passing second, my thoughts are pulled into the refrain of missing you.
Your Villain.

I couldn't stop smiling as I kept reading the note over and over again, filling my heart with infinite warmth and happiness. I clutched the note to my chest as if burying the words into my heart while I carefully touched the rose petals with my fingertips.

I placed the note back as I made my way upstairs to my bedroom with the flowers. I wasn't going to leave it in the living room or on the dining table for my mother to see. If there was one thing I would like to keep to myself, it was my relationship with Damiano.

She wasn't thrilled when she found out that Cara was marrying into la Famiglia Bellavia. Her reaction didn't exactly make me want to jump up and down in eagerness to tell her I was dating someone from the family as well.

The Mafia Boss to make it worse.

I placed the vase on my desk, pulled out my phone, and snapped a photo of the flower arrangement to send to him.

Althaia: Thank you.
I love them so much!
But I love the words even more.

Damiano: Hmm, if I knew you would
like the words this much,
I would have written you a hundred more.

Althaia: Oh, really?
That would have been quite some
extra work with your busy ass.

Damiano: I'm never too busy when
it comes to you.
Speaking of ass, I miss looking at yours.
Touching it too...

Althaia: Getting blue balls already?

Damiano: *Been having them ever since you left.*
Those damn pictures you sent didn't make it better.
I'm warning you – when you return,
will make sure you won't be able to walk
for a week when I'm done burying
myself deep inside of you.

I sat down on my bed, and I bit my lip a little as I squeezed my thighs together. I knew I would miss him terribly, but I didn't exactly think of how... *desperate* I also would be to feel our bodies move against each other.

Every night, before I went to sleep, I would talk to him, and my body would burn with a desire to listen to his deep voice. I also never thought I would be the type to send vulgar pictures of myself.

At first, it was only one picture; a teasing one where I was in bed, in my red lace nightgown, and took a picture of my body posing a bit seductively and sent it to him. His reaction was priceless when he called me right away, demanding to FaceTime him and give him a show.

Althaia: *I look forward to*
being on top of you.
To feel you deep like that...

Damiano: *Fucking hell, Althaia.*
I'm in a meeting.

Althaia: *Aw, too bad.*
I was about to send you a picture
of my tits as a thank you.

Damiano: *Fuck the meeting, send the picture.*

I let out a laugh at his text and stopped my flirting to let him be at his meeting in peace.

Althaia: *Too late.*

Talk to you later ;p

Damiano: *You deserve to be punished for being such a tease.*

I chuckled and let out a blissful sigh. Words couldn't describe how happy he was making me.

"I have something to tell you." My mother smiled after we ordered our food.

We were sitting in a nice restaurant to have dinner and spend some quality time together. Luca and Giovanni were in the restaurant too, seated close to our table. They have been good at staying out of view, but this was an exception, as they needed to make sure I was safe.

I ignored them so I wouldn't draw any attention to them.

"What is it?" I asked, taking a sip of my water.

"I got you a date." My mother beamed, and I choked on my water. Tears blurred my vision as I violently coughed, and she quickly came over to me and patted my back.

"A what?" I asked after calming down.

"A date!" Her green eyes were twinkling in happiness.

I was the spitting image of my mother with the same green eyes, though she was taller and had faint freckles on her cheeks. People would always mistake us for being sisters and would be shocked when they learned we were actually mother and daughter.

My mother had me when she was my age, twenty-four, but she was keeping herself in good shape and taking good care of her health. And me? I was filling myself with garbage and barely did any exercise.

"Why? And with whom?" I looked at her, shocked.

"I was having a chat with one of our regulars the other day. Her son came by, a very handsome young man, and I asked him if he was single because I have a single daughter. So, I gave him your number." She said proudly, and I just gaped at her.

"What?! Mom, you can't just give my number out like that." I hissed quietly.

"And why not? You will like him, trust me. He's very smart, good-looking, and has his own business." She took a sip of her wine, looking satisfied with herself trying to play cupid.

My phone buzzed on the table, and I looked to see a text message from Luca.

Luca: *Turn it down.*

Well, no shit. I sighed, and I looked at my mother, trying to figure out how to get out of this date.

"Mom, I can't go on a date with… what's his name?"

"Liam."

"Liam… I'm sure he's a nice guy, but no, thank you."

"Why not? You have been single for a long time. Isn't it time for you to go out and see what's out there?" She questioned.

My phone buzzed again, and I glanced down to see another text message.

Luca: *Shut it down.*
Tell her you're seeing someone.

I really wanted to glare at him right now, but I couldn't when my mom was looking at me. I couldn't tell her I was dating someone. She would ask too many questions I wasn't ready for.

"That phone of yours has been buzzing a lot lately… Oh my, did you find someone?" My mother gasped, excitement showing in her eyes.

Oh, crap.

"I- Uh… Well." I struggled to come up with any words as I tried to think of some kind of excuse.

"My goodness, you did! Tell me, who is he?" She leaned forward, resting her elbows on the table, ready to hear whatever I had to spill. "Is it Michael?" She asked, helping me with the perfect excuse.

"Yes, it's Michael." I could feel both Luca's and Giovanni's gaze on me as soon as another man's name left my lips.

"I've always liked Michael. He's a good kid. It's cute though, you always had a thing for him when you were younger, and you said you were going to marry him. Maybe it will come true." My mother chuckled and totally exposed my ass without knowing it.

My phone buzzed again.

Giovanni: *I am telling Damiano ;)*

Althaia: *Shut it.*

I looked back at my mother; her face brightened with happiness.
"It's still new..." I trailed off, feeling completely awkward.
"No reason to hurry! At least I know he's a good kid."
"He's a good guy." I smiled.

Giovanni: *Damiano is going to love this.*

I quickly flipped him off when my mother wasn't looking, which only made him smirk.
"How's Cara? Is she doing all right?" My mother asked as we finished dinner with dessert.
"Yeah, she's good. Quite demanding with her endless list of things she wants to have done for the wedding, but she deserves it." I chuckled, and my mom gave a small nod.
"Which one is she marrying again?"
"Lorenzo."
"Hmm."
"Something's wrong?"
"He's the younger brother, right?" She asked. I just nodded, confused about where she wanted to go with it. "I was just wondering why she is getting married to the younger brother and not the oldest... But I guess it's for the best. I heard he's quite the monster, and that's saying it mildly." She scoffed.
I felt myself frowning when she called Damiano a monster, but I had to be careful with my words.
"I wouldn't say that. I've met him a few times, and he seems ... nice?" I was beating myself mentally for being such an idiot. Out of all the words in the world, I settled on nice.
"Are you making jokes now?" My mother frowned.
"I just mean that he hasn't done anything to me to think otherwise, so..." I trailed off when I should have just shut the fuck up already.

"Be careful. Don't get too close to him. I don't want anything to happen to you. Or I swear to God, I will kill him with my own two hands." Her voice was low and threatening. I looked at her in shock, and I noticed Luca and Giovanni react as well at the mention of my mother promising to kill their Boss.

"Don't worry, I will stay away." I tried to give her a reassuring smile as guilt flooded me. I didn't want to lie to her, but now I could hear there was no way she would approve of me being with Damiano.

"You have been working really hard lately, mom. How about you take some time off while I take over?" I tried to change the subject.

"Yeah? I have been thinking about it, going away for a week or something. My back has been killing me lately." My mother sighed.

"I know. I feel bad for leaving you alone with all of this. You and Mrs. Park can go somewhere nice, get drunk, and have massages. Maybe get laid for once." I snickered, and she did not look amused when I said the last part.

"Eat your cake." She said sternly. I laughed when she mumbled about me being a cheeky child.

We sat quietly and chatted as we finished our desserts. Then my mother's eyes kept drifting towards Luca and Giovanni. At first, I didn't think anything of it as she casually scanned the restaurant, her eyes darting from person to person. But this time, she took a few extra moments to study them closely. For so long that Luca even made eye contact with her and gave her a small smile and nod, to which she returned.

Nervousness crept over me. Did she figure out who they really were?

"Want to leave?" I asked, trying to distract her.

"Sure. Let me just use the restroom before we leave." She rose from her seat. Before she walked to the restroom, she looked at Luca and Giovanni with a big smile.

"I apologize for staring at you earlier, I wasn't trying to be rude. I'm just very happy that we live in a time where we can love whomever we want. And if I may say, you two look absolutely gorgeous together!"

I brought my hand up to my mouth, trying to contain the laughter that threatened to escape. My mother was looking so happy for them!

"Thank you! We just got married. Isn't that right, honey?" Luca said with a bright smile and placed his hand on top of Giovanni's. Giovanni was giving him a look that could kill.

"Yes, *dear*." He forced out between gritted teeth.

"Oh, that's lovely! Congratulations."

"Thank you so much, ma'am." Luca's lips curled into a joyful smile. My mother wore a wide grin before excusing herself to the restroom.

Once she was out of sight, I turned my attention to them and immediately started laughing. The sour look on Giovanni's face and his glaring eyes only made it funnier.

"I fucking hate you all." He grumbled.

Forty-Two

ALTHAIA

Things at work had calmed down. I was taking a lot of stress off my mother's shoulder now that I was back because, other than her, I was the only one skilled enough to sketch customers' wishes. We had seamstresses working for us, but they were not always in the boutique with us, only when it became busy.

Time seemed to fly, and before I knew it, weeks had already gone by. It felt like time was going by even faster because as soon as I would get home from work, I would pass out the second my head hit the pillow.

I haven't been talking to Damiano as much, only squeezing in a text message here and there. He called me last night, and I was so tired that I fell asleep while talking to him, but he knew how busy things have been.

I felt guilty that I barely had any time for him when he always made sure to have time for me. And he was the one with multiple businesses and running a Mafia.

Lately, I was feeling like I couldn't get enough sleep, even though I was getting more than eight hours. It was so bad that I would hit snooze way too many times and be late for work. And because of my many late mornings, Luca had to drive me to work. He even had coffee and breakfast ready for me in the car since it became a routine. He would drop me off a block away from the boutique so my mother wouldn't notice.

"Are you sure you can keep the boutique open while I'm gone?" My mother asked for the hundredth time.

"Yes, I'm sure I can. You just focus on relaxing because you're seriously all tensed up." I chuckled. "Besides, things have calmed down a lot, so I can manage."

"Okay, good. If not, you call me, and I will come back right away."

"Nope. I can't believe I have to force you to take a break!" I shook my head and made a tsking sound.

It was evening, and my mother would leave for her trip with Mrs. Park tomorrow morning. Mrs. Park and my mother have been friends ever since we moved here, and I was also close friends with her daughter, Jenny, who was currently on a very hot vacation. And by hot, I was referring to her being with one hot guy after another.

She sent me pictures of them and even rated them from one to ten on how good they were in bed. And other detailed information I didn't need to know. She was definitely going to be the hot, single, rich Asian auntie in the future.

"Hey mom, what's this?" I furrowed my brows at the document in my hands that I found in her purse. She turned to look at me, stopping in her tracks when she noticed what it was.

"You were not supposed to see that. Not yet." She sighed.

"You bought a property?" I asked, confused, as I read. My eyes suddenly went wide when I read where. "You bought a property in Greece?"

"I did." My mother smiled and took the document from me.

"But why?"

"Because we are moving." She stated calmly. I looked at her in complete shock.

"Moving to Greece?"

"Yes."

"Why? We can't just do that!" I exclaimed.

"Why not? We have always talked about how it would be nice to live there whenever we are there on vacation. And trust me, it's for the best. Everything has already been taken care of. Once Cara gets married, we are out of here." My mother left no room for discussion and went back to packing her things.

Cara was getting married soon. Was she expecting us to move so suddenly? And across the world even, just like that?

"Why do we need to move?" I asked again.

"I'm tired of staying here. I want a new start. The sooner we can get out of here, the better." She didn't look at me as she spoke.

"No." I said. "We can't move to Greece, mom. I can't do that!"

"Oh, yes, you can! I'm not leaving without you." She now stood in front of me and furrowed her brows at me.

"No, mom. I can't just leave everything behind and move across the world like that. What about Cara? Am I supposed to leave her?" There was no way I would leave Cara like that again.

"I have just reconnected with my family. I can't abandon Cara. And what about my father?"

My mother scoffed at the mention of my father, which had me narrow my eyes at her.

"Like he cares. Trust me, it's for the best once Cara gets married. Listen, we will talk more about it when I come back." She said dismissively.

"There isn't more to talk about. I'm not moving."

"And why not?!"

For a while, I just stood there and looked at my mother's furious expression, not knowing how to tell her that there was so much more to it.

It wasn't just about my father or Cara.

"...Because I'm pregnant." I held my breath as my mother looked at me in shock. She was silent, her eyes wide with disbelief. I had to bite down on my lip so it wouldn't tremble.

"...What?" She breathed out, shaking her head as if she heard it wrong. I took a deep breath, calming my nerves as I spoke.

"I'm pregnant. I can't leave." I said in a whisper.

"You're pregnant?" She asked, and I gave a small nod, confirming it once again. "With Michael's...?

"No." I shook my head quickly. I had completely forgotten about the lie.

"Then who?" She looked almost scared to know the answer.

"I - Mom, I don't know how to say it, but I never dated Michael..." I trailed off, watching her reaction closely before I continued. "I am seeing someone. It's just not Michael."

She gestured for me to continue.

I swallowed down the knot in my throat that was building up. My heart was beating so much, and my chest was moving up and down fast.

"It's Damiano Bellavia." I held my breath as I watched my mother's face turn into one of horror. She took a step back, not believing her own two ears.

"No... it can't be true... How? When?!" She shouted.

"Mom, please calm down." I tried to tell her with my trembling voice.

"Calm down?! You're telling me you're pregnant with that monster's child?!" She screamed at me.

"He's not a monster!" I snapped back. My mother looked taken aback at my reaction. "He's not a monster, so stop saying that." I said more calmly.

"Did he force himself on you?" Her voice went ice cold, making me widen my eyes in shock.

"No!"

"My God... what have you done, Althaia?" She ran a hand through her hair, looking distressed as she paced back and forth.

I bit down on my lip nervously as I watched her, my heart clenching by her reaction.

"Does he know?" My mother finally broke the silence, facing away from me.

"No... I found out a few days ago." I admitted. I had missed my period, and I didn't even notice it with how busy I had been with everything.

"Okay... okay... He doesn't need to know. We can get this fixed. Get rid of it and pretend it never happened."

"Yo–You can't decide that." I breathed out, looking at her with wide eyes as my heart pumped violently inside my chest. I took a few shaky steps away from her, clutching my stomach suddenly feeling the need to be protective.

"You're not keeping it." She looked at me with a sharp look.

"That is something we will decide, and not you." I said angrily, and she scoffed at me.

"There is no you and him. Do you really think someone like him is capable of being a father? Someone like him could never!" She spat out.

"You don't know him!"

"And you do? You have barely known him for a blink of an eye!"

"I know him way better than you think." My whole body was shaking. Shaking in anger as she kept on insulting him. I could feel tears wanting to build up in my eyes, but I took a deep breath and clenched my fists.

"He cares about me, and I care about him, mom. I really do... I–I love him." I kept swallowing down the sob that so desperately wanted to escape my lips as I stood my ground in front of my mother.

Tears escaped my eyes when she looked at me with so much disappointment. She was shaking her head in disbelief and disgust.

A sob escaped my lips when I opened my mouth to say something, but I couldn't. I turned around and walked out of her room as fast as I could and made my way to the door. I slipped into my shoes clumsily and ran out of there.

I ran as fast as I could down the street. Tears were blurring my vision for a split second before rapidly streaming down my cheeks with my choked-up sobs painfully escaping my lips. I kept running even though I wanted to collapse and crumble. But I pushed my legs to move faster, wanting to escape everything.

Wanting to escape the look on her face.

I collapsed down on a bench, trying to calm down as I angrily wiped my tears away, but they stubbornly continued to run down my cheeks. I hid my face in my hands as I just let it all out. The lump in my throat wouldn't go away, and the more I sat here crying, the more I felt my heart was breaking.

For the first time, I felt I had let my mother down by falling in love with someone I shouldn't have been involved with in the first place.

And now, I was carrying his child.

I didn't notice the footsteps that came closer to me as I continued to sob into my hands. Arms wrapped around me, and I was pulled into their chest, their hand caressing my back as my sobs continued to fill the silence.

We stayed like this for what felt like hours, grateful for being held, as I felt heartbroken. At some point, I stopped crying, but the pain in my chest didn't seem to want to go away.

"You told her?" Luca asked, still holding me. I nodded. He was the one who had gotten me the pregnancy tests when I had called him to do me a favor.

"Luca!" I whispered once the call was answered.

"Shit, is something wrong?"

"No. I mean yes. Fuck, I don't know..." I panicked, pacing my room.

"I'm coming."

"No, no, it's not like that." I told him quickly. I took a deep breath before asking him. "Do you think you can grab me something?"

"Did you have to say it like that? I thought something happened to you." He breathed out. "Sure, what do you need?"

"I... can you get me pregnancy tests?" I asked carefully. He went silent, and I closed my eyes.

"All right. Any specific ones?"

"No. Just... if you could get different kinds that would be great." I said, trying not to panic any further.

"Give me ten minutes."

"Okay."

"Are you okay?" He asked, and I could already feel the tears forming.

"I don't know." I whispered.

"Hey, it's okay. Whatever happens, we're here for you, okay?" He tried to calm me. I nodded before realizing he couldn't see me.

"Thank you, Luca."

All three of the pregnancy tests turned positive.

I leaned back as I wiped the remaining tears from my face. Giovanni was standing next to me, hands in his pockets, as he looked at me. I looked straight ahead at the little lake, feeling more broken and emptier than ever.

"Damiano is calling." Giovanni said, making me snap my eyes at him.

"Don't answer." I said in a panic. They would have to report to him about my whereabouts, and I didn't want to explain what happened right now. He would immediately know I have been crying if I talked to him.

"You know he's going to think something is wrong if I don't pick up." Giovanni pointed out. I looked at him, defeated, with tears in my eyes. "Ah, fuck. He's going to have my head for this." He sighed and picked up the phone.

I stayed quiet, barely daring to breathe as Giovanni talked to Damiano. He tried to come up with some excuse that I was probably in the shower and that I would call when I got out. He had to say twice that he was sure I was home and safe. It sounded like Damiano didn't believe him, but after some time, Giovanni ended the call and looked at me.

"You will need to save my ass for this one."

Forty-Three

Althaia

We were slowly making our way back to the house. I didn't want to go back, but I had to if I was going with the excuse that I was in the shower because I knew he would call again. I just had to calm down entirely and make sure my voice didn't sound off when I talked to him. Hopefully, I could end the call by saying I was too tired to talk just to keep it safe.

"Do you think he will be mad, or...?" I asked them quietly while keeping my eyes down. Maybe they would be able to prepare me for his reaction when I get the courage to tell him.

"Why would he be mad?" Luca asked, and I shrugged at his question.

"I don't know... It's not like this is planned." I murmured. Hell, I didn't plan to fall in love with a Mafia Boss either.

"I don't think he would be mad." He said, thoughtfully. "He's not allowed to be mad when he was the one who got you pregnant." Luca tried to lighten the mood. He even got a pathetic chuckle out of me.

"Damiano as a father... Shit, I didn't think I would live to see that happening." Giovanni commented.

"Is that a good thing or a bad thing?" I turned to look at him, but he kept looking straight ahead.

"My guess is just as good as yours."

"You're so helpful." I said sarcastically.

"What I mean is, Damiano is private and a mystery, even around us. But...it's you. Even a blind man can see he's crazy about you." He added, giving me hope that maybe Damiano would be happy about it. "I don't know what he sees in you, honestly. You're barely average."

My smile dropped immediately.

"You're such a mean bitch!" I threw a punch to his stomach. Giovanni was taken by surprise and let out a restrained breath. Luca laughed, and Giovanni looked at me with an amused look on his face.

"And she's back." He patted my head. A smile slowly formed on my lips again when I realized he said that to get me in a better mood.

Giovanni and I had that sibling relationship where we sometimes wanted to kill each other. Luca and I were the type of siblings that never bumped heads with each other. We shared the same humor, and he was pretty cool about everything. And we loved to gang up against Giovanni because he was constantly grumpy, which made it even more fun to mess with him.

My mood dampened when I saw my house, and I purposely walked slower, not ready to face my mother again. I just hoped that she had somehow calmed down or just gone to bed.

I let out a sigh when we were near, and I stopped to look at them.

"I know you're just doing your job, but...I'm glad you are here. I don't think I could do this if I was alone." My voice cracked, and a lump formed in my throat. I swallowed down hard and took a deep breath. I didn't want to cry anymore. "Anyway, thank you." I gave a small smile, thankful for them.

"Don't worry about it. You are family now, and we will do anything for the family." Luca smiled, and Giovanni gave a small, firm nod. It made me tear up a bit. They saw me as a part of their family. I smiled, grateful for their words that eased my heart.

I quietly shut the door behind me. The house was completely silent and dark. Maybe she went to bed? Either way, I was happy I wouldn't have to face her right now as I made my way upstairs to my room.

I let out a breath when I closed my bedroom door and searched for my phone. Sure enough, I had a few missed calls from Damiano. I took a final deep breath and cleared my throat a few times to make sure I would sound somewhat as I usually do.

"Althaia." Damiano's voice never failed to make me shiver.

"Hi."

"What's wrong?" He asked immediately. The way he had said it made me tear up, and I bit down on my lip so a sob wouldn't escape. I closed my eyes, trying to get it together before I talked.

"Nothing's wrong." I let out a forced chuckle.

"You have been crying." He stated. He knew me too well already to tell.

"I'm fine, trust me." I squeezed my eyes shut as my voice decided to crack. "I was just watching a sad movie, that's all."

"... I see." He replied, not convinced, but he didn't pressure me to tell him, and for that I was thankful.

I settled comfortably under my covers as exhaustion washed over me, and the banging headache I had been ignoring was now in full force.

"I miss you. So much." I whispered into the phone. I longed for the feeling of his arms wrapped tightly around me. I longed for his closeness, craving the soothing sound of his heartbeat and the familiar scent that filled the air when he was near.

"I miss you too." His voice was soft, and it had my eyes welling up with tears.

"I need you. I wish you were here with me." A tear escaped my eye. He was the only person I desperately wanted to comfort me right now and to tell me everything was going to be okay. I just hoped he wouldn't leave once he found out that I'm pregnant.

My heart ached at the thought.

I woke up with tears in my eyes, my pillow damp from crying. I stayed in bed, just staring at the ceiling. It was early, the sun barely appearing on the horizon.

I let out a tired sigh and got up and made my way to the bathroom. I saw my reflection; tired eyes, red, and puffy, and my hair was a mess. I washed my face with some cold water to make my puffy eyes disappear, but it wasn't helping that much.

I still looked like a hot mess.

I made my way downstairs, hearing movements from the kitchen. I looked at the time and saw that it was almost time for her to leave. Mrs. Park would be here with a cab, and they would leave for the airport together.

My mother was leaning against the counter while drinking her coffee. I walked past her, feeling her gaze on me as I poured myself a cup. Neither of us said anything as we drank our coffee in silence with tension so thick it was almost suffocating.

"You were with those two men from the restaurant." She said quietly. I looked at her with a blank look on my face. If she had seen me with them, then she had already connected the dots. I didn't bother to answer.

"You've gone too far into this. Get out of it while you still can."

"I'm not going anywhere." I said calmly.

"It's a world you don't know a thing about. I have been in your situation. Don't make the same mistakes I did."

"So now I'm a mistake?" I let out a humorless laugh.

"Don't you *ever* say that!" My mother placed her mug to the side. "You are the biggest blessing of my life. Your whole life, I've tried to protect you from that world. And I am trying to protect you by telling you to get out of it before it's too late." Her voice was firm, with a hint of desperation.

"It's already too late, mom." I said.

"It's not. You can still get it fixed." She urged.

"There is nothing to fix." I hissed, feeling anger taking over. I placed my mug on the counter, afraid I might break it in my hands with how tight I was holding it.

"You can't be happy with him. Don't you realize many people would love to get to him through you? He's a Don, for God's sake! And you're an easy target for all his enemies! Is that a life you want? Constantly fearing for your life?" My mother raised her voice again, anger showing on her face.

"What difference would it have made if you didn't leave my father? I would have been an easy target, no matter what." I pointed out, startling my mother when I brought it up.

"I left for a reason. To protect you." She insisted.

"Was it really to protect me, mom? If it was to protect me, then why did you let me go there? Why did you let me stay there for so long when you knew what kind of people were involved? You knew I stayed at their place with Cara, so don't give me that bullshit!" My voice rose with each sentence, almost making me shout the last part.

There were certain things we never talked about, and one thing was why she left my father in the first place. For some reason, it was something she didn't want to talk about.

My mother stared at me with a cold expression. This was a whole different side I was witnessing from her. Never in my life have I ever seen her like this. That look on her face was something I have learned to recognize with the time I had spent with Damiano and his men.

"I have booked an appointment with the doctor for you once I come back. This ends then, prepare yourself." Her voice was calm, but the look on her face was cold and dark.

I stared at her retreating form with wide eyes, refusing to believe what I just heard. I let out a shaky breath as I stood frozen in place. My heart was beating too fast. So much it was pounding in my ears.

The sound of the door closing and the car driving away made me snap out of it. I grabbed the coffee mug in anger and threw it to the floor, watching it break. But it did nothing to satisfy the fuming anger inside of me.

I grabbed anything I could get my hands on and smashed it on the floor. Dishes flew and crashed on the walls, watching them shatter into pieces. Drawers were pulled out and their contents spilled, creating a disastrous mess in the kitchen. I was panting as I continued to empty the cupboards, smashing and breaking everything.

But it still wasn't enough to relieve the pain in my heart.

I grabbed my hair and screamed at the top of my lungs; anger, sadness, emptiness, pain. I let it all out.

I stumbled around on my feet as an intense wave of fear took over my body. My body shook. I couldn't catch my breath, and my heart was pounding out of my chest. Everything spun, and I looked frantically around to hold on to something. Instead, I crashed right onto the broken pieces on the floor.

I felt like I was dying.

I couldn't breathe.

My ears were ringing. I couldn't hear anything. My body continued to shake as I gasped for air. But nothing was filling my lungs. My vision blurred. The ringing in my ears intensified and my chest was rapidly heaving, desperate for air.

"I can't breathe...I can't..." I choked out.

Arms grabbed me and made me look up, but it felt like everything was in slow motion. I tried to focus, but I couldn't make out who it was. I could faintly see lips moving, talking to me, but I couldn't hear anything.

Breathe, Althaia.

Damiano's voice rang out. I rapidly blinked and gasped, trying to take deep breaths while I focused on his voice. Slowly, my vision was getting clearer and the ringing in my ears suddenly disappeared.

"Deep breaths, Althaia." Luca instructed with a frown on his face. I held onto him tightly as I tried to match my breathing with his.

"You're okay. You're safe." He kept talking to me, reassuring me as he helped me calm down.

I was sitting on the couch as the paramedics measured my blood pressure. Giovanni had made the call when Luca tried to get me back to my senses. I had gotten cuts on my hands and knees from falling directly onto the glass and plates I had shattered all over the kitchen. Most of them were just surface cuts, but there were a couple of deeper cuts they cleaned and bandaged.

"Your blood pressure is high, but I wouldn't worry too much about it right after a panic attack. Do you have those often?" The paramedic asked, and I shook my head at him.

"I haven't had them before."

"Do you know the cause of it, or did it just happen?"

"I was just...upset." I said, while keeping my eyes down. My body was feeling weak and heavy as I sat there and continued to answer their questions like a robot.

"There's nothing serious, but make sure you get enough restful sleep..." I nodded mindlessly as he continued to talk while packing his things.

I felt empty. Like there was a deep hole inside of me that wouldn't close. I rose from the couch once the paramedics left but was stopped by Giovanni.

"I have to go to work..." I mumbled quietly, keeping my eyes down when he blocked my way.

"The hell you are! Go back and sit down. You need to rest." He sat me back down, and I didn't even protest. I was too weak to do anything. Too upset. Too much in pain.

I lay down on the couch, closed my eyes, and listened to the hushed voices of Luca and Giovanni as they talked to each other. A blanket was pulled over my body, and I soon let sleep take over me to escape my reality.

A feeling of something caressing my stomach woke me up. It took me a few tries to open my heavy eyelids, and I tiredly blinked a couple of times before my eyes adjusted to the darkness in the room.

A sob immediately escaped my lips when I saw him.

"Damiano..."

FORTY-FOUR

ALTHAIA

I quickly sat up and wrapped my arms around his neck. Damiano held me tightly in his body with his strong arms as I sobbed into his neck.

I couldn't believe he was here, right in front of me and holding me.

He caressed my back as we were in each other's arms. Something I had missed so much for the past weeks. Something I desperately needed right now.

"Althaia." Damiano spoke softly and had me look at him. He cupped my face, wiping the tears away. He looked around my face with concern before meeting my eyes. "Tell me what's wrong."

I looked at him with teary eyes, not knowing how to even tell him. Where do I even start? This whole thing had gotten out of control, and I didn't know what to do.

"I -" I bit my lip when my voice cracked and I looked down, trying to breathe before I continued. "I had a fight with my mom..." I decided to say, and I let out a breath before I looked back at him.

He looked at me with furrowed brows, waiting for me to elaborate, but I didn't know how to break it all down to him.

"Because you're pregnant?" He asked, and I held my breath. Fresh tears went down my cheeks as I looked at him with a defeated look, but I gave him a small nod, confirming it to him. "Why?"

"Because it's with you..." It came in a whisper. "She... she wants me to... to get rid..." I broke down, refusing to finish the sentence.

Damiano stilled, his expression hardened, a storm of rage unfolding in his eyes before he pulled me into him again.

"Shh, don't worry. No one is going to take our baby away. I promise." He told me quietly.

"Did Luca and Giovanni tell you?" I asked as Damiano sat against the headboard with me on his lap.

"No. I found the pregnancy tests in your purse when I packed a bag for you." He said, and then I looked around. We weren't in my house anymore, but in what looked like a hotel room. I had been so disoriented that I hadn't even noticed where we were.

"I had to get you out of there." He spoke softly and continued to rub my back. I gave a small nod, wrapping my arms around him tightly.

"Luca called, telling me they had called the paramedics because you were not doing well. Fuck, Althaia, for a minute I thought I was losing you. I was driving like a madman from the airport to get to you." Damiano held me tightly, almost as if his life depended on it.

"It was just a panic attack." I sighed.

"That was more than just a panic attack." He gently lifted my bandaged hand, revealing small spots of blood that had soaked through. "I told you not to get hurt." He kissed my palm.

"I know, I'm sorry." I felt guilty about having him worry like that.

"I'm here now. I won't let you get hurt anymore." Damiano promised. "Did you go to a doctor yet?" His hand went down to my stomach, caressing it.

"No, not yet. I haven't really had time to process the fact that I'm…pregnant." I admitted. It was such a strange word to use about myself. "I was worried about telling you."

We were in the early stages of our relationship, and it was not like talking about babies ever occurred to me. We were still getting to know each other, and I was living in the moment. I honestly didn't know his thoughts about kids or if he even wanted them one day.

"You shouldn't have worried about that."

"I didn't know if you would be happy about it." I said quietly. I tried to control my breathing, feeling my heart beat faster as I waited for him to say something.

Damiano's eyes softened, a beautiful smile on his lips.

"My Althaia, why wouldn't I be happy when it's with you?" He spoke warmly. His eyes held everything my soul thirsted for.

Certainty and joy.

I moved to straddle his lap and placed my hands on his cheeks, caressing them. My heart overflowed with warmth and happiness. He was happy about it. It was the only thing that mattered to me.

"We are having a baby." I whispered.

"We are." Damiano smiled, his eyes were bright and filled with so much tenderness. "No more tears." He wiped away the tears that had escaped, and I couldn't help but chuckle a bit. These were tears of happiness.

"Se agapó." I whispered with a smile on my lips, and I let myself get lost in his eyes.

God, I loved his eyes so much. And I loved him even more.

Damiano looked deep into my eyes when I said those words to him. I didn't expect him to know what it meant. I just had to tell him.

"E ti amo." He whispered back. For a split second, I held my breath, trying to figure out if I heard him correctly. "Ti amo, Althaia." He said once again.

He knew what I said.

My heart went still for a second before furiously pounding, sending me over the edge as everything in me fluttered. I let out a breath, shuddering because of the tingles that shot right through me when he slid his fingers into my hair and cupped my face.

"My Althaia, I love you." Damiano confessed again. I bit my lip to avoid another tearful round.

"And I love you, Damiano."

He let out another one of his beautiful smiles before slowly leaning in. His lips brushed against mine ever so lightly before he kissed me. It was a small, soft peck, yet it had me gasping. It was electric and pulsing when his tongue ran across my lips before completely sealing me with his lips.

I was desperate for more. I wanted to feel all of him, just to make sure I was truly in his arms again, and it wasn't a dream I would wake up from. I leaned in closer, deepening the kiss and tasting his tongue.

My body was burning, our passionate kiss turning wilder, desperate, hungry; so much that our kiss was only broken when we undressed. We had been away from each other for too long, and it showed as we held onto each other as if one of us would disappear.

Damiano laid me flat on my back with him on top of me. His lips trailed to the side of my face, plastering small kisses as he went down to my neck, kissed and sucked my skin. It had me softly moaning, my whole body feeling electric. So much it was almost unbearable. I have missed his touch, and the way he would roam my body, and touching me all in the right places.

"Fuck, how I have missed your moans..." Damiano's voice was low, deep, and husky. It made me feel like I was on fire; even more when he positioned himself at my entrance.

I exhaled a moan when he slowly entered me.

"So fucking tight..." He grunted in pleasure.

Damiano rested his head against mine as he slowly moved his hips against me, giving me time to adjust to him after so long. He filled me up to the brim, stretching my walls completely.

"Don't hold them back. Let me hear you." He groaned, and hungrily went to my lips, pulling my lip with his teeth before shoving his tongue inside as his thrusts went faster and harder.

I moved my hips against him too, getting a satisfying sound from deep in his throat. Our breathing was loud and heavy as our bodies moved flush against each other.

"Perfect. You're so fucking perfect." He growled, and I whimpered when he pulled my legs higher around his waist, gasping at how deep he went at this angle.

The familiar, tightening feeling in the pit of my stomach built, taking me higher and higher as he pushed his thick cock into me. In and out, faster and faster as he panted and grunted, close to his own release.

"Oh God, Damiano!" I cried out. The intense climax rippled through me, having me gasp and arch my back as my pussy trembled in pleasure.

"Piccola, fuck!" His hand gripped my thigh tightly as I felt his warm release.

Damiano buried his face into my neck, plastering small kisses on my skin as he laid next to me. He pulled me into his chest, immediately caressing my stomach again.

"You have lost weight." He said unhappily when he felt my ribs.

"Thank you."

"It wasn't a compliment." Damiano frowned.

"I know." I gave a small smile. "I may have skipped a few meals, but it wasn't intentional. I was just too busy and too tired." I explained. At least now I know why I was tired all the time.

"You need to be more careful. Our baby needs to grow."

Our baby.

His words had me smiling and a wave of butterflies erupted in me.

"I didn't know I was pregnant at the time, but don't worry, I will eat. Now I have an excuse to stuff my face all the time. I'm going to be so fat." I chuckled.

"Good. The bigger you get, the happier I will be." He smiled and placed a small kiss on my lips. "Hopefully, it's going to be a mini version of you and with your green eyes."

"Oh, are you sure you can handle two of me?" I teased with a smile.

"No, but I'm up for the challenge." He said with a chuckle. "A girl or a boy, as long as the baby is healthy, I'll be happy."

I placed a hand on my stomach, a smile on my face as I imagined Damiano carrying a tiny baby in his arms.

"I'm going to shower you both in diamonds." He whispered, placing a hand over mine.

"You can't do that." I laughed. "That is going to be one spoiled child!"

"Of course. That's my baby. I'm going to make sure she is spoiled as hell, so she knows no one will ever be good enough for her." Damiano smirked.

"I don't think anyone would dare to approach her once they see you." I chuckled, and he looked happy about it.

I rested my head on his chest as I traced his skull tattoo with my fingertips. It was a truly captivating work of art, the way the hooded skull wore a crown atop its head, its colossal angel wings adding an enchanting touch.

I raised my head, frowning as I stared at the crown, trying to figure out whether my eyes were playing tricks on me.

"Do you like it?" Damiano asked. My eyes widened.

"Damiano!" I gasped and looked at him in shock.

"Yes, my love?" He smiled softly. I looked back down and traced my fingers across the base of the imperial crown tattoo as I stared in shock at the new ink on his chest.

Αλθαία

It was my name in Greek.

"You're insane." I said breathlessly.

Damiano looked satisfied, pulling me into a kiss that left me even more breathless.

"I told you, only for you, baby."

Forty-Five

Damiano

I continued to gaze at her as she slept in my embrace. Finally, after so long, she was back where she belonged, in my arms, where she fit so perfectly.

Althaia went to sleep after I made sure she ate something, and I made sure she ate enough. Another thing I noticed was her decreased appetite. She could barely finish her plate.

One of the things I adored about her was her love of food. Her eyes would dance with excitement every time she was about to savor something she loved. The way she would close her eyes and wear an expression of sheer joy when it exceeded her expectations.

It never failed to bring a smile to my face. And, fuck, it frustrated me endlessly that she hadn't been looking after herself, whether she knew about the pregnancy or not. But I was here to take care of her now and make sure she was safe and happy. Not like how I found her.

I had to take a deep breath to calm down as I remembered that phone call.

"Luca." I said, accepting his call while en route to my next meeting. "Update me."

"Boss, I think you better get your ass down here."

My blood went cold.

"Where is she? Is she safe?" I asked in a sneer, my knuckles turning white on the steering wheel.

"She's with us and safe." Luca's words had me slightly relax. "But we had to call the paramedics."

I slammed my fist against the steering wheel.

"You were supposed to fucking watch over her!"

"We understand, but it was unavoidable. She had a panic attack." He sighed.

"Let me talk to her." I said as I made a sharp U-turn, speeding up to get back to the manor as fast as possible.

"She's asleep right now."

"Fine. Don't let her out of your sight. I'm coming." I ended the call and made another. "Antonio, I want wheels up in thirty minutes and cancel everything I have. I'm going to Florida."

"Noted."

Parking haphazardly in front of Althaia's house, I rushed inside, and my eyes landed on her body curled up on the couch.

I crouched down, softly caressing her cheek when she let out a small whimper, her lashes wet with tears. Fuck. I had already planned to come and see her, but I should have come the second I heard her tear-stained voice last night.

I went to Luca and Giovanni.

"Why the fuck is she crying?" I hissed low to not wake her up.

"I think it's best if you talk to her about it." Giovanni said, and I stepped up in his face.

"Are you refusing to answer me?" My voice went cold as I wrapped my fingers around the gun tucked behind my back.

Giovanni watched the gun in my hand, then shifted his gaze to Althaia before letting out a small sigh.

"It's not my place to say." He kept his eyes down, accepting his fate without resistance. My eyes narrowed on him before shifting to Luca, who also kept his gaze lowered.

I raised a brow and turned to Althaia, a thoughtful expression on my face.

Interesting. They have silently pledged their loyalty to her.

"Stay here." I told them and tucked away my gun. I went upstairs to find her room to pack a bag. I already knew she had a fight with her mother, and I wasn't going to let her stay here.

I found a bag in her closet and filled it up with clothes and what I thought she would need. I took her purse, to make sure everything was in there before I left. That was when my eyes landed on the pregnancy tests.

I held all three of them in my hands and took a seat on her bed as I read the bold letters.

Pregnant

I let out a long breath. I couldn't believe what I was seeing. Shit. I have never thought of having children before, not even when I was with... Sienna. Still, a smile was tugging at the corners of my lips.

She's having my baby.

I let out a sigh when I realized she must have had a fight with her mother because of this. I grabbed her bag and went downstairs. Once I had her in my arms, I held her tightly and got her out of here.

Now, I couldn't stop looking at her in my arms and caressing her stomach. The thought of her mother wanting to get rid of our baby had me seething with rage. Pissed couldn't even begin to describe the fury boiling within me. If she weren't her mother, I would have hunted her down and made her vanish without a trace. I was going to do anything to make sure Althaia and our baby would be protected and healthy.

As if my protective instincts weren't already strong enough, they seemed to intensify, and I couldn't resist caressing her stomach. I knew it was early, and it would be a while before she showed, but the mental image of her with a pregnant belly made me feel like the fucking king of the world.

That image stirred a different kind of... *excitement* within me. The mere thought had my blood racing down, and there was nothing more I wanted than to bury myself deep inside of her.

Althaia shifted, and I watched as the blanket moved and exposed her naked breasts.

As if I wasn't horny enough already...

"Why are you still awake?" Althaia mumbled, her eyes still closed. She stretched her arms above her head and arched her back, which made her chest rise and her breasts bounce.

Fucking hell.

She wasn't even doing this intentionally, and all I could think of right now was to fuck her.

"I want to look at you."

"Creep." She smiled and opened her eyes to look at me. I chuckled. How I have missed her snarky comments.

"You have been away from me for weeks. I am simply catching up on the time I haven't been able to look at you."

"Hey, I sent you pictures." She grinned, and I raised a brow.

"Which gave me blue balls." I pointed out and faintly brushed my fingers across her breast, watching her nipple harden under my touch. She shivered, her body responding immediately to me. It pleased me to no end that I had this much effect on her.

"Well, you have hands."

"I do..." I whispered in her ear, grazing her earlobe with my teeth. Her breath hitched in her throat as I slid my hand down her stomach. "Though I prefer something warmer, wet, and... *tight*." I smirked as I cupped her pussy.

I nibbled her earlobe, a faint moan exhaling from her lips.

"Go back to sleep." I kissed her cheek before leaning back. She turned her head sharply, her scowl aimed directly at me.

"After you did all that to me?" She scoffed in disapproval. "You're such a tease!"

"It's called payback, my love." I winked. "And you need to rest." I reminded her, and she rolled her eyes at me.

"I have slept almost the whole day." Althaia swung her leg to straddle me and placed her hands on my chest for support. "Besides, what kind of girlfriend would I be to leave you like this?"

I grunted when she took hold of my cock and gave me that sultry look with her eyes.

"Hmm, girlfriend, you say?"

"Mhmm, that's the title I've given myself, unless..." She bit her lip and leaned in, her long hair cascading around us like a curtain, and her teasing gaze held a touch of enchantment. "You want to make me your wife?" She whispered, and amusement twinkled in her green eyes.

I swiftly enveloped my arms around her waist and instantly sat up with her straddling my lap. She let out a small squeal at the sudden motion, her laughter bubbling up as she wrapped her arms around my neck.

"Marry me." I whispered, my gaze locked with those enchanting green eyes that had captivated me long ago.

"Sure." Althaia smiled.

"Marry me." I repeated. Her eyes slowly widened as the weight of my words settled in.

She was for me, as I was for her. If she desired the title of wife, I would happily make it happen. To wed her, to be her husband, for her to be my wife, to have children together, it was all that I desired.

"You can't be serious?" Althaia looked at me in shock.

"I am." I affirmed, meeting her gaze with sincerity.

"Are you only saying it because I'm pregnant?" Her eyes narrowed slightly.

"No. I'm saying it because I love you." I told her softly, stroking her hair as I gazed into her captivating eyes.

Althaia's stunned expression lingered as she observed my face until a gentle smile graced her lips.

"I love you, Damiano. But maybe we should slow things down a bit and have the baby first?"

"Are you saying no?" I frowned, but she continued to smile.

"I'm saying not now. I've barely had time to process that we're going to have a baby. It's all happening so fast. Let's take it one step at a time. I'll be ready the next time you ask." She replied.

Her emerald eyes glistened with love as she gazed at me, fueling my eagerness to make her my wife. But I would wait for her.

Always.

"Althaia Bellavia." I voiced, loving how our names sound together.

"Hmm, now that you say it like that, it does sound good." Althaia grinned and rested her head against mine. "Just wait for me." She whispered before pressing her lips to mine.

I tightened my hold around her, her soft lips driving me crazy as I bit her lips to taste her tongue. A breathy moan escaped her as I grabbed her ass. Althaia slowly moved her hips, making her wetness coat my cock.

"Piccola." My voice was strained and filled with lust.

"Yes?" She breathed out.

"I want you. Now." I growled out. She chuckled but moved to position my length right at her entrance. I grunted when my cock slipped inside her sweet pussy.

I leaned back and watched her take all of me in all of her naked glory.

"You feel so good." Althaia moaned in a whisper, taking her lip between her teeth as she rode my cock like she was born for it. The sight alone made me almost cum.

"Fuck, baby." I groaned, watching her perfect full breasts bounce.

I took her nipple between my fingers, giving a slight pinch, enough to have her eyes closing in pleasure. I slid my other hand down to her pussy, my thumb rubbing her clit as she rolled her hips, her pussy clenching around my cock in the most delicious way.

"Move with me..." Althaia breathed out, but I wasn't done looking at her.

She was the most captivating woman I had ever laid eyes on. Her long, wavy hair was cascading around her like a waterfall, and her astonishingly innocent emerald eyes made her appear even more bewitching.

She was mine. And mine only.

"Damiano...!" Althaia moaned out, and I grabbed her hips to give her what she wanted.

I slammed my cock inside of her, fucking her as I grabbed her breast, kneading her nipple before slapping it.

"Fuck... yes... please..." Althaia threw her head back in pleasure. I smirked. Despite her innocent look, she was a freaky one in bed and let me do whatever I pleased with her.

"Let me see you touch yourself as I fuck you." I growled. "Atta girl." I praised, watching her play with her breasts and clit.

The room was filled with the sound of our skin slapping against each other with her loud moans and my grunting. A deep, throaty sound escaped me when she clenched around my cock.

"Damiano, I'm -" She didn't finish as her entire body shook, her orgasm crashing over in a wave. I slammed myself harder and faster into her, my body tensing as I filled her up with my cum.

Althaia collapsed on top of me as we caught our breath, our bodies covered in a light coat of sweat.

"Fuck, baby. You know how to empty my balls." I breathed heavily.

"That's how I ended up pregnant." She snickered tiredly, making me chuckle with her.

She closed her eyes and gently cupped my cheek, her thumb tracing soft patterns on my skin.

After what felt like an eternity, I had finally found happiness. She had breathed new life into my existence, filling it with new meaning.

She was my missing piece.

FORTY-SIX

ALTHAIA

"Trust me, Damiano. I'm fine to go to work. I've even slept so much that I'm awake this early." I said as I got dressed.

"Keep it closed." Damiano had a frown on his face as he sat on the end of the bed.

"You're a businessman. You, out of all people, should know that it's bad for business if I just keep it closed." I raised a brow and walked towards him. I stepped in between his legs and his hands rested right on my ass.

"I will write a check for your losses. Keep it closed." He insisted.

"Look at you; throwing money at the problem." I laughed.

"Usually works." He smirked.

"Yeah? Well, it doesn't work for me. People have their orders ready, and I kind of need to be there to hand them their purchases." I pointed out.

"You're pregnant. You shouldn't be working at all."

"It doesn't mean I can't work. You know what, I'm not even going to discuss this with you anymore." I shook my head, but still smiled. We had been going over this ever since I said I was going to work.

"The minute you get tired, you're closing." Damiano ordered firmly.

"Fine." I agreed to it just so he would drop it already.

"Good."

I took a step back, but Damiano pulled me back into him. He didn't say anything and raised my shirt to place a kiss on my stomach.

I couldn't help but break into a wide grin at his actions. He was already obsessed with my stomach even though I wasn't showing yet, and always wanted to touch me more than he usually did. And I didn't mind it one bit.

A knock sounded on the door, and I already knew it was Luca and Giovanni coming with breakfast. I was slowly getting my appetite back, and I had pretty much demanded a long list of food I wanted. I had to add a 'please' and some cute emojis at the end of my long message to Luca because it sounded very bossy.

"I might have gotten carried away with the food..." My eyes went wide when I saw the coffee table that was now made into a whole breakfast buffet. All three of them just stared at the pile of food I ordered.

"No judgment from me, but can you eat all that?" Luca looked kind of both shocked and impressed at the same time.

"No! What do you think I am? I just didn't know what I wanted, and it turned out I wanted everything." I laughed. "Oh well, get comfortable and eat!"

I settled on the couch with Damiano sitting next to me and Luca and Giovanni in the armchairs in front of us.

"What are you doing?" Giovanni frowned as I took a sip of my iced caramel macchiato, my favorite drink.

"Drinking?" I said as if it wasn't obvious.

"You can't have that." He got up and snatched it out of my hand before I could even react.

"Hey, give it back!" I got up from the couch to take it back, and him being the mature man he was, held it up high above his head so I couldn't reach it.

"You can't have any caffeine." Giovanni practically scolded me.

"Yes, I can!"

"No, you can't!"

He stared down at me and I scowled.

"Give it back!"

"Giovanni." Damiano called after him.

"She can't have caffeine. That's what the paramedics said." He stated and still held it up high. I considered kneeing him in the balls, but then he would spill my coffee.

I could see Luca leaning back with his food as he watched us like some kind of entertainment.

"I can have that one. It's mostly milk and ice, anyway." I tried to convince him.

"I don't care. Listen, I'm trying to prevent you from having another psychotic episode."

I dropped my jaw.

"Excuse me? Psychotic?"

"Yes. It almost cost me my head, and I don't want to die for you, woman." He scoffed and went back to sit. "Go, drink water, it's healthier."

"Drink water, it's healthier." I mimicked, as I continued to scowl at him. He just looked at me with a stupid smirk on his face as he drank my iced coffee.

"I'm only helping you. Shouldn't you be on a healthy diet, anyway?"

"Shouldn't you be minding your own business?" I snapped. I was very serious about my morning coffee, and the fact that he took it from me... Oh, I was about to give him *hell!*

"Althaia, eat." Damiano called out for me, but I ignored him as I sat down, watching the idiot who was still drinking my iced coffee. He was even making 'ah' noises now and then to agitate me.

"I hope you choke on it and die." I spat out.

"The pregnancy has made you meaner. First, you punch me, and now, you wish for me to choke and die." Giovanni looked amused while he finished *my* coffee.

"That woman of yours is abusive." He said to Damiano, and I flipped him off, which didn't exactly help my case as Giovanni gave a 'see what I mean?' look.

"What's wrong?" Damiano frowned when he saw I was rubbing my stomach as I took deep breaths.

"I don't know, there's this weird smell in the room." I didn't know what it was, but it made me feel nauseous.

I walked around to see if I could spot what it was.

"Oh my God, it's you." I said with disgust to Giovanni.

"How am I smelling bad when I took a shower before coming here?" Giovanni gave a blank look.

I leaned in closer to him and sniffed. The smell came from his clothes.

"It's your clothes..." I tried to wave the smell away from my nose, but it was as if it was stuck in my nostrils. I stepped away from him and at this point, I had to take deep breaths through my mouth to keep my nausea down.

"Giovanni smoked before coming up. That's probably what's triggering you right now." Luca said just as I had to run to the bathroom. I made it just in time for me to throw up.

Damiano pulled my hair back and rubbed my back as I continued to empty my stomach.

"Are you okay?" Damiano looked at me with worry.

"I think I need to lie down for a bit." I said after chugging some mouthwash.

I closed my eyes and tried to calm down because somehow, I still felt nauseous even though I almost threw up my organs. At least it felt like that.

"Gio, go change. You stunk up the entire room." I yelled out to him right as Damiano came back with a bottle of water for me.

"As if she wasn't a pain in the ass before. Now I can't even smoke in peace." Giovanni complained.

"I heard that!"

"You were supposed to." He said grumpily and walked out. I chuckled.

He was so going to be called Uncle Grumpy.

"God, this sucks." I took a bite of some dry toast as I felt sorry for myself. I had to spend another day in bed since I couldn't stop throwing up.

"It shouldn't be like this for long." Damiano tried to comfort me.

"What if it does? I tend to be unlucky, you know." I sighed and leaned back against the headboard. "This is your fault. You did this to me." I blamed him with a scowl.

"I meant to pull out, but then I looked at you and thought you would make a great mother, so I didn't." He joked, and I burst out laughing.

"You're unbelievable."

"I'm sorry you have to go through that, but I'm not apologizing for getting you pregnant." Damiano smiled smugly.

"Ha, you're not sorry. I know you're secretly happy about me not going to work." I said, taking another bite of my toast since it was all I could keep down.

"True. This way, I know you're not overworking yourself, and I can keep an eye on you. Eat more." He handed me more bread.

"You're so bossy." I chuckled.

"I know." He winked. "It reminds me, I have something for you." Damiano got up from the bed and pulled something from his bag.

"What is it?"

"Open and see." He said and handed me a velvety box.

I carefully opened it, and I held my breath as I looked at what was inside. Completely mesmerized by the beauty of the most extravagant jewelry my eyes had ever seen.

The Tiffany Yellow Diamond was right here.

In front of me.

In my hands.

"Try it on." Damiano's voice got me out of my trance from the exquisite sparkling necklace.

"No way, I'm not touching it! I'm afraid to even breathe near it." I exclaimed. I carefully placed it down on the bed so I could admire it from a distance.

"It's just a necklace, piccola." Damiano laughed.

"It's a necklace worth fifty million dollars." I reminded him.

"Why are you whispering?" He looked at me, amused that I had whispered the fifty-million-dollar part.

"What if someone hears and tries to break in to steal it?"

"I happen to be very fast on the trigger. Now, let me see it on you." He took the necklace out of the jewelry box, and I pulled my hair to the side. I let out a breath when the cold diamonds touched my skin.

"Beautiful." Damiano smiled, having me blush. He wasn't even looking at the necklace.

Despite being scared to move, in case I would break it, I still went to the mirror to have a look. Damiano came to stand behind me, wrapping his arms around me as I continued to admire the incredible jewelry around my neck.

A fifty-million-dollar necklace.

Holy shit!

"I can't…" I said breathlessly when I met his eyes in the mirror. It was too expensive, too elegant. It was just too much for someone like me to wear.

"You can, my love. It's all yours." Damiano kissed my neck, tracing a path up ear as he whispered. "Remember what I told you at the auction?"

As if I could forget.

Forty-Seven

ALTHAIA

I could finally open the boutique after two days of being sick in bed. Of course Damiano wasn't too happy about it, but guess who won that round?

Then he insisted on staying with me in the boutique, and that started another round of discussion. I couldn't have him or my assigned bodyguards in the boutique because I knew they would make my customers feel uneasy. I had to remind him he looks scary as fuck to other people.

"Good." He said.

"Good for you, but not for my business. Don't you have a Mafia to run or something? Go do that so I can work in peace." I told him.

That may or may not have resulted in him spanking my ass until it was as red as a cherry, saying I need to be fucked into obedience; a reminder that I was also dealing with a Mafia Boss.

Damiano chose to do some work, while Luca and Giovanni stayed close, but not too close to the boutique to not look shady. I promised I would call if I needed anything.

Luckily, today had been one of the slower days, so I could use the time to keep track of the inventory. As I was in the middle of scribbling down in the workbook, the door to the boutique opened.

"Hi and welcome! How can I help you?" I smiled at the couple, hoping I could help them as fast as possible so I could close. I was hungry and have been thinking about food for the past thirty minutes.

"I need a dress for her." The man's voice had a cold edge to it as he looked me up and down. The way he spoke sent a chill down my spine, and the coldness in his eyes made me uneasy, but I managed to keep a smile on my face.

"I can help with that. Anything particular in mind?" I turned to the woman with auburn hair that beautifully contrasted with her warm, ochre complexion.

"It needs to be long." The man replied instead of her. I had to try my best not to frown at him.

"Of course." I let out a forced smile and turned to the woman. "Do you know what size you are? If not, it's fine! I can measure you." I told her with a warm smile.

"Unfortunately, she's a size six. Someone hasn't been watching her diet and has gained weight." He gave her a disapproving look, and I noticed a slight tremble in her hands until she clasped them together.

"A size six isn't big. I would be concerned if she was smaller." I couldn't help but frown at him as I stared into his eyes. "Let's go find you something, shall we?" I smiled at the woman and led her to the back of the boutique.

We had a spacious area in the back of the boutique for our customers to try on dresses, and their companions could relax in a comfortable waiting area with complimentary drinks.

I grabbed a few dresses I thought would look good on her and led her into the dressing room; the one furthest away from the shady scumbag as he took a seat on the couch.

"You shouldn't have talked to him like that." She whispered so quietly I almost missed it. I was getting a dress ready for her to try but stopped when she looked at me with wide eyes.

"Well, he was being disrespectful." I whispered back. He was being more than that, but she already knew.

"He doesn't like when *women* talk back."

I wanted to scoff loudly, but she looked concerned for me, and her whole body was shaking.

"What's your name?" I smiled and took her hands in mine, trying to give her some comfort.

"Laila."

"Laila, are you in any danger? Do you need help?" I asked softly, letting her know it was okay to tell me. She was hesitating to say anything.

"What's taking so long?" The man suddenly erupted. She flinched, squeezing her eyes shut.

"Just a minute!" I said loudly, not hiding my annoyance with him. "Listen, Laila, I can help you. You don't need to be with someone like that. Stay here while I get help, okay?" I gave her a reassuring smile. There was no way I was letting her go with that dickhead.

I didn't exactly have a plan, but all I had to do was to make a call and Luca and Giovanni would come in here instantly.

She stopped me before I could step out of the dressing room.

"H–he has a gun." Laila looked at me hopelessly, on the verge of tears. Even I had to take a moment and not let her know that I was scared now. I had to be the strong one.

"Don't worry, I can get help." I gave her hand a tight squeeze before getting out of the dressing room. The man's cold eyes snapped at me when I stepped out, sending a chill down my back, but I held my head high.

"I took the wrong size for her. I will be back with the right one." I gave a tight smile and hurriedly went to the desk to grab my phone.

Only to find it missing.

Panic surged through me as I desperately looked around for my phone in my purse, the drawers, under the paperwork. But it was gone.

Fuck!

"Looking for this?"

I jumped and turned around. He let out a sinister smile and waved my phone in front of my face.

I backed away when he slowly inched closer, trapping me between the desk and him. I glared at him even though my heart was furiously beating. But I wasn't about to give him the satisfaction of seeing me scared.

"Give me my phone back." I frowned, but he just let out an evil snicker. He shook his head and made a tsking sound while pressing himself against me. His face came so close to mine that I had to turn away from him.

"You were only supposed to get us a dress. And now look at what you have done in a pitiful attempt to masquerade as a strong woman. You are only designed to spread your legs and please us." He hissed.

My eyes widened when I felt a gun against my stomach, wincing when he pressed the gun harshly into me and violently grabbed my hair.

"Now, go back and get us a dress, and I won't shoot your guts out." He pushed me roughly in front of him and followed closely behind me as I walked back to Laila.

He had his gun pressed against my back, and it filled my body with fear. I put my hand to my stomach and took a deep breath. I couldn't even run out to alert someone. I had to think of something fast.

I quickly glanced at the clock on the wall. Damiano would be here shortly since I was supposed to close soon. We just had to hang on tight until then.

"Okay, let's get you into a dress." I gave Laila a warm smile, trying to let her know everything was going to be okay, but she looked like she was about to pass out.

"You keep that open." He said before I could close the curtain. I glared at him, but he just waved the gun, daring me to defy him. I slowly let go of the curtain and turned my back to him, trying to cover Laila as much as possible as she shakily undressed.

I clenched my jaw. No one deserved to be stuck with a douche like him.

I moved out of the way after she finished getting dressed, allowing him to see her. He looked her up and down, not impressed with what he was seeing, and all I wanted was to spit at him in the face.

"If only she had the body for it." He looked at her with disgust. "You! Let me see it on you." His sinister smile returned as he looked at me. He leaned back on the couch with his arms and legs spread, still holding the gun in his hand.

"That's not a service I provide." I spat out.

The smirk slowly faded from his face, and was replaced by an icy, lifeless expression as his eyes bore into mine. In an instant, he sprang from the couch so fast I had barely time to react as he stood before me. Laila let out a gasp and backed away, and I tried to step away from him, but he gripped my arm and pressed the gun against me again.

"You do as I say, you fucking whore! Get undressed and let me see those fucking tits." He yelled, his grip tightening and making me clench my jaw in pain.

"Then let go of me." I hissed out. He released me but remained up in my face to watch me. My heart was about to burst out of my chest, and I was trying my best to keep calm, but it was so fucking hard.

I slowly untucked my shirt from my jeans. Right now, I couldn't be happier with the outfit I wore and not a dress; even happier when I felt I had my pen tucked in my back pocket.

I grabbed the pen and looked anywhere I could try to stab him hard enough to cause damage to run away.

"Hurry up!" He loosely waved the gun around, and I acted without thinking. I swung my arm out and pushed the gun away from his hand, making him drop the gun to the floor with a loud clang.

"You little–" He hissed out between his clenched teeth and lunged after me.

My eyes shot open wide and backed away when he came at me. I gripped the pen tightly in my hand and aimed right for his eye when he was close enough.

"Fucking bitch!" He screamed with his hands up to his face while stumbling back.

"Laila, run!" I yelled, and she made a run for it with me behind her. Only one of us had to make it out for help to get here.

A sharp, agonized cry tore from my lips as my hair was cruelly yanked, wrenching me to the ground. My groan was silenced when the back of my head collided with the floor. Before I could recover, he grabbed me, hoisted me up, and forced me onto the couch with a brutal shove.

"Look what you've done, you little slut! You should have minded your own business! But no, you wanted to play the hero." He let out a sadistic laugh with one eye open. He was on top of me, his lower body on my legs while he held my arms down.

My breath came fast and heavy as I tried to get out of his iron grip, but every time I moved, he added more of his weight, almost crushing me. It made me panic in fear that he would crush my stomach.

"I fucking bought her! She is my little toy to fuck, and you let her run!"

"You deserve to rot in hell." I sneered, but it seemed he only took pleasure from the words. He had the scariest smile on his lips and leaned closer to my face.

"And I will bring you with me for making my possession escape." He malevolently laughed. "You will replace her and succumb to my needs. You will call me Master as I fuck you and tear you apart." His tone was cruel and so sadistic.

I looked at him with disgust. So much I spat at him right in the face.

My head whipped to the other side with a searing bolt of pain on the entire right side of my face. I struggled to focus, trying to blink away the dizziness. I snapped back to reality when I felt him tear my shirt open.

"Get off me!" I screamed at the top of my lungs, thrashing around to break free. My voice was silenced when he stuffed my mouth with a piece of clothing. He forcibly pulled down my bra and his hand roughly grabbed my breast. Tears ran down the side of my face as I tried to fight.

But he was too heavy and too strong.

"You look so breakable." He fucking moaned. "I can't wait to break you, my Crystal."

I froze and stopped breathing when I felt him trying to unbutton my jeans.

No... Please, no.

My throat tightened, and I felt like I couldn't breathe. I squeezed my eyes shut, not wanting to witness what was about to happen to me.

The weight on top of me suddenly disappeared. I lost my balance and fell to the floor. I spat out the piece of clothing as I shakily got up on my hands and knees, gasping for air.

"No!" I flinched when a pair of hands grabbed me.

"It's me." I relaxed when I saw it was Giovanni.

He had a frown on his face as he looked at me, but he quickly looked away as he took off his jacket and gave it to me. I looked down and immediately tried to cover myself. He had completely exposed me.

I slipped my arms into the jacket and pulled it around me tightly to make sure I was covered. The sound of shouting, groans, and hissing made me look.

Only to see Damiano furiously punching the man's now bloodied face.

"I. Will. Fucking. Kill. You!" Damiano sneered out with each powerful punch. I heard bones crack as he made his face completely unrecognizable.

"Don't look." Giovanni pulled me into his chest and covered my ears. I jumped when I heard multiple gunshots echoing in the room.

Giovanni stepped away when Damiano stood in front of me, splattered in blood.

"That fucking son of a bitch." Damiano's eyes were blazing with anger, holding such a murderous look on his face. "Are you hurt?" He pulled me into him, holding me tightly, and felt around my body to see if I had any injuries.

"I'm okay." I breathed out. I was shaking as I held him tight.

I was somewhat... okay. It was a close call. A really fucking close one. I took a deep breath as I tried my best to compose myself. I had to find out if Laila was okay.

"Damiano, I'm okay." I leaned back to look at him, even though I was sure it didn't look like I was.

"He touched you. He fucking touched you!" Damiano cupped my face, his chest rapidly rising and falling with anger the more he looked at me. "Are you in pain? Fuck! Do you - Let's get you to a doctor."

"I'm okay. I don't need a doctor. I need to find Laila." I stepped away from him before he could carry me. "Oh, God..." I gagged when I made the mistake of looking over at the man. He was in a massive pool of blood, his face decorated with bullet holes.

I had to try my best not to puke.

"Who's Laila?" Damiano asked, blocking my view and led me away from the mess.

"Did you see a woman run out?" I asked Luca. He was standing near the door, making sure everything was okay from his end. I stopped in my tracks, confused, when he shook his head.

If they didn't see anyone go out, then where did she go?

"Althaia." Damiano grabbed my hand and turned me to look at him. I let out a sigh.

"Laila, she was -" I stopped, noticing a shadow from the desk. I hurried over there and crouched down. "Hey, Laila. It's okay, you're safe now." I said quietly and got down on my knees to be on her eye level.

She had her ears covered and eyes squeezed shut. I carefully placed a hand on her shoulder, trying not to scare her too much, but she still flinched.

"I-I'm so-sorry." She whimpered, opening her teary eyes. My heart couldn't take it anymore and I embraced her tightly, whispering she was safe.

Laila sobbed in my arms, and I glanced at Damiano, who met my gaze with a frown before turning his attention to Laila.

"She needed help. I had to do something."

Forty-Eight

ALTHAIA

After she had calmed down a bit, I handed Laila a bottle of water. We remained on the floor under the desk, not wanting her to witness the awful sight of that man.

"Are you okay?" I asked her quietly. She clutched the water bottle to her chest as she kept glancing at Damiano but would quickly look away again.

She nodded, taking a deep breath before speaking.

"You have blood on your face..." She whispered.

"Oh..." I said in surprise and blindly tried to wipe my face with Giovanni's jacket.

"Did..." Laila swallowed hard, then whispered. "Did he do this to you?" Her wide eyes darted quickly to Damiano. I followed her gaze, forgetting his hands were covered in blood.

"Oh, no! No, he's with me. He won't do anything to harm me. Don't worry, we're safe with him." I promised with a smile.

She let out a breath of relief, and her whole body seemed to relax.

"Laila, stay down here for a bit, okay? I'll be right back." She nodded and pulled her legs into her chest. It was obvious to see how broken she was, and I didn't dare to imagine what she must have gone through.

I pulled Damiano away to talk to him quietly, being careful not to look into the other room.

"You should probably wash your hands. You look kind of scary right now." I grimaced as I looked at his hands and clothes. "And I need you to take us back to my place."

"Why?" He frowned.

"She needs a safe place to stay for the night, and all my things are at home." I told him quietly, but he wasn't liking it at all.

"You don't know her. Why are you helping her?" Damiano questioned, making me look at him in shock.

"She was *sold* to him." I could barely believe my own words. Damiano had his blank expression on his face, not allowing me to see what he was thinking. "Can we talk about it later and just go home?" I pleaded.

"Fine. Get her, but don't look in the room." He said sternly, and I gave a nod, keeping my eyes down as I returned to Laila under the desk.

"Laila, would you be comfortable coming home with me? Get cleaned up, eat, and have a good night's sleep? I promise you will be safe."

Laila stared at me with hesitation.

"Why are you helping me?" She was suspicious, and I didn't blame her one bit.

"I was almost a victim of human trafficking. The only reason I'm not, is thanks to Damiano, the man who was here before. He... took care of it and kept me safe. I can't imagine what you must have gone through...but if I can help you, even if it's just a little, then I will." I gave her a warm smile.

Her eyes watered, sniffing before wiping her tears away and taking a deep breath.

"He... he won't come after me?"

"He won't."

"Are you sure?" Laila's voice was laced with so much fear.

"I promise you. You will never see him again." I assured her. It was a promise I could be sure of, and I hoped the scumbag was burning in hell as we spoke.

"Thank you...I don't know your name." She mumbled in embarrassment.

"I'm Althaia."

"Thank you, Althaia."

The ride back home was quiet as I sat in the backseat with Laila. She clung to me and kept her head down whenever the others came close.

"This is the guest bedroom, and the bathroom is right there. I will get you some clothes to change into. Take all the time you need, okay?" Laila nodded after I made sure she would be all right.

"Come here." Damiano closed the door to my bedroom and pulled me into him. I let out a relieved breath and let myself relax in his arms. "Are you really okay?" He asked softly.

"Yes, just shaken up. I'll be fine." I reassured him. He took a step back to look at me, a crease between his brows.

"You're helping the girl. Why?"

"What do you mean, why? She was being mistreated by him, and not to mention sold to that sadistic bastard." I explained with a frown.

"At the expense of your own safety? What were you thinking?!" He was fuming with anger, and I watched him in shock.

"I saw a woman who needed help, so I helped!"

"You put yourself at risk, Althaia. It wasn't just your life at stake, but our baby's as well. He could have pulled that fucking trigger, and I would have found you dead." Damiano clenched his fists.

"It's not like I tried to take him down. I wanted to call for help, but he took my phone. He didn't shoot me, and I'm fine now." I said dismissively and tried to walk away, but he caged me between his arms against my desk.

"No, thank God he fucking didn't. What you did was reckless!"

"Did you expect me just to turn a blind eye to it and leave her with that psychopath?!"

"Yes. You had absolutely no business interfering." He simply said, and I gaped at how little he cared.

"I can't believe you right now." I shook my head and stepped away from him.

"What chance did you stand, Althaia? That fucking bastard touched you. He fucking touched you! And he was going to end you once he was done with you. What would you have gained from putting yourself at risk for some woman?" He questioned with venom in his voice.

"Don't you think I know that?! But I only suffered for a bit while she had to suffer for God knows how long." I felt my eyes water as I spoke. "Maybe you can shut it all down and not care, but I can't. If I can help someone, then I will, and I will not apologize for it." I snapped and angrily wiped away the tears that had escaped.

Damiano slowly walked up to me. He placed his hands on my cheeks, wiping away the tears that didn't seem to want to stop.

"You're right. I don't care about other people. I care about you only, and I don't fuck around when it comes to your safety. You put yourself and our baby in danger, and that is making me really *fucking pissed* at you." He said the words with a quiet voice and a blank stare before leaving my room.

I stood frozen, my throat tightening as I fought back tears.

I sat in the living room in front of the lit fireplace with Laila after we had gotten something to eat. With the sound of crackling from the burning wood, we drank a calming herbal tea I had prepared, both of us lost in thoughts.

I wrapped myself in a blanket after giving Laila one. I was feeling cold. It was probably due to the shock and being upset about the argument with Damiano.

After he left, I felt sick and threw up until nothing came out anymore. I took a hot shower after and made sure my skin was scrubbed raw and cleaned myself from any blood that had gotten on me.

I hadn't seen Damiano since we fought, and I didn't know where he went either. He was pissed at me, and I didn't know what to do. It was not like I couldn't understand where he was coming from, but I still didn't regret trying to help Laila.

"He...cares about you." Laila quietly broke the silence. She was more relaxed after seeing she was truly safe here.

"I know." I smiled.

"I haven't seen a man look at a woman like that before." She kept her gaze down at the mug in her hands.

"What do you mean?"

"He can't stop looking at you. His eyes follow you everywhere... Not in a sexualized way but in a caring way. I haven't seen that from a man before." She gave the tiniest smile and looked at me. I gave a sad one back, my heart breaking for her.

"I hope I didn't get you in too much trouble. I didn't mean to, but I overheard you a bit when I wanted to ask for a towel." Laila looked back down at the mug.

"Don't worry about it. He's just very protective of me and is a little upset with me for putting myself at risk. Maybe a little more so because I'm pregnant." I let out a small chuckle to lighten the mood.

Laila gasped, looking at me with big eyes.

"Pregnant or not, I still stand by my actions, and I don't regret it one bit." I said before she could say anything about it.

Her eyes started to glisten, and I scooted closer to her, holding her hand in mine.

"I don't know how to thank you enough. You've saved my life. No one has ever tried to help...and even sitting here feels unreal. I'm scared it's all a dream, and I will wake up soon. Back with him."

"He won't ever hurt you again. You're free. You can do whatever you want now. Go wherever you want."

"I–I want to go back to my family. I haven't seen them in years." Her voice cracked, and she broke down.

I placed our mugs on the coffee table and pulled her into me as she sobbed. I had to bite down on my lip as it trembled, but tears still escaped as I couldn't hold them in.

How can people be so cruel?

Laila slowly opened up and told me she was from Portugal and came to New York to study. She was out with some friends and left earlier than the others because she felt unwell.

"I didn't know it back then, but I got drugged. I don't know what happened, but I blacked out. When I woke up, I was with a ton of other girls." She whispered. I closed my eyes, preparing myself for what I was about to hear.

"...We... We were... prepared to be sold. They trained us how to be a good slave for our... Master." Laila's voice was shaking, her eyes wide and traumatized.

I couldn't believe my ears as I listened to everything. I cried with her about the inhuman things she had to go through to survive. It made me hold her tightly, desperately wanting to comfort her as much as possible.

Laila was exhausted, and I walked her back to the guest bedroom to make sure she would sleep okay. I sighed as I walked downstairs again as Damiano was on my mind.

I looked out of the window at the backyard, surprised to find Damiano there. He had taken a seat in the lounge chair, his eyes already on me.

I grabbed a blanket and wrapped it around me as I stepped out, slowly walking up to him, but stopped when I saw the pack of cigarettes on the table. He had stopped smoking since I couldn't tolerate the smell. I hated that I had pissed him off to the point he needed to smoke to calm down.

"I didn't smoke. Come here." Damiano's deep voice rang out as he held out his hand for me to take. I walked up to him, placing my hand in his, and stepped in between his legs.

"Are you still mad at me?" I asked quietly.

"I am." He replied, but sat me down on his lap, his hand immediately caressing my stomach. I sighed and rested my head on his shoulder.

"How are you feeling?" Damiano asked.

"Still okay."

"Nauseous?"

"Not anymore."

Damiano let out a sigh of relief, his touch gentle as he caressed the side of my head.

"I'm still not going to apologize for what I did." I said quietly. "I kept thinking 'what if it was my daughter?' I would be so grateful if anyone stepped in to help." I explained softly.

"I know, baby." Damiano kissed the top of my head. "Where does she want to go?" He asked and I looked at him.

"Her family is in Portugal. She wants to go there."

"Fine. I will have Raffaele get her documents ready by tomorrow morning. Whatever she needs, I'll make sure she has it, and is brought safely to her family."

"Really?" I breathed out, afraid I heard wrong.

"On one condition." He looked at me with a dead-serious expression. "This is the last time you pull shit like that." He scowled, but I couldn't help but smile.

I wrapped my arms around his neck as I looked into his still firm expression.

"Okay." I whispered, wanting to put it behind us already. "Thank you."

"I'm only doing it for you."

"I know." I placed a small kiss on his lips, and his hold tightened around me. "I love you." I caressed his cheek with a smile, and his expression softened.

"And I love you. You reckless woman." He scoffed, having me laughing before pulling him in for another kiss.

Forty-Nine

ALTHAIA

Laila was finally on her way to rejoin her family, and we had sent Giovanni with her to ensure her safe arrival. I had packed a bag for her, containing all the necessities and some money, so she wouldn't have to worry for a while and could simply reconnect with her family. I made her promise to keep me updated and let me know if she needed anything.

My heart swelled with happiness knowing that she was finally free, and I hoped that she would receive all the help she needed to live her life to the fullest.

I was getting ready for bed while Damiano was downstairs on the phone with Lorenzo. Since he was here, Lorenzo was to make sure everything went smoothly.

The velvety jewelry box on my desk caught my eye, and I opened it carefully. Once again, I found myself entranced by the breathtaking and opulent necklace.

When was I ever supposed to wear this? I snorted when I imagined myself casually walking around and doing grocery shopping with this around my neck.

I bit down on my lip as I thought of what Damiano said to me that night.

"I want you to wear it. And nothing else."

I listened for any movements coming toward my bedroom. When I heard nothing, I pulled my nightgown over my head and took out the Tiffany Yellow Diamond necklace.

I let my hair fall around me as I gazed in the mirror, in awe of how it sparkled beautifully against my naked body.

I turned off the light, only leaving my bedside lamp to illuminate the room. I lay down in the middle of the bed with my legs bent to pose seductively.

My heart was beating fast when I could hear his faint footsteps coming closer. For some reason, I was nervous to lie here with only the necklace around my neck, even though I shouldn't be.

Damiano has seen me naked hundreds of times already but waiting for him with a fifty-million-dollar necklace around my neck made me feel shy.

My heart fluttered when the door opened, his eyes immediately finding mine as he stopped at the door. Then they slowly trailed down on my body, taking his time, drinking in the sight in front of him.

He stepped closer, his eyes never once leaving my body as if to make sure he saw it all. He grabbed a chair from my desk and took a seat at the foot of the bed.

"Spread your legs." Damiano's deep voice went low in command, and that was enough to send a pool of heat down between my thighs.

I slowly spread my legs for him, his eyes watching intently at my most intimate part. I never took my eyes off him either, watching how he continued to drink in every inch of my body.

"Fucking gorgeous." He whispered, making me blush at his words.

Damiano gave me that half-smirk that made him look so devilish. His eyes were dark and filled with hunger, ready to pounce on his prey. My tongue swiftly wet my lower lip before taking it in between my teeth. It didn't go unnoticed as his eyes immediately looked at my lips, making my entire body tingle with excitement.

"Touch yourself." Damiano leaned back, looking into my eyes, and my heart was still beating fast at the intensity of his stare. "Let me see how you play with that sweet pussy of yours."

My mouth opened slightly at his request, and I could feel my cheeks getting warm. I swallowed down my shyness and slowly trailed my fingers down my stomach, making sure his eyes were following my every move, and came to a stop right between my legs.

I slid a finger along my slit, feeling how wet I already was.

"Oh, fuck baby." Damiano lightly grunted, spreading his legs, and I saw the hard bulge in his pants.

Feeling more courageous, I slipped a finger inside. Then a second. I slowly worked my way to my clit, pleasuring myself the way I knew best. Damiano was watching every single move as I switched between fingering myself and circling my clit.

"Tell me, piccola, what would you think about when you pleasure yourself?" His voice was deep and laced with so much lust, I moaned. He grunted, unbuckling his belt as he freed his hard cock. I watched as his hand moved up and down his shaft in slow strokes.

"I would think of you…" I breathed out. "Every time." I moved my fingers faster as I felt hot from his gaze and the way he was stroking himself. I was burning with so much desire and need to feel him inside of me. Now.

"Damiano…" My breath quickened as I felt the familiar tension building up in the pit of my stomach.

"Keep going. Tell me what you would think about."

I let out a moan as I rocked my hips along my fingers.

"I would think of the way you'd suck my clit and slap my pussy until I came." I panted, watching the tip of his cock glistening with pre-cum.

"I would think of how you would suck my breasts…" I said, grabbing a handful. "Pinch my nipples." I continued, trailing my fingers over my nipples before pinching them as he would.

Damiano's breathing was heavy as he gripped his cock as the pre-cum dripped down. I licked my lips, wanting nothing more than to take him in my mouth.

He got up and removed his shirt, exposing all of his tattoos and his incredibly rock-hard body. He slid out of the rest of his clothing, leaving him naked at the foot of my bed, stroking himself faster.

"Oh, fuck…" I moaned, my orgasm nearing.

"Come for me, baby. Let me see how you make yourself come to the thought of me." Damiano growled.

I played with my clit until my toes curled and my back arched as the wave of pleasure rippled through my body, making me tremble as I let out a small cry.

"Atta girl. You came so beautifully for me." Damiano praised.

I let out a smile as I closed my eyes, calming down from my high. I opened my eyes when I felt the bed dip. He held my gaze as he spread my legs further apart, trailing his lips on the inside of my thigh, giving small kisses as he made his way to my pussy.

My hands fisted the sheet when I felt his hot breath on my pussy, gasping as his tongue tasted me and making my legs tremble even more.

"So sweet…" Damiano grunted and shoved his tongue inside my pussy.

"Please…" I moaned, throwing my head back into the pillow. I wanted him to take me already, filling me up with his thick cock.

Damiano continued his way up, plastering small kisses on my stomach till he reached my breasts. My eyes rolled to the back of my head as his tongue swirled around my nipple, sucking hard and giving that mixture of pleasure and pain that I loved so much.

I moved my hands to touch him, only for him to grab my wrists and pin them above my head while he sucked my breasts. He made his way up, kissing my neck and jaw before stopping right at my ear, grunting.

"You have no idea how fucking beautiful you are." He whispered, his voice hoarse.

Damiano nibbled my earlobe before trailing his nose down to my neck again, sucking hard on my skin and having me squirm in excitement and impatience.

He looked at me and softly caressed my cheek with his fingertips.

"I love you, okay?" He said.

"I know you do." I smiled.

His eyes darkened, leaning down to my ear.

"Good. Because I'm about to fuck you like I don't and watch your pussy drip with my cum." He growled and slammed his cock inside of me. He caught me off guard and made me gasp at the sudden feeling of him filling me up.

He caught my moan in his mouth as he hungrily invaded my mouth and dominated my tongue as he continued to thrust inside of me with hard and fast moves.

Damiano pulled out, and flipped me around.

"Fuck, come here, piccola." He pinned my arms behind my back and pulled me up on my knees with my back tightly pressed against his chest so I couldn't move. With one arm around my waist, he roughly entered me from behind.

"Oh, God!" My head fell back on his shoulder, letting the intensity of the pleasure take over while his hands roamed my body. The way he touched my breasts while the other went down to my pussy and played with my clit.

It was all so overwhelming I could barely keep up and catch my breath. His thrusts were fast and hard; like a beast that had been unleashed as he kept fucking me relentlessly from behind.

"Say my name, baby." He growled, sounding more like a beast than a man. And it had me going fucking crazy.

"Damiano..." I moaned, and I trembled when my second wave of orgasm was near.

He sent a sharp slap on my clit.

"Again!"

"Fuck, Damiano!" I cried out, my entire body jolting at the intense wave of pleasure that erupted in the pit of my stomach. He let out a strangled grunt as I clenched around him.

He let out a roar as he filled me with his cum.

I looked at Damiano's sleeping form next to me, grinning that I had finally woken up before him. His hair was messy, making him look so boyish.

"Morning, my love." Damiano greeted with a smile as his eyes remained closed. "Done staring at me?"

"I thought I had woken up before you for once." I chuckled. "How long have you been awake?"

"A while." He finally opened his eyes and placed a small kiss on my lips. "My love?"

"Hmm?"

Damiano let out a sigh.

"Your mother is home."

Fifty

ALTHAIA

I jolted up in a sitting position and looked at Damiano with wide eyes as fear and panic took over my body.

"Breathe, Althaia." Damiano reminded me as he held me, and I drew in a shaky breath.

"She's home early, and–and you're here!" I suddenly realized, now feeling the blood drain from my face.

"I need you to calm down, baby." Damiano placed his hands on my cheeks, and I immediately clung onto his arms as I felt myself panicking like the day before she left. "Slow down... breathe... that's it..." He guided, and I closed my eyes and focused on steadying my breathing to calm down my hammering heart.

I kept listening to his soothing voice, focusing on the way his thumbs were lightly caressing my cheeks and slowly calming me down.

"I'm okay." I let out a breath and opened my eyes again. "She's going to freak out if she sees you here. How am I supposed to sneak you out when you're a giant?!"

"She already saw me." Damiano informed me and didn't look concerned at all.

"Huh? She... what?"

"Your mother came in to see if you were here. I told her to be quiet so you could sleep."

"She saw you, and you told her to be quiet." I stated slowly as I registered his words in my mind.

At this point, I didn't know whether to laugh or cry. My mother saw me in bed with the man she despised. And it wouldn't take a genius to figure out what we have been doing since we were both naked under the blanket.

"God, why?" I groaned. I was fucking mortified.

I headed to the bathroom, thinking it was time to face her and get it over with, like ripping off a band-aid on a hairy spot.

"Damiano!" I hissed at him when I saw my reflection. He just crossed his arms and leaned against the doorframe, looking at me with a smirk.

"Yes, baby?"

"You can't keep doing this!" I gestured to my neck and chest. They were once again covered in red marks.

"Since you don't want to wear a ring yet, I have to be creative." He shrugged and looked at my neck and chest with a satisfied look. "Looks fucking good on you."

"I can't deal with you right now." I huffed and stepped into the shower, a light chuckle escaping his lips as he joined me.

I had Damiano stay in the room as I made my way downstairs to talk to my mother. He wasn't pleased, insisting on being with me in case something happened. I had to explain that his presence would only add to my stress, and I wanted to have a calm conversation.

I felt my nerves building up rapidly, reminding myself to take deep breaths to prevent feeling sick. I had also chosen to wear a turtleneck to conceal the embarrassing red marks. While she had already seen me in bed with him and knew what we had been doing, it didn't mean I had to flaunt it.

Quietly, I made my way to the kitchen in search of her, but it was empty. The freshly brewed coffee suggested she had been there recently.

I continued to the living room and spotted her sitting on the couch, cradling a mug of coffee while her gaze remained fixed on the unlit fireplace. Taking a seat on the opposite couch, I waited for her to say something.

Silence hung in the air, broken only by the sound of her sipping coffee. My stomach churned with unease as we continued to sit in wordless tension.

"How come you're back so soon?" I asked quietly. I couldn't sit in this tense silence anymore and had to say something.

Finally, my mother looked at me, still expressionless, but her eyes were less cold than before she left for her vacation.

"You brought him into my house." She stated calmly, and I stopped breathing again. "How long has he been here?"

"He came the day you left."

"Why?"

"I wasn't feeling well." Her eyes slightly furrowed at my reply. "Did something happen since you're back so soon?" I asked quickly before she could question me about it.

"No."

"Then what?"

My mother let out a sigh before placing her mug on the coffee table.

"I didn't like the way we left things. It's unlike us to be fighting like this."

"I know." I gave a faint smile. The closest we would come to a fight would just be minor disagreements but would always put it behind us minutes later.

"However, I still stand by what I said."

"Why?" My voice came out in a shaky whisper, feeling a lump forming in my throat.

"Non mi fido di te." She said. I looked at her in shock for a split second when hearing that she didn't trust me, then followed her gaze.

Damiano stood right at the entrance to the living room, sending a chilling glare towards my mother.

"Neanch'io" *Likewise.* He replied.

The air in the room grew heavy with tension as their eyes remained fixed on one another.

"Mom, please... you can't mean that." I was trying my best not to cry, as I felt my heart aching once again.

"To be with him will always put you in danger, and bringing a child will only make it worse. Not only would his enemies want you, but also the child. Is that what you want?" My mother replied harshly.

"Why is that the only thing you can think about?" I snapped in frustration.

"Because it's reality." She stated, rising from the couch.

"You don't think I will keep her safe?" Damiano's voice was almost threatening.

"Safe?" She scoffed. "Worked great for you last time, didn't it?"

The sight of him suddenly storming towards my mother with a murderous look on his face made my eyes widen in horror. I quickly stood in front of him, preventing him from getting closer.

"You don't know shit." Damiano sneered, his body tense as he spoke.

"Oh, I know enough." My mother slowly approached us, not fazed by his actions.

"What are you talking about?" I asked.

"You haven't told her?" She made a tsking sound and shook her head.

"Tell me what?" I looked at Damiano, but he continued to ignore me. I clenched my fists tightly, feeling my frustration bubbling.

"What are you doing in my house?" My mother snapped at him.

"Taking care of your daughter since you're failing to do so." He retorted.

"Who do you -"

"Stop!" I shouted while trying to keep them apart before they killed each other. Both of them had me going through a new emotion every two seconds, something my body couldn't handle right now.

I hunched over slightly when nausea overwhelmed me.

Damiano cursed and pulled me into him to look at him.

"Are you okay? Do you feel sick?"

I got out of his hold and rushed to the bathroom, as I couldn't keep my nausea down anymore. Hands pulled my hair away from my face as I puked my guts out. I already knew it was Damiano. It had become his new job to do so whenever I felt sick.

I washed up and went to lie on the couch, feeling stressed and exhausted. The two of them wanting to kill each other wasn't helping one bit.

My mother sighed.

"Already having bad morning sickness?"

"I don't know if it's morning sickness, or if it's because you two are making me upset and stressed to the point I feel sick." I spat out, letting them know how pissed I was.

Damiano placed a hand on my forehead and frowned.

"You're hot. We should get you to a doctor."

"She doesn't need a doctor. She just threw up. It's fine." My mother said, which earned a glare from Damiano, and she glared right back at him.

"If you don't stop, I will make sure neither one of you will see me for the rest of your lives!" I yelled, which caught their attention. Their eyes narrowed with disapproval as I made my threat.

I took a deep breath and rubbed my stomach.

"Ice cream helped with my nausea. Maybe it will help you too?" My mother suggested.

"I will get you some." Damiano said and turned to leave. Suddenly, he paused and glanced back at my mother.

"What kind?"

"Low-fat. Also, vitamins and some ginger help too. Hold on, let me write you a list." She gestured for him to follow her, and they both disappeared into the kitchen.

"What the fuck?" I sat up and stared at their retreating forms. One minute they were ready to kill each other, and the next they were making a grocery list.

I lay back down and placed a hand up to my head.

"I think I'm going crazy..."

"Why are you helping when you're so unhappy about me being pregnant?" I asked my mother after she had sent Damiano away with a list.

"The way we had left things... I'm not proud of it." She admitted. "The need to protect you took over, not having me think clearly. I kept thinking about you and...*him*. Try to understand where I'm coming from as well. He is the most dangerous and feared man. Knowing he has taken a liking to you, and now you're pregnant with his child... It made me panic." Her eyes narrowed as she spoke.

Her words guilt-tripped me because I hadn't considered her perspective. Spending time with Damiano, I have witnessed his gentle and caring side, which often made me forget the fearsome reputation he held.

"To have a baby, it's a blessing, regardless. I'm just concerned that it's with him."

"Mom, I understand, I do. But he cares about me. If I thought he would hurt me, I wouldn't be with him." I explained.

"If he cared about you, he shouldn't be keeping you in the dark. That's not making me want to trust him at all." My mother frowned.

"I know he doesn't tell me everything. He has several times made it clear to me he doesn't want me to get involved. If you could just give him a chance and get to know him, I think you will like him." I said with a smile. It was a long shot, but hell, I just needed them to tolerate each other and get along.

"Just please, don't make me choose between the two of you." Tears welled up in my eyes, and a lump formed in my throat.

My mother pulled me into a tight hug, and I couldn't help but let out a sob as I had longed for her comfort.

"My sweet Althaia, as a mother, it's my job to protect you. But it's also my job to make sure you're happy." She wiped my tears away. Her eyes were glistening too as she gave me a small smile.

"I am happy. I really am. But I don't want to do this without you. I need you." I sniffed.

"I know, honey. You're having a baby... I can't believe you're already making me a grandma." She chuckled and embraced me again.

I held her tightly, a weight lifted from my heart.

Fifty-One
DAMIANO

"Are you staying with me tonight?" Althaia asked as she came out of the bathroom.

My gaze traced down her figure, admiring the way the black nightgown hugged her curves. It was short, showing off her beautiful legs, and the top showed a generous amount of cleavage.

"My eyes are up here." She placed her hands on her hips and raised a brow.

"You don't want me to look?" I grabbed her hips, pulling her in between my legs as I was sitting on her bed.

"Haven't you looked enough?" She wrapped her arms around my neck, giving me a teasing smile.

"Never. I can't get enough of you. Or your tits." I looked back down and buried my face in her breasts. I placed small kisses, making my way up to her neck, feeling her shiver under my touch until I reached her soft lips.

"How are you feeling?" I sat her on my lap and rubbed her stomach. Althaia let out a tired sigh, resting her read on my shoulder.

"Better. I'm happy I got to talk to my mom about it all. She's less upset about the pregnancy, which is good...but I think it will still take some time before she can wrap her head around that it's with you." She said with a hint of guilt.

I shrugged. I didn't give two shits about her mother.

"I don't care what she thinks of me. All I care about is how she treats you." I told her.

Or so help me God, I will lose my fucking shit on that woman.

"You could also try to have an open mind and put your differences aside. Maybe try not to kill each other every single minute."

I smirked, thinking about how her mother would be one less problem if I made her disappear.

"How's your nausea?"

"The ice cream helped a lot!" She said with surprise. "Finally, something that works because I'm tired of throwing up." She groaned, and I placed a kiss on top of her head.

"I will stock up the freezer for you."

"Thank you, you're the best." Althaia smiled brightly, giving me a quick peck on the lips.

"Anything for you, baby." I let out a small smile when I watched her cheeks get flushed. Fuck , I loved it so much.

"I will be round and rolling before you know it." She let out a tired chuckle.

"I wouldn't mind. Shouldn't you be showing by now?" I asked. I couldn't help but constantly glance at her stomach, hoping for a sign of a growing belly.

"You need to be patient." Althaia shook her head in amusement and looked down at her stomach. "It isn't much, but something is happening." She raised her nightgown around her waist.

My lips curved into a smile, and my heart swelled with warmth. It was subtle, but definitely there.

"It's cute, right?" She grinned and pulled down her nightgown again.

"Very cute." I chuckled, having never used that word before.

"Can't wait for the ultrasound. It's probably so freakishly tiny, don't you think, agápi mou?" She asked.

My smile never faded as I gazed down at her, hearing her excitement as she talked about our growing baby.

"You should call me that more often." I told her.

"My love?"

I nodded.

"I like it." I admitted. She never called me anything besides my name. Even though I loved whenever she called my name, there was something about it when she called me that in her tongue.

"I can do that." She smiled. I pulled her into me and kissed her softly as she smiled against my lips.

There was a gentle knock on the door, and Althaia quickly grabbed the small blanket from her desk chair, wrapping it around herself to hide the red marks.

She closed the door, her eyes catching the frown on my face. Her mother was someone I needed to discover who she truly was. I didn't believe for a moment that she had entirely abandoned her former life. She possessed too much knowledge to be out of the world.

"You know, you have to at least try to get along with my mom." Althaia urged again with a small smile.

"What did she want?" I didn't bother hiding my dislike toward her mother.

"Just asking if you were going to spend the night, which I'm assuming you are?"

"I'm not going to leave you here alone." My frown deepened. The last time they were alone, I found her crying.

"You know I'm not alone."

"I don't trust her." I told her. Part of me wanted to tell her why, so she would understand, but that would only distress her and possibly make her sick again.

I had to be mindful of the impact my words could have on her and our baby. She didn't need the extra stress, especially with everything she was already going through.

"So stubborn..." Althaia muttered under her breath but then looked at me with a hesitant expression. "Earlier, my mom said something that made you...angry."

"Let's go to bed. You're tired." I rose to my feet to undress, ignoring what she was trying to ask.

"What was it about?" Althaia asked. I turned my back to her, closing my eyes for a second.

"It was nothing." I dismissed her, but knowing how strong her curiosity was, she wouldn't let it go before she got an answer.

"It didn't seem like nothing when you reacted like that -"

"Althaia, drop it!" I snapped.

I briefly closed my eyes to calm down before I faced her. Shock was written on her face.

"I'm sorry. I didn't mean to raise my voice." I stepped closer to her, but she backed away from me. Althaia avoided making eye contact with me as she silently made her way to the bed and slipped under the blanket.

"Don't be like that." I sighed.

"I'm not being anything. I'm tired and I want to sleep." She turned off the bedside lamp and turned her back to me, lying as close to the edge as she could.

I clenched my fists, pissed at myself for reacting like that and making her upset. I couldn't tell her about it. I wasn't ready to share that part of my life with her yet. Not when it still made my blood boil.

I slipped into bed with her. Althaia still had her back turned to me, which was unlike her. She liked to sleep in the middle of the bed, and preferably in my arms. But she was letting me know she was pissed at me.

I wrapped my arm around her and pulled her closer to me. She tried to move away, but it only made me tighten my hold on her.

"I'm sorry. Just let me hold you tonight." I whispered to her. She was about to move away again but decided against it and finally relaxed against me.

"Goodnight, my love." I kissed her bare shoulder as I caressed her body, knowing it would make her fall asleep faster.

I knew she deserved to know so much more, but right now, I couldn't get myself to let her know about that part of my life.

Not yet.

After dropping Althaia off at work, I headed straight to the airport. I arrived just in time to see Lorenzo, Arianna, Cara, and Antonio get out of the private jet.

Althaia had mentioned several times that she was missing Arianna and Cara. Naturally, I would go above and beyond to ensure her happiness. That was why I arranged for them to come for a surprise visit. Plus, she was upset with me, and I hoped this might help her forgive me.

However, there was a deeper purpose behind their visits, and that was why Lorenzo and Antonio were also here.

"I need to talk to you." I told them when they were close.

I sent a look in Lorenzo's way, and he responded with a curt nod, gesturing for Cara to step into the vehicle. I took a few steps away, creating enough distance so she wouldn't hear anything.

"Antonio, I need you to follow Jacinta wherever she goes and report everything back to me. Don't let yourself be seen. Not even to Althaia." Giving a quick nod, he made his way towards the car I had sent for him.

"Did you get the decryptor from Raffaele?" I asked Arianna once Lorenzo had joined us.

"I did, but what's going on?" She asked.

"I need to know what her mother is doing. We know she's definitely still in the game, but the question is with whom." I told them.

"What set you off?" Lorenzo asked.

"She knows too fucking much. She knows about... *Sienna*." I clenched my jaw.

"What? How?" Arianna raised her brows in surprise.

"I don't know, but that's what I want to figure out. Whoever those contacts of hers may be, I want them gone." I sneered. "Lorenzo, see if you can get something out of Cara. Maybe she knows something that can tip us off. Arianna, there is a safe in their boutique that only her mother has access to. It's a digital one. Use the decryptor to get the password. Lorenzo and I will take care of the rest."

I was ready to figure out who Jacinta Celano truly was.

Fifty-Two

ALTHAIA

"...Is she being for real..."

"...Should we wake her up?"

"...Let her sleep."

I let out a loud and annoyed sigh by the hushed voices that disturbed my dreams. I turned around, hoping to resume my peaceful sleep.

"How charming."

I frowned at the voice. Why were there people talking, and what were they doing in my room? As I tried to drown out the noise and drift back to sleep, my eyes shot open as reality crashed down on me.

I was in the boutique, not my own room.

In an instant, I sat up and blinked rapidly, trying to fully awaken my senses.

"So unprofessional of you, Thaia!"

Still in a confused daze, I turned to the voice and saw Cara, her eyes filled with amusement.

"Huh...?" I said, trying to figure out what was going on and if that was truly Cara who had magically appeared in front of me.

"Shit, that must have been one good nap."

I turned to the other voice and saw that Arianna was also here. I rubbed my eyes, hoping to clear my blurry vision. My eyes slowly widened when I realized I wasn't dreaming, and they were truly in front of me.

"Oh my God!" I squealed and jumped up from the couch. I immediately embraced them both tightly. "What are you doing here?!"

"I could feel you were missing us. Me the most, so I thought, why not come and visit you? I have a sixth sense or something." Cara grinned and Arianna playfully rolled her eyes.

"Your man said you were miserable without us." She said with a smirk.

"I didn't say that." Damiano looked blankly at Arianna.

"I'm paraphrasing." She gave him a dismissive wave.

I chuckled and went to him, feeling the warmth of his embrace as I wrapped my arms around him.

"Thank you." I whispered, grateful for the effort he had put in to surprise me with a visit. Damiano gave me a small smile and kissed the top of my head.

"Lorenzo." I greeted him and gently patted his arm, causing a slight upward curl of his lips as he met my gaze.

"Althaia." He replied, patting my head in return.

"I have never seen two people being so awkward with each other. For fuck's sake, you are family now! Just hug each other!" Arianna practically yelled.

I felt a strong shove from behind, making me lose my footing and nearly fall over if it wasn't for Lorenzo's quick reflexes. I turned around to scowl at her, only for Damiano to hold me, checking if I was alright, before shooting a menacing glare at Arianna.

"Careful. Don't push her."

"Oh, relax! You're acting as if she's made of glass." Arianna scoffed and gave Damiano a disapproving look.

"It's fine." I reassured him before looking at Arianna. "Just remember, karma is a bitch, and you might just trip down a staircase." I gave her a wicked smile.

"I dare you. I will knock you out in a second." She winked, making me laugh. I had truly missed them. Arianna and Cara became the sisters I never had, their presence bringing me so much happiness.

"Where's mom?" Cara asked.

"I think she went to the bank or something. I wasn't really listening. She should be back soon." I looked at the time, and my brows raised when I saw I had slept for a good hour.

"How long have you been here?" I grimaced, hoping they hadn't been watching me for too long.

"We came like half an hour ago. How can you just sleep at work like that?" Cara laughed at me, making me let out an awkward laugh as I scratched the back of my head.

"I was tired, and it's a comfortable couch."

"You snore."

I whipped my head to look at Lorenzo. A small smile played at the corners of his lips, revealing his slight amusement.

"No, I don't!" I felt my face getting hot as I frowned at him.

"You do." Arianna and Cara said at the same time, making me gape at them.

"Shut up! I don't." I looked at Damiano, who had a small smile on his lips. "...Do I?" I half-whispered to him.

"Just a bit." He confirmed, and I blushed with embarrassment.

"Well, thank you all for visiting. You may now go back home." I walked away from them, not being able to handle the embarrassment.

"Hey, get your ass back here. I'm a customer!" Arianna called after me.

"For what?" I asked.

"First of all, my brother is getting married soon. Second, I just want to spend money." She said and went through the racks of dresses.

"All right, then." I shrugged as I went to grab my things.

After measuring her, I picked out a few different styles for her to try that I thought would look great on her. And for Cara too, since she also wanted to fill up her closet. I loved that we didn't only specialize in custom-designed dresses, but we also offered a wide selection of high-end dresses for sale.

Damiano and Lorenzo got comfortable on the couch and watched me go back and forth between the two changing rooms. Lorenzo either nodded or shook his head at whatever dress Cara had tried on, while Arianna tried to get an opinion out of Damiano.

"Uh, this one is sexy!" Cara pulled the curtain to the side and stepped out.

She wore a tight burgundy dress that hugged her curves. It was *very* short, and the cups were too small for her breasts, making them look insanely huge. Before I could give my opinion, Lorenzo walked so fast over to Cara, blocking her from the rest of us.

"Change. Now." Lorenzo almost growled out. He gently nudged Cara's back inside the changing room and closed the curtain.

"You don't like it?" Cara laughed, knowing exactly what she was doing.

"You can't wear it." Lorenzo said firmly. He was still standing in front of the curtain, making sure she was changing.

"I wasn't planning on wearing it in public, you know." She popped her head out for a second and winked before handing him the dress.

"Ew, gross! Other people are present, Cara." I gave her a disgusted look before making my way to Damiano. In an instant, he took hold of me and seated me on his lap.

"Why are you acting all innocent? As if you haven't been fucking like crazy after being away from each other for so long."

"Cara!" I shouted after her.

"How about you don't talk about sex and my brothers in the same freaking sentence? You're making my ears bleed!" Arianna yelled out to Cara, which only made her laugh as she continued to talk about it.

"You're overworking yourself again." Damiano frowned while rubbing my back.

"I'm fine." I gave a reassuring smile.

"You fell asleep. If you're tired, close and get some rest."

"I was bored and had nothing better to do, so I took a nap. Trust me, I'm okay." I gave him a quick kiss on the lips. Damiano still didn't look convinced, but let it go.

"I think this is the one!" Arianna pulled the curtain open.

She came out in a breathtaking one-sleeved, shimmering lucite green dress. The bodice hugged her waist, highlighting her figure, while the skirt cascaded gracefully with a generous slit on the left side. The dress looked absolutely stunning against her sun-kissed skin and golden-brown hair.

"Wow!" I said, stunned at how beautiful she looked.

"I know, right?" Arianna stepped onto the small stage to get a good look at herself in front of the large mirrors and even spun around so we could see all of it.

"This is definitely the one! Right, Damiano?" I asked, and he took a quick glance at the dress.

"Sure." Damiano shrugged.

"Would it kill you to give a compliment?" Arianna scowled and placed her hands on her hips.

"Yes." He smirked. Her gaze suddenly shifted to my stomach, watching as Damiano tenderly rubbed it.

I quickly grabbed his hand to stop him and rose to my feet. I had gotten so used to him doing it that it made me forget it looked odd when they didn't know the reason.

"Let me see!" Cara came out of the dressing room, gaping. "Yes, that's definitely the one!"

"So, which one of my brothers is treating me today?" Arianna asked, looking back and forth between Damiano and Lorenzo with a bright, sweet smile on her lips while I packed their dresses.

"Didn't I tell you not to depend on a man to buy you anything?" Damiano said.

"And I'm not. This is my brothers spoiling me." She held her hand out, wiggling her fingers and waiting for one of them to give her their credit card.

"More like demanding." I pointed out. She shushed me as she continued to smile sweetly.

"Here." Lorenzo handed her his card, and she happily snatched it out of his hand.

"That's why you're my favorite brother! You're so cheap, Damiano."

"I bought you a car last week. Which you crashed." He crossed his arms, a crease forming between his brows.

"You were in a car accident!" I shrieked out in shock.

"Not really. Raffaele purposely drove into my car for being a sore loser."

"Why in the world would he do that?"

"We were racing, and I beat him. He was jealous that my car was faster than his, so he crashed into it." She shrugged.

I shook my head in disbelief.

"Thaia, remember that one time we took mom's car, and we accidentally dented it in a parking lot?" Cara laughed, making me smile at the memory.

"Don't you mean *you* dented it? You were the one who drove the car, yet I was the one who got spanked with the wooden spoon." I scoffed.

"Your mom hit you with a wooden spoon?" Arianna looked at me, both surprised and amused.

"Mhm. My mom is not shy with the wooden spoon and would pull it out whenever we misbehaved. Cara, being the favorite child, got out of it almost every time. By the way, how does it feel to be the favorite child?" I asked with a fake, sweet smile.

"Amazing! You should try to be one." She grinned with a wink, and I flipped her off.

"It was always me and Michael who got in trouble. Actually, Michael got spanked the most." I chuckled.

As soon as I mentioned Michael, I could already feel Damiano's gaze burning into me. I purposely kept my eyes down as I bagged the last dress.

"Who's Michael?" Arianna asked.

"Just a friend we grew up with." I said dismissively. "Here you go!" I handed them their bags, not wanting to talk about Michael when, clearly, Damiano had strong opinions of him.

Arianna grabbed her bags and practically shoved them into Damiano's arms for him to carry.

"You're too spoiled." Damiano frowned but still carried them.

"I'm your baby sister. I deserve to be spoiled!" She said and dramatically flipped her hair back.

"See, this happens when you spoil them too much." I shot him a look, and he returned it with a wink.

"With the shit I had to go through, this is the least they can do for me. I deserve to be spoiled for life for beating my ass in training." Arianna scoffed and handed me Lorenzo's black card.

"I bet he regrets giving you his card now." I chuckled.

"Please, this isn't even going to make a small dent in his bank account. While you're at it, give yourself a hundred percent tip."

"You are seriously enjoying spending someone else's money, huh?"

"It's fine." Lorenzo said, not caring about the amount Arianna was spending.

"No, thank you. You bought half of the boutique and that is more than enough." I smiled.

Just as we finished, the sound of the door opening caught our attention. My mother, who was distracted with rummaging through her purse while walking toward us, didn't notice the rest of the company present.

"Hi, mom." I greeted, trying to get her attention.

"Hi, honey." She said while still distracted by whatever she was trying to get from her purse. "I have just put my phone in my bag, and now it has disappeared! How does that even work?" She said, frustrated, and let out a sigh of relief when she finally got her phone.

Finally, she looked up and stopped in her tracks. She looked at Lorenzo first and then at Arianna, confusion written all over her face.

"Mamá!" Cara called excitedly, making my mom look at her and gasp in surprise.

"Cara, my love!" My mother opened her arms and hugged Cara tightly.

"You see what I mean with her being the favorite child? I didn't even get half of that when I came back home." I joked to Arianna. She chuckled and patted my back to comfort me, making me let out a small laugh.

I knew my mother loved us both equally. She just showed it more toward Cara since she rarely saw her. It didn't bother me because Cara didn't have a parent who showed her love the way my mother did.

"Look at you! My beautiful Cara." My mother leaned back to look at Cara with a big smile, her eyes twinkling with happiness. "When did you get here?"

"Couple of hours ago. Thought we would make a surprise visit for Thaia." Cara explained, making my mother look back at Arianna and Lorenzo with slightly raised brows. "And since I'm getting married soon, I thought you should meet my fiancé, Lorenzo."

"I see. Hello." She gave a smile to Lorenzo without stepping closer to him. Lorenzo gave a curt nod in return with his blank face. Not that I was expecting him to smile back.

"And I'm Arianna." She went up to my mother to give a handshake with a big smile on her face. "I'm the younger sister and also the prettiest one." Arianna grinned, making my mother chuckle at her comment.

"Nice to meet you." My mother shook her hand and observed everyone carefully.

I didn't know whether I should be annoyed with the way she was looking at them or if I should try to be more understanding. Damiano and Lorenzo were both very tall, intimidating men, and together, they were taking the word terrifying to another level.

"How long are you staying?" My mother asked Cara, giving her a soft smile as she spoke.

"Just a few days before we have to go back. There are still things I need to get done before the wedding." Cara explained and talked about the wedding.

"How about you all come to dinner tonight?" My mother asked, making me look at her in surprise. "Since we're all going to be family, there is no reason we shouldn't get to know each other." She smiled, and her gaze lingered on me and Damiano for a little while longer.

"That would be lovely!" Arianna replied on behalf of everyone, and Cara talked about the type of food she wanted as she had missed her cooking.

"It's settled then. Althaia, let's close so we can do grocery shopping and prepare for dinner."

I pulled Damiano slightly away from the rest and waited for them to exit the boutique. My mother went downstairs to lock up anything important in the safe, as she usually did before we closed.

"I was thinking maybe we should keep the pregnancy to ourselves for now? It's still too early to tell anyone, and I want to make sure everything is fine."

"Why? Do you feel something is wrong?" Damiano's body tensed and placed a hand on my stomach. My eyes widened a bit because I didn't realize my words had come out as if something was wrong.

"No, nothing's wrong! I just meant we can tell them after we have been to my doctor's appointment." I said quickly. The tension from his shoulders slowly disappeared when I reassured him I was fine.

"That's fine. Whatever you want." He gave me a small smile.

"Oh, and also, can you at least try to get along with my mom tonight?" I gave him my best innocent, sweet look.

"Get along with your mom?" He raised a brow, not liking the idea.

"You keep glaring at her. Can you stop doing that? She's my mom and your baby's grandmother. So please, try not to kill each other tonight." I pleaded.

Damiano looked at me for a while, saying nothing, making me think he was going to dismiss the whole idea.

"...Fine." He sighed with a frown.

"Thank you! I love you." I wrapped my arms around his neck and placed a soft kiss on his lips.

"Only for you, my love." He muttered against my lips.

"I know." I chuckled.

Hopefully, it will be a peaceful dinner with my mother.

Fifty-Three
Damiano

"Her mother seems nice, but it didn't go unnoticed how she looked at you." Arianna snickered and took a seat on the couch.

We went back to my hotel room until we had to leave for dinner. Cara had joined Althaia and her mother to help them prepare. I was suspicious about her motives for inviting us, but I decided to go along with it. The closer I got to her, the faster I could find out who she was.

"She doesn't even try to hide the fact that she hates you." Arianna laughed, and I smirked; if only she knew why her mother hated me this much.

Not only did she hate me for who I was but also for getting her daughter pregnant. That alone was giving me satisfaction because I knew she hated that her daughter was carrying my child. And there was absolutely nothing she could do about it.

"Did you talk to Cara?" I asked Lorenzo.

"She doesn't know much, either. She noticed Althaia's parents were growing cold towards each other and were fighting more. They had one big fight; she left and never looked back."

"There is definitely something interesting about that story. I will suggest a sleepover and see what I can dig out. Who knows, maybe even her mother will open up." Arianna suggested.

"What makes you think you will get her mother to talk? She's wary of you, too." I raised a brow.

"Yes, but not as much as the two of you. I have my ways and you have yours. Mine is to slowly get them all drunk, let her warm up to me and she will talk. If she's anything like Althaia when she's drunk, she will definitely talk." She snorted in amusement.

"The good old spiking trick?" Lorenzo looked at Arianna, giving a half-smirk.

"It has proven to be very effective in the past." She said smugly. It was her favorite trick whenever she wanted to lure valuable information out of people.

It was only effective because of the way she looked. Arianna has mastered the art of appearing innocent when she wants to. Since not everyone knew she was our sister, her presence raised no suspicions. I had watched her in action, and though I wasn't pleased with her methods, she always managed to get the job done.

Casually, she would make her way to the bar, her eyes scanning the room until they settled on her victim. She would subtly flirt with them, exchanging glances and occasional smiles, until they mustered the courage to approach her. And without fail, they were easily deceived. Intrigued by the beautiful woman who stood alone, they couldn't help but be captivated.

Once captured by her, it was game over for them.

The only reason I let her do her own thing was because I knew she was highly skilled with weapons and knows how to defend herself. Otherwise, there was no way in hell I would have ever let her go near anyone.

"That's fine, but you can't spike Althaia's drinks." I told her firmly, and a frown formed on her face.

"I can't only let one person get drunk. I need them all drunk, so they don't get suspicious of my questions." Arianna argued.

"She's right." Lorenzo commented, but I only shook my head at them.

"I said don't do it." I gave her a harsh look to drop it already.

"Listen." She sighed. "I get that you're protective of her, but I won't get her drunk to the point she gets fucked up and dies."

I pinched the bridge of my nose, annoyed she couldn't follow a simple order.

"Arianna, I said no." I snapped.

"Why not? Don't you want to find out what's going on with her mother?"

"Find another way then." I hissed.

"No. I'm going to do it whether you like it or not." Arianna challenged. I stepped closer to her, towering over her, my eyes cold as I stared down into hers.

"I said no. What I say fucking goes. Don't defy my orders." My voice turned low in warning.

"Don't talk to me like I'm one of your men." Arianna's persistence in not backing down only increased my annoyance at not listening.

Lorenzo clicked his tongue in annoyance as well. This wasn't unusual. She had a habit of challenging me whenever she didn't like the answers I gave.

"You're working right now, so I'm going to treat you like the rest." I told her sharply.

"Exactly! I'm working. Let me do my work!"

"Do your work, but you can't get Althaia drunk."

"And why not?" Arianna huffed in frustration. I rubbed my jaw, feeling the anger rise for being a pain in my fucking ass right now.

"She's pregnant." I finally said. I couldn't risk her spiking Althaia's drinks behind my back. This was the only way I could make sure she wouldn't do anything reckless and cause Althaia and our baby any harm.

Arianna went completely silent in shock, even Lorenzo gave me a look.

"She's pregnant?" She asked carefully, both of them not sure how to react. But when a smile formed on my lips, it was enough to let them know it was great news.

Arianna's face transformed into a picture of pure joy, her lips curling into a bright smile.

"A baby!" She screamed and immediately wrapped her arms around me. "Oh my God, I can't believe it! This is going to be so great! Lorenzo, did you hear that? I'm going to be an aunt, and you, an uncle!" She kept exclaiming in excitement.

With a smile on his face, Lorenzo walked up to me and playfully slapped my back a few times.

"Congratulations, brother."

"Thank you."

"I'm so happy for you. You're going to have a little one!" Arianna sniffed and went to hug me again.

I put an arm around her, offering a gentle squeeze to let her know I understood why she was feeling emotional. She had been there during my darkest moments, and she had witnessed the light that Althaia brought into my world.

"I was wondering why you kept rubbing her stomach. By the way, you were not doing a good job being discreet about it." She smiled while wiping away her tears.

"I wasn't trying to." I shrugged. "But Althaia told me she wanted to keep it on the down low for now. So, keep your mouth shut about it." I glared at Arianna. I knew Lorenzo would say nothing because he knew how to mind his own business.

Unlike our dear baby sister.

"Okay, relax! No need to kill me with your glare." She rolled her eyes at me and then resumed beaming in happiness at her becoming an aunt.

I stepped away when my phone buzzed in my pocket.

"Antonio."

"Jacinta went to several banks and also made phone calls. I had Raffaele look into the calls she made, but as usual, they are untraceable." He reported, making me furrow my brows. Whoever she was making calls to was doing everything in their power to cover any trace. Even someone like Raffaele hasn't been able to crack the code yet.

"Did she go anywhere else besides the banks?"

"No. Straight back to the boutique." He reported.

"I will look into it. Keep your eyes on her at all times."

"Copy."

I hung up and faced Lorenzo.

"Let's go. We have some digging to do."

The sun was already set low on the horizon when we arrived at the boutique. To avoid drawing attention, we discreetly went behind the shop towards the back door. I went straight to the keypad and punched in the code I had watched Althaia do several times. Except this time, it denied me access and remained locked.

"She fucking changed it." I scoffed and pulled out the decryptor.

Placing it on the keypad, I watched as the screen of the device shifted through a series of numbers before disclosing the six-digit code that Jacinta had updated it to.

Once inside, I made my way downstairs to where the safe was while Lorenzo checked the desk and computer to see if there was anything new. Arianna checked it earlier and sent a picture that there wasn't anything to be suspicious about. Now, I was almost certain there would be something.

As I opened the safe, my eyes immediately landed on the new file. Grabbing it, I examined the papers closely, my frown deepening as I continued to study them.

Lorenzo came to a stop next to me, and I turned toward him, presenting the papers.

"Of course." He tsked out as he looked at the papers, familiar with this kind of work.

"She's still in the game. Now the question is with whom." I said, turning my attention back to the file.

Jacinta was using the business for money laundering.

Fifty-Four

ALTHAIA

We were almost done making the perfect dinner. Well, my mother made the food while Cara and I helped. Actually, we were bickering more than helping make dinner.

I suddenly craved mac and cheese, and we decided to make some at the very last minute. I put Cara on the job since it was the easiest thing on the menu. But somehow, she was screwing it up.

"That's not how you make it. You're turning it into soup!" I told Cara, staring down at the pot of whatever she had going on.

"This is how you make it! It just needs to boil for a bit, and it will reduce." Cara said, annoyed, looking focused as she stirred the pot.

"No, it's literally soup! It looks disgusting." I scrunched my nose. I had no idea what it was, but it sure as hell wasn't mac and cheese. It looked like poison.

"It's not!"

"I can't stand listening to you two anymore! Get out and go set up the table." My mother scolded and pushed us out of the kitchen.

"This is your fault." Cara continued as we moved to the dining area, which was joined to the living room where the siblings were.

"You're the one who can't cook to save your life!"

"You were the one telling me how to make it. You're the one who fucked up, bitch!" Cara said loudly, making me look at her with wide eyes. She then gasped and slammed her hand up to her mouth when she realized her mistake.

We heard my mother's footsteps approaching us, and I quickly went to escape into the living room, and Cara followed closely behind.

"Young lady! I did not just hear such words coming out of your mouth." My mother frowned, pointing her beloved wooden spoon at her.

I bit down on my lip so I wouldn't burst out laughing at the scenario in front of me. Cara, being a grown-ass woman, was being scolded like a child by my mother. And in front of her fiancé.

It was uproariously funny that tears welled up in my eyes as I struggled to stifle my laughter. Arianna leaned forward on the couch, watching us with a grin as she witnessed the infamous wooden spoon in action.

"Is that such language your father teaches you?" My mother raised her brow, and Cara was on the verge of breaking out laughing at the question.

"Ah, you see, my dad doesn't talk much these days." She said casually, making me snort a laugh. My mother shifted her gaze back and forth between us, her eyes narrowing.

"What do you mean? That man never stops talking." Cara couldn't hold it anymore and laughed, making me burst out laughing, too.

Damiano had a small smirk on his lips. He was, after all, the one who made sure my uncle couldn't talk anymore.

"You two are not making any sense." My mother shook her head.

"A lot of shit was coming out of his mouth." Cara continued, which earned a quick slap with the wooden spoon on her arm, making her let out a yelp and rub her arm.

"And yours too! Don't use that language under my roof." She warned and pointed the spoon at her. My mother then looked at me and gave me a whack on the arm with the spoon too, making me gape.

"I didn't even do anything!"

"Oh, you know what you did." She shot me a look and quickly glanced at Damiano before going back to the kitchen. Her words had me fighting through a blush of embarrassment.

"I forgot how hard she hits with that stupid spoon." Cara lightly laughed, still rubbing her arm.

As dinner was served, we all took a seat around the table.

"Oh, none for me." I told Cara when she was about to pour a glass of wine for me.

"That's a first." She looked surprised.

"I'm on a cleanse." The words rolled out before I had the chance to think it through.

"I don't think you know what a cleanse is." She gestured to my plate of food, which consisted of everything that you shouldn't eat if you were on a so-called 'cleanse'.

"Well, I'm doing it my way. First, you get rid of the alcohol, then you slowly work on your food." I explained, hoping she would buy it, but she just scoffed.

"It would have been more believable if you said you were pregnant than on a cleanse." She joked, and I stopped eating. I slowly raised my head to look at her, and her eyes started to widen.

"...Are you pregnant?" She half-whispered. The room fell silent, making it seem she had said it loud and clear for everyone to hear.

"No!... Maybe...just a little...?" I stumbled on the words.

Cara's mouth went slightly ajar, and her brows raised in surprise. It took her a full minute to realize that I wasn't joking before letting out the biggest grin on her face.

"You're pregnant!" She screamed and jumped out of her seat, ran around the dining table, and gave me a bone-crushing hug.

I rose from my seat as well to give her a proper hug with a smile on my face. Cara leaned back to look at me, and I noticed her eyes were glistening with tears and so much happiness.

"Oh, well, this was bound to happen sooner or later with the two of you going crazy -"

"Okay, too much information." I interrupted her by quickly placing my hand to her mouth to stop her from talking. She just laughed at me and gave Damiano's shoulder a small squeeze, congratulating him as she went back to her seat.

"Dear Lord..." My mother commented, taking a sip of her wine. Her cheeks were getting flushed by Cara's words, making me clear my throat in awkwardness. Luckily, it was saved by Arianna getting up and hugging me, too.

"Congratulations! I am so happy for you! I'm finally going to be an aunt!" Arianna beamed.

"You're going to be the crazy aunt who will teach the kid how to use a gun. And I will tell them all about how to practice safe sex since you can't!" Cara laughed loudly.

"Cara, shut up!" I hissed, feeling my face getting hot.

"Dinner is getting cold. Please, help yourself." My mother cleared her throat, almost chugging down her wine.

"Sorry, mamá." Cara chuckled.

Before I could get back to my seat, Lorenzo made his way to me. He smiled before embracing me, leaving me shocked. It took me a few seconds before I reacted and hugged him back with a smile.

"Congratulations, Althaia. I'm happy for you."

"It's happening! Someone take a picture!" Arianna exclaimed.

We stepped away from each other just as the sound of a picture being taken rang out.

"No! Hug again, I didn't get the picture." Cara called out, ready with her phone.

"That's enough." Damiano said unhappily, making Cara look at him with a brow raised.

"He's your brother."

"I don't care. I don't hug you, do I?" He said with slightly furrowed brows. Cara leaned forward and rested her arms on the table as she grinned at him.

"Do you want one?"

"No." He said immediately.

"It's okay, Damiano. I will give you a hug." She quickly went over to him and hugged him while he remained seated and as still as he could. I laughed when Damiano's frown only deepened when she wrapped her arms around him.

Now I understood what they meant when they always cringed at me and Lorenzo. I could just see how awkward Damiano was feeling right now.

"See! It's not that bad, is it?" Cara was smiling right in his face, and he responded with a blank look.

"I had no idea my brothers were this awkward. This hurts too much to look at." Arianna sighed and shook her head when Damiano still had no intention of returning Cara's hug. It even made my mother have the faintest smile on her lips as she watched us.

"Let's get out before they notice we have been gone for too long." I took one last glance in the mirror to make sure I didn't look like someone who just got fucked in the bathroom. Even though it was exactly what had just happened.

I unlocked the door and swung it open, only to stop. My eyes immediately met with Lorenzo's.

He was slouched against the wall, his arms crossed and a teasing smirk on his face. He made a tsking sound as he shook his head.

"Had fun?" Lorenzo asked with a raised brow. My face was burning to the point I was sure I looked like a bright red tomato.

"What are you doing here?!" I scowled, trying to fight through the embarrassment.

"I was looking for my brother, but it seemed he was rather busy. I didn't want to interrupt."

"So, you just thought you would stand here and listen, you pervert!" I whisper-yelled so that the others wouldn't hear.

"I wouldn't have heard a thing if you weren't being so loud." He pointed out and then looked at Damiano. "I see you got yourself a screamer, brother." Lorenzo's smirk widened, making me want to scream at him for saying such things.

"You have no idea." Damiano replied with a smirk. I turned around so fast to face him and slapped him on the chest.

"D-don't say that!"

"Are you done?" Lorenzo asked Damiano, still with his stupid smirk.

"For now. Just had to make sure she stays pregnant." Damiano winked at me, and my jaw dropped. "So eager to please me today, aren't you?" He chuckled, placing a finger under my chin to close my mouth.

Words refused to come out at this moment. I felt completely mortified. Without saying anything, I walked away from the brothers, only to feel a hand grab me and turn me around.

Damiano placed his hand behind my neck and leaned down to kiss me.

"I love you. Now, you can go." He whispered against my lips. If it was possible to blush anymore, I would have.

My body was so hot it was unbearable as I turned around once again to walk away. I let out a surprised gasp when he slapped my ass hard, making me almost run away from them.

"Horny bastard." Lorenzo chuckled, and I wanted to die on the spot.

The sound of laughter reached my ears when I entered the living room, a smile immediately on my face when I saw them all sitting close together. They had opened a new bottle of wine while they were looking through the family album.

"Look who decided to show up." Arianna commented as I took a seat. Cara wiggled her brows at me.

"She totally just had a quickie with your brother."

"Cara!" I almost screamed her name, and Arianna looked at us with disgust. Cara quickly clamped her mouth shut and looked at my mother, completely forgetting she was there.

"I'm going to pretend I didn't hear that…" My mother uncomfortably cleared her throat, and I avoided making eye contact with her.

"Tell me about it." Arianna muttered in disgust and poured more wine for my mother.

"I'll get drunk if I drink any more tonight." My mother tried to stop her.

"Well, I am trying to get drunk to forget. Do you want to remember the words that came out of her mouth?" Arianna glared at Cara, to which she returned with an innocent smile.

"You're right." My mother raised her glass. "Salute."

The longer we sat in the living room, the more drinks they had. They were drunk to the point that they laughed at every single meaningless thing. But I was happy to see my mother happily chatting with Arianna.

"Are you also attending the wedding?" Arianna asked. My mother scoffed and shook her head.

"No. I'm not going anywhere near those bastards." She gulped down the rest of her wine.

"Bad blood with your ex-husband?" Arianna casually asked, leaving me taken aback. I kept quiet, curious to see if my mother would tell us anything.

My mother remained silent, frowning a bit as it looked like she was remembering back to those days with my father.

"…We didn't exactly end on good terms." She answered.

"What happened?" I asked. It was something I have been dying to know, but it was something we never talked about because she refused to, and I learned to let it go.

She let out a sigh, staring at the fireplace with a distant look.

"It was an arranged marriage. We never loved each other."

My brows raised. I had no idea their marriage was arranged.

"But you always looked happy together?"

"We had to make it work for the sake of our families. My father married me off because he didn't have a male heir to take over. It's a 'man's world' as he put it." She laughed bitterly as her expression turned cold. "It's all about power, and of course, your father accepted. That's what it's all about in the end. Power."

We were all at a loss for words, feeling sad for her that she was married off to someone she didn't care for.

"There's no one like lunnyy svet…" She muttered quietly under her breath. Her expression softened while lost in her thoughts, then vigorously shook her head and abruptly rose from the couch.

"Don't mind me, girls, I'm talking nonsense. I had a bit too much to drink." She let out a chuckle. "I'm heading in now. Goodnight."

"Goodnight, mamá." My heart squeezed at the look of sadness that washed over her face.

Fifty-Five

ALTHAIA

"So, pregnant, huh?" Arianna started, spinning around in my desk chair. After my mother called it a night, we headed upstairs to my room so we wouldn't disturb her.

"Yeah, I know. I can barely believe it myself." I smiled, changing into the t-shirt I had stolen from Damiano.

"Were you not on the pill?" Cara asked, coming out of the bathroom.

"Yes, but I forgot to take them with me. I thought I would be fine since I was only supposed to stay for a week, anyway. It was not like I was expecting to, uh, mess around with anyone during my stay." I explained, feeling my cheeks get warm.

"Really?" Cara shot me a mischievous look. "I thought you would hook up with Michael since the two of you were constantly flirting." Cara chuckled, making Arianna look at me with a raised brow.

"You were flirting with someone else?"

"No!" I exclaimed. "Okay, yes, but it was before I even got with Damiano." I admitted and glared at Cara for opening her big mouth. She was completely oblivious to it and flopped onto the bed.

"Michael as in your childhood friend? Does my brother know?"

"Why would I tell him about my past relationships and flirting?" I asked. "If he asks, I will tell him. Just like I'm not pressuring him to tell me about his past relationships, even though I know he was engaged at some point in his life."

Arianna whipped her head to face me so fast I was afraid she would break her neck. She looked at me for a long time with furrowed brows, and even Cara sat up on the bed with a shocked expression.

"Damiano was engaged?"

"How do you know?"

Arianna and Cara asked their questions at the same time, though Arianna was tense with a firm expression on her face.

"I wasn't too sure about it, but you just confirmed it for me." I said, raising a brow at her. "I have known for a while, actually, but he doesn't know that I know." I observed her closely, trying to figure out why she had reacted like that.

"Why didn't you ask him the minute you learned about it?" Arianna played it off by checking her nails as if she wasn't interested in the conversation anymore.

"I don't know." I sighed. "I figured he would tell me if he wanted to. I'm not exactly eager to hear about the women he has been with."

"Why did they break up?" Cara asked.

"That's not my story to tell. If you want to know, ask him." She smirked at Cara, making her roll her eyes at her before getting comfortable on the bed again. "But you're right, it doesn't matter. I can't believe you two are going to have a little one." She gave me a soft smile.

"Ever heard of a condom?" Cara suddenly asked, making Arianna groan.

"We used protection!" I said to my defense. "Well, the first time at least…" I mumbled quietly.

"Damiano was so eager to get his dick wet that he forgot to wrap it up." Cara snickered.

"I fucking hate you right now." Arianna shuddered in disgust.

I let out a laugh when Cara did hip thrusts to provoke Arianna, and it was only a matter of seconds before she would have Cara in a headlock to shut her up.

I sat up with a grumble, stirred awake by my rumbling stomach. It was early enough that everyone else was still asleep.

I looked at Cara's sprawled body on my bed. It made me want to smack her face with a pillow for all the times she has barged into my room at the crack of dawn. But it would have to be another time since I was so hungry that I almost felt sick.

"Oh, it smells so good!" Cara appeared with Arianna just as I finished making a breakfast buffet and placed everything on the dining table.

"I'm starving!" Arianna said and took a seat.

"Well, dig in!" Just as I was about to take a seat, the doorbell rang. "Who would come at this hour?" I said to myself as I went to check.

"Hello there, beautiful! Missed me?!" Raffaele's voice filled the room with joy as he yelled out and wrapped me in a tight hug the instant I opened the door. It took me a full minute to process that Raffaele was here. I hugged him tightly, letting out a laugh as he caught me off guard.

"Oh my God! What are you doing here?" I leaned back to look at him with a smile.

"Everyone just left me and I was feeling lonely. So, I thought why not join you here!" He grinned from ear to ear and pulled me into a tight hug once more.

"Careful, Raffaele." Damiano's voice came out of nowhere when Raffaele squeezed me a bit too much.

"Don't worry, you will get her to yourself in a moment." Raffaele teased but stepped aside for me to see Damiano and Lorenzo. I hadn't even noticed them as Raffaele practically ambushed me.

"You came at the right time. I just made breakfast." I gestured for them to come in, and Raffaele eagerly skipped toward the mouthwatering aroma of the food. Lorenzo shook his head at Raffaele's behavior as he followed him.

Damiano halted right in front of me with a frown on his face.

"You answer the door dressed like that?" His eyes narrowed in on what I was wearing.

"I wasn't expecting anyone to come." I shrugged. Damiano's shirts were big, almost knee-length on me. I have worn dresses more revealing than this.

Which he ruined by cutting and cuming all over it.

I wrapped my arms around him, giving him a sweet smile.

"I've missed you." I gave him a quick peck on the lips, which melted the frown away from his face, and a small smile appeared on his lips.

"I've missed you too, piccola." Damiano said against my lips, having my heart flutter every time he called me that.

"...It's like I can't get a break from your annoying ass. Why did you come?" Arianna scowled at Raffaele when we stepped into the dining room.

"Don't flatter yourself. I'm not here to see your stupid face." Raffaele scoffed and snatched a hash brown off her plate.

That started a war.

They continued with their bickering, their voices growing louder and more animated, while the rest of us savored our breakfast. We watched them as if it was live entertainment.

"I can't remember the last time I drank this much..." My mother groaned, almost stumbling in with her eyes closed as she held her head in her hands.

Just seeing that made me laugh. It was such a rare sight to see my mother like that. Her eyes fluttered open, and she immediately twisted her face into a frown directed at me. She then noticed everyone was present, until her gaze finally settled on Raffaele, who stood tall with a mischievous smile.

"Damn, Althaia! You didn't tell me you had a sister." Raffaele let out a low whistle as he approached my mother, his eyes scanning her up and down.

"I don't. That's my mom."

"Who are you and what are you doing in my house?" My mother's eyes narrowed in suspicion.

"It depends. Do you like young meat? If so, I can be your future baby daddy." Raffaele winked.

I gaped. Was he seriously hitting on my mother?

My mother gave him a blank look.

"I don't like you, whoever you are."

"Don't worry, la mia bella rosa. An hour with me and you will love me." Raffaele's low, flirtatious voice made my jaw drop again. My mother scoffed, clearly unimpressed, and gave him a scrutinizing look from head to toe.

"I bet you can't even last for thirty seconds." Turning around, she walked away, leaving Raffaele's smug smile to drop.

"This is the best shit I have ever witnessed in my life!" Arianna exclaimed as we all laughed.

Raffaele's scowl deepened as he crossed his arms over his chest, not finding it funny.

We ended up heading out since Arianna and Cara still hadn't quenched their thirst for shopping. As soon as we hit the boutiques, ten minutes passed, and Arianna was already carrying five bags in her hands. I thought I had a shopping addiction, but Arianna's obsession with shopping put mine to shame.

My mother joined us, hoping to spend more quality time with Cara, but Raffaele's presence made it anything but joyful for her. For some reason, he wouldn't leave her alone, and she was desperately trying to escape him and his shameless flirting.

I felt Damiano slow, and I looked at him, seeing him focused on something. Before I could ask if something was wrong, he gently tugged me in a different direction and came to a stop in front of a shop.

A baby shop.

A big smile spread across my face as I watched him pick up a pair of baby shoes he had seen in the display window. The tiniest shoes I have ever seen were covered in red roses with a big red bow in the middle.

"We don't even know if it's going to be a girl." I chuckled.

"We'll keep trying until we get a girl." Damiano said in all seriousness.

"Even if we end up with five boys, would you still want to try for a girl?" I raised a brow and Damiano gave me a soft smile. He tucked a strand of hair behind my ear and rested his hand on my cheek, his thumb softly caressing me.

"I meant every word when I said we should have as many children as we can. My love, you have no idea how much I want this life with you." Damiano spoke quietly and placed a sweet kiss on my forehead.

"We'll see if you still want many children after we have this one."

"I hope they will drive me crazy like you do." He playfully winked at me, laughing as I called out a 'hey' after him while he went to buy the shoes.

"This is seriously so cute. Imagine tiny baby feet wearing these!" A beaming smile spread across my face as we exited the shop. I couldn't stop looking at how small these shoes were.

"Are you happy?" Damiano suddenly asked, making me stop and look at him in surprise. "With me. Are you really happy with me?" He had a small frown etched on his face.

My brows raised, then I realized why he was asking. I let out a small laugh, finding it adorable that it was coming from him.

I stepped on the tip of my toes, pressing my lips to his, and his frown slowly disappeared.

"My heart has never felt happier, my love."

Fifty-Six
Damiano

Her stunning emerald eyes gazed up at me, sparkling with brightness, as she smiled with a touch of amusement playing on her lips.

"Do you really not know how happy you make me?" She asked, her fingers intertwined with mine.

"I want to make sure." I told her honestly.

She was happy now, but as her mother made clear several times, she would constantly be a target for my enemies; especially now that she was carrying my child. What if she came to resent me for it?

This was one of the reasons her mother left her father; to protect her from the brutality that comes with living this life. Yet I dragged her right into it because of my obsession with her.

"I guess it's my fault for not telling you enough." Althaia chuckled, making me smile at the sound. Her face beamed with joy and innocence, swelling my heart with a need for closeness, a desire to protect that radiant happiness she exuded.

"I wouldn't mind if you told me from time to time." I gave her a small smile, pulling her closer to me.

"Is my big bad Mafia Boss feeling a little insecure?" She whispered in a teasing tone, biting down on her lip to not burst out laughing.

"Are you calling my ass insecure again?" I raised a brow. I adored her newfound boldness. With her fiery personality and sharp tongue, she constantly called me out on things. She was a person who couldn't be tamed, and she would give you hell for it if you tried.

And I fucking loved it. She made me feel alive in a whole different way.

"Maybe... what are you going to do about it?" Althaia gave me that one smile that made her eyes sparkle with mischief, transitioning from innocence to irresistibly sexy in an instant.

It made my cock hard.

"Fuck, baby, not here." I let out a groan and my hands on her waist tightened. Her eyes widened with surprise when she felt my hard cock against her.

"There you are! We have been looking for you." Arianna's voice rang out.

"Fucking hell." I muttered under my breath when the others were nearing us. I closed my eyes, trying to suppress the visible evidence of my intense arousal. If it wasn't because my baby sister was present, I wouldn't have cared.

Althaia turned around but stayed in front of me to give me time to calm down.

"We were doing our own little shopping. Look what Damiano found." She said happily and showed them the ridiculously small baby shoes that couldn't even cover the palm of my hand.

"Are those baby shoes?" Raffaele asked with a confused look. Althaia let out a sigh and looked at me over her shoulder.

"You didn't tell him?"

"Why should I?" I gave her a half-hearted shrug. I never shared much of my personal life with anyone, and they would all eventually know when she would start showing.

Althaia narrowed her eyes and shook her head slightly before turning to face him.

"We're having a baby." She announced with a soft smile.

Raffaele went silent.

He was dead quiet for a long time, the longest I have ever seen him without talking. I frowned, wondering why the hell he was reacting like this to the news. As if he read my mind, he suddenly jumped forward.

"You're having a baby?!" He tightly embraced her, lifting her off the ground while shouting with happiness as Althaia laughed at his reaction.

My fingers twitched. I had to resist the urge to snatch her away from his grasp, reminding myself that it was only Raffaele. Arianna had lashed out at me, claiming that my possessiveness had no limits, all because I dared to get annoyed when Lorenzo embraced her.

Brother or not, I didn't like other men touching her.

"Holy shit, you're going to be parents!" Raffaele said as he finally let go of her, barely believing the news. "Congrats, man! I'm really happy for you." He expressed his congratulations by giving me a firm pat on the back.

"Thank you." I replied, pulling Althaia back to me.

Raffaele went back to her mother, placing an arm around her shoulders. Jacinta took a deep breath to calm down. She was done dealing with his shit today.

"Can you believe *our* daughter is going to have a baby?" Raffaele smiled big at her. She rolled her eyes and tried to get away, but he held her firmly.

"If you don't let go of me right now, I will smack you." Jacinta threatened him.

"La mia bella rosa, you know me so well already. I enjoy getting smacked." He wiggled his brows.

I closed my eyes and pinched the bridge of my nose. I had no idea what his game was, but he told me to trust him. He better have a good plan for all the shit he was doing, and it wasn't one of his games to get her into bed with him.

"Raffaele! Stop being disgusting and leave my mom alone!" Althaia marched over and pushed him away, coming to her mother's rescue as she let out a breath of relief.

"Your mother is hot! I can't help it!" Raffaele continued to annoy the shit out of them, chasing them while they tried to escape him.

Arianna fell in step with me, and I looked at Lorenzo, signaling him to follow them with Cara to leave us alone.

"What did you find out?" I asked once they were out of hearing distance.

"Turns out her parents had an arranged marriage. Jacinta got married off because her father didn't have a male heir to take over, and you know what that means."

I nodded as we walked at a slow pace. Althaia's grandfather from her mother's side was some kind of mob boss, meaning Jacinta knew this world way better than I initially thought.

The moment I learned Althaia was alive, I quickly skimmed through her family history on her mother's side. Since they were a small family and all were deceased, I had no interest in them, as they were of no concern.

Now it was worth looking more into it to see if any of their old associates were in contact with Jacinta.

"Jacinta admitted they never loved each other, but had to make it work for the sake of their families."

"I see. Anything else?" I looked at her when she hesitated. "What is it?"

"... Althaia knows you were engaged." She muttered. My body tensed, and I could feel the heat of anger rising inside me.

"Did you fucking tell her?" I sneered, clenching my fists.

"Do you take me for an idiot? I was just as surprised as you are!"

"How does she know? Does she know anything else?" I asked in frustration.

"I don't know." Arianna sighed. "She caught me off guard when she revealed it, and then she got suspicious of how I reacted."

"Fucking hell." I rubbed my jaw in annoyance.

"She only knows that you were engaged, but not any details about Sienna." She tried to reassure me. I rolled my neck, trying to relieve the tightness in my muscles.

Did her mother tell her? No, it couldn't be if she had known for a while. Who the fuck told her about Sienna? My frown deepened as nothing came to mind.

"Damiano, she said she has known for a while." Arianna continued. "Don't you think it's time you tell her?" She asked softly, almost carefully.

"No." I said immediately.

"You don't have to tell her everything but come clean that you were engaged. That's it."

I let out a humorless laugh. She doesn't know Althaia the way I do. The second I tell her, it would pique her curiosity, and she would ask more questions that I wasn't ready to answer.

"No." I shut her down and started walking again. Arianna let out a tired sigh and matched her pace with mine.

"Do I have to remind you what happened when you didn't tell her about Sofia?"

"That's not the same." I shot her a piercing glare to mind her own business but she ignored me.

"Damiano, listen to me." Arianna grabbed my arm to look at her. "You don't know who told her, and there's still a chance her mother might talk to her about it. It's better that you talk to her than anyone else. If she truly loves you too, she will understand." Arianna gave me a small smile.

A long silence lingered as my gaze remained fixed on her. I raised a questioning brow.

"Are you an expert in relationships now?"

"What can I say? I give the best relationship advice, yet I remain single." Arianna sighed. I placed my arm around her shoulders as we walked again.

"I know you're with Dom, even though I told you to end it." I gave her a playful smile when she looked shocked.

"How did you find out?" She breathed out, and I scoffed.

"You don't think I know what's going on with my men?"

"I thought I did a good job hiding it..." Arianna groaned out before quickly shooting me a look. "I will get so pissed at you if you hurt him! I won't forgive you."

"If I wanted to hurt him, he would already have been at the bottom of the sea. And not in one piece." I laughed as she rolled her eyes at me.

"I'm not marrying him, if that's what you're hinting at." She crossed her arms tightly, her gaze fixed straight ahead. "Actually, I will marry him if you get married." Arianna gave a smug smile.

She knew I had no intention of getting married after what had happened with Sienna, but she didn't know the newfound hope Althaia had brought into my life.

"I asked Althaia to marry me." I revealed. Arianna froze in her tracks, her mouth gaping open, and her eyes widening in sheer shock as she stared at me.

"Are you serious?"

"I am. But she turned me down." I frowned, my words tinged with disapproval, leaving her even more shocked to hear that. "She wants to take it slow and have the baby first." I explained. But it was okay, I will wait for her, no matter how long it takes for her to be ready to marry me.

Arianna had gone silent as she processed my words.

"She has changed you a lot." Arianna murmured quietly as we were about to catch up with the others. "But for the better. I have never seen you this happy before and after so long... I finally feel like I have gotten my brother back." Her voice cracked, and she hid her face in her hands as she broke down.

"Arianna." I chuckled lightly and pulled her into me. She sobbed into my chest as I rubbed her back in comfort. She was a tough person, and I often forgot that she had witnessed my lowest moments and had been affected by them, too.

We were close enough to the others that they noticed Arianna was crying. Lorenzo's brows furrowed as he cast a questioning gaze from her to me. He was about to make his way toward us, but I signaled to him with a reassuring shake of my head that everything was okay.

Arianna didn't cry for long and wiped her tears away once she had calmed down. Suddenly, all I saw was my vulnerable baby sister that didn't know any better, instead of the tough woman she had grown up to be.

"I know I've been fucked up for a long time, but don't you dare spill your tears over a man. Even if he's your brother. Understand?" I placed my hands on her cheeks as I talked to her softly. She nodded and took another deep breath.

"You know what would make me feel better?" Arianna asked, looking at me with tears still glistening in her eyes.

"Tell me." I smiled.

"That jewelry store right there." Arianna pointed somewhere behind me.

A chuckle escaped my lips as I reached for my wallet to hand her my card. Grinning, she swiftly snatched it out of my hand and hurried towards the store.

"I love you! You're my favorite brother!" She yelled. Lorenzo's face twisted into a scowl as he scoffed at her.

"Don't even try to compete with me, brother. I always win." I shot him a wink, and I knew he wanted to shoot my ass for it.

It made me laugh as I walked toward my mesmerizing green-eyed woman, desperate to have her close to me again.

Fifty-Seven

ALTHAIA

We had been walking for what felt like hours, and Arianna and Cara still hadn't satisfied their shopping thirst. My mother left a while ago once she had bought what she needed and desperately walked away from us; most likely from Raffaele, who wouldn't leave her alone.

Eventually, we decided to ditch the rest because I got too tired, and Damiano took me back to his hotel room.

I ran a bath, creating a mountain of bubbles while Damiano ordered food. The moment I slipped down into the hot water, a sigh of pure bliss escaped my lips.

"Take a bath with me." I moved forward so he could sit behind me. I leaned against him, and instantly, his hands glided across my body to wash me.

"Piccola?" Damiano broke the comfortable silence.

"Hmm?"

"We're leaving the day after tomorrow." He said, making me turn around to face him.

"Already?" I didn't even try to hide my disappointment. Deep down, I had hoped he would stay until Cara's and Lorenzo's wedding, but I knew he couldn't.

"You're coming back with me." His brows furrowed when I shook my head.

"I thought we had already talked about it? I'll be there one week before the wedding."

"You think I'm going to leave you here when you're pregnant?"

"You're talking as if I'm in the middle of a war zone!" I gaped.

"You might as well be."

I wanted to roll my eyes at his exaggeration.

"Damiano, trust me, I'll be fine. Besides, Luca will be with me." I argued. Giovanni wasn't back yet; he was staying a bit longer in Portugal to make sure

Laila would be safe. He saw this as the perfect chance to escape babysitting me and enjoy a mini vacation for himself.

I was happy that Laila kept her promise and updated me whenever she could. She had finally reunited with her family, and she promised she would get all the help she needed.

I wrapped my arms around Damiano, giving him a sweet smile.

"It's only two weeks, then I will be there. I haven't had the chance to spend a lot of time with my mother." I told him. He said nothing, visibly unhappy about it.

"Permanently." Damiano said after a while. "You're coming back permanently. We will find a home for us where you and our baby will be safe."

"You're expecting me to leave everything behind in two weeks' time?" I raised my brows in surprise.

"Yes." His expression told me he was dead serious about it. I took my lip between my teeth as I thought about it. I loved the idea of living with him, but two weeks was no time at all.

"How about we talk about this another time? I'm too hungry to have this conversation right now." I moved to get up, but Damiano held my waist to stop me, and I was met with his intense gaze.

"It's not up for discussion, piccola, but fine, another time." He gave me a quick kiss before he let me go. I let out a small sigh, knowing it was going to be one hell of an effort to convince him.

I was still in the bathroom, brushing my hair when I heard that room service had arrived.

"Good evening, Mr. Bellavia. Are you still enjoying your stay with us?"

I stopped brushing my hair, frowning as I heard the sultry voice of a woman.

"Yes, is there anything we can do for your stay to be more...*satisfying*?"

I let out a small gasp when I heard another woman.

With a scowl on my face, I walked across the bedroom to get to the lounge area. I stood by the doorway, watching the scenario in front of me. The sight of those women with their tops unbuttoned, revealing their cleavages, made my blood boil.

"I'm fine." Damiano replied with an icy tone, completely ignoring them as he focused on his phone. My jaw clenched as I saw what he was wearing. Gray sweats and no shirt.

It almost felt like smoke was coming out of my ears in anger when they were hungrily eyeing him. Their eyes went down his body, resting on his bulge that was quite visible in his gray sweats.

*I'm going to kill them **and** him!*

"Maybe we should have gotten me a change of clothes before coming here." I said as I walked out to them while looking down at the tank top I had taken from Damiano, pretending to be fixing it. I was actually fixing it because my nipples were almost showing.

Damiano looked up from his phone. His eyes slowly trailed down my body and his gaze stopped at my barely covered breasts. Whatever he was doing on his phone could wait as he carelessly tossed it on the couch.

He gave me a lazy smirk and motioned for me to come closer to him. With a gentle yet firm grip, Damiano wrapped his arms around my waist, pulling me flush against his body.

"What's the need for clothes when I plan to have you naked the entire time?" Damiano said with a mischievous grin on his lips. I blushed, not expecting him to say something like this in front of them.

As if remembering there were other people in our room, he looked at them with a blank look.

"What are you still doing here? Get out." He told them sharply. They had been taking their sweet time setting the dishes on the table, thinking it was only him in here.

I grabbed some money from Damiano's wallet to tip them. Unlike me, Damiano always carried a shitload of cash on him.

"Is there anything else we can get for you?" One of them asked once they were done, daring to sneak a glance at Damiano before resting her eyes on me.

"No, thank you." I approached them with a smile on my face and handed over the money. Before she could take it, I pulled my hand slightly back and dropped my smile. "Oh, and don't worry, I am making sure he is more than just *satisfied*."

I shot them a sharp look and handed them the money. Their eyes dropped in shame and they scurried out. I shut the door with a bang and spun around to fix a fierce glare on Damiano.

"What the hell were you thinking?" I snapped. He raised a brow in surprise at my sudden outburst and tilted his head in confusion.

"What do you mean?"

"You seriously think it's okay for you to be dressed like that in front of other women?" I hissed. "Shirtless and wearing *gray* sweatpants?"

"What's wrong with gray sweatpants?" He looked down at his sweats.

"You've got to be kidding me right now! Everything is visible!" I exclaimed in a furious tone, pointing directly at his crotch, where his rather impressive size was clearly visible. He wasn't even wearing any underwear, and his sweats hung low on his hips. It only added to my frustration of them seeing so much of him.

Damiano looked at me with an amused expression as I practically shouted at him.

"Oh, so you think this is funny? How about I just pop outside like this for men to see?" I said. I had barely opened the door before his hand forcefully slammed it shut. He spun me around to face him, his glare murderous, while I gave an innocent smile.

"Do it, and I swear I'll turn these walls into a horrifying canvas of red, painted with their blood for daring to lay eyes on you." He growled, a menacing glint in his eyes.

"You see what I mean? It's not funny." I scoffed and crossed my arms.

"Don't play that game with me, Althaia." Damiano clicked his tongue. I leaned into him and jabbed my finger into his chest.

"You started it. I was about to commit my first murder." I said, deadly serious about it.

"Hot." He responded with a mischievous smile. He leaned down, his face inches away from mine. "Your eyes are so green right now. Green with jealousy." Damiano laughed when I smacked his chest.

"You are seriously unbelievable." I moved past him. I didn't get far when he grabbed me, my toes barely touching the floor, and sat us down on the couch with me on his lap.

"I'm sorry, baby." He kissed my cheek, making me a little less angry with him.

"I'm going to burn your pants. You're not allowed to wear gray sweatpants around others. Your dick was showing, and that is for my eyes only." I gave him one last firm look to make sure he got the message.

"And for your pussy."

"Just stop talking." My cheeks grew warm as I quickly grabbed a slice of bread and forcefully fed it to him. He shot me a wink but stopped his playful teasing so I could finally eat.

As we savored our meal, my mind drifted back to the question I had asked at the start of our relationship. The things I had witnessed left me even more curious.

"Speaking of, how many have you actually killed?" I asked. Damiano gave me a blank stare, but I didn't let it stop me. "I remember asking you if you had killed like five or thirty people, but now I know it's definitely more than five."

"I know you've killed two from the amusement park, the guy who attacked me, and that one scumbag, so that's four." I was thinking out loud while counting on my fingers, as if I was trying to solve a math problem.

"Didn't I tell you not to go down that road with me?" He said sharply, but I just gave a dismissive wave.

"That was like the beginning of our relationship, but I have seen stuff now. Besides, I already know what you're capable of, so..." I trailed off with a grin. Damiano ignored me.

"Then at least tell me what it feels like to ki- okay, I will shut up now." I clamped my mouth shut, my lips pressed tightly together, as I met Damiano's terrifying gaze. His gaze lingered on me, filled with a warning that I had crossed the line.

"I don't like you asking these kinds of questions. It's not a detail you should concern yourself with."

"I'm just curious. That part of the world is filled with darkness and so many secrets. It's intriguing." I explained, leaning into him as I felt tired once again. I don't know why I bother getting out of bed when this pregnancy has me feeling like I could sleep for days.

"You're curious about the wrong things, piccola." Damiano said, ending the conversation. "You should eat more."

"I will burst if I eat more." I said, patting my stomach. Then my eyes landed on the mouthwatering piece of chocolate cake. "Actually, I have room for a bite."

Damiano chuckled softly as he handed me the chocolate cake, his eyes brimming with such affection that I almost found myself shyly looking away.

I woke up in the middle of the night, drenched in sweat and feeling unbearably hot. I ripped the blanket away from me, and my body felt incredibly heavy. I bit down hard on my lip to stifle any sound so I wouldn't disturb Damiano.

I quietly got up from the bed when I felt a wave of nausea hit me. It felt like an eternity before I finally reached the bathroom and closed the door behind me. I hunched forward with my hand pressed against my stomach, feeling the intense cramps. I tried to ease the pain by taking a couple of deep breaths but it didn't help.

I stood by the toilet, feeling like I had to throw up, but nothing was coming out. I let out a small groan, my breath coming in short, labored gasps as I sank to my knees.

The pain was so intense that I had no choice but to lie in a fetal position. I closed my eyes, trying to focus on how the cold tiles felt on my hot skin.

My eyes fluttered open at a continuous sound of knocking on the door.

"Althaia... Althaia..." Damiano kept calling after me, pulling down the handle, but it remained shut. I tried to get up, but a low groan slipped from my lips as the sharp pang in my stomach intensified.

"I can't... I don't feel too good..." Tears welled in my eyes. I couldn't even move.

"Are you close to the door?"

"No." A pained moan escaped my lips as I clenched my eyes tightly. There was a sudden, forceful burst as the door swung open, banging loudly against the wall.

"Shit." Damiano cursed when he found me lying on the floor. "What's wrong? Did you fall? Where does it hurt?" He helped me up into a sitting position, but I was so weak my body was almost completely limp against his.

"Fuck, you're burning."

"Something's wrong, Damiano... It hurts too much." I whimpered, hugging my arms tighter around my stomach. Suddenly, a wave of nausea washed over me, and I barely made it to the toilet in time to vomit.

It felt like it went on forever as I continued to empty my stomach. Tears streamed down my cheeks as I couldn't take it anymore, and my stomach kept cramping.

Damiano wiped my face with a wet towel, making me moan in relief at the coolness. He carried me in his arms as I closed my eyes. I felt like I was dying.

Hearing Damiano's authoritative voice barking orders had me opening my eyes. The sight that greeted me was blindingly bright lights and walls painted in pure white. A woman in a white coat rushed towards us and guided us to a room.

The doctor examined me on the hospital bed, and I groaned in pain as she stuck a needle in my arm to draw blood. I really hated needles.

"You have food poisoning." The doctor said once she was back, and I looked at her, dumbfounded.

"I feel like dying and it's just food poisoning?" I asked, half-expecting her to say 'just kidding' before giving me the actual answer. "But we had the same food. How come you're not sick?" I wondered as I looked at Damiano. He was next to the hospital bed, gently caressing my hair in comfort.

"Did you have anything else for breakfast?" Damiano asked, and I shook my head. I looked at Lorenzo, who had come with us.

"Is Cara sick?" I asked, but he shook his head.

"When you're pregnant, your immune system undergoes changes, which can make you more susceptible to certain infections." The doctor explained. "While your body prioritizes the baby's growth and the baby's immune system is still developing, it's important to pay attention to what you eat and how it's prepared. Contracting food poisoning during pregnancy can pose serious risks, including the possibility of miscarriage."

I felt like I got punched in the stomach and my heart beat felt like it was going to jump out of my chest. I tightly gripped Damiano's hand, feeling his body tense in response to the information.

"We're going to check if everything is okay." She said while she got the ultrasound machine ready. "Have you experienced any spotting?"

"No, I don't think so." I said, my voice shaking with nervousness. Overwhelmed by fear, I squeezed my eyes shut as the cool gel made contact with my stomach, and the transducer gently roamed around.

Please be okay.

I felt my throat tighten and my eyes burn with unshed tears.

"There you go. Everything is as it should be."

I opened my eyes to see the doctor's warm smile, and she turned the screen so we could see. Tears streamed down my face as I let out a small sob at the tiny circle.

Our baby is okay.

Seeing the tiny fetus on the screen brought me instant relief and made me momentarily forget about the pain I was experiencing.

I glanced up at Damiano and saw his expression soften as he kept his eyes on the screen. He then looked at me, a swirl of emotions visible in his eyes as he smiled lovingly before leaning down and kissing me on the forehead.

"Would you like a picture?" The doctor asked, and I nodded immediately.

"Yes, please."

Fifty-Eight

ALTHAIA

"Watching you suffer like this is making me wonder if it's really worth it to be pregnant." Cara made a face at how horrible I was looking; sweaty and exhausted while I was trying to carefully sip some water to rehydrate.

Thankfully, it wasn't anything critical, and we were able to leave the hospital once I received IV fluids. Cara had been worrying and waiting since Lorenzo left in a hurry after he received Damiano's call to drive us to the hospital. I usually don't see much emotion from Lorenzo, but tonight I saw a flicker of worry in his eyes for me and the baby.

"One look at this, and it's making me forget about everything else." I handed her the sonogram and rested my head on Damiano's shoulder.

"Funny how it's the size of a pea and it can make you feel like that." Cara's smile lit up her face as she looked at the picture.

"Yeah, so funny. I'm laughing so hard right now." I said sarcastically, which only made her chuckle.

Lorenzo took the picture out of her hand to have a closer look. I smirked as I looked back and forth between them.

"Hey, Lorenzo." My face broke into a wide grin when he looked at me. "Keep your aim sharp. My baby is going to need a BFF soon." I gave him a playful wink, and he responded with a subtle smirk before shifting his gaze towards Cara. Slowly, Cara looked at him with a blank face.

"No."

"It's going to happen, Cara mia."

"Do you want me to suffer like this?" She pointed at me with her brow raised.

"I have food poisoning." I retorted.

"Which you wouldn't have gotten, but since your immune system is weak because of the pregnancy, you did! I can only think of why one should never get pregnant; you get nausea, you throw up, you get back pains..." She kept on with her list, making me glare at her.

"You are being a real fucking delight right now." I grumbled.

"... and don't get me started when you have to give birth." She ignored me as she continued with her listing. "I saw a birthing video once and it ain't pretty. I am traumatized for life." Cara shuddered.

"Why?" I asked. She shifted to the edge of the couch, her expression serious as she explained.

"You're pushing out a baby that's the size of a huge watermelon! Not only that, your vagina gets all torn up and your butthole explodes."

I blinked a few times, trying to process her words before sitting up straight.

"I'm sorry, what?" I said, hoping I heard wrong.

"Yup. It gets all fucked up down there and they have to stitch your vagina *and* your butthole." I dropped my jaw, and she gave me an 'mhmm' as she leaned back on the couch.

I turned to look at Damiano with a terrified look on my face.

"What have you done to me?" It came out in a scared whisper, and for once, I think he was lost for words by what Cara said.

"I'm sure she's exaggerating." He gave her a disapproving look, but she shook her head.

"I'm not! I will even send you the video so you can see it for yourself."

"I don't want to see that! Why would you even tell me all of that?" I groaned and rubbed my stomach as I felt nauseous again.

"I thought you knew..." Cara made a face of regret. "But I'm sure it won't happen to you!" She tried to cheer me up, which only made me glare at her even more.

"Lorenzo, go make her pregnant right now! I will not suffer alone." I said to get back at her. He actually rose to his feet and went to grab Cara's hand, which she smacked his hand away like a fly.

"Uh, no, thank you." She leaned all the way back on the couch to get away from him.

"Let's go. She needs to rest." Lorenzo grabbed her by the waist, picked her up, and carried her over his shoulder as he made his way out the door.

"I don't want my butthole to explode!" She tried to wiggle out of his grasp.

"Oh, I'm sure it won't happen to you." I snickered, and she flipped me off.

I rested my head back on Damiano's shoulder.

"What time are you leaving tomorrow?" I asked, wanting to prepare mentally for the short time we would be apart.

"It will have to wait, baby. You're too sick to travel."

"Damiano, I can't." I sighed tiredly. Damiano gently held my chin to make me meet his gaze.

"I can't let you out of my sight, not after tonight. We could have lost…" He didn't finish his sentence; instead, he held me tightly.

"I know." I whispered. "I'll be careful." I tried to reassure him.

"Althaia, baby, listen to me." He gently cupped my face. "I can't leave you alone. I will go fucking crazy if I can't have you close to me where I can make sure you're safe."

"I understand you're worried, I really do, but I won't be alone. I have my mother and Luca is here too. I know you have to leave because your phone has been going off like crazy, and you have been trying to work from here. Whatever it is, it sounds like it needs your attention." I pointed out.

I have noticed the constant buzzing and ringing of his phone from text messages and phone calls. Whenever he was on the phone, he would get annoyed or angry with them and kept giving out strict orders.

"Have you been eavesdropping on my phone calls?" Damiano raised an amused brow, his lips curling into a slight smile.

"No." I puffed out. Damiano leaned back, crossed his arms, and tilted his head, as if questioning me.

"Okay, yes, but only a little!" I confessed. "It's not like I could understand much of it anyway. Turns out my Italian sucks." I huffed. I thought my Italian was still pretty good until I heard Damiano speak.

"You just found out?" He gave me a teasing smile, making me gape at him.

"You think I suck, too? Damn." I mumbled.

"Considering you haven't spoken the language in years, I would say it's pretty good." Damiano tried to cheer me up. "I'll speak to you in Italian so you can improve." He offered after seeing how bummed I was.

"Deal! But speak slowly. Seriously, you sound like Eminem rapping in Italian." I said, earning a laugh from him.

"You always surprise me with your choice of words." He shook his head. "You will be ready when I take you to visit my family in Italy." Damiano smiled softly when I looked at him in surprise.

"I would love that!"

"I know. You're going to love my mother and my Nonna. They're going to give me hell for not telling them I have found someone. Nonna is going to be after my ass for getting you pregnant before marriage, but she'll be happy. She's been nagging about babies for years." He scoffed, making me laugh as

I could picture it perfectly. I suddenly had an idea that could hopefully help me negotiate to stay.

"I was thinking that maybe you could pick out a few places for us to look at before I get there?" A crease formed between his brows, and I hurriedly continued before he could brush off the idea. "I just need some time to explain everything to my mother. I can't simply drop everything and say, 'see ya, I'm moving out.' Give me two weeks, and I promise I'll be by your side for good."

Damiano didn't agree, but he didn't reject my idea, either. I knew he needed time to think about it, so I let him be and resumed resting my head on his shoulder.

Damiano extended his stay and spent the next two days taking care of me. He did everything he could to make me feel better, and despite my body feeling a bit sore from staying in bed all the time, I was already better.

I didn't know how, but I had finally, somehow, persuaded him to go back without me. It took some convincing, but he finally gave in.

"I'm heading over to Cara's room to borrow some clothes." I said to Damiano as I slipped on a robe.

"I'll go with you."

We made our way down the corridor as their room was a few doors down. I had texted Cara a while ago, and she left the door unlocked, so I could just come whenever I felt like it.

Coming to a stop in front of their room, Damiano pulled down the handle and swung the door open. He quickly shut the door, and my jaw dropped. My entire face burned hot at the sight I had witnessed.

Lorenzo stood butt naked, his back turned towards the door, as he pounded himself inside of Cara, who was bent over the armchair.

I put a hand up to my mouth, and what started as a giggle turned into a full-on fit of laughter, making it hard for me to breathe with tears blurring my sight. Damiano, on the other hand, had his eyes closed and pinched the bridge of his nose.

"I guess we should expect pregnancy news soon." I managed to get out between laughs as I tried to calm down and wiped away the tears. Suddenly, the door opened, clothes were thrown at us, and it got slammed shut. This time, we heard it lock.

"Keep it sharp, my brother!" I yelled to Lorenzo through the door. Damiano shook his head at me before grabbing my hand.

"I need to wash my eyes with fucking bleach." He said with a scowl on his face and a mix of disgust. I burst out laughing again at the sight.

Fifty-Nine

DAMIANO

Althaia said her goodbyes to the others, and I drove her back home. Not ready to let her go just yet, I walked with her inside. She greeted her mother, and she received a curt nod from me as we made our way to her room.

"What time are you leaving?" Althaia stepped between my legs as I took a seat on her bed. She wrapped her arms around my neck. I held her against my body, savoring the moment, knowing I wouldn't be able to hold her for a while.

"Once the others are ready, we will leave." I sighed, still not happy that I was leaving without her. But I knew I had to be patient and give her the time to sort things out before having her all to myself.

"You'll be fine." She spoke softly before moving to straddle my lap and leaning in to kiss me.

The moment her lips met mine, I was overcome with desire, and I eagerly responded, losing myself in the intensity of our kiss. I held on to her tightly, unwilling to let her go, and wondered how the fuck she had successfully convinced me to leave without her.

The only thing that was keeping me sane was knowing Antonio would be here as well, keeping an eye on them both as an extra precaution.

"Althaia..." I gently held her hands to prevent her from removing my shirt. "You're still sick."

"It's not contagious, if that's what you're afraid of." She frowned.

"No, I meant that you're tired and recovering; you should rest." I didn't want to deny her, but she was still not fully recovered. Her body was weak, and she would get out of breath easily.

"I know what I'm doing. I can handle it." Althaia gave a playful smile. I shifted and laid her down on the bed with me on top.

"Only because I won't be seeing you for a while." I let out a small, teasing smile before capturing her lips.

I had to force myself to leave.

Althaia walked me to the door, and I hated every step as we got closer, only reminding me that I wouldn't be close to her for two fucking weeks.

We came to a stop by the door, and I turned my gaze towards her, pulling her into a tight embrace. The thought of kidnapping her was so damn tempting.

"Be careful and stay safe. Luca will be with you at all times, and Giovanni will be here tomorrow. If you get sick, call me and I will come right away." I placed my hands on her cheeks, captivated by the mesmerizing depth of her beautiful green eyes.

"Don't meddle in people's business, or so help me God, I will be absolutely furious with you." I warned her, but she grinned back at me, her mischievous eyes sparkling.

"If you say 'don't do it', it only makes me want to do it."

"Althaia."

"I'm kidding." She laughed. "I will mind my own business. I've learned my lesson."

"Good." I let out a small sigh of relief and pulled her into a kiss. "I love you." I whispered against her lips.

"And I love you. Here, take it with you so you don't miss us too much." Althaia handed me the sonogram, and my heart swelled with joy as I saw the tiny life growing inside her.

"I will be back to get you in two weeks." I ran my fingers through her hair as she embraced me for one final hug. I glanced upwards to see her mother had made an appearance.

"Keep them safe." I told her. The only thing I could trust her with was to protect her daughter. Jacinta's eyes softened at my words and gave a nod.

With every step away from Althaia, my body grew tense, as if a voice inside me warned against leaving her alone. I paused before getting inside my car. I turned around to steal one last look at her, seeing her smile as she gave a small wave.

Soon.

I reminded myself. Soon, we wouldn't have to do this, and I would wake up with her by my side every day for the rest of my life.

"Her mother is fun to hang out with. I totally see where Althaia got her personality from." Raffaele commented while working on his laptop. "She's quite hot, too."

"Did you come to flirt with her, or did you do something useful?" I gave him a blank look.

"Ah, sorry. I actually forgot she's your mother-in-law." He laughed as if he had cracked the funniest joke.

I rolled my neck in annoyance.

"Raffaele." I snapped at him to get to the point.

"Right. I've been working on cracking the code to track those phone calls she's been getting. Whoever she's in contact with is doing everything they can to make sure their cover is not blown." Raffaele said.

"While you all disappeared and left me alone, I came up with an idea. Since none of you would have been able to do it, I decided to do it myself." He smiled big and looked proud of himself.

"I don't need to hear your life story. Get to the point." I said impatiently, and he gave me a sour look.

"Someone's cranky..." He muttered under his breath, making me shoot a glare at him. "I worked my usual charm to get close to Jacinta because I needed her phone. I installed this software I developed on her phone, and the next time she gets a call, I will be able to trace it. Well, that's what I hope... I haven't exactly tried it out yet, but I'm a genius! I'm sure it will work." Excitement filled his eyes as he rubbed his hands together.

"Good. I want to get to the bottom of this as fast as possible. Antonio has been keeping track of her, but she never met up with anyone, only making trips to the bank." I frowned, wondering about her motives for using the shop to launder money and who she was doing it for.

Jacinta wasn't laundering the money for her own pleasure. We have checked the entire house and the boutique for any unusually large amounts of money stashed away. There wasn't anything.

"We need to check the banks she has visited. She probably has a safe with documents somewhere we don't know about." Lorenzo commented and I nodded in agreement.

"I will see what I can do." Raffaele worked on his laptop as the door creaked open, and Arianna stepped inside.

"We're ready to leave."

"You will have to leave with Cara. We have something to take care of." I told her, and she let out an annoyed sigh.

"Why are you the only ones allowed to have fun? I want to kick someone's ass, too." She scowled and crossed her arms.

"I need you to go back. We're having issues with the shipments, and I need you to deal with it. Dom could use your help." I explained, knowing she wouldn't leave if I didn't assign something to her. Her slow grin and excited eyes were proof that it worked.

"Wait, does that mean you're cool with me and Dom now?" She asked. I smirked and then faced Lorenzo, who had a displeased look on his face.

"What do you say, Lorenzo? Are we cool with it?"

"I need to have one more talk with the fucker before I decide." He sneered, not happy about the fact one of our men had taken a liking to our baby sister.

"Lorenzo, no! Your 'talk' involves anything except talking. It's not fair that you can be with someone, and I can't." Arianna challenged.

He walked towards her, staring intently, and the silence between them was filled with glares.

"If he hurts you or makes you cry, I will cut his throat open." He promised, and Arianna let out a scoff.

"You don't think I will get to him first if he does?" The raising of her brow resulted in a wicked smile from him.

"Good." Lorenzo said, showing his acceptance by kissing the top of her head. I smiled when I saw how happy she looked about it.

"Great! We will leave then." She smiled brightly and turned to leave, but stopped when Raffaele made a sound that caught our attention.

"What's going on?" I went over to him and looked at the screen where pages were scrolling quickly with a mix of letters and numbers.

"She got a call. It got disconnected after five seconds, but that's enough for me to make it work." Raffaele said, focusing on typing in code after code to finally trace the call while muttering words and numbers under his breath.

"I think I got it." He stopped typing, and a map showed up, a red dot blinking at the location. "Mastermind Raffaele did it again!" Getting to his feet, he punched the air and kept praising himself.

"Get ready to move." I told them.

We headed to the location on the other side of town once Arianna and Cara were up in the air. Stepping out of the car, I carefully scanned the surroundings on my end.

The sun had already set, making it almost entirely dark. The location was in the middle of nowhere, with a beat-down warehouse and trees surrounding the place.

Guns were drawn out as we silently moved forward, making sure we wouldn't be spotted by whoever was in there. Once we neared the warehouse, we split up. Lorenzo and Raffaele went around the left side of the warehouse, while I took the right side. Everything was quiet as we continued to move around.

Too quiet.

I met with Lorenzo and Raffaele at the back of the warehouse where a rusty door stood. With a quick nod towards Lorenzo, he pulled down the handle. The door swung open easily, and I entered the room, gun raised in front of me.

I moved forward into the dark warehouse. The only thing I could see were rows of empty shelves, barely illuminated by the faint moonlight seeping in through small windows.

I neared an open space when I stopped, the others following suit. I lowered my gun, my blood boiling at the sight of what was on the wall.

Hanging on the wall across from us were large pictures. Not just any pictures.

Pictures of all of us.

They were from during our stay here; of me and Althaia together, of Luca and Giovanni, Lorenzo and Cara, Arianna and Raffaele. There were even pictures of Antonio and Jacinta. Someone has been keeping track of us, managing to do so without being detected.

I looked at one particular picture that had me see fucking red.

Althaia and Jacinta with their faces crossed over with red spray paint. With the words R.I.P. right in the middle.

"It's a setup. It's a fucking trap!" I shouted. My body was shaking in anger as I turned to look at Raffaele and Lorenzo. "We need to get to Althaia now!"

Before I could even take a step towards the door, we heard several cars pulling up, their headlights streaming into the warehouse through the windows.

"Shit. Get down!" I shouted. I threw myself to take cover behind a shelf just as gunshots were fired into the warehouse.

We were surrounded, and shots were coming from all different directions, shattering the windows.

SIXTY

ALTHAIA

I slipped into my favorite midnight blue satin nightgown with a matching robe and made my way downstairs. My mother had made a small fire in the fireplace for some coziness. It was a bit funny that we had a fireplace, even though it was unnecessary in Florida. But my mother loved them, and they had grown on me.

"I made some tea. It's ginger to help with the nausea." My mother smiled warmly as she handed me a steaming mug, then settled down next to me on the couch, cradling her own cup.

"Thank you." I said gratefully.

We sat quietly together as we sipped our tea in a comfortable silence with the burning wood crackling. I faced my mother when she let out a sigh.

"I must say, they are a lot more different from what I had expected." She admitted. I raised my brows in surprise before a smile appeared on my lips.

"They are. Especially Arianna and Raffaele." I chuckled, and she rolled her eyes at the mention of Raffaele.

"That boy needs a good smacking or two with my wooden spoon. Shameless boy." My mother scoffed, making me laugh.

"You have no idea how many times he has teased me with his stupid comments." I shook my head, amused as I remembered his dumb jokes. "One time, he made such an inappropriate comment that Damiano threatened to shoot him." I laughed before I quickly realized I probably shouldn't have shared that.

To my surprise, my mother was smiling about it.

"It's obvious he cares about you. They all do, and..." She took a deep breath. "I know I haven't been supportive of your relationship with him, but I got scared for you. You are my priority. I want you to be safe and happy." My mother gave me a soft smile as she spoke, and tears formed in my eyes.

"I can see you're happy, and if it means you're happy with him, then there really isn't much I can do about it. I don't want to stand in the way of your happiness."

"Thank you." I said as relief washed over me, grateful that she had embraced our relationship and witnessed a different side of him.

"And now you're going to have a baby. My God, when did you get so grown up?" My mother chuckled with tears in her eyes, and she pulled me into a hug.

"I know. I still can't believe it." I sniffed, my eyes welling with tears. "I have something I need to talk to you about." I told her, feeling my nerves build up.

"He wants me to live with him when I go back for Cara's wedding." I said quietly.

"So soon?" My mother asked, gazing into the fireplace. "It only makes sense that you should live with him. But I need to talk to him before I let you go."

"Talk to him about what?" I asked. She looked at me again, giving me a small smile.

"Oh, you don't need to worry about it." My mother gave a small dismissive wave.

"I hate that answer. Damiano always gives me that answer." I sighed, but she just let out a small chuckle.

"You have always been too curious for your own good." She teased.

"I guess." I smiled. "Then can you tell me what it feels like to give birth? Cara said one's butthole explodes, and I'm mortified." I asked.

My mother was sipping her tea but choked as she accidentally laughed at the same time.

"That child talks too much. Don't listen to her. Your butthole won't explode." She shook her head in amusement. "It feels like bad period cramps. Just a hundred times worse and then it just progresses into something far more painful." My mother made a small grimace as if remembering the pain.

"That is not helpful at all, mom!" I looked at her in shock. Something worse than period cramps? My period cramps were already bad enough.

"But don't worry! You will get the epidural and you won't feel a thing. As soon as I got it, I slept through most of it, feeling no pain at all." She quickly reassured me.

"Thank God!" I put my hand up to my chest as I breathed out in relief.

We chatted for a while about everything as we drank our tea. It felt good to be able to talk to her about my relationship with Damiano, not having to keep it a secret anymore.

"Goodnight, I love you." I placed a kiss on her cheek, and she gave me a soft smile.

"I love you, too. Goodnight, honey."

Once reaching my room, I grabbed my phone, only to feel disappointed when I didn't see any text messages or calls from Damiano. They landed hours ago as Cara had texted me that they had arrived safely. Did he get busy with work the minute he got back?

I got comfortable under the blanket, placing my phone next to me in case he called, though tiredness quickly washed over me as soon as my head hit the pillow.

I jolted up in bed, a sudden loud sound startling me awake. My heart was pounding, and I could hear the thumping in my ears as I anxiously scanned my room.

The sound of hurried footsteps echoed towards my room, sending my heart pounding with fear, leaving me paralyzed and unable to move. The door swung open, and there stood my mother, her breath coming out in rapid gasps as she rushed towards me.

"We need to leave. Now!" She grabbed my hand, dragging me out of bed in a hurry. I gasped when I saw blood on her face and a gun in her hand.

"Mom, what's happening?" I said in a panic, my trembling voice barely able to form the words. My mother hushed me with a hand over my mouth and moved us away from the door as we heard another set of footsteps getting closer.

I clung tightly to my mother, feeling her tense muscles as she focused on the door, her finger on the trigger.

She quietly pulled me behind her when someone stopped in front of my door. The door was nudged, opening it wider than before. The sound of my pounding heart drowned out all other noise when I saw a pair of black gloves holding a gun.

My knees almost gave out on me when he stepped inside.

He was dressed in all black with his head covered, not allowing us to see what he looked like. Without hesitation, my mother pulled the trigger, and I watched him drop dead in front of us.

I couldn't even scream as my mother grabbed my hand again. We ran out of my room while she scanned our surroundings before running downstairs. My eyes went wide, and a gasp escaped my lips as I saw two more dead bodies on the floor; one with a knife deep in his chest. If it wasn't for my mother dragging me behind her, I would have collapsed right on the floor.

We burst through the door, making a beeline for the car, only to realize that the entire street was pitch black. None of the streetlights were working, which filled me with even more fear.

The moment we climbed into the car, my mother slammed her foot on the gas, causing the tires to screech. A scream escaped me when someone jumped on the hood of the car, aiming a gun at us.

"Hold on!" My mother yelled to me, and I quickly reached for the grab handle to steady myself as she made a sharp turn, causing the man to fly off. "Seatbelt on, Althaia!"

It took me a few tries to fasten my seatbelt with how hard I was pulling it. At this point, I had trouble breathing, and my entire body was shaking in fear and panic.

"That damned bastard took me by surprise! I should have known he would do this sooner rather than later." She said angrily to herself while driving so fast everything was a blur.

"W-what's going on? What's happening?!" I screamed as I looked at her. Then my eyes widened even more when I remembered Luca. "Where's Luca? Did you kill Luca?"

"No! I haven't seen him. I don't know where he is."

"Oh my God, what if he's dead?!" I went to reach for my phone, only realizing I didn't have it with me. "I need a phone!"

"There's a phone in the glove compartment."

I quickly opened it and grabbed the phone, my fingers trembling as I tried to remember his number, but my mind went blank.

"You've got to be fucking kidding me." My mother hissed when something caught her eye in the rearview mirror. Glancing over my shoulder, I saw two cars racing towards us.

"Althaia, get down!"

She forcefully pushed me down into the seat just before the sound of gunshots was heard. My mother tried to swerve to avoid them, but it was difficult since we were on a long empty road with only trees surrounding us.

I had my eyes squeezed shut, trying to calm down so I would be able to remember anyone's phone number.

"They are aiming for the tires." My mother continued to swerve sharply from side to side, making me snap out of it and quickly dial a number.

"Luca!" I yelled into the phone when he picked up.

"Althaia! Are you okay?!" He asked frantically. I let out a breath of relief when I heard his voice.

"Thank God you're alive!" I sobbed into the phone. "I don't know what's going on. People broke into the house. We're in the car, trying to get away, but two cars are following and shooting at us." I quickly tried to explain the situation to him, stumbling over my words.

"We're driving as fast as we can to get to you. We got ambushed. They came out of nowhere!" He growled in anger. I swallowed hard. We were fucked.

"We can see the cars now. We will take care of them from here." Luca said as I heard the gunshots coming from his end through the phone. Glancing in the side mirror, I saw the cars behind us swerving frantically to dodge the bullets, but it still didn't stop them from shooting at us.

"Luca -" My head collided with the car door with violent force, causing the phone to slip from my grasp as the car spiraled out of control.

With the rear tire shot, my mother struggled to regain control, but it was useless. The car kept forcing us to the side of the road and into the woods, violently shaking as it sped over the bumpy ground.

My throat closed, not allowing me to make a sound before we crashed into a tree.

I let out a pained groan as my head throbbed and the wetness of something warm seeped through my trembling hands. I struggled to lift my head as my entire body felt heavy.

The door beside me swung open, and I squinted to see my mother's lips moving, but her words were muffled, as if my head was underwater.

"Althaia, we need to run!" Her voice pierced through. The adrenaline kick-started my body into action, temporarily numbing the pain as I got out.

We sprinted deeper into the woods when we heard the sound of car doors slamming and footsteps behind us. Gunshots rang out, causing me to scream in terror and instinctively cover my head with my arm.

"Keep running!" I heard Luca shout.

I was breathing heavily, my chest heaving with each labored breath, but somehow, I found the strength to push myself to run faster.

My mother held my hand tightly, her breathing coming out faster too as she led us into the woods, trying to get away as far as possible from whoever was after us.

Sixty-One

DAMIANO

Bullets flew over our heads while we stayed on the floor. I focused on listening to how many were currently firing. Based on the direction of the bullets coming through the windows, my guess was around eight people; two people on each side of the warehouse, surrounding the building.

Now, the question was how many were out with them, not firing at us.

The fire suddenly stopped, and I glanced over at Lorenzo and Raffaele to find them unharmed. I signaled to them to spread out as I silently rose to my feet.

In these situations, the best strategy was to play dead. It would give us time to work quietly and take them down once they came for confirmation of our dead bodies.

I looked around the warehouse and made my way to a corner where I would be able to take cover. It was now completely dark outside, with no light to be seen from streetlights or headlights.

It was perfection, for I was the Devil, and within my heart, darkness reigned supreme.

I crouched down when the door slowly opened, but no one entered to make sure there wouldn't be any attacks from our side. At this point, I was fucking furious, ready to get my hands on them as fast as possible so I could get to Althaia.

Althaia.

The thought of her being in danger right now ignited a fiery rage within me, and I could feel my body trembling with anger. I closed my eyes, taking in a deep breath and forced my body into a cold zero.

Eliminating all emotions.

I couldn't allow myself to feel anything right now and make any rash decisions. I wanted this to be quick and efficient. We were outnumbered, but with how many, I still wasn't sure. I needed my head in the game.

Arianna's words about Althaia having great survival instincts echoed in my mind, and for once in my life, I prayed she and our baby would be okay.

They have to be.

I let out a long breath, shutting my body down from feeling anything. My complete attention was on taking down those bastards who had the audacity to make such a move against us.

I was thirsty for blood.

I was going to make sure every single drop of theirs was going to be spilled. I wanted the head of the motherfucker who wrote that shit on the wall.

I snapped my eyes open when I heard movements. They were slowly entering the warehouse; one by one, carefully searching to see if they could find our dead bodies on the ground.

I almost wanted to scoff out loud at the naivety of their belief that it would be this easy to kill us. But I was about to show them just how easy it will be to kill them.

Eight of them walked in and split up. Just the number I thought they would be. One came closer in my direction, but I was out of his view. I was still crouched down, remaining still and silent as I waited for him to come closer.

I was molded for this my entire life; born to lead, raised to kill. Whoever was behind this thought they could take me down with a mere trap and a surprise attack. They severely underestimated the apex predator they were dealing with. This wasn't my first time and won't be my last. I wanted to laugh if they thought they would be successful.

He was inches away from me as I observed him to see what kind of person I was dealing with. The way he moved immediately let me know that this wasn't a person who was skilled enough; his movements were clumsy and uncertain.

For the first time in a situation like this, I fucking rolled my eyes. They had hired a group of useless shitheads to get the job done.

I was fucking offended.

He was jittery, constantly glancing over his shoulder in paranoia, fearing that someone might have snuck up on him. I shook my head in disappointment.

I lunged forward and grabbed his head. I covered his mouth with my hand and snapped his neck without making a sound. His body fell limp against mine, and I quietly moved him into the dark corner. I took his gun, tucking it into my waistband behind my back.

I moved along the wall, staying low and hidden in the shadows to get to the next one. I knew Lorenzo and Raffaele had taken care of some already, as I only spotted four now. One of them whispered something to his comrade. I frowned when I didn't recognize the language, but I couldn't care less about it right now.

This was going to end. Now.

I picked up a piece of broken glass and threw it across the warehouse to distract them. They immediately reacted to the noise and split up in two. The others went in the direction of Raffaele and Lorenzo, leaving the two closest to me completely unaware that I had sneaked up behind them.

I grabbed my knife and slit his throat open. In a split second, I moved to the next one when he turned around. He had no time to react before I stabbed my knife deep into his right eye. I watched him drop to his knees, and when I took my knife out, he fell dead to the ground. At the same time, I heard another body drop on the other end.

I moved quietly between the shelves, scanning my surroundings to make sure there were no more inside. I saw Raffaele and Lorenzo coming out of the shadows, signaling to me it was clear from their side.

Now, the question was how many we would face outside.

As we moved closer to the door, Lorenzo grabbed a dead body close to him and threw it out of the door. In an instant, gunshots erupted from outside, alerting us to the fact that there were definitely more than five other people. None of them had the courage to approach the door and kept a safe distance.

I looked over to Raffaele and motioned for him to go to the window from his end, while I made my way to the broken window on my side, and Lorenzo stayed near the door.

With a nod at Raffaele, he sprang to his feet and rapidly fired several rounds out of the window. He took cover once the others found him and shot in his direction. While they were distracted, it allowed me to look out of the window and scan the situation outside.

Ten more people were outside. It wasn't a problem as I took down three men with my gun. They scattered around, trying to hide behind the trees and out of my view. Little did they realize they were still in Lorenzo's line of sight as he shot at them from the door.

They sprayed gunfire everywhere, hoping to hit us. It was useless; the warehouse was much sturdier than expected. It annoyed me endlessly that we were dealing with a bunch of amateurs. The upside was, we would be done with them soon.

Their firing stopped, and I pulled out the extra gun I had as I moved along the long window, firing at them. Impatience welled within me. This had already taken too long.

"Cover me!" I yelled to Raffaele and Lorenzo as I jumped out of the window.

I sprinted towards one of the cars, throwing myself to the ground to seek cover behind it. Swiftly, I reloaded my gun before springing back to my feet.

Darting between the trees, I fired shots to create a distraction, giving Raffaele and Lorenzo a chance to escape the warehouse. The last person in my line of sight fell to my gunfire, and suddenly, the entire area went silent. I strained to listen for any further movements.

"To your right!" Raffaele shouted, and I quickly turned to see that I had missed one person who had taken cover behind a large tree.

A stinging sensation sliced through my upper arm as he moved faster than I could evade, giving him the opportunity to slash me. Fueled by fury, I grabbed his arm, twisted it, and landed repeated punches to his face.

"Piece of shit." I sneered.

I pressed him against the tree, forcefully smashing the back of his head against the trunk. I grabbed his knife, and I stabbed it into his throat with such force that it pierced all the way through and into the trunk of the tree.

I looked at my arm. The cut was deep, and thick blood trickled down my arm, but I ignored it as we ran towards our car, getting in quickly as Lorenzo sped away.

I grabbed my phone and called Luca, only for it to go straight to voicemail.

"Raffaele, track Althaia down. She's wearing the earrings." I told him as I tried to call Antonio. It kept ringing, letting me know it was bad on their end.

Fuck!

"Antonio! Tell me what's going on." I spoke as soon as I heard it pick up. His breathing was heavy, and I gritted my teeth as I knew I couldn't expect anything good.

"Fuck, man. I have no idea what happened. We got ambushed. They broke into the house, but Althaia and her mother got out and drove away. We followed as soon as we could." He said hurriedly, but stopped talking as I heard more gunshots coming through the phone.

"Althaia?" I growled out, feeling my heart beating faster as I waited for his answer.

"I… I don't know. They fled into the woods. I tried to follow, but more of these bastards kept coming!"

"Fuck!" I yelled out and punched the dashboard. I tightened my hold on the phone, my fingers trembling with frustration, as I felt completely powerless in the car.

"I got their location!" Raffaele turned to Lorenzo, giving him directions as he drove as fast as he could.

"Hold them off! We're on our way." I ended the call by throwing the phone to the bottom of the car. Gripping my head in my hands, I felt a whirlwind of emotions now.

Althaia, baby, hang on. I'm on my way.

Sixty-Two

ALTHAIA

We kept running deeper into the depths of the dark woods. Our bare feet pounded on the forest floor, trying to escape the people chasing us and the bullets flying by. But my pace had slowed down. My body begged for even a small gulp of air, my lungs burning for a break, but I had to keep going.

I still hadn't fully recovered despite what I told Damiano. My body was weak and heavy, covered in sweat as my legs threatened to collapse. If it wasn't for my mother's tight grip on my hand, pushing me to keep going, I would be dead.

"Over here." My mother led us behind a towering tree, its trunk wide enough to hide us.

My body gave out, and I crumpled to the ground. I gasped for air, feeling a sharp pain with each breath. Nausea threatened to overpower me, but I somehow held it at bay and shifted my attention to calming my breath. My mother sat down on the ground and rubbed my back, trying to help me as best she could.

I rested my back against the tree, closing my eyes when I felt lightheaded.

"It looks like we lost them. For now." My mother whispered.

The woods were silent. Not a single gunshot or rustle of movement reached my ears, making me question how far we had run into the depths of the forest.

"Are you okay? Are you hurt anywhere?" My mother asked. I opened my eyes and gripped her hand tightly in mine.

"I think I'm fine." I panted. I couldn't tell if I was hurt or not because right now, I couldn't feel a thing. It was as if my body had gone numb.

"Are you okay?" I asked her, and she nodded silently while her eyes darted around, scanning our surroundings. "Mom... what's going on?" I whispered.

She looked at me with a pained expression on her face as she swallowed hard.

"I'm so sorry..." She whispered back, her eyes glistening while holding my hand in hers. "This was not supposed to happen. I just wanted to protect you. Everything I did was for your protection. But I failed." A tear escaped her eye, and she pulled me into her, hugging me tightly into her body.

I already had tears streaming down my cheeks as I sobbed into her shirt, wrapping my arms tightly around her.

"I'm so sorry. I didn't know what else to do. He was threatening to hurt you. I had no choice but to follow his orders to protect you." She explained, and I leaned back to look at her.

"What's happening? Who are you talking about?" I anxiously scanned her face.

"I should have told you the truth from the beginning." My mother's eyes were filled with regret. "Althaia, honey, listen to me. Whatever happens to me, you stick with Damiano. He's the only one who will protect you from him."

"Don't say that! Mom, please, you're scaring me. Who are you talking about?" My breath halted as I waited for her answer, and my body grew colder with each passing moment.

"Make him swear to always protect you no matter what. Do you promise me, Althaia?" She looked at me firmly, and all I could do was nod.

"We don't have time to go into detail, but–" The sound of a twig snapping interrupted her, causing her to snap her head quickly toward the noise. My body froze, not daring to move an inch or make a sound, not even to breathe as I cupped my hands over my mouth, afraid to give away our hiding place.

Light movements could be heard, the crunching of leaves letting us know we were no longer alone. I heard hushed whispers as they came closer. I strained to listen in on the conversation, realizing that they weren't speaking English.

Korean?

I frowned the more I tried to focus on their conversation, but I couldn't make out what they were saying.

We rose to our feet as quietly as possible, prepared to face whatever awaited us. My heart resumed its rapid pounding, and my legs trembled with fear. I had to force myself to calm down; this wasn't the time to freeze up.

I pressed against the tree trunk, trying to catch what they were saying. Suddenly, I was shoved aside so hard I fell to the ground. The abrupt crack of a gun made me snap my head toward the sound, only to find my mother aiming at the spot where I had just been standing.

My eyes widened when I spotted another person coming from behind my mother.

"Behind you!" I screamed just in time for her to turn around and pull the trigger.

But it was empty.

"Althaia, run!" She yelled just as he lunged after her, but she blocked his attack and used the gun to smash him in the head.

I scurried to get up on my feet to help her, only to feel a strong kick coming out of nowhere, hitting me right in the ribs. It forced me onto my back and the air completely left my lungs.

I drew in a sharp breath and rolled to my side, violently coughing while gasping for air as pain radiated throughout my body. A scream escaped my lips when a fistful of my hair was grabbed, forcing me onto my feet.

"Let her go!" My mother screamed at him. She tried to get to me, but she was fighting off two people at the same time.

I clenched my hand into a fist and aimed for his face. He grabbed my arm and twisted it so painfully behind my back.

He forcefully pushed me against a tree, his body completely pressed up against mine, with his forearm against my throat, choking me.

I tried to claw his arm to break free, but he was so much bigger and stronger than I was. His arm crushed my windpipe, making me gag as I desperately tried to gasp for air.

I tried to push him away, but my push was too weak. I looked into his eyes; they were the only visible feature, and he observed me, tilting his head slightly to the side.

My eyes were slowly drooping, black spots appearing in my sight, when he suddenly removed his arm from my throat. I immediately took a sharp breath. The moment was short-lived when he grabbed me again.

My back was against his front as he held me in a headlock, my arms behind my back. I slowly blinked, my body growing weaker by the second. I regained some focus, seeing my mother being held by the two men, a knife against her throat, forcing her to stay still.

"It's me who you want. She has nothing to do with anything. Let her go!" She glared at him and tried to break free, but the more she struggled to move, the deeper the knife dug into her, cutting her skin, and blood trickled down her throat.

"You should have thought about that. Now, she has to pay for your mistakes too." I could hear his sinister smile as he spoke. He sounded almost amused.

"It's a pity, really. She's almost too pretty to die. Maybe I'll take her. I can make a fortune off her." He let out a laugh as if it was the funniest thing ever, making the other two chuckle along with him.

"Let us go!" I screamed, thrashing in his hold.

"She's a feisty little one." He tightened his hold on me, almost crushing me. "I will enjoy you before I snap that pretty little neck of yours." He whispered in my ear, dragging his nose alongside my cheek.

I gagged.

"H-he's going to kill you." I choked out.

"And who's going to kill me? Your boyfriend? I have some news for you; he's already dead." He laughed.

My body froze in shock.

"You're lying…" My voice was barely audible. With tears in my eyes, I looked at my mother. She too went silent at his words, her eyes wide in shock.

"I have no reason to lie. Don't worry, you'll reunite with him. In Hell." He said, and the other one plunged a knife deep into my mother's stomach. She let out a breathless gasp, her mouth slightly open as she gazed at me, tears escaping her eyes.

I stared at her in horror. The little strength I had disappeared, and my body went limp against his with tears streaming down my face. My mother closed her eyes, and she winced in pain as he pulled out the knife, only to plunge it right in again.

"Mamá" I screamed at the top of my lungs, watching her slowly slip out of consciousness as he stabbed her one more time.

A hand clamped on my mouth to stop my screaming, and I vigorously thrashed around, moving my entire body to break free while I cried for my mother.

I watched her fall to the ground, blood soaking her shirt fast. She slowly blinked, looking at me for the last time before closing her eyes entirely.

My throat tightened completely, and I stopped moving, my body going numb. I blocked everything else around me out, only seeing her and feeling my heart being ripped out as I stared at her numbly.

I was in shock, waiting for my mother to get up on her feet, to show me she was okay and still alive. But slowly, my mind understood why my mother was lying on the ground, unmoving.

I didn't realize I had been laid down on the ground. I was still looking at my mother. I felt a pair of hands slowly creeping up my legs and slipping under the nightgown I had on, making their way towards my underwear and pulling it down my legs.

Turning my gaze away from my mother, I looked up at the night sky. My view was blocked as he leaned over me.

My gaze pierced his eyes, my own eyes empty of emotion while his were wicked and consumed by lust as he positioned himself between my thighs.

"I'm going to kill you." I told him, my voice monotonous. I felt his chest vibrate against mine as he let out a small chuckle, ready to proceed with his intentions when I spoke again. "I don't think you understand. I said I'm going to kill you."

I clenched the rock under my hand and brought it crashing into the side of his head.

He yelled out in pain as he fell to the side, holding his head in his hands. Moving quickly, I kept him down by straddling his waist and grabbed the rock with both hands. I lifted it high above my head before bringing it down on his face.

And again.

And one more time.

I screamed at him as I watched the blood flow out from his face, watching him become lifeless underneath me.

And I didn't stop.

I kept going, hearing the sickening thud as the rock smashed into his face. Again and again, until his brain mass splattered out.

"Let go of me!" I screamed as a pair of hands grabbed me from behind, dragging me up. I kept screaming, tears blurring my sight as I tried to break free from their grasp.

"Althaia, stop!"

I stopped, my breaths coming heavy as I was turned around to see it was Luca.

"Luca... help me... my mom." I cried out to him desperately, turning to look at her, only to see Antonio by her side. My eyes darted around, taking in the grim sight of the two lifeless bodies sprawled on the ground.

"Antonio is doing his best. Are you hurt?" Luca asked. Before I could answer him, I let out a strangled breath, squeezing my eyes shut in pain.

I collapsed onto Luca, my hand clutching my stomach. Painful cramps were all I felt, as if I were being stabbed over and over again.

"Althaia!"

I opened my eyes, crying in relief when I saw his face as he ran towards me.

"Damiano..." I let out a pained cry and Damiano abruptly stopped running.

"Shit..." Luca whispered.

I looked at Damiano in horror when I felt it. His expression mirrored mine. I looked down, seeing large streams of blood flowing down my shaking legs.

"No..." Damiano breathed out in a whisper.

Tears silently made their way down my face as he closed the distance between us. He pulled me tightly into his body, his arms around me as if he was trying to shield me.

My eyes closed, and darkness enveloped me, releasing me from the torment of my reality, and leaving behind a heart shattered into irreparable pieces.

Sixty-Three
DAMIANO

I couldn't take my eyes off her as she lay on the hospital bed. Needles were injected into her arms, while her forehead, legs, and feet were all bandaged. Her feet were badly cut up from running through the woods barefoot. Her entire body was bruised and slowly showed discoloration.

She looked almost... lifeless.

"When will she wake up?" I asked Ellie while she changed Althaia's blood-soaked bandages.

"It's hard to tell. Her body shut down and is trying its best to recover after experiencing extensive trauma. And with the blood loss, too, I wouldn't be surprised if she needed another day or two." Ellie sighed, and I gave a short nod.

I couldn't help but look down at Ellie's small baby bump and then glance at Althaia's flat stomach. My chest tightened at the sight. I averted my eyes and looked out the window, trying to shut down from feeling anything at the moment.

But fucking hell, it was hitting hard.

I was happy for Antonio and his wife. Still, the universe was laughing in my face by doing this to me. I knew I was being punished for every sin I had committed; punishing me for every single life I had killed and taken pleasure in doing so.

I was being punished through the one I loved, and the universe took away our baby.

"There's something else I need to discuss with you." Ellie said carefully. "I'll need to perform a dilation and curettage to remove the remains from the uterus."

"Ellie."

"Yes?"

"Get out."

"Of course; however, it's urgent to minimize the risk of infection and toxicity. I'll be back in a bit." Ellie closed the door behind her, and my gaze returned to Althaia.

I let out a breath as I slowly approached her, taking a seat beside her.

"What have I done to you?" I whispered as I cradled her in my arms. I promised to protect her, and I failed. "I'm sorry, baby, I'm so sorry."

"I've brought you a change of clothes." Arianna said as she walked in, carrying a garment bag with her. Ellie and Giovanni followed right after, his fist clenching as he looked at Althaia. He didn't want to leave her side. The furthest he would go was right outside the door.

The entire area was heavily guarded with my armed men at every entrance. I couldn't risk another surprise attack while Althaia was trying to recover.

"Damiano, you need to get some rest. It's been two days." Arianna sighed.

"I'm not leaving her." I snapped. I refused to leave her. I felt like if I let her out of my sight, she would die.

"She's going to wake up soon, and you won't be of any help if you pass out from sleep deprivation." She spoke softly.

"We'll be here." Giovanni assured me.

"Or at least take a shower. You don't want her to freak out when she wakes up." Arianna said, and after a while, I agreed.

"Let me just have a look at your arm first." Ellie said once she was done changing Althaia's bandages. I got slashed pretty deep on my arm and had to get stitched up. "Are you feeling better?"

"It's fine." I replied. I had a high pain tolerance, and it didn't bother me much.

"I mean, are you still experiencing any symptoms of food poisoning?" She asked, making me look at her with a frown.

"I didn't get food poisoning."

Ellie raised her brows a little in surprise.

"Oh, so you didn't have the same food then?"

"We did, but only Althaia got it. The doctor said she caught it easily because of... a weakened immune system." I spat out bitterly. I couldn't get myself to say that it was because she *was* pregnant.

"Hmm." Ellie grabbed her tablet and tapped around.

"What is it?" I asked.

"Are you sure you had the same food?" She asked once again.

"We had the same food for breakfast, and we didn't get sick either." Arianna commented, making Ellie sigh with a frown as she continued to look at her tablet.

"... No, that can't be it." She muttered to herself.

"Ellie." I said impatiently, making her look up at me.

"When she got food poisoning, did you go to the hospital immediately?"

"Yes."

"Then that can't be it. Unless..." She kept on muttering under her breath.

"You think Althaia was specifically poisoned?" I asked, getting straight to the point. My own words had me clenching my jaw in anger.

"Maybe. If you all had the same food, everyone would have been affected. The blood test they took of her showed nothing, either. While pregnancy weakens the immune system, it's not to a point where only she would get sick."

I had to move my neck from side to side to ease the tension in my body before I exploded.

"What do you think it is?" Giovanni asked, his tone dripping with fury.

Ellie grew quiet, her thoughts consumed by studying Althaia's medical journal.

"She had cake." I said, suddenly remembering she ate something I didn't. "She only had a small bite of it."

"What kind?"

"It was chocolate cake, her favorite." I tried to remember if there was anything unusual about it, but there wasn't.

"Did it have powdered sugar on top?" Ellie asked. I nodded, and the realization instantly crossed her face.

"Arsenic." She said confidently. "That's my suspicion. It was likely mixed with the actual powdered sugar. Since she only took a small bite, she experienced cramps and vomiting - typical signs of food poisoning. If they intended to kill her, they would have used a larger dose." Ellie explained.

"I think someone tried to induce a miscarriage, but what doesn't make sense is that Arsenic would have shown up when they did a blood test, which is making me believe her test was swapped out with another."

I turned around and faced the window, my hands gripping the windowsill, my veins pulsating throughout my body. The overwhelming fury inside me begged for release. My head was burning as if I had a fever, wanting to explode. Instead, I closed my eyes and tried to calm down.

"I can't help but think that it was an attack on you, Damiano." Arianna said. "They've been keeping track of us all, and they found out she was pregnant. I think they're trying to prevent you from having an heir by putting the poison on something she would definitely eat."

I was itching to punch the wall, my hands twitching with the desperate urge to unleash this anger within me.

"The guy who attacked Althaia at the hotel was Asian, too. We know her mother was laundering money, but we never found out for whom. Could it really be for Asians?" Giovanni was thinking out loud, trying to connect the dots.

"But why Asians? It doesn't make sense." Arianna questioned.

"She wasn't working for the Asians." I said and faced them. "The ones we faced were mercenaries and not only of Asian descent. Whatever her mother was doing, it was ending, and they wanted to get rid of her."

My initial suspicion was that she was working with Asians. However, after that night, it became clear they were just hired to cover up for the one who ordered the hit. The money laundering wasn't for some random street gang but for someone much more powerful.

Jacinta could take care of herself, too smart to be blackmailed by a couple of lowlifes. It must be someone with something greater and more valuable to hold against her, making her act the way she did.

Such as her daughter.

The door swung open once more, and Antonio and Lorenzo entered, offering a nod in greeting. Antonio and Luca had done the best they could. We arrived just in time before it would have been too late for them as well.

They were able to hold them off with the extra weapons hidden in their car. Still, Antonio needed stitches from being slashed and Luca got shot in the leg, but nothing more than a flesh wound and would be back on his feet soon.

Ellie checked on her husband's stitches before stepping out, leaving us to our discussion. I didn't want to feel bitter about it, but there was a subtle relief when she left. I didn't want to have to look at the painful reminder of her bump.

"Cara talked to Althaia's father. He'll be here in a few hours." Lorenzo informed us. I didn't want anyone from outside to be here, but he was still her father.

"How's Cara holding up?" I asked him.

"She's been out of it. I had to give her something to calm down. She's asleep now." He let out a small sigh, and I could tell he hadn't slept either.

"What do you want us to do?" Giovanni asked, determined to put a plan into action.

"Nothing. For now." My response caught them off guard.

"You can't be serious?" Arianna exclaimed loudly.

"Keep your voice down." I sneered at her with a glare. "If we go into action now, not knowing exactly who to target, word would spread out that we are looking for someone, and it will force them to go underground."

"We'll keep a low profile for now, but I want eyes and ears everywhere. Some fled during the fight, and there will always be one fucker or two who will run their mouth and brag about being hired to take down la Famiglia Bellavia. Once we have given them enough time to let their guard down, we'll strike." I explained.

With time, they will think they have broken me, but little do they realize the storm of vengeance I will unleash.

The Devil's wrath.

Sixty-Four

ALTHAIA

I was surrounded by an impenetrable darkness, my entire body burdened with a crushing heaviness that imprisoned every limb. There were muffled voices in the distance, but my mouth refused to let out a sound for help.

What's happening to me?

An overwhelming fatigue swept over me. Too weak to fight it, I let it drag me into a deep slumber, leaving my question unanswered.

I was slowly waking up, but my body still felt heavy and... in pain. Aches resonated throughout my entire body. My head pounded, and my stomach writhed, making it hard for me to move.

A distinct weight pressed down on my hand. It was a different heaviness from the rest of my body. I tried to move my hand, but only a finger responded. I heard some shuffling before my hand received a gentle squeeze, and something brushed against my face. I leaned slightly into the touch; a small sound escaped my lips as I attempted to speak.

"Althaia baby, wake up."

"Everything hurts." I wanted to say, but my lips weren't moving.

"You're doing well, baby. Take your time." He spoke gently to me, and I felt his hand caressing my head as I gave it a small squeeze.

After a while, I slowly opened my eyes, blinking a few times with my heavy eyelids while trying to let my eyes focus on my surroundings. Confusion settled in when I realized it was a hospital room. I turned my head to the side and saw Damiano.

We didn't say anything as our eyes met, and I saw him visibly relax. His expression carried a hint of pain, leaving me with a slight frown as I wondered why he would look at me like that.

Lifting my hand, I gently placed it on his cheek, caressing him and noting the exhaustion etched on his face. Damiano closed his eyes as if he had longed for my touch, placing his hand over mine and kissing my palm.

"Wha -" I winced in pain, halting my words when my dry throat hurt intensely.

"Shh, don't talk if it hurts. I'll get you some water." Damiano poured a glass and put a straw in it as he handed it to me.

"Small sips." He instructed. I tried to follow, but the cool water running down my parched throat felt so soothing that I emptied the glass a bit faster than I should have, now feeling a little nauseous.

I immediately groaned in pain when I tried to move to sit up. It felt like I had been hit by a truck over and over again.

"Don't move, you have a bruised rib. I'll call for Ellie and let her know you're awake." He pressed a button on the side.

"Wh-what happened?" It came out as a half-whisper. My voice was hoarse and cracked a little as I tried to speak. Licking my dry lips, I tried to piece together why I was in so much pain.

"...You don't remember what happened?" Damiano frowned slightly as I shook my head. He kept my hand in his when the door opened quietly, and Ellie walked in with a smile.

"Good to see you're awake. I'm just going to examine you and ask you a few questions." I gave her a small nod as she flashed her penlight into my eyes, causing me to blink rapidly at the sharp light.

"Do you know who you are? When is your birthday?" Ellie continued to ask me questions about myself, and I answered them all.

"Do you know what happened to you?"

"No."

Damiano gave my hand a small squeeze, making me look at him.

"Can anyone tell me what happened?" I asked.

"Althaia." I turned back to Ellie, who wore a serious expression, causing my heart to beat faster. "You were in a car accident."

I instinctively reached up to touch the bandage wrapped around my head. Swallowing hard, I tried to recall the events, and my body tensed despite the pain. Fragments rushed back, and my breathing quickened. I squeezed Damiano's hand as panic set in.

All those men.

The woods.

My mother!

"Mom ..." I whispered. Panic surged through me, and I tried to get out of bed. I had to see if she was okay.

Ellie tried to calm me, but I pushed her hands away, determined to find my mother.

"Althaia stop. You're hurting yourself." Damiano urged as I groaned in pain. He had to hold me gently to prevent me from moving. Tears welled up as I looked at him.

"My mom... where is she? Is she okay? Tell me she's okay." I clung tightly to Damiano's arms, desperately searching his face for any sign. But the longer he remained silent, the more the truth settled in.

Images of my mother being stabbed repeatedly flashed in my mind, and I let out a shocked gasp. Tears streamed down my face uncontrollably. I shook my head, hoping against hope that Damiano would say it was all a terrible nightmare and everything was still okay.

"I'm sorry..." Damiano's words confirmed the nightmare was real. Sobs escaped from me, and I crumbled as he held me.

"You're lying!" I choked out, wanting to break free from his grasp, but he held me tightly as I sobbed into his chest.

My mother, who had cared for me my whole life, was gone.

My entire body trembled as Damiano held me close. The tears showed no sign of stopping, and with each passing moment, my heart seemed to shatter a little more.

I lost track of time as I cried, but eventually my sobs subsided, leaving me feeling numb.

"Baby... our baby?" I asked, my tone detached as I placed a hand on my stomach. Memories of the pain in the woods and the sight of blood flooding down my legs rushed back.

Damiano looked at me, his hands cradling my face, sadness clear in his eyes.

"The trauma was too much... your body couldn't handle it." He explained gently. I took a sharp breath, my heart squeezing so much I was sure it would stop beating. "You had a miscarriage." He whispered, his voice heavy with sorrow.

His words hung in the air, and I struggled to understand. Pregnant with his child, the baby we had seen on the screen, the one we had grown to love and cherish... it was all gone. Everything we had excitedly expected had vanished in the blink of an eye.

"Our... baby... is... gone?" I couldn't register the sudden crash of despair and mourning; instead, I felt numb and paralyzed.

Why?

The question lingered, but I hesitated to voice it, afraid of the answer. Instead, I was consumed by an overwhelming sense of loss.

I lost everything.

"I'm sorry. I'm sorry I couldn't get to you in time." Damiano buried his face in my neck, his hold remaining firm as I stared blankly out the window.

His repeated apologies echoed, but everything still felt surreal. Somehow, I clung to the hope of waking up from this nightmare, longing for an end to this unbearable torment. But as time passed, the harsh reality of my nightmare settled in.

"But... why?" I whispered. He lowered his shaking head, unable to meet my eyes. "My dad... I want my dad." I muttered.

"I will get him." Ellie said, leaving the room.

Damiano leaned back, his eyes reflecting a turmoil I had never witnessed before. I wanted to comfort him, but I felt so lost, confused, and empty.

The door opened again, revealing my father with Michael trailing behind him. I broke down once more.

"Papá..." I cried out, reaching for him instinctively, much like I would have when I was a kid. My father hurried to my side and enveloped me in his embrace. "They took my mom from me." I sobbed, clinging tightly to him, terrified of losing the only parent I had left.

"They are going to pay for it. I promise you, figlia." My father assured me, his hand rubbing my back comfortingly. Michael stepped closer, holding my hand for support, his eyes reflecting the same sadness I felt.

I knew my mother meant almost as much to him as she did to me. She had cared for us all, offering a love that couldn't be replaced. And now she was just... gone. A part of me resisted accepting it, holding onto a sliver of hope that it wasn't true. Yet, deep down, I knew the painful reality.

"God, why..." I cried. The loss of my baby, whom I loved and cared for deeply, multiplied the pain in my body; it was a constant reminder of my misery.

"My mom and my baby... they're gone." I whispered between sobs. Michael tensed at my words, a frown creasing his forehead.

"Your... baby?" Confusion colored his expression.

I remained silent, wrapping my arm around my stomach. His eyes followed my movements until realization dawned on him. Michael's hand squeezed mine, and he shot a cold, questioning look at Damiano.

Overwhelmed, I closed my eyes and leaned into my father, wanting to go back to that impenetrable darkness.

Sixty-Five

ALTHAIA

"She's going back with us." Michael asserted firmly.

"No." Damiano replied in his cold tone.

"No? Who do you think you are to make that decision?!" Michael erupted angrily.

"If you don't keep your voice down, I will kill you." Damiano's voice was low and calm but filled with promise as they continued to argue about me.

I wasn't sure if they were aware I was awake and could hear them. My back was to the door, but I guess it was slightly open as I heard everything they said, arguing about where I should stay.

It made me realize I didn't have a place I could call home anymore. Even though I had stayed a few weeks in my father's mansion before, I still didn't consider it home because for a long time, it wasn't.

"She's staying with me." Damiano stated firmly, giving no room for discussion. I could hear how Michael was getting frustrated until my father ended their argument.

"Michael, it's fine."

"She needs to stay with her family. Not him." He pressed on.

"Enough!" My father raised his voice, and Michael went silent. "She will stay with him."

I heard him make a sound of disapproval before hearing him walk away. My father let out a sigh.

"I apologize for his behavior. Understand that they grew up together, and he is only looking out for her." My father tried to explain.

"I don't care. If he steps out of line one more time -"

"He won't." My father quickly said. "I will make sure he knows his place."

The door closed, and Damiano came into my view. He sat on the chair beside the bed, looking at me. I didn't hide the fact I heard everything they talked about. Not that it was something I cared about.

My mind was a relentless reel of the horrifying events in the woods. Each night was tormenting. Exhaustion clawed at me, but the nightmares held me captive. My eyes burned with lack of sleep, yet the haunting images continued, leaving me trapped in a relentless cycle of misery.

"Ellie will change your bandages, and then we can leave." Damiano said quietly. I didn't reply and continued to stare straight ahead, still feeling numb and so lost.

He helped me sit up on the bed when Ellie came in. My body still felt incredibly heavy but with minimal pain, thanks to the drugs I had been given.

I sat on the edge of the bed while she checked the wound I had on the side of my head. As I kept my eyes down, I saw the small baby bump behind her loose doctor's coat.

Ellie's pregnant.

A lump formed in my throat as I continued to stare at her stomach. Was she trying to hide that she was pregnant with loose clothing so I wouldn't notice? I wanted to let out a humorless laugh at life slapping me in the face right now.

"Everything is healing as it should be, and you won't need the bandages anymore. You're all set and free to go." Ellie said.

I was healing on the outside, but inside, my soul remained broken.

"Congratulations..." I mumbled out to her and tried to give a small smile, but not much happened. It felt more like a painful grimace than a smile.

Ellie looked at me in surprise and then noticed I was staring at her stomach, unconsciously fixing her coat in a way that didn't show that she was pregnant.

She stood still, hesitating before giving a quick smile and walked away. They were all walking on eggshells around me as if I would break down at any moment. I was already broken to the point I wasn't feeling anything anymore.

I was dead on the inside.

"I've got some clothes for you." Damiano picked up a bag that was on the chair. He helped me get out of the hospital gown I was wearing and dressed me in some comfortable clothes.

"I want to walk." I muttered and stopped him from trying to carry me.

"You shouldn't be moving around just yet." He said, but I ignored him and got up on my feet. Damiano quickly held onto me to steady me as my legs wobbled from still being weak.

"Let me carry you." He insisted, but I shook my head and held onto his arm instead, carefully taking a step towards the wheelchair.

I needed to distract my mind from the constant thoughts and images that wouldn't stop haunting me. It was working, as the only thing I could think about was how heavy yet empty my body felt, and how tired I became from taking just a few steps.

His men heavily guarded the hallway, almost forming a complete circle around us for protection as Damiano wheeled me through the corridors.

Finally, coming outside to the parking lot, a pair of shoes stopped in front of me. I looked up, seeing it was Giovanni. He scanned my face, a slight frown appearing as he studied me. Then his eyes went down to my stomach.

"Don't. Please...just don't." I said to him before he could say anything. I couldn't handle hearing about it. The pitying looks they gave me were already too much for me to handle. I just didn't want to talk about it or have anyone ever mention it to me.

I know what I lost.

Giovanni gave a slight nod before stepping aside so I could get into the car. Damiano held my arm as my legs wobbled towards the vehicle.

Completely exhausted, we sat silently in the backseat. I rested my head against the window, desperately wanting to close my eyes and sleep, but I couldn't. My mother's face was all I saw when I closed my eyes, so I had to distract myself by continuously looking out of the window.

"How many days...?" I asked quietly, watching as we drove past the fields.

"You were out for three days." He said, surprising me with his answer. "Eight days have passed."

I swallowed hard at the information. Eight days had gone by. Eight days I had somehow survived and lived without a mother. How was I supposed to continue living my life like this?

"We'll figure it out." Damiano said softly to me, as if he had read my thoughts.

We arrived at the manor, and it seemed unusually quiet when I stepped out of the car. Or maybe it was just because I was in deep sorrow that everything appeared dark and gloomy. Even the majestic manor didn't seem very majestic at this moment. It was as if I had lost all vision of color, and all I could see was dark gray.

Cara was there when I entered. She looked at me with her sad, red eyes and her disheveled hair. Quickly walking up to me, she embraced me as she broke down.

My arms were down by my sides. I stared numbly over her shoulder, avoiding eye contact with anyone. I don't think there were any more tears for me to spill. I was a standing empty hollow.

I felt her tears seep into my shirt, and I slowly patted her on the back, attempting to offer some comfort. I had no idea what to say. I wasn't sure if there was anything I could say that would make things better.

Cara leaned back to look at me, but I avoided her eyes and stared down. I didn't want to be reminded that I had lost both a mother and a baby simultaneously.

"I...uh...I'm tired." I said, offering the only excuse I could think of to be left alone. I made my way to the stairs, looking up at them and realizing, in my current state, I wouldn't be able to handle walking up on my own.

"Allow me." Damiano said, and he carried me in his arms. We ended up in his room where he gently placed me on the bed.

"The bathtub is ready if you want to wash up now." Damiano said. I nodded, desperately needing to scrub myself clean and erase all evidence of what I had been through.

I kept looking down at my hands. Even though there was nothing on them, I felt like they were covered in thick blood, unconsciously wiping them against my clothes to somehow rid myself of the feeling. But no matter what I did, the feeling always came back.

Damiano helped me undress, careful not to move my arms too much as my ribs still ached. It was impossible to lift my arms above my head without wincing in pain.

I made the mistake of glancing in the mirror, only to be shocked by the sight of my own appearance.

I swallowed hard. I looked as though I had been beaten black and blue, with bruises covering my entire body and face. My eyes appeared hollow, and my skin was unusually pale. Drawing in a shaky breath, I touched my throat with my trembling hand. The nasty dark purple color revealed the evidence of having been choked.

I looked like I had died and been brought back to life.

Damiano stepped in front of me to prevent me from seeing myself in the mirror. Seeing my reflection was horrifying. If this was how I looked after eight days, I didn't want to dare to think how I looked when he found me. How could he even stand to look at me?

"Come." He gently led me to the bathtub. The hot water enveloped me, providing a soothing sensation that made me let out a small sigh.

Damiano was being careful and gentle with me. He washed and dried me, then brushed my hair once I was dressed.

"Althaia, you have to eat." He insisted, continuing his efforts to coax me into eating. The sight of food was unappetizing, making me feel nauseous.

"I'm not hungry." I replied, moving away, and lying down on the bed. I turned my back to him and closed my eyes.

The pills he had given me made me extremely sleepy. I struggled to keep my eyes open, not wanting to be trapped in the nightmares again, even though they haunt me when I am awake too.

Damiano sighed, placing the untouched food to the side. He joined me in bed, gently caressing my head. Unable to fight it, I allowed myself to succumb to sleep.

Sixty-Six

DAMIANO

"Are you getting any sleep?" Arianna asked me, a concerned expression on her face.

"How do you expect me to sleep when she's going through hell?" I snapped at her.

I had stepped outside to smoke once Althaia fell asleep. She hadn't slept properly, and I had secretly given her a sleeping pill just so she could get a little rest. I had never been this stressed or lost in my life before. I had quit smoking because she couldn't tolerate the smell of it when she was pregnant, but I picked it up again.

It was the only thing that could help me relax a bit and prevent me from going out and slaughtering people. I couldn't be a ticking bomb right now. I had to be patient, even though it was killing me to wait and watch her suffer like this.

"How are *you*?" Arianna asked again, and I let out a humorless chuckle at her question.

"Does it even matter?" I inhaled the cigarette smoke deeply, but it was not giving me the fill I wanted.

"It does. You lost -"

"I know what I fucking lost!" I stared at her with an enraged glare. My hands were trembling in anger at the painful loss. But I had to keep it together for the sake of Althaia. "Mind your own business." I sneered.

"You are my business! You need to talk about it, so you don't bury all of your feelings into that deep, dark hole like you always do." Arianna exclaimed in frustration, looking at me with a frown.

I flicked the cigarette bud away, my eyes were cold as I stepped so close to her that she had to take a step back.

"I will handle it the way I want to. I don't need you or anyone else to tell me what to do." My voice was low as I looked at her furiously.

A hand on my shoulder pulled me slightly back, and I glanced back to see it was Antonio who had stopped me. I hadn't noticed that I kept walking toward Arianna, forcing her to back away from me.

I directed my glare at him when he tried to pull me away.

"What are you stepping in for? You think I'm going to hurt my sister?" I roughly pushed his hand away and took a couple of steps back. Despite being angry, I wouldn't lay a hand on my sister, no matter how fucked up I felt.

"No, but you have pent-up anger and frustrations that you're taking out on your sister. If you don't want to talk about it, fine, but get your ass in the ring, and we'll take it from there." Antonio said calmly with his emotionless face.

I let out a scoff.

"Fuck off." I ignored him, making my way back inside when Antonio once again grabbed me.

"Or we can just settle it here." He said and threw a punch at my jaw. It made me take a step back; my head whipped to the side from the impact. I let out a low laugh as I moved my jaw and spat out when I tasted blood.

"Antonio!" Arianna gasped out in shock and tried to step in between us, but he stopped her from intervening.

"Trust me. He needs this before he fucking explodes." Antonio looked at me as if he hadn't just punched me in the face.

"I won't go easy on you." I smirked, and he mirrored my expression.

"I don't expect you to." He said and threw another punch my way.

This time, I blocked it and sent him a strong kick to the side of his stomach. He grunted in pain as I hit him where I knew he got stitched up. Quickly composing himself, he lunged at me again.

We kept going, throwing punches, kicking, and slamming each other to the ground, not giving either of us a break before making the next move.

By now, we had gathered a small audience with my men forming a circle around us to make it more interesting and wilder as we continued to punch and kick each other furiously.

"Okay, that's enough! You're going to kill each other if you keep going." Arianna yelled out and stepped in to stop us.

We had been at it for a while now, and both of us were breathing heavily. At some point, we discarded our shirts after they got ripped from throwing each other to the ground.

I glanced at Antonio, noticing that some of his stitches had gotten messed up and were now bleeding. I got him pretty good, just as he had landed quite a few punches on me. He also had opened up the stitches on my arm. Blood was trickling down my arm and onto the grass.

"Go get yourself fixed." I told him. Without saying another word, I turned around and walked inside.

Instead of heading to my own room, I went to the guest bedroom where Althaia had previously stayed to take a shower. Even though I had given her a sleeping pill, I didn't want to risk her waking up.

I removed the remaining suture from my arm and used staples to close the wound, then bandaged it. It throbbed from the pain, but I didn't care.

I made my way to my room, carefully opening the door to avoid waking her up. I felt relieved to see her still in bed, sleeping.

I went to lie next to her, pulling her closer to me and caressing her body. Her eyelashes were wet, letting me know she had been crying in her sleep, and my chest tightened at the sight.

She had barely stepped a foot into my world and had already become a target. This wasn't a life for her. It never was. I now understood why her death had to be faked.

I took a deep breath and closed my eyes as I held her close, fearing she would disappear if I didn't.

Two days had passed, and I had arranged a funeral for her mother. I looked at Althaia standing next to Cara and Michael as they watched the casket being lowered into the ground. She stared at it numbly.

Since the day she woke up at the hospital, she hadn't shed a tear. It was as if every ounce of emotion within her had vanished, and I detested every moment of it. I could see and feel her, but she wasn't truly present. Her once bright and lively green eyes had lost their spark.

She was like a ghost.

The tan that once graced her skin had faded, leaving her skin pale. She wasn't eating anything either and was losing weight. Only sometimes I could persuade her to eat a spoonful or two of something.

Cara couldn't stop crying and clung tightly to Althaia's side, seeking comfort. However, Althaia barely reacted, her gaze fixed on the lowered casket as it was gradually covered in dirt.

I glanced around at the people present; her father, his men and people that knew her mother. They were informed that it was a car accident, and her death was instant to prevent any further questions.

I kept my gaze on Althaia, barely letting my eyes leave her. Her legs gave way after they finished burying the casket. I moved instinctively towards her but a hand stopped me. It was Lorenzo, shaking his head at me. I clenched my hands but remained still. I turned my gaze back to Althaia, only to see that blonde bastard's arms wrapped around her.

She needs to be with her family, too.

I kept telling myself and watched her go to her father for comfort. It was killing me to see her like this, and it was destroying me that she wasn't seeking me for comfort. But this wasn't the time nor the place to be possessive and jealous.

Instead, I stayed put and watched her.

Althaia had gone straight up to the bedroom when we came back. She had barely uttered a word the whole day, walking around with her eyes down like a lost ghost. She avoided everyone, not wanting to look at anyone.

Especially me.

She couldn't look me in the eyes and always tried to distance herself from me, just wrapping her arms around herself when I stepped too close to her. I wanted to give her the space she needed, but I couldn't bring myself to leave her alone.

I opened the bedroom door, only to find her sitting on the floor by the balcony doors. I stepped closer to her and sat down on the floor as well on the opposite side.

"I get it now…" Althaia said quietly, continuing to look out of the window. I didn't say anything, desperate to hear her voice. "It does fuck you up in a different way. How…could I lose everything like that?" Her voice went into a whisper. She sniffed when tears made their way down her cheeks.

"I see her face everywhere now. At first, it was only when I closed my eyes… but now, it feels like she's everywhere, haunting me because I couldn't do anything to help her. I can't look up because I think it's her among people. And when I look down, all I can see is blood on my hands." Althaia let out a choked chuckle.

"I'm not a killer... he wanted to do unimaginable things to me. I shouldn't feel guilty that I took his life because he deserved it... but I can't. All I see is his blood on my hands, no matter how many times I wash them!" She broke down. I went to her, placing her on my lap and holding her tightly as she cried into my chest. It broke me with every single tear that she shed.

"I can't do this anymore. I can barely stand being in my own skin, much less endure everyone's looks of pity."

My heart hammered in my chest at her words.

"I can't... I just... I can't stay here. I need to leave." She cried out in desperation. My throat went dry, and I swallowed hard.

"I can't..." I whispered. She looked at me with her tear-streaked face. Her eyes showed me how shattered she was.

"Damiano... please, don't keep me here." Her hands fisted my shirt while she kept crying to me.

"Are you leaving me?" I wanted to ask her, but the words died in my throat the more I looked at her. I couldn't bear to watch her like this; broken and in so much pain. I had no idea how to ease her suffering.

"I'm begging you..." She whispered. I couldn't bring myself to say anything and simply held her in my arms.

Maybe for the last time.

After the sleeping pill had kicked in and Althaia fell asleep, I made my way to the office. Pouring myself a drink, I downed it in one go before filling the glass again. I moved to my desk, only to feel my heart drop at the sight of the red baby shoes. I picked them up before angrily tossing them across the office.

"You wanted to see me?" Arianna walked in just as I downed another drink and slammed the glass down on the desk. Placing my hands on the desk with my back still facing her, I let out a breath before speaking.

"I need you to take her away."

"What?" Confusion marked on her face as I looked at her.

"Althaia. She wants to leave, and I need you to take her to a safe house." I ordered. It was what she wanted, and it was for the best.

I had already ruined her.

"You can't be serious? Are you letting her go?" She asked in disbelief, searching my face for confirmation.

"Just do it."

"Damiano, you can't -"

"What the hell am I supposed to do?!" I yelled at her. "Hasn't she suffered enough because of me? I would rather watch her walk away and be safe than watch her die. I can't live through that again. I won't survive if it happens to her too, especially to her." My chest rose and fell rapidly as I spoke. I ran a hand through my hair in frustration. There was nothing I could do for her.

"I need you to take her away because I know I won't be able to let her go." I declared, leaving no room for discussion.

Arianna didn't know what to say but gave a small nod before leaving my office. I grabbed the bottle, took a long swig, and sank into the couch, hoping to drown out the unfamiliar feelings within me that only she could extract.

I glanced across the office, my eyes settling on the baby shoes on the floor. Chuckling to myself, I leaned back on the couch and stared at the ceiling.

"You fucking idiot. You really thought you could have it all." I should have known better. I wasn't meant to be happy.

I was meant to be alone.

My office, once a haven of order and control, now bore the scars of my internal storm. The air was thick with the scent of spilled alcohol and shattered dreams.

The room seemed to pulsate with the aftermath of my rampage. The silence that followed was deafening, broken only by the occasional creaking of damaged furniture.

Today was the day she was leaving.

I couldn't see her off because I wouldn't be able to let her go. I went to the window, observing the cars ready to take her away. Antonio, Giovanni, Luca, and more of my men were to escort her to the safe house.

I stayed back, hidden in the shadows of my office as Althaia followed Arianna out to the car. I clenched my fists.

I stormed towards the door, swinging it open, only to be met by Lorenzo, who blocked my way.

"Move." I sneered when he didn't budge.

"No."

"I said *move*, before I fucking kill you."

"You're not getting past me. You're drunk." He shoved me back inside the office.

"She can't leave."

"Yes, she can. If that's what she needs."

I shook my head, heading for the door when he blocked my way again. I drew out my gun, aiming it at him.

"If it will make you feel better, shoot me, but you're not going after her."

"Lorenzo!" Cara's voice rang out, and I snapped my eyes towards her. She looked worried as my gun aimed at him.

I gripped the gun so tightly in my hand that it trembled. For the first time, jealousy filled my body that my brother gets to be happy while I lost everything.

Slowly, my gun moved to point at her.

Lorenzo's hand clasped around the muzzle of the gun, turned it away, and gripped my shoulder tightly as he spoke harshly in my ear.

"I'll give you the benefit of the doubt because you're my big brother and assume that you weren't about to aim at my fiancée. Because if you were, I will lose my damn mind and fucking kill you. Then I'll have to break it down to Althaia that I've killed you because you were out of control, and it would leave her shattered into even more pieces. Get it fucking together." Lorenzo ripped the gun out of my hand and tucked it behind his back.

"Get out." I spat out, returning to the bottle I was drinking earlier, wanting to numb the pain.

A long silence followed, but he was still here as I heard him release a sigh.

"She'll come back to you. You can't separate two souls meant to be together." Then he left, the soft click of the door closing behind him echoing in the heavy silence.

I wanted to laugh in his face at the empty words. Instead, I scoffed and looked out the window. The cars were gone. And so was she.

"I hope I can find it in myself to truly release you. Because forgetting you is a torment my soul refuses to endure."

Sixty-Seven

ALTHAIA

"You're leaving?" Cara asked. Her words made my stomach knot, and a lump formed in my throat at the way she looked at me.

"I... just need to be alone for a bit." I muttered to her. She bit down on her lips as her eyes glistened.

"I understand. Take care of yourself." She embraced me in a tight hug, and this time, I hugged her back just as tightly before saying goodbye.

I took a deep breath and made my way outside. Arianna was standing next to an SUV, waiting for me, but she wasn't alone. Antonio, Giovanni, Luca, and more men were outside as well.

"Ready?" Arianna asked, and I gave her a small nod before she opened the backseat door, waiting for me to get in.

Before sliding into the backseat, I couldn't help but look around, and a pang of sadness hit me even more when I didn't see him anywhere.

"Damiano is... busy." Arianna said, noticing my gaze.

"I'm never too busy when it comes to you." His words echoed in my mind, but I guess that day became today.

I gave one more look around and slid into the backseat. I couldn't help but feel hurt about it, but maybe it was because he couldn't bear the sight of me anymore.

Why should he when I failed to protect our baby in my own body?

I let out a sigh and looked out of the window as we drove to wherever the safe house was located.

The drive took way longer than I expected. It was hours away, and it felt even longer since the car was filled with silence; no one attempted to make conversation.

We came to a stop in front of a large, two-story beach house. I stepped out of the car to look around. It was windy, but I welcomed it. I closed my eyes, took in a deep breath, and savored the salty, fresh air.

Following Arianna inside the house, the others trailed close behind me. I quickly scanned the very spacious living room as I made my way to the floor-to-ceiling window and looked out. The beach was in full view, and I could faintly make out the sound of the waves. It was so... peaceful here. It was just what I needed.

"Everything has been prepared for you." Arianna spoke, making me turn around to face her.

"The fridge has been stocked and the closet is filled with clothes, so you don't have to worry about any of that."

"The windows are bulletproof, and the doors have bolts going into the ground, making it impossible to break in." Antonio explained. I gave a small nod, impressed by the information. It was a safe house, after all. I shouldn't have expected anything less.

"Also, there's an alarm system and security cameras. You can see what's going on outside. Let me show you how they work." Arianna said, guiding me to a small screen on the wall, explaining what to do, how to activate it all, and what codes to use.

"I guess this is it..." She trailed off, and they were all looking at me. I bit the inside of my cheek, feeling slightly awkward with their eyes on me.

"Uh... thank you." I said to them. It might not have sounded like it, but I was truly grateful for them doing this much for me.

"You shouldn't stay here." Luca suddenly snapped, making me look at him in shock. I noticed he didn't seem very happy during the whole trip here. His face, which was typically filled with friendliness when I was around, now displayed a deep frown.

"Luca." Antonio warned him, but he didn't care and continued to look at me with a disapproving expression.

"He's hurting too, you know. Staying here won't help either of you." His words felt like daggers stabbing into my heart, making me take a couple of steps back. My throat closed, and I looked down at the floor, feeling my eyes burn with tears.

"That's enough, Luca!" Antonio sneered, silencing him. Arianna and Giovanni didn't say anything, making me wonder if they were silently agreeing with him.

Without saying another word, Luca stormed out, and Giovanni was right behind him. I didn't know what they were expecting of me. What I was going through... no one should ever have that happen to them. But it did to me, and I had no idea what to do with myself.

I could barely breathe, let alone think. I just wanted to be alone, to have a chance to figure things out for myself.

"You can always call, remember that." Arianna said, giving my shoulder a small squeeze before she went out, leaving me alone with Antonio.

"Here. Keep this with you." A gun entered my view. My eyes widened a little before I looked at him. "Do you remember how to use it?"

I gave a slow nod.

"Yes."

"Good. I don't expect you to use it, but it eases my mind a bit to know you have a weapon on you." Antonio placed the gun on the table. I had absolutely no intention of using it either.

"Damiano?" I wanted to ask him about it but hesitated, fearing I would get the same reaction Luca gave me.

"He'll be fine."

"Is he mad at me? Is that why he didn't want to see me off?" I held my breath as I waited for his answer, feeling my heart beat faster.

Does he hate me?

That was what I wanted to ask, but I wasn't bold enough to ask, nor ready for an answer.

"It doesn't matter what he thinks. We all heal differently, and this is what you need. Just get better, that's what we all want." His words made me feel a little better about the situation, and I was thankful he wasn't scolding me for staying here.

"Take care, Althaia." Antonio said softly.

"Thank you for doing this for me. And take care of him...please." My voice cracked, and I took a deep breath. I didn't want to cry.

"Don't mention it. He's in good hands." Antonio gave me a small smile. He closed the distance between us and embraced me. "I can't imagine what you're going through, so please, do what you have to do to get better."

I couldn't hold it in anymore and I cried into his chest.

I cried and cried, and not once did it stop for a week.

Sixty-Eight

DAMIANO

My fist connected with the punching bag, making it swing before it came back to me once again as I kept throwing punch after punch. Sweat dripped down my face, and my muscles were sore from the relentless workout.

I wasn't giving myself a break. I knew I was overworking my body by spending hours in the gym, but it was the only thing that could keep me from going to her.

One week.

It had been one agonizing week since she left, and not once had I heard from her. I had no idea why I had expected to hear from her when she had begged me to let her go. She left the next day as if she couldn't wait to get away from me.

Her tear-streaked face was still burned into my mind, and I felt guilty for letting her go through this much pain.

I kept punching the bag, throwing one powerful punch after another, but no matter how much I worked out or how hard I hit the bag, the tension and anger wouldn't subside. Sweat continued to drip down my face as I continued, pushing myself to go harder and faster, desperate to divert my mind from her.

At least she's safe now.

It was for the best for her to leave. She couldn't be happy with someone like me. She had only ever been in danger since we got together. I almost lost her too many times already, and I still had no idea who had been behind the attack or what kind of mess her mother was involved in.

I was going to get to the bottom of it, make sure no one was ever going to hurt her again, and let her live a quiet and safe life like she was meant to; one that was far away from me because that life didn't exist with me.

My world wasn't for her. She was too pure, too innocent to have shit like this happen to her. It had broken her to the point where her once-bright green eyes, the ones I fell in love with, had lost their entire spark.

I hoped she was doing better and healing, even if it wasn't with me. I just wanted her to be happy, and I knew it couldn't be with me.

I wanted to see her, even if it was just for a mere second. Just one last time. *Damn it*. Even working out for hours couldn't distract my mind completely from thinking about her.

The bag hit the ground with a loud thud, making me snap out of my thoughts. I let it be on the ground and sat down on the bench as I wiped the sweat off with a towel and tried to calm down my heavy breathing.

I picked up my phone and looked at the picture I had saved of her. It was the one she had sent to me after I had gifted her the earrings. It was my favorite picture; the way she was smiling, and her eyes had so much life in them.

My phone rang, and the caller ID interrupted my gaze at the picture, a habit I had developed since she left. I kept staring at it, fully aware that I couldn't see or hold her, but I clung to it for my sanity, even though it was simultaneously tormenting me.

"What?" I snapped into the phone.

"Hello, handsome." Raffaele replied with a chuckle.

"What do you want?" I didn't hide my annoyance that he had disturbed me.

"Are you in the gym again?" He said in a disapproving tone. "Are you trying to become a bodybuilder?"

"If you have nothing useful to say, keep your mouth shut."

"What's the fun in that?" I could hear his grin through the phone as I made my way out of the gym, not in the mood to listen to his bullshit.

"Fuck off."

"Now, wait a minute!" He said quickly before I could hang up the phone.

"Get straight to the point before I fuck you up."

"That sounds hot." Raffaele laughed.

I hung up the phone and went upstairs to take a shower. My phone continued to ring when I didn't pick up, but after the fifth time, I had enough.

"What's the point of working out this much if you're still going to be an ass?" He said once I had answered his call.

"Where are you?"

"Warehouse by the port. Why?"

"So I can come and fucking kill you." I sneered.

"Calm down! I was just trying to make a joke, geez…" He kept on mumbling something about me being an unbearable ass these days. I closed my eyes, imagining smashing his skull into a wall over and over again.

"We might have found something."

I snapped my eyes open.

"What is it?" I said impatiently. If there was one thing I hated, it was not getting straight to the point and wasting my time.

"Get your ass over here and you will find out. You could use some fresh air." Raffaele hung up before I could curse at him.

After a quick shower, I got ready and drove to the port where our products were shipped. The warehouse was the central hub where everything was weighed, counted, and repacked before distribution and sale.

We had the most sought-after product in the game, giving our competitors no chance to even come close to what we have. Our cocaine boasted the highest purity, making it far more potent than the inferior cocaine others sold due to their lack of knowledge about the quality of their own products.

If the cocaine was very diluted or if the user had developed a tolerance, they would experience little or no rush. The purer the cocaine, the better the experience was. Just one line of my product delivered that surge of calm euphoria, along with a sense of power, energy, and happiness; all sought after by the users. A second line wasn't even needed to achieve the desired kick.

I stepped into the warehouse, quickly assessing the smooth operation. Making my way to the back, I found Antonio and Raffaele. I shot a glare at Raffaele, still wanting to crush his skull for his incessant phone calls.

"Whatever you have to say, it better be good for your own sake." I gave him a cold stare.

"It is. Turns out you were right; someone eventually bragged about what had happened." Raffaele said.

"I made sure there were eyes and ears everywhere as you wanted. Emilia was the first one to report back, and it looks like the Koreans were involved." Antonio added, and I furrowed my brows at him. "She couldn't get much more information since they spoke in their tongue, but Emilia found out they are going to The LuxePalace for a celebration."

"The LuxePalace." I scoffed.

The LuxePalace was a high-end casino hotel exclusively for the elites, which meant that a bunch of lowlifes like those wouldn't be able to get in. They could only imagine the allure of such a place, their dreams of entering shattered by the insurmountable wall of wealth and status.

Unless someone with a higher influence was involved. Whoever had ordered the kill was getting them in as their fucking reward.

"They're probably attending the Untamed Event. Should be insane this year hence the name." Raffaele grinned, looking excited about it.

"Looks like we have a party to attend. You know what to prepare." I told them.

"You don't find it weird that Koreans are involved? They usually keep to themselves." Raffaele wondered.

"That's what we are going to find out at the Untamed Event. Make sure we have people there and our girls working specifically in the private section." I ordered and turned around to leave.

"Where are you going?" Raffaele called after me, but I continued my way out.

"None of your business." I said curtly and got to my car.

"I'll drive." Antonio said behind me before I could open the door. I turned slightly to face him, raising a brow at him.

"Get a ride with someone else. I'm going somewhere." I opened the door, only for him to block me, preventing me from getting inside.

"I know where you are going. Let me drive." He gave me a blank look as I stared him down. "When was the last time you got some sleep?" Antonio raised a brow at me when I didn't answer. I couldn't remember the last time I had a decent night's sleep.

"That's what I thought, because you look like shit. You will end up falling asleep behind the wheel and crashing on your way. Can't let that happen. I made a promise that you'll be in good hands."

"Fine." I said, knowing he wouldn't give up. "Any new updates on her?" I asked as we drove off.

"No. Still in the same condition." He said. I gave a nod and leaned back in my seat.

The drive was long and silent. I could feel the lack of sleep was getting to me, and I almost wanted to close my eyes to rest a bit. But I couldn't fully rest without having her by my side.

"She's going to hate you for keeping this from her." Antonio broke the silence.

"I know." I replied and looked out of the window. "I don't expect her to forgive me for it, but it's for the best." I had considered every single possible outcome from this, but it had to be done. Even if it meant she would hate me.

He didn't say anything else and continued to drive in silence. Soon, the beach house entered my view, and Antonio stopped the car further down the street to keep it out of sight.

I stepped out of the car and made my way toward the house, glancing around, seeing no lights were turned on and no movements. She was most likely asleep now.

I came to a stop in front of the door, disconnecting the alarm system before unlocking it. I closed the door quietly behind me and waited for a minute, listening for any movements, but it was as quiet as it could be.

I stepped further inside the house, moving silently before a sound made me stop. The noise came closer, and I looked down when I felt something rub against my leg.

Is that... a kitten?

It made a high-pitched sound and kept circling me, rubbing its head against my leg before standing on its paws and climbing on me. I watched as it continued up before I took hold of it. I shook my head a bit, amused that she had gotten herself a kitten.

"Are you keeping her company?" I whispered. It started making purring sounds when I rubbed its head with my finger.

It didn't seem like it wanted to leave me, so with the kitten still on my arm, I made my way to the master bedroom on the ground floor to see if she would be there before checking the upstairs floor.

The door was open, and I saw her sleeping peacefully on the bed. The kitten jumped down from my arm, ran to the bed, and made itself comfortable next to her.

I let out a slow breath as I walked closer, my heart racing at the sight before me. Gently, I sat down on the bed and the longing I had felt so intensely made me place my hand on her cheek, lightly caressing it. I had almost forgotten how soft her skin was, and I felt relieved that she was finally taking care of herself.

A bottle of pills on the nightstand caught my attention. Frowning, I picked it up and saw it was sleeping pills. She was still having trouble sleeping on her own.

I let out a small sigh as I brushed some hair away from her face.

"How are you killing me, yet keeping me alive at the same time?" I whispered.

I was only supposed to see her for a second to ease my mind a bit, but now that I was here and able to touch her, I couldn't get myself to leave. Not yet. I had missed her too much.

I lay next to her and carefully pulled her closer to me as I wrapped my arms around her. It felt like an eternity had passed since the last time I had been able to hold her like this, and it filled the void inside of me.

I placed a kiss on her forehead and continued to caress her head, watching every single feature of her perfect face. There was no woman who could compare to her beauty, especially when it came to her captivating green eyes.

Her eyes suddenly flew open, and she looked at me. I stayed still, watching her unfocused green eyes as her brows slightly furrowed before she closed her eyes again. She snuggled closer to me, and a smile formed on my lips. I closed my eyes, listening to her soft and deep breathing.

A small, high-pitched sound woke me up, and I saw the kitten moving around on the bed, attempting to wake her up. Glancing over at the window, I noticed it was already light outside.

Fuck, I fell asleep.

Althaia stirred in my arms, letting me know she was waking up. I moved as quietly and carefully as I could and slid off the bed, and I rushed out of the bedroom before she could see me.

"Hi." Her voice made me freeze in my step, and I felt my chest warming at the sound of her voice. "Are you hungry? All right, let's get you some food." She chuckled when the kitten continued to make those high-pitched sounds.

I walked into another room to hide when I heard her move and cursed myself up for falling asleep.

"You must have been really hungry." Althaia let out a small laugh.

I rested the back of my head against the wall, closed my eyes, and listened to her voice. It stirred a whirlwind of emotions within me, making me shift slightly for a better glimpse of her.

She was sitting on the floor, watching the kitten eat while stroking its fur. The sight of her made my throat dry, and I desperately wanted to go to her. Instead, I stayed put and observed her from afar.

She let out a sigh, looked out of the window, and gazed at the beach waves.

"It almost felt like he was here…" She said quietly. "I miss him… but I'm not sure I'm ready to face him yet."

My chest tightened at her words, but I couldn't blame her. I was probably a constant reminder that I was the reason for her losses.

I watched her as she opened the door to the back porch and stepped outside with the kitten. I took this moment to get to the front door while she had her back to me. I quietly made my way out and reconnected the alarm system.

Antonio was leaning against the car when I made my way down the street.

"Feeling better?" He asked, making me stop before I could get inside the car.

I looked back at the house, feeling more at ease now that I had got to see and hold her. I gave him a brief nod before we drove away.

Sixty-Nine

ALTHAIA

"Kiara!" I yelled after her when she once again ran over to the neighbor's house.

I had found Kiara all by herself when I had gone for a small walk on the beach. Out of nowhere, she ran to me. I looked around to see if she belonged to anyone, but she was just a stray kitten.

She was all alone, and my heart couldn't take it. I took her in, nurtured her, fed her, and she turned into the happiest and most affectionate little kitten I had ever met. She gave me a purpose again.

I never went far from the house, always staying close in case something were to happen. The chances were slim, as I was pretty sure some of his men lurked somewhere, out of my view, but constantly watching me. He wouldn't have allowed me to stay here if he didn't have someone to report back to him that I was safe.

Now, with Kiara in my care, I needed to explore the town to gather all the necessities for her. It was a small and quiet town, not much happening, but I liked it; it seemed everyone knew each other in one way or another.

I still hadn't retrieved my credit card and was left with Damiano's, but I wasn't comfortable using it. Luckily, I found some cash in one of the drawers. Some was an understatement.

The entire drawer was stacked with hundred-dollar bills, and I supposed it couldn't be called a safe house without emergency stacks of cash. Since I hadn't sorted out my own card yet, I thought I could borrow some until then.

"Kiara!" I called after her once again, but she ignored me and sneaked inside the neighbor's back door that was slightly ajar.

I sighed, walked up to the back porch, and lightly knocked on the glass door. This wasn't the first time she had done this; for some reason, she loved visiting the neighbors whenever we were out for our daily walk.

"I'm so sorry! I don't know why she keeps sneaking into your house." I gave Samantha an apologetic smile when she opened the door with Kiara in her arms.

"Don't be! It's a pleasant surprise, and she is so cute!" Samantha chuckled and rubbed Kiara's head as she kept purring.

Since Kiara kept going into the neighbor's house, I was introduced to Samantha, who lived here with her roommate, Ava. They were extremely nice and would always greet me whenever we crossed paths during my beach walks.

"She really is." I agreed with a smile, shaking my head as I looked at Kiara, who was thoroughly enjoying being in her arms.

"Would you like to come in? I've just baked some chocolate chip cookies."

"You know I can't say no to that. It smells amazing!" My mouth watered a little at the delicious aroma of freshly baked cookies.

Samantha was very much into baking and constantly tried out new recipes. I had now become her designated taste-tester since Ava had grown tired of it. I had the biggest sweet-tooth, so of course I couldn't pass up the opportunity.

"Make yourself comfortable." Samantha gestured to the couch as she continued her way to the kitchen. "Would you like a glass of Cabernet Sauvignon? It goes well with chocolate chip cookies."

"Sure." I smiled and got comfortable on the couch with Kiara on my lap, playing with her until Samantha returned.

"Is she making you taste-test her baking again?" Ava asked and took a seat on the couch.

"I don't mind. It's not like I have any self-control either." I chuckled, and Ava shook her head just as Samantha walked in with a plate full of cookies and wine.

"Well, I need someone to tell me if it's good or if it's crap." Samantha said in her defense.

"Shut up. You know you're a good baker. Also, I think Althaia is scared to give you an honest opinion and just says it's good to be polite." Ava raised a brow at me and sipped her wine.

"That's not true! I didn't like that lemon cake." I pointed out.

"Only because we found out you don't like anything with a citrusy taste, and yet, you said it was good." She gave a small smirk, attempting to prove her point.

"It was still good despite that." I shrugged, making her shake her head in amusement.

"If you have nothing useful to say, don't say it at all." Samantha scolded her and handed me a plate with a big cookie, which I happily took.

It was still slightly warm, and I didn't waste any time taking a big bite, almost closing my eyes in happiness.

"This is probably the best cookie I've had in my life." I praised, taking another bite. It was soft yet had a crunch on the outside, and the big chunks of chocolate melted right on my tongue.

"Eat as many as you want." She said with a pleased smile, enjoying one herself. Samantha was only a couple of years older than me, but she had a motherly demeanor, while Ava was like a wild teenager.

"I've been meaning to ask; do you live alone in that big house?" Ava asked, and I grabbed my glass of wine, hesitating with my answer.

"I'm just here on a little getaway." I replied, which wasn't entirely a lie.

"Got a boyfriend?" Ava gave a playful wink.

"Ava, don't pry into her life. It's rude." Samantha frowned.

"What? It's a normal question." Ava argued, innocently shrugging her shoulders.

"It's okay." I smiled at Samantha before addressing Ava. "And no, I don't have a boyfriend."

I didn't want to give out too much information about myself, and I certainly didn't want to risk them asking why I was alone without my boyfriend. I didn't want to go down that road.

"Good for you. Men suck anyway, and they cheat on you while saying they love you." Ava said bitterly, almost chugging down her wine.

Ava was a very open person and had talked about her ex-boyfriend cheating on her when one day I found her crying on my walk on the beach. I couldn't simply walk past her without asking if she was okay. That was when she opened up to me, and I just listened as she poured her heart out.

"Did I tell you that I found his dick deep into some girl's ass in our bed?!" She said angrily while Samantha rubbed her arm comfortingly.

"Should have cut his dick off and flushed it down the toilet." I shrugged my shoulders. They both looked at me, a bit shocked at my answer before bursting out in laughter.

"I knew I liked you the moment I saw you." Ava said, and I let out a grin.

After indulging in too many cookies and some wine, I thanked Samantha for the invite and made my way back home as it was getting late. Ever since that day, I found it uncomfortable to be outside in the dark and would immediately retreat inside the house to feel safe.

I turned on the security alarm, which I had been doing religiously every single day. I went to the bedroom and plopped down on the bed, feeling tired from all the sugar I had consumed in one sitting.

It has already been two weeks since I got here, and while I was feeling myself getting physically better, mentally I was still struggling. Sometimes I felt lonely, and I strongly longed for him, but I wasn't courageous enough to face him just yet.

By day, I functioned relatively normally, but the nights were the worst. Each time I rubbed my stomach, I couldn't help but wonder what it would have looked like now. That was why I had taken down every mirror in the house; I couldn't bear to look at myself.

My body was still experiencing slight cramps from the miscarriage, often driving me to tears as I mourned the painful loss. I had to find a way to let it go, but how was I ever going to?

I opened the drawer on the nightstand and grabbed my phone. From the moment I arrived, I deliberately switched off my phone to prioritize my healing process.

My phone started buzzing constantly, as soon as it turned on, from the many text messages and missed phone calls I had received. All were from Michael.

I had a knot of anxiety in my stomach as I debated whether to dive into my notifications or keep ignoring them.

The buzzing continued for a while, and I couldn't do anything except wait for it to pass before I could use my phone. Just as it had stopped, my phone buzzed in my hand and showed me an incoming call.

I answered.

"Hello?"

"What the fuck, Althaia! I thought you were fucking dead!" Michael yelled at me, and I bit down on my lip as guilt filled my body. I had completely forgotten all about Michael and my father.

"I'm sorry..." I muttered to him.

"Why haven't you been answering my texts or calls?!"

"My phone has been off. I just needed to clear my mind." I explained to him. He went quiet before letting out a sigh.

"How are you doing?" Michael asked softly, and I took a deep breath before answering him.

"I'm doing... better."

"That's good." He sounded relieved, and I got comfortable under the covers.

"How are you? And dad?" I asked.

"We're all right. Don't worry about us. You're definitely missed around here. If you'd like, I can come and get you tomorrow?" He sounded hopeful. I hesitated, not knowing what to tell him about my situation.

"I, uh, I'm not staying at the manor right now…" I trailed off, and he went quiet for a while.

"What do you mean you're not staying at the manor? Where are you?" Michael asked firmly, and I hesitated again, as I didn't know if it was okay to tell him where I was. But it was Michael, not a stranger.

"I'm somewhere safe, I promise. I just needed to be alone." I tried to reassure him, but it wasn't too much of a help.

"Are you fucking kidding me, Thaia?! Did he leave you alone? That son of a -"

"Michael, that's enough." I said, not liking how he was talking. Fuming with anger, Michael's voice boomed with a string of profanities.

"Where are you? I will come and get you right now."

"Michael, I understand you're worried, but I promise I'm safe. I just had to get away for some time to myself. Please, understand that." I explained softly to him, and it calmed him down.

"I'm sorry. I didn't mean to get angry and yell at you." He sounded apologetic as he spoke. "I was just worried since I couldn't get in contact with you, and it's not like *he's* providing us with any information." He spat out, and guilt filled my body even more for not at least giving them a heads up they wouldn't be able to reach me.

"Can I at least come and see you? I just want to make sure you're okay. Please?" Michael asked.

"Okay." I said, giving in as it didn't sound like he would take no for an answer. I kind of owed it to him since I just disappeared with no warning.

"Just send me the info, and I will be there tomorrow. I've missed you."

"I've missed your goofy ass, too." I let out a small smile as he laughed.

"Of course, you have! It's me we're talking about." I could hear his grin through the phone, and I rolled my eyes at him, even though he couldn't see me.

"I will see you tomorrow, then. It's late and I'm kind of ready to go to sleep now." I said, a yawn escaping me.

"See you tomorrow! Stay safe and sleep tight."

"I will. Goodnight." A slight sense of relief washed over me after our conversation, lifting the weight of guilt for cutting off contact.

I scrolled through my phone, reading the text messages he had left me and seeing how worried he had actually been. I opened a text message from Cara, telling me she was doing better, and they had moved the date of the wedding. I had distanced myself from everyone that I had completely forgotten that there was supposed to be a wedding. But I was happy when she said she was doing better.

Staying here had me missing everyone at the manor, especially a certain person with golden-brown eyes. I bit down on my lip, thinking about if I should make a call tomorrow after Michael's visit.

Maybe it was time to go back and figure things out?

I was nervous to see Damiano again; scared I would see on his face how much he despised me. It made my heart squeeze that we might never recover from the loss, and we would have to live separate lives.

I opened the photo album on my phone, swallowing hard as I looked at a picture of him, and tears welled up in my eyes.

"I'm sorry." I whispered out, my voice trembling as tears streamed down my face and soaked the pillow beneath me, my grip on the phone tightening. "I'm so sorry for losing our baby."

Seventy

Althaia

I have never been a morning person, but since I got here, I have turned into one. I went to bed early, mainly to avoid my mind spiraling into a darker place, and I would wake up early to watch the sunset rising above the water. It was an amazing view and made me feel at peace.

I had been drawing a lot more as well, unable to resist capturing the beauty of the beach with the sun rising on the horizon, casting a shimmering glow on the water.

Each morning, I would sit outside with a cup of coffee, relishing the tranquility that surrounded me. This simple routine became a source of gratitude, slowly helping to heal my soul, mending it piece by piece.

I bought blank canvases and paint supplies as drawing was my escape, and I would always stumble upon something breathtaking here that begged to be immortalized in my sketches. I couldn't resist sketching Kiara a few times; she was too adorable when she curled up next to me and dozed off, or when she would lie on her back while playing with a mouse toy.

There were moments when my hand seemed to have a mind of its own, producing a drawing that surprised me once I finished. It would be of him, more specifically his piercing golden-brown eyes. I would have several pages of him in my sketchbook and not miss a single detail when it came to his tattoos.

Not a day passed without thoughts of him filling my mind. Each time his image surfaced, an overwhelming sense of shame would wash over me, reaching a point where nausea set in, making me push him out of my mind. Despite my efforts, the lingering guilt continued, leaving me at a loss on how to face him when we would inevitably cross paths again.

Dark thoughts would cloud my mind, leading me to believe that his easy acceptance of our separation was tied to the tragic event. I had carried his child, and I lost it. The internal conflict of guilt and shame consumed me, and I couldn't imagine what he must be thinking about it.

My one job, my sole responsibility, was to protect that precious life, and I failed miserably. How could he not blame me for it?

I shook my head, trying to get rid of the relentless thoughts that threatened to consume me. I didn't want to fall into that painful territory, especially when Michael was going to be here any minute now.

Stepping outside, I caught sight of Michael's car pulling up, and a smile formed on my face. Maybe it was a good idea to have Michael come over. It was a welcome distraction from the haunting darkness.

"Thaia!" Michael greeted cheerfully, giving me a tight hug.

"Good to see you, too." I replied, my voice muffled by the hug that practically crushed my head into his chest. Michael leaned away slightly, a smile gracing his features.

"You look better now."

"Are you saying that I looked bad before?" I teased, raising a brow at him. His smile fell with my words.

"No, I was just saying—what I meant was—" Michael stumbled over his words, looking distressed. I couldn't help but laugh at his reaction as he continued to fumble.

"I know what you meant; I was just messing with you." Michael's shoulders sagged in relief, and he shook his head slightly, a small smile playing on his lips.

"You did me dirty there. God, how I have missed you." He pulled me into another hug.

"I've missed you too." I smiled.

"Did you have breakfast yet?" Michael asked when he walked back to his car.

"Not really."

"Good, 'cause I bought some on my way here." He reached into the car and took out a brown paper bag. "And your iced coffee! I think this is the one you usually get, right?" He showed me the iced caramel macchiato, and my eyes widened in excitement.

"Oh, yes! It's my favorite!" I rushed to him and grabbed the coffee out of his hand. "You're the best, thank you!" I grinned at him, and he shot me a wink.

"Not bad." Michael commented, glancing around the living room as he settled on the couch. I joined him, grabbing my iced coffee and taking a sip through the straw.

"You should see the view on this side; it's breathtaking." I gestured towards the beach as I retrieved bagels from the bag.

"It's nice." Michael agreed, looking out the window. Just then, Kiara decided to make her appearance, leaping onto the couch. "Wait, you got yourself a pet?" He stared at her with a funny expression as she sniffed him.

"She was a stray, and I decided to take her in. I couldn't leave her alone." I said with a smile, giving Kiara a gentle rub on the head. "She keeps me company."

"She's a cute one." He chuckled, giving her a small pet. "How are you holding up?" Michael asked once we had finished eating. I shrugged and leaned back on the couch.

"I have my days, you know. Sometimes I feel I'm doing okay, but then the next moment I feel like I'm hitting rock bottom."

"I'm sorry you have to go through this." His expression filled with sadness as he gently held my hand.

"It's just... I miss her so much." I looked down at my lap. "Everything happened so fast, and there wasn't anything I could do to stop it..." A lump formed in my throat, and I took a deep breath to calm down.

"You can't blame yourself. It wasn't your fault." He tried to reassure me, and I gave him a half-smile, not saying anything.

If I had just been stronger, I would have been able to help her. Instead, she was the one who died trying to protect me, and for that, I couldn't forgive myself.

"Just so you know, your father is doing everything he can to find those fuckheads." He said firmly.

"There hasn't been anything yet?" I asked, and he shook his head.

"No. We would probably have found something, a clue of some sort if Damiano just wanted to cooperate with us, but he is shutting us completely out." He frowned, and I looked at him in surprise. Damiano wasn't letting my father in on this?

"Why is he shutting you out?"

"Beats me. He's a fucking mystery and didn't even give a reason."

I knew why. This was personal.

Michael let out a sigh.

"I know I shouldn't be asking you this, but is there anything you can tell us that might help?"

"I'm just as confused as you are." I mumbled. "One moment I was sleeping, the next we were running for our lives."

"It's okay, you don't have to think about it." He gave a comforting smile.

"Wait, maybe there is something?" I said as I remembered something.

"What is it?" He shifted on the couch to sit closer to me.

"I think I heard some of them speak Korean?"

"Korean?" He looked surprised, but then his frown deepened when I gave a nod.

"Yeah, but it doesn't really make sense. Why would Koreans be after my mom?" I wondered out loud. Michael looked in deep thought as he processed the information.

"Definitely weird, but this is a good start and I promise I will look into it."

"Thank you" I expressed, giving his hand a small squeeze. I was genuinely grateful for everything they were doing to help me.

I had been trying to connect the dots, to see if there was something I could do to help them find out who those people were, and why they were after us - or more specifically, my mother. But no matter what I did, I would always come up empty-handed. It was not like I had sensed anything suspicious going on with my mother.

"Can I ask you for a favor?" I bit down on my lip, unsure of how to ask him.

"Of course!"

"I want to go back to the house."

"What house - wait, you don't mean yours?" He asked in disbelief.

"Yes."

"Absolutely not, Althaia!" He erupted angrily with a scowl.

"Calm down, I didn't mean that I want to stay there." I quickly said to calm him down, but he continued to shake his head at me. "I just want to grab a few things of my mom's belongings to keep. I don't have anything of hers, and I thought if I had some of her things around me, it would help me feel better." I explained to him.

It seemed like he was weighing something in his mind as he stared at me for a long moment.

"I don't know, Thaia. It's risky for you to go back, and I don't want to take that risk." He shook his head. "I can go there for you and grab whatever you need?"

"No, I want to do it. I've been thinking about it for a while, and I know I can't go there by myself. And since you're here... so, please?" I asked him, hoping he would help me with it.

He let out a sigh and ran a hand through his hair.

"I don't think it's a good idea." The little hope I had in me died at his words. "But I guess if we had to do it, it would have to be during the daytime to be on the safe side." He said, and I felt hopeful once again.

"Do you think we can go today? I know it's a long drive, but I thought the sooner, the better."

"I'm not driving there." Michael said, checking the time on his watch.

"Oh…" I said, disappointed, and he looked at me with a playful smile.

"Come on! Think a bit highly of me. I've got connections and can get us on a flight in no time."

"Really?" I asked, cheerfully. I hated flying, but I was willing to do it if it meant we could be back as fast as possible.

"Just need to make a phone call, and I can get us on a private flight. It's small, nothing fancy, so don't get disappointed." Michael joked.

"Yeah, because I know what it's like to be on a fancy, private jet." I rolled my eyes as I chuckled. I was feeling a little anxious about going back, but I knew I would be okay with Michael.

"Quick question." I said before he could make the phone call. "How can you get on with your gun?" I asked. Michael laughed at my question.

"You're such a newbie." He teased me. "It's private for a reason. If you're ready, we can leave now."

"Let me just grab a coat, and we can go. I just need to ask my neighbors if they can watch Kiara."

Michael gave a nod and made the phone call.

I went into the bedroom to get a small bag for Kiara's toys and food. I opened the drawer on the nightstand, biting down on my lip as I looked at the gun Antonio had given me.

Not giving it much thought, I grabbed it, making sure the safety lock was on before tucking it into the waistband of my jeans behind my back. I put on a coat to make sure the gun wouldn't be noticeable.

It felt strange to have a gun on me like this, but after everything that had happened, I didn't want to take any chances, and I certainly didn't want to be defenseless this time.

I grabbed the bag, took Kiara in my arms, and went to Ava and Samantha. I rang the doorbell, hoping someone would be home.

"Hi, Althaia." Ava greeted with a bright smile. She seemed to be doing better today than when I left last night.

"Hi, Ava! I know this is sudden, but I just wanted to ask if it was possible for you to watch Kiara for a few hours?" I asked with a hopeful smile.

"Yeah, sure. Are you going somewhere?" She looked over my shoulder, and I followed her gaze, seeing Michael leaning against his car, waiting for me. Ava gave me a small smirk when she looked back at me.

"I thought you said you didn't have a boyfriend? He's hot." She winked, and I rolled my eyes at her.

"I don't. He's my friend and just visiting."

"Right." She dragged the word out and wiggled her eyebrows at me. "I'm just messing with you; we will take good care of her."

"Thank you so much! Again, so sorry about it being so sudden." I said once again, but she just gave a dismissive wave and took the bag and Kiara.

"Don't mention it. Have fun." Ava winked at me again before laughing. I just shook my head and walked over to Michael.

"Ready?" He asked with a smile and opened the door for me.

"As ready as I can be."

Seventy-One

ALTHAIA

I could feel myself growing more anxious the closer we were. The gun tucked behind my back did little to ease my nerves. The idea of having to use the gun to defend myself didn't sit well, but I knew it was a necessary precaution. I was not a killer; the trauma of what I had done still haunted me. The image of the man's bloodied face lingered in my mind.

I took a deep breath, forcing down the rising nausea.

"Hey... hey, you're going to be fine." Michael glanced at me and took my hand in his as I kept tapping my hand against my thigh in uneasiness.

"I don't know... I'm starting to think it's a mistake. What if something happens?" I rambled on, sharing my fears with him instead of keeping them to myself.

"I won't let anything happen to you. Trust me." He gave my hand a small squeeze, but I still wondered if we should have brought extra protection with us.

Just as the thought crossed my mind, I checked the side mirror, trying to spot any cars following us. I hadn't seen any of Damiano's men so far, making me wonder if anyone was watching me, or if they were truly keeping themselves out of my sight.

I had no idea if they had managed to follow us. We had taken a flight and now we were in the car on our way to the house. I also just realized they would report every detail back to him.

Great.

"It's highly unlikely someone would do anything during the daytime. It's too easy to get caught like that." Michael said, pulling me out of my dark thoughts.

"I hope you're right." I sighed and tried to relax.

I felt my heart beating just a little faster as we neared my house. I squeezed his hand in an attempt to comfort myself in some way. We drove closer and closer, only for confusion to set in when he drove past the house without stopping.

"Why are you not stopping? You just missed it." I looked at him, but he remained focused, scanning the area.

"I'm just going to drive around the block to make sure it's safe before we get out. Just in case." He slowed down a bit as he kept looking around. I did the same, my eyes scanning the area to see if anything looked suspicious.

Michael was being careful and thorough as he drove around a few times, then stopped and parked further away from the house to see if someone had followed us.

Fortunately, there wasn't anything, and he pulled up in front of the house. My heart was racing when I got out of the car, and I could feel my legs losing a bit of strength as I looked around.

Every single thing came rushing back to me; gunshots, screaming, running, and blood. I knew this would be hard, and I hadn't even taken a step inside the house, yet already, I was feeling like this.

Michael pulled me close to his side, keeping a vigilant watch. I noticed he had his gun in his hand, though hidden if anyone were to look our way.

I let out a breath as we stood in front of the door, hesitating a little before pulling the handle down. Only to find it locked.

"Huh, that's weird..." I muttered and tried the door again in case it was just stuck. It remained stubbornly locked. "Who could have locked it? It's not like we had the time to lock the freaking door before running for our lives." I frowned, and then it hit me. It could have only been him.

"Don't you have a key?" Michael turned his head to look at me while keeping an eye out.

"No..." I sighed in frustration. We came all the way here for nothing. "I didn't expect it to be locked." I said, glancing around the front porch.

"Want me to kick it open?"

"That doesn't sound like a good idea." I raised a brow at him, and he just shrugged his shoulders at me as if saying 'I tried'.

"Actually... No, wait! Maybe there's still a spare key out here?" I rushed to the small bench on the porch.

"I just remembered she used to put a spare key here because there was a time when I kept forgetting my keys."

"Why doesn't that surprise me?" He grinned, and I flipped him off in response. Crouching down, I reached under the bench, feeling around until my fingers found the tiny hole my mother had made to place the spare key.

"Found it!" I exclaimed happily and pulled the key out. I unlocked the door, only to be halted just before I could turn the handle.

"Let me go in first, but stay close behind me." Michael cautiously opened the door, gun at the ready in case someone were to suddenly appear.

We stepped into the house, listening intently for any signs of movement, but all was quiet. I released a breath when Michael declared it safe. At least for now.

Scanning the surroundings, I found the house surprisingly clean. Damiano must have taken care of that.

Being back inside the house flooded me with so many emotions that I had to bite my lip to keep it from trembling. I swallowed hard as I made my way to my mother's bedroom. Neither Michael nor I said much as he checked out the house. He didn't push for conversation, recognizing the difficulty of the moment, and I appreciated that.

Reaching my mother's bedroom, I turned to him.

"Can you stay out here, or maybe grab the photo albums for me while I go in? I just want to do it alone." He nodded and headed to the living room after I directed him to where the albums were.

Closing the door behind me, I shut my eyes and took a deep breath. The weight of being back in this place hit me hard.

I pushed my emotions aside, trying to clear my head, knowing time was limited. I searched the room, my main goal being to find anything that could provide answers or at least a clue. Until recently, I had never suspected my mother of anything, but now I knew she was involved in something; something that ultimately led to her death.

I continued my search in her closet, sifting through her clothes and feeling for any hidden compartments. I couldn't shake the feeling that if there were secrets to be kept, they would be hidden somewhere in her bedroom.

I kept looking around, my eyes darting in every direction, but the more I searched, the more my frustration grew as nothing came into view.

With a huff, I placed my hands on my hips and looked around in the room, trying to think from my mother's perspective. Where would she hide something she didn't want anyone to find?

I almost gave up when I stared at the large carpet that was under the bed. I mentally groaned when I realized I had to move her gigantic bed *and* the large carpet to see if there was anything there.

"Well, you want answers, so you better get to work." I mumbled to myself. I moved the bed and grasped the corner of the carpet. Kneeling down, I began feeling around the wooden tiles, hoping to find a secret hiding place. I had no idea if it were even possible to hide anything under the tiles, but then again, I had already experienced enough to know that anything was possible.

I kept pressing the tiles with my hands, but they all seemed firmly in place, glued to each other. Frustration welled up within me. Maybe I was reading too much into this? What if it wasn't as deep as I had imagined?

Despite these doubts, a nagging feeling persisted, urging me to uncover the truth. I needed something, just one piece of evidence that could lead me to answers.

"Give me one damn thing!" I exclaimed, slamming my fist down in frustration.

I rapidly blinked away the tears when I felt one of the tiles move slightly when I slammed my fist down. I touched it again, trying to shake it just to make sure I wasn't tricked. It moved!

My heart was beating faster, now knowing that I might have found something. I was so anxious that my hands shook, and I had to take a moment to calm down.

It wasn't easy to remove the tile, and I had to use my nails to get underneath it to get a hold of it. After a few tries, I finally did.

A knock on the door jolted me, and I nearly let out a scream before realizing it was just Michael on the other side. I was so focused that I had forgotten about him.

"Thaia, are you okay?" He asked. He didn't open the door and stayed outside.

"Yeah, I'm just taking a moment, processing everything." I grimaced at the terrible excuse. "I'll be out in a minute."

"It's fine. Take your time." He said softly before I heard him walk away from the door, probably to give me a bit more privacy.

I breathed a sigh of relief and returned to the now-removed tile. Peering into the shallow darkness, I wasted no time reaching down to blindly explore its contents.

My hands moved from side to side until I finally felt something solid. Pulling it out, I found a small wooden treasure chest adorned with engravings on the lid; details that were unfamiliar and unreadable to me.

The chest was just large enough to hold a few items. Luckily, it lacked a lock and only had a simple metal hinge to keep it shut since I wasn't supposed to see it, or anyone else, for that matter.

I quickly opened it to see what it contained. Just as I opened it, I saw some papers and something that seemed to look like letters and… was that a picture? I picked it up to see it was an old picture of my mother when she was younger, and she wasn't alone. A man was next to her, and not someone I had seen before.

I kept rummaging through the small chest before deciding this had to wait. I didn't want Michael to become suspicious about why I was taking too long, especially since I was only supposed to grab a few things. I also didn't want to risk our safety by staying here for too long, so I suppressed my curiosity and quickly arranged everything back to how it was.

I grabbed a small box from my mother's closet and placed the chest at the bottom before adding a few more of her belongings around it. I made sure to fill the box enough to hide the chest, wanting to keep this a secret until I had the chance to look through it.

I glanced around her room one last time, hoping I would somehow be able to avenge her death in one way or another.

"I'm ready to leave." I said to Michael once I stepped out of the bedroom. He looked at me as if trying to see if I was okay, and I gave him a small smile to let him know I was.

"Do you need anything else besides these photo albums?" He asked, holding them up.

"No, I don't really care about the rest. I just took the stuff that I knew my mom… liked." It was still weird to talk about my mother in the past tense, and it made me slightly uncomfortable. I knew it was because there was still a part of me that refused to believe that I had lost her.

"Okay." Michael gave me a comforting smile before we left.

I locked the door but kept the spare key with me. Michael was scanning around the area once again, but I wasn't as worried as I was before. If someone intended to attack, they would have likely done so while we were in the house to avoid getting caught.

"Can you take me to the boutique while we're here? I should put up a sign or something to let customers know we're permanently closed." I asked him once we were in the car.

There was no way I would want to run the boutique alone, and for some very obvious reasons, I couldn't stay here. As much as I enjoyed my job, it wouldn't be the same without my mother.

Michael looked at me with a frown on his face.

"…You don't know?"

"Don't know what?" I looked at him, confused.

He sighed as he ran a hand through his hair and looked at me with a sad expression.

"It was burned down."

Seventy-Two

ALTHAIA

My throat closed when I saw the burned building. I stepped out of the car, barely believing what I was seeing in front of me. The boutique my mother had worked so hard for was just gone.

Gone like she was. Vanished, leaving only memories behind.

"I'm so sorry, Thaia." Michael wrapped an arm around my shoulders while I still looked at the boutique in disbelief.

"Why would they do that?" My voice was nothing, but a mere broken whisper.

"I don't know, but I promise you I'll find out whatever I can and let you know if something comes up. They're all going to pay for this." Michael promised me, but right now, it all felt like empty words to me. "Come, let's go now."

"Do you want to take a walk with me on the beach? The sun is about to set, and it's a beautiful sight to witness." I asked Michael. He decided to keep me company for the rest of the day, even though I hadn't said much since we came back.

He made sure I got something to eat and tried to lift my spirits. It did help that he was here. I had forgotten how goofy he could be, and I was happy that I was able to spend some time with him since it had been so long since the last time.

"Sure." He smiled, and we made our way outside. "Are you sure you don't want to stay at my place instead of here?" Michael asked again, trying to convince me not to stay here on my own.

"I appreciate the offer, but I just need some time for myself." I explained to him as we walked down to the beach.

"I don't like you staying here by yourself."

"It's literally a safe house. Do you really think they would send me out here if it wasn't safe for me?" I pointed out. I rolled my eyes at him when he scoffed at my answer but said nothing else.

We walked alongside the water, watching and enjoying the incredible view of the sunset. There was something incredibly peaceful about watching the warm colors of red and orange in the sky. With the water reflecting everything, it created an even more majestic sight.

My hand reached up to touch the necklace that I always wore, only to be reminded again that I had lost it. I let out a sigh; it was a necklace I had received from my grandfather before he passed away—the only thing I had from him.

I stopped walking as I faced the water, and closed my eyes while taking a deep breath of the fresh, salty air. I loved it here. The sounds of the waves made me feel calm as I embraced the serenity.

"Is it true?"

I turned around to face Michael, seeing how he looked troubled while still gazing at the water.

"What is?" I asked him, curious about why he was suddenly wearing such a grim expression. He let out a breath and looked at me, his ocean-blue eyes gazing intently.

"You and him... is it really true?"

I faced away, feeling my heart ache at the mention of him. I wasn't even sure if he still wanted me, and I couldn't blame him if he wanted to leave me. I had lost a life that was precious to him too.

"Something like that..." I muttered, and my throat went completely dry. Michael grabbed me and turned me around to look at him.

"Why him?" He asked firmly, his brows furrowed, and seriousness in his expression that took me by surprise. He stepped closer, his hands slowly sliding up and resting on my cheeks. "Why him and not me?" He whispered.

I was too stunned to say anything as he caressed my cheeks.

In the silence, the sound of the waves crashing on the shore seemed to intensify, creating a backdrop of the unspoken emotions swirling between us.

"W-what?" I breathed out, and my eyes widened.

"Althaia, I've loved you since day one. I've always wanted you."

My body was completely frozen in place, unable to say anything at all as I watched his face coming closer to mine.

"Michael, I'm sorry, but I don't…" I shook my head and tried to take a step back, but he wrapped an arm around my waist, preventing me from moving away from him.

"Don't say you don't feel anything for me either, because I know you do." He stated. I swallowed hard at the way he was affectionately looking at me.

"I'm sorry, Michael, but I don't. I-I love him." Even if he didn't love me anymore, my heart would still belong to him.

I put a hand on his chest and slightly pushed him away from me while I took a couple of steps back.

"You can't be serious. He's not good for you, Thaia!" Michael's eyes turned angry as he glared at me, a deep frown etched on his face. "He can't make you happy. I can!" His words had me completely shocked.

"You don't know anything about him or our relationship." I frowned, anger bubbling up at his words.

"I know what type of man he is. I've been around him longer than you have. Trust me when I say that he's just toying around with you." He spat out his words, a venomous tone in his voice.

"Listen to yourself! You sound completely insane." My voice rose as I shot him an angry look.

"It's the truth." He insisted, his anger matching mine.

"Stop it!" I yelled at him. He looked taken aback by my sudden outburst. "You don't know him the way I do. I'm sorry Michael, but I don't feel the same way about you. I love you, but not the way you want me to. I'm *in love* with him."

"All that time we've spent together when you came for the engagement party, all the flirting between us. Are you saying you never once felt anything for me? Because I don't believe it."

"I will not lie and say I didn't have a crush on you before, because I did. But he made me happy, whether you want to believe it or not." I said to him softly, watching the play of emotions on his face. His brows were still furrowed.

"You're my best friend. I would hate to lose you over something like this, and you deserve someone who loves you, too. And it isn't me. Not the way you want me to."

"When did it happen?" He masked his emotion with a blank expression.

"It doesn't matter when it happened." I sighed.

"It does when we suddenly found out that you were pregnant with his child. So, when the fuck did it happen?"

I stopped breathing, my heart clenching at his words while he looked at me with cold eyes.

"You carried his child. How could you be that reckless with someone you barely know?!" Michael erupted.

I slapped him hard across the cheek.

"How could you, Michael?" My voice was shaking in anger, and unshed tears burned in my eyes. I turned around and walked away from him as fast as I could.

"Shit! Althaia, stop! I didn't mean it like that." He ran after me and grabbed my arm, but I ripped it out of his grasp and pushed him away from me.

"Don't fucking touch me!" I screamed at him, a tear falling down my cheek. The anger and hurt were etched on my face as I struggled to contain my emotions. "After I've lost... how could you say that to me?" A sob escaped my lips, my shoulders shaking with the weight of grief.

Michael looked at me with regret written all over his face.

"I'm sorry, I didn't -"

"Leave." I told him abruptly, not wanting him to be here anymore.

"Thaia, please..." He tried to reach out to me, but I moved away.

"Leave, Michael." I said again. He ran a hand through his hair, and I was trying my best not to break down entirely.

"I'm sorry." He gave a defeated look and went around the beach house to get to his car. I stood still, not going inside until I heard him drive away. I put a hand down to my stomach, feeling the loss even more now.

I wiped away my tears as I went inside. After a moment, I heard a knock on the door, and rage filled my body as I made my way to the front door, ready to scream at Michael for all the things he had said.

I swung the door open, about to say something, but clamped my mouth shut.

"Arianna?" I said in surprise. She raised a brow at me and walked past me into the house. I shut the door and followed her into the living room. "Is there something wrong?" I asked anxiously, thinking something had happened to Damiano.

"Yes, there is." She turned around to look at me, and I felt my heart drop.

"Did something happen to -"

"It's best if I do the talking here." She interrupted me. Her entire demeanor towards me was different from what it usually was, and it didn't go unnoticed that she was talking to me in a harsh voice.

"I don't know what your game is, but you begged Damiano to let you go because you needed to be alone, so he did. We put you in this house for you to stay safe and do whatever healing you needed to do, *alone*. But now, I find out that you invited another man over, and also went back to the house where you almost got killed without informing any of us. What if something happened to you, huh?" She snapped at me.

"Michael was with me, and he made sure everything was clear before we even went inside the house." I said quickly, trying to let her know that I wasn't being completely reckless about it.

"You see, that's what I don't understand. Why were you with another man?" Arianna tilted her head slightly to the side. I frowned at her accusing tone.

"It's Michael. Someone I grew up with, someone who was close to my mother, not a stranger as you're making it sound to be." I crossed my arms, not liking how I had to explain myself with whom I was hanging out with.

"Wasn't he the childhood friend you flirted with before Damiano? So, you're telling me nothing is going on between the two of you? Because it sure did look like you were having a cute moment on the beach together - *just friends,* right?"

"Nothing is going on between us. He *is* just a friend." I said through gritted teeth.

"Right. Does he feel the same?"

I glared at her, not saying anything, as she already knew the answer to her own question.

"Why are you here, Arianna?" I didn't like the way she was toying around with me with her words.

"I came to see what was going on when I heard a man was visiting you. You're lucky I'm the only one who knows about this because you know Damiano would kill him on the spot if he knew what had happened."

"Nothing happened between us." I clenched my jaw, as she kept going on about it.

"I don't really understand you, Althaia. How is this fair to Damiano? You left him when he needed you the most." Arianna said sharply.

"I didn't leave him!" I snapped.

"Then what do you call this?" She gestured to the house.

"I just needed some time alone. None of you know what the hell I'm going through!" I exploded. She gave me a blank look in return.

"You're right. I don't know what you're going through, but you're not the only one who lost someone." Arianna spoke calmly. "I know you're suffering from a greater loss, and I'm so sorry. But did it ever occur to you how Damiano is feeling? He lost a baby, too, and every day I am watching him suffer. We're all hurting, and it's tearing us apart."

My lip started to tremble, and my heart broke into a million pieces. Of course I was constantly thinking about him and his feelings, but I didn't know how I was supposed to help him when all I felt was shame about it.

"You know what? Stay away from my brother. He doesn't deserve this." Arianna gave me one cold stare before she made her way out of the house.

I didn't move from my spot in the living room, completely broken by everything she said. I fell to my knees when I couldn't hold it in anymore and broke down.

The cold floor pressed against my trembling knees, the harsh reality of Arianna's words echoing in my mind. Was this really it? Was it truly for the best that I stayed away from him?

All these thoughts made me sob out loud, hiding my face in my hands as I cried hard, feeling completely shattered that I had failed to be there for him.

The little progress I had made vanished, and I felt myself being sucked back into the deep, dark hole with no way out.

Seventy-Three

ALTHAIA

Hours went by as I remained on the floor, lying on my back while staring emptily at the ceiling. It never occurred to me just how much I had fucked up by staying in the safe house.

He had always been there for me, taken care of me, and I just left him all by himself. I knew I should have been there for him. I wanted to be there for him, but I was afraid to look at him, terrified to witness him blaming me for everything. I ran away because I was scared that the longer I stayed around with a flat stomach, the more he would despise me for it.

Slowly, I stood up and made my way to the bathroom. I uncovered the mirror and looked at myself, seeing how red and puffy my eyes were.

What a fucking mess I have become.

I washed my face with cold water, hoping it would take the worst away and make my eyes less puffy. I grabbed an oversized hoodie and pulled the hood over my head as I walked to Ava and Samantha's place to get Kiara.

I knocked on the door, making sure I kept my eyes lowered to the ground to avoid any questions about it because I knew it was visible to see I had been crying.

"Hey, Althaia. Here to get Kiara?" Samantha asked with a smile.

"Yeah." I had to clear my throat a little as my voice sounded off. "Thank you for watching her." I tried again, sounding better.

"Are you okay?"

"Yep." I dismissed her question just as Ava made an appearance with Kiara. I took her in my arms, happy to see the little furball rub her head against my chest with a purring sound.

"Thank you again for watching her."

"No problem." Ava said, and I turned around to leave, only to stop after a couple of steps before I turned around to look at them again. The warmth of Kiara's purring provided a small comfort, easing the heaviness in my chest.

"How come you reported to Arianna and not to Damiano?" I decided to ask since it went through my mind ever since she left.

I had my suspicions about them the moment we bumped into each other, but I wasn't too sure about it. Now, I was completely sure they were working for him when I hadn't been able to spot any of his men.

It only made sense he would put someone close to me but also someone I wouldn't recognize, so I wouldn't feel like I was being watched. I just didn't know why they reached out to Arianna first.

"Huh? Who?" Ava raised her brows, faking confusion, but I saw right through it. Samantha was quiet as she was still observing me ever since she asked if I was okay.

"I know he sent you here to keep an eye on me. I just want to know why you reported to Arianna today and not him?" I was looking directly at Samantha, who now had a corner of her mouth tilted a little upward, confirming that they were, in fact, working for him.

"I guess there is no point in keeping this a secret from you..." Ava trailed off and looked at Samantha.

"I think you know why we reached out to Arianna instead of Damiano." Samantha replied, and I gave her a slight nod. "It doesn't seem like you're ready to see him either, since you didn't mention him once to us. If we reported to him, he would have come." She added, and she was right. If we were to see each other again, I would rather have it be under different circumstances.

"I see. Thank you for not telling him." I didn't wait for them to say anything else and went back to the house.

I stayed locked inside the house for days, or maybe even weeks. I didn't know how many days had passed since Arianna and Michael were here. I had turned off my phone again, hoping Michael would get the message when he continued to call me and send me endless messages. I wasn't interested in whatever he had to say to me when he so brutally brought up the pregnancy.

The rooms were shrouded in a heavy silence, broken only by the occasional meow from Kiara, who seemed to sense my despair. I haven't gone outside a single time, and if Kiara hadn't needed attention, food, and water, I wouldn't have left my bed.

I was also pretty sure that if Ava and Samantha couldn't see the lights being turned on and off in the house, they would probably have thought I was dead. I kind of was already.

I let out a sigh after filling up Kiara's bowl with food, seeing I would need to get out and buy some more for her soon. Just as I was picking up some of the cat toys on the floor, I stumbled upon the box I had filled with some of my mother's things.

I took the box and got comfortable on the couch as I went through the stuff. It was a bittersweet moment for me, feeling sad that this was how I would feel closer to her now, yet happy that I was able to get some of her things, and extremely grateful that they didn't burn down the house. That would have destroyed me.

My heart skipped a beat when I saw the chest at the bottom of the box. I had completely forgotten about it! I quickly picked it up, feeling my nerves kicking in as I opened the chest.

I emptied it and laid everything out in front of me on the couch and went through the papers. It looked like they were all letters from someone, but it wasn't anything I could read.

It was in a different language, and not one I recognized. How many languages did my mother know? I had only ever heard her speak three languages, but not once has she mentioned that she knew more.

My eyes scanned the letter I was holding, trying to see if there was anything I could recognize, but to my disappointment, there wasn't anything. I came across the picture and took a closer look to examine it.

It was definitely my mother when she was younger. I had seen enough pictures of her to know what she looked like back then. My mother was looking directly at the camera, smiling. The man next to her had an arm wrapped around her waist while he had a soft expression on his face as he looked at her. It was actually a rather cute picture, making me smile at it.

As I examined the picture closer, I couldn't help but wonder about the man; he had blue eyes, light brown hair, and was quite handsome. Perhaps he was an old flame? The tenderness in his gaze suggested a closeness that intrigued me. Could the letters be from him?

I turned the picture around, seeing something was written on the back. A date was written on, letting me know that my mother was around her early twenties in the picture. Further down something more was written.

Lunny svet & Solnishko

I noticed this one word that was written several times in the letters. The more I looked at it, the more I felt like I was familiar with it. Where had I heard this word before? My brows furrowed as I went through my mind, hoping something would click.

"No way!" I gasped out loud, my jaw dropped in the process. There was absolutely no way.

"She will always be my Solnishko."

Realization struck me like a lightning bolt. The shock on my face mirrored the astonishment at what I had just uncovered.

His words echoed loud and clear in my mind as I looked at the picture in complete surprise. I examined the man in the picture again, and it slowly dawned on me that this man must be Mr. Alexei Vasiliev.

"There is no fucking way!" I almost yelled out, my eyes widening in surprise. Had my mother been in a relationship with the Boss of the Russian Mafia?!

Holy fuck!

"Wow... I did not see that coming." I mumbled to myself, barely believing my eyes.

The more I looked at the picture, the more I thought he actually looked like Mr. Vasiliev. This new piece of information made me realize my mother was so much more than what she had made me believe.

I went through the papers, trying to gather them neatly, so I could put them back in the chest again. I would definitely have to find someone who could translate these letters for me.

Just as I was stacking the papers, my eyes caught a small envelope that I hadn't checked. Curious, I opened it and looked inside, seeing there was another letter. I unfolded the paper, and at the same time, something dropped into my lap.

I picked it up, discovering a rather fancy black card with silver writing on it. I looked back at the letter.

Attend the Untamed Event at the LuxePalace. You'll meet him there.

— N.

My gaze shifted to the black card, seeing the name LuxePalace written elegantly in silver. Was this card some sort of invitation and would it have gotten her access to the place? What even was the LuxePalace? I had never heard that name before.

As curiosity tugged at me, I quickly got up from the couch, retrieved my phone from the nightstand, and turned it on. Ignoring the missed phone calls and messages from Michael, I went straight to the browser to do some research.

It didn't take me long to find out that it was exclusively a place for the stinking rich people. LuxePalace was some sort of fancy casino hotel, and much more, just for billionaires.

A mix of fascination and confusion washed over me as I searched for the Untamed Event, trying to see when that was supposed to happen since nothing else was written on the note. It seemed my mother already knew that place and when it was supposed to be, as there was no more information about it.

Shit, my mother did a fucking good job in hiding this side of her life.

I guess you were that kind of person if you were still a part of that world. I thought she had left it for good when we moved away.

I found the date for the event and checked on my phone; I saw that the Untamed Event would be in four days. For some reason, my heart was beating fast at the thought of going there to check out the place.

I bit down on my lip, wondering if it would be a good idea or not. Glancing back at the note, questions lingered in my mind; who was N, and who was she supposed to meet there?

Maybe it could be Mr. Vasiliev?

As I kept wondering, I only ended up with more questions that might be answered if I went to the LuxePalace.

Four days.

I had four days to come up with a plan and get my ass to the LuxePalace.

Seventy-Four

ALTHAIA

Four days passed in a blink of an eye, and I had spent every single day trying to come up with a plan. Yet, the reality was far from the simplistic scenario I had envisioned in my mind.

First of all, I was being watched, and it was not as if I could casually announce, 'yeah, I'm just going to the LuxePalace to snoop around a bit because I think I might get some answers about my mom.' Nope. I couldn't risk getting caught and having them call Damiano.

I had to come up with a bulletproof plan and think like them. Spending enough time around Damiano and his men had given me insights that could guide me in the right direction.

Second, I didn't know what to expect at the LuxePalace. I had told myself always to expect the unexpected, but in the underworld, that saying held no real meaning. They always take shit to the next level with no limitations to their imagination.

Third, going to such a place without expecting at least one of Damiano's men being present would be naïve. I needed to become unrecognizable.

Bits of memories came back to me about what happened in the woods. When I woke up in the hospital, everything was a blank slate, a protective mechanism, according to Ellie. Now, details were resurfacing, some clearer than others.

I remember my mother said *he* attacked sooner rather than later. Someone was after her, and she was aware of it. However, the attack in our own home caught her off guard.

I let out a small gasp when it hit me.

Maybe she wanted to talk to Mr. Vasiliev for protection?

Well, there was only one way to find out.

I grabbed the basket I had filled with delicacies and a nice bottle of wine, making my way over to Ava and Samantha. As soon as I reached their front porch, the door opened. Since I knew they worked for Damiano, they didn't bother hiding that they were watching me; hence why they opened the door before I even had the chance to step close enough to knock on the door.

"Sup, Althaia!" Ava said happily, making me smile at her chipper mood.

"You're really watching my every move, huh?" I joked, to which she laughed.

"Yeah, I don't feel like being discreet anymore now the cat is out of the bag, anyway. Plus, a certain someone would have my head if I wasn't being thorough." She gave me a knowing look.

"I guess you're right." I chuckled.

"Come on in. Cecilia has just baked you a chocolate cake."

"Cecilia?" I asked.

"Oh, shoot! I forgot you didn't know her real name. Samantha was just a cover name in case you would get suspicious of her name sounding Italian." She explained with an innocent grin on her lip.

"That makes sense. Wait, is your real name Ava, then?" I squinted my eyes at her, making her laugh.

"It sure is. I'm not Italian anyway, so I thought it was pretty safe." She said as we made our way to the living room. "But we had a feeling you were already onto us the moment we bumped into you."

"I had my suspicions, but I wasn't too sure. When you asked if I had a boyfriend and I said no, you seemed surprised, like you already knew the answer." I pointed out, and she looked impressed.

"Damn you're good! And here I thought you would be easy to trick. I totally underestimated you." Ava shook her head in amusement.

"I learned from the best." I winked with a smile.

Cecilia made an appearance in the living room, her apron covered in flour.

"I thought I heard your voice! I had my headphones in while baking because Ava wouldn't shut up about being bored." She said, glaring at Ava, who gave her a sour look in return.

"I guess I haven't given you much to do lately." I said a bit awkwardly. I stayed inside most of the time, except when I went out to do some shopping for the house and Kiara.

"Which is a good thing, but Ava seems to forget that." She kept scolding her, and Ava just rolled her eyes at her while mumbling something under her breath.

"By the way, this is for you guys." I said, coming to Ava's rescue and holding up the basket. "I just wanted to thank you for watching Kiara that day." I smiled softly at them, to which they returned.

"Well, I'm not about to turn down that bottle of wine! I will get the glasses." Ava turned around and made her way to the kitchen.

"I made a chocolate cake for you. I heard it's your favorite." Cecilia smiled.

"Chocolate cake or not, I'm not going to say no to whatever you've baked." I said, making her face brighten before she followed Ava to the kitchen.

I placed the basket on the coffee table and decided to look around the living room. They had made it look like they had been living here for a while, with many personal touches and frames of pictures scattered around. They really thought of everything to make things as believable as possible.

A vibrating sound caught my attention, and I looked over to see a phone ringing on the couch. I picked it up to hand it over to either of them but stopped in my tracks when I saw the name flashing on the screen, causing my heart to pound.

Damiano.

Damiano was calling, making me stand still and just stare at the phone. I really wanted to answer the call, just to hear his voice for a second. My finger hovered over to accept the call, but Arianna's words stopped me. Still, I kept debating if I should answer the call, but it was already decided for me when the call ended for taking too long.

I let out a breath, my heart squeezing as I placed the phone down on the couch. The phone buzzed again. I couldn't resist and peeked at the screen. It was a text message from him. But when Ava and Cecilia returned quickly, I moved away from the phone and sat on the opposite couch.

"There you go." Cecilia handed me a plate with a large piece of chocolate cake, vanilla ice cream, and some cut-up strawberries on the side.

"This looks amazing, thank you!" I said excitedly, genuinely thrilled about the dessert. Cecilia always seemed pleased with my reaction whenever she handed me a plate of her heavenly baked goodies. "No wine for me." I told Ava when she was about to pour me a glass.

"Why not?"

"Last time, the wine and sugar knocked me out in a second, and I'm planning on having a second plate of this." I said, digging into the chocolate cake. Ava just shrugged and picked up her glass, taking a sip.

Cecilia glanced at the phone on the couch and quickly sent a text back. It didn't go unnoticed that she rolled her eyes at whatever Damiano had texted her, leaving me curious about their conversation.

"Thanks for the cake, guys." I said and then faked a yawn when the bottle was halfway empty. I knew it was my cue to bid them goodnight. "I've been going to sleep early these days, so I'm already tired."

The sun just dipped below the horizon when I made my way back. The safe house was next to theirs, so it wasn't far, yet they kept watching me until I reached the house safely.

Now it was time to get ready.

I went to the bathroom where I had already laid everything out so I could get ready faster. I had about an hour before the cab would be here, which was also enough time for Ava and Cecilia to be knocked out cold.

I wanted to look different as much as possible, so I got myself some colored contacts, making my eyes blue instead of green. I also did heavy eye makeup and red lips. Last, I grabbed the short, black wig with bangs and put it on.

"Damn, I really do look different." I said, in awe of my own reflection.

I had four days to devise a plan, and this was the best I could come up with. Going to LuxePalace was undoubtedly risky, especially using my mother's card, and that was why I had to look different for my own safety.

The strategy was simple; blend in, avoid drawing any attention, and search for Mr. Vasiliev, hoping that was the person my mother wanted to talk to. If I don't find him within an hour, I will be out of there.

Easy peasy.

I slipped into a royal blue satin dress with a slit leg. I chose this dress strategically; I could wear a garter belt, concealing my gun discreetly while still being able to reach it with ease. If I was going to meet the Boss of the Russian Mafia, I sure as hell wasn't going without a gun.

Satisfied with my appearance, I threw on a pair of sweatpants and a hoodie over the dress. I stuffed my heels into a bag along with a clutch filled with a shitload of cash I had taken from the emergency drawer.

I looked out of the window facing Ava and Cecilia's back porch, allowing me to keep an eye on them. I couldn't see inside, but their silhouettes would be visible if they moved since the light was still on. With binoculars, I checked for any activity, but it seemed quiet. No movements.

They were out cold, and this was my cue to leave.

I kept the television on to give the illusion that I was watching. I went to the other side of the house, to the window facing away from their place. After making sure no one was around, I opened the window, jumped out, and left it slightly ajar for my return.

I crouched down low on the grass, staying hidden in the shadows as I moved down the street where I had ordered the cab to pick me up. Constantly scanning my surroundings for any sign of Damiano's men or familiar cars, I quickly made my way to the spot where the cab came into view.

"Cab for Lily?" The driver asked as I got inside. To be extra cautious, I had given a fake name. Damiano had numerous businesses, and his people were everywhere. I couldn't risk anyone recognizing my name and reporting back to him.

"Yes."

"Cool! I'm Chad. Where are you off to?"

"The LuxePalace." I said, a little out of breath from basically playing a spy on a mission. My heart was also pumping like crazy as I continued to look around anxiously, but it seemed I had made it safely and unnoticed.

Chad made a whistling sound as he drove off.

"Fancy! Not to be rude or anything, but I don't think you're allowed in, wearing that." He took a quick look at me and my comfortable clothes before returning his focus to the road.

I ignored him as I started to take off my hoodie and sweatpants and put on my heels. I grabbed a small mirror I had packed with me to make sure everything still looked okay and that my wig wasn't out of place. It freaked me out how different I looked.

"Damn! Now you look like someone who can get in!" Chad glanced at me again when he realized I was wearing a dress underneath.

"That's the plan." I chuckled. If Chad thought I looked like someone who could get into the LuxePalace, then I had done my job pretty well.

My nerves were getting to me when I saw we were getting close to my destination. My eyes widened at the large and luxurious building with lights on it, making it even more extraordinary and expensive looking.

Shit, now I was scared I was underdressed for this.

Chad drove around a large, round lake with sprinklers shooting water high in the air. I told him not to park the car in front of the building but rather further down the street. It was still close, but I wanted to assess the situation before going inside.

"This is for you." I said, and his eyes widened when he saw the stack of money I wanted to give him.

"That is way too much!" He shook his head, but I just placed the money on the passenger seat for him.

"Take it because I need a favor from you. I need you to stay here and wait for me to come back. I don't know how long I'll be gone, but you're kind of my personal driver tonight. And if you wait for me, I will double the amount when I'm back. Deal?" I smiled, and he was shocked that I would give him more money.

"You have my word, Lily! I will wait for you." Chad said excitedly, making me chuckle at his enthusiasm.

"Thank you!" I got out of the cab, only grabbing my clutch, leaving the rest in the car with Chad.

Luxurious vehicles lined up in front of the opulent casino hotel, dropping off people dressed in fine clothing as they ascended the grand staircase to the entrance. I took a deep breath and blended in with the people at the entrance.

"Welcome to the LuxePalace." The doorman greeted me as I handed him my card. He scanned it, casting a brief glance at his computer screen. "Enjoy, and have a pleasant evening, Jacinta."

"Thank you." I replied with a smile, stepping inside.

This was it.

I took a moment to inhale deeply, steadying my nerves, and strode forward with confidence.

I've got this.

Seventy-Five

ALTHAIA

The LuxePalace overwhelmed my senses with opulence and grandeur, leaving me in awe as soon as I entered. The floor was adorned with a glossy beige marble, reflecting my surroundings vividly with its mirror-like sheen. Above, the ceiling reached astonishing heights, adorned with chandeliers that dripped with glistening crystals.

I did my best not to appear too lost, as everyone around me seemed familiar with the place. Deciding to take a seat at the bar, I figured it was the best way to observe my surroundings without giving away my confusion or discomfort.

I ordered a glass of wine and nearly choked when I learned it cost several hundred dollars. Just for a single glass! It was a good thing I was only pretending to be rich for an hour, because keeping up with this lifestyle would leave me broke and on the streets in no time.

Yes, my mother provided me with a comfortable life, but this was a whole new level of extravagance.

As I sipped my wine, I scanned the room, observing people gathered by the casino tables; gambling, chatting, and reveling in the atmosphere. I kept an attentive eye, hopeful of spotting Mr. Vasiliev. However, the longer I lingered at the bar without catching a glimpse of him, the more my hope sank.

After finishing my wine, I decided it was time to explore the venue. For a moment, I thought of the possibility that he had changed his mind and decided not to attend the event. The note suggested he would be here, but then again, I was just assuming and hoping it was him. I was curious about his history with my mother.

Making my way toward the elevators to explore other floors, I paused. His dominating presence filled the room; tall, intimidating, and surrounded by a few men. He was impossible not to notice.

Adrenaline surged through my veins as soon as I spotted him, and I quickly walked toward Mr. Vasiliev. I found myself at the far end of the room, desperately hoping to reach him before he stepped onto the elevator. I was

THE DEVIL'S FIRE

practically half-running as the elevator doors opened, and I just managed to slip inside before they closed.

Trying to calm my pounding heart, I realized I was now standing right next to Mr. Vasiliev. With three of his men present, I was relieved to find a random couple in the elevator, which made my sudden entrance go unnoticed.

The couple exited on the fifth floor, and I noticed the button for the sixteenth floor was pressed. I remained still and quiet, facing away from them, pretending that the sixteenth floor was my stop as well.

The elevator came to a stop, and all four of them stepped out. I walked behind them at a measured pace, leaving enough distance to avoid sparking suspicion. I glanced around the hallway lined with hotel rooms, a perfect cover, as I pretended to search for a specific room number.

Mr. Vasiliev and his men reached the end of the hall, turned a corner, and after a brief pause, I followed suit. I turned around the corner, and I was suddenly slammed against the wall with a force that emptied my lungs of air.

I winced, squeezing my eyes shut and letting out a yelp of pain as the back of my head collided with the wall. My eyes snapped open as something cold pressed against my forehead. I stared into cold, emotionless eyes, a gun held firmly, pointing directly at me.

"Now, tell me, young lady, why are you following me?"

I turned towards the voice, finding Mr. Vasiliev looking at me calmly, hands tucked into his dress pants.

Words lodged in my throat as I was caught completely off guard. He nodded to one of his men, who approached me and began to pat me down.

I remained frozen, my heart threatening to burst out of my chest. The tension escalated as the man discreetly shifted the slit of my dress, revealing the gun securely tucked into my garter belt.

Mr. Vasiliev briefly glanced at the exposed weapon before returning his gaze to me, his brow slightly raised.

"Who sent you?" His demeanor had shifted significantly from the auction. It was understandable, considering he had approached me then, and now I looked different, armed with a concealed weapon.

"No one." I stammered, hating the tremor in my voice. "I had hoped I could talk privately with you."

"Explain the gun." Mr. Vasiliev remained calm and collected as he questioned me. He remained visibly unfazed as he spoke. It was painfully clear that I stood no chance against them.

Yeah, no shit. You have no experience, you fool.

I made a small grimace as he and his men glared with cold, expressionless eyes.

"It's for my protection." I answered honestly. "I just want to talk." I added quickly to reassure him that my intentions weren't malignant. Despite my words, he remained unconvinced.

"I don't have time for this." Mr. Vasiliev sounded bored, glancing at his watch. He then looked at the man holding the gun against my head. "Get rid of her." He ordered, turning to walk away.

My eyes widened as the man removed the gun from me, only to attach a silencer.

"W-wait! Wait!" I screamed out in pure fear, but he ignored me, continuing to walk away. "Y-you said you called her Solnishko!" I yelled out in desperation.

Everyone stopped in their tracks, turning to look at me again. My breathing was heavy, and my legs begged to give out on me, but I fought to pull myself together.

"What did you just say?" His expression shifted to one of curiosity as he focused on me. I glanced at the other men; it was visible that they were all familiar with the name.

"You called her Solnishko, right? Did she, by any chance, call you Lunnyy svet?" Even his men turned to look at him. I held onto a tiny hope that this revelation might save me, praying they wouldn't decide to end my life then and there.

Mr. Vasiliev studied me for a long moment before furrowing his brows.

"Who are you?" He demanded.

"If we could talk somewhere privately, I'll explain." I said firmly, attempting to mask the fear that threatened to overwhelm me.

"Follow me."

I let out a breath, keeping a wary eye on the man who had held me at gunpoint making sure he tucked away his weapon. He trailed closely behind as I followed Mr. Vasiliev and his men into a room.

I expected it to be a suite, but it turned out to be an office. Mr. Vasiliev took a seat on the couch, gesturing for me to sit in front of him. I hesitated, glancing at his men to ensure none of them would suddenly pull a gun on me.

Once convinced it was safe, I took a seat, perching on the edge in case a quick escape became necessary. My hand rested on my thigh, close to the gun they hadn't taken away. Mr. Vasiliev noticed, his gaze shifting from my hand to meet my eyes.

"Care to tell me now who you are?"

"I don't know if you remember me, but we talked at the auction. I'm Althaia."

"Althaia…" He mused, as if recognizing the name. "I remember her looking differently." He added, with a hint of skepticism.

"Well…" I trailed off, removing my wig to reveal my real hair and taking out the colored contacts. "I was just trying out a new style." I said, attempting to inject a bit of humor to ease the tension. It seemed to work, as he looked amused.

"Why the disguise?"

"I didn't want to be recognized."

"So, you're telling me you're here on your own?" He raised a brow.

"I am." I nodded.

"Were you not with Damiano Bellavia? I have a hard time believing he would let you be here on your own." Mr. Vasiliev leaned back on the couch, eyeing me with a newfound interest. The mention of Damiano caught me off guard; I hadn't expected him to be asking about him.

"It's… a long story." I replied.

"You shouldn't be here. It's not safe for you, especially under disguise."

"I can take care of myself." I said defensively, and he gave me a skeptical look. "Okay, you caught me off guard." I admitted, and he chuckled.

"You were a second away from being killed. You have no idea what kind of headache you would have caused me if I had you killed and Damiano found out. He tends to go insane when it comes to someone he cares about. Especially after last time."

"What do you mean?" I asked. His eyes narrowed a bit, and he remained silent for a while.

"You don't know?" He smirked, adding to my curiosity.

"Don't know what?" I pressed for more information.

"If he hasn't told you, then it isn't my place to say." His smirk widened, and I let out an annoyed sigh.

"You can't say that and not even tell me!" I practically scolded him.

"I suggest you talk to your man, then." He shrugged.

"He doesn't tell me much. He doesn't want to involve me in all of this." I sighed.

"Good." He smiled, and I gave him a blank look.

"My curiosity can't handle being left in the dark."

"Your curiosity can get you killed."

"That's what he told me!" I exclaimed loudly.

"You should listen to him."

"This is not how I imagined this conversation would go." I mumbled quietly, leaning back on the couch and feeling more at ease. "I don't get it. Knowledge is power, right? It would help me if I knew more."

"Knowledge is power to a certain extent, yes. It also depends on what kind of person you are. For someone like me, it's power. For someone like you, not so much. It will do you more harm than good." Mr. Vasiliev got up from the couch. My eyes followed him as he grabbed a bottle and two glasses before returning to the couch.

"This world is anything but nice. You're with a powerful man, and people love to play dirty tricks just to get to him, to see him crumble to the ground." He spoke as I watched him pour vodka into the glasses.

He handed me a glass, which I took, but eyed it suspiciously. Mr. Vasiliev let out a small laugh as he observed me examining the clear liquor.

"You know damn well if I wanted to kill you, I would have already put a bullet in you. It's not poisoned." He had a point, but I still hesitated.

Mr. Vasiliev shook his head at me before downing his drink in one go, showing me it was safe. I followed suit; the liquid burned my throat as it went down. It was very strong, and I made a small grimace at the taste.

"Impressive. Not many would have handled it that well."

"I happen to like vodka." I half-shrugged. "So, you really think I should be left in the dark?" I asked, wanting to continue our conversation.

"Most certainly. Enemies and competitors are always seeking ways to destroy la Famiglia Bellavia, making you an easy target for potential kidnapping and torture. There was a time I thought they had succeeded, but Damiano surprised us all. In his twenties, he took over his father's position and rapidly expanded the family's influence, making it more powerful and feared."

"Then, a turning point happened that seemed like it would be his downfall. However, Damiano defied expectations. No one has shown such little regard for their own life as he did, establishing an empire that now strikes fear in everyone. Not bad for someone so young." Mr. Vasiliev remarked, clearly impressed by Damiano's accomplishments.

It felt like he was describing a completely different person than the Damiano I know. While I knew Damiano was powerful and feared, I had no idea to what extent.

"You seem to know a lot about him." I raised a brow, chin resting on my palm, leaning forward.

"I keep ears everywhere."

"How do I know it wasn't you who tried to destroy him?"

"I don't fuck with Italians, and they don't fuck with us. He poses no threat to my businesses right now, but he might be at some point, and then it's a different story." He replied, as if it were the most obvious answer.

"Also, I don't play dirty. If I want him removed from the face of the earth, I will target him and him only, not someone close to him." He pointed out, making me squint my eyes at the word 'someone.'

"Who was it? His father, mother?" I guessed, but he smiled at me and shrugged his shoulders.

"Ask him." He replied pointedly, and I snorted, doubting Damiano would answer.

"Enough about that. I want to know how you know she called me Lunnyy svet." His blue eyes looked at me sternly.

I opened my clutch and handed the picture to him. I decided to take it with me in case he didn't believe me.

Mr. Vasiliev looked at the picture for a long time, not saying anything, and his expression was blank as he stared at it.

"How did you get this?" He asked, still examining the picture. It sounded as if he already knew the answer but needed me to confirm it.

"She's my mom." I said softly. I looked at his men, noticing their surprise, except for one.

He looked at me as if he already knew who I was. Reaching inside my clutch again, I pulled out the note and walked up to him.

"Was this from you?" He didn't look at the note, continuing to study me, confirming that it was from him.

"You look so much like her."

Seventy-Six

ALTHAIA

His comment made me smile, and pride filled my chest. He looked around at my face with a slightly soft and pained expression. A lump slowly formed in my throat.

He knew.

Mr. Vasiliev got up and snatched the note out of my hand, his eyes scanning over the words before he looked at the man in front of me with an angry look.

"What is this, Nestor?" He glared at Nestor, demanding an answer. I took a couple steps back, but Nestor didn't seem bothered by Mr. Vasiliev's angry tone and took a quick glance at me before looking at him.

"She reached out to me." He said, and I noticed Mr. Vasiliev's body tensed.

"Why?"

"She said she needed to see you. I sent her a message that she could meet you here."

"And why didn't you inform me of this?" He was angry, and I felt a twinge of worry for Nestor now.

"She didn't want you to know, considering how you left things the last time." He explained, giving Mr. Vasiliev a knowing look, leaving me confused as I observed their conversation.

"What happened?" I asked. Mr. Vasiliev turned around to face me. He had a stone-cold expression, but his eyes showed anger.

"That damned woman tried to kill me!"

I dropped my jaw in shock.

"Are you talking about my mom?!"

"Who else? She's the only person crazy enough to pull that kind of shit on me." He scoffed, and my eyes widened.

"To be fair, you tried to kill her, too. She was just faster." Nestor pointed out, making Mr. Vasiliev whip his head to him so fast with a frown on his face.

"After all these years, you're still loyal to her?" He spat out. Nestor gave a small smirk and shrugged his shoulders. "I should kill you for being loyal to someone else."

"It's not someone else. It's Solnishko." He said, as if he hadn't just been threatened to be killed.

"Whoa, whoa, back up! You tried to kill my mom?!" I exclaimed in shock.

"Nothing new about that. We tried to kill each other many times." Mr. Vasiliev said casually.

"We all know if she really wanted to kill you, she would have." Nestor added, making Mr. Vasiliev scowl at him.

"That damned woman stabbed me." He erupted. One of his men chuckled but immediately stopped when he got one sharp glare from him.

"I need to sit down." I was overwhelmed by everything they said. "That doesn't sound like my mom at all. Well, not that I would know because I just found out she had a whole different side to her life I had no idea about." I sighed.

Had I really been that naive and oblivious to everything that had been going on?

"Where is she? Why isn't she here?" Mr. Vasiliev looked at me. I looked at Nestor, seeing his expression darken.

I let out a breath as I faced Mr. Vasiliev, feeling my eyes fill up with tears.

"She's gone..." My voice came out in a whisper, and the room fell silent. It was so quiet that I could hear a pin drop.

"Pust' yeye dusha pokoitsya v mire." Nestor and the two other men said in unison.

Mr. Vasiliev was silent, his face and eyes blank as he looked at me. But the look on my face was enough for him to close his eyes, face away from me, and go to look out of the window.

Nestor sat in front of me on the coffee table, letting out a sigh.

"What did that mean?" I asked him quietly.

"May her soul rest in peace." He explained. I gave a small nod, grateful for their words. "She was an amazing woman. She may have hidden many things from you, but she wanted you to live a normal and quiet life. And she did a good job raising you." He smiled, which I returned.

"Were the two of you close?" I asked.

"If there was one woman I would happily take a bullet for, it would be her." Nestor said, making me smile with him. "You look better now."

"What do you mean?"

"I was at the funeral when I found out." He said, glancing at my stomach.

I swallowed hard when he did, fighting the urge to wrap my arms around my stomach.

"How?"

"I have my ways." He explained, and I didn't question it any further. My gaze landed on Mr. Vasiliev's back as he continued to look out of the window.

"I don't understand. I remember him saying he cared about her, but why would they try to kill each other?"

"They had a rather... complicated relationship. He's a stubborn man, and she was an even more stubborn woman. They drove each other crazy all the time but still loved each other." Nestor said, and I just let all the information sink in, still in shock that my mother had been in a relationship with Mr. Vasiliev.

"Last time I saw her, she tried to kill me." Mr. Vasiliev spoke, his back still facing us. "Then she disappeared. She loved to do that to me, and she was good at it, always going by different names to make sure I wouldn't be able to find her." He turned around and made his way back to the couch, pouring himself a drink before he continued.

"Eventually, I stopped caring and left her alone to live whatever life she wanted. A couple of years later, she appeared in front of me again. Now I realize how she was able to always find me." He gave a look to Nestor, who just shrugged him off.

"At some point, I found out she married Gaetano Volante. An Italian. That pissed me off. But I was more pissed at myself for letting her go, which resulted in her getting married." He downed his drink with a somber look on his face.

After hearing this from him and remembering what my mother had said when Arianna and Cara were over for a sleepover, made my heart ache for both of them. My mother never truly loved my father. Maybe that was why she decided enough was enough and left with me.

"I think it's safe to say she never stopped loving you. She wouldn't have kept the picture and all those letters if she did." I spoke softly to him. He let out a small smirk at my words.

"She kept the letters?"

I nodded, and he shook his head a bit in amusement.

"Tell me what happened. How did she die?" Mr. Vailiev's eyes went cold in a second, and I told him what I could remember, intentionally leaving some parts out. I wasn't ready to talk about it yet.

Mr. Vasiliev's expression only darkened with each word that came out of my mouth, his men mirroring his expression, and I had to try my best not to cry while talking.

"And you haven't found those people yet?" He asked once I was done. I shook my head.

"Not to my knowledge." I said. One of his men started to speak in Russian, and Mr. Vasiliev listened to him while looking at me, nodding his head.

"I see." He simply said to him. "You really shouldn't be here, Althaia."

"I know, but I really wanted to see you and figure out why she wanted to meet you." I said and looked at Nestor. "She didn't tell you why she wanted to see Mr. Vasiliev?"

"Alexei. Call me Alexei." I nodded at him and returned my gaze to Nestor.

"No, she didn't tell why and only said she needed to speak to him."

I let out a sigh at his answer. I guess that would forever remain a mystery.

"How did you know when the funeral was?"

"I didn't. She gave me her information to get her an invitation here. Once I found what name she went by, I found out where you lived and the boutique you were running. I wanted to check up on her but found the house empty, and then I checked the boutique to find it burned down. From that day, I checked the cemetery every day, hoping to be wrong. That's when I found you." Nestor ran a hand down his face, looking distressed and sad about it.

"You should have told me." Alexei glared at Nestor; the angry look was back on his face.

"You would have gotten involved, and you know we can't. She's not your business anymore."

"She will always be my damn business!" Alexei roared out, making me jump in my seat. He started to speak rapidly in Russian, and Nestor only nodded at him. Whatever he said to him didn't sound very good, and it kind of felt like Nestor was in trouble.

"Althaia, I have something I need to attend to, and you're not safe here. I need you to go up to the twenty-fifth floor, to room 2509. You will be safe there." Alexei said to me, making me furrow my brows at him in confusion.

"Why?" I asked. But one sharp look from him let me know not to question him.

I put my wig back on and got out the extra set of colored contacts I had brought with me in case anything went wrong with the ones I wore. Luckily, I had a small mirror with me in my clutch to check if everything was in place.

They walked me out to the elevator once I was ready.

"Thank you for telling me about my mother. I feel like I know her more now." I gave a small smile.

"Take care of yourself and stay safe." Alexei said, and I bid them goodbye and stepped into the elevator.

What a night this had turned into, and I couldn't help but chuckle a bit to myself for being able to sneak away and pull this off. I felt like the Mafia.

"I'm the Mafia. We do it like a Mafia." I started to sing quietly to myself.

I reached the twenty-fifth floor and walked down the hall, searching for the room number. It now occurred to me Alexei didn't give me any key card to the room or even told me how to get in. Was I supposed to just knock, and someone would let me in?

"Hmph." A sound came out of me just as I crashed into someone.

"Watch where you're going."

My eyes immediately went up to his as I recognized his voice, but quickly looked down once I saw who it was.

Fuck, Gio is here!

"Uh, sorry. Wrong floor." I said quietly, but he didn't bother to spare me a glance.

I was about to turn around to walk away when I noticed that the door next to him was room 2509. The door opened, and my heart pounded like no tomorrow.

It was Damiano.

My breath halted at the sight of him. My body started to tingle and at the same time, my stomach churned in nervousness.

I walked towards the elevator as fast as I could.

Fuck.

Fuck!

Fuck!!

I repeatedly pressed the elevator button, hoping the doors would open faster. Frustration built up within me as it seemed to take an eternity. The footsteps approached, and it was too late for me to escape to the exit stairs.

I almost wanted to scream in frustration.

Finally, the elevator doors opened, and I quickly stepped inside, pressing random buttons and the one to close the doors as quickly as possible.

That damn Russian set me up! He knew Damiano was here!

Relief washed over me as the doors started to close. However, it was short-lived when a hand appeared between them. I pressed myself into the corner, watching Damiano enter with Giovanni and Luca. Panicking, I kept my gaze down, hoping he wouldn't recognize me. After all, I looked different now, and there was no way he would know.

I tried to take a deep breath to calm my racing heartbeat, worried that the sound might give away my nervousness. Peeking through my eyelashes, I saw that none of them were looking in my direction. Trying to compose myself, I couldn't resist stealing a glance at Damiano.

The sight of him, tall and intimidating with a muscular build, sent a flutter through me. He looked so unbelievably good in his well-fitted dress shirt.

Suddenly, he looked directly at me. I averted my gaze and faced the elevator doors, trying to maintain a neutral expression. Despite my efforts, I could feel his intense gaze on me.

My throat went dry, my body heated, and the elevator ride felt like an eternity. I barely breathed, fearing they might recognize me.

When the elevator finally came to a stop, I quickly stepped out. I felt a wave of relief as no one else exited on that floor.

When I heard the doors closing, I couldn't help myself and turned around just to catch another glimpse of him. My eyes met his as he was already looking at me, but I couldn't look away. He tilted his head slightly to the side before the doors closed and broke our eye contact.

I let out a breath and leaned on the wall for support, feeling my legs were about to give out on me. Placing a hand over my thumping heart, I rested the back of my head on the wall and closed my eyes.

I didn't know how long I had been waiting, but it was long enough to be sure I wouldn't bump into them again. It was time for me to get the hell out of here and back to the safe house. I quickly made my way out and towards where Chad was, thankfully, still parked.

"Thank you so much, Chad!" I quickly handed him the promised money.

I grabbed whatever I could in a hurry, giving him more than I had promised. But I didn't care as I quickly got out and ran to the house in my dress and heels. I went to the side window, jumped to get through, and fell inside with a loud thud in my clumsy hurry.

"Ow..." I winced as I landed painfully. Scrambling to my feet, I let out a breath of relief as I went to the living room when I heard Kiara's small voice. "You have no idea how close that was." I said to her, giving her a pet.

"Was it?"

The light switched on, and I quickly pulled out my gun, aiming it in the voice's direction.

"Oh, fuck." I said, and quickly hid the gun behind my back.

"Oh, fuck indeed." Damiano said in a low, dark tone.
I'm in deep shit.

SEVENTY-SEVEN
DAMIANO

The LuxePalace, adorned in opulence and glittered with the glow of wealth, presented an ostentatious display of grandeur. Yet, it still failed to impress me. I wasn't here to make an appearance; in fact, I entered discreetly through a staff entrance.

I was here to hunt and not to startle the prey into flight.

Exiting my hotel room, I made my way to the secluded back corridors to avoid prying eyes. I reached a hidden service elevator that required a special card that Raffaele had secured for me. I scanned the card, stepped in, and pressed the button for the top floor—an exclusive area where those fuckers were celebrating for killing the life that was growing inside of the woman I love.

This day couldn't have come fast enough. My hands have been uncontrollably twitching, wanting to get my hands on them so badly, but I had to be patient, and usually, I was anything but.

For my Althaia.

For her, I would be anything she desired.

I closed my eyes, losing myself in thoughts of her. Who was I fooling? I couldn't find it in my heart to ever let her go when she had thoroughly infiltrated my heart in every conceivable way.

So much time has passed since I last held her in my arms; the ache in my heart remains, leaving me feeling emptier with each passing moment as the hollowness within me deepens.

I shoved the thoughts of her aside when the elevator doors opened.

I stepped onto the top floor, taking a quick scan of the situation. Men were drinking and having the time of their lives with women on their laps. A stage was present with women entertaining them on poles while waitresses glided through the space, catering to their insatiable appetites for drinks, drugs and flesh.

Unbeknownst to them, each one of them worked under my command.

"Shut down the elevator." I instructed Raffaele into the comm link hidden in the collar of my dress shirt.

"Copy."

The lights of the elevator went out, and the exit sign extinguished where my men were waiting behind the door. I sauntered in, hands in the pockets of my slacks, as their eyes turned toward me. My presence startled them; recognition spread across their faces, but they kept it together, pretending to continue enjoying the party.

My aim was the biggest table where their so-called leader was sitting, enjoying himself with his closest comrades.

I slid into the booth in front of them, catching their attention.

"Gentlemen." I greeted with a short nod. "I hope you don't mind me joining you." I smirked. One of them turned to their leader, speaking in their native tongue, before returning their gaze to me once he replied.

"He says, of course not, and would like to get you a drink." He spoke for his leader, making me raise a brow. Was he his spokesperson?

"How generous of you. I'll take you up on that offer." I waved over a waitress, and she placed a bottle of fine whisky along with four glasses on the table. "Allow me." I said when he was about to reach for the bottle.

I poured the glasses, raising mine.

"Un brindisi... al il tuo funerale." *A toast... for your funerals.*

I downed the drink and slammed the glass onto the table.

The music stopped, and complete silence followed right after. All their eyes were on me after my toast. I grabbed my pack of cigarettes and took one between my lips, offering them one, but they declined. Tension filled the air as they watched my every move.

I took a drag of my cigarette, the smoke curling around me as I glanced to the side, observing his men closing in. A humorless chuckle escaped my lips.

"I wouldn't do that if I were you." I warned, exhaling the smoke.

"This is an exclusive area. You have no business being here." The spokesman declared.

"Really?" I challenged. "Then let's get right into it, shall we?"

They drew out their weapons just as my men stormed through the doors, aiming guns at them. The women seated on their laps held knives to their throats.

"I warned you that it wasn't a good idea, no?" I laughed, taking a final drag before extinguishing the cigarette in their leader's drink. "I'm not interested in staying long. I have one question, answer it, and you won't have to suffer. Much."

Their leader and his comrades exchanged glances as they scrutinized me.

"We owe you nothing." The spokesman spat out.

"I disagree." I replied calmly. "Just one question, and I will leave."

Whispers circulated among them in their native tongue. I checked the watch on my wrist before slamming my fist down on the table, cutting their hushed conversations short.

"I'm not a patient man, so tell me, which one of you fuckers hung the pictures on the wall." I asked.

"Whoever you're looking for is not here. None of us here threatened to kill them."

"Oh?" I raised a brow. "I never mentioned anything about killing. I was referring to the lovely portraits, but it seems you're all too eager to jump to conclusions." I grinned. The spokesman, uneasy, glanced nervously at his leader.

"It seems that you know an awful lot about what I'm talking about." My tone remained eerily calm, accentuating the sinister tension in the air.

I leaned in, the shadows dancing on my face as I fixed my eyes on the spokesman.

"You thought you could lay hands on what's mine and get away with it?" I sneered, relishing the fear that began to etch itself across their faces. "Now, the reckoning has arrived."

I grabbed the spokesman by the shirt in a swift motion, hauling him across the table as I rose to my feet. Gripping his face tightly, he winced in pain as I leaned in.

"You can't fathom how much I've daydreamed about tearing your head off." I hissed. "You'll wish you were never born."

He shook his head vigorously, his entire body trembling with fear. A commotion ensued, with his leader and comrade attempting to reach him, shouting at me.

"Restrain them. I want those two alive." I commanded my men as they bagged their heads and dragged them out.

"I was just following orders!" The spokesman stammered out.

"Who gave the order?"

"I don't know! I don't know anything!"

I tightened my grip on his face, my anger intensifying.

"You're telling me you did all this without knowing who gave the order? You're either a pathetic pawn or a lying piece of shit." I sneered.

His eyes darted around, desperation in his gaze.

"Give me a name, or I promise your suffering will make you beg for death." I growled.

"I swear, I don't know." He pleaded, his voice shaking.

"Wrong answer." My lips curled into a sinister smile, unveiling a darkness I had been waiting to unleash.

I flipped him around in a headlock as I grabbed my knife, holding it to his throat and cut the skin. I couldn't hear his pleas, consumed by my own thirst for his blood. I could have slit his throat and gone on with my day.

But no, I wanted his head.

I dug my fingers into the slit of the cut I made, blood pouring like a waterfall down his body as he thrashed in an attempt to flee. There was no escaping me once I had caught my prey.

I pushed in deeper and deeper, clawing my way inside his throat, leaving a gaping hole open and ripped out his trachea. I discarded it like a piece of trash when he fell to the floor, and I gripped his head with both hands. I pressed down a foot on his chest and snapped his head from side to side.

The sickening sound of bones snapping filled the room, a nauseating symphony that sent tingles down my spine. The heavy and disturbing crunch mirrored the sight of a body contorting and breaking in ways it was never meant to.

My lips curled into a sinister smile, warping the familiar contours of my face into a mask of deranged delight as I watched his skin tear from his body.

My eyes sparkled with unhinged excitement, reflecting the pleasure that had seized me as his head finally separated from his neck.

I grabbed his head by his hair, showcasing it to everyone. The gruesome sight made a few vomit. I examined the head in my hands, tossing it back and forth with a sardonic smile playing on my lips.

"Reminds me of when I was a boy. It's been a while since I've played ball." I said. With dark amusement, I started to bounce it on my feet before catching his head in my hands again.

"Looks like I still got it." I chuckled, my men laughing with me. Those who didn't know me looked at me with a mix of horror and disbelief etched on their faces.

"Let's keep it." I said, tossing the head to Giovanni. He caught it, holding it up to his face.

"Shit, he's ugly." He remarked, tossing it into a bag.

I observed the room, taking in the sight of terror-stricken eyes, soiled clothing soaked in vomit, and pants tainted with piss and shit.

"Kill them. Fill the room with their screams and paint the walls with their fucking blood." I commanded.

In an instant, a chorus of terrified screams filled the air, their voices choked as blood filled their throats.

All for you, my Althaia.

"Burn the entire floor with their bodies. It is called the Untamed Event, after all." I said and made my way to the elevator that Raffaele enabled again.

Giovanni and Luca followed me to my hotel room, standing guard while I took a shower. The warm water cascaded down, turning from clear to red as it circled the drain. Once again, I closed my eyes, the thought of Althaia evading my mind at every given chance.

I turned off the water and stepped out of the shower, drying my body before dressing in a fresh dress shirt and pants. I swung the door open, ready to get the hell out of here to interrogate the bastards we captured.

"...Sorry." A small voice said before scurrying off. I looked at Giovanni's annoyed expression and raised a brow.

"I'm a damn tower compared to her, yet she fucking crashed into me." He grumbled. Luca shook his head, a playful smile on his lips.

Ignoring him, I made my way to the elevator, sticking my hand between the doors before they closed and stepping in. I glanced briefly at the woman present, who shuffled into the corner and kept her head down. Luca couldn't help but smirk at the disapproving glance Giovanni shot her way.

I watched in the reflection of the elevator doors how she slowly raised her head and looked at me. My eyes narrowed subtly as I continued to look at her. She looked familiar.

Way too fucking familiar.

My head snapped towards her, and she looked away in a hurry. I observed her, recognizing the familiarity in the set of her jaw, and the shape of her lips that I had captured many times with my own.

My gaze descended to the unique contours of her body, her figure holding memories, curves and lines that spoke of intimate moments we have shared. Her chest rose and fell rapidly, clutching the purse tightly in her hands before she suddenly rushed out of the elevator when it came to a stop.

My eyes remained fixed on her, tracing every step as she walked away. The doors were closing when she spun around, her eyes locking onto mine. I tilted my head, clenched my fist, and the doors sealed shut, separating us once again.

"What's going on?" Luca asked, noticing my reaction.

"Call Cecilia and Ava. Now!" I growled at them.

"No one's picking up." Giovanni informed me, and I clenched my jaw.

"That woman." I gritted. "Was Althaia."

"What the hell?"

"Call them again!" I fished out my phone from my pocket and made a phone call once I was out of the elevator.

"No one is to set fire to anything until you've gotten the all clear. I will have your fucking head if there's even the slightest spark."

"Understood."

I hung up and called another number.

"A woman on the seventh floor, blue dress, short black hair. Ensure she safely leaves the LuxePalace, and do not draw any attention to her. If she gets as much as a scratch on her, it will be your funeral."

"Yes, sir."

"Still no answer." Luca said.

"They better be dead for letting her slip out on their watch." I sneered, storming through the back entrance where a car was already waiting.

I walked around the car, getting into the driver's seat, and Giovanni and Luca slid inside. I slammed my foot down on the gas, the tires screeching as I raced towards the safe house.

My hands clenched around the steering wheel, anger surging through me from that reckless woman.

"What?" I snapped into the phone when I answered.

"She got out safely and is taking a cab."

"Follow that cab, but keep a distance."

"Yes, sir."

I parked the car out of view when I reached the safe house.

"Go figure out what happened to Cecilia and Ava." I told them, storming towards the safe house Althaia was staying in.

Despite my anger, I still entered quietly, hoping to be wrong, but I was fucking right when she was nowhere to be found.

I turned off the TV, sitting on the couch in complete darkness as I waited for her return. The kitten jumped on my lap, circling, and it made itself comfortable.

"Your owner is about to get her ass spanked raw." I whispered, stroking its fur.

Some time passed before I heard a loud thud coming from the other bedroom.

"Ow…" I heard her wince. The kitten recognized her voice, made a sound and sprung in her direction.

Quietly, I rose to my feet, watching her silhouette entering the living room.

"Damn, you have no idea how close that was." She said with relief in her voice as she talked to her kitten.

"Was it?" I asked, flipping the switch to turn the lights on.

Her whole body straightened and aimed a gun at me. She had a gun, and that set me into a blinding rage.

Her eyes widened and hid the gun behind her back.

"Oh, fuck."

"Oh, fuck indeed."

Seventy-Eight

ALTHAIA

"Damiano..." I swallowed hard as I looked at him, feeling my heart rate going up once again. "I...uh..." My mind went completely blank when I tried to come up with some kind of excuse. But who was I kidding? I was in deep shit no matter what.

"Quiet." He growled out, and I clamped my mouth shut.

Damiano looked at me with his darkened eyes. I had seen that look on his face before, moments before he was about to end someone in the most brutal way.

And now it was aimed at me.

He slowly walked up to me, his eyes scanning my body, before he met my eyes. I had to tilt my head up to be able to see his face when he stopped in front of me.

My breath hitched in my throat at how close we were. He still had that effect on my body, making it flutter and tingle without even touching me, and his face was so close to mine that it almost felt unreal.

It also took everything in me not to turn around and make a run for it, not ready for what I was about to face.

I didn't notice when he reached for the gun I was hiding behind my back before he ripped it out of my hands. Damiano looked at the gun, turning it over as he examined it.

"How did you get this?" His voice was laced with so much anger, making me gulp a little.

"I, uh, bought it?"

He placed the tip of the gun under my chin to tilt my head up higher.

"Don't lie to me. This belongs to me, so tell me who the hell gave it to you?" He sneered. I stayed quiet.

"Fine. I will find out in a second. Go sit your ass down and take that shit off." His eyes were cold as he looked at me. I swallowed hard.

Damiano's eyes followed me as I sat down on the couch. At the same time, the door opened and Antonio, Giovanni, Luca, and Raffaele walked in with Ava and Cecilia, who were still half-asleep and had to be carried by Luca and Raffaele. They all gave me disapproving looks, and I looked away, taking off my wig and contacts to hide my nervousness.

"What happened to them?" Damiano asked, looking at Ava's and Cecilia's drowsy state.

"We found them asleep." Antonio reported.

"Didn't I say to keep an eye on her at all times, and you fell asleep?" Damiano snapped at them. Cecilia looked at him and blinked a couple of times as she tried to focus.

"It just happened. We suddenly got tired after she left. It must have been the wine." She mumbled and leaned into Luca.

"Did you drug us?" Ava asked, making all of them look at me.

"You drugged my girlfriend?" Luca hissed at me. My eyes widened at his words. Cecilia was his girlfriend? That meant she was Damiano's cousin.

Fuck. Me.

"I wouldn't call it drugged, per se... I just crushed some sleeping pills and put them in the wine..." I awkwardly trailed off and squirmed in my seat. If Luca wasn't pissed at me before for staying in the safe house, he definitely was now for, well, drugging his girlfriend with sleeping pills.

"Badass." Ava half chuckled and rubbed her eyes.

"Take them away." Damiano ordered, and Luca and Raffaele carried them out. Even Raffaele, who was usually playful, was quiet and looked at me with a pissed-off expression.

Damiano held up the gun, making Antonio look at it.

"I gave her the gun."

"And why the fuck would you do that?"

"In case she needed it for extra protection." He said calmly while Damiano glared at him with a murderous look.

"She barely knows how to use it. What if she hurt herself with it?"

"I'm not that stupid." The words came out before I could stop them, making him whip his head at me so fast.

"Didn't I tell you to stay quiet?" He growled out, and I frowned.

"This is getting ridiculous." I mumbled under my breath and crossed my arms, but he heard it.

"Do you think this is a joke? What the fuck were you doing at the LuxePalace?!"

I was startled when he raised his voice at me. He stepped closer and stared me down.

"I'm not going to talk to you if you're just going to yell at me." I stood up to get away from him, but he grabbed my arm firmly to face him again.

"You're going to tell me before I really lose my fucking shit." His expression made my heart drop.

"Please, let go. You're scaring me." My voice came out in a whisper. He let go of me as if I had burned him and stepped away.

I didn't want to feel this way, and I knew he would never hurt me, but the way he was talking to me and looking at me was not something he had ever done before.

Damiano let out a string of curse words as he ran a hand through his hair before turning around.

"Fuck!" He yelled and punched the wall. His fist went through it before he left the house, slamming the door shut.

I bit down on my lip as I looked anywhere but at Antonio and Giovanni, hating that they were witnessing this. I glanced in the direction of the door, contemplating whether I should follow him or not.

"Let him cool off. He'll be back." Antonio said. I nodded, swallowing the lump that had formed in my throat. I knew I fucked up, and I really hated how angry he was with me.

I sat back down on the couch, took my heels off, and waited for Damiano to come back. They said nothing and just watched me while I was lost in my thoughts.

I didn't know how long it was before the door opened again, and Damiano walked in. I couldn't tell if he had calmed down or not. His face was completely expressionless, void of any emotions.

"Leave us." He ordered them. Antonio looked at me, and I gave a nod, letting him know I would be okay. It didn't go unnoticed by Damiano, but he said nothing.

We looked at each other, no one saying anything, as his intense gaze was on me. I shifted around on my feet, feeling anxious. His emotions were masked, and I didn't know what awaited me. Now I wish he would yell at me. That way, I would at least know what went through his mind.

"Did I hurt you?" Damiano's deep voice broke the silence, looking at my arm where he had grabbed me.

"No." I said softly.

"I didn't mean to scare you." His brows furrowed.

"I know."

"Althaia..." A shiver rippled through my body when he said my name. I let out a breath, and my heart beat faster. "You're getting on a plane first thing tomorrow. You're leaving the States."

I felt my heart drop, and my chest rose and fell in shock.

"W-what?" I managed to get out, but he just looked at me calmly with a straight face, which I hated so much right now.

"You heard me. It's for the best." He simply said, and as I looked at him with wide eyes, he turned around to leave. My mind was like a chaotic storm, crashing with questions.

Why did he want to send me away?

Best for whom?

Me?

Him?

Was he sending me away because he couldn't bear having me around because of...?

"Is it because I lost the baby?" My voice was shaking, laced with sadness and fear; fear that it was because of our loss, and fear that he would leave me for good.

"*What?*" Damiano turned to face me so fast. "What did you say?" His eyes narrowed.

"I-I didn't mean to. I know it was my fault, but I didn't..." My voice was cracking, and my entire body was shaking. Tears were already streaming down my face before I could stop them. I bit down on my lip, which so badly wanted to tremble.

"I didn't mean to lose our baby." I broke down crying, unable to hold it in anymore as my choked-up sobs escaped my lips.

"Althaia, no." Damiano closed the distance between us, embracing me tightly to his body as I sobbed into his chest.

"Look at me." He placed his hands on my cheeks, wiping away my tears as he looked at me firmly. "Don't you dare blame yourself for what happened. It was not your fault; it *isn't* your fault, you hear me?"

"Then why do you want to send me away?" I stammered out. There was no end to my tears as I looked at him with a defeated look. He scanned my face before letting go of me, leaving me with a feeling of loss.

"For your own sake. Do you have any idea what kind of danger you put yourself in by showing up at that place? Alone?" Damiano's anger returned, and his eyes went cold.

"I did it for a reason, and you wouldn't let me go there if I told you."

"Damn right, I wouldn't let you!" He roared out, making me look away.

"You have no idea what kind of people were in that place. They wouldn't hesitate to kill you! And because of that, I need to send you away so you don't pull that kind of shit again. Don't you understand that I want you to be safe? I want you to live a safe and quiet life away from here, away from *me*, because I can't give you that." Damiano looked pained by his own words.

I frantically shook my head in panic.

"I don't want that! I want to be with you!" I cried out. He let out a dark chuckle as he looked at me.

"You're the one who wanted to get away from me, and I'm helping you to do so."

"I didn't mean it like that! I... I was scared you would blame me and despise me for losing the baby. I didn't know what else to do but to go away. Everything got too much for me, and I just needed some time for myself." I explained, feeling my heart about to explode.

Damiano was quiet as he continued to look at me, his eyes softening a bit.

"I wanted to come back to you. I never wanted to stay away for so long, but I was told it was better to stay away from you. I know I hurt you, and I fell apart again. For days, I felt like I had nothing, but every time I thought that, I thought of you. It made me realize that for me, home is with you. You are where my heart is." I poured my feelings out to him.

"All I wanted was to be with you, to start a family... I know I shouldn't have left. I should have been there for you, as you've always been for me. And I'm sorry. I'm so sorry!" I sobbed, my heart aching as I finally let everything out, fearing this might be the end of us.

"Fucking hell..." Damiano took me in his arms. I held him tightly, not wanting to let him go. Damiano sat on the couch with me curled up on his lap.

"Who told you to stay away?" He asked softly. I closed my eyes and took a deep breath.

"Arianna visited me." I said quietly and looked down at my lap.

"Why?"

"Because Michael was here." I faced him, seeing that he was already looking at me with a frown as his hold slowly tightened.

"He just wanted to check up on me, and eventually, I agreed. But I... uh, went back to the house with him to grab some of my mom's stuff." I held my breath as I nervously bit down on my lip.

"You what?!" Damiano furiously erupted.

"You're only going to get angrier from here…" I mumbled.

I could feel him trying to contain his anger as he formed his hands into fists and looked at me like he was ready to send me away for good.

"I found something." I went to the room I had jumped into.

Damiano followed me as I grabbed my clutch. I went to get the small treasure chest I had hidden before sitting back on the couch again.

I laid everything out on the coffee table. Damiano picked up one of the letters, his frown only deepening as he looked it over. I handed him the picture, scooting closer to him as he observed it. He turned it around, reading what was written on it.

"That's Alexei Vasiliev." He raised a brow as he looked at the picture. If he was surprised, he didn't show it. I then handed him the note Nestor had sent to my mother. "I went to the LuxePalace, hoping I would find him to talk to him."

Damiano glared at me, but I tried to ignore it as I continued to speak.

"When we were at the auction, we had a small chat. He said I reminded him of an old girlfriend, and I remembered him calling her Solnishko. That's why I thought it was him."

I started to tell him everything I had learned about my mother and her relationship with Alexei, and he listened carefully.

"You should have told me about this." Damiano said.

"I know, but you would have left me completely out of it -"

"Damn right I would have!" He interrupted me, making me let out a sigh of frustration.

"Let's be real for a second. You wouldn't have gotten that information if you went to talk to him about my mom. And to be honest, you would probably have tried to kill each other because he said Russians and Italians don't fuck with each other." I pointed out to him, and he knew I was right about that.

"Can't you hear how damn reckless you are? What if he killed you after you were done talking?" Damiano got up and paced the floor in anger.

"He had no intention of killing me." That was until I revealed my identity to him, but I wasn't going to tell him that part. Damiano would start a war if he knew I was held at gunpoint. "Besides, he set me up by sending me up to the room you were staying in. He wanted you to find me."

"You didn't know that after he let you go! You had no idea what you were getting yourself into. You do whatever the hell you want without thinking of the potential danger you could have been in. And don't get me started on that fucking gun. Are you asking to get killed?" He yelled. I stayed quiet, letting him get his anger and frustrations out.

He was right, and I had nothing to say to argue his point. I acted recklessly because I was desperate for answers, and no one was going to give them to me if I didn't seek them out myself.

"I know -"

"No, you don't! I'm trying to keep you safe, Althaia. I'm doing everything I can to protect you because..." Damiano's breathing was heavy as he looked at me with a pained expression. "I don't want to watch you die like I watched Sienna die."

Seventy-Nine
DAMIANO

Althaia raised her brows in surprise and recognition of the name, making me wonder just how much she actually knew about Sienna.

I took a seat in front of her, rubbing my jaw in frustration while my gaze fixated on the floor.

"Sienna was your fiancée..." She stated, almost carefully. I nodded, my gaze returning to her.

"Who told you about her?"

"Mr. Roberts' wife, Elena. She was taken aback when you showed up with a date. She mentioned you had come a few times with someone else, but she wasn't certain about the engagement until she saw the ring on Sienna's finger." Althaia explained, having me raise a brow.

"Why didn't you ask me about her?" My eyes narrowed slightly. Althaia was a curious woman, too curious for her own sake, and it surprised me she hadn't asked me about Sienna the minute she learned about her.

"I just figured you would tell me whenever you felt ready to talk about her." She shrugged her shoulders. "I mean, it's not like I'm itching to hear who you have been with."

The corner of my mouth twitched slightly upward as I observed her scowl, witnessing the unmistakable surge of jealousy in her eyes. I enjoyed it when she got jealous; it revealed a possessive side I found alluring, and I enjoyed teasing her with it.

"Now that I think of it, I don't believe you would have mentioned her even if I had asked. That day, when my mom returned early from her trip, she was talking about Sienna, wasn't she?"

"Yes." I kept my gaze on her, noting the way she looked down at her lap, biting down on her lip; a nervous habit of hers.

"Do you... still care about her?" Althaia asked. I understood the reason behind her question, considering my reaction that day.

"Not in the way you might be thinking." I observed her as her brows furrowed ever so slightly before she met my gaze.

"What does that mean?"

"Come here." I extended my hand, inviting her to take it. She rose from her seat, placing her hand in mine, and I grabbed her waist, pulling her down onto my lap.

For weeks, I have been feeling a void inside of me because she wasn't near, and it almost felt surreal that I could hold her now.

Her green eyes, the ones I cherished, gazed at me, patiently awaiting the words I needed to share. It was time to tell her about that part of my life. I had moved on, and there was no woman I desired more than her.

"I've been groomed to take over from my father, shadowing him as he taught me everything. At eighteen, I took on a partial leadership role, working tirelessly to boost profits, expand territories, and invest wisely. By the age of twenty, my father saw the results and reputation I had built. He stepped down, passing the family legacy to me." I looked at her, her eyes gleaming with curiosity, evoking a subtle smile from me.

Always so curious.

"I formed alliances with a family that would benefit us, and to strengthen those ties, my father suggested I marry their daughter. At twenty-three, I eventually agreed, and we got engaged. It wasn't out of love; it was arranged purely for business purposes because, at the time, that was all that mattered to me." I continued.

"You kind of sound like a dick." Althaia blurted.

"You think?" I raised a brow in amusement as she gave me a half-shrug, smiling.

"Just a little."

"I know, but it wasn't always like that. The more time I spent with her, the more I started to care for her, and at some point, I began to love her. I stopped postponing the wedding and made the decision to finally marry her. We were three years into our engagement when she died in my arms." Althaia took a sharp intake of breath, looking at me in shock.

"There was nothing I could do as I held her in my arms, witnessing her take her last breath before life left her. It... it fucked me up. So much so that I stopped caring and killed my way through the underworld until I found him." I said, staring off into the distance.

That day haunted me day and night. I could never forget the feeling of her blood splattering on my face when she was shot in the neck. Sienna, choking on her blood, as I desperately tried to stop the bleeding. Her fearful gaze lingered before her eyes turned blank and lifeless. I shouted for her to wake up, but she didn't, and I held her in my arms for hours before being pulled away.

I didn't sleep. I couldn't, haunted by the image of her face and the sound of her choking on her blood.

"But all of that is over now, and I've made peace with it. A part of me still cares about her, but not in the way you think, because I love you. I didn't love her the way I love you." I confessed softly. She had no idea that she was the one who made me whole.

Althaia suddenly wrapped her arms around my neck. She hugged me tightly, taking me by surprise as she pulled me out of my thoughts. I wrapped my arms around her too when I felt something wet soaking through my shirt.

"Are you crying?" I tried to get her to lean back to get a look at her, but she only tightened her hold on me and hid her face.

"No." Her voice cracked.

"You silly woman, why are you crying?" I couldn't help but chuckle at her reaction. Her heart never failed to impress me.

Her capacity for caring extended even to people she had never met. Her heart was so pure, brimming with compassion, and that was what made me fall in love with her. She became my light and my fire, gradually dissolving the icy remnants of a past I had sought to forget.

"I'm not silly." She sniffed.

"I beg to differ."

"Shut up." She murmured, leaning back and wiping away tears with a furrowed brow. "How can I not cry? It's just so… heartbreaking. It's cruel! Why would they do such a thing?"

I placed my hand on her cheek, understanding why she was reacting so strongly. She could relate.

It suddenly became clear to me that her longing to be alone was a way for her to find healing, rather than an attempt to distance herself from me permanently. I felt a pang of guilt for not realizing that sooner.

"They wanted to break me and force me to step down. They used her to get to me and made sure I wouldn't be able to have an heir soon. Now, they're doing it again… with you."

"Me?"

"Someone has been keeping an eye on you and found out you were pregnant. That night, when you fell ill, it wasn't because of food poisoning.

They intentionally poisoned you to induce a miscarriage." I held her tightly, anger rushing through me.

Althaia let out a gasp and looked at me with wide eyes, her hands going down to her stomach.

"Poisoned?" She whispered and swallowed hard at the information.

"With arsenic. It mimics the symptoms of food poisoning. It should have been detected in the blood test, but we believe it got swapped out." I explained.

"Oh..." She let out a shaky breath. I sighed and placed my hand over hers on her stomach. "Does that mean if..." She struggled to finish her sentence as she held onto my hand tightly.

"If not for that, there might have been a chance it wouldn't have happened." I said to her gently.

Even though she had started to recover, her entire body remained weakened, leaving her in a vulnerable state. When they were being chased, it pushed her body to the edge, and it shut down, unable to hold on to the pregnancy.

"So don't you ever dare blame yourself for what happened." I told her firmly. It pained me that she had carried the weight of self-blame for the miscarriage when it was entirely out of her control. That attack was aimed at me, and once again, the story was repeating itself.

Now with Althaia.

She looked down at her lap, a frown creasing her face, lost in her thoughts.

"Tell me, what's on your mind?"

"How I want them to suffer." She declared, lifting her head, her eyes ablaze with a fire I hadn't seen before. "I want them to suffer so badly for everything they've done to us, for making me lose so much." She said it without hesitation, her voice firm and clear as anger continued to burn within her.

I was witnessing a different side of Althaia. She usually had the eyes of innocence, a face of an angel, and a personality that shone brightly. But at this moment, it was as if the fire inside her had been unleashed and was ready to reduce everything to ashes. I recognized that look on her face.

She was thirsty.

Thirsty for revenge.

I positioned her to straddle me, locking eyes with her still fiery green gaze. My hand slid to the back of her neck as I drew her face closer to mine, looking deeply in her eyes.

"Ask me to destroy the entire world for you, and I will happily oblige. If you want me to put their heads on a fucking flagpole, or serve them to you on a gold platter, I will. Whatever your heart desires, consider it fulfilled." I promised her.

I drew her nearer, my other hand tracing a path up her thigh, our lips nearly brushing against each other. Her breath quickened, and her lips parted, a tempting sight that drew my gaze downward.

It took every ounce of self-control to resist the urge to claim her lips with my own. The mere thought of it accelerated my heartbeat, making every passing moment feel charged with an irresistible tension.

"You sound unhinged." Althaia said in that breathy voice that always makes me lose all control.

"You drove me to the brink of madness." I whispered back, my gaze locked on her green eyes.

"Don't blame me. You were a madman long before you met me." She countered.

"Maybe you've just refined my lunacy." I mused.

She smiled softly.

"I guess I love you, even in your certifiable derangement."

"I'll be whatever you want, piccola. You're mine, and no other man can ever have you." I declared quietly, completely mesmerized by her eyes.

Every fiber of my being ached to close the remaining distance and taste the sweetness of her lips. But I didn't. A hesitant force restrained me, a lingering doubt that wrestled with the pulsating desire within.

"And you belong to me. No woman can ever take you away from me." Althaia whispered as she leaned in, her own hesitation clear as she glanced at my lips.

"Damn fucking right I do." I reached for her face, gently cupping it with my hands, as I was unable to resist the pull any longer.

Her eyes locked on mine. Time seemed to slow and the world outside disappeared as our lips met. The feel of her lips was soft and warm; a sensation I had longed for and missed.

I swept my tongue across her lips, and her mouth parted for me to taste her tongue. I gripped the back of her neck, unwilling to let her slip away.

Althaia let out a small moan, stirring the beast within me. Her fingertips traced a tantalizing path down my chest. Each touch felt like a flame, igniting a fire that had been smoldering for far too long.

A low growl escaped my throat as the warmth of her touch left a trail of desire in its wake. Her fingers gripped the fabric of my dress shirt, and in one swift, almost primal motion, she tore it open, buttons scattering like sparks in the darkness.

The cool air caressed my exposed skin, contrasting with the heat of the moment. It was a declaration, a physical manifestation of the passion that had been building between us. Her touch spoke with a hunger that matched my own.

Althaia pulled slightly away, catching her breath while her hands remained exploring my chest.

"So beautiful." I said under my breath as my hands slipped down the straps of her dress, exposing her full breasts.

She took in a sharp breath when I pinched her already hard nipple, my other hand finding its way under her dress, pulling her thong to the side. I let out a grunt when I traced my finger along her slit, slowly pushing inside her wet pussy.

"Damiano..." Althaia moaned, resting her head against mine.

"Fuck, piccola. I've missed your voice." I whispered a groan as I circled her clit, loving the sounds she was making. My cock was begging to sink into her pussy, needing a release so fucking badly.

"Althaia, I need you." I searched her eyes, waiting for her to tell me we were okay.

"You have me. Always." She said with a subtle smile as she caressed my cheek.

I grabbed her ass and rose to my feet with her legs around me as I went to the bedroom. I lay her down on the bed, tearing the dress from her body. I had to take a moment to admire her beautiful naked body. Her chest was rising and falling fast in anticipation as I discarded my clothing, her eyes drinking me in as I freed my cock.

I leaned over her, savoring the taste of her lips as I kissed and nibbled on them. I wrapped her legs around me, the heat of our bodies melding together. Every second felt like an eternity, and I couldn't bear to wait any longer.

I glided my cock along her slit, coating myself in her arousal, causing a low, pleasurable sound to escape my lips. It drove me to madness, and I thrust myself into her in one go.

I halted when she winced and clenched her eyes closed.

"Shit. Am I hurting you?" I panted out.

"I'm fine. It's just been a while." She opened her eyes, giving me a reassuring smile. "Please, don't stop." She breathed out.

"I'll be gentle." I moved slowly, letting her adjust to me, and soon her body relaxed. I dove deeper, wanting my entire cock to be enveloped in her sweet pussy. Her nails scraped down my back, sending shivers through me at her touch.

"Keep going. Mark me, baby." I groaned, her nails digging deeper into my back, and I welcomed the pain. I quickened my pace and closed my eyes, savoring the feeling of her pussy clenching on my cock.

I massaged her clit with my thumb, watching her eyes close as her pretty mouth moaned for me.

"Damiano..." Althaia panted, making me grunt as I felt her tightening around me.

"Fuck, keep saying my name, baby."

I leaned back, firmly gripping her hips, slamming my cock inside of her as I watched her breasts bounce to the rhythm and listened to the melodic sound of her moaning my name over and over, inching me closer to my own release.

"Oh, fuck!" She cried out, arching her back, and her legs trembled as I felt her come undone around me.

"Fuck!" I grunted, pulling out and releasing on her stomach.

I dropped to my arms above her, catching my breath as I rested my head against hers.

"Don't leave me again." I whispered. Her eyes shimmered with unshed tears, one slipping down her cheek, and I gently kissed it away.

"Never."

EIGHTY

DAMIANO

"We isolated them and kept them awake. They will talk when exhaustion hits them." Antonio reported to me.

"Good." I replied over the phone.

I sat down on the living room couch to avoid disturbing Althaia, who was asleep. I flipped open the sketchbook she had on the coffee table, curious to see what her mind had created.

"You should get some sleep. You're a pain in the ass when you're sleep-deprived." Antonio commented. Before I could tell him off, I heard Raffaele in the background.

"Is that Damiano? Let me talk to him real quick." I heard some rustling before he got on the phone. "Damiano! Damiano, please, just please listen to me!"

"What do you want?"

"Please, get laid!" He cried out desperately. "You've got too much pent-up sexual frustration, and all kinds of frustrations that exist. So please, for the love of God, get laid! I'm tired! I am so tired! I haven't worked this much in my life, and you have been up everyone's ass, not giving us a break. I want a break! So, please, stay there for a week, have lots of sex and sleep, and come back happy. I'm begging you on behalf of everyone!"

"I'm fine." I chuckled at him for being dramatic.

"He's laughing! Guys, he's laughing! My man got laid!" He shouted in happiness, making me shake my head at him.

"Shut up. You can all take a break until I come back." I told him, and it sounded like he cried out in relief at my words as he continued to shout to the others in pure contentment.

"Tell Althaia I said thank you. She has some serious power over you, and I'm going to kiss her feet in gratitude."

"Fuck off." I hung up just in time for my phone to buzz with a message saying that Arianna would be here soon.

I stepped outside to see her arriving with two of my men. I had assigned security to everyone as an extra precaution.

"You could at least have put a shirt on." Arianna grimaced, but her expression shifted when she saw my face.

"You have some fucking nerve." I sneered at her. She crossed her arms in defense and frowned. "You had no business coming here and telling her to stay away." I gritted my teeth. I didn't want to raise my voice and wake up Althaia.

"I wasn't about to have you keep suffering. You were hurting too, and she left you alone!" My sister snapped back.

I stepped closer, looming over her.

"You don't know what the hell is going on. If you believe I was suffering, then imagine her pain. She physically suffered when it happened and now carries the burden of blaming herself for the loss of our baby, not to mention the loss of her mother. So, who gave you the right to stick your nose in our business?" I hissed.

Arianna looked away from me, keeping her arms crossed.

"Don't think I will turn a blind eye to this because you're my sister. Starting today, you will be trapping the streets." I ordered her. Her head snapped towards me, and her eyes widened in disbelief.

"You can't be serious?! Do you know how humiliating that is?"

"Good." I retorted and looked over at my men. "Make sure she does her job."

"Yes, Boss."

I turned around and went inside, not sparing my sister another look when she protested.

I tossed my phone on the couch, returning to the sketchbook, and flipped the pages to see what Althaia had created. I loved taking a sneak peek into her creative mind, and she never ceased to impress me.

I flipped through colorful sunsets and drawings of her kitten playing with toys until I stopped at a drawing of me. A warm feeling washed over me as I flipped through the pages, a smile tugging at the corners of my lips at the sight of countless drawings of me.

I came across a small drawing, running my thumb over it as I looked at it; a tiny baby curled up in its angel wings. The loss was still painful, and my chest always tightened whenever I thought about it. I couldn't imagine what it must have been for her. I should have reassured her from the beginning, making it clear that it was in no way her fault.

It could never have been.

I let out a sigh as I closed the sketchbook, thinking how it was possible to love something so fast, only to be gone in a blink of an eye.

"Damiano?" Althaia's panicked voice reached me, and I quickly rose to my feet.

"What's wrong, baby?" I took a quick scan around the room as I approached her.

"Oh, uh…" She suddenly looked embarrassed. "I thought I dreamt it and you weren't really here."

I smiled as I got in bed, pulling her close to me.

"I'm here." I placed a kiss on top of her head, feeling her relax in my arms. "I was on the phone with Antonio, and I didn't want to wake you. Go back to sleep."

"Later. I want to watch the sunrise." Althaia said as she rose from bed, calling after Kiara while getting dressed before heading out to the back porch.

The sun was slowly making its presence known on the horizon, and I found myself watching with amusement as Althaia briskly walked after her kitten on the beach. She was laughing as they played together, and then the roles reversed; the kitten darting as swiftly as its tiny paws could carry it, chasing after her. I laughed, well aware that Althaia would go to any length to avoid running.

My eyes lingered on her, a tender smile gracing my lips as I reveled in the sight of her carefree and blissful demeanor. In just one day, she had effortlessly swept away all the tension from my body.

Fucking hell, she has me whipped.

And I fucking loved it.

Althaia crouched down, showering Kiara with affectionate pets and scratches, who was purring in bliss. She rose when she saw me coming, gracing me with a loving smile as I wrapped my arms around her. The sun's rays hit her face, and her eyes sparkled with a vibrant green hue, making her look even more breathtaking.

"Having a pet made me realize just how out of shape I am." She said, a bit out of breath.

"You're in better shape than you think." I told her and she raised a brow.

"You think so?"

Softly cupping her chin, I leaned down to her with a sly smirk on my lips.

"The way you rode my dick proves it well."

Her face instantly flushed, and she looked at me with wide eyes, too stunned to speak. She lightly smacked my chest repeatedly as I laughed at her reaction.

"Why would you even say that?" She scowled at me, her expression cute as she tried to fight through the embarrassment my words had caused.

"My innocent Althaia, nothing to be embarrassed about. It's all true."

"Did you have to say it like *that*?"

"Say it like what? That you ride my dick well?" I winked, watching her gape at me as her face flushed even more.

"You are seriously too much!" She exclaimed and tried to get away from me. I held her in place, encircling her with my arms and promising to stop teasing her — for now, at least.

The sunrise painted the sky with bright colors, and the sound of waves filled the tranquil silence. I stole glances at her, seeing the soft expression on her face and the gentle smile that adorned it.

"You like it here." I said, and she faced me.

"I do. It's nice here."

"We can stay for a few days if you want." I offered.

"Really?" A radiant smile crossed her face.

"Yes. Besides, I was told to stay away for a few days."

"I'm guessing it was Raffaele." Althaia chuckled, and I nodded.

"Who else? He's the only one who loves to complain." I sighed. He was an annoying piece of shit, and even though he was my cousin, I had never wanted to shoot someone as much as I have with him. One day, it was going to happen if he kept annoying me.

She shook her head in amusement before letting out a blissful sigh.

"You know, I never thought I would like a beach house this much."

"Let's get one." I told her. She raised her brows in surprise. "For you and me." And when we were ready, for our children, too.

I wanted to see her and our children running around on the beach, laughing and being happy, like I had witnessed her doing with Kiara.

"I would love that." A smile spread across her face before she turned her gaze back to the water. "I have a question." Althaia broke the silence after a while.

"I'm listening."

"Sienna... you're not with me because I look like her or resemble her in any way?" She asked, a small frown etched on her face.

"No, you're nothing alike. Not in appearance or personality-wise." I said, and she seemed to relax at my words. "Sienna had short hair, brown eyes, and was the quiet type. She only ever spoke when spoken to and was very obedient. But you? You are one fucking chaotic woman. You never listen and love to drive me insane. So no, you're far from alike."

"That's such an exaggeration! I'm not chaotic, and I do listen!" Althaia looked at me with complete offense. I shot her a blank look. "Okay, I sometimes listen..." She trailed off.

"I don't recall any moment where you've followed my orders." My hands slid down to her ass and lifted her, making her wrap her legs around me.

"Well, I do the opposite when I get ordered around, so that's on you! Don't order me around, and I might just listen to you." She grinned, and I clicked my tongue at her as I walked toward the water.

"You have no idea how strong my urge gets to punish you for not listening." I told her in a low voice, taking her lip between my teeth, gently tugging before letting go.

"Punish me, how?" Althaia breathed out, and my cock got instantly hard at the lust swirling in her eyes.

"You will see." I gave her a playful grin as her smile dropped when she heard the splashing sounds of me walking into the cold water.

"What are you doing?" She eyed me suspiciously, tightening her hold on me. I continued walking deeper into the water until it reached my thighs.

"You don't want to go for a swim?" I asked.

"No! The water is ice cold!"

"Sounds like a problem. For you." I gave her a devilish smirk, then grabbed her waist and tossed her into the water. Althaia screamed before disappearing under the water.

I made my way out of the water, but turned around when I heard her resurface.

"I-I'm going to kill you!" She shouted at me, her teeth chattering, and her body shivering from the cold.

"I would like to see you try." I taunted. She was half my size, and the only real physical damage she could ever cause me was kicking me right in the balls.

"Get back here so I can drown you!"

I watched her as she tried to run out of the water, only to trip and fall face first, right back into the water.

I laughed out loud at the amusing sight, which only made her angrier with every step she took toward me. I didn't move, waiting for her to come closer. Once close, I grabbed her by the waist to carry her.

"No! You better not throw me in the water again!" She squirmed in my hold, attempting to break free, but I held her tightly against me.

"You did that perfectly on your own." I teased, earning me a glare from her. She shivered against my body as I walked back with her to the house, calling for Kiara to follow us.

"Why w-would you do th-that?" Althaia struggled to talk with her teeth chattering. I chuckled, and she gave me a sour look in return.

"Part of your punishment."

"What did I do to be punished?!"

"Fuck, piccola, where should I even begin? The list is long." Her eyes went wide, and I laughed before kissing her cold lips. "Now, let me get you warmed up and fuck you to sleep."

"Someone's looking quite relaxed." Raffaele snickered when I entered my office.

We had returned to the manor after a few days at the safe house. Althaia wanted to catch up with Cara, and I left to give them privacy.

"It's amazing what it does to you when you finally get to fuck." He continued with a smug grin. I shot him a blank look.

"Are you done?"

"Yeah, I'm saving some for Althaia later." He laughed and sprawled out on the couch. Antonio shook his head at Raffaele's comments.

"Did she tell you why she was at the LuxePalace?" Antonio asked once Lorenzo came into the office.

"She did. She went to talk to Alexei Vasiliev." I revealed. Raffaele sat up straight, letting out a whistle.

"Yo, she got some balls of steel!"

"For what reason?" Lorenzo's brows furrowed, his voice carrying a hint of suspicion.

"Turns out her mother had a romantic history with him." I said. I proceeded to share everything she told me about Jacinta and Alexei Vasiliev as they listened attentively.

"Could he be the one who was after her mother?" Raffaele wondered.

"It's a possibility, but I don't think it's him." I then explained my thoughts since I learned about their history. "I want whatever needs to be gathered to see if it's a match." I finished, receiving nods from them.

"We can do that at the wedding with no suspicion and get the results immediately." Antonio added.

"This situation is getting crazier." Raffaele commented, scratching his head. "Does she know?"

"No, and not a word about it to anyone. I want to be sure first." I ordered before dismissing them.

I walked to the balcony doors and watched Althaia strolling in the garden with Cara.

"Any new reports about her?" I asked Antonio, who remained behind.

"Some improvements, but it's a slow process." I nodded, and he joined me, both of us watching her. "If it turns out to be true—"

"I don't care." I interrupted him. "She belongs to me, and there's no way in hell I will ever let her go."

EIGHTY-ONE

ALTHAIA

"I'm sorry for leaving you like that. I know it was hard for you too, and I haven't been the most considerate person." I apologized to Cara as we strolled through the garden.

"Don't worry about it." She replied with a soft smile. "It wasn't much of a surprise. You've always been the type to isolate yourself when upset."

"I know, but it wasn't right of me to do that. I abandoned everyone, especially Damiano." I sighed.

"You were dealing with a lot, you still are. Trust me, I understand what that feels like. Besides, Lorenzo was a great support; he never left my side." Cara reassured me. Her words stung, and guilt consumed me for not being there for her.

"I'm sorry."

"If you apologize one more time, I will hit you." She threatened, glaring at me.

"Sorry—I didn't mean it! It just came out." I quickly added, covering my head as she was about to smack me.

"Well, it sounds like things are still going great with Lorenzo?" I asked as we watched Kiara explore the new territory. With so much space for her to run around, I had to keep a close eye on her to make sure she didn't suddenly disappear.

Cara's face lit up with a smile at the mention of Lorenzo.

"It is. He's genuinely the best man I've ever been with. A big softie, really." She chuckled, her entire demeanor brightening as she spoke about him.

I smiled as I witnessed the twinkle in her eyes.

"A softie? Tank Man can't be a softie." I remarked, struggling to imagine him in such a light. "Weren't you scared when you first saw him? All I could think about was how intimidating he looked."

"You still call him Tank Man?" Cara laughed.

"He's literally the size of a tank!" I exclaimed.

"Oh, he sure is." She gave me a cheeky smile and a wink, gaining a groan from me as I rolled my eyes.

"I don't need to know that."

"Don't pretend Damiano isn't a big softie when it comes to you. That man is head over heels for you. Like, you're the reason for his existence or something." Cara chuckled.

Her words made me go silent.

"I'm not sure I deserve him." I whispered after some time. "He's done so much for me, and I've given him nothing." I confessed, feeling tears welling in my eyes.

"Oh, babes, don't ever think you don't deserve him. You've given him so much, and you don't even realize it." She reassured me.

"I'm not sure." I sighed.

"He's a different man because of you. That man was the uptightest dick I had ever met in my life. Then you came, and he's been on cloud nine ever since. So, yes, you've given him so much that he can actually enjoy life for once."

I kicked my head back in laughter at Cara's passionate rant.

"I've missed you so much!" I wrapped my arms around her in a tight hug.

"But to answer your question, I suppose I was scared when I first saw *Tank Man*." She gave me an amusing look before continuing.

"I saw him first from a distance, and all I could think was, 'If that man hits me, one blow and I'm as good as gone'. Then I got to see him up close, and it hit me just how enormous he was. That's when I started thinking about how I wanted to climb him." She bit her lip, wiggling her brows at me.

"Only you, Cara." I said with a laugh as she chuckled. "I'm happy for you, and soon you'll be Mrs. 'Tank Man' Bellavia."

"I can't wait for that. To get a new name, a fresh start, and just leave that crappy name behind for good. No offense."

"None taken." I gave her a dismissive wave. I would have felt the same if my father had abused me.

"It wasn't always like that, you know. I gave Lorenzo a lot of hell in the beginning. I didn't want this engagement and tried to get out of it by being a psycho-bitch to him. But I guess along the way, I just fell for him." Cara chuckled to herself, and it had me smiling.

"You being a psycho to Lorenzo? I would pay to see that!"

"Yeah, you should have seen when I set fire to his car." A mischievous look was on her face.

"You set his car on fire?!" My eyes almost bulged out of their sockets.

"Sure did. Yet, he still asked me to marry him."

"Holy shit." I said, processing the things she had just said. "You know, when Damiano visited me back home, he asked me to marry him." I revealed.

"He what?" Cara gaped at me with her eyes wide in shock. "And you said no?" She asked, barely believing her own two ears.

"I didn't say no. I just suggested waiting because I had barely wrapped my head around the fact that I was, well... pregnant." I kept my gaze down, taking a deep breath, as talking about it was still painful.

Cara wrapped her arm around my shoulders to offer comfort, and I responded with a small smile to assure her that I was okay.

"I was overwhelmed and felt like everything was moving too fast. I wanted us to take one thing at a time, take it slow, because why should we rush?" I continued.

"But?"

"With everything that has happened, it made me realize more than ever that there is no one else I would rather be with than him, so why wait? Everything can be gone in the blink of an eye."

"Sounds like it will be a yes next time." She said with a smile, and I couldn't help but smile at the thought.

My eyes went to the manor when I felt someone watching me. I found him immediately standing on the balcony. My entire body fluttered at the sight of him, and my heart beat just a little faster, too. I gave a small wave, and he returned it, a smile playing on his lips.

"Definitely."

I walked back inside the manor, now in search of Luca. I felt like I owed everyone an apology, given the tension that lingered between us. He was upset with me for leaving and furious about the incident with his girlfriend.

I knew that wasn't going to help my case, but I hoped he would eventually soften up. Luca was like a brother to me, supporting me when I confided in him about my pregnancy. Despite my initial freak-out, he remained excited and tried to calm me down.

I made my way to the kitchen, following the sound of voices, only to find Ava and Raffaele, who was busy flirting with her.

"I know you like it wild, baby. I can rock your world." Raffaele was standing close to Ava, who leaned against the counter with a raised brow, clearly amused.

They hadn't noticed my presence, and I had to put a hand over my mouth to stifle a laugh at Raffaele's attempt at a seductive voice.

Part of me considered leaving them alone, but for the sake of amusement, I decided to stay and witness how he played his game.

"I don't do small dicks." Ava teased with a playful smile.

"Nothing small about me, and you know that. You can even check for yourself now if you want." Raffaele caged her in between his arms with a smirk.

"I will." Ava's hands went down his waistband, pulling it towards her as she took a look down. "Impressive." She commented, and Raffaele's smirk widened at her words.

"I know, and your mouth will look so good wrapped around my cock -"

"Uh, this is a common area." I said, making them snap their heads toward me. They seemed unfazed that I had caught them, but my cheeks were starting to flush at how straightforward he was.

"Althaia!" Raffaele groaned at me when Ava stepped aside with a chuckle. "You cock-blocked me!"

"How did I cock-block you? Were you seriously about to do it in the kitchen with so many people in the house?" I asked him, my face scrunched in disgust.

"You think I care? I was about to dip it!" He said, almost childishly. I half-expected him to stomp his foot too.

"Now you're definitely not going to *dip it*." Ava rolled her eyes, and he let out another groan. He wore an annoyed expression as he looked at me.

"What did I ever do to you to deserve this? I've never cock-blocked you. In fact, I made sure no one would disturb you at the safe house so you and Damiano could fuck."

"Excuse me?" I gaped at him, feeling my face getting warmer by the second.

"You are excused. Now, go so I can get back to business." Raffaele looked back at Ava; his flirty expression returned, but she just opened a bag of chips and started to munch on them, not looking impressed with him at the moment.

"Sorry, you've missed your chance." She said with a smirk and made her way out of the kitchen.

"Playing hard to get? Okay, I see you, no worries! I can work hard."

"I'm really not, but better luck next time." Ava sang and disappeared from our view.

"Wait! So, I do have a chance?" He shouted after her but received no response.

"Wow, Raffaele, could you sound any more desperate?" I shook my head at him, and he shot me an annoyed glare.

"I am desperate! You have no idea what kind of torture Damiano has put me through, keeping me busy all the time, never giving me a break, and not once letting me bust a nut."

"I really don't need to hear about all that..." I trailed off, but he ignored me as he continued.

"Do you know how painful it is for a man to have blue balls and not be able to get a release? It's fucking painful, and you ruined it for me." He huffed out as I awkwardly stood and listened to him.

"My goodness, just use your hand if you're in that much need!" I turned around and walked out of the kitchen, eager to escape the conversation.

"It's not the same!" He yelled out as he followed me. "You should at least offer me something."

I stopped in my tracks, turning around to face him, and saw him grinning at me.

"Have you lost your mind?"

"Just a little. So, what kind of service would you like to offer me? Your mouth, your hand, or even spread your legs for me - wait, why are you smiling like that?" Raffaele was confused as my smile got bigger with every proposition.

I didn't say anything as I continued to smile sweetly at him, and his smile immediately dropped when it hit him.

"Fuck, Damiano is behind me, isn't he?"

"Yup." I grinned, and he let out a sigh, mentally preparing for whatever was going to happen.

"Damiano." Raffaele let out a nervous laugh and slowly turned around to face him. Damiano was looking at him with deadly eyes, and I couldn't help but feel sorry for Raffaele this time.

"What happened was -" Raffaele quickly made a run for it, sprinting out of our view while shouting for mercy.

"Are you going to run after him?" I chuckled as Damiano continued to glare in Raffaele's direction.

"No, I'll get him when he least expects it." Damiano grabbed my waist, pulling me in for a kiss. "I have to go take care of something. Don't wait up."

"Where are you going?"

"I'm going to have a chat with some people." He replied, and that was when I noticed the change in his outfit, figuring out what kind of 'chatting' it was going to be.

"Well, do you know where Luca is? I need to talk to him, Gio, too."

"They're right behind you."

I approached them, feeling nervous that they wouldn't accept my apology. Coming to a stop in front of them, they both wore blank expressions, making me even more nervous.

"I just want to say I'm sorry. For everything." I said. I chewed on my lip when neither of them said anything, and I was ready to accept that they were still mad at me and be on my way.

Then Luca let out a sigh.

"Come here." He said and embraced me, bringing a smile to my face as I returned his hug. "As long as you're okay."

"I will be." I assured him. Luca gave me a soft smile as he let go of me. I turned to look at Giovanni, who now had his arms crossed as he stared at me.

"You owe me an apology."

"I just said I was sorry." I replied in confusion, but he shook his head.

"You walked into me at the LuxePalace, and you didn't say sorry. So, where's my apology?" Giovanni practically demanded, and I dropped my jaw.

"I did!" I exclaimed, frowning at him.

"I didn't hear you."

"That's not my problem! I said sorry, and you were just straight-up rude. Who says to a stranger, 'Watch where you're going'?" I said, trying to imitate his voice, and he frowned at me.

"I'm a whole foot taller than you. How the fuck did you miss me?"

"I was distracted! Why do you always have to be so grumpy?" I scowled at him.

"Maybe if you had the courtesy to look where you're going, I wouldn't have to channel my inner grumpiness. Manners, ever heard of them? They're not just for show, you know."

I gasped.

"Oh, hell no!"

"Here we go again." Luca sighed and shook his head as he watched us continue to bicker back and forth like we used to.

EIGHTY-TWO

DAMIANO

"If it turns out to be true, then we can go ahead with our plan as we wanted to from the beginning. We know Gaetano wants access to the weaponry, like that wasn't fucking obvious." Raffaele rolled his eyes. "We now know his associates and how he works. I say let us just go ahead and kill him like we always wanted and take over his territories. He's a bastard, but damn, he knows how to make money and make an even bigger demand for the products."

"It's not that simple anymore." I told him. Leaning back in my seat, I closed my eyes as we headed to the storage facility, accompanied by Luca and Giovanni.

"Oh, right, Althaia. Maybe she doesn't care?" He wondered.

"Are you that dense?" Giovanni shot him a look to see if he was serious.

"We know Cara won't care." Raffaele replied, thinking he made a valid point.

"Cara was abused, almost beaten to death. Althaia wasn't." I reminded him.

Gaetano was only using Cara to gain access to my weaponry, and I was taking advantage of it as well, making him believe he could.

The plan was to understand the infrastructure of his organization and dismantle it entirely. He was steadily recruiting more men and expanding his influence. I couldn't allow that to happen. I had to get rid of him before he could pose a serious threat to my organization.

It was a game I enjoyed; to kill them and seize control of what they had spent their lives building.

Cara had the freedom to go wherever she pleased when it was over. As it turned out, she and Lorenzo developed a relationship. It wasn't an issue; it meant she was fully under our protection as we executed our plan.

Then I fell for Althaia and had to put the plan on hold

"Even if it is true, he's still the only father figure she has known her whole life. I already have enough reasons for her to hate me. I will not give her another reason by killing him like that." I stated.

"Maybe that's why her mother left?" Luca suggested, trying to find a clue.

"It's a possibility." I replied. Until I had the results, anything was possible at the moment.

Althaia might not even be the daughter of either of them. There was still a chance of a third person being involved in this mess. Perhaps that was why Jacinta decided to disappear; to ensure Alexei Vasiliev wouldn't find out about it, given they might have had something going on.

"Whatever it is, I hope we figure it out soon. I feel like I've aged ten years already." Raffaele groaned, slumping forward and resting his head on the driver's seat.

Then he suddenly straightened up and looked at me with a mischievous grin.

"By the way, does Althaia know you hid cameras in her hotel room?"

"No." I glared at him as his grin widened.

"I bet she was naked a lot. Did you jack off to the footage?"

"I will beat the shit out of you again if you don't shut the fuck up."

"About that, why did you go for the face? My face hurts, and I can't have it bruised. I need to stay pretty." He rubbed his jaw where I had punched him.

"I will kill you if I hear you talk like that to her again." I warned him.

"I just need to get laid." He sighed and leaned back in his seat.

"I gave you time off. You have enough money to pay for someone." I raised a brow while he gave me a sour look.

"No, I can't do that. I'm trying to get Ava. Have you seen her? She's so damn beautiful and wild in every way. I want her."

Everyone turned to look at Raffaele.

"What?" Raffaele asked, confused that the attention was on him. I shared a look with the others before shaking my head and getting out of the car.

"You're crushing hard on her." Luca grinned, voicing what we were all thinking. He only ever called women hot or sexy when he wanted to get them into bed.

Raffaele had no problem finding a woman to satisfy his needs, and he has been trying to shoot his shot at Ava ever since she returned from the safe house.

Ava, a close friend of Cecilia, found herself in trouble, and I helped her get out of it. Since then, she has been loyal to the family. She returned the favor by keeping an eye on Althaia, as I needed people she wouldn't recognize.

Though I kept underestimating Althaia, as it turned out she was onto them from day one.

"I mean, she's fun and doesn't shy away." Raffaele shrugged, attempting to cover up his actual feelings for her.

"You're not fooling anyone. We know you like her. You haven't fucked anyone since she showed up." I said as we made our way down to the underground passage.

"Shit, that explains why I'm in so much pain…" He muttered. "I will wait because I know she will be worth it. I just hope it's soon."

I glanced at him, clearly seeing that he wanted her for more than just one night. It will do him good to settle down and not cause me any more headaches.

I opened the door to The Chamber of Torture, revealing the two bastards tied up in chairs, beaten and groaning as Antonio threw water at them to keep them awake.

"Still not willing to talk?" I tilted my head. One of them began speaking in Korean and shook his head vigorously.

"They barely know any English words. He tried to say something earlier, but nothing made sense. We need someone to translate." Antonio informed.

"We need to find someone reliable right now." Raffaele went into thinking mode. I turned around when Luca cleared his throat.

"We already have someone who can speak Korean. Althaia." He suggested, and I glared at him, knowing damn well I didn't want to involve her.

"I agree." Antonio said, approving of the idea. "Think about it. We can get her here to translate and be out again in five minutes."

I remained silent, staring at the scumbags, rubbing my jaw as I pondered the situation. It was the safest and fastest solution, and I needed to know who was behind this. I just hated the idea of her being here, fearing it would scare her.

"Fine." I decided and headed back to the manor.

It was late, and she should be asleep by now. I carefully opened the door, trying to minimize any noise, but to my surprise, the room was dimly lit. My eyes were immediately drawn to a pair of green eyes as I spotted her sitting on the bed with her sketchbook.

"That didn't take long." She smiled.

"I told you not to wait up. It's late." I said as I took a seat next to her.

"I wanted to wait for you. I sleep better when you're here, anyway." She gave me a half-shrug. I couldn't help but smile as I admired just how stunning she looked with her long hair cascading around her in waves.

"You look beautiful."

"Thank you." She said shyly and wrapped her arms around my neck before pressing her lips to mine.

Fuck. There was no way I wanted her to do this, but she was our only choice now.

"Are you okay?" Althaia looked around my face, her brows slightly furrowing when I let out a sigh.

"I am. I need your help." I said. She looked at me in surprise, which only lasted a second before panic showed in her eyes and her hands felt around my body.

"Are you hurt somewhere?" Her voice was laced with worry. I chuckled and stopped her from trying to pull my shirt off to see.

"I'm not hurt." I reassured, and she relaxed again.

"What can I possibly help you with?" Her curiosity was back on, and I just hoped this wouldn't fuck her up.

"You know Korean, right?"

"Yes...?"

"The ones we caught only speak Korean, and we need a translator."

"Me?" Althaia pointed to herself, and I nodded.

"You don't have to if you don't want to." I stated firmly.

"Wait, wait. You are asking me for help?" She pointed at me before pointing at herself again.

"Yes." I raised a brow when she suddenly looked excited.

"Well, what are we waiting for? Let's go!" Althaia rolled out of bed in a hurry and almost ran to the door.

"My love." I called after her, making her stop to turn around and face me. "Change first." She looked down, realizing she was only in her nightgown.

"Oh, right. I'll be ready in a minute!" She ran to the closet, and I chuckled at her enthusiasm.

I held her hand as she looked around in the underground passage. We came to a stop in front of the door, and I turned her to face me.

"Are you sure you want to do this? I can still find someone else." I asked her one last time to make sure she was truly fine with it.

"I want to." Althaia said, looking determined to help.

"This is not a normal room. We call it 'The Chamber of Torture', and you will see many weapons and tools present." I observed her facial expression, but she gave a small nod, not showing any sign of discomfort.

"Okay."

"Althaia, if you get the slightest bit uncomfortable, you'll tell me right away." I told her firmly.

"Don't worry, I will." She gave me a reassuring smile. I let out a sigh before kissing the top of her head.

I opened the door, making sure I held her close to me to give her a sense of comfort. My men gave her a nod in greeting, and she glanced around before her gaze landed on the two tied up in the chair.

Althaia looked at me, and I gave her a nod. I had already explained to her on the way what I wanted to get out of them.

She started talking to them, and they eyed her as she spoke in their language. One even let out a grin and said something back to her. I watched her facial expression closely, noticing a slight frown as she reacted to what he said.

"What did he say?" I asked her when she rolled her eyes at him.

"… He called me a bitch."

"That piece of shit." I nodded to Giovanni, who held the aluminum bat. I wanted to keep it minimal with her present. "Althaia, don't look."

"No, I want to watch." She insisted.

Giovanni's powerful swing of the bat struck the bastard's kneecap with full force. The room filled with his cries of pain, and he jerked around in the chair in agony. I glanced at her and caught a glimpse of a subtle smile forming at the corner of her mouth. I couldn't help but smirk at her reaction, noticing the twinkle in her eyes that mirrored my own delight.

Althaia started questioning the other one.

"He says they know what their fate is going to be in the end, whether or not they talk. I tossed him the choice between a quick, painless way and a drawn-out torture session."

I slightly raised a brow that she was taking control and negotiating with them. I glanced back at the scumbag, and he looked to be in thought. I let her do what she wanted as she talked to them again.

"He's saying they have nothing to lose."

"Nothing, you say?" A malicious smile crept onto my lips as I looked at them. "We'll see." I nodded to Luca and turned Althaia away from them, covering her ears.

Luca pulled the head of their spokesperson from the bag and displayed it to them. Their voices filled the room with horror, shouting as they stared at the severed head.

Althaia was startled by their reaction. She held onto my wrists with her eyes narrowing in confusion. I kept her in place, her ears covered, until Luca concealed the head again.

I spun her back around as Antonio rolled a video of their families; the ones they thought they hid so damn well from me. In this Devil's realm, there was no secret dark enough to elude my grasp.

"What is it?" Althaia asked me quietly.

"A video of their families." I said, watching the color draining from their faces. "Tell them they will taste the same fate."

Althaia translated with her head held high and a demeanor that left no room for doubt about her resolve, and pride surged through me as I observed her.

"They don't know who ordered the kill, but it's someone who has a lot of power. All communication happened through untraceable calls. They were provided with a phone and were instructed how to use it to orchestrate the setup..." He spoke rapidly, and the more Althaia listened, the tighter her hands clenched into fists.

It all made sense now with the phone call Jacinta received. Although she never answered, the brief five-second ring was sufficient for Raffaele to pinpoint their location. They were aware we were keeping an eye on her, and they exploited it to divert us, ensuring we couldn't reach them in time.

Althaia swallowed hard before talking.

"They were instructed to specifically target my mom, with the freedom to do as they pleased with me... on the condition that my pregnancy be terminated."

"That son of a bitch!" Giovanni was about to swing the bat again, but Althaia stopped him.

She moved in closer, leaning slightly down, and spoke to them in a hushed tone. A smile crossed her face, and whatever she had said made one of them lunge forward in response.

I yanked her back and delivered a powerful kick to his face, sending him sprawling to the ground.

"Make sure they suffer. They deserve it." Althaia walked out of the door. I exchanged a surprised glance with the others before letting out a wicked smile.

"You heard her." I left the room to follow her. I immediately pulled her into me, holding her tightly. "Are you okay?" I placed my hands on her cheeks to make her look at me.

"I am." She gave me a small smile. I looked around her face to see if she was lying, but she was fine.

"What did you say to them?"

"I warned them that time was running out and their loved ones' lives hinged on their cooperation. I may have hinted they could say their goodbyes by providing valuable information. Once they confessed everything, I promised they would suffer for killing my mom and our baby." Her eyes glowed with satisfaction.

I couldn't be prouder.

I gently tilted her chin and kissed her.

"Good girl." I whispered against her lips, watching her blush at my words. "My innocent Althaia, welcome to the Darkside."

Eighty-Three

ALTHAIA

I didn't feel remorse. In fact, I felt a sense of satisfaction. I hoped the consequences they faced would truly make them suffer for their actions, not just against me, but against us.

They had ruthlessly snatched my mother from me and poisoned me, causing me to lose our baby. I was enraged by their success in taking away the life we had created and the one person who had been by my side my entire life.

Their blood deserved to be spilled, and I wished for them to rot in hell.

"Althaia." Damiano pulled me out of my thoughts, realizing we had made it out of the underground passage. He looked at me with concern, taking my hand in his as I had unconsciously clutched my stomach.

"I'm okay." I reassured him, giving his hand a small squeeze and taking a deep breath of the fresh night breeze.

"Talk to me. What's on your mind?"

"It's just that... now that they've confirmed they wanted to make me lose..." I couldn't even finish the sentence, clenching my jaw as anger fumed inside of me and pain pierced my heart.

"I know, baby, I know. I promise you, we will get them all and make them pay for it. Whatever you want, I will do it. You call the shots." He spoke softly, yet his expression was deadly serious.

"Does that make me your boss now?" I joked, and he cracked a smile. Damiano pulled me into him, and I rested my hands on his chest as I looked at him with a teasing smile.

"If only you knew just how much power you hold over me." He gave me one of his beautiful smiles as he lightly caressed my cheek.

"Oh, is it a good idea to actually tell me that?" I grinned.

"Are you planning my downfall?" He asked quietly, leaning closer to me, our faces only inches apart. My body tingled at how close he was.

"Hmm, then who will be pissed at me for doing something reckless and stupid if I do?" I said, pretending to think about it.

"You mean to punish you?" Damiano's voice dropped to an alluring depth.

He flashed that devilish smirk, transforming him into the sexiest Devil alive. My body immediately responded to his words, a wave of excitement surging to the pit of my stomach.

"Perhaps... I happen to enjoy it when you tie me up." I slid my hands slowly down from his chest, tracing the contours of his rock-hard body until my hand rested on his crotch.

I smirked when I felt his excitement growing from my touch. Licking my lower lip, I pulled it between my teeth, and he exhaled a small grunt as I teasingly palmed him outside of his pants.

"You are quite the intoxicating trouble." He grabbed the back of my neck before forcefully capturing my lips in a heated kiss. Forgetting everything else, I responded eagerly. My hands explored his body as he emitted a soft groan at my touch.

His kiss was intense and unrestrained, making me clench my hands on his shirt, wanting to tear it off. I craved the feel of all of him; his warm skin, his muscular shoulders, the rhythm of his movements within me. The heat intensified, becoming almost unbearable, and he was wearing far too many clothes.

He bit down on my lip, and a moan escaped me as my hands ventured under his shirt, tracing the ripples of his abs.

"This just proves my point that psychos attract psychos. They got all horny after sentencing those dickheads to death." I heard Raffaele say. I pulled away, facing him with a glare as he showed up with Antonio and Luca.

"Now, who's being the cock-blocker?" I scowled, annoyed that they had disturbed us. If they hadn't, I might have just dragged Damiano to the car to have my way with him.

"Payback is a bitch, isn't it?" He said with a smug grin.

"Not really. I'm still going to get some either way. So, tell me again, when was the last time you got to 'bust a nut'?" I crossed my arms, wearing a playful smirk. His smug grin faded and was replaced with a glare.

"That is such a low blow, Althaia. Making fun of a man's suffering." Raffaele shook his head.

"I'm not making fun, just stating facts. Here's a piece of advice: maybe don't say, 'Your mouth will look good wrapped around my cock,' and you might get some."

"Dude." Luca looked at Raffaele in disbelief, and Antonio shook his head in pure disappointment at him.

"I really don't like you right now." Raffaele huffed out, and I chuckled.

"I'm just saying it wouldn't kill you to try and be a little romantic. Women like that. If you don't know how to be romantic, ask around! You're surrounded by people who are in a relationship." I gestured to Antonio and Luca.

Raffaele looked like he was thinking about it before he glanced at Damiano.

"I want to know what Damiano said to you, because I still have a hard time believing he can be romantic."

I blinked a few times, feeling my face growing hot before facing Damiano. He looked to be amused and tilted his head, waiting to hear what I had to say.

"That's private." I crossed my arms, facing away from them as I tried to hide my flushed cheeks.

"Oh, don't tell me you fucked the second you laid eyes on each other?" He threw his head back in a laugh.

"No!" I scowled, feeling my face getting warmer by the second.

"That came out a bit too fast, didn't it?" Antonio commented and the others agreed.

"You know what? It's none of your business." I turned around to face Damiano, who seemed to enjoy the conversation and had no intention of rescuing me from it.

"What did I say to you?" He raised his brow with a teasing smile on his lips.

"They don't need to know." I hissed out slowly to him, trying to signal that he damn well knew why.

"Hmm, If I remember it correctly..." He softly cupped my chin, leaning closer to my face. "I told you to spread your legs, and you complied like a good girl."

I wanted to fucking scream.

Damiano chuckled as he stepped away. Laughter erupted from the others as I helplessly blushed. I stared at him in shock, my jaw dropping without words.

"I don't blame you, Althaia." Raffaele wrapped his arm around my shoulders. "Damiano is one hell of a sexy man. I would immediately spread my legs for him, too." He wiggled his brows at me.

I pushed his arm away from me, cleared my throat, and looked at Damiano.

"If that's how you want to play with me, then fine! Just know I definitely *won't* be spreading my legs for you, and you can join Raffaele in having blue balls." I huffed out. Damiano frowned, clicking his tongue at me.

"Pussy power for the win!" Raffaele shouted.

"Raffaele, if you don't shut up, I will cut your dick off and shove it down your throat." I glared at him and made my way to the car.

"She's low-key scary." Raffaele mumbled as they followed me to the car.

"That's my girl." Damiano said with pride, and a small smile appeared on my lips.

I looked over my shoulder, seeing his gaze was already on me, and he winked. I rolled my eyes before facing straight ahead again to hide the fact that his wink had me blushing. It even sent a wave of butterflies to my stomach.

"Damiano." Arianna called after him when we arrived at the manor.

"Go to bed. I will be up soon." He kissed my head before I made my way inside, completely ignoring Arianna when she came up to talk to him.

I was still hurt by her words, and I had no intention of talking to her. It was not like she was attempting to talk to me, either.

"Did we just forget Giovanni?" I asked Antonio, only now realizing he was missing.

"No, he kicked us out. He wanted to have them for himself."

"Why?"

Antonio gave me a small smile.

"Believe it or not, but he lost it when he came back and found out what happened to you. He wouldn't leave the hospital and stayed close to you to make sure you would be okay."

I was shocked, too stunned to say anything.

The grumpy Giovanni, who had more than once threatened to throw me out of the car if I didn't stop singing? The one who saw me as a pain in the ass and scowled for being my assigned babysitter?

That Giovanni?

"Are we talking about the same person?" I asked.

"Trust me, we were all surprised."

"Aw, he cares about me! I am so going to tease him with that." I grinned as I rubbed my hands together, already planning on how to annoy the hell out of him with the new information I have.

"Of course, you are. I wouldn't have expected anything else." Antonio shook his head at me with a smile. It dawned on me just how well they all knew me, and I was forever grateful to have them all in my life.

"Reminds me, I don't think I ever got to congratulate you on becoming a father soon." I muttered, embarrassed that I had known for a while and hadn't even congratulated him.

"Don't worry about it. You had other things on your mind." Antonio gave my head a light pat.

"Do you know if it's a boy or a girl?"

"It's a girl." His blue eyes twinkled in happiness at the mention of their baby girl, and my heart warmed in pure joy for him and his wife.

"That's amazing! I'm so happy for you!" I beamed and surprised him with a sudden hug. "You're going to be a great father."

"You think so?" Antonio chuckled and embraced me back.

"I know you will." I smiled at him.

"Thank you, Althaia. Well, I better get going before Damiano rips my arms off for hugging you."

I stepped away, only to see Damiano's disapproving face as he walked up to us. I rolled my eyes and exchanged a look with Antonio before he bid us goodnight, dismissing Damiano's glare.

"Didn't I tell you not to let other men touch you?" Damiano scowled.

"They work for you. They also happen to be your friends, and, well, they are friends of mine now." I crossed my arms, trying not to smile, as I wanted to have a little fun with this.

"I don't like it."

"And what are you going to do about it? Punish me?" I retorted, tilting my head to the side. His eyes darkened as he stepped closer to me, and my heart accelerated just a little at the way he was looking at me.

"If it wasn't because you're tired, I would have fucked you so thoroughly that your voice would go hoarse, and you wouldn't be able to walk straight."

I drew in a sharp breath, squeezing my thighs together.

"I don't feel tired anymore." My voice was a mere whisper, almost out of breath.

A subtle, almost sinful, smirk played on his lips, showcasing a mastery over the art of seduction. His gaze was an alluring blend of danger and desire, sparking a thrilling sense of excitement.

"Let me take you to bed, then." Damiano had that devilish smirk on his lips. In one swift motion, he hoisted me over his shoulder, effortlessly carrying me inside.

"Damiano!" I gasped.

"Atta girl. Keep saying my name." He teased and delivered a sharp slap to my ass, leaving me completely mortified that his men were watching.

Eighty-Four

ALTHAIA

I rested my head on Damiano's chest, feeling his fingers play with my hair as I traced his tattoos with my own.

"Damiano?"

"Yes, piccola?"

"Their families… what are you going to do to them?" I looked up at him, finding his eyes closed before he opened them to meet mine.

"Nothing. I don't hurt innocent people. I only use them as bait."

"Okay." I said with relief in my voice.

"I shouldn't have let you go there." He sighed.

"I didn't do a good job?" I propped myself up on my elbow.

"You did well." Damiano caressed my cheek with a smile. "I'm worried I'm fucking you up with all of this."

I moved to straddle him, a teasing smile on my lips.

"You are." I whispered, looking at him playfully as my hand traveled down his body. "With this." I gave a sly grin when I wrapped my hand around his cock.

"As long as it's the only way." Damiano winked as he slapped my ass. I bit down on my lips as his hands explored every curve of my body, sending shivers down my spine as I felt his cock getting hard.

"Let me take care of you…" I moved down, but he stopped me.

"No, it's okay."

"Why not?"

"I don't want you to do that." Damiano shook his head.

"I don't mind, you know." I said. It was not like I hadn't noticed that he wouldn't let me go down on him before. Every time I wanted to ask, he would distract me with something else, and I would forget about it.

"I don't… care for it." He replied.

"Huh?" I looked at him in surprise. "I don't think I've ever heard of a man not liking it."

"I have my reasons." Damiano tried to dismiss me and get me to lie on top of him again, but I stopped him and squinted my eyes at him.

"And what are those reasons?"

"Piccola, I'm not going to tell you with your jealous ass and with my dick in your hand. I'm afraid you might just bite my dick off if I do."

A wave of amusement washed over me, making it hard to hold back a laugh. "You had a bad blow-job experience?"

"Big time." He scowled, slightly shuddering as he remembered it.

"That bad?" I chuckled.

"You have no fucking idea. I tried it once, and I got traumatized for life."

"I want to know."

"You really want to know?" He raised a brow in question, and when I nodded, he shook his head. "You are quite an unusual woman. Fine, but first."

I laughed when he removed my hand from his length.

"I was fifteen, and I hooked up with some girl. She wanted to go down on me, and since I was horny as fuck, I let her. I wish I hadn't." Damiano had a traumatized look on his face, and it took everything in me not to laugh.

"She went down on me, and I had no idea what the fuck she was doing. She was pulling on my dick so fucking hard and used her teeth. I'm surprised she didn't leave a bite mark. I was in pain. It felt like I was about to get castrated. I was so desperate to get away from her that I faked a phone call and ran away. That was my first and last time. I wasn't horny for weeks after that."

Damiano wore a grim expression, and although I should have felt sorry for him, I couldn't hold back my laughter.

"I'm glad I can humor you with my suffering." He scoffed, but still smiled.

"I'm sorry, it's just not what I expected to hear. You're telling me that something that happened around fifteen years ago made you never want to do it again?"

"Yes, I didn't give it much thought after that. I get by without it just fine." He said, shooting me a wink, which made me roll my eyes at him.

"What if I can change your mind?" I suggested, leaning down so that I was close to his lips. "I happen to be very skilled with my tongue." I added, slowly running my tongue across his lip.

He looked skeptical.

"Just relax." I whispered, placing a soft kiss on his lips before making my way down. I took my time, kissing his chest, the ripples of his abs, in case he changed his mind. He didn't, so I continued.

I wrapped my hand around his cock again, adding a bit of my saliva, and moved up and down in slow strokes. Damiano let out a soft sound and relaxed completely. I leaned forward and slowly trailed the tip of my tongue along the underside of his cock, watching it twitch in my hand.

He groaned as I teased him, and I looked at him, seeing his eyes were closed. I ran my tongue across the tip, tasting his pre-cum, before wrapping my mouth around his cock. He was so long, I had to use my hand for the rest of his shaft.

I moved my head up and down, creating suction by tightening my cheeks to give him the best experience. I quickly found out what gave him the most pleasure and focused on those sensations, my tongue exploring every inch of him.

"Fuck, that's good." Damiano groaned out. His hands fisted in my hair as he thrust into my mouth and kicked his head back. "Yes, baby. Keep taking my cock with that pretty mouth of yours."

I let out a soft moan as I continued to swirl my tongue around, keeping a steady rhythm and adjusting the pressure in my hand.

"I'm close." The sound of his growl intensified, driving me to go just a little faster, to squeeze a little tighter, as he continued to thrust into my mouth. It didn't take long before he let out a primal sound, his hands gripping my hair tightly as he released himself into my mouth.

I licked my lips, a smile spreading across my face as I looked up at him. His eyes were barely open.

"So, how was it?"

"I didn't think it was possible, but I just fell even more in love with you, piccola."

I grinned in victory.

The next morning surprised me when I saw Damiano was still sleeping next to me, considering it was almost lunchtime. I was happy he was finally allowing himself to sleep, and I guess this time I was the one who had tired him out.

"Well, good morning to you." Cara's voice broke through the lively chatter in the dining room where most of the group was present, savoring their lunch.

"Yeah, yeah, morning." I said and took a seat. I was so hungry that I didn't have time for small chitchat as I grabbed myself a bagel.

"Someone woke up hungry." Ava gave a teasing smile.

"I had a long night." I replied, giving a quick thanks to Cara when she poured me coffee.

"Has anyone seen Damiano? I need to talk to him." Arianna walked in with a frown, her footsteps heavy with frustration, and let out an annoyed huff when everyone said no.

I stayed silent and sipped my coffee, pretending I didn't notice their piercing gazes, all directed at me as they waited for me to tell them where Damiano was.

"Do you know where he is? He's not answering his phone." Arianna directed her question to me, but I just took a bite of my very delicious, toasted bagel with cream cheese.

"Althaia?" She tried to get my attention. I took another bite. I was deaf until she gave me an apology.

"Okay, fine!" Arianna huffed and plopped down in the chair across from me, causing me to shift my gaze towards her.

"I'm sorry! I'm a nosy bitch, and I stick my nose in people's business because I get protective, but it still doesn't excuse that I was a bitch to you. I said things I shouldn't have, and for that, I'm sorry."

I popped the rest of my bagel into my mouth, taking my time chewing my food, and took a long sip of my coffee.

"You were a bitch." I stated.

"I know."

"Did you mean any of it?"

"No. I was mad and talked nonsense."

"Are you going to stay out of our business?"

"Yes. Trust me, I've learned the hard way. What I said that day was out of line and you didn't deserve it. I'm really sorry."

"Then apology accepted. Bitch." I smirked behind my mug of coffee. Arianna rolled her eyes playfully and gave a smile.

"Wohoo, there you go! Finally, friends again!" Raffaele erupted.

"Can you now tell me where Damiano is? He's been sending me on crappy jobs, and I just can't do it anymore." She groaned.

"He's asleep." I said, and they all fell silent in confusion.

"Damiano's asleep?" Lorenzo checked his watch in surprise. I guess it was really unlikely for him to sleep in.

"Oh, so that's what you meant by a long night." Ava chuckled.

"Just keeping my man happy." I gave an innocent smile.

"And happy he looks! There's my man! Look how well-rested he is!" Raffaele wiggled his brows.

My heart skipped a beat at the sight of Damiano, his muscles flexing beneath his perfectly tailored dress shirt and slacks. He leaned in and pressed a soft kiss against my cheek before settling next to me.

"When did you get up?" Damiano asked, ignoring everyone else as I poured him a cup of coffee.

"An hour or so. I thought I would let you sleep." I could see how well-rested he was, with his eyes sparkling and a content smile on his face, and that gave me another ego boost, knowing I was the reason.

"Good, because he's a dick when he doesn't sleep." Lorenzo commented.

"If you can't handle the heat, you know where to fuck off to." Damiano retorted, unbothered, as he ate.

"I can't do this again. I'm not staying for another round of them taking a hit on each other's pride. Let's go, Lorenzo, we got stuff to do." Cara tried to drag him with her, but he barely budged.

Lorenzo clicked his tongue at Damiano, who wore a taunting smirk, before finally following Cara.

"Ugh, what am I supposed to do if everyone has plans? Cecilia is still all glued up on Luca." Ava groaned and slumped in her seat.

"I can think of something we can do." Raffaele gave her a cheeky smile, and I let out a small sigh at him trying to flirt with her.

"You don't have any plans? Cool, let's go then." She said, and he looked stunned by her answer.

"Wait, you're serious?"

"Yeah. Come on, you're so slow!" She grabbed his arm and pulled him out of the chair. "There's this farmer's market I've been wanting to check out with Cecilia, but she's too busy sucking Luca's dick...." Ava continued to talk as they made their way out, making me chuckle. It was definitely not what he was expecting.

"Damiano, we need to talk. I'm done. I can't do it anymore!" Arianna said desperately to him. He barely glanced her way as he leaned back in his seat and looked at me.

"Did she apologize to you?"

I nodded.

"Are you content with it?"

"I am. It's all forgiven now." I reassured him, and he gave a small nod before facing Arianna.

"I've learned my lesson. I promise to never interfere with anything that has to do with your precious love."

"Good, because if you do, I'm sending you back to Italy and you can live with Nonna." He warned, and Arianna looked a little scared about it.

"Yeah, no thank you. Trust me, I'm all out of your business." She put her hands up in surrender and quickly left the room.

"Is your Nonna scary?" I asked.

"Not really. She's just a very traditional and religious woman."

"So, how traditional and religious are we talking about?" I wondered.

"She saw my tattoos and said I was going to hell." He said casually, and my eyes widened. "I almost gave her a heart attack the last time I was in Italy. Nonna saw I had gotten more tattoos and prayed to God to forgive me." Damiano smiled as he talked about her.

"She sounds fun." I chuckled. "When was the last time you saw her?"

"It's been a while. When you and Cara first got here."

"Oh, the day after you freaking marked my body and then disappeared?"

"Yes, to let other men know you were taken." He smirked.

"What men? You had the whole place in lockdown, anyway."

"I had to let my men know to fuck off when they saw you." Damiano gave a smug smile. I shook my head at him with a playful smile.

"Did you suddenly decide to go on vacation?" I asked.

"No." He said slowly. "It was the anniversary of Sienna's death."

My smile fell as I went silent.

"I'm sorry. I didn't mean to pry like that."

"I visit her grave every year on her anniversary, along with her family, to share my condolences. I returned the belongings I still had of hers and her pictures. When I did, her family didn't question why; they realized I was finally trying to move on."

"Because of me? I wouldn't have minded if you kept her things." I said, feeling a slight guilt.

"It was about time I did. I was holding on to someone who wasn't going to come back. When I saw you for the first time, I was intrigued. I returned her things because I wanted a new start. With you." His words sent a flutter through my body, intensifying as he leaned in, bringing his lips incredibly close to mine.

"And the way you sucked the life out of me, lets me know I have the right woman by my side."

"Damiano!" I groaned, making sure no one heard him. It only made him laugh more when my cheeks flushed.

Eighty-Five

Althaia

Since everyone had plans today, and Damiano had work to catch up on, I decided to visit my father. I passed the time playing with Kiara until it was time to go.

I lightly knocked on Damiano's office door, mindful not to disturb him in case he was on an important call.

"Come in."

I opened the door and poked my head in, checking to see if he was busy. He hadn't looked up yet and was still engrossed in some papers.

"Hi." I greeted, and his eyes immediately met mine.

"You don't need to knock. You can come in whenever you want." Damiano said, putting down the papers in his hand and gesturing for me to approach him.

"I didn't want to disturb you." I replied, walking around his desk. He took hold of my waist and placed me on his lap.

"You will never be a disturbance to me. Next time, just walk in."

"I will try to remember that." I placed a small kiss on his lips, making him smile. "Doing anything interesting?"

"No, just paying bills."

"Don't you have someone to handle your finances?" I asked as I glanced at the papers on his desk, once again filled with endless lists of numbers.

"I do, but some things require my attention." He said.

"Jesus. How are you not broke?" I knew he had *money*, but I still get surprised every time because it turns out to be way more than I would have imagined.

"I would be one hell of a lousy Don if that was going to make me broke." Damiano said, amused by my reaction as I let out a whistle.

"Not too shabby of a career path. I should form my own gang and make a shit ton of money."

"Really?" His voice let me know he was trying not to laugh at me.

"Yes, I would be really good at it." I said cockily, holding my head high, and he just scoffed.

"Baby, you won't even last ten minutes before getting your ass shot."

I crossed my arms and looked at him in complete offense.

"I would definitely last longer than ten minutes! I will just rule over a few streets and keep it low-key. Who would shoot me for that?" I questioned.

"Me. And you wouldn't even see it coming." Damiano leaned back in his seat and smirked at me.

I did a dramatic gasp and put my hand to my chest as I looked at him with an exaggerated, shocked face.

"Why would you shoot me? I thought we were homies!"

"Don't take it personally, my love. It's only business. You would walk around in *my* territories, trying to take *my* money." He leaned in closer to my face, his voice low. "*No one* takes what's mine. You will have to kill me for it."

"Oh, really?" I placed my hands on his chest, offering him an innocent smile. Damiano's gaze penetrated deep into my eyes, making my breath quicken at the intensity of his golden-brown eyes.

I bit down on my lip, noticing his eyes immediately following the movement. Taking it as my cue, I swiftly reached down to his waistband, where I knew he kept his gun.

One moment I was on his lap, and the next, he had me bent over his desk with my arms secured behind my back.

He tsked, not impressed at all.

"Many have tried to kill me and failed. What makes you think you would be any different, piccola?" Damiano whispered in my ear, his body pressing against mine. There was something so exhilarating about this position that had me grinning.

"Thought I would give it a shot, you know. See if I could take down the big, bad Don Damiano Bellavia."

"I have to admire your courage." He chuckled, his chest vibrating against my back. "Under normal circumstances, you would have been shot before you could even blink. However, it would have been a waste since you look quite enticing right now like this."

Damiano's hand trailed down my spine, making my body tingle in response. I bit my lip when he reached around and stopped at the front of my jeans. He unbuttoned and slid his hand inside, his fingers gracing the lace thong I was wearing, following the slit of my pussy.

"You look so fuckable bent over my desk, piccola." Damiano slid my thong to the side, continuing to tease me and making me wiggle to feel more.

"Well, are you going to fuck me, then?" I breathed out, getting wet at the thought of him fucking me from behind like this.

"Want me to fuck you bent over my desk like this?" He asked, pressing his cock against my ass.

"Yes." My answer came out embarrassingly fast. Damiano slid down my jeans, just below my ass. I was excited, wanting him to fill me up already.

Then he spanked me.

So. Fucking. Hard.

It brought a loud scream out of me.

"If only you hadn't reached for my gun, I would have. Such a pity." His voice was taunting as he rubbed me where he spanked me. Then he fucking slapped my ass again.

"Fuck!"

"Learned your lesson?" I could imagine what kind of dark look was on his face right now as he watched me at his mercy.

"You suck." I huffed out.

"No. You suck, I eat." Damiano pulled up my jeans, laughing.

I rolled my eyes and faced him, rubbing my sore ass cheek.

"And here I thought you would do anything for me." I faked a scowl.

"I will, but go for my gun and there will be consequences. Don't pull that shit on me again, and there won't be problems. Understood?" His voice was serious but carried a playful smirk on his lip.

"Yes, Sir!" I straightened up and did a salute, having him shake his head at me in amusement.

"Now that you're here, I have something for you." Damiano led us across the office and stopped in front of a wall. Before I could ask, he placed his hand on the wall, and a square shape opened up out of nowhere.

"There's a transparent sensor on the wall designed for my hand shape and fingerprints to unlock the safe hidden inside this wall." He explained.

My mouth hung slightly ajar, genuinely fascinated.

He opened the safe and pulled out a large envelope when something in there caught my eye.

"Wait." I said and reached into the safe.

"I couldn't bring myself to get rid of them." Damiano spoke softly at the red baby shoes and sonogram in my hands.

My heart squeezed a bit painfully at the sight of it all, but I still smiled, grateful that he saved them.

"Thank you for keeping them." I gave him a kiss and placed them safely inside again. I just hoped that one day we would be lucky. "Is that the Tiffany Yellow Diamond?!" I let out a small gasp of happiness as I recognized the jewelry box.

"Yes, it was still in your room when we cleaned your house."

"Thank God! I thought I had lost it." I said, relieved. "Keep it in there. I don't want to be responsible for losing fifty million dollars."

We returned to his desk as he handed me the envelope.

"You fixed the insurance for the boutique?" I asked when I read the documents.

"I did."

"Thank you, but the numbers are a bit off, don't you think?" I showed him the documents, but he didn't look as he asked me.

"Why are they off?"

"You're kidding me, right? I'm pretty sure the boutique is nowhere worth this much!" I gaped at him. "I know you made sure I got a nice settlement for it, but even this is too much. Did you write a check?" I eyed him suspiciously, finding it hard to believe the valuation on paper matched the actual value of the boutique.

"I didn't write a check. Keep looking." Damiano urged. I went to read how they had concluded the amount of insurance money.

"It still doesn't make sense." I mumbled, as I frowned while reading. "I know we did well, but we were nowhere near this value." I looked at him in confusion.

"You're right, it doesn't make sense. I did make sure you got a nice settlement, so you wouldn't have to worry about it. The numbers are off because your mother used the boutique for laundering money."

"Sorry, what?" I shook my head, hoping I heard him wrong.

"Your mother was involved in money laundering. I believe it's connected to those who were after her. I'm convinced they are the same people who burned down the boutique to get rid of any evidence." He explained.

I let out a sigh, rubbing my forehead. I felt a wave of overwhelm as I continued to uncover new information about my mother.

"Althaia." Damiano drew me into him when I had been silent for a while.

"I'm okay. It's just... I feel like I don't even know her." My voice was heavy with sadness. I rested my head on his chest as he soothingly rubbed my back.

"I know, baby." He whispered softly. "She probably had a good reason and did whatever she could to keep you safe."

"There is still nothing new that can help us?"

"Nothing yet, but don't worry about it for now. I will tell you if there is anything useful."

"Thank you. Well, I should get going now. Are you giving me a ride to my dad's house?"

"Gio and Luca will take you there. They are waiting for you. I have something I need to prepare, but I will come and get you."

"Oh shit, they have been waiting for me all this time?"

He nodded, and I made a face, knowing Giovanni would have something to say about being kept waiting.

As we walked out to the driveway, sure enough, Giovanni already had a scowl on his face.

"Please, take your time. It's not like we have been waiting for you to come out." Giovanni glared at me. "It's bad enough that I have to babysit your annoying ass once again." He continued to complain.

"Drop the act, Gio. I know you like me." I grinned, and he shot me a disgusted look.

"I really don't."

"Yes, you do! Your secret has been revealed to me. You care about me." I continued to tease him, prompting a frown.

"I don't know who's filled your head with nonsense, but I don't."

"You care about me."

"No."

"Come on, give me a hug." I smiled widely and opened my arms. He placed a finger on my forehead, stopping me from getting closer.

"I don't get paid enough for this."

I scoffed at him when he pushed me away with his finger and got inside the car.

"You shouldn't have done that, Gio! Have you forgotten how great my singing voice is? I'm going to give you one hell of a concert now!" I shouted after him. I tried not to laugh when he opened the car door again and got out.

"Dario. You go with them. I will take this car."

"Oh, no! Don't think you can escape me now!" I jumped on his back, making him stumble in surprise.

"What the fuck are you doing? Get down!"

"Not before you admit you actually care about me!" I tightened my hold on him when he tried to get me off him. I know he wanted to fling me off, but he couldn't because Damiano would have his head in a second if I as much got a scratch on me.

I grinned, totally taking advantage of it.

"Over my fucking dead body." Giovanni growled in annoyance.

"Wrong answer!" I started to painfully pinch his cheek, laughing as he let out a frustrated sound.

"Fine! Just get down before I flick you away like the little gnat you are."

"So?" I retorted when I hopped off his back.

"You are... *tolerable*." His response wiped the smile right off my face. "This is the best you will get out of me. Now, get in the car and let's go. I don't have time for this." He said quickly before I could say anything and slid inside the car.

"You just earned yourself a concert with me!" I shouted after him.

"Torturing my men once again?" Damiano wrapped his arms around me.

"He's such a drama queen. My singing is not that bad." I said with the utmost confidence. I had never seen Damiano try to hold back a laugh as much as he was right now, making me gape at him. "You think my singing voice is bad?"

"You should get going before it gets too late. Stay safe." He gave me a quick kiss on the lips before walking away.

"That wasn't an answer!" I called after him.

"I love you, baby. See you later." Damiano called over his shoulder, and now it was my turn to click my tongue.

"My voice is great." I grumbled under my breath before getting inside the car.

Eighty-Six

Althaia

The familiar driveway welcomed us with its smooth asphalt and neatly trimmed hedges. My father's mansion, a place I hadn't seen in what felt like a lifetime, stood before me, and memories of both of my parents in this house came flooding back.

My heart sank as the weight of having only one parent settled in.

"Hey, you okay?" Luca's voice brought me out of my thoughts. "You've been staring at the house for a good five minutes and haven't made signs of getting out."

"Oh, sorry. I didn't even notice." I let out an embarrassed chuckle and got out of the car.

"I'm going inside with you." Giovanni said while he scanned our surroundings.

"No need for that. I'm pretty sure I'm safe in there." I assured him. He suddenly frowned, and I followed his gaze. It was Carlos, his jaw clenched as he returned the glare before entering the mansion.

"Isn't that the cunt who gave you a cut on your face?"

"How do you know about that?"

"Damiano made sure he got the same treatment. With a lil' extra surprise." Luca smirked.

"He did?" I asked, suddenly remembering that he said he should have put a bullet in him instead.

"We normally never question Damiano's actions, but we found it strange that he randomly went up to him and fucked up his face." Luca laughed.

"If Damiano got to him, then I'm sure he won't try to do anything to me again." I said. I still didn't know why Carlos hated me so much. All I did was show up. Was it maybe sibling jealousy?

"Damiano will have our fucking heads if you return with even a scratch on you. Can you please, for once in your life, try not to do anything stupid? I happen to like my life and would like to live another day." Giovanni crossed his arms as he practically lectured me.

"Why are you all acting like I do something stupid all the time?" I said defensively. They all shot me a blank stare as if saying, 'really?' Even the extra men Damiano sent with us. "I don't!"

"But you do." Luca retorted.

"Name me one stupid thing I have done." I challenged.

"The LuxePalace." They said immediately at the same time.

"Anything other than that." I rolled my eyes at them.

"You drugged my girlfriend."

"You went back to your house unprotected."

"You met up with the Russian Mob Boss with a gun."

"You tried to save that girl on your own and almost got yourself killed in the process."

"You never listen."

"You -"

"Okay, I got it!" I almost shouted when they kept going. "I said *one* thing, not a whole damn list."

"It just proves how stupid you are." Giovanni shrugged and leaned against the car.

"You're stupid..." I muttered under my breath and made my way inside the mansion.

Okay, so I had done my fair share of stupid things, but one thing I sure as hell would never regret was helping Laila get away from that scumbag. I hoped the piece of shit was having a fun time, rotting in hell.

"Althaia, darling!"

Oh, fuck me already.

"Hi, Morella." I gave a tight smile. I have not missed her high-pitched voice, or her constant 'darling' calling.

She grabbed me by the shoulders and gave each of my cheeks a kiss.

"Darling, how are you? I heard what happened, and I am so sorry, darling. Are you feeling better?" Morella asked.

"I'm doing better, thank you." I tried my best to keep a smile on my face and not cringe at her high-pitched voice.

"Oh, darling, I know how hard it all can be. I went through something similar as well."

"You did?" I asked in surprise, and she nodded.

"Yes, darling. A few years ago, my mother passed away in her sleep. It was the worst thing I have ever gone through." Morella clutched the pearls around her neck.

I tried to see if she was taking a piss on me, but the sadness in her voice said otherwise. I was completely stunned, unable to utter a single word. How in the world could she think it was the same thing?

"I'm so sorry to hear that." I muttered, holding my tongue back. Losing a parent was hell, but I would prefer my mother passing away peacefully in her sleep over being murdered in front of me.

"Thank you, my darling."

"So, is my dad around?" I asked before she could continue.

"He will be here shortly. Do you want to grab a cup of coffee while you wait for him?"

"No, thank you. If I have any more coffee today, I won't be able to sleep." I forced out a chuckle. "I will wait for him in his office."

"All right, darling." Morella's high-pitched voice went an octave higher, and I hurried to my father's office before I lost my hearing.

I grew restless waiting for my father for thirty minutes. Rising from the couch, I wandered around his office, scanning the bookshelves, but nothing caught my interest.

Sighing loudly, I plopped down on his desk chair and began spinning around in boredom until the idea struck me to find blank papers. Since I had to wait anyway, I might as well kill time by drawing.

"That looks familiar…" I muttered, looking at the necklace that was in the drawer. It was a necklace that looked awfully like the one I had lost.

I grabbed it, turning it over in my hands, only to gasp loudly when I realized it was mine.

"What are you doing in here?" Carlos' voice rang out by the door, already glaring daggers at me.

"Waiting for my dad. What else does it look like I'm doing?" I replied, not caring if it came out bitchy. After all, he didn't deserve niceties after backhanding me across the face.

"It looks like you're snooping around." He snatched the necklace out of my hand.

"It's mine." I reached for it, and he tried to push me away, but I quickly grabbed his arm before he could.

"Touch me and see what happens to you." I warned him.

Carlos made the smart decision to back away from me.

"What is going on here?" My father's voice boomed, frowning as he looked back and forth between us.

"Nothing's going on. I was just waiting for you, and Carlos was about to leave." I said, as neither of us showed signs of backing down.

"She was being a nosy bitch and snooped around." Carlos held up the necklace to show it to my father.

"I dare you to call me that one more time, and you might just accidentally drop dead to the ground." I took a step closer to him, ready to remind him just how precious his balls were.

"Enough!" My father roared, grabbing Carlos by the shoulder.

He forced him away from me and spoke to him rapidly in a low tone in Italian. Whatever my father was saying to him, it didn't look like Carlos was very happy about it. He walked out of the office without saying another word.

My father let out a sigh and looked at me.

"I'm sorry, figlia. How are you?"

I smiled and went in for a hug.

"I'm doing better." I said, closing my eyes and enjoying the comfort of my father's arms wrapped around me.

"You do look better. Are you being taken good care of?" He leaned back to look at me.

"I am. I went away for a little while... I just needed to process everything." I explained as we moved to take a seat on the couch. "Sometimes I find myself holding my phone, about to call her, and then I remember I can't." My throat tightened, and I took in a deep breath to avoid crying.

"I understand. I can't say it will get easier or better with time. Eventually, you just learn to live with it. But you will heal, and you will be whole again. One thing is certain; grief changes you. You will never be the same, nor would you want to be." My father sighed as he looked deep in thought.

I realized just how accurate it was. I didn't feel the same at all, nor did I ever want to be as helpless as I had been. I was too weak, and it would forever weigh on my conscience. If only I had been a little stronger, maybe I could have saved her, but no.

She died to protect me.

"Sounds like you've had your share of grief as well?" I asked. He let out a chuckle, but not a humorous one. He rose from the couch and walked over to the bar to pour two drinks, handing me a glass of Scotch before resuming his seat.

"It's a tough industry. It was difficult at first, but now people come and go, and you just get used to it." My father said with a shrug and sipped his drink.

"I don't like the sound of that." I muttered.

"No one does, but it's reality. It's better to get used to it to protect yourself." My father tapped his head.

I took a sip of my drink, feeling my heart twist at the thought of losing more people I cared about.

"You were never supposed to be a part of this world, figlia. You care too much." He chuckled.

"I can't help it." I smiled.

"Because your mother did an excellent job of raising you." His words filled me with pride as he gave me a small smile. "I meant to ask you something but didn't, since you were in a completely different state. Did your mother tell you anything before she... passed?"

"Such as?" I asked.

"Perhaps anything useful that could help us investigate?"

"I don't think so. I only remember bits and pieces from that night. I'm not too much of a help, unfortunately." I said sadly.

"I see."

"Why?" I asked when it felt like he didn't believe me.

"I'm just trying to help, figlia. Your mother and I may have had our differences, but she's still my ex-wife and the mother of my child." His expression softened, making me feel guilty.

"Sorry. I wish I could be of more help." I sighed in defeat, truly hating that I couldn't be more useful to anyone.

"No, don't worry about it. But if you do remember something, even something minor, let me know."

"I will keep that in mind." I gave a small smile as he nodded in approval.

"Good. Now tell me, how's the wedding coming along?" He suddenly asked in joy.

Excited about the mention of Cara's wedding, I told him everything that she had caught me up on, and he listened to every word, smiling now and then.

"That also reminds me, I don't even have a dress for the wedding." I said when I was done.

"You still have two weeks, plenty of time to find something." My father gave a dismissive wave.

"That is not something you can say to a woman, papá." He chuckled at my gasp.

"It's just a dress. They all look the same anyway, just in different colors."

"Such a man thing to say." I shook my head in amusement. "How can you say that to someone who literally worked in a boutique as a gown designer?"

"All right, all right, my bad." My father put his hands up in surrender.

"By the way, wasn't that my necklace I found in your desk drawer? I was looking for some blank papers while waiting for you and found it there. I wasn't trying to snoop around, I promise!" I quickly said when he frowned.

"Ah, yes, the necklace." He retrieved it from the pocket of his suit. "You forgot it in the hospital, and I didn't have a chance to give it to you."

"That's a relief. I thought I had lost it when... well, I'm just happy to see it again." I said as he handed it to me. I almost dropped it when I jumped in my seat as someone barged in.

"Damiano! Good to see you again." My father rose to his feet, unbothered that he barged in. Damiano gave a nod to my father as they shook hands. "I'm assuming you're here to get my dear figlia."

"I am." Damiano looked at me and then looked at the coffee table, frowning at the empty glasses, before looking at me again. "Let's go."

"It was nice to see you again. Take care, papá." I hugged him and placed a small kiss on his cheek.

"You too, figlia." He smiled. Damiano barely glanced at my father when he bid us goodbye and placed an arm around my waist.

I couldn't tell if something happened that got him in a mood, or if it was just me who was used to him being different when we were alone.

As we descended the stairs to the driveway, Michael was on his way up. He stopped, as if he wanted to say something to me, but refrained when Damiano pulled me tighter into his body as we passed him.

I never thought my friendship with Michael would turn into this, but he punched me with his words when I was already at my lowest. For that, I couldn't even bring myself to look at him.

Damiano opened the car door for me, and just before I could step in, he gently cupped my chin and pressed his lips to mine. The kiss was soft, yet dominating, stealing all the air from my lungs. He leaned back with a smirk on his lips.

"Tastes even better when I know you're mine."

Blushing, I slid into the car, now eager to get away from Michael's eyes on us.

Eighty-Seven

ALTHAIA

"Where are we going?" I asked when I realized we weren't heading in the direction of the manor.

"It's a surprise." Damiano gave a teasing smile.

"I don't like it when people say that."

"I know." He winked, making me groan.

We made it to an airport, and he stopped right in front of a private jet. My head snapped so fast towards him.

"You said you wouldn't send me away!"

"I'm not sending your ass away. Who else would suck the life out of me if I did?" He retorted with a smug grin.

"You're such a dick." I scoffed. Damiano chuckled and kissed the back of my hand.

"We're going to Italy, my love."

A smile spread on my lips.

"Are you serious?"

"No, I took you to the airport for the fun of it." I gave him a blank look, and he obviously found his reply funny as he chuckled. "I told you I would take you to Italy to meet the rest of my family. Now is a good time before the wedding."

"Well, now I feel a little nervous." I admitted, feeling a knot tighten in my stomach.

"Don't worry, I know they will love you." Damiano reassured me.

"I'm talking about flying." I said, looking at the jet.

"Nothing to be worried about, my love." Damiano lightly caressed my cheek with his thumb before leaning in to softly kiss my lips. My stomach erupted with a fluttery feeling, making me smile against his lips.

"How much did you drink? Your cheeks are flushed." He pointed out as his tongue went across his lip.

"Maybe a little more than I should have, but it was surprisingly good!"

"You liked the vanilla Scotch?"

"You can tell what it was?"

"I can still taste it on your lips. It's also what your father usually drinks."

"Hopefully it will calm me down when we get on that thing." I commented, casting a skeptical glance at the aircraft. "Oh, that also reminds me. Can you help me put it on so I don't lose it again?" I pulled out the necklace from my pocket.

Once clasped around my neck, Damiano touched the small pendant as if examining it.

"My dad kept it safe since I forgot it in the hospital."

"Did he now?" He raised a brow as he played with the pendant.

"Ellie must have taken it off while she tended to my wounds." I said, relieved that it was back in my possession.

Instead of responding, Damiano offered a small smile and took my hand.

"Let's get going."

We boarded the jet, finding Giovanni and Luca already settled comfortably in the plush leather seats.

"If you need to rest, there's also a bedroom. It's going to be a long flight." Damiano mentioned as he settled across from me, with a small table between us.

"How long does it take to get to Italy?"

"Around twelve hours."

My eyes widened in shock.

"I have to stay in this metal coffin for twelve hours?!" I shrieked.

"You have been to Italy before, yes?" Damiano looked at me with a touch of amusement.

"When I was younger, but I don't remember flying for so long."

"It's nearly the same duration as flying to Greece." He pointed out.

"It's been so long since I last went there, and I take sleeping pills so I won't think about flying." I said nervously.

The thought of being stranded thousands of feet above the ground, with no power to prevent a disastrous crash, sending you straight to your death.

The fear was overwhelming, draining the color from my face and causing my heart to race uncontrollably.

"Hey, come here." Damiano spoke gently, taking my hand and guiding me to sit beside him. "Nothing is going to happen. I promise you it's safe." He reassured me, looking concerned when my hands slightly trembled.

"That is not something you can promise..." I mumbled, feeling my anxiety spike. "If something goes wrong, can you at least shoot me so I don't have to witness crashing to my death?"

Damiano's expression darkened at my request.

"Don't be ridiculous, Althaia."

I turned to look at Luca.

"No." Luca said before I could even ask him.

"Gio?"

"I will happily shoot you. Don't worry about it." He said, barely acknowledging my existence as he kept his gaze fixed on his phone.

"Thank you. I knew I could count on you."

"I got your back on this."

Luca kicked Giovanni's leg, making him shoot a glare in his direction. With a warning look from Luca, he turned his attention to me and then to Damiano.

"I was just kidding." Giovanni's words were rushed, making me immediately shift my attention to Damiano, whose face bore a hauntingly fearful expression.

"You better watch your mouth, or I will throw you out while we're flying." Damiano practically growled. His tone sent a shiver down my spine as his voice dripped with promise.

Giovanni nodded in response before resuming his focus on his phone.

"And you." Damiano gently held my chin, guiding my gaze to meet his. "Don't you dare joke around with something like that again. I won't tolerate it." He stated firmly, fixing me with a deadly glare.

"Sorry." I whispered.

Holding Damiano's hand tightly in mine, I could feel my heart racing as we were catapulted into the air. Damiano did everything to distract me, talking to me about his family as he massaged the inside of my wrist.

He shared so many stories that I was completely engrossed that I hadn't realized we had been flying for a while.

"Did you have a good time with your father?"

"Yeah, it was nice to see him again." I said happily, and he grinned at my reaction.

"That's good." He smiled.

"He asked me if I could remember anything that could help him find who killed my mom." I let out a small sigh, feeling down that there wasn't anything new.

"What did he want to know?" Damiano furrowed his brows.

"If my mom mentioned anything before she passed away."

"I see." He replied, concealing what he was thinking as the blank expression settled back on his face.

"It's just one big blank space whenever I try to remember anything.... Well, maybe she did?" I suddenly said and sat up straight, my heart beating a little faster.

"What is it?" His demeanor caught the attention of the others.

"My mom said how she should have known how *he* was going to do this sooner rather than later." I told him, completely forgetting to tell him about that part.

Damiano exchanged a brief glance with the others before turning his attention back to me. I didn't know if it was something useful.

"As much as I would rather have you not remembering that night at all, do you remember anything else she said?"

I furrowed my brows, deep in thought.

"Something about I need to stay with you... because you're the only one who can protect me from *him*."

Damiano's expression turned into an icy, terrifying glare, causing shivers to run down my spine as his intense gaze locked onto me.

"... But it could be anyone. She didn't get to finish what she meant by it." Defeated and disappointed, my shoulders slumped as I realized it was likely a dead end.

"I don't want you to worry about it now. Leave it to me." Damiano said before I could ask how we were ever supposed to get to the bottom of this.

"You will let me know if you find something, right?" I looked at him with hopeful eyes.

"Of course, my love." Damiano's strong arms pulled me closer, his lips gently brushing against the top of my head.

The hours flew by, and with each passing minute, my anxiety about flying vanished. I even moved to sit across from Damiano so that I could gaze out at the breathtaking sunset. Looking down from above, the scenery stretched out in all its magnificent glory.

Damiano still had work to do, so I busied myself with my sketchbook, which he luckily had packed. Taking a small break from drawing, I grabbed the small bag of chips and munched on them. Luca had fallen asleep in his seat, but Giovanni was awake and still on his phone.

His eyes were always glued to the screen of his phone these days. He didn't notice I was staring at him, but then my eyes widened when I saw a small smile on his lips. I gaped in shock as he texted back to whoever had him smiling like that.

I took my phone out and quickly sent a text to Damiano.

__Althaia:__ Does Gio have a girlfriend?

Damiano looked at me with a brow raised, wondering why I was texting him, but I signaled for him to text me back.

__Damiano:__ Why the sudden interest?

I rolled my eyes at his jealous ass.

__Althaia:__ He has been on his phone non-stop, AND he is smiling. Look!

Damiano discreetly glanced at Giovanni, observing the faint smile still lingering on his face.

__Damiano:__ Not that I know of.

__Althaia:__ Sounds like a job for me. I'm going to find out!

I grinned at Damiano, and he responded by shaking his head at me before returning to his paperwork.

I sat comfortably, swinging my legs over the armrest, pretending to sketch while waiting for Giovanni to return to his phone.

"I need to pee." I announced to no one when Giovanni went back on his phone.

I walked past him, taking a few steps, only to sneak back to right behind his seat, and looked over his shoulder.

I held my breath, trying to be silent as I strained to catch a glimpse of the person who had managed to put a smile on his grumpy face.

"Oh my God!" I gasped loudly, making him jump in his seat.

"What the fuck?!" Giovanni gave me a disapproving look, but I just stared at him in shock.

"When did that happen?" I pointed to his phone.

"You were reading my texts?"

"Uh, yeah?" I said, as if it was no big deal. "When did that happen?" I asked again.

"I don't need to tell you anything." He scoffed and hid his phone.

"Scoot over." I pushed him to make room for me in his seat.

"There's no room for your fat-ass here." He groaned as I wiggled to get comfortable.

"Aw, you think my ass is fat? I have been doing some squats lately. Does it show?" I stood up, and his eyes widened as a faint blush tinted his ears.

"Why are you trying to get me killed today?" Giovanni looked at the ceiling, avoiding looking at me.

"I'm not. Is my ass fat or nah? It's a serious question."

"A single glance, and your eyes will be carved out." Damiano warned before his eyes met mine. "And you, my hand has been twitching for hours now. Stop testing me."

I bit my lip at his so-called threat.

"Has it now?" I wiggled my brows, earning a small smirk from him.

"Now I wished I was dead." Giovanni let out a groan of disgust.

"Oh, shut it. Now, tell me how long you have been talking to Laila?" I once again made him scoot so I could wiggle my way next to him. "You know I won't leave you alone until you tell me." I grinned.

He ran a hand down his face in annoyance.

"For a while now." He sighed in defeat.

"I need details. Tell me everything!"

"It's not what you think. You were the ones who sent me to Portugal to make sure she would be safe, so I did. Now she just texts me to let me know how she's doing."

"Bullshit." I said immediately. There was no way he would have given her his number if he wasn't interested or had some level of concern. "You like her. You have been smiling at your phone like crazy."

"I haven't." He gave me a blank look.

"But you have." Luca yawned and stretched his arms. "Your endless bickering woke me up. What did I miss?"

"Gio has a crush on Laila." I replied.

"Who?" Luca looked confused at the name.

"The girl Althaia foolishly tried to help on her own in the boutique and almost got herself killed in the process." Damiano filled him in.

I shot Damiano a blank look for explaining it that way, but he merely arched an eyebrow, silently asserting, 'I'm right.'

"Oh, that girl." Luca said in realization.

"Now tell me, how did it happen?" I went back to Giovanni, excited to hear the story.

"It's not that deep, okay? I was with her to make sure she got to her family safely. She then admitted that she still felt unsafe and asked if I could stay for a couple of days. I hung around for a bit and helped her out with some stuff." He shrugged and tried to dismiss us.

I shared a brief look with Damiano and Luca, and I could tell they weren't buying it either.

"Yeah, he likes her." Luca mused in a playful tone.

"Totally." I grinned.

I was thrilled that Laila could find comfort after everything, and I knew Giovanni liked her since she had him smiling like that already. Maybe she could make him a lot less grumpy.

"You're in over your heads. I'm just checking on how she's doing." Giovanni tried to defend himself.

"Whether you admit it now or later, we know you're into her because you don't care about people's well-being." Damiano stated.

"Seconded. The only person you've shown any concern for is Althaia." Luca added, making Giovanni look at him as if he wanted to strangle him.

"She's the last person I would care for."

"Don't lie." I scoffed.

"Don't be delusional." He retorted.

"Antonio told me you never left my side at the hospital." I smirked.

"He must have confused me with someone else."

My jaw hung open, and he pulled down his hoodie over his face, shooing me away so he could pretend to sleep.

I took a quick shower before we landed and got ready since we would drive directly to Damiano's family home. My nerves kicked in, and my stomach felt like a tangled mess as I struggled to decide on an outfit. I wanted to give a good impression.

"Is this fine? Am I showing too much skin?" I asked Damiano.

I had slipped into a stunning nude midi dress with ruched details and an asymmetrical hem. It added a touch of sophistication, and the single sleeve lent it an alluring charm, leaving my other arm gracefully bare.

"You look absolutely beautiful." Damiano smiled, pulling me into him by my waist, a tender admiration in his eyes.

"Thank you." I placed a quick kiss on his lips. "Are you sure I'm not showing too much skin?"

"No, you're fine. You're overthinking this." He chuckled.

"Well, I don't want your Nonna telling me I'm going to hell for showing too much skin!" I tried to convey the seriousness of the situation. Then I gasped. "She can never know I've spread my legs for you before marriage. She will surely tell me I'll burn for eternity! What if -"

Damiano stopped my rambling by squeezing my cheeks together with his hand, making my lips pout.

"My love, you will be fine. More than fine because you're you. You have a way to make people love you."

"Do you think so?" It came out muffled.

"I know they will love you. Come, it's time to go." He held my hand, and I took a deep breath as we made our way out of the jet.

This was it.

I was meeting his family.

When we stopped right in front of a beautiful estate, my nerves kicked in full force. I had to remind myself to breathe.

"This way." Damiano led me to the garden, and that was when I heard voices getting closer. "Stay behind me." He smiled at me as we rounded the corner.

"Dio mio, Damiano!"

I heard gasps and sounds of excitement, making me smile at their reaction to him.

"My beautiful son is back." His mother spoke in Italian and hugged him with tears in her eyes. It allowed me to see just how much they resembled each other.

Damiano embraced her back before she stepped away, and he greeted whom I assumed was his Nonna. His mother was smiling at him, and then she turned to look in my direction, only now realizing he had brought someone with him.

"Damiano?" She gasped and put her hand to her chest. His Nonna had the same reaction when she spotted me.

Damiano's touch was tender as he clasped my hand, his lips curved into a gentle smile.

"Madre, Nonna. Meet Althaia, the love of my life."

EIGHTY-EIGHT

ALTHAIA

My heart thumped nervously in my chest, yet as I stole a glance at Damiano, a soft look and a smile graced my lips at how he introduced me.

The love of his life.

At that moment, the world around us seemed to fade away. The way he looked at me made everything else inconsequential.

I could see the resemblance between Damiano and his mother; her golden-brown eyes and dark, shoulder-length hair reflected the beauty that ran in their family. She wore a light copper-colored halter-neck dress, enhancing her tan skin and radiating an incredible beauty.

His Nonna, an elegant presence, stood tall with dark brown eyes and black hair pulled into a bun. She donned a long-sleeved dark green satin dress, an attire befitting royalty.

Not intimidating at all.

"It's a pleasure to meet you." I greeted them with a warm smile, squeezing Damiano's hand to conceal my nervousness.

"My goodness, aren't you a beauty!" His mother beamed with happiness and pulled me into a warm embrace. I was surprised but chuckled in relief.

"Thank you." Her compliment made me feel shy, and I could feel my cheeks flush.

She gently placed her hands on either side of my face, looking at me with a soft smile. Her eyes sparkled with genuine happiness, creating a moment that felt heartwarming.

"Così bella. Don't you think, madre?" His mother stepped aside, allowing his Nonna to appraise me. Her dark eyes swept over me from head to toe, giving me a slightly intimidating feeling.

I bit down on my lip nervously when she didn't say anything, my heart thumping faster. I looked at Damiano, but he appeared calm and relaxed, which I took as a good sign.

His Nonna approached me slowly, placing a hand under my chin and turning my face slightly from side to side as she examined me. Then she released a smile and turned to look at Damiano.

"Very beautiful. You did well, my child." She winked, making Damiano release a smirk as he turned to look at me.

"I know I did." Damiano placed a tender kiss on my forehead and lightly caressed my cheek. He drew me in with his golden-brown eyes, and everything else faded away again as my heart filled with warmth.

"He's completely captivated by her." His mother whispered with a chuckle, breaking the spell Damiano had cast over me. I helplessly blushed when I noticed they had been watching us in our little bubble.

"Take a seat. I want to hear all about how this happened and how long you've been hiding her from us."

Damiano pulled out a chair for me, and we both took our seats. Unseen servers swiftly arranged plates and glasses, serving us a delightful meal. The sight and aroma of the food made my mouth water, and I suddenly realized how hungry I was.

"Eat, baby, I know you're hungry." Damiano whispered quietly to me, gesturing towards the enticing food on my plate.

He didn't have to tell me twice before I dug in as elegantly as I could. The dish was cheesy and saucy, and as it touched my tongue, I felt my eyes wanting to roll to the back of my head in pure bliss.

"Buon appetito." His mother smiled, offering me more food.

"Now, tell us, Damiano, when did it happen, and why haven't you told us?" His Nonna took a sip of her wine, ready for interrogation.

"I'm telling you now." Damiano rested his arm behind me, a sly smile playing on his lips as he addressed his Nonna.

"For how long?" His mother asked eagerly.

"She was already in my life the last time I was here."

"Damiano!" His mother scolded him. "All this time and you didn't even bother telling your mother that you have found someone?" She made a tsking sound, clearly unimpressed.

"As long as he has found someone, I'm happy. I'm not getting any younger, but I refuse to die before you give me some great-grandbabies." His Nonna's words had me momentarily pausing, but I quickly tried to cover it up by reaching for my glass of water.

Damiano's hand gently caressed my shoulder, and as I looked at him, he wore his blank expression. He took a subtle glance at my stomach before grabbing his glass of wine and swirling it around without saying a word.

To offer him comfort, I placed my hand on his lap and tried to give him a small smile when his body was slightly tense. It was an innocent remark from his Nonna, who couldn't have known what we had gone through.

"Don't say that. You're going to scare her! There's plenty of time to think about babies, and Damiano's still young, so let them take their time."

"Plenty of time for whom? Certainly not for me! Damiano's not getting any younger either. He's almost forty!"

I snorted out a laugh before clamping my hand over my mouth, chuckling at his Nonna's comment.

"I'm thirty, Nonna." Damiano sighed tiredly.

"She will lecture him for a while about not getting any younger." His mother shook her head and moved her chair closer to me.

"Damiano did tell me how she's trying to get him to have some babies as soon as possible." I chuckled, watching Damiano patiently listening to his Nonna's rant.

"Don't worry, honey. Since Lorenzo is getting married soon, some of the pressure has gone to him and Cara."

"That might take a while since Cara hasn't gotten over the fear of giving birth."

"You've met Cara?" She asked in surprise.

"She's my cousin." I grinned, and her eyes widened slightly.

"Oh, so you're a Volante?"

"She's the daughter of Gaetano Volante." Damiano informed them as he sipped his wine.

"How interesting." Nonna commented, tilting her head slightly to the side as she looked at Damiano.

"Well, at least you're Italian, or part of you is... Tell me, dear, what are you?"

"Ay, madre..." His mother sighed and shook her head.

I chuckled at his Nonna's choice of words.

"My mother is Greek. Is it that obvious that I'm not fully Italian?" I grimaced a bit, feeling embarrassed that my Italian wasn't as good as I would have liked it to be.

"You have a slightly different accent, and, well, it's not the best Italian I've heard! But don't worry, spend time with me, and you will have no trouble." She smiled. "You're family now, so you may call me Nonna from now on."

"And you just call me Eleonora. No need to be formal with me; you're practically my daughter." She gave my shoulder a small squeeze, smiling warmly as she looked at us.

This made me feel emotional. I had spent weeks thinking about how I didn't have a family anymore, but I did. Every single person in Damiano's life had made sure I could always count on them, and I was forever grateful for that.

I ended up telling how we met at the engagement party, joking about feeling like I had met the Devil and fearing he was after my blood. It wasn't a joke back then, but now I could at least jest about it since it didn't turn out to be true.

"I never threatened to shoot you." Damiano raised a brow when I mentioned his sudden appearance in my hotel room.

"You said you could easily put a bullet in me through the door." I reminded him, making him smirk.

"That wasn't a threat, my love. I was stating a fact." He said casually, earning a scoff from me.

"Wait, were you really planning on shooting me?" I asked, and Damiano pretended not to hear me.

"What made you change your mind?" Nonna questioned, amused by our banter.

"She fell face-first when she tried to run away from me. Never in my life have I seen anything like that before. It made me laugh." He looked at me teasingly.

"So, me trying to run for my life and falling on my face saved me from getting shot?"

"Funny how things work in your favor." He gave me a cheeky wink before getting up from his seat. "If you'll excuse us for a moment, I'd like to show Althaia around." Damiano said, extending his hand for me to take. I expressed my gratitude for dinner before he led me away.

"... Isn't she just wonderful?" I overheard Eleonora saying, bringing a smile to my face.

The estate was truly enchanting, with lights illuminating our surroundings. My eyes were drawn to the various flowers and blooming trees, their pink blossoms standing out against the green foliage. I found myself envisioning sitting under one of those trees during the day, recreating the beautiful scenery in my sketchbook.

"I told you they would love you. You can relax now." Damiano reassured, pulling me into him as we strolled around the garden in the comfortable night breeze.

"I never expected such a warm welcome. You have a wonderful family." I mused, resting my head on him with a smile. "I know I don't say it enough, but thank you." I said softly as I looked into his eyes.

"For what?" His brows slightly raised.

"For everything. 'Thank you' feels like nothing for all you've done for me. No one has ever gone to the extent you have. No man has ever loved me as deeply as you have, and you continue to show me endless love, which I'm not even sure I'm deserving of."

No words could fully express the deep gratitude I felt for everything he has done for me. He consistently went above and beyond, and I knew I didn't deserve him, but there was no way I was ever going to let him go.

He was mine.

I went up on the tips of my toes, placing my hands on his stubbly cheeks that I loved so much. He pulled me close, wrapping his arms around my waist, as we stood under the pink flower tree, gazing into each other's eyes.

"I love you." I whispered to him with a soft smile as I lovingly caressed his cheeks.

Damiano rested his head against mine and closed his eyes.

"Say it again." He whispered.

"I love you, agápi mou. So much that sometimes, I fear my heart might stop because of it."

Under the gentle glow of the moonlight, he stood captivated, his eyes gazing at me with an adoration that I hadn't seen before.

I planted a tender kiss on his lips, a sweet embrace that made my heart flutter as if it were the first time I had ever tasted his lips. His hand found its place behind my neck, deepening our kiss as our tongues danced in a rhythmic harmony. In that moment, he claimed me with a passion that left an indelible mark on my soul.

"We have to stop. They might see us." I said breathlessly.

"Let them." Damiano pressed me against the tree and worked his way down to my neck, sucking on my skin.

"My love..." I breathed out a moan.

"Fuck, piccola!" He grabbed the back of my thighs and hoisted me up around his waist. "You expect me to stop when you say that to me *and* make that sound?" He growled out and pressed himself against me, making me feel his excitement.

"I want to believe I've left a good impression. I don't want to ruin it by having your mother and Nonna find us fucking against a tree." I chuckled, sensing his frustration. "I will make it up to you, I promise." I gave him a quick kiss before wriggling my way out of his hold.

"Fine." Damiano scowled as he watched me adjust my dress. He gently lifted my chin, the lingering lust still visible in his eyes. "You owe me a round with that mouth of yours." His voice was low and deep as he ran a thumb over my lips.

"Oh, look who's loving the skills of my tongue." I wiggled my brows at him. He let out that smirk that made him look like the sexiest Devil alive.

"I'm surprised and amazed. I'm afraid to ask how you've learned to use your tongue like that."

I shot him a sidelong glance as we strolled around the garden, finding his lack of discretion rather amusing.

"I've only been with two guys before you. And a woman. But, you know, the real practice comes from popsicles." I chuckled.

"What did you say?" Damiano halted and turned me around to face him.

"Popsicles?"

"No, before that."

"That I've been with a woman?"

"You've been with a woman before?" He repeated slowly.

"I was curious and went for it." I shrugged. "Is that a problem?" I crossed my arms and tilted my head when he said nothing.

"No." He said slowly, a smirk forming on his lips. "It explains how you can use that tongue so well." He winked, and I shook my head playfully at him before we walked again.

"Hmm. Sounds quite hot, actually. Who knew my innocent Althaia was a pussy eater?"

I yelped out when he smacked my ass.

"How about you stop being so horny for once?" I hissed out to him, afraid someone might have heard or seen us as we were close to the house.

I hurriedly tried to walk away, but he swiftly pulled me back and effortlessly tossed me over his shoulder.

"I can't. My cock gets hard every time I see you. Just like it is right now. Let's find a room so I can fuck that mouth and pussy of yours."

"Don't say that so loud!" I gasped, looking around to see if anyone was watching us. "Put me down!"

"No." He slapped my ass again and tried to slip his hand under my dress.

"Damiano!" I struggled to get out, but he held me in a pretty firm grip as he ascended the stairs to enter the house.

"You know I love when you say my name, baby." I could hear the smugness in his voice.

"You won't get laid if you don't put me down this instant!"

"Are you threatening me?" He said with amusement.

"No, it's a promise. I'm never going to suck your dick again." I hissed in a whisper, and I suddenly found myself back on my feet.

"You are getting a bit too comfortable making those threats to me." Damiano remarked with an unimpressed raised brow.

"You know what they say; hit them where it hurts." I grinned. His eyes slightly narrowed as he towered over me.

"Yeah? Then I'm going to show you just how fuc -"

"There you are!" Nonna appeared out of nowhere, and I quickly took a step away from Damiano, trying to fix myself so it didn't look like he was about to *destroy* me.

"Let me show you to your rooms." She gestured for us to follow her, and we obediently trailed behind as she led us through the house and up the stairs. "This is where you will stay, dear." Nonna opened the door for me.

"Thank you." I smiled.

"And you." She turned to look at Damiano. "You'll stay downstairs in the guest bedroom. No sleeping together before marriage. It's a sin!"

I let out a chuckle, but it slowly died down when I saw the stern expression on her face as she looked at Damiano.

Shit, Nonna is serious.

"If you want me to have babies, then I have to get in there." Damiano retorted. My eyes widened, and my jaw hung open in utter embarrassment.

"Oh, Dio mio." Nonna's hand swiftly slapped his arm as she scolded him. All he did was give a nonchalant shrug. "It's a sin to commit fornication! Do you want to displease the Lord?" She looked at us with a terrifying glare.

"No, Nonna, absolutely not! I am definitely waiting... for marriage. No reason to worry." I tried to reassure her with a smile, and Damiano raised his brow at me in amusement.

I shot him a look, signaling him to keep quiet when I received an approving nod from Nonna. There was no way I was going to let her find out that we had fucked way too many times already. Hell, we had even put the bedroom in the jet to use.

"Excellent. Now, Damiano, it's time for us to pray and cleanse those impure thoughts. I have Holy Water for you to use." Nonna declared and grabbed his arm to drag him with her downstairs.

Damiano shot me a mischievous look, mouthing, 'fucking you later,' followed by a wink. I had to cover my mouth to muffle my laughter while Nonna persisted with her talk about praying.

She was going to need way more than Holy Water if she wanted to turn the Devil into an Angel.

EIGHTY-NINE

DAMIANO

I strolled out to the backyard and settled into one of the sunbeds beside the pool. Retrieving my pack of cigarettes, I lit one, my gaze drifting upward to the balcony where Althaia's room was.

My Nonna had made it abundantly clear that I should steer clear of Althaia's room in the evening because, according to her, the Devil would lure and tempt us into committing unimaginable sins.

Too bad that indulging in those forbidden desires was my favorite sin when it came to the love of my life.

I was well aware she was keeping a watchful eye on me, which was why I was out here, killing time and waiting for her to fall asleep. That woman never ceased to treat me like a boy instead of the man I had become.

"Why is my son sitting out here by himself?" My mother approached, wearing her usual warm smile.

"I'm waiting for Nonna to fall asleep." I said, taking another drag as she settled on the sunbed in front of me.

"Of course you are." She chuckled.

"She made me pray and splashed Holy Water on my face." I shook my head, and my mother tried to hide her laughter behind her hand.

"That's Nonna for you. You know how she feels about doing anything before marriage. She wants you to be 'pure' for your better half."

"I will have to disappoint her on that part." I gave her a smug smile, to which she shook her head in amusement.

"As long as you keep it to yourself. She's going to have a heart attack if she hears that!"

"I know." I laughed, taking a final drag before putting out the cigarette.

"Althaia's wonderful. She's such a bright person, and I can see just how happy you are with her. I've never seen you this carefree before with..." She trailed off, unsure if she should say it or not.

"It's fine, madre. You can say her name." I told her. Her brows slightly raised at my answer.

Her name no longer stirred the same emotional turmoil within me when it was mentioned. There was a time when it invoked anger, a result of the pain I felt at her untimely death.

I had done her justice. I caught every single one behind her death, ensuring they met a grim and horrifying end. Now, it was time for me to move beyond that chapter in my life.

"Does she know about Sienna?"

"She knows." I nodded. My mother smiled warmly, her eyes reflecting a sense of relief as she recognized I had finally let go of the past.

"I can see why you fell for her. She must keep you on edge." My mother chuckled.

"You have no idea how many times she's made me question my sanity. She's stubborn, barely listens, and is too curious for her own good. Everything that I hate, but it's her. I don't know how she did it, but she captured me, especially with those mesmerizing green eyes." I smiled as I talked about her.

"She does bring out a different side of you that I haven't seen before. It's been too long since I've seen you this happy, and words can't express how overjoyed I am to witness it."

"She made me whole." My mother's eyes welled up with tears as she gazed at me with a gentle smile. "Ma, don't cry." I chuckled, wiping away her tears.

"Oh, hush! There's nothing in the world that makes a mother happier than seeing her children happy. My job is done." She said, giving my cheek a light pat. "But I won't forgive you for not letting us meet her sooner." She added with a stern glare.

"I wasn't trying to keep her a secret." I said, gazing up at the balcony where the light illuminated her room. Althaia's silhouette moved around, likely unpacking her things.

"Someone is after her." I turned back to my mother, who raised her brows at the information. "I had planned on bringing her here to meet you sooner, but..." My gaze shifted to the ground, and I rolled my neck to release the tension building up in my body.

"She was attacked. I had Antonio and Luca watch her, but they were taken by surprise. Mercenaries broke into her home, chased her and her mother. She watched her mother get stabbed in front of her, and she..." I let out a breath, and my mother looked at me with concern. "We lost a baby that night."

My mother let out a small gasp, placing her hand on her chest.

I suppressed every emotion that threatened to surface, pushing them into a dark corner. I tried not to think about it, as it often led me to wonder what it would have been like right now if it didn't happen. She would be showing now, something I so desperately wanted to witness.

The image I had painted in my mind of how she would look with a pregnant belly had me close my eyes for a bit before I shoved it away.

"She was pregnant?" My mother looked at me in shock. "You were going to have a baby?" She whispered, and I nodded briefly.

Neither of us said anything after that.

"Did you get them?" Her voice dripped with anger, and her eyes hardened.

"Some of them." I frowned, displeased that it was only some.

"That's why I brought her here, to keep her safe for a little while. I almost lost her, madre." I shook my head and ran a hand through my hair. "I can't go through that again. Not with Althaia."

"Listen to me." My mother placed her hands on either side of my face to make me look at her firm expression. "You won't lose her. I know you'll do everything in your power to keep her safe. Sienna's situation was different, and you've changed since then. You've grown and become wiser. You are Damiano Bellavia, my son. Don't forget that." She finished with her usual warm smile and a soft look in her eyes.

Her words brought a small smile to my face.

"Grazie, madre." I embraced her, placing a kiss on top of her head.

The sound of a balcony door opening drew my gaze to Althaia's room. She was nowhere to be seen in the darkness, but the door was ajar. I took that as my cue.

"Are you going to climb up to her?" My mother chuckled, and I smirked.

"I am. If you don't mind, I would like to go to my woman now."

"She's all yours. I will make sure your Nonna doesn't know, but you better be out before she wakes up." She sang out as she made her way back inside.

I waited, smoking another cigarette and scanning my surroundings. I scoffed and shook my head in amusement that my Nonna was making me behave like a fucking hormonal teenager.

I walked to the wall I needed to climb to reach her balcony as I did one last scan. I had done this many times as a young boy when I wanted to go out unnoticed. Back then, it was a workout, but now, it was a piece of cake.

I jumped to get a grip on a windowsill. Hanging from it, I swung my body to the right to secure a hold on the edge of the balcony. With a smooth pull, I hoisted myself up and climbed over the railing.

The curtains gently swayed with the cool night breeze, and I moved them aside as I entered the dimly lit room.

Only for something to hit my face.

I directed my gaze downward to see a pillow. Looking back up, I saw Althaia sporting an innocent grin.

Did she just hit me with a fucking pillow?

"I'm sorry. I definitely thought you were a kidnapper." She said, biting her lip to stifle a laugh at her own joke.

"Did you, now?" I moved closer, aware that she had another pillow hidden behind her back.

"Yes, but I can see how it's not a kidnapper but rather the Devil paying me a visit." She swung the pillow at me again, aiming for my head. I blocked it with my arm, snatched it from her grip, and tossed it aside.

"The Devil, you say?" I flashed her a devilish smirk as I approached, noticing the amusement in her eyes. Coming to a halt in front of her, I pulled her into me.

"A beautiful one, if I should say so myself." Althaia spoke softly, placing her hands on my chest. "Took you long enough." She whispered before pressing her soft lips to mine.

I kissed her slowly, savoring the taste of her lips and tongue, as if there was no place I would rather be.

Althaia wrapped her arms around my neck as my hands slid down to her ass, lifting her as she wrapped her legs around me. I fucking loved it when she did that.

"I don't know if that's a good idea." She leaned away, breaking the kiss when I walked us to the bed. "I, uh…happen to be kind of…loud." Althaia's cheeks flushed.

"You are loud." I agreed, and I watched with a smile how she looked shy about it. "Nothing to be shy about, baby. You know how I love hearing you." I chuckled when she hid her face in the crook of my neck.

I laid her on the bed and hovered over her.

"I have something in mind." My hands trailed up her thigh, to her underwear, before sliding them down her legs. "Open up." Her brows raised, but she still opened her mouth, and I stuffed her panties into her mouth. It was enough to make sure no one would hear her.

I grabbed the hem of her nightgown, pulling it over her head but stopping right at her wrists and tying them together.

"Now, be a good girl and try not to make a sound." I whispered to her.

Althaia's chest rose and fell faster as my gaze traced over every inch of her exposed skin. I savored the sight of her full, round breasts, the gentle curve of her waist, and the enticing shape of her full hips before finally meeting her gaze again.

And those eyes were my favorite.

The way they sparkled exuded innocence, making her utterly perfect with a soul so beautiful that it illuminated my once dark world.

I slowly removed my clothing, her gaze fixed on my every move, taking in my presence, just as I had absorbed hers. Casting aside my dress shirt, I unfastened my belt and slid off my pants.

Her green eyes went down, focusing on my hard cock. I sensually stroked myself at a deliberate, almost agonizingly slow pace. Her eyes traced every movement with intense focus, and she slowly opened her legs for me.

"Yes, that's my girl, wider." My voice emerged in a low, rough tone.

I hovered over her, my lips finding her breast as I sucked and explored her nipple with my tongue. My lips explored her body, gliding down to her stomach and resting between her thighs. With each kiss I placed on her thigh, she squirmed with excitement, urging me to where she yearned for my touch.

I traced the line of her pussy before sliding a finger inside of her, and a moan escaped her lips.

"No sounds, baby." I reminded her. She gave me a disapproving look before biting down on her underwear.

I inched my lips closer to her pussy, spreading her lips and stroking her clit with my tongue. Althaia's hips bucked, and I held her thighs to keep her from moving. Her sweetness coated my tongue as I thrust it inside of her before latching on to her clit.

I watched her struggle against the nightgown tied around her wrists as she struggled to keep quiet. I smirked and traced my tongue in slow strokes, adding two fingers inside her pussy, making her throw her head back.

I pumped my fingers as I sucked on her clit, feeling her legs tremble as I brought her closer to a sweet ecstasy.

"Come on my tongue, piccola." I growled hungrily against her pussy, savoring every drop of her essence as her body convulsed with the power of her orgasm.

I grabbed the back of her knees, pushing them to her chest as I watched her pussy spread for me. I slid my cock along her slit before slowly entering her, making a small grunt as I felt her tight and warm walls of her pussy envelop my cock.

"You feel so fucking good..." I whispered, driving in deeper. I could see the pleasure consume Althaia, her eyes rolling to the back of her head as I took my time burying myself in her pussy.

I swiftly turned her over onto her stomach, firmly gripping her hips to get her onto her knees. I pressed her face into the pillow as I shoved my cock in with deep, powerful thrusts. My hand traveled down her spine, her back curving so beautifully as I fucked her from behind.

I spanked her ass, hearing her muffled moans as I thrust faster and harder. I grunted quietly as the room filled with the sounds of our skin slapping against each other. I played with her clit as I was close to my own release.

"Fuck!" I gritted. Her tight pussy walls clenched around my cock as her orgasm rippled through her. I pulled out at the same time, almost a second too late, and came on her ass.

Althaia slumped down flat on her stomach while I caught my breath.

"Don't move." I went to the bathroom and grabbed a damp towel before returning to bed. I cleaned her up and untied her wrists. She rolled onto her back with a lazy grace. I removed the underwear from her mouth, and her eyes slowly fluttered open.

"I should tell Nonna the Holy Water didn't work." She chuckled.

I leaned in closer to her with a smirk, my lips brushing against hers.

"Tell her how good you were fucked by the Devil." I winked.

I watched Althaia as she struggled to stifle her laughter, but her attempts were in vain.

"So, your Nonna is really assuming you're a virgin? A thirty-year-old virgin?" She asked in between chuckles but couldn't stop and was now full-on laughing.

"Apparently." I said with a shake of my head.

"That is too funny!"

"Nonna was always after us when we were younger, warning us to not get involved with anyone until marriage." I lightly scoffed.

"I understand the idea of preventing hormonal boys from fucking around to avoid accidental pregnancies. But you were engaged! Surely, she wouldn't expect you to be a virgin when you were in a serious relationship, right?" Althaia looked at me with a raised brow, amusement clear in her eyes.

"Sienna was... different." I said, resting my hands behind my head and closed my eyes.

"Different how?"

"Sienna was a proud Catholic woman." I answered.

"... You're telling me you didn't have sex?" She asked. "Come on, just tell me! I'm not going to get jealous if that's what you're worried about." I knew she rolled her eyes when I didn't reply right away, which made me slightly smile.

"We didn't have sex."

"Weren't you engaged for like three years or something?" I felt her move and hover over me, but I still didn't open my eyes.

"Yes."

"You want me to believe that?" I opened my eyes to see Althaia giving me a blank look.

"It's the truth. She wanted to wait for marriage, and I respected that." I replied. She looked at me for a long time before slowly realizing I wasn't joking.

"So, three years and you didn't... did you cheat on her?" Her question came out accusingly, and it was my turn to shoot her a blank look.

"I'm many things, but a cheater isn't one of them, piccola." I stated firmly, my words leaving no room for doubt.

"It's just that you have such a high sex drive! You're constantly horny. I can barely keep up with you!" She exclaimed, making me raise a brow.

"My love, you're just as horny as I am." I smirked as I pulled her to lie on top of me.

"No, I'm not."

"Hmm, your pussy seems to be wet and ready when I'm around. That's the definition of horny." I winked.

"Oh my God, just stop..." She muttered, placing her hand over my mouth to stop me from teasing her. "I was just wondering how you stayed in a relationship for three years and, well, didn't *dip it*."

I chuckled at her choice of words.

"I took care of it myself whenever I needed to."

"Ah! That's why your biceps are this huge! It totally makes sense you're this strong if you have been jerking off like crazy for three years." Althaia bit down on her lip to not laugh again when she squeezed my biceps.

I laughed, entertained by her jokes.

"Well, my hands have been on a pleasant break since you came around. I don't even need them anymore, especially now that I have your mouth to use too." I gave her a smug grin as she scoffed at me.

"You're such a dick."

"A dick that you blow."

Laughter burst out of her before she quickly clamped a hand over her mouth to muffle the sound.

"It's getting bright outside. Will you be sleeping here?" Althaia asked as she sat up in the bed.

"As much as I would love to, I can't. Nonna will be up soon, and the first thing she will do is check if I'm in my room." I sighed in annoyance.

"You will be fine." She leaned down and placed a quick kiss on my lips before getting off the bed. "Want to take a quick shower with me?" She looked over her shoulder, a mischievous smirk on her face as she noticed me ogling her naked ass.

"You know where my gun is if I ever say no." I said and followed her to the bathroom.

Drying my body, I heard the subtle sigh that escaped her lips. Althaia stood before the full-length mirror, draping a robe around her body.

"What's wrong?" I asked when I saw her slightly rub her stomach.

"Nothing." She gave a tight smile, her eyes darting away from mine, and exited the bathroom. I followed her and quickly got dressed, noticing the shift in her mood.

"Come here." I reached for her and made her look at me. "Tell me what's wrong." I spoke to her softly.

Althaia bit down on her lip, a sign of her nervousness, and looked away.

"Nothing's wrong. It's just... do you ever think about it? What it would have been like if we hadn't..."

"I do. All the time." I responded right away, knowing what she meant. A flicker of surprise crossed her face at my answer.

"You do? But you don't talk about it."

"I know. I try not to think about it, but sometimes it creeps into my mind. There was nothing more I wanted when I found out."

"Me too." She sighed, and I pulled her into me. "When Nonna mentioned babies, it just made me wonder what it would have been like now. I would probably be way too big because you would force me to constantly eat." Althaia chuckled.

"Most definitely." I smiled. The image of her being pregnant invaded my mind once again, and this time, I let it linger for a bit.

"Do you... do you still want one?" She shifted around on her feet, another nervous trait of hers.

"No."

"Oh..." Her expression fell and disappointment filled her face. She tried to look away, but I softly grabbed her chin to hold her still.

"One is not enough." I let out a playful smile when she scowled before slapping my arm.

"Why would you say it like that?!"

"I wasn't done talking. Your fault for assuming I was." I joked.

I intentionally did it to help her relax when her body started to get tense as we talked about it. It worked because her body slowly relaxed against me, but not before commenting how I was a jerk for pulling that on her.

"So, how many are we talking about? Three?" Althaia asked, and I scoffed at the number.

"No, my love. At least ten." I told her.

"Ten?!" She exclaimed with her eyes wide, and I nodded.

"Yes. I want as many as possible with you." I said in all seriousness.

"But ten is a lot... I'm still the one who needs to push them all out! Let's say four for now." She stated as if we had come to an agreement.

"No. It's too little. Six children, and I won't ask for more." I said as a final offer.

"I will meet you in the middle and say five." She offered, and I shook my head.

"No, it needs to be an even number, so six."

"Why six then? Four is somewhat of a manageable number."

"Go big or go home." I winked.

"I would say that too if I wasn't the one pushing them out." She pointed out and raised her brow.

"I'm the one who needs to keep my aim sharp every time we have sex. That's a lot of pressure." I joked.

"Yeah, I don't think that will be a problem. You got me pregnant without even trying." She chuckled.

"It was partially your fault. I meant to pull out, but you felt too good not to come inside of you. The way you clenched your pussy around my cock..." I lowered my voice, giving her a sly grin as I trailed my hands down and playfully squeezed her ass.

"My God, it's a miracle you don't faint considering your blood rushes to your dick several times a day." She placed a hand on my chest and pushed me away. "Besides, you need to get going before Nonna wakes up."

"Fine." I sighed, the heaviness in my voice reflecting my discontent at the thought of her not sleeping in my arms.

I turned around to steal one last glance at her before stepping out. Placing my hands gently on her cheeks, I caressed them, allowing myself to become entranced by the depths of her green eyes.

"Will you be okay?" I asked, worried her thoughts would wander to a dark place after I had left.

"Yeah, don't worry about me. I'm fine." She gave me a reassuring smile, making me relax a bit. "What about you?"

"Whether we have children or not, having you by my side for the rest of my life is more than enough for me, my love." Her big green eyes sparkled like emeralds as she slowly released a shy smile.

Ninety

ALTHAIA

I woke up feeling refreshed. After Damiano left, I fell asleep immediately, and our conversation left me with a much lighter heart. The fact that he still wanted kids made me feel so much better.

I made my way downstairs and took my time to look around the estate. The interior was beautifully decorated with a mix of modern and antique elements, creating a classy and cozy atmosphere.

The walls were adorned with paintings, and I stopped by each of them to appreciate the art. Of course, I couldn't help but notice the humongous display of 'The Last Supper' by Leonardo da Vinci that had a wall for itself. That could only be Nonna's doing.

I found it quite amusing how there was such a stark difference in religious beliefs within Damiano's family. His Nonna was a devoutly religious woman who strongly believed in God, while Damiano seemed to be practically the Devil incarnate.

I let out a snicker.

"Do you find the painting amusing?" A slightly humorous male voice interrupted my thoughts, making me turn around.

A tall man with piercing dark brown eyes stood beside me, his hands tucked into the pockets of his slacks as he observed the painting. There was no mistaking that this man was Damiano's father. Lorenzo was the spitting image of him.

"Oh, no, I wasn't laughing at the picture..." I said, embarrassed that it had looked like I was.

"I won't tell. It'll be our little secret." He replied, still gazing at the painting. "Do you know the story behind this painting?" He asked, and I turned to look at it again.

"Jesus telling his disciples that one of them is going to betray him, or Leonardo da Vinci's new paint experiment technique when he made it?"

He turned to look at me, a brow slightly raised.

"And what about this painting experiment?"

"He used tempera paint on a dry plaster surface instead of the traditional fresco technique. The experiment wasn't quite successful as it flaked within a few years, and then later it got completely ruined." I explained.

"Interesting. Are you an artist yourself?" He asked, eyeing me as he spoke.

"I wouldn't say that, but it's an interest and a passion of mine." I offered a small smile, and he responded with a brief nod.

His gaze traveled over me, but the blank expression he wore made it difficult to discern his thoughts, causing an unexpected sense of nervousness.

"Oh, sorry, I'm -"

"Althaia Volante." He interrupted before I could finish introducing myself. "I'm Riccardo. You thought I wouldn't know who you are? I found out as soon as I heard my son brought a woman with him. *Especially* a Volante." The corner of his mouth twitched ever so slightly, and I felt a subtle urge to frown at his words.

What the hell does he mean by that?

"I wouldn't have expected anything less." I offered a tight smile, and he tilted his head slightly to the side. His gaze bore into me, as if he were trying to peer into my soul and unveil my darkest secrets.

"You do look quite well for someone who is supposed to be dead, no?" He smirked.

Like father, like son.

"That was me telling death, 'not today'." I tried to joke to ease my nervousness, but his piercing, cold eyes made it challenging.

The corner of his mouth turned up just the tiniest bit, and I had no idea whether to interpret that as a good sign or not.

"Why don't you join me outside? I'm sure you could use some breakfast, and we'll get to have a little chat together." Riccardo didn't leave me much of a choice as he turned around, heading in the direction of the garden. I followed quietly behind him.

We stepped outside where a table was already set up with food. I took a quick glance around, noticing two unfamiliar men standing close by, presumably working for him.

"Have a seat." He gestured to the chair in front of him.

"Thank you." I sat down and looked around once again, but there was no sign of Damiano or anyone I knew, for that matter.

"Damiano is not here, but I'm sure he'll be here shortly." Riccardo looked at someone behind me, making me turn and see Luca present. He was on the phone, likely speaking with Damiano, and ended the call after seeing Riccardo.

"Tell me why your death had to be faked." Riccardo wasted no time and cut right to the chase.

"That was my father trying to protect his daughter. I'm sure you can understand that." I retorted, attempting to relax as much as possible. I had a feeling this was going to be an interrogation rather than a conversation. Any trace of hunger I had felt before disappeared with his intense gaze on me.

"What an odd way to do so, wouldn't you say?" He questioned while pouring a cup of coffee.

"I agree. However, I do believe my father did whatever he thought would be best for me at the time." I said truthfully.

"If you say so." He took a sip of his coffee as I eyed him. "I hear your mother is Greek."

"Yes."

"That's going to be a problem for me." Riccardo said in all seriousness.

This man didn't beat around the bush at all.

"And how is that a problem?" I responded defensively and frowned at him. I glanced to the side, seeing Luca standing closer now, able to hear our conversation.

"You surely can understand that I would prefer my son to be with a full-blood Italian and from a family that would be beneficial to him."

"That's your preference, Mr. Bellavia. If Damiano wanted that, he would have done so." I offered a sweet smile, causing him to slightly squint his eyes.

"Damiano doesn't know what he wants." He stated firmly.

"I respectfully disagree. We both know Damiano is a man who goes for what he wants. And I am the one he wants." I could tell my words had an impact when he furrowed his brows. If this was how he wanted to play, then so be it.

"You seem quite confident about it."

"Why shouldn't I be? Damiano hasn't given me one single reason why I shouldn't be secure in our relationship." I replied.

Riccardo suddenly burst into laughter and leaned back in his seat.

"Let's just get to the point. How much do you want?" He asked, amused.

"Excuse me?"

"How much money will make you leave? Name your price."

I looked at him, completely taken aback, and he just smirked and sipped his coffee.

"With all due respect, Mr. Bellavia, but this 'chat' of ours has turned rather ridiculous." I remarked, giving him a blank look. I didn't want to give him the pleasure of getting a reaction out of me, even though I was pissed.

"I'm merely expressing what I believe would be best for this family. It isn't you." He gave me a smug grin. "I've already found a woman from a powerful family for him that would be far more suitable and beneficial." He continued.

I scoffed. As if I would ever let Damiano be with someone else.

Over my fucking dead body.

"Is that all you care about? Power? What about his happiness?" I tilted my head, my brows furrowing in distaste.

"He will learn to live with it, just like everything else in life." Riccardo signaled to one of his men to approach him and handed him a checkbook. "This should be enough for you to leave my son and never show your face again, yes?" He said, scribbling down an amount before sliding the check across the table to me.

Right now, I was wondering how much damage I could do to his face with a fork before getting shot by his men.

He gestured for me to pick up the check, so I obliged. I saw the exorbitant amount of money he was offering for me to leave Damiano. Still, I couldn't help but smile as I stared at the check.

"I see you're pleased with the number." Riccardo remarked, content. I said nothing; my smile widened as I locked eyes with him.

And then I ripped the check into tiny pieces.

"I'm not interested. You'll just have to get used to me because I'm not going anywhere. Whoever you have in mind, consider them out of the picture. If I can't be with him, then nobody will because I will be going on a killing spree." I threw the small pieces on the table, raising a brow to see what else he had up his sleeve.

"Wouldn't it be easier to kill Damiano then?"

"Nah, he's impossible to kill." I waved my hand with a sigh.

Riccardo let out a booming laugh, leaving me looking at him with confusion and surprise.

"It was a pleasure to meet you, Althaia." He smiled as he got up from his seat and left the table with his men.

"What the hell just happened?" I said out loud to no one in particular. Before I could call after him, Luca blocked my view and took a seat where Riccardo had previously sat.

"He was testing you." Luca explained while grabbing a cornetto from the pastry platter.

"Testing me for what?" I asked.

"To figure out your intentions with Damiano. In other words, if you're a power-hungry gold digger." He said, taking a bite and nodding in satisfaction. I let out a snort.

"Well, if I were on a gold digging expedition, don't you think I would've aimed for, I don't know, someone who *isn't* a criminal and *kills* for a living?"

"That would make sense. It would be insane if you stayed around just for money after everything you have been through. You would be one hell of a desperate gold digger." He chuckled.

"You knew he was testing me?" I asked.

"Yeah, I caught up on that pretty quickly, and I wanted to see what you had to say. Not that I think you're a gold digger, but many women would do anything to be with Damiano because of the wealth and power he possesses." Luca said as he finished eating.

"Well, he could have done it differently." I muttered.

"Your true colors show when you're angry, which made me realize you're kind of psychotic." He smirked, leaning forward to rest his arms on the table.

"How so? I didn't even do anything." I remarked, grabbing a cornetto as my appetite returned.

"You wanted to stab him with a fork, didn't you?" Luca laughed when my eyes widened.

"How did you know?" I whispered.

"You tend to look at things for too long, giving away what you want to do. Plus, you were eyeing your fork like you *really* wanted to stab him. That's bold to do so in front of the former Boss." Luca grinned, and my face paled in mortification.

"Maybe he didn't notice?" I asked. Luca shot me a 'really' look. "I know, long shot..." I sighed.

"Don't worry about it." He tried to reassure me.

"Easier said than done! I apparently just showed a former Mafia Boss that I wanted to stab him! *With a fork!*" I exclaimed.

"It's not that big of a deal. No offense, but you're not really... a threat." Luca gave an apologetic shrug. I opened my mouth, about to say something before clamping it shut.

"Eh, true." I agreed, acknowledging his point. I had no fighting skills whatsoever, at least none that could ever be compared to theirs.

"I will teach you how to be a bit scary. Though your height makes it a bit difficult." He snickered.

"So funny." I gave him a sarcastic smile and flipped him off. "Anyway, where's Damiano?"

"He should be here soon. I was told to make sure you got something to eat, and you should also wear something comfortable that you can move around in."

"What are we doing?"

"A small hint; you're going to get your ass kicked." Luca smiled slyly.

"I'm going to get my ass kicked?"

"Big time." He said confidently, leaving me to wonder what it could be.

"Dare to make a friendly bet?" I suggested.

"It'll be the easiest money I'll make." Luca grinned, making me playfully roll my eyes at him. "How much are we talking about?"

I took a few seconds to consider. I didn't want to throw in a high number in case I actually lost.

"Hmm, let's say fifty!" I extended my hand, and he shook it, sealing the deal with a smug grin.

"All right, fifty grand." He said, and I choked on my spit as he leaned back in his seat once again.

"Wait, what?!" I gaped at him with my eyes wide.

"You just said fifty?"

"I meant *fifty* dollars! Not fifty *thousand* dollars!" I exclaimed. Was he out of his damn mind?!

"What am I supposed to do with only fifty dollars? I can't even buy a decent meal with that. You already shook on fifty thousand. A deal is a deal." He lounged back, hands behind his head, wearing a stupid smirk.

"Are you insane?! That's a lot of money!" I tried to reason, but he just shrugged.

"You better not lose then." Luca stuck his tongue out teasingly.

"I'm not betting that much!" I frowned and crossed my arms.

"A deal is a deal. Do you know what happens to those who don't pay what they owe?" Luca leaned forward, resting his arms on his thighs as he spoke.

"I think I have an idea." I muttered, unsure when I saw Luca's demeanor change. He stared at me with a psychopathic intensity I had never witnessed before.

"Trust me, you don't. I fucking torture them. I slowly cut into their skin until they scream and beg for me to stop. But I love it when they beg. I feed off their screams. It only makes me want to keep going."

His voice was low and cold, his expression turned dark and sinister as he looked at me like I was his very next prey.

I was startled by the sudden shift in his personality. Hell, he even made me want to run away.

"And that's how you do it. Scary, right?"

I blinked a few times as I watched him return to his normal expression, with his usual smile.

"What the hell?! There's no way it's normal to switch personalities just like that." I shrieked. "You definitely belong in the Mafia. You're a lunatic!"

"I didn't get to my position by being a softie. Why do you think Damiano assigned me to be your bodyguard? It's because I'm *very* good at my job, actually better than good."

"I've just never seen that side of you." I chuckled.

"I know. I decided to keep it low-key after that night at the amusement park. You were pretty freaked out and almost fainted. I wanted to make it easy for you."

"Aw, look at you being so considerate of me." I gave an exaggerated, flattered look.

"Yeah, what can I say? You grew on me." He let out a dramatic sigh with a teasing look.

"Well, since we have established that, you should -"

"No. I'm not letting you win. I don't care *that* much about you to purposely lose the bet. My pride won't allow it." Luca gave me a smug smile.

"But I don't have that kind of money!" I protested. That was a lie. I had that kind of money from working my ass off in the boutique, and I definitely had a lot more now since Damiano had fixed the insurance. But Luca didn't need to know that.

"Not my problem." He shrugged, ignoring the glare I was giving him.

"What a bitch." I muttered under my breath as I left the table to return to my room.

"Heard that!" He called after me.

"Good." I replied, frowning as I tried to think of how not to lose fifty thousand dollars.

I found a pair of leggings and a shirt to get dressed in. Just as I pulled the t-shirt over my head, a knock sounded on the door before it quickly opened.

"Hi." I smiled as I saw Damiano, my heart skipping a beat at the sight of him. He looked as handsome as ever in a fitted t-shirt that showcased his incredible physique.

"Ciao, amore mio." He gave me one of his beautiful smiles as he approached me. Placing a kiss on my forehead, he made my body flutter at his actions.

"How did you sleep?" He asked.

"I slept well, and you?"

"Could have been better."

"Is that why you were up early?" I chuckled.

"Part of it. I had to take care of something. Also, this is for you." Damiano handed me a beautiful bouquet of pink lilies.

"They're beautiful. Thank you, my love." I stepped on the tips of my toes and placed a small kiss on his lips.

"You're welcome." He smiled at my words, looking at me with his softened eyes. "Are you ready? I'll have someone put them in water for you."

"I just need a different pair of shoes." I put the flowers on top of a dresser. "So, where are we going?" I asked as I put on my sneakers.

"It's a surprise." Damiano teased with a playful smile as I shot him a displeased look. "It has also come to my attention that you wanted to stab my father with a fork."

I stopped in my tracks and stilled. I met his gaze to find him looking at me with an amused expression.

"I don't know what you're talking about." I said, searching for a hair tie and avoiding eye contact.

"Really?" Judging by his still amused tone, I knew he didn't buy it.

"Mhmm." I replied as I turned my back to him.

His arms enveloped me from behind, drawing me close. His lips traced a path along the side of my neck, reaching my ear. The rhythmic beat of my heart quickened in response, and I closed my eyes as he playfully nibbled on my earlobe.

"Have you forgotten that you're a lousy liar?" He whispered, his breath sending shivers down my spine.

"Yes." I breathed out before quickly snapping my eyes open. "Uh, I mean, no." My response sounded more like a question than a confident statement.

Damiano chuckled, his amusement clear as I turned around to face him.

"Fine, maybe I did want to stab him with a fork, but he kept talking about finding a more suitable woman for you. If I had a gun, I would have shot him *and* that woman he was talking about. But I didn't, so I contemplated the fork. You're mine. No one can have you but me. You hear me!" I jabbed my finger into his chest as I looked at him with a frown.

Damiano's smirk widened as he grabbed my chin, drawing me in until our lips were close.

"Crystal clear, my possessive Althaia." He whispered, brushing his lips against mine. "No woman has my heart, but you."

"Good, or I might just fork you too."

"You're more than welcome to *fork* me." Damiano playfully tugged on my lip with his teeth, sending a jolt of tingles through my body. "Come, let's go, piccola."

"Where are we going?" I asked again as he led me outside to the driveway.

"You'll see." He chuckled when I let out an annoyed sigh. "Maybe this will put you into a better mood until then."

As we stepped outside, I let out a gasp. My eyes could barely believe what was in front of me.

"Of course you would own this car!" I *almost* ran to the Maserati Alfieri in pure awe, examining every single side of the car. The sleek lines, the elegant curves - it was a piece of automotive art.

I couldn't resist running my fingers delicately over the smooth surface as Damiano joined me, wearing a satisfied smirk.

"Like it?" He asked, his eyes gleaming with amusement.

"I do! I love it so much. I have a weakness for supercars." I sighed dreamily at the car.

"You can drive it."

"Really?" I gaped in shock. "Wait, you're not joking, right? Because if you are, I will never suck your dick again."

"For fuck's sake." A familiar, grumpy voice spoke out. I turned in its direction, completely oblivious to the fact that Luca and Giovanni were also present.

"Whoops..." I let out an awkward laugh while Giovanni shot me a disapproving look.

"Keep that shit to yourself. I don't want to hear it." He glared grumpily, a disgusted expression on his face.

"Oh, shut up, Gio. You're the one who's perverted and eavesdropped on our conversation. Be like Luca and don't listen." I pointed at Luca, who seemed like he couldn't give two shits about my comment.

"You're the one shouting about sucking dicks. Maybe don't shout, and I won't hear it." Giovanni shot back.

"How many dicks do you think Damiano has because I've only sucked one so far."

"I don't wanna hear it!" He shouted, and I laughed at his reaction, watching him retreat into a different car and slam the door shut.

Ah, poor, grumpy Gio.

"As long as my Boss is happy, I'm happy." Luca commented with a laugh.

"Right? I'm actually doing you all a favor." I joked. "Gio should get his dick sucked; maybe he will be less grumpy."

I looked at Damiano, seeing him with his eyes closed as he pinched the bridge of his nose.

"What?" I asked innocently, and he just sighed with a shake of his head.

"Just get your ass in the car. You're driving."

I let out a joyful squeal and wrapped my arms tightly around him.

"Thank you! I love you so much!" I gave him a quick kiss before sliding into the driver's seat.

"I will direct you. Don't go too fast." Damiano said once he got inside the car. I looked at him with a raised brow.

"You put me in a car with a top speed of 189 miles per hour with an acceleration of 4.4 seconds, and you want me not to go fast?" I scoffed and got the car started, making it roar as I pressed down on the gas a few times. "What a fucking beauty!" I beamed in happiness and continued to make the engine roar like a beast!

"Althaia -" Damiano warned, and I just laughed.

"Too late!" I stomped on the gas, and we were thrust back with the surge of acceleration.

I screamed in excitement, my heart racing, adrenaline coursing through my veins as we shot out of the driveway.

Ninety-One

ALTHAIA

I was driving fast!

The smooth glide of the car, the harmonious purr of the engine, and the commanding sound it generated when I accelerated filled me with pure joy. This beauty was making me feel unstoppable.

"You can slow down now." Damiano said while scanning our surroundings as usual.

"Are you scared?" I grinned.

"No, but you lost Luca and Giovanni." He replied. I glanced in the rearview mirror, only to find an empty road behind me.

"Oh, my bad. I just can't get enough of this car!" I exclaimed with enthusiasm, tenderly caressing the steering wheel as I slowed down to give Luca and Giovanni a chance to catch up.

"At least you can't be mad at me for losing them when you're with me. You really got pissed when I lost Antonio that time." I laughed.

"My hand was twitching badly that day. You had no idea how much I wanted to punish you for it." Damiano said, making me take a quick glance at him when I realized something.

"That day was the first time we were together... Was that why you were so rough with me and slapped my ass so fucking hard it was sore?" I gaped.

"Yes, and it turned out you loved it." He gave a smug smile and winked.

"Whatever…" I responded. Of course, I loved it, but that man didn't need any more ego-boosting.

"Since you're letting me drive this car, does it mean I can drive your Bugat-"

"No." Damiano cut me off sharply, not even allowing me to complete my sentence.

"Worth a shot." I muttered.

Luca and Giovanni had caught up with us, and Damiano directed me to wherever we were going.

"What are we doing here?" I asked when we came to a stop. Our surroundings didn't give away anything, as we were out in the middle of nowhere.

"You'll see." Damiano took my hand and led me to a field. I couldn't contain my excitement when I saw it was an outdoor shooting range.

"Are you really going to teach me how to shoot?!" I exclaimed loudly. He smiled at my enthusiasm.

"I am. You need to learn from the best." With a playful wink, he guided us towards a table where an assortment of weapons were displayed. "Do you remember what Arianna taught you?"

"I do." I nodded. It was one of those unforgettable experiences, and I recalled everything as if Arianna had taught me just yesterday.

"Show me." Damiano switched into boss mode, speaking firmly as he gestured to the gun with its magazine already out and bullets ready to be loaded.

I was a bit nervous, not because of the gun, but because Damiano was a literal professional, and I didn't want to fuck up in front of him.

I grabbed the gun, loaded the magazine and pushed it in, took off the safety, slid the rack back, and rested my finger on the trigger guard.

"Good." Damiano had watched intently at my every move before giving me an approving nod, and I couldn't help but feel a little prideful about it. "Let's see how you do."

"Please, don't make fun of me." I said as we faced the human-shaped paper targets ahead. I felt a wave of nervousness with three pairs of eyes watching me, all of whom were incredibly skilled.

"I won't make fun of you." Damiano chuckled.

"I know you won't." I turned around and gave a warning glare to a certain person. "But Gio will."

Giovanni gave a taunting smirk, and I just knew he was waiting for me to do badly.

"If he does, you can shoot him."

Giovanni's smirk fell and shot a blank look at Damiano.

"Deal!" I grinned.

Damiano stood close by as I held the gun firmly with both hands, aimed at my target, and then fired. I took a slight step back from the recoil before lowering the gun. I made a face when I saw a small hole in the bottom corner.

"At least I hit the paper!" I scowled at Giovanni, who laughed but disguised it as a cough.

"Keep going." Damiano instructed.

I shot a few more times, and the results were more or less the same. I sucked, *big time*, and I could feel how badly Giovanni wanted to laugh at me.

"Not too bad." Damiano commented as he looked at the paper.

"You don't have to be nice about it." I sighed, my confidence plummeting.

"It's not that bad for a beginner. Let me show you." He moved behind me, adjusting my stance. "You're too tense. You need to relax your body, especially your shoulders." As soon as he mentioned it, my shoulders sagged.

"Oh, I see." I rolled my shoulders to ease the tension.

"Both eyes open and take a deep breath." He instructed me, adjusting the gun in my hand and making me aim a little higher. Just as I was about to shoot, he placed his hands on my waist and trailed his nose alongside my neck.

I squinted my eyes, trying to focus, but his actions were making my entire body tingle, and my heartbeat spiked.

"You're not really helping right now." I said and lowered the gun.

"Good call. Never shoot if you're distracted."

"I'm really being tested today..." I muttered, rolling my shoulders before focusing again.

I made sure to relax my body, kept both eyes open, and took a steady, deep breath before pulling the trigger again. After a few more shots, I lowered the gun, and my eyes widened when I saw I was only two lines away from hitting the red dot in the middle.

"Did you see that?!" I turned to look at Damiano for him to confirm that my eyes weren't deceiving me.

"Good girl." He smiled. I bit down on my lip as it sent tingles right to my core. I wanted to jump on him just for calling me that.

"... Althaia."

"Hmm?"

Damiano looked at me, amused.

"I said, let's keep practicing."

"Oh, right. Okay." I turned around fast to hide my blushing face. Damiano quietly chuckled as he stood behind me to help with my stance once again.

"Don't worry, I'll give you what you want later." He said lowly. I guess it really was that obvious that I wanted him.

I kept practicing while Damiano observed my every move. I still had a long way to go, but I could quickly see a clear improvement with his expert help.

"You're a fast learner. That's good." He praised me while he studied my target papers.

"I have a good teacher." I shot him a cheeky wink, making him smirk.

"I know I am. Soon, you will have decent aim."

"Are you ready to get your ass kicked, Althaia?" Luca approached with a grin.

"This is our bet? Oh, hell no! You know I will lose."

"A deal is a deal."

"No. I'm not betting that much on this."

"Then I will have to shoot you." He casually shrugged.

"How much did you bet?" Damiano asked, but not before giving a warning look to Luca.

"I said fifty! He's the one who said fifty thousand *after* I shook his hand." I explained, but Damiano just shook his head.

"You didn't clarify how much, making the bet valid."

"Are you taking his side? He tricked me!" I argued, trying to emphasize that I was the victim.

"I wasn't there. It's your word against his."

"Why would I lie, hmm?" I placed my hands on my hips.

"Why would I question my men?" Damiano tilted his head, looking at me with a raised brow.

I didn't have a response, so I scoffed.

"Better cough up those fifty G's." Luca laughed and pulled out his gun. Without even blinking, he casually aimed at the target paper, firing his gun a few times as if it were the easiest thing ever.

I glared at him, watching every bullet hit right in the middle.

"I smell victory." He practically sang out. I clicked my tongue in annoyance.

"Well, since we didn't clarify the rules..." I dragged out and looked at Damiano with a grin. "Hey handsome, wanna earn some money?"

"No, you can't do that. The deal is you do the challenge." Luca protested.

"I don't recall we ever clarified that. Unless you have proof?" I smirked.

That's right, I can play dirty too.

"She has a point." Giovanni backed me up for once, and Luca wasn't looking too pleased about it.

"Damiano, will you pretty please help me?" I clasped my hands together and gave him my best puppy eyes.

"Sure." He gave a sly smile and looked at Luca before drawing out his gun.

"Best out of three." Luca declared, facing the target with the utmost seriousness.

"Fine. If that's how many times you want me to destroy your ego." Damiano let out his devilish smirk as he got ready.

"You might have just started a war between the two most competitive people." Giovanni remarked, watching them with amusement.

"Opps." I grinned, not sorry at all, because there was no way I was losing fifty thousand dollars.

I watched in anticipation, noticing Luca was a lot more focused now than he was when he thought he would be challenging me. Damiano took a quick glance at me and gave me a wink that gave me a rush of butterflies.

I couldn't resist biting my lip as my eyes slid down to his ass, giving an impressive nod as I checked him out. Even his ass was so fucking perfect.

"You're unbelievable."

I looked at Giovanni, finding him with a brow raised.

"What? He's hot, and he's got a nice ass." I shrugged, giving one last glance at Damiano's ass before focusing on what they were actually about to do.

I fixed my attention on Damiano, studying his posture and how he held his gun. He was standing slightly sideways as his entire body exuded relaxation. I wouldn't be shocked if his idea of unwinding involved shooting targets.

Shortly after, they both fired their guns. Without a pause, they continued firing. Three bullets sailed through the air, hitting their target, and I watched in pure fascination. Once done, both of them tucked away their guns, and Giovanni retrieved the papers to declare the winner.

"That's embarrassing." Giovanni laughed.

"Who won?" I asked, a bit nervous. It was not that I lacked faith in Damiano, but this was coming down to the very last detail, and he did shoot almost carelessly while Luca remained focused.

Giovanni presented the papers, and I noticed that one hole was just outside the red dot.

Luca snatched them from Giovanni's hand to examine them closely.

"One more round." Luca tossed the papers away while Gio patted his shoulder in comfort.

"I think you've embarrassed yourself enough." Damiano said, crossing his arms and smirking at him.

"By the way, I would like it in cash." I taunted.

For the first time, the look in his eyes showed me he wanted to shoot my ass.

Ninety-Two

DAMIANO

"That's enough for today." I told her after watching her fire the last bullet. Althaia let out a breath and rolled her shoulders to relieve the tension. She still had to learn to loosen up her body.

I watched as she confirmed there were no more bullets in the gun and the magazine before securing the safety. I was impressed. She proved to be a quick learner and adept with her hands. I had no doubt that she would excel in no time.

"You did well." I praised her.

"You think so?"

"Better than Arianna when I was teaching her." I remarked.

"Really? I am so going to throw that in her face. Who knows, maybe I will even be better than you. Better watch out, Damiano. I am coming for your throne." Althaia winked.

"Keep dreaming big, my love." I teased, grabbing the gun from her and placed it back on the table.

"You never know."

"I do. And no, you can't try it." I said firmly before she could voice her question. She looked at me with her brows slightly raised in surprise.

"What are you, a mind reader today?"

"You were eyeing the machine gun like it was a piece of chocolate cake— almost salivating too." I crossed my arms as she laughed.

"But I would look badass with this one!" She insisted.

"You wouldn't. It will have you flying back on your ass from the recoil."

"I feel like you're exaggerating."

I shook my head.

"I will show you." I picked up the M249 SAW and went back to the shooting range. This one was considerably heavier and louder than what she had been practicing with.

I positioned the SAW, bracing it against my shoulder, took aim, and fired. My shoulder jolted back from the force, and if she tried it, she would end up on her back and shoot us all, given her lack of experience.

Returning the machine gun to the table, her mouth was slightly ajar.

"I see what you mean. That's a powerful one." She said in awe.

"It is. This is an M249 Squad Automatic Weapon; a reliable, belt-fed light machine gun with a length of close to forty inches and a loaded weight of around seventeen pounds." I explained, setting the SAW back on the table.

"Oh, I want one!" Althaia exclaimed, fascinated.

"This isn't something civilians can get their hands on." I informed her.

"Then how do you have access to these weapons?"

I stepped closer to her, enclosing her between my arms as I leaned down.

"I may love you, but there are certain things I won't share." I spoke in a low tone, locking eyes with her green gaze. I was especially cautious about what was being said around her now that she was wearing her family heirloom. I had warned the others about it as well.

I needed to get rid of it.

"Worried I'll spill the secrets on how to access your weaponry to my father?" Althaia wiggled her brows, making me smirk as I slightly shook my head.

"No, I'm not concerned about your father. We have a deal." I said, stealing a quick glance at her necklace; a deal that led him to believe he could gain access if he played his cards right.

I stepped away and pulled out my phone when it buzzed in my pocket.

Antonio: *I just received an update.*
There are signs she might wake up soon.

Damiano: *Good.*
I'll call you later.

"You're not going to ask how I know about your weaponry?" Althaia continued.

"I assume someone ran their mouth to you." I put the phone back in my pocket and looked at her. I knew it was that shitface who told her.

"That was awfully specific for an assumption." She crossed her arms, giving me a suspicious look.

"Is it?"

"Yes. You don't assume; you know things for certain." She slightly squinted her eyes at me.

"There's a first for everything." I half-shrugged, dismissing her, and began reloading my gun with the bullets I had fired off earlier.

"No, wait a minute. You know who told me, otherwise you wouldn't have made that so-called 'assumption.'"

I ignored her and tucked my gun into my waistband.

"Did you bug my hotel room?"

I sighed. Of course, she went there.

"And what if I did?" I raised a brow, tilting my head a little. Althaia's face contorted into a scowl, her cheeks getting flushed.

"How much could you hear?"

I stepped closer to her.

"Everything." I whispered. She didn't know I had planted cameras in her room as well, allowing me to see everything she did, and I had no plans of telling her either.

One night, I was working late in my office, the computer running with live footage of her in the hotel room. I didn't pay much attention since she was in bed, tossing and turning, unable to sleep.

Just as I was finishing the paperwork, I halted in my tracks when a sound caught my attention. I thought I had misheard, but then the sound came again. I looked up, finding her naked with her legs spread, moaning while she played with that pretty pussy of hers.

"Your voice is like a sweet melody to my ears."

"You were listening?!" She hissed.

"Yes." I leaned in to whisper in her ear. "And I fucked my fist to the sound."

Althaia's eyes widened, leaving her momentarily speechless.

"You're such a creep!" She huffed out and walked away from me.

I chuckled and grabbed her arm to stop her.

"We're not done yet."

"You just said it was enough for today?"

"Shooting, yes. Now, you need to learn how to fight." I told her.

"Fine. As long as I don't have to run." She scrunched up her face at the thought.

"You have to if you want to survive. Come." I led her to the middle of the field. "Tell me what you remember."

She listed everything Arianna had taught, and I gave a nod in approval.

"Good. Now, listen carefully to me. Fighting is the absolute last resort for you. I want you to hide, and it's not up for discussion." I stated firmly. "You may have gotten lucky in previous situations, but that will not always be the case. I want you to focus on your surroundings, and if you can hide, then do so until help arrives. Understood?"

Althaia nodded.

"You still need to outsmart your attacker. Tell me, Althaia, if you can't hide and you know you won't stand a chance in a fight, what do you do?" I watched her as her brows slightly furrowed in thought. It didn't take long before she let out a smirk.

"Easy. Seduce him." She said proudly, and I gave her a blank look.

"No." I said immediately.

"Why not?" Althaia stepped closer to me, placing her hands on my chest. "I'm pretty sure it would work." She gave me a seductive look, her hands trailing down, coming dangerously close to my length as she pressed her breasts against me.

"You seem like someone who knows how to touch a woman like me in all the right places." Her sultry voice and innocent gaze tempted me to explore her body.

It was stirring a reaction within me, and all I could think of was all the ways I would make her come.

Those thoughts vanished when pain erupted on the inside of my thigh, causing me to slightly lose my balance. Simultaneously, her fist went flying toward my face. Just before it could connect with my jaw, I blocked it. Turning her around, I twisted her arm behind her back and held her in a loose headlock.

"Nice try." I smirked.

"You have to admit it was good. I almost got you." Althaia laughed. "All men are the same. You can't think once all the blood has rushed down."

"You won't be doing that. Now, show me how you're going to get out of this."

"Easy." She looked at me with a playful grin. "Hey, handsome. Fancy hitting it from the back?" She said, pressing her ass against my dick, rubbing while she bit down on her lip and shooting me a wink.

Fucking hell.

"Focus, Althaia." My voice was strained as I held her tightly around the waist to stop her from rubbing against my cock, which was getting hard. "What do you do?" I repeated.

It didn't take her long before she instinctively turned her head to the side, safeguarding her airway from being cut off. Mentally, I applauded her quick thinking.

Her grip on my arm tightened, fingers finding their place on the inside. She tucked her chin and threw her shoulders into a forceful shrug, creating space between us.

Althaia was doing exceptionally well, especially considering her lack of training.

With one arm still secured behind her back, my curiosity piqued about how she planned to free herself. Then she did something I didn't see coming.

She bit me.

So. Fucking. Hard.

"Shit, Althaia!" I hissed as she continued to bite down hard on my arm.

I tightened my hold around her, testing to see if it would affect her. Instead, it only made her shake her head like a damn dog while still clamped onto my arm.

Althaia took that small window of opportunity when my hold loosened and jabbed her elbow right into my ribs. A grunt escaped me, and she swiftly pulled herself out of my grasp.

"Good job." I praised her with a smile. "I haven't seen anyone get out of a headlock like that."

"Well, I've been choked a few times now. I have a hunch of what to do." She chuckled at her own joke.

I cracked a smile. For some reason, she used humor as a coping mechanism, but if that was what it took for her to deal with it, I was on board.

"Is your arm okay? I didn't mean to bite that hard." Althaia asked with concern, and quickly grabbed my arm to look at it.

"It's fine. Don't worry about it." I reassured her, but a gasp escaped her lips when she looked at the bite mark.

"It's bruising and swelling! We need to get it checked!"

"It's fine, piccola." I repeated, but she remained unsure, taking another look at it. "It's all part of the training. I'll get it cleaned, and it will be fine. Next time, bite harder, and you'll get out faster." I kissed the top of her head, knowing she was feeling guilty.

"Lorenzo has slashed me many times. This is nothing." I added.

"Does it hurt?" Althaia asked, still reluctant to let it go.

"No, it tickles, actually."

She let out a small scoff.

"Wow, Don Damiano is so hardcore." She playfully rolled her eyes. "All right, what's next?"

"I'll teach you a few more moves. First, never keep your body completely upright. Have your legs spread and bend your knees slightly. This way, you won't get thrown to the ground easily..."

I explained everything that would benefit a newbie, and I observed her attentively absorbing the information I was giving.

"...You've got some good strength in you, so remember when you throw a punch, put your weight behind your shoulder for a more impactful strike. And I want you to always keep your jaw clenched. If not, it will easily get broken if you get hit." I finished.

"Okay... That was a lot, but I think I got it." Althaia seemed determined to learn, which was promising. In case something were to happen, she would have a chance of defending herself and reaching safety.

"Good. For this round, you'll spar against Luca and Giovanni." I turned around to look at them and called them over.

"Both of them?!" She exclaimed, almost in horror.

"Yes. I'll be observing to figure out your strengths and weaknesses. Before you start, you need to take off your necklace."

"Good idea. I forgot I was wearing it."

She moved her hair to the side for me to unclasp her necklace. I took hold of the chain, pretending to unclasp it. Instead, I made one quick, sharp pull and broke the chain.

"Sorry, piccola, it broke. The chain must have gotten loose when I held you." I removed the necklace to show it to her.

"Oh, no... I just got it back." Althaia held the necklace in her hands, looking upset about it.

"I'll get it to a jeweler and have it fixed for you." I promised and placed it in my pocket. "Luca and Gio, you're up now."

"Cool. Ready to run?" Luca grinned, and Althaia gave him a disgusted look.

"No thanks. I don't run."

"We'll see about that." He smirked and pulled out his knife.

Ninety-Three

ALTHAIA

"Hold the fuck up!" I shouted as Luca and Giovanni brandished their knives. "Why do you have a knife when I am completely unarmed?"

"You stole fifty thousand from me. I'm here to teach you a lesson." Luca declared, a crazy look in his eyes.

"I won that money fair and square." I managed a nervous laugh.

"No." He advanced, and I shifted my feet, uncertain if he was serious or mocking me.

"Come on, Luca! You can't be serious. Put the knife away." I tried to appear unbothered, but the reality was anything but that.

"No. You played dirty, and I don't like when people play dirty." He gave me a maniacal smile, closing the distance.

My eyes widened as I took several steps back. What the hell was I supposed to do? How could I fight them when they were armed?

I looked at Damiano, finding him observing us with his arms crossed and his expression completely blank. He wasn't going to say anything to save my ass? Was he really going to let them skin me alive?

"Your man can't help. You're on your own." Luca said as he got extremely close.

"Okay, listen -" My eyes went wide when he swung his knife at me. I screamed and ducked to avoid getting slashed in the face. "Are you fucking crazy!" I yelled at him, backing away to create as much space as possible, but he continued to step closer.

"Yes, I am. Now, run." He sprinted towards me, barely giving me time to turn my body around and run.

I raced as fast as my legs would carry me, trying to create as much distance as possible between Luca and myself. I despised running, and I would do anything to avoid it, but you best believe I would definitely run for my life.

Like right now.

I could feel Luca close behind me, urging my legs to go faster. Desperation set in as I frantically scanned the field for anything that could help my escape, but we were in an open field with nowhere to hide!

My lungs were starting to ache, but I kept going, pushing myself to move my legs faster as I tried to think of a plan. I made a sharp turn to throw Luca off, gaining a few seconds of a lead. Just as an idea came to mind, Giovanni appeared in my view, blocking the way to the table with weapons.

Fuck, fuck, fuck.

I completely forgot about Giovanni. At this point, I just wanted to lie down and give up, but I kept running, even though my lungs and legs begged me to stop. I had to think of something fast.

Running around Giovanni wasn't an option; it would only slow me down, and I could almost feel Luca's breath on my neck.

Do anything to survive.

Summoning the last reserves of energy, I sprinted toward Giovanni, who wore a smirk and prepared to grab me. Just as I neared, I threw myself to the ground, sliding between Giovanni's legs.

"What the fuck?"

Swiftly getting back on my feet, and before he could fully turn around to face me, I kicked him.

Right in the crotch.

"Motherfucker!" Giovanni let out a strangled grunt, cupping himself as he bent over.

I kicked the back of his legs, making him fall to his knees. I pushed him and sat on his back to keep him from moving. I grabbed his gun from his waistband and aimed it at Luca.

"Back the fuck up." I said with my heavy breathing as I held the gun shakily from the adrenaline pumping through me. Luca ignored me and took a step closer to grab me.

Then I pulled the trigger and shot right above his head as a warning.

"You could have shot me!" Luca shouted after he threw himself on the ground.

"Then back up! And don't worry, I'm not that good yet." I said tiredly and lowered my arms.

"I know! That's why I said you could have shot me!"

"My fucking balls..." Giovanni groaned underneath me.

"Yeah, Yeah... Oh God, I think I'm going to throw up..." I slid off of Giovanni to lie flat on my back when I felt nauseated. My heart was beating like crazy, and I was seeing stars. It wasn't even nighttime yet.

Damiano blocked my view as he looked down at me.

"I don't know whether to be impressed or to be fucking pissed at you for firing that gun."

"You sent me into battle defenseless. I wasn't about to be cut." I groaned.

"For someone who doesn't run, you're fast. That's good." Luca commented. I glanced at him, seeing he looked completely fine while I felt like dying.

"Why did you have to kick me in the fucking balls?" Giovanni slowly rolled onto his back, wincing as he did so.

"Sorry, I panicked." I got up on my feet. "My legs are trembling, and *not* in a good, mind-blowing, post orgasm kind of way." I complained and slumped against Damiano.

"You can take a break before we continue." Damiano wrapped his arm around me to keep me upright.

"Nope! No way! I'm not training anymore today." I protested.

"I need to ice my balls..." Giovanni winced as Luca helped him up to his feet. "You just wait, Althaia. Next time, I won't go easy on you." He glared at me, his voice filled with promise.

"Agreed. Since you have proven you can think fast under pressure, there is no need to go easy on you now." Luca retorted with a mischievous smile.

"You call that easy? Running after me with a knife?!" I dropped my jaw.

"These are retractable knives." Luca laughed and pushed the 'blade' into the palm of his hand for me to see it was practically a toy.

"I hate you all."

"This was merely to assess how you handle pressure, observe your stamina, and evaluate your ability to think under stress." Damiano explained. I groaned, already dreading what kind of torture awaited me next.

"And here I thought you brought me to Italy for a nice vacation and to meet your family." I muttered grumpily, fatigue washing over me.

"Since you performed better than expected today, you can rest. Luca, Gio, you can have the rest of the day off." Damiano practically ordered, to which they replied with a firm nod and went on their way.

"Carry me, please?" I had no energy left, and my legs wouldn't stop trembling when I tried to stand on my own.

"Next time, we'll start with a small round of laps to avoid your legs trembling after a sprint." Damiano said as he carried me in his arms and walked towards the car.

"Why do you hate me?"

"I don't hate you." He chuckled.

"Then don't make me run." I said in all seriousness.

"It's not avoidable, but I will make it up to you. Anything you desire, just let me know, and consider it done." He vowed.

"Anything?" I asked to be sure.

"Anything, piccola."

I had to bite down on my lip to not let out a smirk as I knew exactly what I wanted.

"Your Bugatti when we get back home."

"No." Damiano scoffed immediately.

"Too late. You said anything I want." I pointed out.

"Anything but that. If you want a diamond necklace, I will get you one. If you want the Maserati, you can have it. But you can't drive my car."

"Ah, but you see, you always say you're a man of your word. Are you not going to honor that?" I said smugly as I watched him scowl at me.

In the Mafia, they held honor in the highest regard and never tolerated any disrespect towards it. That was why I used it against him.

"Just a small ride, I promise!" I said.

"Fine."

"Really?" I asked, surprised he had given in this fast.

"Sure." Damiano smirked, making me squint my eyes at him.

"Why are you smirking?"

"You want to ride my Bugatti? Fine. I will have 'Bugatti' written on my dick so you can ride it." Damiano laughed.

"Oh, fuck." I sighed when I realized my mistake. "I will steal it then."

"Try, and you will see what will happen to you." Damiano placed me on my feet when we were by the car.

"Are you going to spank me?" I mocked.

"No, my love." His low tone sent shivers down my spine. "Something you're not ready for yet, but you will be soon." His thumb went along my jaw as he pushed me up against the car.

"Just the thought of it makes my cock hard." He whispered, pressing his lower body into me so I could feel his excitement in his pants.

"What is it?" I asked, almost breathlessly, when he continued to rub his length against me.

"Are you getting wet at the thought of it?" His hand trailed down my stomach and stopped right between my legs. "The thought of me giving you sweet tortures to your wet pussy?"

My body instinctively responded, and I slightly spread my legs to give him better access. He nibbled my earlobe while applying more pressure, and I let out a small sigh of enjoyment.

Then he stopped.

"Why do you always stop when it starts to get good?!" I huffed in annoyance.

"Payback for teasing me out in the field." Damiano smirked.

I muttered something under my breath and slid into the car with a scowl.

Ninety-Four

Damiano

"How come you want to train me all of a sudden? You didn't seem too happy when Arianna wanted to train me." Althaia asked as we drove.

"I know. Arianna suggested training you after the night of the auction, but I was stubborn, thinking I could always protect you. I had to face the reality that I can't control everything. Training you will make me feel at ease that you know how to defend yourself and stand a chance."

That night in the woods haunted me for weeks. The sight of her lifeless body against mine, the flow of blood between her legs — it all felt too familiar and paralyzed me on the spot.

I feared she wouldn't wake up and die in my arms, just like Sienna did. Clinging tightly to her, I resisted letting go or allowing anyone else near as I shook her awake, but her eyes remained closed. The only thing that kept me somewhat sane was when I felt her pulse.

Althaia's touch on my hand brought me back to reality, making me release my tight grip on the steering wheel. She gave me a warm smile as she pulled my hand to her, caressing it in her lap. It made me feel immediately relaxed.

"Thank you." She whispered gratefully.

"However, it doesn't mean you can do stupid shit just because I've decided to train you." I reminded her.

"How else would I show off my new skills, then?" She grinned.

"Althaia." I warned.

"I'm just kidding." She laughed. "For now."

I glanced at her, seeing her snicker to herself. I let out a sigh and shook my head at her in amusement. She was going to be the death of me.

We drove for a while as I had another surprise for her, and Althaia was already curiously looking out of the window as soon as we drove onto a dirt path.

"Is this your vineyard?" She gasped when she saw the rows of grapevines.

"It is." I said, smiling at her excitement.

The vineyard grounds were a village of its own, boasting a beautiful landscape of nature wherever you looked. Those who lived here were the same people who worked tirelessly to craft the wine into its current exceptional quality, positioning it as one of the most expensive wines on the market.

"This is so beautiful!" Althaia beamed as I parked the car in front of a familiar house.

"Come, I will show you around." I went around and opened the car door for her. At the same time, a short, older woman came out of the house.

"Oh, my heart, I knew it was you!" She gasped when she saw me. "Vico! Vico! Come quick!" She shouted over her shoulder, walking as fast as she could towards me before embracing me in her arms.

"Ciao, Chiarina." I chuckled when she tried to squeeze me harder with her short frame.

"Ay, Chiarina, what are you shouting for?" Vico came out of the house with his eyes narrowed before they went wide when he spotted me. "Dio mio, Damiano!"

"Ciao, Vico. How have you been?" I chuckled when he slapped my back during our embrace.

"Oh no, we haven't seen you in months. We're curious about how you've been." Chiarina half-scolded, placing her hands on her hips.

"My apologies. It wasn't my intention. I've been good. Great, actually." I turned around and noticed Althaia with a smile on her face as she observed everything.

"Who's the young lady?" Vico asked. I extended my hand to Althaia, and she placed hers in mine, coming to stand next to me.

"Vico, Chiarina, this is Althaia, my love. Althaia, meet Vico and Chiarina Mancini."

"Buonasera, Mr. and Mrs. Mancini." Althaia greeted. Both Vico and Chiarina were momentarily baffled, staring at Althaia as if she were not real.

"Finally!" They both exclaimed simultaneously and pushed me aside to welcome her.

I shook my head with a bemused smile as they gathered around her, holding her hands and showering her with endless compliments. Althaia smiled shyly at them, and a blush crept onto her face.

"Can I get my woman back, please?" I stepped in to rescue her from being overwhelmed. Vico and Chiarina might be older, but their energy rivaled that of kids on a sugar high.

"Well done, son!" Vico slapped my back again, his grin widening.

"Beautiful, dear!" Chiarina pinched Althaia's cheeks.

"I know." I smiled. I gently took her by the waist, coming to her rescue. Otherwise, they wouldn't let her go.

"Come inside! Let me cook you dinner. Look how skinny you are! Ay, Damiano." Chiarina's forehead creased as she gave me a disapproving look. I couldn't help but laugh at being called skinny.

"Another time, Chiarina. I just wanted to check up on you and show Althaia around for a bit."

"Don't make us wait for months to see you again, understood?!" Vico added.

"I promise."

They nodded approvingly before bidding us farewell. I led Althaia in the direction of the grapevines to give her a tour.

"They seem like lovely people." She chuckled.

"They are. I've known them since I was a kid. They've been working for the family for over thirty years and practically helped raise us." I explained.

Vico and Chiarina had always been in the picture for as long as I could remember. They were loyal and pure-hearted people, essentially part of the family. When I took over, I made sure to check in on them regularly. It was the least I could do for their hard work and loyalty.

"The way their faces lit up when they saw you, it's clear they love you." Althaia looked touched. "So typical of grandparents to scold you for not eating enough." Althaia laughed.

"I apparently need to spend more time in the gym."

"Are you insane? Are those muscles not enough for you? You already have an impressive body!" She exclaimed, her eyes tracing down my physique.

"She called me skinny. In other words, she called me small." I pointed out, making her scoff.

"Please, there is nothing small about you - oh, zip it." She said when I smirked.

We ascended a small hill, coming to a stop at the top to give her the best view of the vineyard landscape.

"This is amazing. It looks like something straight out of a painting." Althaia's eyes sparkled with admiration, and I found myself captivated as she beheld the landscape in awe.

The setting sun painted her face with a soft, golden hue, and in that moment, her eyes shimmered with a radiant light. Her gaze wandered over the endless rows of grapes, reaching as far as the eye could see, with charming houses scattered across the land. In that tranquil scene, she was the one who stole my breath.

"Among all my achievements, this is the one that fills me with the greatest sense of pride, and it wouldn't have happened without the hard work of Vico and Chiarina. Their dedication makes sure that everything is meticulously crafted to perfection." I shared and told her more about the process of winemaking, watching her absorb every piece of information.

"Italy was among the countries that were hit the hardest by the economic crisis, resulting in a significant rise in unemployment. You were right about vineyards favoring technology over manpower. I wanted to change that; to help improve the economy by creating jobs for the community. Before I knew it, we had to expand. Do you see all these houses present? People loved the job, the bond, and the community so much that we had to build houses for them to stay close to what they love doing."

"I can hear the pride in your voice." Althaia said, her mouth curving into a smile as she wrapped her arms around my waist.

"I'm proud to be able to give something back to my people." I replied, caressing her hair as she looked at me with her beautiful green eyes.

"You're a good man for caring about your people. Many who possess power like you wouldn't even have cared."

"I'm far from a good man." I admitted quietly. I have done unimaginable things to people. I still do.

"I strongly disagree. Look what you have created!" She gestured to the vineyards. "This wouldn't have happened without you. You have built an entire village for people who love working for you. You are a good man with a good heart, and I love you for it." She smiled, stepped on her toes, and kissed me with her soft lips.

"And I love you." I whispered against her lips.

"We're spending the night here. Just the two of us." I said as I parked in front of a mansion.

"Is this your way of rebelling against Nonna?" She teased with a chuckle.

"I won't spend one more night without you in my arms. If I can't do that under her roof, then I'll just find another roof." I replied as I led her inside and upstairs to the master bedroom. "Everything you need is here. Also, I've got the hot tub ready for you to ease your soreness after today's training."

"God, I love you!" Althaia grabbed my hand and pulled me with her to the bathroom where the hot tub was.

After a quick rinse in the shower, she let out a sigh as she lowered her body into the hot water. I settled into the hot tub behind her, the jet streams creating a pleasurable massage-like effect.

"Just what I needed after you made me run today." Althaia sighed in bliss and closed her eyes.

"I'll have the hot tub ready again tomorrow after your training."

"I'm going to pretend I didn't hear you."

I chuckled as her body completely relaxed against me, massaging her shoulders to ease the tension.

"That feels nice." Althaia moaned quietly as my hands wandered her body.

I kissed her shoulder, trailing up to the side of her neck, and lightly sucked her skin. My cock was getting hard as I touched her breasts before sliding a hand down her stomach to between her thighs.

"Piccola?" I called after her quietly as her breathing got heavy.

Is she serious right now?

"Of course, you fell asleep." I sighed before letting out a small laugh as I shook my head. "I guess that's my punishment for making you run."

I had to adjust my length, which was painfully pressed against her back, and waited for it to die down.

I closed the door behind me to the office after I had put Althaia into bed. She didn't wake up once and was completely knocked out.

I sank into the chair behind the desk, and I pulled out the necklace to scrutinize it. My eyes narrowed, suspicion gnawing at me as I held the heirloom under the light. My gaze penetrated its every detail, searching for the elusive mystery that hid beneath the surface.

And there it was.

I opened the drawer to retrieve a magnet. Placing it near the pendant, I disrupted any concealed signals and brought the pendant down onto the desk, shattering it into pieces.

"Fucking bastard." I clicked my tongue. The real pendant had been swapped out with a fake one, crafted from glass, with a small, concealed device.

Leaning back in my seat, I examined it closely. It wasn't a tracking device, but a microphone. This discovery could only mean one thing, and it complicated matters even further.

I grabbed my phone when it rang.

"Antonio."

"She's awake."

"Good. And?"

"She's suffering from memory loss at the moment."

"I need her clear when I get back."

"We'll do whatever it takes to make her remember." He assured me.

I nodded, twiddling the microphone between my fingers.

"And one more thing." I said, squeezing the microphone until it snapped in half. "I need you to prepare *every single one* of my men and get everything ready. When I return, there will be war."

"Understood."

I ended the call and swept the shattered fragments of glass off the desk. Retrieving the small box concealed in the drawer, checking it one more time.

For her, I'm going to burn the world.

Slipping the box into my pocket, I left the office, making my way toward the bedroom where she was peacefully asleep.

Ninety-Five

ALTHAIA

"Damiano?" I called out his name when I found the space next to me empty. I didn't get a response, so I called out his name again and listened for any movements, but the entire place was quiet.

I switched on the lamp on the nightstand next to me, seeing a note attached to it.

Come find me.
D.

I smiled at the note and went to the bathroom to wash my face and brush my teeth. Once done, I headed to the walk-in closet to find something to wear, but to my surprise, I found another note attached to a hanger.

I grabbed the note, loving this playful side of him.

Let me see you in this, piccola.

Even when he wasn't around, he could make my heart flutter with just written words.

I dressed in the attire he had chosen and took a glance in the mirror. The outfit was a vibrant red, captivating two-piece with a mesh mini skirt. It had an off-shoulder crop top adorned with charming, ruffled sleeves and a cute front lace-up.

Of course, he would pick this color. It was his favorite color on me.

As I made my way downstairs, the place was dimly lit, but Damiano was still nowhere to be found. I looked for him until I found another note on the door.

Good girl. Now, follow the pathway.
Your Villain.

I bit down on my lip. Even through his writing, he had a way of making me blush.

Wait a minute.

"I will bite your dick if this is a test." I called out in case he was hiding to see if I was able to follow orders. Everything was still and quiet. After deciding he wasn't inside the house, I stepped outside.

Sicily was unusually hot this time of the year, but right now, the temperature was perfect as I breathed in the fresh air as I followed the pathway.

It was graced with in-ground lights, creating a magical nocturnal scene. The soft illumination gently traced the route, revealing the rustic beauty of the vineyard. Rows of grapevines were subtly lit, casting shadows that danced in the darkness. This place was stunningly beautiful, even when darkness fell and the night came alive with twinkling lights.

I let out a groan when the pathway turned into a hill, and my legs were sore from running earlier.

"God, you really hate me today; first running and now climbing a hill?" I complained to myself, but stopped when I found a single rose in the middle of the way with a note attached.

You're almost there, amore mio.
Your Devil.

My heart warmed at the sight of rose petals that now covered the entire path, their delicate fragrance mingling with the night air. It had me smiling big and excited about what was awaiting me.

As I neared the summit of the hill, the warm glow at the top became more apparent. When I finally reached the peak, a small gasp escaped my lips at the breathtaking sight before me.

Lanterns hanging from the large tree cast a warm tone over the area, and beneath the tree, blankets and pillows were cozily arranged, accompanied by delectable food and drinks.

And there, at the end, stood Damiano with his back facing me.

He turned around, and the warm glow from the lanterns accentuated the golden hue of his eyes. His gentle gaze and smile had a way of making my heart skip a beat, no matter how many times I saw it.

"You made it." Damiano approached me with both a massive smile and equally massive bouquet of red roses. "You look beautiful as ever, my love."

His eyes traced down my body before he leaned in, planting a sweet kiss that sent tingles throughout my entire being.

I was left speechless.

"What is all of this?" I asked. For some reason, my heart was pounding faster.

"A date. I never took you out on a proper date, and this is me trying to make up for it. Do you like it?" He asked.

"I absolutely love it!" I couldn't help but gaze around, appreciating all the thoughtful details he had arranged for our date. "Thank you so much!" I exclaimed with excitement, eliciting a smile from him as I leaned in for one more kiss.

"Come, you must be hungry." Damiano held my hand, leading me to the large fuzzy blankets.

"Oh, I'm starving!"

"You will love this one." Damiano poured us a glass of red wine. "To you." He said and clinked our glasses together.

"To us." I corrected him with a smile. "For being bad bitches and outliving our enemies."

Damiano threw his head back and let out a hearty laugh, completely taken aback by my words. My cheeks were hurting from smiling so much. I loved the sound of his laughter; so deep and carefree.

"Salute, for being called a bad bitch for the very first time in my life." Damiano chuckled as he raised his glass.

"There is a first for everything." I laughed and raised my glass in agreement.

"Indeed, there is." He said, his eyes twinkling with amusement.

"Oh, wow! This is good." I exclaimed after sipping the wine.

"I knew you would love it. This is one of the sweeter wines we produce."

"I would love to know how you make this one; it tastes almost like juice."

"You will. Mr. Roberts is coming to visit. He wants to witness with his own two eyes the place you have talked so highly about. If all goes well, he will be making a much larger purchase, and you will receive fifty percent of that."

"What? No!" I almost shouted at him.

"Yes. You made it happen." Damiano insisted.

"I didn't even know what I was talking about back then." I tried to explain to him, but he only gave a half-shrug.

"It doesn't matter."

"It does! Look at what you've accomplished. You've not only created jobs for all these people, but made a community. They all have a roof over their heads. This is all your doing." I gestured to the beautiful landscape. The view from the top of the hill was breathtaking, with the lights from the houses below sparkling like stars in the night sky.

"I am well aware of it, my love. It still doesn't change the fact that you gave him a different perspective." He said as if it wasn't up to discussion.

I slightly frowned before an idea came to mind.

"Okay." I agreed. "Then I want to invest the money in this place, and whatever money that will be made from that, I want to reinvest. Then use the money to create more jobs and housing for the people."

These amazing, hard working people have transformed this place into what it was today. They deserved everything.

"I had a feeling you would say that." Damiano said with a soft smile. "Will that make you happy, my love?"

"Without a doubt. Yes!"

"Then so be it." Damiano cupped my chin, tilting it upwards before pressing his lips to mine.

This night was unforgettable.

My heart overflowed with emotions, and words failed to capture the depth of my feelings at this moment. Being with the man I loved and talking about everything and nothing at the same time.

Damiano rested his head on my lap as I fed him chocolate-covered strawberries. He shared more about his family and upbringing in Italy, and I loved how big of a family he came from.

"Thank you for bringing me here. This place is like something out of a fairytale." I stood by the hill's edge, with Damiano's arms embracing me from behind. The landscape unfolded before me, and the night sky adorned itself with a myriad of stars.

"Anything for you." He whispered, planting a gentle kiss on the side of my head, and I sighed in bliss.

This night couldn't have been more perfect.

"Are you happy, my love?" Damiano asked.

"I don't think 'happy' will ever capture this feeling." I replied with a smile. "And what about you? Are you happy, agápi mou?"

A hush settled over us as Damiano released his arms from around me. I turned, wondering why he had gone quiet, only for my heart to thump faster.

There, before me, Damiano knelt on one knee, a box clasped in his hands. His eyes, brimming with an abundance of affection, met mine.

The world stood still, encapsulated by this moment.

Ninety-Six

ALTHAIA

Damiano's beautiful smile illuminated his face, his golden-brown eyes sparkling with boundless affection.

"Althaia, your presence in my life has touched me on a level that words alone cannot capture. It's more than you may ever realize. The first time I saw you, you took my breath away. You were the most beautiful woman I had ever seen, and that sentiment hasn't changed; every time I look at you, I'm captivated and hypnotized by your beautiful green eyes."

Tears welled up in my eyes. I was stunned and speechless, hardly able to believe that this was happening.

"You, my love, are and forever will be the most enchanting woman my eyes have laid upon. You, my love, are the fire who warms the coldest corners of my soul. You, my love, are the very heartbeat of my soul, the melody in every breath I take. Althaia, will you marry me?"

My heart raced uncontrollably, and tears streamed down my face.

There was no one else I would rather be with.

There was no one else I would choose to share my life with.

He showed me the true essence of love, and in his arms, I found my place where I truly belonged.

"Yes..." I breathed out in a whisper. "Yes, yes, yes!" I exclaimed, leaping forward and wrapping my arms around his neck. Damiano, caught off guard, laughed as we tumbled, with me ending up on top of him.

I looked into his alluring golden-brown eyes as I placed my hands on either side of his face, gently caressing his stubbly cheeks.

"You will marry me, piccola?" He asked once more.

"Of course, I will marry you. I don't want to spend my life with anyone else but you." I whispered.

Damiano responded with a breathtaking smile, placing a hand behind my neck until our lips met in a kiss that made my heart flutter and my body tingle.

THE DEVIL'S FIRE

The way his lips met mine was a symphony of sweetness and passion, an intensity that lifted me higher and higher, as if I were soaring through the air with the hum of the world around us. In his arms, I held him closer, surrendering completely to the perfection of this moment, melting into the embrace that felt like an exquisite dance of souls.

"I love you. Words alone can never express just how much." I told him, struggling to hold back tears.

"And I love you, my Althaia." The softness in his eyes, brimming with affection, brought fresh tears to my eyes. "Don't cry." Damiano chuckled, sitting up with me straddling his lap.

"I can't help it. It's more than anything I could ever imagine." I half-sobbed.

The moment felt like a magical dream; one I wish to never wake up from.

"I thought I would step up my game, and at least make sure you were dressed when I asked. Unlike last time." He said, a playful glint in his eyes, earning a laugh from me.

"You did well." I replied, sealing my words with a small, tender kiss.

"Here, let me see it on you." Damiano reached for the ring box and opened it. My eyes widened in awe as I saw the extraordinary, yet exquisitely beautiful oval-shaped cushion diamond ring.

The centerpiece, an immense diamond, possessed a captivating brilliance that seemed to dance with the play of light; the band was adorned with a delicate row of meticulously set tiny diamonds, forming a sparkling halo.

Its breathtaking beauty left me speechless, and under the gentle glow of the lantern lights, the ring took on a truly magnificent allure.

"Damiano." I gasped.

"Do you like it? I selected each diamond and had it handcrafted."

"You designed this ring?"

"I did, but if you don't like it, that's okay. We can find something else." He said it casually, as if the considerable investment, time, and thoughtfulness he put into it weren't a concern.

"This is the most gorgeous ring I have ever seen! But Damiano, I would have been happy with any ring. You didn't have to get me a diamond this big." I expressed.

"Don't be ridiculous, piccola. I need people from a mile away to see you're taken." Damiano said firmly, without a hint of a joke.

"Oh, you made sure of that big time." I chuckled.

Damiano took my hand and slid the ring onto my finger, taking his time to admire it.

"Beautiful." He smiled before placing a tender kiss on the back of my ring finger, as if he was sealing the ring in place with his lips.

"I can't believe this is happening." I wrapped my arms around his neck as he pulled me closer to his body. Resting my head against his, I closed my eyes, savoring this moment. My heart was warm and excited about this new chapter of our lives.

Together.

"Soon you will belong to me in every way." Damiano whispered, his lips brushing against mine.

Our lips sealed in an embrace as my fingers moved skillfully, undoing the buttons on his shirt one by one until it slid off his shoulders. I felt a subtle shiver under my touch as my hands explored his muscular body. The reciprocity of desire between us was a beautiful dance; one where he had a bewitching effect on me, just as I did on him.

The moonlight bathed us in its ethereal glow as our clothes slowly disappeared, one by one.

"Look how beautiful you are." Damiano whispered, the softness in his eyes mirrored by the gentle trail of his fingers; from my jaw, down the valley between my breasts, and lingering between my thighs.

His lips closed around my nipple, his tongue swirling and sucking hard as he created a cocktail of pain and pleasure. He pushed the tip of his finger inside my pussy, caressing along the slit to feel my arousal.

"Damiano." I moaned softly when he gently circled my clit. My soft moans were captured by him as he slid two fingers inside, his thrusting and curling motion making me gasp.

"Let me make you feel good." I breathed out and pushed him to lie flat on the blanket.

I gripped his thick cock in my hand, darting my tongue across the tip and tasting his pre-cum.

"Fuck, baby." Damiano let out a long breath as I took him in my mouth. I hummed, feeling my arousal drip down my thighs as I watched the way his eyes closed in pleasure.

I slowed down, replacing my mouth with my hand, knowing it would make him crazy.

"I need to feel you." He growled impatiently, thrusting his hips to make me go faster.

"Yeah?" I bit my lip as I positioned myself on top of him, slowly grinding along his length. The way it stimulated my clit caused me to let out a moan, while he responded with a groan and a tight grip on my ass.

"Fuck, piccola! Don't be a fucking tease." Damiano delivered a sharp slap to my ass, and a small cry escaped my lips from the searing pain that he rubbed away with his palm. "That's what you fucking get."

"So impatient." I grinned.

His fingers dug into my ass until I finally slid down onto his cock that spread my walls so perfectly, it made me close my eyes and let out a sigh of pure bliss.

"You feel so good..." I panted as I moved back and forth, riding him and feeling all of him in this position. Damiano was grunting underneath me, muttering about how tight my pussy was around his cock.

Slowing down, I opened my eyes and leaned in, feeling the warmth of his lips against mine as I planted a gentle kiss.

"Damiano?"

"Yes, my love?"

I gazed into his eyes while gently running my fingers through his soft hair, my heart thumping with the weight of my next words.

"Let's make a baby." I held my breath as his golden-brown eyes looked deeply into mine.

"Are you sure?" Damiano asked softly, his hold tightening around me.

"Yes." I replied, with no trace of hesitation. "Let's start a family, my love."

He suddenly moved, laying me on the blanket as he hovered over me, and I wrapped my legs around him.

"Then let's make a baby." Damiano's eyes lit up before he claimed my lips and wildly thrust himself inside of me, making me gasp against his lips.

The way he pounded with a savage strength as I clung onto him, crying out in pleasure while he kept calling out my name like a prayer, was unlike anything before. I was close, my pussy clenching around his cock, and he pushed me over the edge when he rubbed my clit with his thumb.

I screamed out his name, my eyes rolling back as waves of pleasure washed over me.

"Althaia." Damiano growled out, thrusting one last time until I felt his cum filling me up.

We lay still for a moment, catching our breath as our eyes locked. Then, a devilish smirk spread across his lips, and a swirl of lust danced in his eyes.

"It's far from over, piccola. We have a baby to make."

"Hey, guys!" I greeted Luca and Giovanni in a joyful tone with a big smile.

Damiano wouldn't let me skip training, but it was okay since I was in too good of a mood to actually complain about it.

"Someone's a little too happy about getting her ass kicked today." Giovanni commented with a smirk as he crossed his arms.

"I came prepared today. Better watch out or I might just accidentally cut your face." I retorted.

"With what? Your nails?" He teased with a smug grin.

"No, with this." I grinned as I held my hand out for them to see my engagement ring.

"It will definitely be a clean cut." Luca whistled. "Congratulations! I'm happy for you." He embraced me tightly in his arms before turning to Damiano.

"And when can I expect you to propose to my cousin?" Damiano asked with his arms crossed and gave a scrutinizing look.

"I'm working on it." Luca replied and scratched the back of his head.

"Shit, that's huge." Giovanni's voice had me looking at him. He looked impressed at the size of the diamond before a smile slowly appeared on his lips.

"Congratulations." He took me by surprise when he half wrapped an arm around me in an attempt of a hug.

"Awh, look at you caring for me!" I laughed. I just had to tease him with it.

"I'm being polite." Giovanni retorted, and I rolled my eyes at him for still trying to deny it.

"Are you ready, piccola?" Damiano asked. I gave a nod, taking my ring off to keep it safe.

Damiano refreshed my memory from yesterday's training and then taught me a few more skills. Once I was confident with it, I had to face Giovanni, who was moving his neck from side to side.

"I'm not going easy on you." He smirked.

"I don't expect you to. Better watch out I don't scratch your stupid face." I snickered.

My smug smile was quickly wiped away when Giovanni moved faster than I could ever comprehend, and he slammed me down to the ground like a ragdoll, knocking all air out of me.

"That's for kicking me in the balls."

Ninety-Seven

ALTHAIA

"I thought you got kidnapped! I was about to send out a search party!" Cara scolded me with a frown as I watched her all cuddled up in bed while we were FaceTiming.

I was by the pool, sunbathing and sipping my iced coffee when I gave her a call, but I had forgotten about the time zone and accidentally woke her up.

"I didn't even know he was taking me to Italy to meet his family. He made it a surprise." I tried to explain to her.

"You could have sent a text or something." She continued to sulk.

"I know, I'm sorry. I've been kind of busy these days."

"Oh, yeah, I can see you're *so* busy looking fucking hot while sunbathing in Italy." Her sarcasm had me giving her a blank look. "Busy fucking Damiano all day?"

"That too." I winked before we burst out laughing. "I've been getting my ass kicked. Damiano has been training me, and Giovanni and Luca showed me absolutely no mercy! This is the first time in days I'm getting a break." I said in relief.

"Well, at least you're getting better." Cara offered as a comfort.

"True."

"Did you meet their father yet?" She smirked.

I let out a scoff in response.

"Let me guess, he tested you?" She chuckled.

"He offered me money to leave Damiano." I rolled my eyes, but I wasn't pissed about it anymore.

"How much did he offer you?"

"A ridiculous amount of twenty million dollars."

"What the hell? Why the fuck was I only offered five?" Cara exclaimed, clearly offended.

"That's still a lot, Cara." I chuckled at her reaction. "I'm interested to know what you did when he asked you."

"I grabbed the check, stuffed it in my bra and said, 'thank you, now I have your money and Lorenzo's money to shop with, then left." She grinned, looking proud of herself.

"Maybe that's why he 'only' offered five million to you, knowing you would take it." I laughed as I tucked a strand of hair behind my ear.

"Wait, what the fuck is that?" Cara pressed her face against the camera.

"What? Oh, this?" I smirked and showed her my enormous engagement ring.

"He proposed?!" She gasped and then screamed in joy when I confirmed with a nod and gigantic smile. "Shit, that ring is gorgeous! And huge! Look, Lorenzo." She rolled to the other side of the bed, and Lorenzo came into view as he looked at the screen.

"He was there the whole time?" I asked, mortified.

"Uh, yeah? Where else would he be?" She gave me a 'duh' look. My cheeks heated in embarrassment that he had heard our unfiltered conversation.

"Hello to you too, Althaia. Sorry to disappoint you with my presence." Lorenzo looked amused, and I let out an awkward laugh.

"I didn't mean it like that."

"I see he finally proposed to you." He remarked, eyeing my ring. "Of course, that bastard would get you a diamond that big."

"You could learn something from him." Cara teased, struggling to contain her laughter when he turned to her with a blank look.

"Is that ring on your finger not big enough for you?" Lorenzo raised a brow, and she gave an innocent shrug.

"Anyway, congratulations, Thaia! I'm so happy for you!" Her entire face lit up with happiness.

"Congratulations, Althaia. Tell my brother he's a dickhead." Lorenzo added.

I laughed and bid them goodnight so I wouldn't disturb them any longer.

Damiano came out in his swim trunks, and my eyes drank in every inch of him before he dove into the water. I sat on the pool's edge as he swam towards me.

"There's my handsome husband." I smiled.

"How's my beautiful wife?" Damiano asked as he drew me into the pool with him.

"She's never been better." I replied, pressing my lips against his, relishing in the fact that I could now call him my husband.

We signed the marriage certificate and had a small, private ceremony at the local town hall the day after he proposed. I have been on cloud nine ever since. Damiano's family was thrilled about the engagement news, but we have kept the marriage a secret from everyone except my bodyguards. We just wanted to enjoy our new titles as husband and wife to ourselves for now.

"Did you talk to Cara?"

"I did. She's happy for us. Also, Lorenzo wanted me to say you're a dickhead for getting me a diamond this big."

"Because I always do better than him." Damiano smirked.

"My God, how big is your ego?" I laughed.

"Almost as big as my dick."

"So, micro?" I teased.

Damiano let out a laugh, but not a humorous one; it was a laughter tinged with promise, his eyes growing darker with a look that suggested I should pray for what awaited me.

"Is that how you want to play, piccola?" He pressed my back against the pool's edge, and my breath quickened when I felt his length getting hard, which was anything but micro. "Seems like you need to be taught a lesson."

"I like it when you do." I smirked as excitement rushed over me and my legs tightened around him when he undid my bikini top. My nipples were already hard, but whether it was because of the water or him wasn't clear. All I knew was that I wanted his mouth on me.

Damiano placed me on my feet on the stairs, pulling my arms behind my back and tied them with my bikini top. His pupils dilated, drawing me in with an unmistakable desire and hunger. It was as if the very essence of passion had taken residence in his gaze, leaving no doubt that his emotions were ignited with an overwhelming sense of lust.

He sat me down at the top of the stairs while he stood with his legs on either side of me.

"I won't be nice." Damiano promised.

"I don't want you to be nice." I said in a breathless whisper. He let out a devilish smirk as he freed his cock from his swimming trunks. I licked my lips, a surge of lust making my mouth water.

I let out a surprised gasp when he grabbed a fistful of my hair, yanking my head back to meet his eyes.

"Then be my good little wife and open your smart-assed mouth nice and wide for your husband." His voice held a deep tone of command. When I didn't open my mouth fast enough to his liking, he smacked his cock across my cheek. "Open your mouth, piccola." Damiano growled at me, and I dropped my jaw in shock.

Before I could even say anything, he shoved his dick right into my mouth, not giving me time to even brace myself. He hissed as he kept my head steady by my hair, pushing in deeper so much that I was gagging.

Damiano pulled out to let me breathe, but it was only for a second before he shoved himself in again.

"Fucking hell, baby, you're so fucking pretty when your mouth is full of my cock." He groaned as he thrust his hips against me. Tears sprung to my eyes, and the only thing that escaped me were gagging and slurping sounds, and fuck, I loved it.

I inhaled sharply when Damiano pulled out, and he looked at me with a sinister expression, still gripping my hair tightly while he stroked his length.

"You sound the best when you're gagging on my cock."

"More like choking." I almost wheezed out, trying to catch my breath.

Damiano gripped my throat, forcing me on my feet as he leaned in close.

"Wouldn't be able to do that with a micro, no?" He let out a low chuckle, not letting me respond before he had me bent over the edge of the pool.

"Damiano!" I let out a cry as he thrust his hard length inside me with a single, powerful motion.

"Louder." He growled, the sound vibrating through me as his hand made contact on my ass with a sharp slap. The sensation made me gasp, but it only fueled his intense rhythm of pounding into me.

I closed my eyes tightly, completely overwhelmed by the feeling of him engulfing all of my senses.

"Open your eyes, wife. Look how I'm fucking you." Damiano wrapped his hand around my throat, pulling me up against his chest to make me look in the window's reflection.

His devilish grin accentuated the shadows in his eyes. His gaze, consumed by an insatiable lust, held an intensity that seemed to penetrate the very essence of desire.

My entire body trembled as I whimpered under his mercy, and he only seemed to revel in it.

"Come for me, wife. Let me hear you fucking scream." Damiano grunted in my ear.

The quick, intense slap on my clit sent waves of pleasure coursing through me, having me undone in a scream of his name.

"I must admit, it is some exceptional wine." Mr. Roberts complimented, and I bit back a smile in excitement.

Chiarina and Vico gave us a tour of the vineyards when Mr. Roberts arrived, and they did an outstanding job. I found it all incredibly intriguing, and my fascination deepened as they walked us through the process of measuring sugar, acid, and tannin levels to shape the style of wine they aim to produce.

"However, I'm not sure if I like the wine bottles. They are a little dull to my taste." He added and looked at the bottles.

Damiano and I shared a look, and I mentally sighed. Mr. Roberts has been trying to drive the price down by finding any kind of excuse, and I found it hilarious how Damiano pretended not to hear him by checking his watch every time he made such comments. It was obvious Mr. Roberts wanted the products; he just didn't want to pay the full price.

"Can I ask what you prefer, Mr. Roberts?" I asked.

"Well, I have several exclusive high-end restaurants that are beautifully and lavishly decorated. I want something that needs to represent that as well as I'm also selling a lifestyle." He said as he swirled the wine around in his glass.

I gave a slight nod and studied him, looking at the way he was dressed and the rings on his fingers. It looked like he and his wife were big fans of jewelry and preferably something that sparkled.

"Can I please have a pen and paper?" I asked Chiarina, which she immediately got for me. I thanked her as I grabbed the notebook and started to draw the ideas I had in mind.

Mr. Roberts took a step closer to see what I was doing when I moved the pen around in quick strokes.

"How about something like this?" I showed him the quick sketch I had made.

"I'm listening."

"Imagine the wine bottles fully covered in any color you desire—gold, silver, or black, each with a shiny finish." I paused, carefully observing his expression, and it seemed my words had captured his attention.

"I assume your restaurants have a dimly lit ambiance, which is ideal. You can create a stunning display with these bottles and illuminate them with spotlights. Picture it; a wall adorned with beautiful gifts, sparkling brightly to captivate your customers." I had to restrain a smirk as I noticed his brows subtly rise at the mention of the word 'sparkle.'

"You can even ensure that the wine is sold exclusively in bottles, and customers are allowed to take the whole bottle home. The label won't be a traditional paper wrap; instead, it'll feature an engraving with not only Mr. Bellavia's brand name but also the name of your restaurant. It will be a one-of-a-kind design that benefits both parties, as customers become walking advertisements for both of you." I presented all the details of the new bottle design, keeping his interest by explaining its benefits for both businesses.

I finished with a smile, but Mr. Roberts was now slightly frowning as he stared at the drawing I had made.

He was quiet for a long time, and I wondered if I had screwed up with this idea of mine. Nervousness started to creep in, and I glanced at Damiano, who was also studying the drawing with his head tilted slightly to the side. His blank expression left me unsure of his thoughts on the idea. In that moment, I realized I should have asked if it was acceptable for me to even pitch such a proposal.

Mr. Roberts surprised me with a chuckle and a shake of his head as he looked at Damiano teasingly.

"I see why you brought her along. She's making me spend money."

"Well, it is money well spent, in my opinion." I grinned, feeling relieved. "You're not just getting exceptional wine; you're also contributing to building a community here." I gestured to the beautiful landscape and the people working with high spirits.

"You are helping create jobs and housing for people who have lost everything but found a second chance here. To me, that is more than enough reason to make a deal." I smiled, my heart warming by the story behind Damiano's vineyards.

"Good thing you kept her around. She deserves that ring on her finger." Mr. Roberts gave Damiano's shoulder a friendly pat. "I would like to have a few words with your workers, and then we'll talk numbers." He didn't wait for a reply as he headed toward the first worker he saw, wineglass still in hand.

"Good job, cara mia." Chiarina exclaimed excitedly before she and Vico followed Mr. Roberts.

"Living up to your name again, Althaia, one who cares. You landed me yet another deal." He winked with a smirk as he wrapped an arm around my waist.

"You're giving me too much credit when this place speaks for itself."

"Your idea is great. It will make his ass feel special."

"I thought so. That's why I said it would be a one-of-a-kind design only for him." I snickered, and he looked amused.

"That's my girl." Damiano said proudly and kissed the top of my head, having me slightly blush at his words.

"I should probably get going now since you're going to talk numbers." I checked the time on the watch around his wrist.

"My mother is waiting for you. She will give me another earful if I keep you any longer. Luca and Giovanni are here to take you." He said, just as I heard them pull up.

Damiano's mother had been scolding him through the phone that he was keeping me all to himself. She then invited me to go out with her to shop since I still had to find a dress for Cara's wedding.

"And this is yours from now on. It's our shared account." He added, pulling out a black card.

I immediately shook my head.

"No."

"You can't fight me on this one, baby."

"I don't like spending your money."

Damiano let out a small sigh and cupped my face with his hand, squeezing my cheeks together as his face came closer to mine.

"We are married. You are *my wife*. It's *our* money, understood?"

"Okay." I gave in but had no intention of using it.

"If you don't use it, there will be punishments." He stated firmly. My brows went up, now intrigued. "I will make you run."

"Diavolo!" I gasped, and the look on his face showed me he was serious about it. "Fine, I'll use it." I said in defeat, and he let out a satisfied smile.

"Good. I will see you later, Mrs. Bellavia." Damiano whispered and placed a small kiss on my lips.

He opened the car door for me and gave my ass a playful smack before I slid inside. I shot him a mischievous wink before the car rolled.

"Jesus, and here I thought he couldn't be more obsessed with you. Turns out I was wrong now that you're married." Giovanni commented.

"I honestly thought we would never see him get married." Luca added.

"I still can't believe we're married." I chuckled, loving that I now could call Damiano my husband; something I once feared wouldn't happen.

I shifted to the middle of the backseat, poking my head out between the headrests with a teasing smile.

"So, what's your excuse for not having proposed to Cecilia yet?" I asked Luca.

"Well, she made it clear she didn't want to get married before we even started to date."

"Oh, makes sense then."

"But lately, she has been subtly talking about marriage, and I guess she has changed her mind." He shrugged.

"You're going to propose, then?" I asked excitedly.

"I have the ring ready." He smiled and I let out a squeal of happiness for him.

I took a look at Giovanni, who had been quiet and very focused on his phone.

"Hopefully, you can too, whenever your girlfriend Laila is ready for you." I teased him.

"Yeah." Giovanni said, then immediately looked at me and straightened up in his seat. "I mean, she's not my girlfriend." He tried to cover up as he scowled.

"Oh, shut it! You're totally a thing! You keep texting each other."

"He called her last night, and they talked for hours." Luca spilled the beans, sending a smirk Giovanni's way.

"Ohhh!" I gave him a playful wink.

"Both of you, shut up." Giovanni said grumpily, making us laugh and continue to tease him. One thing for sure didn't go unnoticed was how his ears turned red.

He was crushing so hard on Laila.

My teasing came to an end as we arrived at the shopping center.

Its roof was a masterpiece, composed of two intersecting glass-vaulted arcades forming a stunning octagon with a burst of captivating colors. While Italy was known for its beautiful architecture, this particular structure stood out as truly magnificent.

I spotted Eleonora and her assigned bodyguards. It was the same two men who were present when Riccardo tested me.

"There she is, la mia bellissima nuora." Eleonora greeted me with her usual warm smile as she opened her arms and embraced me. "How are you, honey? Is my son taking good care of you?"

"Never been better." I smiled. "He's always taking good care of me." I chuckled as she gave an approving nod.

"Good! If he doesn't, you send him my way, and I will teach him a lesson."

"Duly noted." We both laughed, and she linked her arm with mine as we strolled toward the first boutique. "Is it always this empty in here?" I asked when no one was here except for us.

"Oh no, honey. I had them shut down for us to shop in peace."

"You can do that?" I asked in surprise.

"Of course." She shot me a wink and led me to a gown boutique while I was left stunned.

"Buongiorno, Signora Bellavia!" A well-dressed woman greeted Eleonora with kisses on each cheek.

"Buongiorno, Corinna! How have you been?"

"Wonderful! Oh, and who's this with you?" Corinna looked at me.

"This is Althaia, my son's fiancée." Eleonora said proudly with a smile.

"Oh, could it be Damiano's...?" She asked, a bit unsure.

"She is." Eleonora's entire face brightened, and Corinna's brows went up in surprise.

"How lovely! Welcome!" She suddenly embraced me and kissed my cheeks.

"Thank you." I smiled at her cheerful greeting.

"Let's find you some beautiful dresses, shall we?" She gestured for us to follow her to a different section of the boutique.

"I hope you don't mind that Miss Miciela is still here. She came earlier and suddenly, nothing impressed her when she found out you were coming." Corinna sighed.

"Oh, Miciela? Not at all." Eleonora dismissed with a smile. Corinna smiled with relief as we entered the fitting area where refreshments were already arranged on the table.

"What are we looking for?" Corinna asked once we were seated on the couch.

"I need a gown for Lorenzo's and Cara's wedding." I said, assuming she already knew about it.

"We need three new dresses for her." Eleonora added, sipping her champagne.

"Three dresses for a wedding?" I asked.

"Just one dress for the wedding, honey. I want you to come with me to an event tomorrow, and for the third dress, Damiano asked me to get for the ceremony."

"Damiano didn't mention anything about a ceremony to me." I remarked.

"Seems like time will tell. Now, up you go." She chuckled and urged me towards Corinna.

Once Corinna took my measurements, she went to retrieve dresses for me to try. While we waited, I chatted with Eleonora and got to know her a bit more. She was such a warm soul, always had a soft expression, and a smile on her face.

"Are you okay, amore?" She held my hand in hers, looking worried.

"I am. I was just thinking about how you remind me of my mother." I couldn't help but smile sadly.

My throat would still tighten every time I thought of her, and the ache of missing her was overwhelming. Eleonora, sensing my emotions, mirrored my expression and pulled me into a comforting embrace, for which I was grateful.

"Alright, dear. Let's have you try some gowns."

I turned to Corinna, and my smile slowly faded when I saw she had returned with five large racks of dresses.

Ninety-Eight

ALTHAIA

The entire experience of me trying on dresses gave me a strong sense of déjà vu. It sent me right down memory lane when I went dress shopping with Damiano. And now, his mother kept sending my ass back with a new dress for the same reasons Damiano once gave.

"It's unsightly."

"Dio mio! We are not trying to give Nonna a heart attack. That is too revealing!"

"Simply hideous."

Eleonora was a harsh critic, and I feared we wouldn't find anything to meet her approval. Then I accidentally commented that it didn't matter what kind of dress I wore, as long as I was there for Cara.

"Oh no, honey! You have a reputation to uphold. As the soon-to-be wife of Don Damiano Bellavia, it's your responsibility to reflect not only his status but also his wealth and power, all while showcasing your own beauty. The way you present yourself becomes a statement." She explained, causing my brows to rise in surprise.

"I had no idea." I replied, looking at my engagement ring. That must be why he chose such an enormous diamond. I looked at myself in the mirror, wondering how I was going to do that.

"Don't worry, amore. You will learn with time." Eleonora smiled and sent me back in.

"I really hope you like this one because it's gorgeous!" I pulled the curtain to the side for her to see.

I stepped to the circular stage and did a small spin for her to see the entire dress. I was praying she would approve of this dress because we had been here for hours, and this one was the best of them all.

The dress, a sparkling arctic blue, featured an off-shoulder V-neckline. It snugly embraced my waist and then gracefully flowed looser around my hips, complemented by an elegant slit.

This was unlike anything I had worn before, and the color beautifully complimented my tanned skin. The more I looked at it, the more I fell in love with it, but dreaded Eleonora's answer.

"This is definitely the one!" She said happily, and I let out a sigh of relief.

Fortunately, we had already chosen the dress I would wear for tomorrow's event. It was a rich, royal blue gown with a sweetheart neckline, and it came with a pair of matching long gloves that reached my elbows. They kept the third dress a secret for some reason.

"Oh, that's a gorgeous one!"

I turned to look in the direction of the unfamiliar voice. She took off her sunglasses, stepping closer to admire my dress.

"How come you didn't show me this one, Corinna?" She asked.

"Because it was not for you, Miss Miciela." Corinna gave a tight smile, and the woman returned a much more obvious fake smile.

"Buona sera, Signora!" Miciela greeted Eleonora with kisses. "It's so nice to see you again! How's the family? Damiano?"

My brow went up the minute she mentioned his name.

"My fiancé is doing great. Thank you for asking." I replied with a sweet smile. It took everything in me to not say *husband,* but I held my tongue.

"Miciela, this is Althaia, Damiano's soon-to-be wife. And this is Miciela. Her family is in business with ours." Eleonora explained. In other words, an ally to the family.

"Nice to meet you, Miciela." I deliberately offered her my hand with the engagement ring for a handshake. Her gaze lingered on the ring before she shook my hand.

"Likewise, Althaia." She said my name as if she recognized it, having me slightly tilt my head to the side.

"Honey, get changed, and let's head to the jewelry store to find you something beautiful." Eleonora smiled at me, and I gave a small nod and made my way to the dressing room. But not before I shot Miciela one last look, finding her eyes tracing me from head to toe.

Fuck, I really hope she isn't one of Damiano's past lovers.

I immediately pushed those thoughts out of my head. I had to remind myself that it was all in the past and didn't matter anymore. I was his wife now.

"You can go right ahead while I sort this out." Eleonora told me when I was near.

"You don't have to. I can take care of it." I tried to protest, but she ushered me out of the boutique and towards Giovanni and Luca, who had been waiting with Eleonora's bodyguards outside.

"This was one exhausting round." I sighed to them.

"We thought it would be. Here." Giovanni handed me my favorite iced coffee and a sugar-glazed Taralli.

"You're the best. Thank you so much!" I took the iced coffee gratefully and gave them both one big hug. I almost wanted to cry in happiness when I took the first sip.

"There you go, getting recharged." Luca chuckled as he watched me happily eat my Taralli. "Done shopping?"

"Not yet. We're heading to the jewelry store now, and then I think we're done." At least, that was what I was hoping for. It wasn't that I wasn't enjoying my time with Eleonora, but if we had to continue like this with every shop, we would never get out of here.

Once I finished my iced coffee and snack, I went inside the jewelry store while Luca and Giovanni waited outside again.

The jeweler, a kindly older gentleman named Mr. Felini, welcomed me as I browsed. While looking around, my gaze fixed on a particular ring that immediately caught my attention.

"Can I please have a look at this one?" I asked Mr. Felini.

"Of course!" He unlocked the display and carefully presented the ring.

It was a wide, rectangular gold ring with a captivating large green emerald. I listened as Mr. Felini talked to me about the ring. It made me smile and felt even more unique.

"I would like this one, please. Can it be wrapped as a gift?" I asked.

"Absolutely! It's no problem." He smiled, and I handed him back the ring. I handed him my card just in case Eleonora showed up and tried to pay for it.

I signed the invoice and went back in search to find something for the wedding. I didn't want to buy anything until Eleonora was here, in case she didn't approve.

The door to the store opened. I took a quick glance, seeing it was Miciela. I mentally rolled my eyes when she gave me her fake smile.

"So, Althaia." She said as she stepped closer to me while looking at the displayed jewelry. "Are you also attending the ball tomorrow?"

"I am." I gave her one curt answer, not hiding that I didn't want to chit-chat with her.

"I've heard of you." She stopped in front of me. I let out a sigh to show her I wasn't interested in whatever she had to say. "Sofia is a great friend of mine." Miciela smirked.

"Sofia?" I tilted my head, pretending I had no idea who she was talking about.

"She worked for Damiano." She clarified.

"Ah, Sofia, the maid! How is she? Has her nose healed well? And what about her hands? Poor girl didn't know what she was up against." I feigned a sad look with a shake of my head.

The smirk on her face vanished instantly and was replaced with a glare. She opened her mouth to say something, but stopped herself as Eleonora entered the store. Miciela immediately plastered on a fake smile. I couldn't help but frown at her action, disgusted by how phony she was.

"Found anything you liked?" Eleonora asked as she approached me, not paying any attention to Miciela.

"I did! I thought of something like this?" I showed her what I thought would be great with the dress.

"Perfect! We will get you this one for tomorrow." She said excitedly.

"Oh, is this not fitting for the wedding?"

"I have already chosen something special for you. Do you want to see it?"

I nodded, curious to see what it looked like. Mr. Felini opened the jewelry box, and I immediately shook my head.

"Eleonora, thank you, truly, but this is not something I can accept." I protested. The entire necklace was crafted from diamonds, and a larger diamond served as a pendant.

"Nonsense! Damiano already told me you would try to protest, but it's not going to work with me. It's also a gift from me." She smiled. I let out a small sigh and accepted my defeat.

We bid Mr. Felini goodbye, and as we stepped out of the store, a smile was immediately on my lips when I spotted Damiano. I quickened my pace until I was enveloped in his arms.

"Missed me?" Damiano smiled, cupping my cheek as his thumb lightly traced my skin.

"Always." I rose on the tips of my toes until our lips met.

"Look at you, lovebirds." Eleonora chuckled. I pulled away, blushing as I forgot we had a small audience.

I sensed another set of eyes on me, and when I turned, I found Miciela sending glares in my direction.

"Oh, and tell Sofia I said hi." I winked, making my way out with Damiano's arm around me.

Ninety-Nine

ALTHAIA

Since I had to attend the event tomorrow, we had to spend the night at Nonna's place. This also meant we still had to sleep in separate rooms because they didn't know we were married yet.

I tossed and turned in bed, unable to find a comfortable spot. I let out a sigh of frustration and rolled out of bed. I grabbed the wrapped ring box, and since I had no pockets, I shoved it between my breasts.

I carefully opened the door and peeked out into the hallway to see if the coast was clear. It was quiet. I tiptoed through the dimly lit hallway and made my way downstairs. I stopped at the end of the staircase and looked around in case Nonna was up. I almost wanted to chuckle at how two adults had to sneak around to be with each other. But I was having fun with it right now as I played spy and tried to be light on my feet.

I hid behind furniture on my way until I reached Damiano's room. Slowly, I pulled the handle down and opened the door. I even held my breath, making sure no sound could be heard as I sneaked inside.

The nightstand lamp was still on as Damiano lay in bed, his eyes closed. I bit down on my lip as I took in the mighty sight of him; shirtless and with his arms behind his head, making his biceps look deliciously huge.

"Damiano." I whispered as I hovered over him, expecting him to open his eyes, but they remained closed. "Damiano." I whispered again, but he didn't respond.

My eyes slightly narrowed because I knew he wasn't asleep. Then I let out a smirk.

"I'm horny." Damiano's eyes flew open, and he grabbed me so fast that I found myself lying underneath him. I had to bite down on my lip to stifle a laugh. "I knew you weren't asleep!"

"Offer me your pussy and I will even wake up from death." His lips brushed against mine before pulling my lower lip between his teeth. "Spread your legs, baby" His hand was already on its way down before I stopped him.

"I'm not horny. I just said it to get your attention." I chuckled quietly. Damiano clicked his tongue at me, not impressed.

"Shame. I was about to show you a good time."

"I know, but I just wanted to sleep next to you."

"That's just as good, my love." He smiled and gave me a feather-like kiss.

"I actually have something for you." I sat up on the bed, and Damiano raised a brow when I reached in between my breasts to retrieve the ring box I had stuffed in there. "For you."

Butterflies fluttered in my stomach as I watched him unwrap it. He opened it, seeing what was inside the box before his eyes met mine. I gave a shy smile and took the ring, held his hand in mine, and slid it down on his finger.

"I want people to know you're taken too. I thought it looked nice with the green emerald because you always say you love my green eyes. It's said that green represents growth and renewal, being the color of spring and rebirth. The gold represents divinity and power." I explained.

He gazed at it for a while, making me feel nervous if he even was going to like it. It was a risky shot since I hadn't seen him wearing any kind of jewelry.

"I can't remember the last time I received a gift." Damiano said quietly while still looking at it. "But this is definitely my favorite one." His expression softened with a smile.

"You really like it?"

"I do. Thank you, my love." A wave of butterflies erupted in my stomach when he pulled me in for a soft kiss.

"You look even more handsome with that ring on your finger." I gave him a teasing smile.

"Because it lets people know I'm yours." He stated, amused.

"Duh!" I chuckled and got comfortable in bed with him. It did make my jealous ass feel better now he was wearing a ring. "There's also something I want to ask you..." I trailed off.

"I'm listening."

"I met Miciela today, and she asked about you... It made me wonder if you two have -"

"No, never." Damiano shook his head immediately.

"Okay, good. Now I can sleep in peace." I smiled and snuggled into him.

"Is that what kept you awake?"

"Maybe."

"You silly woman." He chuckled. "There's no way I could ever mess around with someone like her. Miciela is known for being a climber."

"The type who fucks her way to the top?" I asked, not expecting to hear that.

"Yes. She thought she could use Raffaele to get to the top, but he was only interested in fucking her. So, he did and left as soon as he was done with her." Damiano explained.

"No way!" I gasped.

"I had to save his ass as he almost got in trouble with her brother. I've told him many times to not fuck anyone important to my business, but he still did." He let out a disapproving sigh.

"I kind of feel sorry that he used her like that, even though she used him too."

"She tried to get to Lorenzo after she failed with Raffaele." He added.

"She tried to get with Tank Man?!" I gaped, and Damiano laughed quietly at Lorenzo's nickname.

"She did, but he didn't even spare her a glance."

"Gotta admire her courage." I admitted.

"My love, don't worry about anyone from my past. I always made sure it was with someone I knew I wouldn't see again. Except for that one mistake." Damiano reassured me.

"I'm trying not to care but thank you for telling me." I smiled, resting my head on his chest as I closed my eyes. "I love you."

"E ti amo, piccola"

It was yet another day of training. Despite having an event to attend later in the evening, Damiano wouldn't allow me to skip my training. Trust me, I tried to get out of it by mentioning the time it takes to get ready, but he simply shut me down. This led to me scowling at him the entire ride to the training field.

"Hey there, pretty lady!"

"Raffaele!" I erupted excitedly when I saw him. He did a small run toward me and gave me a bone-crushing hug.

"Have you missed me?!" He shouted.

"I have!" I chuckled when he let go of me. "When did you get here?"

"Not too long ago. I heard something big happened to you, and I had to come and see for myself. Let me see your hand!" Raffaele grabbed my hand and did a dramatic squeal.

"Holy fucking shit, that is huge! Congratulations!" He picked me up and started to shake me as I laughed. "How did he do it? Was he romantic? Did you spread your legs for him after?" He wiggled his brows.

"As if I'm going to tell you." I laughed, and he actually pouted at me.

"Come on! Just tell me!"

"I will leave it to your imagination."

"Oh, baby, the things I imagine are going to make you feel so dirty -" Raffaele barely got to finish his sentence when Damiano punched him in the stomach.

I just sighed at Raffaele for never learning to keep his mouth shut when Damiano was around. While the cousins were occupied, Antonio walked up to me with a smile.

"Congratulations, Althaia. I'm happy he finally proposed to you." He said and ruffled my hair.

"Thanks, Nino." I smirked when he slightly squinted his eyes at me.

"I told you; you can't call me that."

"Mess up my hair again and I will." I laughed, and he shook his head at me in amusement. "How's Ellie and the baby girl?"

"They're both doing great. Baby girl is healthy and growing stronger every day." Antonio's eyes brightened as he talked about them.

"Just what I want to hear! I can't wait to meet her." I beamed.

I had no doubt she would be one beautiful baby girl with the genes of her parents; her father with blue eyes and her mother with a sepia skin tone. She was going to break hearts for sure.

"Me either. Just don't let her wait for too long. She needs her cousins." He spoke quietly to me. My heart beat a little faster at the thoughts of both our kids running around and playing together.

"I'm already working on it." I whispered.

"Good." He gave a playful wink.

"Not the face! I have to stay pretty for Ava!" Raffaele's voice caught our attention.

"My God, Damiano, just leave him alone." I stopped him before he could land another punch at Raffaele.

"Don't worry about me. I can take it. It keeps me young." Raffaele let out a goofy smile. I shook my head at him. One day, he was going to be unlucky and get his ass shot.

"So, when's the big date?" He asked. I looked at Damiano, and he gave me a nod that I was free to share the news.

"Well, there's no rush actually since we're already married." I revealed.

Raffaele dropped his jaw open, and Antonio just smiled, not looking surprised at all.

"Without me?!" Raffaele erupted in offense.

"We haven't told anyone. You're the only ones who know. So, keep your mouth shut." Damiano spoke sternly to Raffaele.

"Does that mean she -" He stopped talking when Damiano gave him a deadly glare.

"Althaia, get started. We don't have much time today." Damiano gestured for me to get out on the field before I could ask what Raffaele was implying.

"Which one of you losers is fighting me today?" I looked at Giovanni and Luca with a teasing smile.

"Oh, look who's confident! Let me go for a round." Raffaele rubbed his hands together and got ready. "Ready to get that ass spanked?" He wiggled his brows.

Damiano pulled out his gun.

"It's my turn to beat him up." I told him before he could pull the trigger.

"We'll see about that." Raffaele caught me off guard when he grabbed me and put me in a headlock. I had practiced this at least hundreds of times now and knew exactly what to do.

I swiftly moved my head to the side to free my airway. I elbowed him in the stomach and created some distance between us before he could restrain my arms. Next, I firmly gripped his arm, lowered my chin, and bit him as hard as I could.

"Ow, shit! You bit me!" he yelled in surprise and immediately loosened his hold on me. It gave me the chance to get a better grip on his arm before I flipped him over my shoulder.

He landed with a resounding thud, upside down in front of me.

"Don't underestimate me. Look who's my trainer." I let out a taunting smile.

"Don't get cocky!" He smirked and grabbed my ankle. Anticipating his move, I swiftly got down on one knee before he could push me down. Taking advantage of the situation, I delivered a sharp punch to his bicep, causing temporary paralysis.

"Doubting my mad skills?" I teased when he groaned in pain.

One Hundred

ALTHAIA

I did my makeup and set my hair in an elegant low updo, leaving a few strands to frame my face.

Pleased with the result, I stepped out of the bathroom to grab my dress but stopped when I noticed my phone flash before going black. Frowning, I checked my phone and saw several missed calls. Before my mind could dwell on the worst possibilities, it rang again.

It was Michael.

I stared at the phone in my hand, not too sure if I should take the call or not. But I kept thinking something happened to my father, and he was calling to let me know. I took a deep breath to calm my pounding heart and hoped it wasn't anything serious.

"Hello?"

"Althaia! Are you okay?!" Michael asked frantically.

"I'm okay." I said, confused why he was reacting like this.

"Why didn't you answer your phone? I thought something happened to you!" He shouted with frustration.

"I was getting ready and didn't have my phone on me. Is everything okay? Did anything happen to my dad?" I asked nervously.

"Listen, I need to talk to you. Can I see you tonight?"

"We can't."

"Thaia, please... I know I said some fucked up shit to you and I'm sorry. I really am, but I need to see you." He pleaded.

"I can't, Michael. I'm not in the states right now." I muttered.

"What do you mean you're not in the states?"

"I'm in Italy." I said and took a seat on the bed.

"Why? With who..." His voice faded as he realized with whom.

"I'm visiting his family." I revealed.

Michael went quiet, and for some reason, I was nervous about his reaction.

"...Did he propose to you?" His question was barely audible.

I bit down on my lip, wondering if I should tell him the truth.

"Yes. We're engaged." I closed my eyes when I heard him let out a shaky breath. I couldn't help it, but my heart ached for him.

"Congratulations…" Michael mumbled, but I could still hear the hurt in his voice.

"Thank you, Michael." I rose from the bed and noticed Damiano standing by the doorway, his face void of emotion as he looked at me. "Listen, I have to go, but I will talk to you when I can." I said to Michael and hung up before he could reply.

"How long have you been standing there?" I asked Damiano.

"Long enough." Damiano simply replied.

"Eavesdropping, are we now?"

"No, I came to give you this but didn't want to interrupt your phone call." He handed me the jewelry box I had bought with his mother.

"Oh, thanks. Well, now that you're here, can you help me with my dress? I need you to zip it up."

"What did he want?" Damiano asked while he zipped me up. I shrugged.

"I don't know. He asked if we could meet up, but I said I couldn't." I said as I put on my matching gloves. "Is there something wrong?" I asked him. He was unusually quiet when it came to Michael.

"No." Damiano smiled softly and wrapped his arms around me. "You look beautiful as always, Mrs. Bellavia." He whispered, leaning down to capture my lips with his.

"I have one more thing for you." Damiano pulled out a blue garter band. Before I could tease him about it, he pulled something else out, having me look at him in surprise.

"It's an OTF knife. Keep it on you at all times when you're there." He kneeled and slid the garter band on me and placed the knife securely in the band. "It eases my mind if you have something to defend yourself with. And no, you're not getting a gun. You handle the knife better." He immediately said when I was about to ask him. But he was right. I was better with a knife than a gun at the moment.

"It's making me feel badass." I grinned.

"Only for emergencies. I don't want you to play with it and hurt yourself." Damiano stated firmly once again.

"If you're that worried, just give me a fork."

"I might."

"No, too late. You already gave me the knife." I snickered and made a small run for the door.

"Aren't you coming as well?" I asked when we got outside to the driveway.

"No, it's ladies' night." Damiano stuffed his hands into his pockets. "I might get a tattoo while you're out." He smirked and glanced out of the corner of his eye when Nonna and his mother made an appearance.

"You will do no such thing!" Nonna erupted and smacked Damiano's head with her clutch.

I put my hands up to my mouth to not burst out in laughter at the amusing sight. Damiano gave her a blank look and slowly rubbed the back of his head.

"It's the work of the Devil!" She continued to scold him, making a chuckle escape my lips. He took a quick glance at me before his smirk returned.

"Nonna, do you know what Althaia loves to call me?"

My eyes slowly widened.

"Il Diavolo, because of the unimaginable things I do to her -"

"Let's go, shall we?" I said loudly to drown out his voice as I sent him a glare, to which he responded with a wink.

"Yes, but let me see you first." Nonna had me do a small spin. "Beautiful, dear!" She had a satisfied look on her face while giving an approving nod.

"Of course she is! My son has excellent taste." Eleonora complimented me as well, having me slightly blush.

"That's my woman. Have fun, baby." Damiano kissed the top of my head.

"Will do!" I smiled before we got inside the SUV. It was his father's men who were driving, but Giovanni and Luca were following in a different car.

"Eleonora, you mentioned I now have an image to uphold. It made me wonder what exactly is expected of me as a wife?" I asked.

"Traditionally, you would take care of your home and your children; to be a good housewife." Nonna answered.

"That was more in our days, madre." Eleonora smiled and then looked at me. "It would be up to you and Damiano and whatever you agree upon. Ask him what he expects of you, and you tell him what you expect of him as well. It goes both ways, and most importantly, that you're both content with your decisions."

"And of course, your loyalty to him, but we will get to it soon, dear." Nonna added, and I nodded as I thought about what they said.

It looked like we were the last ones to arrive as we stood at the top of a long staircase overlooking the ballroom. Attention quickly shifted to us when

Nonna took a couple of steps ahead, standing tall with her head held high, overseeing them like a Queen with her subjects below.

The power radiated from her as if you could feel it just by the way she carried herself. Eleonora's words made even more sense as I watched them present themselves with their mere presence. Not a single word needed to be said; it made you almost want to bow down to them in pure respect.

It was beyond incredible.

Nonna was the first to descend the stairs, and we followed closely behind as a show of respect for her status as the matriarch.

"Do you understand now, Althaia?" Eleonora asked with her usual warm smile.

"I do. I have never seen anything like this before." I was still in awe, but nervous at the same time. What if I couldn't present myself the same way they had?

"You will learn how to with time." She assured me as if she had read my thoughts.

As we descended the stairs, we got ambushed, or at least it felt that way, when a group of women eagerly approached to greet Nonna and Eleonora. It was almost a mirror of the experience I had with Damiano at the auction.

However, I didn't mind greeting and talking to them as I was introduced as Damiano's soon-to-be wife. They gave surprised looks, and a few raised their brows, scrutinizing me from top to bottom. I didn't pay much attention to them. Instead, I observed Nonna and Eleonora, from how they talked and how they continued to carry themselves.

"Excuse us for a moment." Eleonora smiled and led me away from the group while Nonna was still conversing with some of the older women.

I let out a breath as we had already been here for a while, greeting and talking to what felt like at least a hundred people.

"Sometimes they just don't know when to give you a chance to breathe." She chuckled and grabbed two glasses of champagne, handing me one, which I took gratefully.

"It is quite overwhelming, to be honest." I admitted.

"It will get easier."

"May I ask how long you've been doing this?" I asked as we strolled, admiring the art on the walls.

"As long as I can remember! But it mattered more once I married Riccardo. I was nineteen and had Damiano when I was just barely twenty."

"That's... young." I looked at her in surprise.

"We were young and in love. You have seen how Riccardo's mother is; very traditional and had us married as soon as possible." Eleonora said with amusement.

"I can imagine that." I chuckled lightly.

"I'm so happy Damiano has found you. As a mother, to see him like this fills me with an indescribable joy. Thank you, honey." She gave my shoulder a light squeeze, and my heart warmed up by her words.

Eleonora excused herself to the restroom. I continued to admire the paintings while sipping my champagne.

"So, we meet again, Althaia."

I let out a small sigh at the now familiar voice, turning around to see Miciela accompanied by two other women.

"Miciela." I smiled tightly. There was just something about her that gave me a hard time hiding my dislike towards her.

"Have you been feeling good lately? Any nausea?" She asked with a wide smile. I raised a brow in confusion. "How's the pregnancy?" She faked a sweet smile, but her eyes were cunning while my heart stopped at the mention of it.

"Oh, silly me." Miciela put her hand up to her mouth and let out a chuckle along with the others. "I forgot you lost it. So awful for you." She placed her hand on her chest and exaggerated a sad look on her face.

She took a step closer to me, her eyes turning cold, and dropped her fake act.

"I know what you did to Sofia. I won't let it slide, and you will pay for it." She hissed before quickly flashing a satisfying smile and turning around to leave with the two women.

No words came out of me.

My chest heaved from the sharp intake of breath.

My eyes burned as tears wanted to spill.

But I refused to let them.

Instead, I followed her.

I downed the champagne and took out my knife from my garter band.

Anger consumed me.

I couldn't hear anything.

I couldn't see anything.

Except for red.

I was seeing red.

And she was going to pay.

"Miciela!" I shouted her name, making her turn around to face me. She was standing by a table, chatting with people around her, and her smirk was still present. Until her eyes landed on the knife in my hand.

Miciela tried to step away from me, but I was faster.

My grip tightened around the handle as I forcefully stabbed her hand, the knife meeting the table to anchor her in place. She let out a blood-curdling scream, and I grabbed a fistful of her hair as I violently shattered the champagne glass against the table's edge. Without hesitation, I forcefully shoved the sharp shards of shattered glass into her mouth.

But it was not enough.

I smashed her head down on the table.

One time.

Two times.

I yanked her head, forcing her to meet my cold eyes. Her mouth was split open and blood poured out. I placed my hand over her mouth to keep the glass inside as she wept.

"You should have kept your mouth shut." My voice was low and calm as I looked deep into her eyes. "Sofia should have been an example of that for you. Yet, you decided to ignore it. *I* am the reason she is still alive, and she should be fucking grateful for that. *You do not get to fuck with me!*" My words hissed out, my entire body shaking with anger.

To see her blood wasn't enough. I wanted to see the life disappear from her eyes; to see her body become lifeless as my hand wrapped around her throat.

I snapped out of it, coming back to reality, and shoved her away from me.

"You're lucky I'm not a killer, but mention my baby, and I will gladly become one." I left before giving in to the need to end her life.

Everyone was watching me in shock, but no one dared to interfere.

"I would like to leave now. Please." I said to Nonna and Eleonora, who had made their way to me.

"Let's get you out of here." Nonna said, and Eleonora quickly led me out.

I was hurt, yet an unsettling numbness engulfed me at the same time my legs mechanically carried me outside.

"What the hell happened?" Giovanni frowned when he saw me as he and Luca immediately drew out their guns.

"You need to get her to safety right now!" Eleonora ordered them.

They all moved quickly, ushering me into the backseat of the car with Giovanni. Luca took the wheel, driving us away, while Eleonora and Nonna remained behind with Riccardo's men.

"I need to cut off your glove." He took out his knife, and I followed his gaze, only now noticing I had glass stuck into the palm of my hand.

"Hold her!" Luca shouted. I looked up just in time to see a car coming out of nowhere and hitting us.

Giovanni held me tightly, sheltering my head with his arms as we were violently thrown into the car door.

"Are you okay?" I checked on Giovanni, confirming he was unharmed, before turning my attention to Luca.

Words caught in my throat when I saw a man standing just outside my window, a rifle aimed directly at me.

Then he pulled the trigger.

One Hundred One

DAMIANO

"All preparations are ready." Antonio informed me as we entered my office.

"Good." I replied, taking a seat on the couch.

My gaze swept over the various files and pictures scattered on the table. I was now convinced that each attack was connected, but the lingering questions were how and why.

"So, you're confident he's got something to do with this mess?" Raffaele asked and sprawled on the couch.

"I found a microphone in the pendant of her necklace." I replied. Raffaele sat up straight and looked at me in surprise.

"And you think he did it?"

"I know it was him. He told her she forgot it in the hospital. She wasn't wearing the necklace once we got to the hospital. When we went back to clean the house, it was nowhere to be seen, so either she lost it in the woods, or they grabbed it before we would notice." I explained.

"And suddenly it just happened to have a microphone in it." Antonio added.

"Do you still have the necklace? Maybe I can trace its origin, find out where it was purchased, and identify the buyer." Raffaele said.

"I broke it."

He gave me a blank look.

"And why would you do that? A magnet would have done the job just fine to disconnect any signal."

"I didn't want to take any chances." I shrugged.

"We underestimated the bastard." Antonio sighed, and I nodded in agreement. Gaetano was an eager man, and his eagerness knew no bounds. He would stop at nothing to get what he wanted.

"I still don't understand how he got Koreans to work for him. They don't work with anyone." Raffaele pondered.

I rubbed my jaw as I examined the pictures of the ones we had identified.

"Michael." They both looked at me when I let out a humorless chuckle. "It's that shitface, Michael." I said as I looked at Antonio.

"When you were with her at Gaetano's house, she went with Michael to Koreatown. He must have some kind of contact with Koreans."

"That's fucked up. Didn't they grow up together, and now he's trying to kill her?" Raffaele scoffed.

I took another look at the pictures while they discussed. I grabbed a particular one as I examined it.

"... I'm going to stuff a knife up his ass -"

"Michael is not trying to kill Althaia." I cut off Raffaele. "He might be being used."

"How can we be sure of that?" Raffaele asked.

"Because he's in love with her." I revealed. Althaia had told me everything about it at the safe house, not wanting to keep any secrets from me.

"I fucking knew it." Antonio scoffed.

I put the pictures in order on the table for them to see.

"The drive-by shooting at the church, Michael, was not there. At some point, Gaetano disappeared and left his men behind as a show for us. Roberto said he had a random phone slipped into his bag when he was trapping the streets. It was most likely Michael who did it or had someone else do it to avoid getting caught."

"It would make sense. Michael is respected on the streets, and he's deeply connected." Antonio commented.

"Shit. Gaetano tried to kill Althaia so soon?" Raffaele frowned as he focused on the pictures.

"No. That was aimed at us. She just happened to stand in the way, but he didn't care. If I hadn't gotten to her in time, she would have been shot in the head." I clenched my jaw as I remembered just how close she was to get a bullet in her head.

"My guess is Michael's the one who has contact with Koreans, but he has been unaware of what jobs they were hired to do. Gaetano needed people who couldn't be traced back to him, and they were all hired through Michael. He doesn't ask questions and makes sure the job is done. That would explain the bastard who attacked Althaia in the hotel." I explained.

"And he made sure he wouldn't be able to speak because he knew he would get caught. The pictures hung on the wall were a message; to let us know she was being watched." Antonio finished my thought.

"That tongueless bastard was caught off guard when he saw Althaia and thought he could finish her." Raffaele said, understanding how it was all connected now.

"Most likely. Gaetano has been keeping us busy while he blackmailed Jacinta into laundering money for him, leaving her no choice but to comply, especially with Althaia staying with him."

I continued to explain my thoughts on how it was all connected: from the increased non-traceable phone calls Jacinta received, to the boutique being used for laundering money, and then burning it down to eliminate any evidence left behind.

"Jacinta knew he was going to come after her once he was done using her; that's why she bought that property in Greece to flee with Althaia, but he attacked sooner than expected." I finished.

"He is one sick bastard... He must know Althaia is not his daughter. Or maybe she is, but he doesn't care because he wants to get revenge on Jacinta for leaving him." Raffaele wondered out loud.

"Whatever it is, we're putting an end to it. I'm going to fucking skin him alive for everything he did." I wanted to get my hands on him, make him suffer for all the pain he caused Althaia.

For killing the life we had created inside of her.

"Until then, I still want a DNA test to make sure. What's the status on her?" I asked Antonio.

"She won't talk."

"What about Lorenzo?"

"No. She made it clear she will only talk to you."

"We can always force her to talk." Raffaele suggested, and I gave him a sharp look.

"No. No one is to go near her. I'll make sure she talks when we get back."

"Or I can just charm her with my handsomeness." He wiggled his brows with a mischievous grin.

"What handsomeness? You will send her straight back into a coma." I smirked as he scowled at me.

"You're spending too much time with Althaia. Her personality is rubbing off on you." He scoffed.

"That's definitely something she would say. Shouldn't you be charming Ava instead?" Antonio asked, amused.

Raffaele let out a groan and slumped in his seat.

"I'm trying! One moment I think I have her, and then the next, she plays hard to get. It's confusing!"

"Maybe don't say you want her mouth wrapped around your cock." Antonio raised his brow, having me chuckle.

"I'm never forgiving Althaia for spilling that out to you." He muttered grimly, and I shook my head in amusement.

"Don't talk to her like you talk to the women at the brothels you visit." I pointed out to him. He still had a lot to learn when it came to speaking respectfully to women he wasn't paying to fuck.

"Really, Damiano? Are you keeping an eye on me?" Raffaele shot me another blank look.

"Just making sure you're not fucking anyone important to me." I said and grabbed my phone when it rang. "Luca."

"We need backup!"

I immediately stood up, a frown appearing on my face as I signaled to the others to get going.

"We're on our way. What happened?" My hold tightened around my phone as we quickly made our way out to the cars, Antonio ordering more men to get going.

"Something happened between Althaia and Miciela. Maximo's men want her head in return." He quickly explained. My face darkened and my jaw clenched.

"I will hang their heads on the streets if they so much as misplace one hair on her head!" I growled out in fury as we got into the car and drove off. "What's the situation?"

"We're stuck and they're still shooting after us."

I heard the faint shots from Luca's end. As long as they were inside the car, they would be fine as it was bulletproof.

My frown deepened when I heard Althaia let out a strangled scream in the background.

"Shit, they're going to blow the fucking car!" Giovanni yelled.

"Two minutes. Stall them until we get there." I tossed the phone to the side, grabbed the rifle Raffaele handed me, and got ready.

"Surround them and don't let anyone get past you. Get a car to Luca and Giovanni and let them escort Althaia to safety immediately." I ordered them as I racked the slide.

I moved my neck from side to side and let out a slow breath to calm down the rage inside of me.

We arrived at the scene, chaos unfolding before us. Maximo's men were unleashing a hail of bullets at the car, the air thick with the acrid scent of gunfire. Without a moment's hesitation, I kicked the door open, instantly capturing their attention. In the deafening symphony of gunfire, I swiftly returned the favor, my shots ringing out with deadly precision.

One shot.

Two shots.

Three shots.

Bodies hit the ground, dropping like flies. I moved fast, unloading rounds with each shot tearing through flesh and bone before taking cover behind a car. We had them surrounded, making it easier to take them out with them in the center. They were trying to take cover, but my men didn't allow them.

My gaze landed on the car where Althaia was. Giovanni was shielding her while in the process of getting her to the car to get her to safety, while Luca had their backs covered.

As I prepared to move again, shots rang out from a different direction, and targeted them. I followed Luca's aim and noticed one of Maximo's men taking cover beyond Luca's reach.

While Luca kept him occupied, Giovanni quickly got into the car with Althaia. I moved between the vehicles, crouching low as I approached from behind. The idiot was too focused on taking cover from Luca's gunfire that he was oblivious to my presence.

I gave a nod to Luca to let him know I would take care of it, and they could get out of here.

The bastard was seconds away from pulling the trigger again as they were all getting in the car, but I slammed the back of his head with the rear of the rifle. He crumpled to the ground with a thud as I kicked his gun aside, and I relentlessly pounded his face into the pavement.

"You. Dare. To. Fucking. Shoot. At. My. Wife?!" Each word was punctuated by the merciless blows from the rifle.

His face turned unrecognizable, blood splattering everywhere. I turned the rifle around and pulled the trigger, ending his life with a single shot. The bullet tore through his neck, creating a gaping hole that spewed blood as he choked before becoming lifeless.

I glanced over at my men, confirming that they had finished them all off. The distant noise of an approaching car caught my attention, leading me to aim my rifle in that direction.

"Hold your fire!" I ordered my men as I recognized the car. "What are you doing here? Leave, madre." I glared at her driver for bringing her here when she stepped out.

"Maximo is on his way. I tried to talk to him, but he wouldn't listen." My mother ignored me and looked at the dead bodies spread around.

"What happened?" I asked with a frown. She put her hands on her hips and let out a sigh.

"I don't know. I went to the restroom, and the minute I got out, I saw Althaia in the process of banging Miciela's head against the table."

My frown deepened. Before I could ask anything else, the screech of tires made me turn around.

"Get inside. Now." I closed the car door, making sure my mother was safe before approaching Maximo. His men aimed at me as I walked up to him, but he signaled for them to lower their guns when he faced me.

"Damiano, I demand an explanation!" He roared when I stopped in front of him. "Care to explain why you're protecting a woman who hurt my sister?" Maximo hissed as he brought his sister out.

I looked at Miciela, her face all messed up with blood gushing out of her mouth. I tilted my head to the side before letting out a small chuckle and shaking my head.

My wife is truly a covert psychopath.

My reaction only fueled Maximo's anger, and I half-expected smoke to come out of his ears if that were possible.

"You better deliver that woman's head to me right now!" He yelled. I shot him a sharp look and stepped closer.

"What did you say?" My voice went deadly low, my face darkening as I stared at him.

"That woman -"

"That woman you're talking about." I cut him off. "Is my wife."

His eyes widened, and he began to say something, but I had no interest in hearing it. Moving fast, I grabbed him, locking him in a tight headlock with my gun pressed against his temple. His men aimed at me once again, but they hesitated to fire as I used him as a shield while backing away.

"We have an alliance! You cannot do this!" Maximo wheezed, and I clicked my tongue at him.

"I can. Your sister broke it, and now you have to face the consequences for going after my wife." I growled out. Althaia was not a violent person by any means. Miciela must have done something to make her react like that.

"Tell them to drop the guns or you're dead." I warned him. Instead of complying, he attempted to free himself.

I pressed the gun into his head, my patience wearing thin.

"Now! Tell them to drop them, and I will let you go." My grip tightened around his neck, his face turning red before he finally signaled for them to surrender their weapons.

As soon as the firearms hit the ground, my men shot them, and their bodies dropped lifelessly to the ground one by one. I released my hold on Maximo and pushed him away, making him stumble forward as I aimed my own gun at him.

"Wait, you said -"

I didn't let him finish and shot him in the head.

"I let you go, didn't I?" I scoffed at his dead body.

A weeping sound caught my attention, and I spotted Miciela hiding behind the car. Stepping closer, I took a good look at her. She really got messed up good.

I shook my head in disapproval at Maximo for not getting her medical attention immediately. Instead, the son of a bitch brought her with him.

Miciela tried to crawl away from me but slumped to the ground due to her injuries. To my left, my mother came to stand next to me.

"You're fortunate I taught my son never to harm a woman." My mother remarked, taking the gun from my hand, which made Miciela cry out loudly. Without saying a word, my mother pulled the trigger and shot her in the head.

I arched a brow at my mother as she handed back my gun.

"No one hurts my children." My mother gave my cheek a light pat before returning to the car. Her words brought a slight smile to my face as I followed her.

"Have someone clean up this mess." I instructed Antonio. The once black street was now drenched in blood and scattered with dead bodies. "And find Sofia. I'm putting an end to her for good this time." I firmly ordered before getting into the car, desperate to see my wife.

One Hundred Two

Damiano

I walked quickly through the house until I heard muffled voices coming from the den. The door was already slightly open, and I saw Althaia sitting on the couch with a doctor attending to her hand. Her gaze was on the floor; her usually bright green eyes seemed dull, and her expression was blank.

Stepping inside, her head snapped in my direction. I watched her take a sharp breath, ignoring the doctor as she walked quickly toward me. I immediately wrapped my arms around her, holding her close to my chest, and felt the tension slowly melt away.

Leaning slightly back, I placed my hands on her cheek, examining her face to see if she was hurt anywhere else.

"Damiano, I'm sorry. I didn't -"

"Shh, baby." I gently shook my head as I saw her eyes glisten with unshed tears. "Don't apologize for anything." I reassured her softly.

"Are you hurt anywhere else?" I gently took hold of her hand. She had a few pieces of glass stuck to her hand, and she had several deep cuts, but nothing that would need stitches. I took a deep breath to keep my composure in front of her. She was in a vulnerable state, and I didn't want to add to it.

"No, I just cut my hand, but Gio got hurt. He was bleeding!" Althaia, despite her injuries, looked at me with concern for Giovanni's well-being.

"It was just a flesh wound. No need to cry about it." Giovanni's voice sounded from the door. He walked to us, showing he was okay with his bandaged arm. "You're lucky it hit me, or you would have gotten a pretty nasty scar. And your husband would have detached my head from my body." He crossed his arms with an amused look.

"But you got hurt because of me!" Althaia's voice was laced with guilt.

"It's my job to keep you safe. As if I would let them hurt you." He tsked but let out a small smile. She looked a bit hesitant when she glanced at his arm.

"Is that you admitting you care about me?"

"Woman, didn't I just prove I would take a bullet for you? Do you need me to spell it out for you?" Giovanni scowled.

"Yes." She said immediately and he let out a sigh.

"Fine. Yes, I do care about you. I don't know why, but there's just something about you that makes me care for you. Happy?" He shot her a blank look. She took him by surprise when she suddenly embraced him.

"Very happy. I know it's your job to protect me if anything were to happen, but now I *know* you don't hate me." Althaia told him, and he looked taken aback by her words before he lightly patted the top of her head.

"I don't hate you... I'm just Uncle Grumpy."

"You are." Althaia chuckled, looking relieved by his words.

"Your father wants to talk to you." Giovanni informed me with a look that said it was important.

"He can wait. Leave us." I told him.

I led Althaia back to the couch as the others left the den, and I took a seat where the doctor had previously sat. Taking hold of her hand, adjusting the small light, and grabbing the tweezers, I began removing the rest of the glass.

"Tell me what happened, my love." I spoke to her softly. Althaia let out a breath, taking a moment to compose herself.

"Miciela... she asked how my pregnancy was going." Althaia whispered. I paused in what I was doing, my brows furrowed as I looked at her. "She mocked me for my miscarriage, and I just... lost it. I felt such anger, and the next thing I know, I'm following her and stuffing broken glass into her mouth." Her eyes narrowed as she relived the moment.

"I'm not sure how I was even able to do it, but I didn't mean to cause problems. I'm -"

"Don't you dare apologize." I held her chin, looking at her with a firm expression. "She had it coming for opening her mouth, and you did the right thing to shut her up." If anything, Miciela didn't deserve a bullet in her head; she deserved a painful death.

"It's not that I'm regretting it, just feeling guilty about putting the others in danger." She muttered, and I couldn't help but let out a small laugh.

"You're not putting anyone in danger. Don't underestimate my men. They're all highly trained."

"I guess." She gave me a small smile.

"I'm proud of you, my love." I smiled softly. Her brows slightly rose as she looked at me. Her cheeks started to take on a rosy color as she gazed at me so innocently with her big green eyes. It was hard to believe that it was my innocent woman who had fucked someone up so badly.

"Tell me how you did it." I winked, seeing her eyes almost sparkle and ready to tell me everything as I resumed cleaning her hand.

I listened to every word as she explained. The more I listened, the more I wished I had taken Miciela and tortured her to death.

"I also stabbed her hand with the knife you gave me." Althaia said proudly.

"My little psychopath." I chuckled. She leaned forward, a small smirk on her lips.

"I learned from the best."

"You did." I matched her smirk before closing the distance between us, kissing her soft lips.

"I just don't know how she knew I was pregnant." She sighed as she rested her head on my shoulder.

"We'll figure it out." I assured her. It shouldn't have been possible for Miciela to access Althaia's medical journal since it was secured. I needed to get Raffaele on it to see what was going on.

"Nonna knows about it, too. I had to tell her what happened. She didn't say anything, but she didn't look pleased about it."

"She'll get over it. What we decide to do is none of their business, but only ours." I told her. Althaia's gaze went to the doorway, and I glanced over my shoulder seeing my father there.

"Go to your room. I will be right back." I said to her quietly, receiving a nod in response. I kissed her forehead before getting up.

I followed my father into his office. My Nonna and mother were present, as well as Antonio, Luca, Giovanni, and Raffaele, along with two of my father's men. Taking a seat on the couch, I already knew what he wanted to say.

I looked at the green emerald ring on my finger. It reminded me so much of her eyes, making me love it even more and wearing it with pride.

"Do you have any idea what kind of mess you've made?!" My father erupted.

"I didn't make a mess. In fact, I got rid of the trash." I faced him, my words not easing his anger.

"We had an alliance! They were our important allies in Italy, and that woman ruined everything! You are to get rid of her immediately!"

I abruptly stood and walked up to him, getting as close as I could while staring him down.

"What are you saying, father?" My voice was deadly low, daring him to repeat himself. He didn't back down as he frowned at me.

"She is ruining your business! Isn't she the one who attacked Miciela? Isn't she the reason you still haven't killed Gaetano as you should have long ago?" He spat out.

I let out a humorless laugh and gave a devilish smirk.

"My wife should have killed Miciela for mocking her about having a miscarriage. Althaia is not a killer; however, she has a husband who will happily kill in her name. Only a fool would dare to anger her."

"You married her?" My father asked in disbelief.

"Damn right I did." I turned around and slowly made my way over to my men.

My father went silent because he knew what it meant. Now that Althaia was my wife, she outranked everyone except me, giving her permission to do whatever she pleased with no questions asked.

Something caught my attention, having me look at the bottom of the closed office door, only to see a shadow had appeared from behind it. The corner of my mouth tilted upwards ever so slightly.

"It's a mistake." My father said, making me turn around to face him.

"If anyone has a problem with my wife." I declared, and my men drew out their guns but didn't aim. "They will find themselves six feet under." I finished, daring him to challenge me. Althaia was mine, and no one was taking her away from me.

His men exchanged glances with my father, their hands inching toward their tucked guns, but he shook his head at them.

"Good call." I smirked.

"Enough, you two." Nonna cut us off with a sharp tone as she stood up, giving us both a glare. "No one is to touch the girl! You have to honor the laws." My father received a hard look from her.

"Besides, she just proved she is more than capable of being the wife of a Don. She is exactly the type of woman Damiano needs by his side." Nonna said, leaving no room for discussion.

"I agree." My mother commented. "If anything, she showed she truly is a Bellavia." She looked at me with a wink.

"Tomorrow, a ceremony will be held, announcing Althaia is now officially my wife. I won't tolerate any disrespect towards her." I stated as a final order and walked out of the office.

"Damiano." My mother's voice had me stop and face her. Her eyes were slightly narrowed when she stopped in front of me. "When were you going to tell me you got married?"

"When we have settled on a date for the wedding." I smiled when her eyes lit up.

"Oh, so you are having a wedding? Excellent! I thought I would have to kill my own son." My mother chuckled.

"I thought you might if I didn't have one."

"You are my firstborn; of course, I want a wedding to celebrate my son has found the love of his life." She smiled warmly.

"Thank you, madre." I kissed the top of her head, grateful she wasn't displeased about it.

"Now, go to her." My mother didn't have to tell me twice as I immediately made my way upstairs.

I opened the door, finding Althaia had changed her clothes and was sitting on the bed with her sketchbook.

"How's my curious little psychopath?" I teased and sat on the bed in front of her. Her cheeks started to flush as she gave an innocent smile.

"I don't know what you're talking about. I have been here the whole time."

"Sure you have." I chuckled, grabbing her waist and settled her in my lap. "Have I not said you would be one terrible spy?"

"You really are the Devil! How did you know?"

"Your shadow."

"Oh." She laughed, looking embarrassed about it. I held her tightly to me as I buried my face into her neck, inhaling her scent. "It's not like I heard anything, anyway. That door is thick!"

"For obvious reasons." I chuckled.

"I wanted to know if I caused you trouble." Althaia sounded worried, making me smile against her neck.

"My love, your man is the Boss. We can do whatever the hell we want. If anyone has a problem with it, they can find themselves dead." I said, planting small kisses around her neck, feeling her body shiver as I did so.

She let out a small chuckle as my lips trailed along her jaw until I caught her lips with mine. My hands went down and grabbed her ass with both hands. My length was getting hard and ready to be buried deep inside of her.

"Ahem." Someone cleared their throat along with the sound of a knock on the door.

Althaia gasped, pushed me away, and quickly stood up. I inwardly groaned and looked to the door to see who dared to cockblock me.

It was my Nonna.

Althaia's face turned as red as it could be, and she seemed like she wanted the ground to swallow her whole.

"You should consider closing the door before starting anything." Nonna raised a brow at me, and I gave her a small shrug.

"I didn't know you were the type who peeked."

"Damiano!" Althaia scolded me, completely mortified, looking like she was about to faint. I couldn't help but laugh at the whole situation; getting fucking caught by my Nonna at the age of thirty.

"I will pretend I didn't hear that for your own sake." She sent me a glare, and in return, I gave her a smug grin.

"I'm not here to lecture you, but to acknowledge your pain. It's a unique pain to prepare your heart for a child that never comes."

I stood still, not expecting her to say that. The emotions I had suppressed for so long started to surface. I glanced at Althaia, pulling her into me as her eyes glistened.

"Lord knows I've had my experience with it. It's not something I wish anyone to go through. My dearest, both of you, know that your child is with our Lord in heaven, waiting to be reunited with you." Nonna spoke gently.

I let out a breath. Something inside me felt strange. I wasn't a big believer, but her words made me feel relieved in some way. Some sort of closure.

Althaia sniffed, wiping away the tears that made their way down her cheeks, but she was smiling.

"Thank you." Her voice was filled with relief. Nonna gave her a warm smile and lightly caressed her cheek before looking at me.

"You both will do great when the time comes." She patted my shoulder before turning to leave. For the first time, I was speechless. But one thing was for sure, I was feeling deep gratitude for her words.

"Oh, and just stay in the same room, for God's sake. I am tired of you sneaking around to be with each other." Nonna sighed tiredly. I shared a look with Althaia, whose eyes had gone wide before we both turned our attention to Nonna.

"You knew?" I asked, genuinely surprised. She scoffed and raised a brow.

"Of course, I knew! I know everything that happens under my roof." She gave me a knowing look, making me slightly smirk. "Am I not the one who taught you to keep eyes and ears everywhere, hmm?" Nonna said in an amusing tone before leaving the room.

We both stared at her retreating form before Althaia let out a laugh, and I joined in.

My Nonna was truly an exceptional woman.

One Hundred Three

DAMIANO

Althaia drifted off to sleep on our way to the mansion at the vineyards to get some peace. As I parked the car, I gazed at her sleeping form in the passenger seat, smiling when her lips were slightly parted and let out a faint snore.

Gently cradling her in my arms, I carried her to the master bedroom and tucked her into bed before returning to my car. I drove off once a few of my men pulled up to make sure Althaia was going to sleep with no disturbance. While the mansion was a secure place, I wasn't willing to take any chances.

My eyes landed on her phone that slipped out of her pocket. My brows furrowed at the thought of her phone being hacked after I had gotten rid of her necklace. Again, that shouldn't have been possible when Raffaele made sure her phone should be safe. I grabbed it and turned it off. He would need to figure out what the fuck was happening.

I arrived in front of the large, white building where I typically held my business meetings in Italy. Taking a quick scan around, a few of my men who were outside, greeted me with a nod before I headed inside.

I walked through the double office doors and found everyone already present, including my father, as I was the last to arrive. At the other end of the table sat the Romanos family.

Taking a seat, I leaned back, raised a brow, and waited for them to begin the discussion.

"You must understand why I have requested a meeting with you. I want to understand what has been going on before taking extreme measures." Tommaso's eyes held anger, but frankly, I didn't give two shits about it.

"We have been in business together for a long time. We had a deal, yet you killed two of my children. For what?!" He hissed out. His chest was heaving as he tried to control his anger.

I looked at him for a while with scrutinizing eyes before I let out a small laugh.

"I don't know about you, Tomasso, but I was raised by women. In my family, we don't fuck around when it comes to our women. We *value* them. We *kill* in their names. So, tell me, was I not right in getting rid of your daughter who harassed my wife and mocked her for miscarrying my child? For killing your son, who demanded my wife's head for defending herself?" I tilted my head, a chilling grin stretching across my face.

He exchanged a look with his son, Matteo, at the mention of my wife. They knew it was a promised death sentence if you went after a Don's wife, no matter who the fuck you were.

"This is not something I can let slide." Tomasso decided to say.

"That's up to you. We can settle things right here, right now." I shrugged nonchalantly and drew my gun, my men mirroring my action. The Romanos tensed up, now on high alert, analyzing the situation.

"However, you damn well know you don't want to start a war with me. You need me, but I don't need you. You're replaceable to me, and everything you've worked for will crumble. Your family will be gone too. So, what's your choice? Think wisely, because I won't show mercy after this."

Tomasso looked distressed, understanding he stood no chance against me. They were outnumbered, and I reveled in seeing the sweat form on his forehead.

Everyone has a price they are willing to accept to turn a blind eye to a situation, and he was no exception. He was a money-hungry man, and he proved to be a valuable asset in the business. The results were consistently satisfactory due to his eagerness. However, he knew that starting a war with me would mean losing everything and more because I would destroy anyone who dared to go after my wife.

"You know the saying, 'one bad apple spoils the whole barrel'? I found two and got rid of them. Maximo and Miciela let their ego take over and acted foolishly. My issues were with them and not with you." I told him truthfully.

Tomasso thought about it for a while before looking down at the table in submission, having me smirk.

"Good choice." I got up from my seat and looked at Matteo, who was the next heir. He would gladly continue the alliance because he didn't give two shits about his siblings; all he wanted was to be seen as someone important, and I could grant him that.

"Learn from your siblings' mistakes, and we will have a long partnership. I will meet with you next week, and we can discuss business. Goodnight, gentlemen." Without another word, I left.

My father caught up to me, walking silently by my side before giving my shoulders a few pats. It was his way of apologizing as he was never one to do so directly with words.

As I stepped outside, I found Raffaele next to my car.

"What's the status?" I asked him, and he let out a sigh.

"Her medical journal was hacked and left accessible for anyone to see. I couldn't trace it back to who did it since they have had time to cover their tracks."

I briefly closed my eyes at the information.

"It's most likely his doing. What the fuck is his game with this?" I frowned, rubbing my jaw. "I need you to check her phone. He might have used it as a listening device." I said, handing him Althaia's phone.

"Got it. You can also ask Sofia herself why and how they got that information. She's all cozied up in our lovely Chamber of Torture." He grinned.

"Good."

"Maybe we should have Althaia come and stab her with a fork?"

I cracked a smile at his joke as he laughed. The word about Althaia wanting to stab my father with a fork spread like wildfire among my men. They found it hilarious, given that she was a tiny person with a gentle soul, and they couldn't fathom how she could possibly cause anyone serious damage. However, after seeing how Miciela looked, they were all surprised, and I have never been prouder.

"Here's the necklace, by the way. They did a good job of making a replica." Raffaele handed me the small jewelry box. I took a look and nodded in approval. This was the closest to the original pendant.

"Good. Have the phone sent back to me in the morning." I instructed him.

"Sure thing." Raffaele sang as I got inside my car.

I parked in front of the stone building in the middle of nowhere and made my way through the underground passage. It was the perfect place for soundproofing, tucked deep under the ground to muffle any desperate screams.

I reveled in the isolation of my Chamber of Torture, far removed from civilization. The distant echoes of those who were dragged in there, futilely screaming for help, always filled me with a euphoric sensation.

I opened the door and stepped inside. Sofia was tied up in the center of the room, her face streaked with tears.

"Damiano..."

"Shut it." I told her, my tone cold as I stared her down. I despised the sound of her voice saying my name.

I grabbed a chair and sat in front of her, resting my arms on my legs as my eyes narrowed.

"You have some fucking nerve." I growled.

"Damiano, please! -"

"Did I say you can talk?!" My voice filled the room, and she fell silent, fresh tears streaming down her face. I clicked my tongue in annoyance.

Such a headache.

"You should have kept your mouth shut and lived quietly. The reason you even got out alive was Althaia feeling sorry for you, despite you trying to kill her. I let you live because I want to please her. However, you took advantage of that kindness. So, tell me, Sofia, how did Miciela know she was pregnant?"

"I-I don't know. I told her not to do anything, but she didn't listen!" She cried out desperately, sobbing uncontrollably.

"You dare to lie to my face." I sneered, and she frantically shook her head.

"I'm not lying! Please, Damiano!"

"Tell me the truth."

She sniffed and tried to calm down her sobbing.

"I-I really don't know what happened. She-she received some kind of link, and all of Althaia's information was there. Miciela wanted to do me justice, but I told her not to! I told her to let it go, but she didn't listen!" Sofia cried out, and I let out a chilling laugh.

"Justice for what, exactly? For defending herself when you tried to kill her?" I tilted my head.

"I tried to stop her! I really did! Please, just let me go! I will stay out of your life. Just let me g-go." Sofia continued to beg.

There was no point in talking to her anymore. I got the confirmation I needed.

I pulled out my pack of cigarettes, lit one up, and took a long drag before exhaling the smoke. I rose from my seat just in time for Vittoria to make her entrance, clad in her usual black leather outfit.

She stood ready for whatever torment her heart desired, especially since I had explicitly instructed my men to avoid causing harm to women unless absolutely necessary. Even then, they were permitted to use only enough force to restrain them.

This was precisely why I hired Vittoria. She was a sadistic woman who seemingly took more pleasure in torturing and breaking people than anyone else. She was perfect for the job.

"What sins did she commit?" Vittoria asked. That was her favorite question. The severity and duration of the torture were determined by the shit the person had committed.

"Tried to kill my wife." I said as I smoked. Her smile widened and turned into a sadistic smirk.

"She has earned a round with the whip." Vittoria's eyes danced with excitement as she pulled out her whip, swinging her arm, and a sharp sound resonated in the room when it kissed the floor.

"Whatever you desire, Vittoria." I faced Sofia, whose wailing had gotten louder, choking in between sobs, and looked like she was about to faint. "Your mother will be taken care of. She is, after all, loyal to the family." I told Sofia.

"I'm begging you! Please... please don't do this to me!" She shouted in desperation and tried to break free.

"You will be begging for a long time." Vittoria let out a sadistic laugh before swinging her arm again.

The whip sliced through the air, lashing Sofia's skin across the arm. Her eyes went wide, and her mouth was agape with no sound escaping her. Then the blood-curdling scream came out, and Vittoria closed her eyes to the sound with a smile.

I deeply inhaled the smoke, enjoying the punishment she was getting.

"Her voice makes me so excited." Vittoria said and opened her eyes. I finished my cigarette and turned around to leave.

"She's all yours." I heard the second swing of the whip, and more screaming escaped Sofia just before the door closed entirely behind me.

I would have stayed to watch, but the thought of my beautiful wife in bed, waiting to be cuddled in my arms, made me leave faster than ever before.

Returning to the mansion, I went upstairs to the bedroom, only to find the bed empty. Before I could call out her name, my eyes landed on the nightstand where a note lay. Grabbing it, a smirk appeared on my lips as I read the message.

Can the Devil find me?

One Hundred Four

DAMIANO

I loved a good hunt; especially when it comes to her.

I slipped off my shoes to move silently, attentive to any sounds within the house, but it remained quiet.

I searched the top floor before I made my way downstairs, checking every room before I reached the living room. She was still nowhere to be found. Just as I was about to resume my search, I came to a sudden stop and glanced out of the floor-to-ceiling window. There she was on the other side, grinning sheepishly before running away.

I quickly made my way out, loving she wanted me to chase her. She laughed, increasing the distance by running to the other side of the pool. Tilting my head at her, a smirk played on my lips as I took a step, watching her mirror the movement in the opposite direction.

"I'm going to catch you." I told her, taking a few slow steps in her direction.

"We'll see about that. If you do, I will reward you." Althaia winked, and a particular body part got quite excited at the idea.

"Deal." I faked a sprint towards her, and she released an excited laugh, racing as fast as she could, descending the stairs and heading to the garden.

Instead of following her directly, I took a detour to a part of the garden I was sure she hadn't discovered yet. As I walked along the small path, it led me right to her. She was hiding behind a tree, her back facing me as she kept an eye out for where she thought I would be coming from.

"Where did he go?" Althaia whispered to herself.

I sneaked up behind her, and she let out a noise of surprise as I turned her around, pinning her arms above her head.

"Got you, baby." I whispered.

"Wait—How?" She gasped.

"The Devil's work." I winked, pressing close to her, my thumb running across her plump lips.

"You haven't won yet." Althaia smirked, dropping to the ground to release her arms from my hold, and made another run for it.

I crossed my arms and leaned against the tree, watching her go before she stopped and looked over her shoulder.

"I'm giving you a head start." I said.

"Ha! I don't need a head start!" She grinned.

"Are you sure?" I tilted my head, wearing a teasing smile.

"Positive!" She replied confidently.

We locked eyes for a moment before I slowly let out a smirk.

"Run." I sprinted towards her, watching her eyes widen.

"Oh, fuck!" She yelled, laughing as she sprinted to the other side of the garden. She was fast, but not faster than me. I could have caught her the moment she turned around, but instead, I deliberately slowed down just to relish the sound of her voice.

Her laughter, a melodic symphony, reached my ears, wrapping around my heart with enchanting warmth. The world around me faded away, leaving only her; the source of my captivation. I silently thanked the universe for making this woman mine.

And I don't give a shit about how whipped I sound.

"Getting tired, old man?"

"Who are you calling an old man?" I scoffed.

"You, obviously. You can't even catch me. Perhaps take a nap and see if you can catch me when you've had enough rest." Althaia snickered, and I shook my head, entertained by her words.

"You have it wrong, my love. You know how lions love to play with their prey before killing it? It's to tire them out, making the kill easier." Her eyes narrowed, and she put her hands on her hips.

"What are you implying?"

"I'm toying with you before I kill your pussy with my dick, of course. You will not last for much longer." I gave her a sly grin, and she let out a snort.

"We will see about that!" Then she ran again.

"Oh, we will." I chuckled and sprinted after her, quickly closing the distance between us as she desperately tried to get away from me.

I grabbed her waist from behind, making her scream with laughter as I lifted and held her tightly to me. I placed her down, spun her around, and caged her between my arms against the tree.

"Caught you again." I said, my voice going low. "What's my reward for catching you?"

"What do you want?" Althaia bit down on her lip, and I leaned in closer to her face.

"You."

She gave me that one smile that made me go fucking crazy as her eyes went down to my lips. She closed the little distance between us and swept her tongue across my lip.

"Then take me." She breathed out, almost in a moan. My cock was hard in an instant. I grabbed the back of her legs, hoisting her up as she wrapped her legs around me.

"I'm going to fuck you nice and hard, piccola." I growled out and made my way inside with her.

Althaia wrapped her arms around me, kissing me hungrily as I tasted her tongue. I grunted, feeling like a starved person as my hands found their way under her nightgown.

She wasn't wearing any underwear.

"Fuck, I can't wait." I was too impatient and laid her down on the sunbed.

My hands traced every curve of her body beneath the silky fabric of her nightgown until I gently removed it. I had to take a moment, just to watch her as the moonlight cast a mesmerizing glow on her figure.

"So beautiful." I whispered. Her green eyes sparkled with a moonlit brilliance as if she belonged to a realm untouched by mortal existence.

Althaia smiled shyly at me; she always did whenever I complimented her, and I found it to be one of the most endearing things.

She grabbed my shirt, pulling me closer until our lips met to taste the sweetness of her tongue. I smiled a bit against her lips when her hands wandered around my body impatiently. I chuckled when she ripped my shirt open.

"Too slow." She said and undressed me. She had me switch positions, positioning herself on top of me as she straddled my hips. "Looks like I'll have to fuck you instead." She winked, and my cock twitched at her words.

"I'm all yours, baby."

Althaia grabbed my shirt and tied my hands together, making me arch a brow at her when she attached them to the sunbed's top.

"Enjoy the show." She gave me a sultry look, her eyes smoldering with desire as her lips faintly brushed mine.

Her hands glided down my body along with her, and I exhaled a breath when she wrapped her mouth around my cock.

"That's it, baby." I grunted. The sensation of her tongue swirling around my tip sent waves of pleasure through my body as she eagerly sucked me.

Althaia's eyes were on mine, and I groaned at the sight of her mouth full of my cock. That alone made me want to fill her mouth with my cum.

"Like it?" She smirked.

"Fucking love it."

She returned to straddle me, and she rolled her hips along my length, coating me with her arousal. Althaia moaned as she threw her head back as she continued to grind on me.

"Piccola." I warned through clenched teeth.

"Yes, baby?"

Sweet hell.

My cock twitched.

She bit down on her lip, and a wave of lust engulfed me entirely. I made the move to touch her, but my hands were met with restraint.

"Let me touch you." I growled out.

"Hmm, I can touch for you." Althaia winked and supported a hand behind herself as she spread her legs for me to see her glistening pussy.

"Fuck, you're so perfect." I whispered. I swallowed down another grunt as I watched her fingers trail down her stomach and settled between her thighs.

I was almost panting, my eyes never leaving her fingers as I watched intently how she spread her lips and circled her clit. Althaia moaned, hips bucking when she slowly inserted two fingers inside of her, pumping in and out.

My cock twitched again, and I grunted when she licked off her own arousal, wishing it was my tongue coated in her sweetness.

Finally, she lowered herself onto my cock as she let out that breathy moan I loved so much.

"Keep going." I groaned as I watched her pretty pussy taking me in and clenching ever so slightly around me.

I couldn't take it anymore. I needed to touch her. With one hard pull, I broke the top of the sunbed and released my hands. I grabbed her tightly and slammed my hips against her.

Althaia let out a choked gasp in surprise as I rammed into her pussy, needing to move hard and fast.

"Don't stop... please, don't stop." She moaned, closing her eyes as I felt her clench around me.

"Touch yourself, piccola." I panted, watching her fingers eagerly finding her clit.

"Oh, God... Damiano..."

"Come for me, baby." I gritted out, close to my own release when her entire body tensed. I plunged into her with one powerful thrust, causing her legs to shake with pleasure as she climaxed, and I quickly followed suit.

I took a moment to catch my breath before getting on my feet with her still around me.

"I'm claiming your ass tonight, piccola."

"Can I ask you something?"

"Always, my love."

Althaia shifted in bed to get a look at me.

"Have you visited Sienna yet?"

I slowly shook my head, surprised by her question.

"I haven't."

"I think you should." She smiled softly. "You should buy her favorite flowers and give them to her."

"Why? I have moved on." My brows slightly furrowed. I hadn't even considered visiting her again now that I was with Althaia.

"I know you have made peace with it, but you were still with her until the end. You should visit her when you have the chance."

"You're not jealous?" I asked.

"No." Althaia chuckled. "My jealousy has boundaries, and I can't be jealous of a woman who has passed away. She was in your life, and you cared for her."

I let out a small smile before giving a nod.

"Do you want to come with me?"

"That would be weird." She released a soft laugh. "It should be just the two of you. I don't want to invade that part of your life." Her fingers gently brushed against my cheek, leaving a tingling sensation in their wake, before she closed the little distance between us and pressed her lips against mine.

"I love you." She said against my lips before nestling into the crook of my neck.

"And I love you, baby."

"Oh, and by the way... God forbid, but if I were to die before you, you're not allowed to remarry. I swear to God, if you do, I'll crawl out of the grave, rip her head off, and take you with me. Do we understand each other?"

I let out a laugh at her warning.

"My love, you'll never have to worry about it. If you die, I will simply die with you. We will never be separated. I will follow you from this life into the next. Wherever you are, I'll be there."

"Promise?" She whispered.

"I promise, my love."

One Hundred Five

ALTHAIA

I pulled my hair up to see if I should do an updo or leave it down.

"Leave your hair down." Damiano leaned against the door frame.

"Are you sure?" I asked. He stepped closer and took a strand between his fingers.

"Yes. I love it when you leave it down. I also love it when I can wrap my hand around it like this." He said as he wrapped his hand around my hair, gently tugging it to make me look up at him. He placed a small, sweet kiss on my lips that had tingles erupt inside of me.

"Mind telling me where we are going?" I tried again. Damiano had been so secretive about it, and frankly, my curiosity was gnawing on me to figure it out.

"Somewhere." He smirked.

"Well, what are we doing, then?"

Damiano shrugged, entertained that I have been trying so hard to get just a hint.

"You will see when we get there." He retorted and led me out. "I brought you your dress."

"The dress that was kept a secret?"

"Yes. I picked it for you." Damiano smiled. Excited that he picked it out, I unzipped the gown bag and was immediately stunned by the dress.

"It's gorgeous!" I smiled big as I touched the soft fabric. "Of course, it's red." I chuckled.

"It's my favorite color on you." He took the dress out of its bag and helped me get dressed.

As I looked in the mirror, I admired the exquisite dress he had chosen for the occasion. The dress was a stunning one-shoulder design where a silver beaded band adorned the neckline, extending down to the side of my waist. The dress also had a side split, and a long trail elegantly trailed behind me.

"You look gorgeous, Mrs. Bellavia." Damiano kissed my bare shoulder. It never failed to make me shiver in ecstasy when he called me by my new name.

I took in the sight of him dressed in a snug burgundy velvet blazer paired with a perfectly fitted black dress shirt that embraced his frame.

"And you look handsome as ever, Mr. Bellavia."

Damiano extended his arm, inviting me to link mine through his.

"It's time to go, my love."

Wherever we were heading, a mix of excitement and nerves fluttered in my stomach.

We had been driving for a while, and since I wasn't familiar with Italy, I couldn't even guess where we were going.

Soon, we came to a stop, elevated and overlooking the ocean with a mountain curving around. The sunset glistening on the water made the view even more magical.

"This way." Damiano guided me down a stone staircase adorned with lights on either side.

As we descended, the illumination increased. Suddenly, loud and jubilant noises erupted, making a small gasp escape from me.

"What's this?" I asked once we reached the bottom. The place was beautifully decorated, and so many people were present; it was almost intimidating.

Another gasp of surprise escaped me when I spotted familiar faces; Cara, Arianna, Lorenzo, Cecilia, Ava, and others from back home. They all wore big smiles, and Cara waved ecstatically.

I looked at Damiano, my heart racing with a growing realization of what this was.

"A ceremony for you. It's time to take the oath, my love." Damiano smiled, and I mirrored his expression.

It's happening.

My heart was thumping faster, and my nerves were all over the place, but a soft smile from Damiano made me calm down and take a deep breath.

"Come." He spoke softly to me and led me to a stage that had been set up.

We stopped in front of a podium where a goblet, knife, gun, and card were present. My nerves spiked once again. I had only heard about an oath one had to take, but I had no idea how it was administered.

To distract myself, I scanned the vast crowd and spotted Nonna and his parents, offering warm smiles. My jaw wanted to drop as realization struck me; all these people present worked for Damiano. What struck me even more is that these were not all of them, but those who mainly resided in Italy.

I know Damiano was powerful and had many people working for him, but witnessing a glimpse of it now was truly incredible.

"La Famiglia Bellavia!" Damiano's voice boomed out, silencing everyone and giving us their full attention. It took everything in me not to shuffle my feet, seeing so many pairs of eyes on me.

"I have gathered you all here tonight to witness a new member join our family. My wife, Althaia Bellavia!" Damiano's beautiful smile accompanied his announcement, triggering a round of applause, shouting, and various noises from the assembled crowd. Excitement, nervousness, and a myriad of emotions coursed through me as I waited in anticipation of the next step.

Damiano looked at me.

"Are you ready?"

"Yes." I nodded, shoving my nervousness away, and focused on him.

"Althaia Bellavia, do you swear to be loyal to me as your leader and husband? Do you swear to be loyal to our family, to protect our brothers and sisters, and to honor our code of silence?" Damiano's golden-brown eyes bore into me with intense focus as he spoke loudly, clearly, and firmly, emphasizing the significance of the moment.

And I was ready for it.

"I swear." I responded, which earned a slight smirk from him.

He grabbed the knife from the podium and took my hand in his. I made a small grimace, knowing blood had to be shed since it was a blood oath. I just hoped it wouldn't be painful.

Damiano held my index finger, pinched it, and poked a small hole with the knife. I almost wanted to laugh at how dramatic I had made it up to be in my mind.

He then grabbed the card, and my brows went up when I recognized the image on it. It was the very same one he had tattooed on his chest; the hooded skull, the crown, and the massive Angel wings. It was my favorite tattoo of his; one I had memorized and recreated many times in my sketchbook.

"This drop of blood symbolizes your birth into our family. We are one until death." Damiano said and pinched my finger until blood dropped onto the card.

He flipped the card, showing a saint's picture, and repeated the process. The next thing he did was to take out a lighter and lit up the inside of the goblet. He put the card over the flames to burn.

"May your flesh burn like this saint if you betray me and our family. Repeat after me."

"As the flames burn this saint, so let my soul burn with the same flames for eternity. I enter alive, and only death can release me." I repeated, and Damiano kissed both of my cheeks.

"Benvenuta in famiglia, Donna mia." His golden-brown eyes were bright and filled with pride. I let out a small breath and smiled at him as a new feeling overtook my body.

Damiano grabbed my waist and pulled me into a kiss. Hard, but sweet, which had me melt entirely in the moment. I pulled away in surprise when I heard the crowd chanting loudly.

"Viva Don Damiano e Donna Althaia!... Viva Don Damiano e Donna Althaia!...."

It was an overwhelming feeling that had me feel incredibly warm and emotional inside as I looked at their proud and cheerful faces.

La mia Famiglia.

The sounds of multiple gunshots startled me, and I leaned into Damiano. Everyone had pulled their guns out and was firing in celebration.

"Join them." Damiano stepped behind me and grabbed my hand, guiding me to hold his gun with his hand over mine. Together, we fired a few shots over the ocean, and the crowd erupted in joy again.

"No turning back now. You are bound to me for life." Damiano spoke.

I gave a slight smirk, looking at him over my shoulder.

"Wasn't that my destiny in the first place, hmm?"

"You're right. You belonged to me the minute I laid my eyes on you." He mirrored my smirk.

"Hot." I winked.

"Look at them shamelessly flirting in front of us all like that. And even in front of Nonna!" Raffaele's voice rang, having me roll my eyes at him.

"Don't look if you have a problem." Damiano told him.

I chuckled as we made our way back down from the stage and was immediately enveloped in a tight embrace as Cara squealed in happiness.

"I want to be mad at you for not telling me right away you got engaged, and even more for getting married in secret, but I'm so damn happy for you that it doesn't even matter anymore!" She practically screamed. I laughed as I hugged her back, grateful she was here to witness this moment.

"When did you arrive?" I asked them all.

"Today! We got the news yesterday and left in a hurry. Thanks for the heads up, by the way." Cara said to Damiano in a teasing tone.

"You're welcome." He simply replied. She gave him a bored look before shaking her head.

"Well, congratulations to you both!" Cara said, and with a playful smile, she opened her arms wide to hug Damiano.

A small crease appeared between his brows when she neared him. She wrapped her arms around him, and his arms remained still by his sides, not making a move to hug her back.

"Come on, Damiano. I'm your brother's soon-to-be wife! Gimme a hug!"

I couldn't help but laugh at the amusing sight. Damiano looked at me as if saying I needed to get him out of this situation.

"She has a point. She's your family too." I said. He looked down at her before slowly patting her back.

"That hurts to watch." Arianna grimaced as she looked at them, along with Ava and Cecilia. They all chuckled at how awkward Damiano looked at the moment.

"He needs to loosen up a bit, and I'm helping him to do so." Cara laughed, finally releasing Damiano, and he immediately wrapped his arm around my waist.

Arianna looked at us both with a warm smile.

"Congratulations, big brother. I'm happy you finally found the one." As she hugged him, Damiano smiled and kissed the top of her head.

"Oh, I see, how it is Damiano!" Cara squinted her eyes at him. "Don't worry. We will get there!" She promised.

"I will stab him if his lips go anywhere near you." Lorenzo made an appearance with Dom, who went to wrap his arm around Arianna. It looked like the brothers had finally accepted their relationship.

"Is that a threat, brother?" Damiano smirked.

"A promise." Lorenzo retorted, mirroring his smirk.

"Cara, come here." Damiano called after her, and her eyes lit up.

"Althaia." Lorenzo looked at me, and Damiano's head snapped to look at Lorenzo so fast with a warning look.

"Now, that's a death wish, brother."

"... I don't understand. Are they joking, or do they really want to kill each other?" I asked Arianna when they continued making threats to one another.

"Just their usual pissing contest." She sighed.

"You will see a lot of that." Cecilia said, amused as she came over to us with Ava to congratulate me.

"I guess." I chuckled.

The evening continued with more people coming up to greet and congratulate us. They all made me feel so warm and welcome that I couldn't stop smiling from ear to ear.

Eleonora was so happy that all of her children were gathered, and Nonna was busy telling the others to hurry and get married because she wanted great-grandbabies. She continued to rant about how she was not getting any younger while everyone stood awkwardly.

I chuckled quietly and took a break from the crowd to grab a drink from the bar.

"What's up with the glaring?" I asked Raffaele, finding him sitting on the barstool and glaring into the crowd. He didn't respond as he continued staring daggers at someone. I followed his gaze and saw Ava talking to another man, laughing and touching his arm.

"Oh..." My brows went up.

"I don't like that. I fucking hate it. Why the fuck is she touching him?" He snarled, and I rubbed his back in comfort.

"Are you still being very explicit with your words, or...?" I trailed off, and he gave me a blank look before sighing.

"No. At least, I don't think so." He muttered and rubbed the back of his head in frustration.

I let out a small sigh as I tried to comfort him, feeling sorry for him because it was obvious he wanted her, but it looked like she wasn't interested.

"Oh my God!" I suddenly erupted in a laugh when Damiano walked up to us.

"Yeah, thanks for laughing." He sulked, and I shook my head at him as I chuckled.

"You have it all wrong. She is trying to make you jealous." I told him. This had his attention, and he straightened up.

"What?"

"Remember when we first met? I flirted with you and touched your arm and all that stuff?"

"How can I forget." Raffaele wiggled his brows, and I rolled my eyes at him. I looked at Damiano, who had reached us, before turning my attention back to Raffaele.

"I did it solely to make him jealous. And it worked." I pointed out to him.

"You almost had me kill him." Damiano remarked.

"That's on you. No one told you to be jealous." I grinned.

"Okay, so what do I do? Punch the shit out of him as Damiano did to me?" Raffaele asked impatiently.

"You can. If you're sure you can win the fight." Damiano said as he pulled me into him.

"Are you saying I'm weak?" Raffaele scoffed.

"No, but Renzo is a cage fighter. He has never lost a fight." He added. Raffaele looked back at Renzo and rubbed his chin.

"I could always shoot him."

"Okay, that's enough. No one is punching or shooting anyone." I gave a stern glare to both of them.

"I just tried to help." Damiano shrugged.

"Yeah, by sending him to his death." I replied.

"So far, I'm only getting insults from you both." Raffaele gave us a sarcastic smile.

"Listen, she's obviously doing this to get a reaction from you because she has been glancing your way throughout the evening. You don't need to fight him, or freaking kill him. Just go up to her and show him she's yours; show her you're serious about her." I smiled, and he nodded a few times, taking in the information.

"Okay. How do I look?" He straightened out his dress shirt and made sure his hair was in place.

"Handsome! Now, go get her tiger." I smiled.

Raffaele's gaze shifted towards Ava, who was still deep in conversation with Renzo.

"Ava!" He shouted, attracting attention to him, and practically stormed towards her. My jaw hung open as this was not how I meant he should do it.

Ava turned around to look at him, and Raffaele grabbed her by the waist and kissed her. It didn't take long before Ava wrapped her arms around his neck and kissed him back.

"Huh... I guess he could do it like that." I said in surprise.

"Took him long enough." Damiano commented, and I chuckled in agreement. As I glanced around, something caught my eye. I looked across the other side of the water, and my gaze fixed on the mountain that curved around.

"Damiano, look!" I gasped and pointed.

Luca was down on one knee!

I waited in anticipation as we could only see them and not hear them. It felt like the longest moment before Cecilia leapt into his arms.

"About time. But I still did it better."

"Not everything is a competition." I laughed at his comment.

"You're right. No one can compete with me." He looked at me with a teasing look. I shook my head with a playful roll of my eyes and leaned into him, sighing blissfully.

Everything is perfect.

One Hundred Six

ALTHAIA

I made one last round of checks in the massive banquet hall before the wedding ceremony. Everything looked like it belonged in a fairytale, and Cara deserved every single moment of it.

Her wedding was being held in a gorgeous castle, and the reception banquet was exquisitely decorated in all white; even the floor featured a beautiful glossy white design. The ceiling was stunningly adorned with flowery chandeliers, and long white vine flowers hung down, almost creating a beautiful curtain of white blossoms.

Pleased with the work that had been done, I walked up the stairs and down the long hall in the direction of the master suite to check on Cara.

The moment I opened the door, I was struck speechless by the breathtaking sight that greeted me.

Cara in an off-shoulder Cinderella-esque wedding gown with gorgeous streaks of silver design. It had beautiful diamonds and pearls stitched to it, making the entire dress sparkle.

Her hair was beautifully done in an updo, and she even wore a tiara that completed the look altogether. Her neck was decorated with a classic round diamond necklace, complemented by matching earrings.

"You look absolutely breathtaking." I stared at her in pure awe.

"Thank you, Thaia." Cara smiled warmly before taking in a deep breath.

With a smile playing on my lips, I grasped the veil and made my way towards her.

"How nervous are you?"

"So fucking much, and I don't even know why. I knew this day was coming, and it's all part of the deal." She breathed out and kept twisting her fingers in nervousness.

"Because this is no longer just a business deal for you. You love him." I chuckled.

"I know." Cara said in relief, happiness etched on her face.

"You're finally free; to live the life you want with Tank Man."

"He's never going to hear the end of that nickname, is he?"

"Never!" We both laughed.

With the long veil finally in place, I turned to steal a glance at her, my eyes filled with adoration. She looked like the most beautiful Disney princess ever.

"I wish mom was here to see you. She would have been so proud of you." I said, my voice cracking, tears shimmering in my eyes, as Cara's expression softened into a sad smile.

"I'm happy I got to see her one more time." She sniffed. "Oh no, the tears are coming, and I just got my makeup done!" She quickly looked up, blinking back tears. I chuckled as I blinked my tears away and helped her blow some air to not ruin her makeup.

Once making sure Cara was ready, I went to check on Tank Man to see how it was going on his end. I neared his suite and some of Damiano's men were outside.

"Donna." They greeted me with a nod, and I smiled in return.

"I told you, Althaia is just fine."

"Not going to happen."

I shook my head, a bit amused by them. They insisted on calling me Donna as a sign of respect, and no matter how many times I told them to just call me by my name, they refused big time.

I knocked on the door, waited for a bit before poking my head inside. When I saw it was the usual gang present with Lorenzo, I entered.

"Oh wow, look at you! You cleaned up well." I grinned as I approached him.

He did look impressive in his wedding tuxedo; an elegant silk dress shirt in a deep copper color with silver patterns on the collars to match Cara's dress, his cuffs following the same design, and a tie to bring it all together.

His waistcoat was black with crisscross patterns of the same deep copper color and had a crown symbol in the middle. He finished the look with a black velour blazer and classic black dress pants.

"Thank you, Althaia."

"So, Lorenzo…" I trailed off while I fixed his tie. "Since Cara has a useless father, I have taken the role to say this." I tugged on the tie to have him meet me at eye level, and have it slightly tighten around his neck.

"If you hurt her, I will kill you. I'm not sure how since you're Tank Man, but I will find a way. I promise you that."

The corner of his mouth went up.

"I can assure you, I'm not going to hurt her." He promised.

"Good!" I said happily and released him with a big smile.

"You're lucky you're my brother's wife. Or else I wouldn't have let it slide that you just threatened to kill me." He said with a slight smirk.

"Ah, yes! This kind of power feels amazing! How does it feel to be outranked by someone who has only been around for a few months?" I teased.

Damiano had told me about my new status as his wife, and I may have rubbed it in Giovanni's face that I outranked him. He gave me his usual scowl in return as I continued to make fun of him.

"Only because you're fucking Damiano." Lorenzo scoffed.

"Guilty." I grinned, and he cracked a smile.

"You may outrank me in status, but I outrank you in everything else. Let's have a fight and see who will win."

"Oh, as much fun as that sounds, I will happily give you the win. I'm pretty sure my head would pop off if you put me in a headlock. And I'm definitely not about to have you smash me into the ground Tank Man style and break my back. I would rather have Damiano break my back, if you know what I mean." I wiggled my brows.

My answer had him throw back his head in laughter. I gave a surprised expression but smiled as it was the first time I had ever heard him laugh like that.

"You're really something else. It's good to see you're not scared of me anymore." Lorenzo gave a faint smile.

"I'm almost there. I still get intimidated sometimes. The only reason I'm not right now is because my husband and bodyguards are present." I joked, and he gave an amused look. "Anyway, you look amazing." I gave one more smile before I turned around to leave, but not before giving a cheeky wink to Damiano.

I walked out of the suite and down the hall, smiling as I knew Damiano was following me. Before I knew it, a hand clasped around my arm, and I was pulled into another hallway.

I was pinned against the wall, and Damiano claimed my lips with his. I placed my hands on his chest as he wrapped his arm around my waist, pulling me into him as much as possible.

"Hey, handsome." I said, smiling against his lips.

"Hey, beautiful." He gave one more kiss before leaning slightly back. "You look heavenly, my love." Damiano smiled as his eyes raked over my body.

"And you look magnificent as ever." My eyes went down to check him out. He was wearing an elegant three-piece suit tuxedo with gold outlining, and the inside of his blazer had a beautiful gold flower design. He looked like a royal as always.

"How are you feeling?" Damiano asked, having me look back at him.

"Good. Though I can't wait to hit the bed and sleep." I let out a small sigh. Damiano looked almost concerned.

"You were tired a lot the last time..." He trailed off, and I immediately shook my head.

"Maybe because I have never attended so many parties in such a short time before." I chuckled.

Of course, we had to celebrate Luca and Cecilia's news, and a massive engagement party was held. We also celebrated my birthday in Italy. With everything that had been going on, I had completely forgotten all about my birthday, and Damiano held a surprise party for me. I had never been spoiled that much in my life as I was on my birthday.

Once again, Damiano went above and beyond, leaving me absolutely speechless. He gifted me a Bugatti Chiron. I never thought I would ever be an owner of a Bugatti. I found that situation fitting to make a joke about how we should race to see which Bugatti was faster, to which I received warning glares from him.

What made me cry was when Damiano made me his official designer for his winery business. He wanted to redesign all the wine bottles to have their own unique styles. I also signed a contract to be a part-owner as well. I felt honored that he chose me to be a part of his vineyard's rich history.

Then there was Cara's bachelorette party, which was beyond crazy! It was just us girls having a night out, and it came to a point no one could stand upright from drinking too much. We were laughing at everything, and when Damiano, Lorenzo, Luca, Raffaele, and Dom came to get us home, we tried to run away from them.

"It has been crazy and then dealing with jetlag on top of it all. I also didn't get that much sleep to make sure everything was ready on time." I explained.

Damiano slightly frowned, his eyes landing on my stomach.

"If it will make you feel better, I will take a test when we get home." I offered, and he gave a nod.

"I have been filling you up pretty good." He whispered with a smirk, making me chuckle in response.

"You have. If you're not too busy later, I'm pretty sure we can find a room and have a little fun." I winked.

"Or we can just find a room now."

"Nope. Can't ruin my hair and wrinkle my dress before the wedding. Keep it in your pants for now." I said and pushed a finger into him to make him step back.

"Worth a try." He muttered.

"I will let Cara know you're ready." I informed Lorenzo, who had stepped outside.

Just as I was about to leave, I stilled when I spotted my uncle at the end of the hall with some of my father's men. An involuntary shiver ran down my spine in disgust at the sight of him, and I took a step back.

"What's wrong?" Damiano wrapped his arm around me when I had pressed myself into him to comfort myself.

"He just creeps me out." I muttered.

They all turned to look at my uncle, their expression blank but their gaze so intense. He looked our way for a split second, his eyes meeting mine before he turned his back to us.

"Disgusting perv for grabbing my butt." I shuddered again in disgust as I relived the moment, and the nausea appeared.

They all snapped their heads at me at the same time, and a flare of anger showed in Damiano's eyes as he looked at me.

"What did you say?" His tone let me know he was one second away from storming to my uncle. "When the fuck did he do that?" Damiano's jaw tightened, and his hands clenched into fists.

"At the dinner party." I quickly grabbed his hand to stop him. "Damiano, no. Besides, you already cut out his tongue that day. Let us just enjoy the wedding and deal with him another time." I tried to tell him, but he kept glaring daggers into my uncle's back.

"Did he do anything else?" Damiano almost sneered at his question.

"No." I shook my head. "I need to go back to Cara. It's time for you to go as well." I told them.

"I will go with you."

"Only if you can walk past him without crushing his skull into the wall."

He looked at me for a long time, clicking his tongue in annoyance.

"Yeah, I thought so - oh, look, he's going now, so all good! Hurry up and go to the altar. I will get Cara." I smiled and quickly went on my way. "He's ready." I smiled excitedly at Cara, and she took another deep breath before plastering on a smile.

"It's time to get married."

One Hundred Seven

DAMIANO

"He grabbed her ass. What kind of fucking sick pervert would do that to their niece?" Giovanni spat out as we made our way to the altar. It was taking everything to keep myself in check, and not empty my gun in her so-called uncle's face.

"I should have fucking killed him that day." I said, clenching my jaw. The only reason I didn't was because I needed this wedding to go through; to have a reason to stay close.

"His head is mine. I've waited a long time for everything he did to Cara—the years of abuse." Lorenzo sneered.

"I want that DNA test done as soon as possible." I ordered them.

"Is it necessary to have a DNA test? Just after what she said is good enough proof to me." Luca commented.

"It is, because after putting an end to Gaetano once and for all, I'll need concrete evidence when I come clean with everything to Althaia." I told him.

That aspect would be the most challenging part of all this; revealing the truth to Althaia about everything that has been going on. While she believes I'm keeping her in the loop, in reality, I have been gathering proof to present to her who has been behind all the attacks.

If she knew what had really been going on, she would want to get involved or handle it on her own. Knowing how reckless she could be, I wasn't telling her anything for her own safety. Not until we knew for sure.

Once I tell her the truth, everything else will be out of my control, and the one I fear the most is Althaia's reaction. She was going to hate me for keeping everything a secret.

"Everything is ready and everyone is in position. We'll be waiting for your signal." Antonio informed me, and I gave a nod.

"Good. I want anyone vulnerable out of here as soon as I give the signal."

My Nonna and mother were present, and I wanted them out of here, along with Althaia, Cara, and anyone not fit for a fight and in need of protection. Even though I had been training Althaia, and she had already shown impressive skills and creative thinking, this was a different fight, and it was not something I wanted her to witness.

The plan was to trap them inside the castle, making it easier to have them locked in one place for complete control over the situation. I wasn't going to play games anymore, but I still aimed to take him down as quietly as possible to avoid a larger war. My men were my responsibility, and I intended to carry this out with minimal casualties on our side.

My father was right; this had gone on for too long already. We were supposed to take down Gaetano months ago — quick and easy after gaining his trust and leading him to believe he could have access to my weaponry.

Because that was how it all worked. It was a game of wealth and power, and I relished setting an example for everyone that I was the one running the shit here, and no one else. I eliminated anyone before they could even become a threat.

"Stay alert." I gave one last order before they proceeded to take their seats.

I walked down the aisle with Lorenzo and stopped at the altar with him since I was the best man. Glancing around at the seated people, Nonna and our parents sat at the front on our side, while Gaetano, his wife, brother, and Carlos were on the bride's side, seated at the front.

Those bastards were smiling, thinking this was all in their favor, and it took everything in me not to pull out my gun. Instead, I directed my attention to Lorenzo.

"How are you feeling, brother? Nervous?" I offered a teasing smile when he shot me a blank look.

"No."

"Of course, you're not. You are Tank Man, after all." That garnered an amused reaction from him.

"That wife of yours has a unique way of expressing her thoughts."

"You don't say. She calls me the Devil." I smirked.

"How fitting." Lorenzo snorted.

"I would say Tank Man is quite fitting as well."

"It is, actually. Cara is definitely not complaining." He smirked, and it was my turn to give him a blank look.

"Not interested in hearing about that. I've already seen your ass, and I'm not in the mood to be any more traumatized." I told him.

"Really? My ears were bleeding when I heard you fucking in the bathroom. Besides, I blessed your eyes with my pretty ass." Lorenzo gave me a playful smile.

"There's nothing pretty about your ass, and I bet you were almost wanking to the sound of me."

"Now that's fucking disgusting."

We both stared at each other before we cracked a smile. It was obvious to hear just how much Althaia's and Cara's personality had rubbed on us.

The chatter subsided as the music began playing. All eyes turned towards the large double doors as they opened. A smile spread across my face as Althaia walked out, the first one to do so as the Maid of Honor.

Althaia smiled beautifully, and her green eyes sparkled with majesty. She looked ethereal in her dress, which elegantly embraced her beautiful body as she walked down the aisle, holding a small flower bouquet in her hands.

Our eyes locked, and when I couldn't tear my gaze away, and she responded with a shy smile, her cheeks blushing a rosy hue. I continued to watch her until she came to a stop, and my eyes shamelessly traced down her body. The dress and its color complemented her tanned skin exquisitely, embracing her figure with delicious allure.

I definitely wanted to rip that dress off her later.

The change in the music helped me snap out of my thoughts, preventing me from taking any impulsive actions. Once again, everyone directed their attention to the doors.

Cara, in her big wedding dress with a veil-covered face, started to slowly walk down the aisle. I glanced at Lorenzo, letting out a subtle smile as I observed his reaction; a reaction I knew all too well from experiencing it many times with Althaia.

He looked at her, completely mesmerized, trapped under her spell as she walked towards him. Lorenzo went to her, his hand reaching out to intertwine with hers, and together they stood before the priest to begin the sacred rites and prayer.

As the priest spoke, my eyes found their way back to Althaia, captivated by her cheerful face as she looked at Cara and Lorenzo. Lost once more in my thoughts, I surrendered to the vision of her, imagining her in a white bridal gown. Marriages and starting a family had never held much appeal for me, but it was inexplicable how she made me want it all.

With her, and only her.

Althaia bit down on her lip, trying to stifle her laughter while raising a brow at me. That was when I realized they were waiting for me to give the priest the rings for him to bless.

"Take this ring as a sign of my love and fidelity. In the name of the Father, the Son, and the Holy Spirit."

The place erupted in cheerful applause as Cara and Lorenzo sealed the beginning of their marriage with a kiss.

"Have you seen Michael anywhere? I can't believe he's not attending the wedding." Althaia's brows furrowed as we entered the reception banquet. She scanned the area, but Michael was nowhere to be found.

"I haven't." I replied. His absence caught my attention, given that Gaetano usually had him by his side as his right hand.

Althaia let out a sigh.

"Why are you looking for him?"

"I forgot to call him back in Italy. I thought I would hear him out."

"He didn't call you again?" I questioned, and she shook her head.

Interesting.

"Don't worry about it now. He'll probably show up later." I said, hoping to prevent her from overthinking and asking around for him.

"I guess. Well, I should say hi to my dad. I haven't talked to him since we got here." She let out a small, embarrassed chuckle and headed in the direction of Gaetano.

Gaetano stood with his wife and a few of his men, smiling as Althaia approached and hugged him.

I turned away from them, scanning the surroundings before pressing a small button on the inside of my collar.

"Keep an eye out for Michael. He might be lurking around." I ordered before walking up to Althaia, not wanting her to be alone in their presence.

"Damiano! I see you snatched my little girl." Gaetano smiled happily. I stared at him blankly, noting his unusually cheerful demeanor as he raised his glass. "May this only bring our families closer and more powerful."

One Hundred Eight

DAMIANO

"Oh, darling! The ring is just beautiful!"

My jaw clenched at the horrendous high-pitched voice. Every time that woman opened her mouth, it felt like a bunch of knives continuously stabbing into my ears. I was convinced Gaetano was partially deaf. It was impossible he heard that voice and decided to marry it.

"Thank you, Morella." Althaia gave a tight smile, and I could tell it was taking everything in her not to grimace.

"Wonderful news, figlia! When's the big day?" Gaetano smiled widely.

"Oh, actually…" Althaia started, and my hand squeezed her waist a little, warning her not to let it slip out. She quickly glanced at me before facing Gaetano again with a soft smile. "…We haven't decided yet. Plenty of time to figure it out." She told him instead.

"Good, good. The sooner, the better." He looked at me when he said that, not being discreet about his underlying message to me.

"Congratulations again, darling." Morella smiled big.

"Enjoy the party." I told them with a nod and led Althaia away from them. Hell, I was desperate to get away from that voice.

"We certainly will." Gaetano replied.

Not for too long.

"What was that about?" Althaia asked me quietly when we stepped away from them.

"About what?"

"Why couldn't I tell my father that we got married?"

"I thought you said you wanted to keep it a secret?"

"Yeah, well, we already told your family and everyone who works for you." Althaia scowled slightly.

"It's not the same. My family and men need to know who you are; it changes things. Your status as my wife, and second in rank, lets them know you are the top priority when it comes to safety."

"You're always acting as if my father is going to hurt me." Althaia's brows dipped, looking at me as if trying to figure out what was going on.

"I'm just cautious. That's all." I told her, and that was the truth.

"Is that why you're all tense today? Is there something going on that I don't know about?" She looked concerned, and I gave her a smile.

"No, nothing's going on, my love. Don't worry and enjoy the wedding." I placed a kiss on her forehead, and I saw her visibly relax at my words.

"All right. Oh, get excited about the cake! I know you're not that into sweet things, but I helped choose the filling, and it's freaking delicious!" Althaia's eyes lit up at the mention of the cake, amusing me. Food was truly the way to her heart.

"That's not true." I pulled her into me as I leaned slightly down to her and spoke quietly. "I eat your pussy all the time, and you're deliciously sweet."

"Damiano!" She gasped and looked around to see if anyone heard me while her cheeks started to flush in such an adorable way. "Don't say that! Our families are here!"

"So?" I raised a brow at her as I continued to tease her. "I want them to know I take good care of my wife."

"You're such a shameless man!"

I chuckled when she hurried away from me in embarrassment and joined Arianna, Ava, and Cecilia. I took one more look around, observing everyone chatting as they should, making sure there was still a festive atmosphere.

I joined Althaia and the others as Cara and Lorenzo made their grand appearance. Another round of applause echoed for them, with people cheering as they descended the stairs together.

"I can't believe you're actually married now! Congrats once again." Althaia embraced Cara tightly.

"It's about time." Cara chuckled.

"Yeah, sorry about that." Althaia scrunched up her nose. "But hey, at least you're Mrs. Tank Man now! Better late than never." Althaia grinned.

"How in the world are you coming up with those names?" Arianna laughed.

"Apparently, she thinks I have the same build as Lorenzo. Thanks for that, by the way." Cara gave her a sarcastic smile.

"I never thought I would be called fat on my own wedding day." Lorenzo commented, crossing his arms as he looked at them all.

"No, not fat. Just big." Cara gave him a cheeky wink.

"Ew, gross. Save that talk for your wedding night." Arianna groaned, and I nodded in agreement.

"Congratulations." I wished them both. I gave a small smirk to Lorenzo when I wrapped my arm around Cara's shoulder.

"Oh my God! It's happening!" Cara gasped in excitement. Lorenzo's gaze was focused on my arm around her with a glare.

"I wish you a lifetime of happiness with Lorenzo." I said and kissed the top of her head just to piss him off.

Arianna and Althaia looked at me with surprised looks while Cara stood still in shock.

"Althaia, you look a little tired on your feet." Lorenzo looked at her with a small grin, ignoring the warning glare I was sending him.

"Huh...?" She looked at him confused, but then let out a small squeal when he suddenly swooped her into his arms. Althaia's eyes went wide, and she was blushing uncontrollably.

"I don't care if you're my brother, I will shoot you."

"Likewise."

"Put her down."

"Only if you let go of my wife first."

We stared at each other, waiting until one of us gave in, but I refused to lose. Instead, I pulled Cara closer to me and wrapped both arms around her. Cara didn't care; she was only happy about what was happening and even wrapped her arms around me. This pissed Lorenzo off even more, seeing her like this.

"Althaia, wrap your arms around my neck."

"Fuck off, you bastard." I snarled and grabbed my wife out of Lorenzo's arms.

The evening continued smoothly, with people enjoying themselves. Gradually, people whom I didn't need to be here were escorted out of the castle.

My father kept Gaetano engaged in conversation, ensuring his distraction while we executed our plan. It had to be done smoothly and unnoticeable while I had my men in position.

"I'm going with Cara to help her into her second dress for the cake cutting." Althaia informed me with a smile. I had made sure Arianna kept Althaia distracted as well, so she wouldn't notice why my Nonna and mother were suddenly missing.

I wrapped my arm around her waist and placed a soft kiss on her lips.

"Be safe." I told her quietly. She looked at me, slightly confused, before letting out a smile.

"I will try to make it back and forth safely." She teased with a chuckle. They both went on their way and soon were out of view. I looked around at my men, giving a discreet nod that it was time.

"Dario, they're coming your way now. Escort them quietly and safely out of here." I ordered. They were the last ones I needed to get out of here.

"Cop -"

I stilled when he got cut off.

I looked at Lorenzo, and his eyes narrowed, letting me know it wasn't just me who heard it.

"Dario, answer me." My entire body tensed up when the only response was the sounds of him gagging and gargling.

In his own blood.

"What's going on here?"

"Oh my God, Dario!"

I held my breath at the sound of Althaia's voice.

No...

No!

Fucking no!

My legs sent me in a sprint towards the stairs with Lorenzo in front of me when we heard them scream. My heart was already pounding in fear of not getting there in time. I couldn't let that happen.

Not again!

As we ran, the sounds of whistling and crackling reached my ears. Someone had set the fireworks off.

I halted at the top of the stairs when the power suddenly went out, leaving us completely in the dark.

"Raffaele, what's going on?" I spoke into the comm link, but he didn't answer. "Raffaele!" I shouted, but it was still radio silent.

"I don't have time for this." Lorenzo said and moved again. The only light we had came from the moonlight streaming through the large windows in the hallway.

I sprinted with Lorenzo when suddenly two figures emerged from a connected hallway, machine guns aimed directly at us. I grabbed the back of Lorenzo's shirt, yanking him forcefully back with me as a barrage of gunfire erupted.

We dodged by a hair's breadth, seeking refuge by the staircase with wood splinters raining over us. Lying low, the chaos in the banquet hall grew louder with the relentless gunfire echoing from different directions. Shouts and screams intertwined with the shattering of glasses filling the air, and I dreaded I might already be too late.

"Where the fuck is Gaetano?!" I shouted as I pulled out my gun. Rage overtook my body, and I unleashed a torrent of bullets on anyone who dared to enter my line of sight.

Projectiles were flying from all directions, my men seeking cover and returning fire whenever they could. I joined the chaotic symphony of gunfire while scanning the room.

Gaetano was nowhere to be seen. The blackout was his cue to slip out.

"Damiano, cover me!" Lorenzo shot up, and I swiftly drew my second gun, unleashing a barrage of bullets to divert attention.

My shots created a momentary distraction, and it was enough for Lorenzo to get far enough into the hallway as he moved closely along the wall.

I stopped, giving them time for them to reappear. Just as one of them edged into view, Lorenzo lunged, slamming him mercilessly to the ground. The second one emerged moments later, and I shot him before he could reach Lorenzo.

I sprinted toward the room where Dario was stationed with Lorenzo hot on my heels. I tried to get in touch with any of my men who were positioned on this end, but was met with silence.

"Fuck." I came to an abrupt stop at the doorway at the sight of Dario sprawled on the floor with his throat slit. "Check the rooms." I told Lorenzo, my frustration and anger boiling over as I kicked open doors in the next room.

My heart was pounding as I rushed from room to room, shouting in pure frustration and anger when I found my men lying on the floor.

All dead.

And my wife was nowhere to be seen.

"Damiano!"

I sprinted back to Lorenzo's position, finding him kneeling beside Raffaele, who lay unconscious with a pool of blood around his head.

"He's alive." Lorenzo informed me once he confirmed his condition.

I removed my jacket and applied pressure to the wound on the back of Raffaele's head. He was supposed to oversee the cameras and control the power, a critical part of our plan, but they had reached him before we could put our strategy into action.

The sound of approaching footsteps made me raise my gun at the door, only to lower it when I saw it was Luca.

"Shit!" Luca exclaimed as he saw Raffaele.

"They couldn't have gone far –" I halted mid-sentence, sharing a look with Lorenzo. He heard it too. The fireworks had ceased, allowing us to hear the whirring of helicopter rotors.

"Luca, help Raffaele!" I got up in an instant and rushed toward the front lawn. It was the only place close enough to the castle for a helicopter to land.

Lorenzo and I split ways, each racing down a different hall to get to them before it was too late.

The helicopter came into view through the large windows. I stopped running when I saw Gaetano standing next to the helicopter as they loaded an unconscious Cara inside. A snarl of rage escaped me when I saw Althaia fighting against three men to break free of their hold.

"Don't fucking touch her!" I shot at the window, cracking it before breaking it as I jumped through.

I landed on the ground, rolling to break the fall, not caring about the shards of glass cutting into my skin before I sprang to my feet. The piercing sound of her cries for help pushed me to sprint faster towards her.

"Knock her out already!" Gaetano shouted at them, and one of them pulled out a syringe to sedate her.

"Althaia!" I shouted in desperation.

I couldn't let this happen.

I refused to let this happen to me again!

"Watch out!" She screamed. I quickly followed her gaze and my eyes landed on Carlos, who had been camouflaged among the trees. I aimed my gun at him and fired.

But it was empty.

The sound of gunfire rang out, and I hit the ground. The wind got knocked out of me and an excruciating burning sensation took over my body.

My hand touched the side of my stomach, feeling nothing but blood gushing out of me.

"Damiano! No!" I heard her scream before her voice disappeared.

I struggled to get up; my body was completely heavy. I felt paralyzed and powerless as I lay there.

"Althaia... I'm sorry..." My sight went blurry, and I was met with darkness.

One Hundred Nine

ALTHAIA

"...Althaia..."

A small groan escaped my lips. I felt groggy and completely disoriented. Nausea washed over me, and my eyelids were heavy when I tried to open them.

"Althaia, please wake up." Cara's voice sounded clear, shaking me, and I pushed myself to open my eyes despite their heaviness.

"... I don't feel too good." I whispered as she helped me sit up. Resting my head against the wall, I slowly blinked and looked around. It seemed like we were in a small basement room with a tiny lightbulb barely giving any light. There was an annoying, faint sound of water dripping somewhere.

Where the fuck are we?

"Are you okay?"

I blinked a couple of times and looked at Cara. Her hair was a complete mess, and it looked like she had been through hell.

"I... what happened -" I stopped breathing as everything rushed back to me.

Dario. Blood. Fighting.

"Damiano!" My eyes widened, and I suddenly felt suffocated. The images of Damiano getting shot and lying still on the ground flooded my mind.

Tears started to stream down my face while Cara, in a panic, tried to make me snap out of it.

"Breathe! Please, breathe!" Her voice shook, tears glistening in her eyes. I finally gasped, air filling my lungs as I clutched tightly onto her arms.

"Damiano... they shot Damiano!" I choked out. My entire body was trembling as the image of him getting shot repeatedly played in my mind.

"What...?" Cara breathed out, tears leaving her eyes.

"My God, they shot him!" I cried out, clutching my chest, my heart ached as it shattered into a million pieces.

My love, my life, my everything—the man who was supposed to be the father of my children.

"...He's dead..." I whispered through sobs. Cara stumbled to her feet in shock, clutching her head as she paced the room.

"No... this can't be happening... he can't be dead. This is not happening!" She shouted in frustration. Racing to the door, she banged on it violently while screaming.

"You fuckers! You can't be doing this! You made me miserable for years. You don't get to do this to me again!" Cara screamed at the top of her lungs, unleashing all her frustrations on the door.

I wiped my tears away, took a deep breath, and shakily stood up. My body felt heavy, as if gravity was pulling me down. But I couldn't afford to sit here and wallow in self-pity. We had to take action to get out of this situation. All those hours Damiano had spent training me needed to be put to use now.

I exhaled, attempting to clear my head. I had to figure out what to do. Just like he taught me.

"Cara!" I pulled her away from the door before she could hurt herself, wrapping her in a tight hug. It was her turn to sob, and I gulped down the sob that threatened to escape me. Crying wouldn't help anyone.

"It's going to be okay... we'll be okay." I kept telling her, trying to convince myself too.

Both of our heads snapped to face the door as we heard it unlock. My father stepped inside, staring at me with cold, cunning eyes that held an abundance of hatred.

"Papá -" I began, but he raised his hand to stop and silence me, his jaw clenched.

"Don't you *ever* call me that." He hissed out.

"What?" I breathed out when he looked at me with so much disgust.

I glanced behind him, noting Maso and Carlos present, both wearing the same expression. My heartbeat accelerated, and my breathing grew louder at the sight of Carlos.

"You son of a bitch!" I screamed, lunging at him with the intention of smashing his head repeatedly into the wall.

I felt it coming before I saw it, and the next moment, I found myself on the ground. Blinking, I tried to clear my blurry sight, and the entire right side of my face stung with pain as my father backhanded me before I could reach Carlos.

"What the hell are you doing?!" Cara yelled at him, rushing to my side. I spat, the taste of blood filling my mouth. Before I could catch my breath, I cried out in pain as I got kicked in the back.

"You filthy Russian!" Carlos laughed, and I whimpered in pain as he kicked me again.

"Don't touch her!" Cara punched his face, causing his head to snap back from the force.

I stumbled to my feet as Carlos turned his hateful glare toward her. He pulled his hand back, about to hit her, when Maso grabbed his arm. No words were exchanged, but Maso's warning glare spoke volumes.

Carlos scoffed at him before ripping his arm away. I glanced down at the floor, grabbed my fallen heel, and threw it at Carlos's head. Satisfaction filled me when he winced and grabbed his head.

"You little -" He hissed and pulled out his gun, aiming it at me.

"Enough, Carlos. We can't use her if she's dead." My father intervened, placing his hand on the gun and forcing Carlos to lower it.

I took a couple of steps back, bringing Cara with me.

"Count your days, you filthy Russian." Carlos spat out.

"I don't understand." I frowned, looking at them in confusion. My father gestured for Carlos and Maso to leave, and he clasped his hands behind his back before facing me.

"You should ask that woman you call a mother. Oh, right... I forgot I got rid of her." He chuckled, making me take a sharp intake of breath and grasp onto Cara's arm. Tears filled my eyes, my heart pounded in my chest, and my legs were a second away from collapsing.

"It was you? You - you killed mom?"

"I should have gotten rid of her a long time ago for all the betrayals. But at least she was useful to me in the end—just like how you're going to be useful to me in getting what I want." His face transformed into a cunning expression.

"Although, it would be rude of me to take all the credit for it when it was Michael who made it happen. He was a great kid. A good asset. Such a shame I had to get rid of him as well when he stuck his nose in business that didn't concern him." He sighed as if genuinely saddened, but the malicious grin on his lips revealed the opposite.

Cara screamed at him while I felt numb at his words. My mother, my baby, Damiano, and now Michael. He had taken away everyone I cared about.

I closed my eyes. I felt sick and suffocated.

"You're a dead man walking. He's going to kill you." I spat out, clenching my hands into fists as I glared at him.

"And who's going to kill me? That dead husband of yours?" Gaetano asked, mockingly.

"You sick bastard!" I screamed at the top of my lungs and lunged towards him.

He let out a chilling laugh and closed the door before I could reach him. I banged my fists against the door, kicking it, while I screamed for him to come back so I could kill him with my bare hands.

"It's no use." This time, it was Cara's turn to pull me away from the door. I was breathing heavily, and my mind was spinning out of control.

"He took everything away from me!" A choked-up sob escaped me, and I broke down crying, unable to keep it together.

"I'm sorry. I'm so sorry. This is all my fault." Cara sniffed as she held me tightly in her embrace. "This wouldn't have happened if I hadn't told you to come to that stupid engagement party. And mom would still be alive! I was being selfish because I knew it would piss them off if you showed up... That's what I wanted, after all those damn years of them making me miserable. I'm really sorry, Thaia, I shouldn't have…" Cara's eyes filled with guilt as she looked at me, heartbroken.

"No, no. It's not your fault." I shook my head, holding her tightly as she cried into me, my own tears never-ending as well.

I wiped away my tears and slid down the wall to sit on the ground, patting the space next to me.

"Did you hear what that cocksucker for ice cream called me?" I stared at the ceiling before facing her.

"Russian." Cara said, and I nodded. She was confused, hell, even I was so fucking confused about the whole thing.

"Mom was not exactly who I thought she was… There were many things she kept from me, and it frustrates me so much I can't even ask her what has been going on." I started. "Do you know who Alexei Vasiliev is?" I asked before continuing.

"Who doesn't? He's known to be a lunatic."

"The first time I met him was at the auction Damiano took me to." I swallowed hard at the mention of his name and bit down on my lip to avoid it trembling.

I took a deep breath and cleared my throat.

"He told me I reminded him of an old lover back in his days. At first, I thought it was creepy that he told me that, but then he continued to talk about how they loved each other but were bad for each other. But no matter what, she would always be his Solnishko. And she called him Lunnyy svet."

Cara gasped, her eyes slightly widened, and I knew she recognized the word.

"When I returned to the house, I found a small treasure chest with some letters and a picture. That picture was of mom and Alexei together." Cara continued to look at me in complete astonishment while I explained everything from when I found the picture to my meeting with Alexei at the LuxePalace.

We sat in silence, allowing the information to process. However, my thoughts were all over the place, giving me a pounding headache the more I dwelled on them.

The thought of my mother having an affair with Alexei has crossed my mind, but I didn't allow myself to have that thought, because why would Gaetano pretend to be my father?

I started to chuckle at how fucked up everything was at the moment.

"No wonder my Italian sucks." The chuckle turned into a burst of full-on laughter, and Cara couldn't help but laugh along with me.

"Zdravstvuyte, bitch!" Cara greeted as we laughed.

"Hey, what if you're Russian too? Maybe your mom had an affair as well?!" I gasped at the possibility.

"Shit, I wouldn't blame her if she had an affair. Have you seen how ugly that piece of shit father I have is? I would have cheated in a heartbeat too! Does Alexei have a brother? Maybe she hooked up with him?"

"You definitely didn't get those genes from him, that's for sure." I said, before bursting out in laughter.

The jokes continued, and we laughed as if we had lost our minds. We laughed, then cried, then laughed again as we listed out how miserable we were. Our laughter died down as we caught our breath, sitting once again in silence, each in our own thoughts.

"You know..." Cara broke the silence. "I never told anyone, but one day I snuck out, and I tried to kill myself by jumping from a bridge."

I whipped my head so fast to look at her, seeing her smiling sadly as she spoke.

"I was beaten and broken so much already, and then they wanted to marry me off to someone who was known to be a powerful and skilled assassin, adding to the pile of shit I was already going through. I snuck out of the house, got drunk to lessen the pain in my body, and then I jumped. Without giving it a single thought."

"Cara..." I sniffed, holding her hand tightly in mine.

"I don't know how, but Lorenzo found me and saved me before it was too late." She smiled as she thought back to it. "I just wanted to make one decision about my life, and that was when to end it. I was pissed when he saved me, wanting to be put out of my misery. But I'm grateful he did because, for once, he gave me the will to finally live." Cara sobbed, and my heart broke even more.

"We'll get out of here." I promised her. Whatever I had to do, I had to get her out of here. "You deserve to live a normal...ish life with Tank Man 'cause let's be honest, they're anything but normal." I lightly chuckled, trying to somehow lighten the mood.

"I do want that normal-ish life with my Tank Man." She sighed.

"You will. But first, we need a plan to get the fuck out of here."

One Hundred Ten

DAMIANO

I heard faint voices around me while the persistent burning sensation spread across my abdomen. Someone tapped my cheek, and I slowly opened my eyes. My vision was blurry, and I could see shadows above me. Their mouths moved as they spoke, but I couldn't comprehend their words. I tried to move, but a sharp pain made me clench my jaw and grunt in discomfort.

"I've got you. You'll be fine." Antonio came into focus.

"Althaia… I need to get to Althaia." I felt hands restraining me, but I pushed them away, gritting my teeth as I powered through the pain to sit up.

"We need to get you fixed first. You've lost a lot of blood." Antonio intervened, preventing me from moving further.

"I… don't care… she needs me." I growled out and tried to push them away.

"You can't help her if you're fucking dead!" He shouted in anger. "I have to get the bullet out of you. Bite down on this." He put a piece of cloth into my mouth.

I braced myself for what was about to happen.

Strong arms held me firmly to the ground as Antonio drew his knife. My entire body tensed, and I clenched down hard on the cloth, gritting my teeth through the pain. My voice was muffled as he carved into me, and beads of sweat covered my face.

"Almost there. Hang on."

It felt like enduring a series of powerful blows with a knife, each strike relentless, leaving me breathless and drained. I closed my eyes, letting my mind focus on anything but the excruciating pain coursing through me.

And then, I stopped feeling anything, captivated by something else.

Soft, long brown curls framed my view, swaying in the wind as their ends gently brushed against my face. They belonged to the most entrancing pair of sparkling green eyes I had ever seen. Her rosy, plump lips formed a dazzling smile, laughter filling the air as she ran carefree on the beach.

Warmth spread within me, my heart beating faster as a smile crept onto my lips.

What have I done in this life to deserve heaven sending me the most beautiful Angel to stay by my side?

My breath caught as she turned to look at me, appearing even more stunning than I could fathom, bathed in the hues of the sunset.

An Angel, radiant with fiery colors.

"Can the Devil find me?" She chuckled lightly, a teasing glint in her eyes.

"Always. I will always find you, my love."

"Don't you die on us, damn it!" My head was violently slapped to the side, and I finally opened my eyes, gasping for air. My chest rapidly rose and fell as I took in my surroundings. "Shit, that was a close call." Giovanni sighed in relief.

"We need to get you to the hospital -" Antonio was cut off.

"We found explosives! Get away from here, now!"

Without hesitation, they pulled my arms over their shoulders, hoisting me to my feet. I clenched my jaw through the pain, grunting as they hurried away from the castle.

"That bastard really wants to wipe us out once and for all." Luca sneered.

"Did everyone get out?" My voice strained as my breathing came out fast.

"Save your strength. We have it under control." Antonio said.

As we approached the car, a sudden thunderous sound boomed behind us, and the blasting wave hit our backs, causing us to stumble to our knees. Shards of rocks were flying everywhere, and I glanced over to see the castle collapsing with bright flames.

"Make sure everyone is okay and gets treated." I ordered them as I was laid in the backseat of the car. Antonio was with me, making sure to keep pressure on the wound at all times.

"Worry about yourself now. We need you to get better and get our Donna back." He firmly instructed me, and for once, I listened.

My wife needs me.

I was rushed to the hospital where Ellie tried to convince me to get surgery, but I kept shutting her down while she gave me a blood transfusion and an IV for the pain.

"Give me a temporary solution and whatever meds to keep the pain away." I demanded.

"That's not how it works! You can die if you don't get it treated!" Ellie's eyes pleaded with me.

"If you can't fix it without putting me under anesthesia, then I don't want it. I don't have time for this." I could feel the minutes slipping away, taking me further from Althaia. I couldn't afford to waste time here.

"... Sometimes, I hate working for you." Ellie sighed but still mentioned there might be something she could do. "This won't hold forever, but it should buy you some time."

I lay still on the hospital bed while Ellie began to stitch the wound. She made a makeshift brace, securing it around my midsection to prevent me from straining the gunshot wound.

"You're lucky you work out as much as you do. Thicker muscles make you slightly more bullet-resistant, and thank God it didn't hit any vital organs." She grumbled while she fixed me.

"Ellie?" I felt her gaze on me, but I kept staring at the ceiling. "If Althaia were to be pregnant... what are the chances of the fetus surviving if she was given a sedative?" I felt her still, and she went quiet. I closed my eyes, already knowing the answer to my question.

"The fetus is most vulnerable in the first twelve weeks. Stress and trauma inflicted on the body... It would be a miracle if it survived."

"I see." I answered curtly.

"Is there a chance she is right now?"

"No." As much as I longed for a child with her, every fiber of my being prayed there was no possible way she was pregnant now. The pain after losing the first one... It would devastate her to go through it again. And there was no way on earth I would ever let that happen to her.

Never again.

"What's the status?" I turned to Luca, who appeared by the doorway. He frowned slightly before he spoke.

"No signs of Lorenzo yet, and Arianna... was stabbed." I jolted up to my feet and pushed past Luca.

I barged into the room she was in, my eyes landing on her sleeping form on the bed with tubes and needles attached to her. My mother was by her side, her eyes red from crying, and my father was present as well, a dark look on his face.

I stepped closer to her, my hand shaking in anger as I touched her face. I briefly closed my eyes, leaning down and placed a kiss on her forehead.

"You've got this, Arianna. You're a fighter. Always remember that." I whispered to her. "She'll be okay." I told my mother. She said nothing and just nodded.

I turned to look at my father.

"It's time to make them pay."

"How's your head?" I asked Raffaele, who had a bandage wrapped around his head.

Ellie followed me and finally had me sit still to finish up my treatment. I had gathered Antonio, Giovanni, and Luca in Raffaele's room to get an update on everything. They had minimal injuries, nothing that would significantly affect them, which was good as I needed my best men to fight.

I had lost men, and even though Gaetano took us by surprise by being one step ahead, we still overpowered the ones in the castle as we had prepared for war.

"They knocked the shit out of me before I could warn you." He groaned and winced as he touched the back of his head. Ava was next to him, looking more pissed than ever.

"What happened?" I asked.

"The entire system was hacked. They gained access to the cameras, the power, and even intercepted the comm links we were using. Before I could regain control and block them, I was knocked out." Raffaele explained with a sullen look. "Before that, I got the trademark of who it was. It's Ghost."

I rubbed my jaw at the information.

Now it made sense why we were having difficulty tracking the phone calls in the beginning. Ghost was known for executing schemes without leaving a trace, hence the name.

The intriguing part was that Ghost didn't work for anybody and only performed a one-time task. This meant Gaetano was paying him millions, if not more, to keep him around for longer.

"I should have known, but given that this is unusual for Ghost to do, it didn't cross my mind. My pride is hurt, and I'm going to show him who he's messing with." Raffaele sneered.

If there was one thing about Raffaele, it was that he took pride in what he did. The look on his face right now told me he was ready to go to war with Ghost.

"Good, because I need you to find out where Althaia and Cara are."

"You'll have to find someone else to do it. Raffaele needs to rest." Ellie commented after finishing bandaging me.

"I don't need to rest. Just give me some pain meds, and I'll be good."

"You have a concussion! You can't be in front of screens for at least 48 hours." She scolded him.

"That's not going to happen. Sorry to disappoint you, love." He barely got to finish his sentence before he yelled out in pain when Ava smacked his head.

"Sorry, love. Your head was in the way." She gave him a fake smile, and Raffaele grinned at her.

"Shit, you're hot when you're mad."

"Focus." I glared at him, having no time for their flirtations.

"Your symptoms will only get worse. You need to rest. Why do I even bother fixing you if you're only going to hurt yourself even more?!" Ellie said in frustration.

"Ellie." Antonio pulled her into him, holding her tightly as she became distressed.

"I can help." Ava offered. "Raffaele can guide me. That way, he doesn't have to be exposed to any screens for too long."

"Love the enthusiasm, babe, but that's not how it works. It's about coding." He chuckled, and she crossed her arms, looking at him with a light scowl.

"I know how to code. I studied it."

"What, really?!" He gaped.

"Yes." She confirmed once again. He wasted no time and stood up in front of her, looking at her seriously.

"Listen to me, Ava. The minute this shitstorm is over, I'm marrying you."

I raised a brow, having never seen him look this serious before.

She leaned into him with a slight smirk.

"Then you better get me a nice ring."

"Are you done now?" I glanced at them, letting them know we had more important matters to focus on.

I put my shirt back on and carefully stood up for Ellie's sake. She took a deep breath, fighting against the tears while Antonio spoke to her softly.

"Thank you, Ellie, for everything you do. Now, I need you to go home and focus on your health and the baby." I gently ordered her, and she sighed.

She wasn't supposed to be here, but her passion for her job led her to step in and help. Ellie was the best doctor around here, but I couldn't risk distressing her for the sake of the baby. I knew Antonio was relieved about me making that decision and left with her to take her home.

"Althaia is wearing her ring. You should be able to track her." I told Raffaele and Ava.

"About that." Giovanni said and held out her engagement ring.

"We found it tossed away along with other jewelry." Luca informed. I took the engagement ring, staring at it before my fist closed around it.

"Any news about Lorenzo?" I asked.

"Not yet."

The more they talked, the angrier I became. Nothing was working in our favor, and now it would take us even longer to figure out where the hell Gaetano took them. Lorenzo missing wasn't easing my concerns. There was no way he was still inside the castle when it blew up. I knew for a fact he made it outside, but the question was where the hell did he go?

"I want the premises completely searched –" I stopped when I heard a commotion coming from the hall and quickly stepped out to see what was going on.

Lorenzo was making his way toward me, out of breath, with sweat covering him as he angrily ripped his shirt open. He looked like a bull, ready to attack at any moment, and everyone stepped out of his way to avoid triggering his anger.

"Get him some water." I had him sit down to catch his breath. Luca handed him a bottle of water, and Lorenzo poured it over his head to cool down. "Where were you?"

"I tried to follow them. I ran for as long as I could until I lost sight of the helicopter." He said as Luca handed him another bottle. I waited for him to tell me something useful.

"Hold on, were you able to get the tail number, or anything to identify the helicopter?" Raffaele asked.

"I did. They were headed Southwest."

Raffaele raised a clenched hand in victory.

"Okay, good, awesome! I will be able to trace the helicopter using the air control and radar system. We can narrow it down to identify which helicopters are currently or have recently been flying to the Southwest."

"Just a thought—wouldn't Ghost already have covered for them?" Giovanni commented.

"No. If he removes the tracking from the flight radar, it will attract attention. The system will flag it as missing, triggering a full-scale search party. He wouldn't risk it." Raffaele explained.

"Get at it as soon as possible and gather everyone at the manor." I commanded, a sense of relief washing over me at the possibility of reaching Althaia and Cara sooner rather than later. My body itched to get my hands on Gaetano and make him suffer as much as possible.

They quickly set off to assemble everyone for our strategic planning, while I provided Lorenzo with updates.

"Arianna was stabbed."

Lorenzo rose to his feet with fury etched across his face.

"What?!" He snarled. "Where is she?"

"Down the hall to your left." I told him. He ran a hand over his head before approaching me.

"I swear to God, if she dies, or if my wife dies... hell, even Althaia, I am going to rip that fucking *woman* to pieces." Lorenzo growled.

"I won't stop you." I said to him. If it were to happen, even though I was praying with everything in me that they would be safe, I wasn't going to stand in his way.

He nodded and headed to Arianna's room, but I placed a hand on his shoulder to pause him.

"She'll be okay. There is no way she is leaving us when she lives to annoy the shit out of us." I assured him, patting his shoulder before making my way out.

There was still someone I needed to have a conversation with.

Exiting the car with Antonio, we entered the house, heavily guarded by my armed men. Proceeding down the hall to the living room, I found her seated on the couch, holding a mug.

She stood up when saw me, but I gestured for her to sit back down again. I sat in front of her, and her eyes followed my movements when I pulled out my gun and placed it on the table.

"You're going to tell me everything, or I promise you, I will be the one ending your life. Speak." I declared with a cold stare.

She looked down at the mug in her hands, sighed, and nodded before meeting my gaze with eyes of a color that reminded me too much of my wife's.

"I will tell you everything."

One Hundred Eleven

DAMIANO

"This is what we've found so far." Ava announced, unrolling a map onto the table. Everyone had gathered at the manor once Ava and Raffaele had something useful for us to strategize a new plan.

"Based on the information given, they can't be more than two hours away in flight time. We've narrowed it down to this." She drew a circle around the area, and I frowned. It was still a big region, and it would take us too much time to precisely pinpoint where they were located.

"Our theory is they have to be closer to this area." She drew another, smaller circle within the first.

"What's your reasoning?" I asked.

"The type of helicopter they're using can't fly more than five hours at a time, and since this is not a helicopter that can refuel midair, they have to go to the fuel station, which is two and a half hours away. However, we don't want to rule out the rest of the area completely." Raffaele explained.

"They could already have a truck ready to fill up." Luca pointed out.

"While it's possible to have a truck ready to refuel, I doubt Gaetano would take the chances of having one there because it's one large truck. In case we managed to follow him, the helicopter flying away and the truck being on its way would mess up his hiding place." Raffaele concluded.

I listened carefully, assessing every possibility.

"How confident are you about it?" I needed them all to be entirely sure. We couldn't risk being wrong and wasting time, and we certainly couldn't afford to underestimate Gaetano once again.

"It's the only explanation. Plus, the radar system did show they flew around this area. Now, we just need to find where exactly. It will be easy enough since we have managed to narrow it down." Raffaele affirmed.

"Good." I nodded.

Discussions continued as we crafted a plan. While we could prepare for the worst, Gaetano still held the advantage. We didn't know this location, and he likely had traps set up in the area.

Despite having the manpower and weapons to take him down, the lack of information about the building posed a significant disadvantage. Without knowing how to navigate and find Althaia and Cara, he could catch us off guard once again.

"We will do our best to find it by satellite, but it will take some time." Ava replied.

"In the meantime, everyone, get some rest and prepare yourselves." I instructed.

The room fell silent when the landline phone on my desk rang. I stared at it and let it ring a few times before hitting the speaker.

"Speak."

"I see you made it out alive. What a shame." Gaetano's voice filled the room, and the tension heightened.

My hands clenched into fists on the table at the sound of his laughter. I closed my eyes for a second, forcing my body into a cold zero. I couldn't let my emotions control me, and I needed my head to be clear.

He had my wife at his mercy—the one person who truly mattered to me. I had to shove every single one of those thoughts away and deal with him the way I knew best.

Painting the city fucking red with his blood.

"Let's cut the crap and name your demands." I said, leaning on the desk and faced my men. They all listened intently, staring daggers at the phone.

"Watch your tone with me, boy. I am, after all, the one who can determine the fate of your wife." Gaetano chuckled.

A slight frown appeared on my face. He knew we got married. He must have picked it up either from hacking her phone or from the comm links we wore at the wedding.

"I don't like wasting time, Gaetano." I asserted. My voice was cold and steady. I knew he was playing games, dragging out time to get a reaction out of me.

I wasn't going to make the same mistakes as before and give him the pleasure of me reacting to his nonsense. He knew what she meant to me, but I knew how to play games as well.

And I fucking always win.

"I guess we shouldn't waste time. Time is precious, after all." Gaetano sighed before bursting into laughter. "Hand over all of your weaponry and shipments."

Now, it was my turn to release a dark chuckle.

"Quite a large demand, Gaetano."

"In exchange for your wives."

"Hmm, I see." I said. He fell silent, not expecting my response. I let him sit in silence for a while before choosing to speak again. "And how do I know they're alive?" My voice lacked emotion, signaling that I wasn't bothered.

"You will have to take my word for it."

I laughed at his answer.

"They could be dead as we speak. My wife is of no value to me if she's dead. I'm rejecting your demands." I declared, hanging up the phone.

I met Lorenzo's gaze.

"I will get your wife back." I promised him. He trusted me and knew what I was doing.

A smirk formed on his lips when the phone rang again. I mirrored his expression and let it ring a few times.

"Gaetano."

"You dare to hang up on me?!" He roared.

Just the reaction I wanted.

"Yes." I retorted. Luca and Giovanni suppressed a laugh. They recognized Althaia's personality in the response.

Gaetano was left stunned, not expecting this turn in the conversation.

"Be careful. Disrespect me again, and a bullet will find its way between her eyes." He threatened.

"I don't enjoy repeating myself, Gaetano. If you want me to meet your demands, I need proof they're still alive." I stated.

"Fine. A picture will be sent to prove they're still alive."

"Not good enough. I need live footage."

"No."

"Unfortunately, I won't be able to meet your demands." I said, hanging up once again. I was going to make that bastard go insane.

"Damiano." My father warned.

"He's not going to kill them. He's desperate."

"He can still hurt them." He frowned.

"I know." I said, crossing my arms and awaiting his next call. This was a calculated risk, but I believed Gaetano wouldn't resort to drastic measures after his initial plan failed.

Ten minutes passed, and he still hadn't called back.

"Patience." I urged everyone as they stared impatiently at the phone.

I understood their desperation to get their hands on him, especially now that he had their Donna. While patience wasn't my strong suit, I have learned that anything involving Althaia requires patience. In this situation, it was more necessary than ever.

More time passed by, a few of my men paced the floor, and I popped a few painkillers in my mouth to minimize the pain.

Everyone came to a sudden stop, their attention shifting to me as soon as my phone rang—it was a video call.

"Connect it to the screen." I tossed the phone to Raffaele, who quickly hooked it up to the large screen hanging on the wall in my office.

And there they were.

Gaetano stood at a doorway, filming Althaia and Cara in what appeared to be a basement.

"You piece of shit!" Althaia screamed, hurling a heel at Gaetano. He managed to close the door before it could hit him. "Get back in here!" I heard her shout and bang on the door. Then the camera switched to him.

"Now, it's your turn to deliver. You have 24 hours. I will be tracking you and send you the direction once you're on the move. Come alone. If not, your Russian whore is going to be hanged from the neck."

And the line went dead.

I continued to stare at the black screen, and the whispering escalated into a loud discussion behind me.

"Russian?! Did he say Russian?!" My father erupted furiously.

I slowly turned around and faced them all. The only ones who weren't surprised were my closest men, who had been investigating this with me.

"He did." I shoved my hands into my pockets and looked at them all.

"You're saying we swore to protect a filthy Russian?!" One of my men shouted out. My head snapped in his direction, a dark look taking over my face.

Before I could reach for my gun, the sound of a gun firing filled the room, and he dropped dead with a bullet in his head.

"That's my brother's wife you're talking about." Lorenzo sneered.

"Anyone else?" I cocked a brow at them, waiting to see who else dared to disrespect my wife.

Their eyes flickered around between me and the gun in Lorenzo's hand. Antonio, Luca, and Giovanni drew out their guns as well, challenging them to utter something disrespectful.

"Did you know about this?" My father's cold gaze landed on me, showing me just how livid he was about it.

"I had a hunch. I wasn't completely sure, and I wanted it to be confirmed before I broke the news. Gaetano managed to do us dirty before we could gather a DNA test." I admitted.

"Did you know before you married her?"

"I did." I said, unfazed by his disappointed look.

"You have fooled us all." My father spat out.

I slowly walked up to him, stopping until I was completely up in his face.

"I didn't fool anyone." I asserted in a guttural, low growl. My gaze bore into him with a glare before facing my men. "I didn't keep anyone in the dark. Althaia doesn't even know about this. She believes her father is Gaetano. New information surfaced, and we took time to investigate different possibilities. We found out her mother had an affair during her marriage to Gaetano."

"Who's the father then?" Simone asked.

"It doesn't matter who the father is. What's important here is, hasn't she been treating you well? Has she ever been vile against you? Has she not shown kindness to you and shown how much she cares about you?" I questioned, studying their faces.

They exchanged glances, and a few nodded.

"Althaia has no idea. She's innocent. Don't let her heritage influence your judgment when she has consistently shown care and loyalty for all of you. Her heart is pure, and she wouldn't hesitate to take a bullet for any of you. I won't force you to stay and fight, but you know the consequences if you decide to leave. It's blood in, blood out. Make your decision." I stated, awaiting their responses.

Renzo stepped forward from the group, coming to a halt in front of me. His expression was serious as he placed his fist on his heart.

"I swore my loyalty to you. You helped me and my family get back on our feet. While I haven't had the honor of a conversation with your wife yet, she always had a bright smile and waved when she passed us. I am with you all the way. Viva Don Damiano e Donna Althaia."

I gave him a firm nod and then turned to face the others. They followed Renzo's lead, chanting in unison.

"Father?" I glanced at him. "Either fight with me or against me. Your choice." My father rubbed his jaw before sighing.

"What's the plan, son?"

I smirked.

"I will give him what he wants."

Time flew as I detailed the plan and discussed everyone's role and expectations. Each person listened intently, offering their thoughts; it was an all-or-nothing scenario.

With everyone on board and confident in the plan, we set our actions into motion. As I was about to slide into the car, my attention shifted to the gate. A car sped through, crashing into the fountain in the middle of the driveway.

I signaled my men to hold their fire and approached the vehicle. I stopped as the door swung open, revealing a body slumped to the ground.

It was Michael.

One Hundred Twelve

DAMIANO

My brows furrowed as I observed his motionless body on the ground. I halted in front of him, nudging him with my foot until a groan escaped him.

I watched him struggle to stand, seeing how severely he was beaten. His face bore cuts, bruises, and blood, and his arm was wrapped around his ribs, likely broken, given his overall condition.

Michael winced as he slumped against the car, breathing heavily before meeting my gaze.

"What are you doing here?" I stared at him blankly, waiting for an explanation.

"I... Shit - Althaia."

"You're too late." I scoffed.

"I tried... to warn..." He continued to groan in pain, on the verge of passing out.

"You're wasting my time. Get off my property."

Michael slumped to the ground again, and I signaled for my men to get moving.

"I know where they are."

That grabbed my attention, and I turned to look back at him. He was struggling to keep his eyes open.

"Do you think he knows something?" Antonio joined me, eyeing Michael suspiciously.

"He called Althaia in Italy, but she hung up before he could tell her what he wanted. He never called back, and now I know why."

"He's Gaetano's right-hand man. It could be one of Gaetano's games to throw us off."

"I know." I replied as we stared at him.

Michael could be a setup, providing us with information to make us believe we have an advantage, only for Gaetano to wipe us out entirely when we arrive.

"Get him some medical attention." I ordered, and Antonio glanced at me. "If what he has to say matches with what we have found out already, it will help us prepare logistics. If not, put a bullet in his head."

Time was ticking, and I was going to exploit whatever valuable information I could get my hands on.

Luca and Giovanni grabbed Michael's arms, lifting him without bothering to be gentle.

A grim expression settled on my face, my jaw clenching at the sound of multiple screeching vehicles approaching. I seized Michael by the collar, slamming him against the car, making him wince.

"Who the hell did you bring?" I sneered at him. He was in too much pain to answer. I released him, and he fell to the ground.

Every one of my men was ready, aiming and waiting in the direction from which the intruders would come.

"Fire!"

Bullets flew, hitting the approaching cars that tried to encircle us. I wouldn't let them get the chance, and the firing increased until the cars had to come to a stop. The cars were bulletproof, but we held them back by denying them the opportunity to shoot at us.

But something didn't add up.

I raised my hand to signal them to stop firing. The cars remained motionless, making me narrow my eyes at them.

"Take cover!" I shouted and drew out my gun.

The cars formed a shield, blocking our bullets as more vehicles arrived behind them. Men emerged from the cars, taking cover and aiming their guns at us. Yet, they refrained from firing.

Rage surged through me when I saw who it was. He approached me with a dark expression on his face.

"Where the hell is she?!" He shouted furiously, and my jaw clenched.

I saw red and stopped right before his face with a sinister look. He aimed his gun directly at my head, and I did the same to him.

"You're in my territory. That's a fucking death penalty." I growled, my finger ready on the trigger.

"Where the hell is she, Bellavia?!"

"Leave while I will still spare your life, Vasiliev." I sneered.

In any other circumstances, I would have shot him before he could even step a foot out of the car. However, I didn't have the time to start a war in the middle of my driveway with more pressing matters at hand.

Vasiliev stepped closer, red dots from laser sights dotting him. I knew my men had taken control of the situation from the roof. Still, Vasiliev remained unfazed by the number of guns pointed at him.

"Pull the trigger, and you're all as good as dead. You'll never find her." I promised. Nestor, one of his men, stood behind Vasiliev, his gaze sharp and gun at the ready.

"I'll ask one more time before I create a bloodbath. Where. Is. She?!" He roared.

"Leave my territory. I don't have time to deal with you." I said, my patience wearing thin. I would have to deal with him another time.

"A bloodbath it is, then." The distinct sounds of weapon racks sliding into place filled the air the moment he uttered those words.

"Antonio! Order the kill on Jacinta!" I shouted. Vasiliev clenched his teeth in anger at my directive.

"Are you really going to kill the mother of your woman?"

"Yes. The place is packed and guarded with men. One call, and she's as good as dead." I threatened with a smirk.

Vasiliev let out a laugh, disbelief evident in his expression.

"Let's see what Althaia has to say about you threatening to kill her mother."

"She won't believe you. She thinks her mother is already dead."

He squinted his eyes.

"Tell me why you faked her death, Bellavia."

"That's none of your business."

"Oh, but she is my damn business! I'm not leaving until I get what I want." Vasiliev growled. My jaw clenched. Of all days, he chose today to show up and be a pain in my ass.

"To protect her. From Gaetano." I decided to disclose. Fury flashed in his eyes as a dark look overtook his face at the mention of Gaetano.

The sound of groaning and shuffling caught his attention. His eyes snapped to Michael, who managed to get on his feet.

"Gaetano's dog. Hand him over."

"No." I scoffed. If Michael knew something, I wasn't letting him go.

"Althaia... Cara... We need to go. He's going to kill them." Michael grunted.

Vasiliev looked at me with questioning eyes. I let out a frustrated sigh and pinched the bridge of my nose at Michael's lack of awareness at the moment.

Vasiliev's eyes scanned the area, a crease appearing between his brows.

"Gaetano has taken Althaia hostage." He concluded. "Why?"

My hand gripped his gun tightly in frustration before lowering it. He shouted something in Russian and his men lowered their guns.

"Get him some medical attention before he passes out." I gestured for my men to lower their guns, and the red dots disappeared from Vasiliev. "Follow me." I turned around to get back inside.

I didn't wait for a reply because I knew he would follow me. He was curious to know what was going on, and he wasn't going to leave me alone. He had already wasted too much of my time by showing up.

Now I know where her curiosity trait comes from.

Vasiliev was smart enough to bring only Nestor and two other men with him inside my office. My father was quiet the entire time, observing the situation. I knew he had already connected the dots on who Althaia's father was, and it probably left him stunned.

Hell, this whole situation was a fucking mess.

"I'm waiting. Why is Gaetano holding his own daughter hostage?" Vasiliev asked.

I crossed my arms and leaned against my desk.

"He's been using her to blackmail Jacinta into laundering money for him. Once he was done, he ordered a hit on them. Jacinta was stabbed and on the verge of dying if it weren't for Antonio, who managed to keep her alive. I faked her death and placed her somewhere safe to figure out who was after her. I didn't know it was Gaetano at the time. Now, he has Althaia and my brother's wife, and you're here, wasting our time."

His expression went cold as he took in the information. There was no doubt he still cared for Jacinta; otherwise, he wouldn't have been so reckless as to step into my territory.

"What does he want from you?"

"Weaponry and shipments."

"Of course." He scoffed. "For what reasons other than being a greedy dog?"

"To take you down." All eyes shifted to Michael, who had just entered the room. He leaned against the doorway for support as he spoke. "He's been recruiting and training men to create an army to take you down. But he doesn't have access to weapons like Damiano to do so." Michael continued.

"How cute." Vasiliev shoved his hands into his pockets. "Other than existing and being more well-off than he is, what else have I done to piss him off?"

"You took his woman." Michael pointed out.

Vasiliev threw his head back and let out a loud laugh.

"He's the one who got married to her. Not me."

"True. But you still slept with her while she was married to him." I commented.

"Not my fault he couldn't please her, and she had to come to me." He said smugly, and I gave him a blank look. "So, now he's holding his daughter hostage to blackmail you because of your relationship." He stated, connecting the dots.

"Althaia is not his daughter." Michael continued, and Vasiliev raised a brow at the information.

"Vasiliev, when was the last time you saw Jacinta?" I inquired.

"Over twenty-five... years ago..." He trailed off, deep in thought. Nestor rapidly spoke to him in Russian. Vasiliev's eyes snapped to mine as his frown deepened. "You're telling me..."

"Althaia is the byproduct of your affair, and Gaetano knows. Congratulations, you have a daughter." I said sarcastically. If he was surprised, he didn't show it but remained silent.

"That damned woman!" He raged out, his hands turning into fists. "Where the hell is that damned woman?!"

"Safe. Now, be on your way." I commanded.

"She's... she's alive?" Michael's eyes went wide in shock. "I thought I killed her?"

"You're the one who tried to kill her?" Vasiliev grabbed Michael in a rage and pulled out his gun.

"Let him go." I ordered calmly and approached him. I couldn't risk him shooting Michael when he was our best chance to tell us where Althaia and Cara were.

"I didn't know!" Michael erupted.

"You expect me to believe that?" Vasiliev sneered.

"You know how it works! I don't ask questions; I get the job done. I had no idea I was recruiting men for Gaetano to make a hit on her. She was like a mother to me. I've been trying to find out who was after them, which led me to this condition. Gaetano found me snooping around and tried to get rid of me when I found out." Michael explained, and Vasiliev stared at him with cold eyes before finally letting him go.

"I'm an orphan. Jacinta took me in as her own when my parents didn't care enough about me and left me to fend for myself as a kid. I know the importance of family. Althaia, Cara, and Jacinta—they're my only family. If I knew, I would have done everything I could to stop him." He looked pained as he talked.

"What's the plan? I want in. I want my hands on that filthy dog." Vasiliev said, locking eyes with me.

"I don't need your help." I scoffed.

"You owe me a favor." He retorted, and I frowned.

"I don't owe you shit." I spat out.

"But you do. I delivered Althaia safely to you at the LuxePalace, didn't I?" Vasiliev smirked.

My frown deepened, and I was about to tell him to fuck off when Michael spoke.

"Gaetano wouldn't see it coming. We'll catch him off guard and get them out of there sooner."

"And how would you know?" I asked. Michael pulled out a flash drive.

"Everything you need to know is here. I knew I would get caught and managed to download everything. It's the location, blueprint of the building, and whatever traps he has set up in the area."

I snatched the flash drive from his hand and tossed it to Raffaele.

"You better be telling the truth." I warned him.

"I am." He said, and I stared him down while I waited for Raffaele to check everything.

"Everything is clear. It matches what we already have found out. One problem though."

"What?" I gritted my teeth. My patience had already run up, and I was one second away from shooting the entire place up in frustration.

"Cameras are everywhere, and Ghost is most likely the one controlling them."

My entire body tensed. It meant it would take too much time for Raffaele and Ava to figure out how to get control over the cameras. And we didn't have the fucking time.

"Ah, Ghost. He is *very* good. Even I couldn't get my hands on him." Vasiliev commented.

"I can help with that. I know Ghost." Michael spoke.

"You know him?" I raised a brow.

"I know *her*. We go way back, and I was the one who got Gaetano a deal. I didn't know she was still working with him."

"Wait, Ghost is a fucking woman?!" Raffaele erupted in shock and Michael nodded.

"Yes. Can you get me a secure line? I will get in touch with her and see what I can do. She owes me a few favors."

"Listen up. This is what we're going to do now." I said, coming up with an idea.

After looking through what Michael had managed to get on his flash drive, it gave me the perfect advantage of preparing logistics, and we would get Althaia and Cara out there faster than planned in the first place.

Time was running out, and there was no time to argue with Vasiliev about keeping his distance. We efficiently prepared everything and informed everyone about the impending operation.

For the first time in history, Italians and Russians were working together, all united by a common purpose—the women in our lives.

With the trucks loaded with Gaetano's demanded items, I arrived at the destination. Stepping out of the car, I lit a cigarette, taking in the surroundings. It was a cargo warehouse by the port that Gaetano had bought and constructed underground passages and basements.

"Look what we have here. Good boy, Bellavia." Gaetano emerged from the warehouse, accompanied by armed men.

I looked at him calmly, brushing off the insults he hurled my way.

"I've got everything you demanded in the trucks. Hand over the girls." I said to him.

"Easy there. I need to check if everything matches." He replied and signaled his men.

Shots were fired, taking down the drivers, before gesturing for his men to inspect the trucks. I wasn't surprised; I knew he was going to do that.

And I also knew how to stage deaths for a convincing show.

I had a total of five trucks, and they meticulously checked each one. They took a few tall wooden crates out to demonstrate that I had held up my end of the bargain.

"Excellent!" Gaetano erupted excitedly.

"The girls." I reiterated. He pretended to sigh in sadness.

"I would hand them over, but you see, you were five seconds late, and I told you not to be late. They're currently somewhere, hanging around with a rope around their necks." He announced with a sinister laugh.

I let myself fall deep into my zone, with a red haze clouding my vision.

"Gaetano, do you understand why they say never make a deal with the Devil?" I interrupted his laughter.

He looked at me with narrowed eyes as I blew out the cigarette smoke into the night sky. I flicked the bud away, flashing him my devilish smirk.

"I'm about to show you why." I drew my guns out at the same time men jumped out from the wooden crates.

And a war with fire began.

One Hundred Thirteen

Althaia

The longer we stayed in this shit hole, the more I felt like my sanity was slipping away. The constant ache in my heart deepened, a relentless pain of the haunting thought of Damiano being gone.

The vivid image of him being shot played on a cruel loop in my mind, and no matter how hard I tried to resist, tears streamed down my face like an unending cascade.

I wrapped my arms tightly around my knees, a weak attempt to contain the storm of emotions raging within me. Guilt, thick and suffocating, consumed me. If only I had stayed away from him, he could have still been alive, and spared from the burdens I unknowingly dragged into his life.

Damiano wanted me to be happy, and he did in ways no one else could, but, in return, I burdened his shoulders with a weight that led to his death.

Was this really going to be the end for us?

For him?

For me?

If Damiano wasn't here with me, then I wouldn't want to live anymore. And maybe, just maybe, with a glimpse of hope still in my heart, I would be able to see him again in the next life.

"We have to do something…" My voice was barely audible. I sniffed and wiped the tears as I stood up, my legs trembling a bit from being physically and mentally exhausted.

The sedation left my body all messed up, and my mind wasn't giving me a break with anything.

"I know, but what can we do?" Cara sighed and got up as well. I could see she was just as drained, but we had to shove it all to the side and focus on getting out of here.

I looked around in the basement room we were in. There wasn't anything we could use to try to break out, and the door was being guarded from the other side.

"Wait, I have an idea." Cara whispered and stepped closer to me. "Maso is by the door. Maybe I can convince him to let us out to the restroom?" She suggested, and I thought about it, assessing the possibilities.

"What makes you think you can convince him?" I asked. She drew her lower lip between her teeth, hesitating a bit before she spoke.

"He... kind of took care of me." Cara whispered. I gave her a questionable look, waiting for her to elaborate. "He was the only one who was kind to me and took me to get treated whenever I was beaten to the point I couldn't walk. At some point, we might have had feelings for each other... but he stopped before it could turn into something more. Or maybe I read too much into it and confused his kindness for something more." Cara sighed.

"I don't think so." I told her. Carlos was close to hitting her, but Maso didn't allow it and stopped him before he could. "He still has a soft spot for you, but how big, I wouldn't know. Whatever it is, we have to take advantage of it and at least try to do something." I said.

"It's worth a try."

"Just one problem; we don't know how many of them are out there with Maso." I sighed. If it was only Maso, we had a better chance of taking him down. But if there were more men guarding the door, our chances were slim. Even more so as we had nothing to defend ourselves with.

I let out a small gasp when I realized we were still wearing our hair accessories. It was not much, but at least they were still somewhat sharp enough to stab someone if we put enough force to it.

"Okay, this is what we're going to do." I lowered my voice to make sure no one would be able to hear me.

I carefully explained what I had in mind to get out of here while mentally preparing myself actually to fight. This was not out in the training field with Luca and Giovanni. This was the real deal, and it had my stomach churning.

Our lives were on the line.

We both took a deep breath, preparing ourselves for what we were about to do. We only had one shot, and we couldn't fuck it up.

"Maso?" Cara knocked on the door while I stayed behind. She continued to call after him and knock until the hatch in the door opened. Maso didn't say anything and just looked at her, waiting for her to speak.

"We need to use the restroom."

"I will get you a bucket."

"What?!" She shrieked in disgust. "If you think I'll be willing to pee in a disgusting bucket, then you're wrong!" Cara frowned at the thought.

"I can't help you." Maso replied in a monotone voice.

"Wait, Maso!" She called after him before he could close the hatch. "Maso, please... I really need to go, and I'm on my period. Do you know how dangerous it is to leave a tampon in for so long? I could get TSS. Do you know what TSS is? It's Toxic Shock Syndrome, and if you don't want me to die from bacteria getting into my body, I suggest you let me use a normal toilet so that I can take care of my business."

Cara continued to plead her case in a passive-aggressive tone, holding her ground. She continued to stare him dead in the eyes.

"If you're going to fucking hold women hostage, at least be a bit more considerate of our anatomy."

I looked back and forth between them as they continued to stare at each other for a while. My body was tense, hoping this would get us out of here.

Then, suddenly, Maso shut the hatch, and my heart dropped.

We fucked up.

"Bring tampons!" Cara yelled before turning to me with a small grin. "It worked." She whispered when she neared me, and I looked at her, confused.

"It didn't look like that..."

"That's how he works. He doesn't say anything but will get the job done. Now, we just have to wait until he returns."

Time passed before the door suddenly flung open, and Maso stood by the door. It now dawned on me how big he actually was, spiking my nervousness even more as doubt overtook my body.

"Get going." Maso ordered sharply and gestured with his head in the direction we should go.

I held tightly onto Cara's hand as we stepped out into the long hall. I wanted to curse out loud when I saw one more person out there with Maso. And he was holding a gun.

I stayed close to Cara as we walked down the long hall. She was the one who had to put the plan into action, taking advantage of whatever relationship she had with Maso. I just had to stay close since she was my chance of survival. They couldn't give a fuck about me and would kill me in a heartbeat.

Maso and the other guy were behind us to make sure we wouldn't attempt any escape or resistance. My heart was beating like crazy, and I couldn't help but keep glancing behind me, fearing I would suddenly get shot from behind.

"The fuck you looking at?!" The guy spat out and pushed me hard, causing me to trip over my dress and fall into the wall. I winced as my elbow got scraped, feeling the cuts sting me immediately.

"Don't touch her, you pig!" Cara stepped in front of me.

"What did you call me?" He hissed out and aimed his gun at her.

"Lower your gun." Maso snapped. He stepped closer to him, and Cara made the move to cower behind Maso, pretending to seek comfort with him. Maso's body tensed when her hand touched his back.

"That bitch -" I couldn't see what was happening, but he never finished his sentence. He let out a scoff and kept his mouth shut.

"Leave. I will take care of it." Maso ordered. The guy gave him a stare before turning around to leave.

I let out a breath, feeling the tension easing a bit now that it was only Maso. He turned to look at Cara and handed her something. Only now did I realize he was holding a box of tampons.

"Thank you." Cara gave him a small smile, and he immediately looked away, as if he didn't want to see her smile.

Maybe he does feel more for her than he lets on...

"Are you okay?" Cara asked me.

"Yeah, I'm fine." I gave her a small, reassuring smile.

"Hurry up." Maso once again ordered, having Cara roll her eyes.

"Calm down, will you? We will be back in that shit hole soon enough." She snapped and grabbed my hand.

We continued down the hall, going through a door before we reached the restroom. I was the one to go in first, and I looked at Cara to make sure she would be okay by herself. She gave a small nod, and I swallowed hard before going.

He won't hurt her, I reminded myself.

Shutting the door behind me, I let out a shaky breath. Now, all I had to do was to waste some time for Cara to work her charm on Maso.

I pulled out the accessory I had stuffed in between my breasts. It was a wide, pearly hairpin I had in my hair, and it would be my best shot as a weapon.

As quietly as I could, I broke the pearls off and sharpened the pin against the wall, all while I heard Cara trying to spark a conversation with Maso.

"Why exactly are you doing this to me? Was marrying me away not enough?" Cara was talking to him in a gentle tone, but he wasn't replying. "I didn't expect this from you. You were the only one who was nice to me... Did you ever care about me? Or was it all fake as well?"

"... It wasn't."

I stilled at his reply.

"Then why did you push me away?" Cara asked after a while. She talked quietly, as if she didn't want me to hear. I knew she loved Lorenzo and was happy with him, but it sounded like she wanted some clarity on whatever happened between them.

"What happened shouldn't have happened in the first place. It was my mistake, and I should have known better." Maso replied, still in that tone that didn't hold any emotions.

"Why was it a mistake? Was I too broken and bruised for you? Of course, I was. I was nobody." Her voice was laced with sadness, and my heart dropped for her.

"Cara..." His tone went soft, and I anxiously waited for what he was going to say. "It was wrong of me to get involved with my boss's daughter." Maso said, his tone going back to being emotionless.

"That's it? That's your shitty excuse?" Her voice raised.

I jumped when there was a hard bang on the door.

"Time's up! Get out." Maso ordered loudly to me. I tried to compose myself and took a deep breath, holding the now-sharpened hairpin in my hand.

"Always go for the vital points." I whispered to myself.

I took another deep breath before swinging the door open.

One Hundred Fourteen

Althaia

I swung the door open, holding the hairpin tightly in my hand. I stopped at the doorway, feeling the tension. Cara kept her eyes fixed on Maso while he was keeping a sharp gaze at me. I wanted to shout at Cara for not being ready, and possibly wasting our only chance. I couldn't do this on my own.

"Turn around and put your hands on the wall."

"What, why?" I asked, my heart leaping to my throat and my hands started to get sweaty.

"I said turn around -"

"She can't!" Cara finally snapped out of whatever was going on with her and came to my rescue. "I need help since I can't do anything in this big dress." She continued and gestured to her dress.

Maso's eyes narrowed as he looked at me. His eyes continued down, stopping by my hands where I had them both into fists.

"Hands on the wall, now!" He snapped. I took a step back when he came closer to me, and I sent a panicking look to Cara.

"No, wait, Maso -" Cara went after him but tripped over her dress and crashed into him. Maso was fast and grabbed a hold of her before she could hit the ground.

This was it.

I quickly kicked the back of his leg, having him fall to one knee. His head snapped to mine with fury, reaching for his gun. Cara pushed his hand away from the gun, and in that split-second, I pierced the hairpin straight into his eye.

Maso shouted in pain as he grabbed his head. I tried to silence him by putting him in a headlock to cover his mouth. Cara limited his movements by holding onto his legs to keep him down.

"Grab his gun!" I told Cara to hurry. The second the words came out of me, Maso snapped out of it and elbowed me right in the face.

I let out a strangled scream as I staggered backwards before falling to the ground. A massive, overpowering shock flooded my body before a sharp pain spread across my face like a bitch.

I blinked a few times to regain my vision. I raised my head just in time to see Maso shoving Cara away from him. With a burst of adrenaline, I jumped to my feet.

Only to meet the muzzle of a gun aimed at me, with a very furious Maso behind it.

"You fucking Russian." He sneered, with the hairpin still attached to his eye. His eye was bleeding, and the way it looked had me trying not to throw up all over the place.

My chest rose and fell quicker than ever as I looked right into the gun. This was it for me. There was nothing I could do.

I was mentally preparing myself to be gone, and I hoped, whatever was going to happen, at least Cara will be getting out of here. I hoped Lorenzo would be able to find her and get her all the help she would need after witnessing my death.

I watched as his finger curled, ready to pull the trigger. I closed my eyes, just wanting it to be over already.

I will be with you soon.

I managed a small smile, thinking of Damiano, our baby, and my mother. We will be reunited soon.

A tear rolled down my cheek.

"No!" Cara screamed, and I snapped my eyes open at the sound of gurgling.

I breathed out in shock at the sight.

Maso was choking badly, trying to stem the bleeding from where Cara had plunged a knife into the side of his throat. Her hand was trembling on the handle as he staggered on his feet, crashing into her and they both fell against the wall.

"Ca...ra..." Maso choked out as he stared at her with wide eyes, almost pleadingly.

"I'm sorry..." Cara sobbed, only to be met with a sickening gurgle. His hands were desperately trying to do something, but they were moving slower by the second.

Choked sobs filled the hall, blending with the guttural sounds of his struggle for breath. Maso's blood-covered, trembling hand touched her face. His thumb brushed away a tear while looking at her as if he had just been betrayed by the love of his life.

Maso's final breath escaped in a haunting whisper, his hand falling away from her face before his entire body slumped against her. His eyes closed, and his body stilled.

"What have I done... what have I done?" Cara whispered, her voice trembling in fear.

I stood frozen in place at the gruesome sight, the blood continued to gush out from his neck.

Forcing my eyes away from him, I looked at Cara. She was silently crying, looking pale and her entire body was trembling. I instantly went to her, getting her away from Maso and turned her back to him.

"It's okay, Cara. It's okay." I pulled her into me, holding her tightly, and kept telling her over and over again that it was okay, trying to convince myself as well.

I placed my hands on her face, wiping her tears away.

"You did what you could. It was out of your hands." I spoke to her firmly, concealing the horror that churned within me. Cara looked lost, enveloped in shock; a feeling I knew all too well.

"Listen, Cara. Right now, we need to snap out of it and get out of here, okay? It's our only chance." I talked to her hurriedly, and she nodded, taking a breath to compose herself. "We need to move his body into the restroom before anyone sees." I swallowed hard, looking at Maso.

Luckily, the doors were heavy and thick to not attract any attention to us, but it was only a matter of time before anyone would walk in through those doors. The other guy might come soon to check on what was taking long for us to get back.

I grabbed Maso, forcing myself to think of his body as a heavy bag of potatoes and not a dead body I was dragging. Cara came to help, flinching when his head dangled towards her.

"Just a bag of potatoes..." I mumbled continuously. We got him into the restroom when I saw the trail of blood that followed along with the body.

"The blood!"

We grabbed a bunch of toilet paper and tried to get rid of the blood the best we could, but it was still not enough. I looked down at my dress, getting the idea of cutting it to use as a cloth to cover our tracks.

I searched around for anything sharp I could use to make a tear and, of course, there was nothing. Until my eyes landed on the knife stuck in Maso's throat.

"Oh, fuck... I need that knife..." I said, swallowing hard to keep my nausea down.

"You're not actually thinking of..." Cara trailed off, looking disturbed by the idea.

"I am..." I nodded but made no move to get it. "Okay... okay... You can do it. You smashed a rock into someone's head. You saw his brain mass. This is nothing." I tried to encourage myself. "Nope, not working." I gagged. I put a hand to my mouth, trying my best not to throw up.

I took a few deep breaths and finally mustered the courage to retrieve the knife.

I grabbed the handle with a disgusted look on my face as I tried to pull it out. The feeling of the knife being pulled out was so vile that I almost emptied my stomach on him. It was too much for me and I had to immediately pull it out in one swift motion.

"To think our husbands do that for a living..." Cara was looking just as sick as I was.

"Something I will never understand." I shivered in disgust.

Ignoring the blood on the knife, I cut my dress shorter and tore the material into a few pieces. We wet them and wiped the floor clean in haste.

We were almost done when we both froze in place and looked at each other with wide eyes. The sound of loud voices could be heard, and they were getting closer to us. I quickly wiped away the last blood on the floor before we rushed into the restroom.

"Fuck, the wall!" I whispered in a panic. I was about to get out again when Cara grabbed the back of my dress, pulled me back inside the restroom and closed the door just in time when another door banged open.

Men shouting and footsteps running past the door had us looking at each other with questioning looks.

I quickly told Cara to handle the gun because she had better aim than me, and I was better at handling the knife. The footsteps were fading, and I let out a breath of relief, thankful they didn't notice the blood on the wall.

"Where the fuck is Maso?!"

We both tensed at the voice of the other guy that had been guarding the door.

We pressed ourselves against the wall next to the door when he stopped nearby. Cara and I jumped in fear when bullets were flying in through the door, and I held my hand to my mouth to not let out a scream.

Then it went completely silent.

He stepped closer to the door, and I tried to signal to Cara what to do next and follow my lead. I crouched down, pressing myself to the wall as much as I could and gripped the knife.

The door slowly opened. The second he was within my reach; I plunged the knife right into the side of his stomach. He screamed out in pain and crashed into the door.

"Now, Cara!" I shouted, and she fired, shooting him right in the face.

"We have to run." I said, gagging as I pulled the knife out of him.

"Cut my dress!" Cara lifted her dress, and I went to cut it, but then stopped as we both stared at her wedding dress.

"Such a beautiful dress, though..." I said.

"I know. It's my dream dress." She looked at it sadly. We both took a second to admire it before I let out a sigh and cut the bulky dress.

We sprinted down the long hall after making sure the coast was clear. The others went this way, meaning there must be an exit somewhere.

We entered through another door, finding ourselves in front of a stairway. As I looked up, I counted three floors above us, each shrouded in dimly lit uncertainty.

"We don't know how many we will face up there." Cara spoke.

"I know. But we have to take the chance and see if we can fight our way out." I told her. "Shoot whoever comes in sight, and we can take their weapons to make it out."

Cara was nervous. Hell, so was I. It was not like we had years of training to be doing this.

"Don't think, just shoot, and I will stab any of those bitches who dare come near us." I said, trying to ease the tension. She cracked a small smile and clasped my hand tightly in hers.

Together, we made our way up, trying to keep out of sight.

"They're here!" Someone shouted from below. He sprinted up the stairs, and I heard more footsteps approaching.

"Run!" Cara reacted faster, pulling me along as we dashed up the last few steps to the first floor. There was no time to assess the situation on the other side as we burst through the door.

"They're escaping!" There were more men to the far left of the hall, guarding the floor.

We ran to the other side with them hot on our trail. We ran as fast as we could but stopped when someone appeared at our end with a machine gun. At this moment, I wanted to cry that we were surrounded.

"Get down!"

The words coming out of his mouth barely registered before I reacted, grabbing Cara and throwing us both to the floor as bullets flew over our heads.

When everything stilled, I looked up and rose to my feet, wary of the person in front of us. He was dressed in all black and wore a mask. I held the knife tightly, getting ready to swing as he neared us.

Then he took his mask off.

"Michael?!" Cara gasped.

"Wait, I thought you were…" I trailed off, but then really took a look at him. He looked like he had been through hell.

Cara was about to go to him, but I stopped her as I looked at Michael with narrowed eyes, unsure if we could trust him.

"Look, I know what I have done is unforgivable, and I would like to explain my side of things. But that will have to wait until I get you out of here and to safety. I've got clothes for you to change into, so hurry up. We don't have much time." Michael explained, but I still hesitated.

"Althaia, please. I would never intentionally put you and Cara in danger. Trust me." He looked sincere with his pleading expression.

"Come on." Cara nudged me and I gave in. He looked relieved, and we followed him to where he came from. This place was like a maze with so many passages. It felt impossible to navigate around.

"You can change here. I will keep an eye out." Michael led us to a dim area and handed us the duffel bag he carried with him before turning around to give us privacy.

We hurriedly helped each other get out of our dresses and pulled the clothes out, black leggings and black shirts.

"The vests too." Michael said.

I moved to grab one when I was suddenly pushed against the wall. I swung my knife at the assailant, but my arm was blocked and pinned against the wall. I instinctively prepared to bite his arm, only for a strangled gasp to escape me, and the knife slipped from my grasp in shock.

His lips curved into a beautiful smile as his eyes met mine.

MARIAM EL-HAFI

"Hi baby."

One Hundred Fifteen

Althaia

I felt my heart stop beating.

I was afraid to even close my eyes or blink, in case this was some kind of an illusion; a beautiful one that I would never get to see if I did.

Had I died, and were we now reunited?

With my shaky hand, I reached out and touched his face. He leaned into my touch, and a sob escaped my lips as tears welled in my eyes.

"Damiano?" I sobbed in a whisper.

"I'm right here, piccola." He kissed the palm of my hand and pulled me into him.

I cried into his chest, wrapping my arms tightly around him. It was real. He was right here in front of me, holding me tightly in his strong arms as he buried his face into my neck.

My husband is alive.

Damiano wiped my tears away when I had calmed down, his hands cradling my cheeks before leaning down to capture my lips. As our lips touched, the stress and anxiety melted away, replaced by a deep sense of serenity and relief.

I couldn't breathe.

Only because it filled me with an overwhelming sense of pure joy and love. Our lips met with a desperate intensity, as if our lives depended on that kiss, and my heart raced with a torrent of emotions.

Damiano pulled back slightly and rested his head against mine. It probably wasn't the right place or time, but I couldn't care less as I clung to him in desperation.

"I told you; I will always find you, my love." He whispered.

He always kept his word, no matter what.

"I really thought you had left me." I sniffed with a fresh wave of tears.

"Never. Not even death can do us part." Damiano wiped my tears away with his thumb as he caressed my cheek.

"How bad is it?" I asked and looked down to where he had been shot. I lifted his shirt to see, but he was wearing a bulletproof vest underneath.

"It will take more than a bullet to bring your man down." He smiled softly. "Are you okay? Does it hurt anywhere?" Damiano felt around my body to find any injuries.

"I can't really feel anything." I whispered.

"It's the adrenaline." His brows furrowed as he examined my face. I was sure it was bruised after being elbowed so hard in the face. "Are you bleeding anywhere?" Damiano's eyes were filled with concern for me, and I shook my head.

"I'm not."

"Are you sure?"

"I'm okay." I cupped his face, and I could feel his entire body relax. "But I'm worried about you." My voice cracked. He was looking pale and had small beads of sweat on his forehead.

"Don't be, piccola. It's nothing I can't handle." He reassured me and went to grab the vest for me. "Let's get you out of here."

Damiano strapped the bulletproof vest and made sure it was tight and in place. I looked over at Cara, seeing her wrapped in Lorenzo's arms while he talked to her quietly to calm her down.

She didn't deserve to go through all of this, especially on a day that was supposed to be her happiest day. It wasn't fair to her. It wasn't fair to any of them.

Damiano stopped in his tracks when I sniffed and saw my teary eyes.

"Where does it hurt?" He immediately went to unstrap the vest, but I shook my head before he could. "Tell me what's wrong." He cupped my face.

"I'm sorry."

"What are you apologizing for?"

"For everything." To see him so badly hurt was something I could never forgive myself for.

"You silly woman." Damiano let out a small chuckle. "You have done nothing wrong, and did we not say for better and for worse?" He reminded me.

"We did."

"Good. If I didn't mean it, I wouldn't be here, and I would have let your ass get shot a long time ago." He gave a cheeky wink before my eyes widened when he slapped my ass and gave it a good squeeze.

I was lost for words.

"Sorry to interrupt you all, but we have to go." Michael called out.

After Damiano made sure I was okay and everything was in place, he picked up the knife I had dropped.

"Whose blood?" He looked at the knife with a slight frown.

"Maso's, and some other guy I don't know."

"You took down Maso?" Michael looked at us in shock and I nodded.

"I stabbed him in the eye with a hairpin. He was about to shoot me if it wasn't for Cara who managed to grab his knife and save me by stabbing him in the throat."

Damiano shared a look with Lorenzo before they both turned to look at Cara.

"Honestly, I was more scared of what Damiano would do to me if I let anything happen to you. That thought alone scared the shit out of me. Besides, I took an oath too; to protect my brothers and sisters." Cara gave a faint smile despite the sadness swirling in her eyes.

"Thank you, Cara. I owe you a lifetime." Damiano said gratefully, leaving her in shock. It was not every day you hear a Mafia Boss express indebtedness to you.

"I just want to get out of here." She said.

"Let's get going." Lorenzo urged, keeping a tight arm around Cara. Damiano nodded but then stilled, as if he was listening to something.

"How close, Ava?" He suddenly said, and I was confused for a split second before realizing he had an earpiece.

"More of those fuckers keep popping up." Lorenzo sneered when we heard the faint voices coming closer.

"Here, take this." Damiano handed me a gun and tucked a knife into the front of my vest for easy accessibility. "Your reflexes are good. Next time, swing the knife from below. It's harder to block that way." I gave a firm nod, feeling my heart rate go up once again at the nearing voices.

Damiano gave me an earpiece too so I could hear Ava and Raffaele. They had taken over the cameras in the entire building and were informing us how many men we would face.

"Althaia and Cara, stay close together and follow Michael's lead. Lorenzo and I will take care of those fuckers so you can slip through." Damiano ordered us.

"Will you be okay?" I asked worriedly.

"I'll be fine, my love." Damiano gave me a quick kiss, but it still didn't ease my worry.

"Please, be safe." I whispered as my stomach twisted.

I swallowed hard as we took cover away from the door where those men would burst through at any second.

Damiano and Lorenzo got ready while I held Cara's hand tightly in mine.

"They got this." She reassured me, and I took a deep breath to ease my nerves.

"Once we get the chance, we will have to go through that door, then we should be able to find an exit from there." Michael explained and loaded his gun.

I checked the safety and racked the slide on mine, preparing myself to actually use this weapon.

The door burst open, and the first pair of men barged through. Before they could take more than a couple of steps, Lorenzo, like the Tank Man he is, grabbed them by her necks and smashed their heads together and tossed them aside. Damiano finished them with precise shots of his gun.

"That's my man." Cara said, completely mesmerized by the strength of her Tank Man. I too was watching the duo in awe. It was incredible to see them in action.

They were two highly skilled and lethal men, currently taking down one after another as if it were nothing. I kept my eyes on Damiano, making sure he would be okay. Even while injured, he seemed invincible.

The Devil and Tank Man moved around each other with a smooth synergy, covering one another's backs in a way I hadn't witnessed even in movies. They were truly a manifestation of one mind in two bodies.

"Now's our chance!" Michael shouted to us.

We hurriedly got up and ran down the hall, where Damiano and Lorenzo were distracting the others and trying to barricade their way so we could get through.

"Take the exit to your right!" Lorenzo shouted, and we sprinted to get there, even as more men kept appearing for them to fight off.

Breathless, we reached the exit door, and I struggled to catch my breath on the other side. The bulletproof vest weighed heavily on my body, and it was slowing me down.

"Where to?" I asked, trying to make out our surroundings. The hall was dark, and we had to stay close to the wall to feel our way.

"Ava, any help?" Michael asked, and I had completely forgotten she would be able to guide us.

"Sorry, guys. I can't make out anything. The cameras are busted on that side."

"Great." Cara muttered.

"According to the map, there are two doors. Keep going to the very end, and that exit should lead you to the conveyor room. From there, take the stairs, and you will be able to get out." I absorbed every detail Ava shared while tracing my fingers along the wall to gain a sense of my surroundings.

"Found it!" Cara yelled, and I followed her voice until I could feel her. I squinted my eyes at the sudden bright light when we opened the door.

"And where do you think you're going?"

My jaw clenched at the voice.

"Carlos." I sneered when I found him.

"Going so soon, *sister?*" He laughed and pulled the trigger.

One Hundred Sixteen

ALTHAIA

I let out a scream when I landed on the ground with a force, and an immediate surge of pain shot through my shoulder.

"Fuck!" I clenched my teeth, fighting through the pain as I tried to get up on all fours. Groans reached my ears, and I turned my head towards the source.

"Michael!" I gasped, crawling toward him, ignoring my own pain.

"Why did you do that, you idiot?" Cara sat up and reached him.

He had pushed us away and took the bullet.

"Are you guys okay?" Michael panted, attempting to get up but immediately clutching his ribs and slumping down again.

"We're okay." I said, pressing down on the wound on his leg. I quickly glanced around, seeing we were behind a machine and out of Carlos' view.

This would buy us a bit of time. I needed to figure something out to stop the bleeding.

"Isn't it cute? A traitor is helping the enemies." Carlos' voice rang out, followed by another gunshot. I felt the bullet whiz past me, narrowly avoiding my head.

"Stay down." Michael yanked me to the ground and forced himself to get up. He fired back, forcing Carlos to seek cover. "Fuck!" Michael groaned and slumped to the ground in pain.

"Don't strain yourself. Are you hurt anywhere else?" I scanned his body for other injuries, but it was difficult to determine since he was wearing a bulletproof vest.

"Just a few cracked ribs. The drugs have worn off." He panted with a strained voice before more shots were fired.

"You're not getting out of here! You're all dead!" Carlos laughed, making me grit my teeth.

"Help Michael while I distract that little bitch." Cara said, preparing to move.

"Wait, take my gun with you." I patted myself, realizing I didn't have it on me. "Shit!" My eyes widened in panic.

I searched around for it on the floor and found it. The only problem was, it had slipped to the other side, and there wasn't a chance to get it without getting shot by Carlos.

I reached up to my earpiece to call for any backup.

But it was gone.

"It's okay, I got it." Cara showed she had a gun.

"Are you sure you want to do this?" I asked with concern. I didn't want anything to happen to her, but with Michael unable to move and no one to call for help, we had to try.

"No! You're not doing it." Michael growled in pain. We ignored him as we continued to lock eyes. She gave me a determined look, convincing me she could do this.

"I've hated that ugly bitch from day one."

"Try to keep him away from here while I help Michael."

"Cara, no!" Michael tried to get up to stop her, but it was already too late as she got going.

"Shut up. You're not in charge anymore." I told him and had him lay still so I could put pressure on his leg. "Are you hurt anywhere else?"

"It doesn't matter. Just leave me and save yourself. I'm a dead man either way." He grunted.

"I'm not leaving you here." I glared at him. I knew it was his pain that was talking.

"There is not much time. You and Cara have to get out of here before it's too late. This place is about to blow up." Michael pleaded.

"Then I better get you out of here." I grabbed the hem of his shirt and tried to tear it apart to use as a bandage. I could hear Cara in the background, agitating Carlos by calling him an ugly bitch.

"Please, Thaia... I don't deserve it. Everything I have done, and your mom... I deserve to rot. But first, I need to tell you how sorry I am. I never meant to hurt you, and when I said those things to you... Fuck, I was a piece of shit."

"Michael -"

"No, let me say this first." He looked at me with pleading eyes. "I'm not asking for forgiveness because I don't deserve it. I was jealous when I saw you with him. I believed you were making a mistake, and I thought you were better off with someone like... someone like me. I know you got married and I'm happy for you. And unlike me, I know he will never hurt you and he will do anything for you. I love you, Althaia. I do. But I love you more as my family. You and Cara are the only ones I have left. I -"

"Stop." I felt a lump in my throat grow. He looked at me with eyes filled with regret and sadness. "Stop talking as if you're about to die. We're getting out of here and we'll be fine. Your words hurt me, yes, but you can't control who you love, and I know that very well because look who I'm with." I chuckled lightly to force the tears away, and he even let out a small smile through his pain.

"I also know how miserable life can be when you think you have no one. But you still have me. Us. We're still your family. What happened in the past is forgiven." I said and continued to tear off a piece of his shirt to bandage his leg.

Michael put a hand on top of mine to stop me.

"If only I knew what was going on, I would have done everything I could to stop it."

"I know." I believed him. Gaetano was the piece of shit who deserved to rot. Not Michael.

"I don't deserve it. Save yourselves." He tried to stop.

"Yeah, no." I smacked away his hand and bandaged his leg. He clenched his jaw when I bound it around his leg, making sure there was enough pressure. "I kind of have a reputation of caring more about others than myself." I smiled and gave his hand a small squeeze.

"Can you help me loosen up the vest? I can hardly breathe and it's pressing against my ribs."

I quickly fixed it and he let out a small breath of relief.

I suddenly froze in place, and Michael's expression mirrored my own. Everything was silent. Michael tried to rise, but I placed a finger on my lips to have him stay quiet.

With trembling arms, I crawled quietly to assess the situation. Every fiber of my being prayed that Cara was unharmed.

Swallowing hard, I sat with my back pressed against the machine and slowly peeked out. A gasp escaped me at the sight, followed by the sharp crack of a gunshot. In a panicked reaction, I jerked back, landing on my side in an attempt to take cover. But it was too late; a cry of pain erupted as I clutched my bloodied arm.

"Thaia!" Michael reached out to me.

"I'm fine, I'm fine." I clenched my jaw in pain.

I looked down at my arm, removing my shaking hand to see so much blood gushing out. It was burning in pain and the skin was open, but no bullet was stuck.

"I - Fuck! He has Cara!" I gritted out.

Michael, with newfound strength, rose to his feet, gun at the ready. Before he could pull the trigger, he was sent flying backward onto his back.

"Michael!" I screamed, rushing to him, and quickly felt relieved when I saw he would be okay. If he weren't wearing a vest, he would have a bullet in his chest now.

Carlos' laugh boomed out.

"There is that scream. I've wanted to hear it ever since I saw the video of you screaming after your mommy." He taunted.

I stopped breathing.

"I watched it all, you know. How everything happened. I made them wear a body camera to record you so I wouldn't miss out. The way you cried and screamed after your mommy made me horny."

I could feel my heart pounding in my chest, my breath hitching with each laugh that escaped his lips. My eyes burned with unshed tears. They videotaped my mother's death as if it was some kind of sick entertainment?

"Your reaction was praiseworthy. Screaming, crying, and shouting before going numb. That shit went straight to my cock. It had me almost jerking off to it."

"You're sick... You're fucking sick!" I screamed, but it only humored him some more.

"It's a shame they didn't get to you. I wanted them to cut you open. To cut out that disgusting thing that was growing in your belly."

It felt like time had stopped, and everything stopped moving. I wasn't even breathing anymore as everything shut down within me.

The pain, the anger, the sadness, the shame I felt when my baby was ripped away from me. I was left only with a picture—a painful memory; a constant reminder of how powerless and shattered I was when I couldn't protect my own baby.

"Disgusting?" My voice trembled.

Trembled with anger.

"Did you just call my baby disgusting?" I didn't know what was happening to me as I let out a laugh.

Humorless, dark, and cold.

I grabbed the gun, my hand tightening around it.

"I'm fucking killing that ugly bitch."

One Hundred Seventeen

Althaia

I sprinted while firing, but the distance was too great to land a shot. All the lessons Damiano taught me about maintaining composure and focus seemed to evaporate. My heart pounded, and I trembled in a fury so intense that my sole desire was to reach Carolos and witness the life drain painfully from his eyes.

Disgusting?

The word kept echoing in my mind, a relentless drumbeat of rage and determination.

I raced forward, darting from cover to cover, firing my weapon in Carlos's direction. He, too, seemed desperate to hit me, his own shots erratic and unfocused. I weaved between concrete pillars, closing the distance. My aim wasn't perfect but hitting him wasn't my goal.

Not yet.

He still had Cara, and I couldn't risk accidentally shooting her. Instead, my plan was for him to empty his gun while I inched closer. And at this moment, I was fucking thankful Damiano had made me run at every practice.

"Shit!" Carlos cursed out. I let out a slight smirk when I heard him pull the trigger of the now-empty gun.

I stepped out from behind the pillar, the gun ready in my hand, and aimed for Carlos. My finger rested on the trigger, about to shoot, but stopped when he used Cara as a shield to protect himself.

"Let her go." I snarled. Cara was trying to get out of his grip but stilled when he pressed a knife against her throat.

"Nah. For once, she's actually useful." Carlos smiled cunningly.

"You piece of shit!" I sneered and stepped closer.

"Ah, ah, ah! Don't come any closer. Unless you want to watch me slit her throat open." He laughed, and Cara winced when he slowly made a cut in her throat.

"Let her go!" I screamed, and my hands started to shake as I held the gun, wanting so desperately to shoot him.

But I couldn't.

"Thaia, go... get out of here while you still can." Cara pleaded, and I shook my head.

"I'm not leaving you. Not again." I had already failed her before. I couldn't let it happen again.

Over my fucking dead body.

"It's okay. I wasn't meant to live long, anyway." She smiled sadly while I vigorously shook my head.

"Can you stop being suicidal for just a damn minute and let me help you?!" I yelled, trying not to cry while thinking of how to get her out of this situation.

"Oh, how sad. I would even shed a tear if I actually gave a shit about you." Carlos' voice interrupted. "If you really want her to live, I'm willing to do a trade. I will let her go if you come with me." His sinister smile returned.

"Althaia, no!" Cara shouted.

"Shut the fuck up, bitch!" Carlos hissed and pressed the knife against her neck, more blood trailing down as he cut deeper into her skin.

"Stop it! I will go with you!" I screamed in desperation. "Just let her go."

"Excellent. I'm sure *our dad* will be very pleased about that." Carlos smirked as I glared at him. There was nothing more I wanted to do than wipe his disgusting smirk away.

"Althaia, don't do it!" Cara desperately shouted to me.

"It's okay, Cara." I tried to give her a reassuring smile.

I watched tears glisten in her eyes as she continued to beg me to leave her behind. I ignored her as I lowered the gun and looked at Carlos.

"Let her go, and I will go with you willingly."

"Not so fast. Put the gun down on the ground and kick it away."

My eyes narrowed, hesitating.

"Remove the knife from her throat first."

"Fine." Carlos let out a loud sigh of annoyance but removed the knife. He was still holding Cara tightly, almost hiding behind her to make sure I couldn't shoot him without hurting her too.

"Your move. Nice and slow." Carlos said.

I clenched my jaw, but slowly lowered the gun to the ground as he watched me like a hawk. Once it was down, I kicked it away and I made sure it would be nowhere near that cocksucker for ice cream.

"Put your hands up and slowly approach me." He grinned, and I glared at him but followed his order.

"Let her go now." I hissed.

"Sure." He rolled his eyes at me.

Then suddenly smirked.

"You really are a dumb bitch."

I stood frozen, eyes widening, and the air knocked out of me as he plunged the knife into her. Cara gasped, her eyes filled with terror, mouth open, and choking on the sounds that wanted to escape when Carlos twisted the knife before pulling it out.

"...Cara..." I whispered, shock resonating in me. She looked at me with tears that escaped as her body trembled before falling to the ground. "Cara!" I shouted at the top of my lungs, running to her side.

"You're coming with me!" Carlos grabbed me and pushed me away before I could get to her. I landed on the ground but got on my hands and knees to crawl to her, tears already blurring my sight.

"Please, no!" I cried after her. I almost reached her when I got yanked up by my hair. My scalp was burning, but I couldn't care about it as I numbly tried to push Carlos away to get to Cara.

"I'm sorry... I'm sorry..." I kept sobbing to her.

"It's okay... I just want peace." Cara smiled as tears ran down her face. I watched her slowly close her eyes, making me scream after her.

"Cara, no! Stay awake, please stay awake!"

"Get the fuck going!" Carlos dragged me away from her. "If you don't fucking listen, I will slit her throat and then yours." He hissed, holding the knife against my neck before roughly pushing me in front of him.

I glanced back at Cara, tears covering my face, as Carlos kept pushing me forward toward the stairs of the overhead walkway. He was close behind me, and I could feel the knife against my back, urging me on.

Silently, I cried as I took slow steps toward the exit.

It was all happening again.

First, my mother, and now Cara. I tried to repress my sobs, thinking of how useless I was. What was the point of all the training if I couldn't use it when it mattered? I was powerless and worthless. I couldn't even protect my loved ones. Once again, they were dying in front of me.

I looked down at my feet, wishing I was put out of my misery as my heart ached, mourning every single one I had lost in my life.

Blinking the tears away a few times, I realized the knife was still tucked into my vest.

I stopped walking.

"Hey! Keep going, Russian whore!" I felt him nudge me with the knife.

I shook my head. It was all or nothing.

"Fuck you!" I grabbed my knife and ducked as I whirled around fast.

I blocked his arm with the knife as I struck at him from below as sadness and rage overwhelmed me.

I would rather die knowing I at least tried fighting for my loved ones.

I watched the way my knife slid across his face. Carlos stumbled back into the safety railing as he clutched his face.

"You fucking bitch!" He screamed.

"Shut up already." I lunged after ducking before he could grab me and kicked the back of his leg.

Carlos landed harshly on the grating, and I instantly climbed on top of him to keep him down. Gripping my knife, I raised it high above my head with adrenaline pumping like crazy.

I was ready to end his life once and for all.

I plunged the knife down, aiming for his throat.

Carlos blocked it and delivered a hard blow to the side of my neck. I dropped the knife, choking and becoming dizzy, losing focus on what was going on.

He shoved me away, and I forced myself to cough, struggling to catch a breath and fill my lungs.

But it was short-lived.

Carlos got on top of me and wrapped his arms around my throat.

"You really do make everything so fucking difficult." He hissed. "I wasn't planning on killing you yet, but you deserve to fucking die for what you just did! Sleep tight, *sister*!"

I was gagging, and my airway was almost entirely cut off. He added more pressure, and I knew it was almost over for me.

I tried to move my head to the side to buy myself some time, only to notice we were on the edge of the walkway. With one hard push, we would both fall out of the wide safety railing.

We were at least twenty feet up—enough for the fall to be fatal.

"Then you're dying with me, *brother*." I choked out.

Summoning every ounce of strength, I used my legs to help me, and we both rolled over the edge.

One Hundred Eighteen

ALTHAIA

I cried out in pain as I gripped the edge; it felt like my fingers were on the verge of being sliced off. My body swayed twenty feet up in the air, struggling to hold on as I was too heavy.

Looking down, my heart went to my throat at the height. My life depended on the strength in my arms, which were practically nonexistent since I had prioritized eating over trying to be physically stronger.

"Let go of me, Carlos!" I shouted. He was holding onto my legs, adding more weight, when I was barely able to handle my own.

I could feel the sweat drip down my face as I panted, literally holding on for dear life with that ugly bitch hanging onto me.

"You crazy bitch! If I'm going down, you're coming with me!"

"I would rather kill myself than die with you!" I tried to kick him off, but he clung onto me. I had to be careful with how much I moved if I didn't want to lose too much of my grip.

"I will take you with me!" The bastard started to jerk around, making me gasp as my hold loosened on the edge of the platform.

"Carlos, stop!" I gritted my teeth.

My arms were burning, and I knew they would give up soon. I would be falling for God knows how long until I hit the ground. My spine would break, and my skull would be split open, spilling my brain mass everywhere.

It would be one horrifying death.

"We will both die if you keep moving!" I shouted.

"That's the point, bitch!" Carlos had the audacity to laugh. I could feel my fingers slip and I squeezed my eyes shut.

Life isn't fucking fair at all.

It wasn't fair for Damiano to find me dead on the ground like that. Sienna's story flashed in my mind, and my eyes welled up with tears for Damiano. It wasn't fair that this was going to happen to him again, to have his happiness completely stripped away once more.

Once he found me, he would break, and I was afraid what would happen to him because I knew he wouldn't try to seek that happiness again.

He has already gone through so much.

With Sienna.

With our baby.

Now, me.

I prayed for him.

I prayed he would be okay, no matter what the outcome would be.

I prayed for everyone I had come to love and care for, hoping they would be okay.

"...Fuck!"

I snapped my eyes open and looked down at Carlos, witnessing his struggle to hold on.

Grabbing the opportunity, I tried my best to wiggle one foot out of his grip. I would be able to hang on for a bit longer without him clinging to me.

"Let go already!" I hissed, attempting to kick him off me.

The son of a bitch had the nerve to laugh.

"I'm taking you with me to hell!" Carlos twisted his body, shaking us, and my fingers slipped even more.

"Go suck Satan's cock for ice cream. You will be needing it."

With one hard kick to his hands, he fell.

"You fucking bit -" He never got to finish his sentence as he hit the ground.

I gasped in horror at the gruesome sight that unfolded before me. I had failed to notice the metal poles sticking out of the ground, and Carlos landed directly on top of one, becoming impaled. The metal pole jutted out from his stomach, and I could see bits and chunks of his insides on it. His mouth and eyes were agape, frozen in a macabre gaze that pierced right through me.

I felt sick.

I pushed my nausea aside and focused on hauling myself up. It was only a matter of seconds before I would taste the same fate as Carlos.

"Oh, God... oh, God...!" I gasped as one hand slipped.

My body was swaying too much for me to hold on, and I tried with all my might to regain my grip. However, my arm was too heavy and in too much pain for me to raise it.

I watched helplessly as my fingers slowly slipped from the edge, and there was nothing I could do. I squeezed my eyes shut, not wanting to witness the last moments of my life.

I fell.

I felt the rush in my entire body, almost like the sensation before going on a fast roller coaster. Except, this was the feeling before plunging to my death.

But it only lasted for a split second.

A hand clasped around my wrist, and my eyes shot open.

I couldn't even make a sound as everything got choked up in my throat.

"I got you!" Damiano grunted, almost out of breath.

He was drenched in sweat, his face contorted in a frown, and he groaned as half of his body hung over the edge while gripping my arm tightly. Damiano gritted his teeth, struggling to pull me up as my body swayed in the air.

"I'm slipping!" I choked out, my heart nearly stopping as I fell an inch.

"You're not leaving me!" He growled.

He used the safety railing with his legs for support and reached for me with his other arm. Panting heavily, sweat dripped from his face as he exerted every ounce of strength to haul me back up to safety.

When half of my body was on the platform, he wrapped his arms tightly around me and pulled me in. Damiano was on his back with me on top of him, both of us in an iron grip.

We were both panting, and my entire body was shaking - not from the effort, but from the realization that I had narrowly escaped the same brutal fate as Carlos.

"Are you okay?" Damiano's voice was strained as he spoke but still held me to him, afraid to let me go.

"J-just hold me, please." I cried, burying my face in his neck.

Tears streamed down my face, and I couldn't discern whether it was from fear of almost meeting my end, or from relief that he saved me.

Damiano's arms slowly loosened their hold on me and slid down. I raised my head to look at him. His eyes were closed, and he was looking unusually pale.

"Damiano?" I called after him, panicking when he didn't respond. "Damiano?" I tapped his cheek a few times as I kept calling his name.

But he didn't respond.

He didn't wake up.

"Damiano!" I shouted. "No, no, no, please wake up!" My tears fell down his face.

"Y-you can't leave me... we-we haven't had enough time... please, come back to me." But there was still no response, and his eyes remained shut.

I sobbed as I cradled his head into my arms.

"Come back to me, my love..." I whispered, refusing to accept I was holding my dead husband.

I frantically looked around his body to figure out what was happening to him.

His gunshot wound!

I quickly ripped his shirt up and unstrapped his vest, but nothing prepared me for the sight.

His wound was open, and blood flowed out too fast. I immediately tried to stop the bleeding with my hands, watching the blood seep out between my fingers and cover my hands.

I rapidly blinked away my tears to clear my sight, but they continued to stream down my face as I tried to think how to help him.

Shakily, I grabbed his shirt again, tearing a large enough piece of cloth to wrap around him. I tied it as tightly as I could while still adding pressure. Damiano was still unmoving. He wasn't even making a sound.

I moved up to him again, checking his pulse on the side of his neck, holding my breath as I did. I let out the biggest breath of relief when I felt his heartbeat. It was faint and slow, but it was still there.

"Althaia!"

I looked over my shoulder, seeing Lorenzo with Cara unconscious in his arms.

"Please, save Cara!" Lorenzo looked at me, and then at Damiano. I could see he was hesitating to leave.

"Is he okay?" He asked.

"I got him, Lorenzo. Help Cara." I practically ordered. He gave one small, firm nod before running to the exit with Cara.

"Damiano, wake up." I whispered, caressing his cheek, hoping for some kind of response. I kept calling his name, touching him, and hoping, *praying*, he could hear me and come back to me.

I let out a choked-up sob, and a small smile formed on my lips when I saw movements behind his closed eyelids. He let out a breath as he started to say something, but I couldn't make out what it was.

"What are you saying?" I leaned down, my ear close to his mouth.

"... Beautiful Angel..." He muttered, and my smile got wiped away.

Beautiful Angel?

Who was he talking about? Never once has he ever called me an Angel. I looked at him with a frown, jealousy bubbling in me.

"Who are you calling a beautiful angel? I don't care if you're on the verge of dying, you better not dream about another woman! Wake the fuck up!" With that, I slapped him.

Damiano's eyes snapped open as his head got whipped to the side.

"Fuck, woman!" He suddenly erupted. "How the fuck are you this tiny yet so fucking strong?"

"Who were you calling a beautiful Angel, huh?" I scowled with fury. Damiano let out a lazy grin as he looked at me.

"You're my beautiful Angel. So fiery, my love."

I clamped my mouth shut, feeling my jealousy dying as he cupped my chin. It didn't go unnoticed how his movements were slow, even when he blinked—it was slow.

"I thought you left me..." My voice cracked and my lip started to tremble as I sniffed.

"No, no... I was just... resting my eyes." He started to close his eyes again, and he was looking paler by the second. I had to get him out of here fast to get help.

The explosives!

"We have to hurry and get out of here. Can you move?" I was afraid to even try to move him in case I worsened his condition.

"It hurts like a bitch." Damiano grunted and clenched his jaw. This was bad. He was the type of person who could endure a lot of pain, and this meant it was critical.

I helped him to get on his feet, and the sound of approaching footsteps caught my attention and I looked up.

"Thank God it's you." I breathed out when I saw it was Giovanni. There was no time to be fighting off Gaetano's men in here when the whole thing was about to blow up.

"Shit, are you okay?" Giovanni looked at us, assessing our injuries.

"We're okay. Gio, Michael is still down there. He was shot and needs help." I told him. Giovanni was also injured, and bleeding from the side of his head, but he was still well enough to be able to help.

"No, you need help." Giovanni frowned when he saw Damiano's condition.

"Giovanni, we don't have time! Go help Michael, now!" I shouted, ordering him to get going, but he still didn't listen and stepped towards us.

"I will pull the rank card if you don't go." I gave him one hell of a look and Giovanni gave me one disapproving scowl, but he finally got going.

"That's my Donna." Damiano half chuckled as I helped him to his feet.

He wrapped an arm around my shoulders, leaning on me for support, and I had to use my entire strength to keep us both upright.

"Have I ever told you how hot you look when you're angry?"

"Damiano, this really isn't the time nor the place to be saying such things." I was already struggling to keep his weight on me as we made our way to the exit.

"Sure is."

"Did you hit your head or something? Because you're not thinking straight."

"I'm thinking about my wife's pussy like I always do. I would say my head is just fine."

"My God… is the pain making you high? Never mind. Stop talking and keep walking. You're heavy!"

"It's because of how big my dick is."

"Shut up."

"Yes, baby."

I was panting, my body aching and sweating, as we finally made it out from the building with Giovanni and Michael close behind. The outside was even more chaotic; shouting, gunshots, cars on fire, and dead bodies on the ground.

It was a literal war zone we had stepped into.

I looked around, observing that Damiano's men had the upper hand, and it appeared to be under control. There were so many armed men present, some I recognized, and some I didn't.

My eyes landed on a group of men standing in a semi-circle, guarding someone. My gaze lowered, and I saw Cara's father on the ground, beaten and tied up.

"Did you catch Gaetano too?" I asked Damiano, feeling hopeful that this nightmare was ending.

"No. The bastard is hiding like the coward he is and left his brother out in the open." Damiano groaned. I looked at him, noticing his condition had worsened.

"Sixty seconds! Get away from here!" Renzo shouted, and everyone started to move.

"Shit... Althaia, you have to go. Now." I felt him trying to move away from me, but I held him tightly, almost wanting to slap him again.

"You really need to get that head checked if you think I'm leaving my husband behind. Shut up and keep walking!"

Right now, I didn't care if I caused him more pain as I held him tightly and walked as fast as I could. He would be okay as long as I got him far enough away from here.

"Antonio!" I shouted after him when I saw him.

Antonio spotted us, shouting orders out in Italian, and ran to us with a bunch of men. As soon as they grabbed Damiano, I collapsed to the ground in exhaustion. It was physically impossible for me to get up.

"Forgive me for touching you, Donna." Niccolò said before he picked me up in his arms and ran.

I held onto him tightly when I started to hear low explosions. Looking behind him, my eyes widened in terror when I saw the end of the building erupting in flames. It kept going, one explosion after the other, like a domino effect, coloring the night sky with orange flames.

"Cover your face!" Niccolò shouted to me.

Quickly, I shielded my face with my arms just as a deafening blast erupted. The blast-wave was intense, sending us forward. Niccolò absorbed most of the impact as we tumbled across the ground.

Coughing and squinting my eyes, I rose to my hands and knees, shielding my face from the lingering heat.

"Are you okay?" I asked him, and he gave me a thumbs up.

"All good." He reassured me. I nodded, waving away the smoke that was quickly filling up the area.

I looked around for Damiano, stumbling up to my feet, when I saw him lying on the ground.

"We need to take him to the hospital and get him treated right away." I told them as they helped me get Damiano up on his feet. "Do you think everyone got out?" I asked Antonio as I looked around, luckily seeing many of Damiano's men were present.

"From our side, yes." He said.

"Okay, that's good. Did anyone find Gaetano yet?" I asked. Antonio shook his head, and I sighed.

"I guess he was still inside then." It was the only explanation since the outside was heavily guarded. There was no way he could have slipped out without any of them noticing.

"We will do rounds to check for any survivors." Antonio informed me.

"Please, anyone who is severely injured, send them to get medical attention immediately. To the men who are well enough, let them search the area for Gaetano. He can't have gotten far away." I told Antonio, and the men nearby stood and listened to me as if I was their commander.

"Understood, Donna." Antonio gave a firm nod, leaving me a bit taken aback by how he addressed me. He was Damiano's right-hand man, and I saw him as someone superior.

"I need to get Damiano treated but update me on what's happening. If you need anything, let me know, and I will have someone on their way." I added, and Antonio ordered the men to get going.

"Look at you, ordering them around like a true Donna. They don't even need me anymore." I looked at Damiano and he gave me a half-smirk.

"Of course, they need you. And I need you, too." I gave a small smile, helping him as we were led to a car.

I wanted to feel relieved that it was over, but I couldn't until Gaetano was found. If he had gotten away, who knows what his plan would be next, and this could happen all over again.

I blinked a few times when something caught my attention. I looked ahead, focusing on the ground. The soil seemed softer there, and it appeared as if a section of the ground was moving upwards.

I stopped walking and kept my attention fixed on that spot.

"What's wrong? Are you in pain?" Damiano asked, and I shook my head.

"Something is not right over there…" I trailed off, wondering if my eyes were playing tricks on me because of exhaustion.

But they weren't.

It suddenly shot up, and someone sprinted away.

"It's Gaetano!" I shouted, pointing in his direction. My body tensed, ready to chase after him, but I stopped myself when I remembered I was supporting Damiano.

"Capture him! Alive!" Damiano commanded, and his men pursued Gaetano.

The loud gunshot echoed, causing everyone to freeze. I witnessed Gaetano falling to the ground, screaming in pain as he clutched his leg.

"Wait, what's happening?" I frowned, recognizing familiar faces approaching from the other side.

Alexei and Nestor.

Alexei approached Gaetano with a scornful expression before shifting his gaze to Damiano. His men followed suit, aiming their guns at us.

I felt Damiano's body tense, curses escaping under his breath as he pulled me behind him for cover. My heart started beating frantically as I assessed the situation. We were in no condition for another war, especially against Alexei.

"Now, you're going to tell me where she is." Alexei seethed through gritted teeth. "Where the hell is she?!" He roared, and the loud sound of rifles being racked filled the air.

I stepped out from behind Damiano.

"Althaia, get back!" I ignored Damiano's plea, standing in front of him and his men with my arms wide open, attempting to cover and protect them in some way.

"Alexei..." I stepped closer to him, my heart pounding in my throat when one of his men turned attention to me, ready to fire. Alexei noticed and smashed the back of his rifle into the man's face.

"Don't fucking aim at her!" Alexei shouted, and Nestor barked something in Russian at them, causing their aim to shift away from me.

"I'm not sure what's happening here, but I've already told you. My mother is gone." My eyes flickered back and forth between him and Nestor. "If you want to know where she is buried, I can -"

"I will stop you right there. I went to the cemetery and dug up her casket." He said, and I gaped at him in pure shock.

"You desecrated my mother's grave?!" I yelled at him.

"No. Your mother was not in it." Alexei looked at me with his stormy, piercing blue eyes.

"What do you mean?" I breathed out, scared that someone had taken my mother.

Alexei didn't answer and turned his gaze to Damiano. I turned to face Damiano, who was looking at Alexei with a firm expression.

"Damiano, what is he talking about?" I asked. He kept his gaze fixed on Alexei before finally shifting his eyes towards me.

"Your mother is alive."

One Hundred Nineteen

DAMIANO

Althaia was in shock.

She was so shocked that her body gave out, collapsing to the ground. I gritted my teeth as I shoved my pain aside, grabbing her and pulling her to me.

I didn't give two shits about Alexei at this moment; my only concern was her. She looked numb, lost, as she tried to comprehend what I had just said. For once, Alexei remained silent, and his men stood by as he observed Althaia.

His daughter.

He hadn't expressed his thoughts on the situation, about discovering he had a daughter. However, he seethed with anger toward her mother for keeping their child a secret.

For twenty-five years, he had lived oblivious to the fact that he had a child in the world. To compound his frustration, his daughter believed Gaetano was her father; an Italian man who had married her mother.

"Come on, breathe, Althaia... there you go... breathe." She gasped for air, and I felt her entire body shaking against mine. Despite my own struggle to stand due to the pain, I held her tightly, knowing it wouldn't be long before I lost consciousness again.

"Oh, damn it. Get her a doctor and tend to yourself. You're useless to me if you're dead." Alexei sighed, even rolling his eyes in exasperation.

"If you pull some dumb shit, Vasiliev, you know what the consequences will be." I warned him.

"You are in no position to make any threats to me."

"Does it look like I give a fuck? Fuck up, and the blood is on your hands." That was my final warning to him before we rushed to the car.

In the car, I was slipping in and out of consciousness. My heart raced faster than ever, and I could feel the blood dripping down from my stomach. Althaia was beside me, attempting to keep me awake by talking and tapping my cheek.

For half of the ride to the hospital, I couldn't hear what she was saying; her voice sounded distant, as if she were far away.

I opened my eyes, seeing everything blur past me.

"...Surgery immediately!"

"Help him, please." Althaia's voice sounded out, causing me to frown at the sound of her crying.

"Don't cry, my love."

I felt her lips on mine; soft, light, and feathery, making my heart somehow beat even faster, spreading warmth inside of me.

Like a fire, keeping me alive.

"I love you." She whispered, but I heard it loud and clear.

"And I love you, piccola."

Suddenly, the world was swallowed by darkness.

I rested in the recovery room, listening to Antonio as he provided a detailed report. The surgeons had to work swiftly on me, considering I had pushed my body beyond its limits, and it nearly cost me my life.

"Everything is clear, and people are receiving treatment." Antonio reported, and I nodded.

We had encountered a larger enemy force than anticipated, resulting in numerous injuries among my men. While we had casualties, the toll was minimal compared to the losses Gaetano suffered.

"We have him and his brother locked up separately, and the place is heavily secured."

"And Vasiliev?"

"He's still around but keeping his distance."

"Of course he is." I shook my head. "I want eyes on him at all times."

I turned my attention to the door when it opened.

"You good?" Lorenzo asked as he stepped inside.

"Still breathing."

"You look like shit."

"And yet I'm still better looking than you." I shot back, and he cracked a smile. "How's Cara?"

"She'll pull through." Lorenzo murmured, rubbing his jaw with a frown. I knew that feeling too well; the sense of helplessness when there was nothing he could do but wait and hope for the best. "Althaia is with her now." He said, and I sighed.

It had been over twenty-four hours, and not once did Althaia leave my side until I woke up, ensuring I would be okay. Then she became restless, pacing back and forth, before deciding to check on everyone else.

"How is she handling the news?" Antonio asked.

"I'm not sure. She hasn't mentioned it, yet."

"Denial." Lorenzo commented, and I nodded. Our attention shifted to the door when it opened again.

"Oh... Am I disturbing you?" Althaia asked as she looked at us.

"No. Come here." I extended my hand as she entered.

"We'll give you some privacy." Antonio and Lorenzo nodded respectfully at Althaia as they passed her.

She placed her hand in mine and sat on the chair next to the bed. Her eyes flickered around, showing a conflicted expression before she finally met my gaze.

"How do you feel? Are you in a lot of pain?" She looked at my bandaged torso.

"I'm fine." I reassured her, and her shoulders sagged in relief. We sat in silence, and I watched her play with my fingers while she avoided looking at me.

"Althaia -"

"Cara is going to make it." She suddenly said, still not looking at me. "Michael too. Gio and Luca are getting fixed up as well. Arianna was awake, but she's sleeping now, so..."

She continued to update me on everyone's well-being. I already knew the status, but I let her continue, wanting her to talk instead of remaining silent and drowning in her thoughts.

"And you? What's the status on you?" I asked. A small smile appeared on her lips at my question.

"Well, I did get shot, so I had to get my arm stitched. My nose is not broken, just sore from the hit, so I will say I got pretty lucky." Althaia let out a small breath before finally looking at me.

I looked at her for a while and she squirmed around in her seat. It was obvious she was battling something inside her head.

"What's on your mind?"

"Everything." She forced out a chuckle before biting down on her lip.

"Tell me." I spoke to her softly, and her eyes started to glisten.

"Why would you say something like that to me?" Althaia whispered.

I held her hand tightly in mine. It sent a jolt in my heart at the sight of her innocent green eyes filled with tears. She was vulnerable, conflicted, and broken. It all showed in her eyes like a raging storm.

"That night... I saw her with my own eyes, so why would you say that to me?" She choked out. I cupped her face with my hand, wiping her tears away with my thumb.

"You're right. I shouldn't have said that to you. I should have shown you instead."

"Damiano, please, stop... It's messing with my head." She cried.

I never hated myself as much as I did right at this moment with the way she was looking at me. I wanted to cradle her in my arms, comfort and protect her. To tell her everything would be okay.

But will it be?

I had no idea what would happen after this.

"What are you doing? No, no, you can't do that!" I ignored her as I pulled out the tubes attached to me.

"Can you get me a shirt from the bag?" I asked her while I tried to get up from the hospital bed.

"No! You can't just do as you please when you just had surgery. Stop moving!" Althaia tried to stop me but didn't know how as she was afraid of hurting me.

She placed her hands on my chest, and I grabbed her wrists, pulling her close to me.

"I-I almost lost you, please stop..." She begged.

"Look at me." I had to talk to her firmly before she would listen. "I'm fine. I'm alive, and I'm not leaving you." Her green eyes looked at me with tears threatening to spill.

"Do you promise?"

I gave her a soft smile.

"Always."

Althaia looked around anxiously, barely able to sit still in the car. She thought I had been hit on the head too many times and suffered partial memory loss. I didn't try to convince her otherwise and just let her see with her own two eyes.

We stepped out of the car at the safe house. She glanced around, and her hand tightened around mine when she noticed the heightened security. She gulped as her breathing changed but managed to take a deep breath.

I took a quick look at the car that followed us. It was Vasiliev because he loved to be a pain in my ass and wouldn't let me get anything done in peace. I gave him a warning glare, reminding him to wait outside until Althaia had the time she needed.

"Shoot him if he tries anything." I told Antonio and Giovanni, instructing them to keep an eye on him.

"Don't need to tell me twice." Giovanni kept his gaze on Vasiliev with his gun ready. Vasiliev was leaning against the car with his arms crossed, as if he had not a care in the world. Althaia was too lost in her thoughts to realize what was going on.

I led her inside the house, noticing the slight tremble in her body as she walked. I looked at her when we stopped right in front of the double doors. I wanted to say something to her, to somehow prepare her. But how could I prepare her when she was about to see her dead mother alive?

Instead, I kissed her head in a feeble attempt to comfort her.

I opened the doors, my eyes landing on Jacinta sitting on the couch with her usual mug in her hands. She rose to her feet when she saw it was me.

"I have a visitor for you."

Jacinta's eyes slightly narrowed in confusion. I stepped aside, and she let out a gasp when she saw Althaia.

Althaia remained silent, her eyes wide. She stood frozen, gazing at her mother.

"... Mamá?" She whispered, tears welling up.

"Althaia, my baby." Jacinta cried out, moving closer. She halted when Althaia took a step back.

I frowned, noticing the rapid rise and fall of her chest.

She was having a panic attack.

"Althaia." I reached out for her, but she flinched away from my touch.

"Don't touch me!" She stumbled back, hitting the door before turning around and running away.

One Hundred Twenty

DAMIANO

"No. Stay here." I stopped Jacinta when she tried to go after Althaia.

I gritted my teeth, walking as fast as I could in the direction she ran off. This fucking gunshot wound was limiting me too much.

I stepped outside to the garden, watching her leaning against a tree to catch her breath.

"Althaia." I frowned, taking in her distressed state.

"Stop! Just... please stop. Don't come any closer." She closed her eyes, trying to control her breathing.

I clenched my fists in frustration, angered at myself for causing this. Remaining still, I watched her cry and struggle for air. I would prefer getting shot a hundred times more than seeing her like this.

"How... how could you do this to me?!" Althaia screamed at me with eyes filled with a storm of rage and betrayal.

"I did what I believed was best at the time." I spoke to her calmly, even though my heart was about to race out of my chest, realizing this could be what drove her away from me.

Althaia laughed, but not her usual sweet, joyful laughter that I loved so much; the one that always made me feel like the luckiest man alive.

No.

This laughter was empty, while her eyes showed me just how torn apart she was.

"Do you realize how fucked up that is? How fucking sick that is?" She spat out with a venomous force. "I was completely shattered! I grieved her death to the point where isolation was my only refuge. Even from you, I had to hide away! You witnessed my misery... how could you stand by and watch me drown in such pain? How could you make me believe that my mother was gone from my life forever?"

Althaia's sobs tore through the air, and my heart broke at the sounds of her pain.

"It was killing me inside to see you like that, but it was the only way to protect your mother. She had been in a coma for weeks, and it was uncertain if she was going to make it. If Gaetano knew she was alive, it would have made it easier for him to finish what he started." I spoke to her gently, my eyes observing her reaction to not push her over the edge into another panic attack.

Althaia's eyebrows drew together in a tight frown.

"You knew about Gaetano?!" She shouted.

"I had my suspicions." I admitted. "I wanted a DNA test to confirm it."

"Oh my God..." Althaia whispered in shock.

I came clean with everything, finally telling her the truth.

Althaia clutched her head as I told her every detail of how my investigation had deepened, ever since she first showed me the old photo of her mother with Alexei Vasiliev.

Telling her how I was almost a hundred percent sure that Alexei Vasiliev was her biological father.

Telling her about the fake heirloom and the microphone planted in it.

Telling her how I connected everything back to Gaetano, from the first attack to the last.

Telling her the original plan of taking down Gaetano before she became part of my life.

Telling her the plan at the wedding to take him down as quietly as possible.

I told her everything; I didn't want any more secrets.

But now, I didn't know what the fuck would happen to us.

"I didn't think you would understand if I told you." I said. There were countless times I was on the brink of telling the truth to her, to reveal that her mother's death was a lie to put an end to the torment I was putting her through.

But I couldn't because of fear; fear of losing the only light in my dark world. All because I was one selfish bastard who couldn't fathom a single day without her.

She was my everything. My light. My fire.

"See, that's where you fucked up, Damiano. You always think that I wouldn't understand, but you never even tried to let me in, to see if I could understand." Althaia spat out, her eyes storms of betrayal and hurt.

"I didn't want to involve you."

"This is my life!" She screamed at me, a sound that was filled with rage.

Her green eyes, that were always sparkling with such joy and innocence, now blazed with a burning fury. I had never seen her like this before; she was like a stranger that was created by the pain I had inflicted.

A cold dread settled in my chest, fearing this was the moment that would break us.

"Althaia..." I stepped forward, reaching for her, but she held her hand up to stop me. She leaned back against the old tree, staring up at the night sky.

"I want to understand your reasons." She said, her voice trembling with emotions. "Part of me probably understands what you had to do, but right now... I'm just so... *upset* with you."

Her words pierced through me like stabbing knives.

"I'm overwhelmed and confused." She continued, her eyes distant, lost in a sea of thoughts and feelings. "I just need... space. Some time to think and process everything." Althaia said, wiping her tears away while her gaze remained in a lost state.

The sound of my racing heartbeat drowned out all other noise.

"Are you leaving me?" The words slipped out before I could bury this question in the deepest, darkest corner of my mind.

How could I blame her if she walked away? I had just proven how fucked up I was and what a fucked up world I was living in. This time, anger could have no place in my heart, unlike the last time she needed distance.

I tried to keep it together, but I wanted to crumple to my knees.

Althaia's eyes brimmed with fresh tears, and I exhaled slowly. It was a weak attempt to steel myself for the words she was about to say.

"Damiano..." Althaia whispered, and I briefly closed my eyes.

She slowly walked up to me, and it was incredible how my heart didn't explode at how fast it was pounding. She placed her hands on my cheeks, and I wrapped my arms around her.

I needed to hold her, to have her close to me if this was our last moment together.

"I'm not leaving you." Althaia's voice was soft, making me inhale sharply in relief. "I'm pissed and hurt, but I'm not leaving you. I just need some time to process what's happening."

I rested my head against hers, a feeling so overwhelming was crashing over me.

"You can be angry with me, or even despise me if you must. All I ask is that you stay by my side. I need you, more than anything else." I whispered to her.

"I might be angry for a long time."

"I understand, and I'm going to do whatever it takes for as long as it takes to earn your forgiveness." I promised.

I held her tightly to me and inhaled her scent. It had a way of instantly soothing my mind and body.

"Damiano, please let me go." Althaia mumbled against my shoulder.

"Let me just hold you for now." I said, not ready to let her out of my arms just yet.

"No, I'm about to throw up on you if you don't move now."

I stepped away just in time as she turned and threw up by the tree. I held her hair back as she continued to be sick. Althaia had reached her breaking point. She was visibly exhausted; she had gone through so much without a moment's rest.

"Let's get you inside so you can rest." I told her. She gave a small nod as I led her inside to one of the bedrooms on the other side of the house to make sure she wouldn't bump into her mother for now.

Althaia slumped tiredly on the bed, closing her eyes, and took deep breaths to keep the sickness down. I went back downstairs to grab a few things, a bottle of water and electrolytes to keep her hydrated.

I paused for a moment, closing my eyes and clenching my jaw as the first twinges of pain made themselves known. I pulled out the painkillers Ellie had given me, well aware that they wouldn't do a lot to relieve the pain.

As I made my way back to the staircase, Jacinta appeared, glancing around in search of Althaia.

"How is she?" She asked. Her eyes flickered upstairs, unsure if she should go to her or stay away.

"She will be okay. She needs some time before seeing you again." I told her.

Jacinta nodded as she let out a heavy sigh. I climbed the stairs when I halted by her words that came out next.

"She lost the baby that night, didn't she?"

I glanced at her over my shoulder, seeing the sadness etching deeply on her face.

"Yes." I replied, and she closed her eyes with guilt consuming her. "You have another visitor. Alexei Vasiliev." Jacinta snapped her eyes open in shock before quickly transforming into a cold glare.

"What is he doing here?"

I scoffed at her question.

"You have a lot of shit to explain. What the fuck did you expect?" I countered and made my way to Althaia.

I shut the door behind me, hearing her throw up again in the bathroom. She came out after washing up, and I sat her on the bed and gave her the bottle of water.

"Take this one too." I said quietly. Althaia stared at the pregnancy test in my hand before looking at me, a mixture of emotions crossing her face. "I heard you get sick at the hospital, too. Take it so we can be sure."

"Okay." She finally agreed. I had been wanting her to take a pregnancy test for a while, but she insisted it was too early to tell, especially since it hadn't been long since we decided to try for a baby.

I couldn't shake the strange feeling, and even if the test was negative, I would know it was because she was exhausted and overwhelmed.

Althaia drank the water and went to the bathroom. The second she went inside, I paced the floor. I couldn't stand it. I checked my watch, wondering why she was taking so long, only to see she had only been in there for a minute.

I had to take in a deep breath and exhale slowly to calm down my racing mind.

The door swung open, and I rushed to her side, waiting for her to tell me anything.

"It says to wait three to five minutes." Althaia said, wrapping her arms tightly around herself.

"Okay." I nodded, keeping my eyes fixated on the clock.

We sat together on the bed, her head nestled on my shoulder, and I gently rubbed her back in silence. The three minutes dragged on, feeling like an eternity as I continued to watch the time with my impatience growing with each passing second.

"It's time." I finally broke the silence, and Althaia bit her lip in nervousness.

"Do you mind checking?"

"Are you sure you don't want to?" I asked. With a nod from her, I made my way to the bathroom, spotting the test on the counter.

A whirlwind of emotions rushed through me, and I took a deep breath before picking it up. Staring at the result, I closed my eyes briefly before turning back to Althaia.

"Pregnant." I whispered, my own words feeling almost surreal.

I had to double-check the pregnancy test to make sure my eyes weren't playing tricks on me.

Pregnant

Those bold, black letters stared back at me, and a smile tugged at my lips.

Glancing at Althaia, my smile began to fade when I saw the pain in her eyes.

"Do you not want it? Did you change your mind?" I questioned, unable to comprehend why she looked so devastated by the news.

"... I'm bleeding." She whispered.

Time froze, and my world came crashing down.

One Hundred Twenty-One

ALTHAIA

I hadn't even processed the fact that Gaetano wasn't my father. My entire existence had been nothing but a cruel, damned lie.

I didn't think it was possible to feel more miserable than this. I kept being dragged down into an abyss of darkness and drowning in fear and pure devastation.

I was exhausted.

I had lived for twenty-five years, and I didn't know who I was, or even who my family was.

Now, my mother, whom I had thought I witnessed die, was somewhere in this safe house.

Alive.

And now, I was reliving the same nightmare that had shattered me once before.

My body felt heavy. All I wanted was to curl up in bed and let the darkness take me somewhere else—somewhere where I wouldn't feel so miserable and heartbroken again.

Damiano stood still, his gaze fixed on me as if his entire world had just crumbled, while silent tears streamed down my face.

"I'm sorry…" I whispered to him, my chest tightening as the pain deepened.

I had failed once again.

Damiano's eyes narrowed, and he seemed almost furious with me as he closed the distance between us. He gently cupped my face, his expression firm.

"I don't want you to *ever* blame yourself, do you hear me?"

"How can I not?" I sniffled, overwhelmed by defeat. "You told me before to take a test, and I didn't because I was afraid of disappointment. And now…

now, it's gone before we even had a chance—" I couldn't continue as my voice broke.

Damiano pulled me close to his chest as I cried out my pain while he whispered soothing words to ease my suffering.

"My love, there was nothing we could have done, even if we had known. I'm sorry you have to go through this again." He sighed. When I looked at him, I cried even harder when I saw the sadness in his eyes.

"We'll be okay." Damiano comforted again and wiped away my tears. "How bad is it? Are you bleeding a lot?" His brows furrowed with worry, and I shook my head.

"It's not as bad as last time. It's more like spotting, and I have some cramping. I thought I was getting my period, but then you said the test was positive." I sat down on the bed with Damiano, feeling like my head was about to explode from the headache that had started.

"Let's get you to the clinic." Damiano said quietly. I gave a short nod but didn't make any move to get up.

I rested my head on his shoulder as he wrapped his arms around me and placed a kiss on top of my head. I closed my eyes, mustering the courage to face what was about to happen to me again.

"Can I have Ellie?" I asked.

"I'll give her a call and let her know to meet us there." Damiano said, and I held his hand to give him some comfort too.

I wasn't sure how long we sat in silence until Damiano suggested we should go. I sighed, and we slowly made our way downstairs, primarily because I didn't want him to overexert himself when he just had surgery. He shouldn't even be moving, but he was one stubborn man.

I stopped in the middle of the staircase, feeling my heart beat faster.

It was my mother, standing right by the doorway to the living room.

I swallowed hard, feeling my lips tremble. I walked down the rest of the stairs, closing the distance between us, but stopped a few steps away from her. My mother stood still, watching me, waiting for me to make the first move.

I observed her closely, noting the color in her cheeks, the brightness of her green eyes, and the rise and fall of her chest with each breath. She looked just as I remembered her before I thought I had lost her.

"Mamá!" I cried out and reached for her.

"My baby, Althaia." My mother wrapped her arms around me tightly, holding me as close to her body as she could.

I let out a shaky breath, feeling her arms around me and hearing her heart thumping in her chest.

"My sweet Althaia." She whispered, gazing at me with teary eyes as she placed her hands on my cheeks.

"I thought I had lost you." My voice barely above a whisper, I sniffed, trying to control my tears. My mother gave me a sad smile.

"Your boyfriend took good care of me. It pained me not to see you, but I knew it had to be done this way, for your safety too. He promised me I would see you again, and I've been waiting ever since." She explained.

I wiped away my tears and managed a small smile.

"Husband, mamá. He's my husband."

My mother took in a sharp breath in surprise.

"You got married?" I nodded, and she glanced behind me at Damiano. "Even though she's -" She stopped talking, returning her gaze to me.

"Yes, even though I don't have a drop of Italian in me." I said, letting her know that I was aware of Gaetano not being my biological father.

"As if that would have stopped me from marrying her." Damiano retorted, making me face him. His arms were crossed as he stared at my mother with an expression that said he still wasn't quite fond of her.

It made me let out a small smile.

Damiano's gaze went to meet mine, and his expression softened.

"I know what I want when I see it." He said with a wink. Even in the midst of my emotional turmoil, he had the power to make me blush.

My mother wore a warm smile as she watched us, and I embraced her once more, needing to reassure myself that she was truly here with me.

"Cara... How's my Cara?" My mother's smile faded when she saw the look on my face.

"She'll be okay." I assured her with a small sigh. "I will tell you everything, but maybe we should start with..." I trailed off, unsure how to word it.

"Of course, honey. I'm the one who owes you an explanation." She cupped my cheek, and I gave a small nod.

It was time for me to learn the whole truth.

"Also, he's outside. He deserves to hear it too." I didn't need to clarify whom I was referring to, as her expression already showed she knew.

My mother remained silent, her fingers tenderly brushing through my hair and tucking a strand behind my ear. She offered a small, but forced, smile.

"Would you like me to make you a cup of tea?"

"That would be nice." I smiled back at her. She gave my hand a small squeeze before I watched her retreat from the room.

My mother was nervous and likely needing a moment to collect herself before facing the man she hadn't seen in over twenty-five years.

"We should get you to the clinic first." Damiano urged.

"I know, but I need to do this first. I know it's going to be bad news, but to have it confirmed... I don't think I will be able to have this conversation after." I sighed. For now, I could pretend everything was fine with me.

"Are you sure?" Damiano's eyes narrowed with concern as he studied my face.

"I am, but you should rest, Damiano. You look tired." I said with worry.

"Are you saying I look like shit?" He raised a brow.

"Just a little." I bit back a smile when he clicked his tongue at me.

Alexei and Nestor were still by the car, waiting patiently. I took a deep breath and approached him alone, with the others keeping a watchful eye.

I stood in front of him, feeling a bit awkward after learning who he truly was to me.

"Are you okay?" Alexei asked, surprising me with his gentle tone.

"I... Well, I don't know." I replied truthfully. My thoughts were scattered, and I was doing my best to push through the turmoil. "It turns out she's alive." I decided to say with a forced chuckle.

Alexei and Nestor remained silent, their gazes fixed on my troubled expression.

"Follow me." I told them and went back to the house with them close behind. This time, Antonio and Giovanni followed inside as well.

My mother was in the living room, her back to us as she gazed out of the floor-length window. She turned around when she heard us enter, her eyes immediately locking onto Alexei. Neither of them spoke for a long while, both simply watching each other.

Alexei was stunned at the sight of her. He had likely given up hope of ever seeing her again a long time ago, and now she stood before him for the first time in many years.

Then, his eyes turned icy cold, and he shot her a menacing glare.

"You damned woman!" And he pulled out his gun.

Well, shit.

One Hundred Twenty-Two

ALTHAIA

As soon as Alexei drew his gun, Damiano pulled me behind him, and his men followed suit, fingers on the triggers and ready to fire. Before any shots could be fired, Nestor quickly pushed Alexei aside, and a knife narrowly missed Alexei's head.

Surprised and confused, everyone turned to look in the direction from which the knife had come. My mother had her brows pinched with her gaze locked on Alexei, ready with another knife in her hand.

"Did you forget how she loved to do that to you?" Nestor sighed at Alexei, though his attention remained fixed on my mother, his expression filled with anger.

"Seems like her aim is off." Alexei sneered.

"It's not off; it was simply a warning. I got you once, and I can do it again." My mother spoke calmly.

I gaped in shock as I watched the tense standoff between them — my... *parents*.

"Okay, let's all just take a moment to calm down." I said and moved around Damiano to face both Alexei and my mother. Damiano stopped me, but I assured him I would be fine. I doubted they would do anything if I stood in between them. "Let's try to be normal, civilized people for a moment and lower your weapons." I suggested carefully.

"Stay out of it. This is between your mother and me." Alexei hissed, his gaze never leaving my mother.

"Don't talk to my daughter like that!" My mother snapped at him, and her words only further fueled Alexei's rage.

"Your daughter? Apparently, she's my daughter too! And you hid her away from me for twenty-five fucking years, you damned woman!" He shouted and a tense silence fell over the room. He was seething with anger, but his eyes showed how much he was hurting.

My mother was taken aback by his outburst, and we all shared in the shock of witnessing his unexpected explosion of emotions.

My mother then turned her gaze toward Damiano with furrowed brows.

"You told him?" She asked.

"I did." Damiano replied unapologetically.

"That was not your business to tell." She hissed, and Damiano's eyes darkened in response.

"Oh, but it was when your daughter got kidnapped by the man you let her believe was her father." His voice dropped ominously.

"I found the small treasure chest in your room, and the note from Nestor to meet him at the LuxePalace. I went to meet him." I quickly interjected.

"Alone?" My mother's face drained of color, and I nodded in response. "Althaia!" She scolded, furious with me.

"Yeah, no need to be mad at me about it. Damiano already went bat shit crazy on me for it." I muttered. "What I mean is, it wasn't my first time meeting Alexei, and I told him about you. Then, I guess at some point, he went and dug up your casket." I elaborated.

"Of course, he fucking did." My mother scoffed, and I raised my brows in surprise. My mother never cursed, which was why we were never allowed to do so under her roof. She had made that clear many times, and often with her wooden spoon.

"Mamá, is it really true that he's...?" I trailed off, even though I had already heard it several times, wanting confirmation from my mother. Her gaze softened as she held my hands in hers and let out a sigh.

"Yes. He is your biological father." She confirmed.

I let out a breath and turned to look at Alexei. He, too, gazed at me as if I were unreal.

I could understand why no one would ever have suspected he was my biological father instead of Gaetano. We looked nothing alike.

His eyes were blue, mine were green.

His skin was light, mine was tan.

I resemble my mother entirely in terms of looks, which made me wonder if I had inherited anything from him at all. Then something suddenly crossed my mind.

"Ew!" I blurted out, and my expression contorted with disgust before I could control it. Alexei appeared deeply offended.

"What? Would you prefer that stupid Italian man as your father?" Alexei's Russian accent grew heavier as he frowned at me. "It's bad enough you're married to an Italian." He continued, which caused Damiano and his men to send him menacing glares.

"Watch your mouth, Vasiliev. You're already on thin ice." Damiano almost growled, but Alexei ignored him, still looking offended, which almost made me want to laugh.

"I didn't mean it that way. I just remembered you telling me how I resembled one of your old lovers. That's pretty disturbing now."

"You said what?!" My mother and Damiano erupted in fury.

"How was I supposed to know she was my daughter? I was intrigued when I saw her, and not in a nasty way. She looks exactly like you did at her age, and it piqued my curiosity." He shrugged.

My mouth formed an 'o' as I wondered if that was where my curiosity stemmed from.

"Other than the looks, you're nothing alike. Althaia is pure-hearted, innocent, and bright. But you!" He pointed at my mother with a growl. "You are one crazy woman who tried to kill me! But it's okay. I can see the years haven't treated you well, you old woman." Alexei grinned, a satisfied expression on his face as my mother shot him a deadly glare.

"Who are you calling old, you dusty man?!" She erupted, and I gasped as she threw a knife at him. Once again, Nestor had to intervene and push Alexei out of the way when he stubbornly refused to move.

"Are you really going to let her get you again?" Nestor sighed and shook his head. Then Alexei began speaking rapidly in Russian. Whatever he was saying, my mother's eyes narrowed.

Then she started to speak in Russian.

My eyes almost bulged out of their sockets.

My mother and Alexei continued to exchange heated words in Russian. Even Nestor intervened, but it seemed like he was trying to calm them down.

"This is not how I imagined things would be..." I said to Damiano, who also observed the chaotic scene. I glanced at him, noticing the frown on his face before he raised his gun. "Damiano, wait -" My words fell on deaf ears as he fired.

Horror filled me as I looked at the others, but I breathed a sigh of relief when I realized he had fired above their heads as a warning.

Alexei and Nestor reacted quickly, aiming their weapons at Damiano. I wasn't worried, though, because I knew no one was going to shoot.

Still, a smile crept onto my lips as I noticed that Alexei had instinctively grabbed my mother and pulled her behind him to protect her. She would always be his Solnishko, and he would always be her Lunnyy svet. No matter how much they tried to deny it at the moment.

"Do you want to die?!" Alexei shouted at Damiano.

"Quiet." Damiano spoke calmly with authority. "You can all kill each other for all I care. But my wife is a priority, and she needs answers, and she better get those answers right now before I shoot your brains out."

"Let me just rephrase that real quick." I sighed and patted Damiano's arm to calm him down. "It looks like you have a lot of catching up to do, but before that, can we please get to the point where I'm involved first?" I asked, hoping to divert their attention from potentially killing each other for a moment.

"Of course, honey." My mother replied with a smile, but quickly frowned when she noticed Alexei's arm around her. "Let go of me. I don't need your help." She pushed his arm away.

"Ungrateful woman." Alexei scoffed.

"Stop it!" I snapped at them, having enough of their fighting already. They both shot glares at each other, but fortunately, listened.

My mother sat me down on the couch, holding my hands in hers as she thought of how to explain everything to me.

I knew there wasn't much that could surprise me at this point. I just needed to understand how and why she had made the choices she did. Whatever the truth was, I trusted she had good reasons for every decision she had taken.

"Okay." My mother began, and I was finally going to hear the truth.

My mother came from an influential Greek family, and her father was in fact a mob boss back in the day. However, with the rise of Italians and Russians taking over territories faster than ever, the Cirillo Family, known as Oikogenia Tsirillo in Greek, struggled to maintain a name for themselves.

Over time, they got overshadowed by the many Mafia organizations that were expanding and simply couldn't keep up.

My mother's father refused to let that happen to him. It was his honor and pride, and he would rather die than watch it all crumple like that.

My grandfather firmly believed in traditional patriarchal values, and since my mother was an only child and female, there was no way he would allow her to take over and lead. Even though mother had silently watched everything and gained the skills and knowledge to take over as a leader. It was naturally her birthright, but he refused.

When my mother was young, she was allowed to get an education, giving her the opportunity to travel and explore the world while she took her semesters abroad.

That was when she met and fell in love with a certain Russian man.

They wanted to get married and live their lives together, but life was never that easy. Alexei Vasiliev was next in line to take over the Russian Mafia, and when she proposed the idea to my grandfather, he erupted in fury and refused.

"...because no one likes the Russians, but I do." My mother let out an innocent smile, and a light blush crept on her cheeks. It almost had me giggling. It was the first time I had ever seen her like this.

"That didn't exactly stop me from seeing him. I would sneak out to meet him, and I guess I was living in my own forbidden love fantasy. But then..."

Grandfather had fallen sick, and it was only a matter of time before he would be gone. When my mother's semester ended and she had to go back home, her hand in marriage was promised to Gaetano Volante. Marrying my mother off to Gaetano gave him the power to take over the Cirillo Family as their rightful leader.

My mother couldn't have an opinion on it and the wedding was rushed just in time for Gaetano to take over before my grandfather's passing. My grandmother was a prime example of a submissive wife; always obeying her husband's decisions and never challenging his authority. Hence why she never tried to stand up for her own daughter.

When my grandfather passed, she was in deep sorrow, and a few years later, she followed him to the grave.

"I despised that way of life and their narrow perspective on gender roles. I never saw eye to eye with it. According to those men, I was stubborn, opinionated, and they believed I needed to be put in my place." My mother rolled her eyes.

"I had no way of reaching out to Alexei to explain my situation. Once you become a Don's wife, you have eyes following you everywhere and reporting back on every single thing you did. It took me time to figure out how I could get out without being seen." She continued.

I gave a slight nod in understanding. Damiano made sure I had protection from the very beginning, and they reported everything back to him.

My mother then looked slightly awkward about telling the next part.

"When I did, well, I'm not proud of it, but that was when I took the chance to see him."

"A Russian booty call. Who would have thought?" Nestor snorted out a laugh, slapping Alexei on the back. I choked out a laugh when my mother looked mortified, and Alexei gave Nestor a scowl.

"Shut your face. There is a child present." Alexei said.

"I'm twenty-five, but okay." I chuckled.

"I have a question." I said to Alexei. "Wouldn't you have been able to track her down?"

"I would, if she ever bothered to give me her real name. She loved to play games with me and gave me different names, like a damn spy she thought she was. Back then, you can say I was a bit young and dumb." He shook his head with a slight smile. "I did look for her, but the names never matched her description."

"It's Jacinta." I clarified, and he raised a brow at my mother.

"Is that your real name or something you made up?"

"Jacinta is my real name." My mother confirmed.

"What kind of name is that? Your parents really fucking hated you, didn't they?" He laughed as if it was the funniest thing ever. If my mother had another knife in her hands, she would have thrown it at him.

"But, you know, time passed, and I stopped caring. She was too much of a headache for me, anyway." Alexei gave a dismissive wave, acting like he didn't care. Of course, I didn't buy it. They were both playing hard to get.

"What? Was I too opinionated for you? Did I challenge you too much? Did I hurt that stupid ego of yours? No surprise, since I was this close to being able to kill you." My mother scoffed loudly at him.

"Close. You didn't succeed." Alexei fired back.

"Only because I changed my mind at the very last second." She countered. His eyes narrowed, turning into two cold slits as he stared at my mother.

"You should get checked for psychotic disorders."

"Oh, go cry to your mama, you big baby. That old hag was the reason I went crazy!"

"Mom!" I gasped in shock that she would say that about his mother.

"Careful, Solnishko. That's my late mother you're talking about." He sneered, and my mother rose to her feet in rage.

"The same mother that prevented me from ever telling you we were going to have a child!" She shouted at him.

It went dead silent as they stared at each other.

"…What are you talking about?" Alexei frowned. My mother let out a breath and briefly closed her eyes to calm down.

"I am not a heartless person. I was going to tell you the minute I found out. I knew she was yours because, at that time, Gaetano was away for over four weeks. Two weeks after I saw you, I started to get symptoms, and Gaetano was still not back from his trip." She ran a hand through her hair.

"May she rest in peace, but your mother was doing the most to keep us apart. She never liked me, but in your eyes, she could do no wrong. I showed up to tell you, to figure out what you wanted to do. But I ran into your mother first, and she prevented me from seeing you. I explained to her it was urgent and then had to tell her the real reason. She tried to kill me on the spot." My mother shook her head in disbelief.

"But she knew. She knew I was carrying your child, but she kept it from you. I had no choice but to return to my life with Gaetano. What other options did I have? I couldn't risk your mother going after me to end my pregnancy. I stayed for protection."

"Fortunately, I didn't show after a while, letting Gaetano believe it was his child. Althaia's file says she was born prematurely, but it's not true. I manipulated the dates for it to align the last time I was with Gaetano."

My mother explained, her voice filled with pain, and sadness as she averted her gaze from him.

"…My own mother…" Alexei muttered. He struggled to conceal his emotions, but they overwhelmed him.

He rubbed his jaw and without a single word, he turned around and left.

One Hundred Twenty-Three

ALTHAIA

My heart ached for them both. The fact that my mother was going to tell him, maybe even holding onto the hope that they could finally be together.

But no.

For her own protection and mine even, she had to accept her life with Gaetano. I couldn't fathom the turmoil that Alexei must be experiencing right now. To have been on the verge of learning that he was going to become a father with the woman he loved, only to have his own mother hide the truth and carry it with her to the grave.

Nestor was frozen in shock as he looked at my mother before gaining composure and followed Alexei.

I remained silent, allowing my mother the space she needed to compose herself. My gaze turned to Damiano, who stood leaning against the wall, arms crossed, and a neutral expression on his face. I wondered if he was interested in the story or didn't care at all.

He quickly let me know he wasn't interested when he impatiently tapped the watch on his wrist, urging me to hurry to the clinic. I knew I had to go soon, but I couldn't leave after this. My mother literally dropped a bomb on us all.

"Mamá?" I called after her. She faced me, giving me a soft smile as she returned to sit next to me.

"I know how it all sounds but know you're still the best thing that ever happened to me." She whispered as she caressed my cheek. I smiled, never doubting that for a second.

"The decisions I made are not something I am proud of, but I had to ensure your survival and safety for as long as possible. Thankfully, you resemble me, which made it easier. I never wanted you to carry the Volante name because

THE DEVIL'S FIRE

you weren't his child, but I couldn't use your real name either. Instead, I made an excuse about protection and tweaked the Cirillo name into Celano to give it an Italian ring." My mother continued to explain.

"I actually prefer the name Celano to Volante." I confessed, making her chuckle.

"I just had to continue the lie for a bit longer until I could find a way out. Bit by bit, I saved enough for us to get away. But, of course, nothing was easy. Life never is. You loved him as your father, and it broke me because I was going to ruin it. But your well-being meant more to me, and if it meant you would resent me for taking you away, then that was fine with me. You just had to be safe."

Guilt overwhelmed me. I had been heartbroken when we left, and I remembered feeling a bit resentful toward my mother at the time.

"How did you do it?" I asked.

"Well, for once I felt like I had luck on my side. I found out Gaetano was cheating on me with Morella."

I gasped.

"No! Really? With Morella?"

"I know." My mother scoffed at the choice, making me bite back a laugh. "It gave me the perfect reason to get away from him. I even made a scene to make it look like I was genuinely upset about it, and that was when we left."

"You slapped him." I blurted, and my mother looked at me in surprise.

"How do you know?"

"Cara and I overheard you two arguing. We sneaked out of our rooms, and we saw you slap the fuck - I mean, we saw you slap him." I quickly corrected myself. Who knew if she had a wooden spoon here?

Instead, my mother broke into a smile.

"My biggest regret will always be not fighting harder for Cara." She confessed with guilt laced in her voice. I gave her hand a small, comforting squeeze.

"I know, but we can't change the past, we can only learn from it. What's important is that you can be there for her now." I told her, my gaze briefly shifting to Damiano.

I had learned that lesson the hard way. I never intended to hurt him, but I did when I went away. It was a guilt I would forever carry with me. However, one thing was crystal clear; I would never repeat that mistake.

My mother continued to explain she was keeping taps on Gaetano to always be one step ahead of him. Surprisingly, he had never attempted to come after us after we left. It was at that point that my mother decided to leave her old life behind and start anew in Florida. She worked tirelessly to establish her own boutique, never imagining it would become as successful as it did.

And then the news of Cara's engagement party came.

"I'm not sure if you remember, but you got so angry at me because I wouldn't let you go. I simply couldn't risk it. You begged me for days, asking me why you couldn't go when it was your father we were talking about. You started to ask too many questions. Questions I wasn't ready to answer. I didn't even know how I was supposed to tell you everything after so many years."

"I completely forgot about that. I was too happy to see Cara after you agreed to let me go." I admitted.

"I know. What you didn't know was I followed you to make sure you would be okay."

"Seriously?!"

"I did. I never understood why Gaetano let us go so easily. I went undercover, dressed as a server, to stay close to you in case anything happened to you. But then, things took a turn when Damiano grabbed you, thinking he knew the truth. It nearly gave me a heart attack!" My mother exclaimed.

I leaned back on the couch, trying to process the overwhelming flood of information. This was way, way deeper than anything I could have ever prepared for.

"So... you knew everything?" I asked, thinking back to the phone call where she was angry about Cara's engagement to a Bellavia.

She nodded.

"I had to act like I was completely in the dark. But, to be honest, I didn't know about you and Damiano until you told me. I did recognize that man and the other one, Luca, I think his name was." My mother pointed at Giovanni.

"You thought they were a couple at the restaurant." I said, stifling a laugh while Giovanni gave me a disapproving look.

"I apologize. But you did look great together!" She cheerfully remarked to him, causing his frown to deepen, which made it even funnier.

"Luca's engaged and Gio has a girlfriend, but he won't admit it." I let out a playful smile when he gave me a blank look.

"Shame. I really hoped they would be together." She whispered to me, having me shake my head in amusement.

My mother sighed before continuing with the story.

"That was when I thought I would show up at your hotel and take you back home. But Gaetano caught me before I could get out of there."

My eyes widened.

"I have no idea how that bastard recognized me, but he did." My mother frowned, still visibly angry about it. "He revealed he knew the truth about you, and I was positive he was going to get rid of me right at that moment and go after you next. Instead, he forced me to work for him under the radar, and I was in no position to challenge him."

My brows raised in realization. Now it made so much more sense why he had reacted so angrily when he saw me at the engagement party.

"I was sent back to Florida, and then I was laundering money for him. He needed a business no one would keep an eye on. I had to put in many hours of work for it to even make sense, and that piece of shit always reminded me how easily he could hurt you if I didn't listen. He sent me a picture of you sleeping at his house; gun to your head." She clenched her jaw as she spoke, and a cold shiver ran down my spine.

Gaetano was toying with my mother and had me thinking I was spending quality time with my father.

It had me feeling sick.

"And that was why you bought that property in Greece." I stated. I didn't need to hear anymore. I could connect every single thing now.

My mother nodded.

"Yes. One big mistake Gaetano made when he took over was forcing the elders to retire early as a way out. Most have passed away, but there is still one I have always been close to, and he helped me out with the property. I call him Uncle Belen." She smiled at the mention of him.

"He was one of the very few who actually agreed that I should be the new leader. He's the type of person who sees everything but stays hidden in the shadows. Ask him anything, and he would have an answer for it. That is how I knew about Damiano's late fiancée."

"You threw that in his face at the time. Why?" My tone let her know I was not pleased with it at all.

"I brought her up to see how he would react to it. If he didn't, that means he didn't care, and you had gotten yourself into some very serious trouble. So, not only was I trying to get Gaetano off our backs, I would also deal with la Famiglia Bellavia. Which is a hundred times worse than dealing with any other family." My mother let out a breath, and I could feel all the stress she had to go through.

It suddenly made sense to me why she had such a strong negative reaction to my pregnancy at that time.

I wrapped my arms around her and embraced her tightly, taking her by surprise by the sudden action. My mother had done an amazing job of keeping me safe and living a normal life.

"Thank you for everything, mamá." I whispered.

"You don't have to thank me. I did what any other mother would do — to always protect their child."

Tears welled in my eyes.

"I'm so sorry I couldn't help you." I choked out.

"That's not your job, honey. If anything, I'm the one who should apologize for making you live a lie."

"I don't really care anymore. I'm just so happy you're okay." I wiped away my tears, feeling a new sense of relief wash over me.

"Me too, honey. It's all thanks to your husband. You have a good one by your side." My mother smiled, and I could also see how relieved she was after coming clean with the truth.

"I know." I agreed. In the end, I was grateful that Damiano had saved my mother and kept her safe. I just didn't appreciate the part of him making me believe she was dead.

"There's somewhere I need to go, but I will see you later." I let out a breath and finally rose to my feet, only to wince in pain when my stomach cramped.

"Shit! I'm taking you to the clinic now." Damiano stormed to me while my mother was holding onto me with concern.

"What's happening? Are you hurt?" Her voice was laced with concern. I took a deep breath and forced a smile onto my lips.

"I just found out I was pregnant...But I think I suffered another miscarriage before coming downstairs."

My mother looked at me in pure horror.

"What?!" Antonio and Giovanni erupted at the same time, rushing to my side as well.

"And you let me sit here and babble about this?!" My mother exclaimed. "You need a doctor! I will go with you."

"I will be fine. Besides, you have things you need to sort out with Alexei." I said.

"No. He can wait."

"I think he has waited long enough, mom. Don't worry about me. I will come and see you after." I promised, before Damiano almost went to carry me to get going.

Antonio and Giovanni practically ran out to get the car going to get us to the clinic.

"Fuck, I can't believe I listened to you on this." Damiano growled, angry with himself when I had to slightly lean into him for support.

"Damiano." I stopped him and he looked at me with worry in his eyes.

"What's wrong? Are you in a lot of pain? Let me carry you."

"No, you can barely stand on your own." I said, placing my hands on his cheeks and feeling the roughness of his stubble under my palms.

"Thank you for saving her." I told him, my voice filled with gratitude. "Thank you for everything and for always coming back to me."

His eyes softened.

"No need to thank me, my love." He said, placing a gentle kiss on my forehead before taking my hand as we headed towards the car.

I paused before getting in when Alexei and Nestor approached us.

Alexei stood in front of me.

"I'm not sure what I'm supposed to do, but I would like to get to know you, if you'll have me." He said, a small crease forming between his brows, as if he were nervous about his request.

"I would love that." I replied with a warm smile, and he returned it. Then he looked at Damiano, his expression turning serious.

"We have something that needs to be discussed. It's about her birthright."

"I know. I will set up a meeting." Damiano responded, and Alexei gave a firm nod before making his way inside the house.

"Nestor?" I called after him, and he turned to look at me. "Make sure they don't kill each other, please?" I asked with a small smile.

"That's been my job ever since they met each other." Nestor let out a playful sigh but promised me he would.

"Come on, let's go." Damiano said. I took another deep breath, preparing myself for the worst, again, as we made our way to the clinic.

One Hundred Twenty-Four

ALTHAIA

Ellie was already at the clinic, waiting for our arrival. The closer we got to the examination room, the more my anxiety spiked. I dreaded it more than ever; the confirmation of another miscarriage.

The thought that another life might be lost was suffocating.

Damiano, Antonio, and Giovanni were just as worried. No one bothered to mask their emotions as they were concerned for my well-being and what was going to happen.

"So, what are we dealing with?" Ellie asked once she closed the door to give us some privacy while Antonio and Giovanni waited outside.

"I took a pregnancy test. It was positive, but... I'm bleeding and cramping." I swallowed hard as Ellie listened carefully to me.

Damiano stayed close to me, his grip tight on me as if I were on the verge of collapsing.

"Okay, we will do a blood test to confirm the pregnancy, and then do a transvaginal ultrasound for a more detailed view."

I followed her instructions and laid on the hospital bed, focusing on Damiano while she drew my blood. My thoughts swirled in a chaotic storm, and a wave of dread washed over me like never before.

My heart raced when Ellie examined me, and I had to remind myself to breathe. Damiano held my hand and caressed my head for comfort.

"Whatever happens, we'll get through it, okay?" He whispered softly to me.

Words were stuck in my throat, unable to say anything. Instead, I nodded and tightly clung to his hand, feeling as though time was stretching endlessly, while I struggled desperately to hold back tears.

"Oh." Ellie suddenly said, causing both of us to immediately turn our attention to her. Her brows were slightly furrowed as she focused on the screen.

"What is it, Ellie?" Damiano asked, his anxiety mirroring my own.

"Well - actually, you should see for yourselves." She turned the screen around to show us.

I let out a shocked gasp.

"Everything is fine." She smiled.

"But what about the bleeding and cramping?" I stumbled on my words, afraid to get my hopes up in case it was a false alarm.

"You have nothing to worry about. What you're experiencing is implantation bleeding, which is normal. The cramping is due to hormonal changes as your womb is preparing itself." Ellie explained.

"Everything is okay, then?" Tears had already welled up in my eyes as I asked once more, just to be sure.

Ellie's face lit up with a genuine and warm smile.

"Everything is absolutely fine. Congratulations, guys! You're going to be parents." She beamed.

I covered my face with my hands, sobbing at the news as Damiano wrapped his arms around me.

"I'll give you a moment alone." Ellie said, before I heard her exit the room.

I looked at Damiano, smiling through my tears.

He cupped my face in his hands, his golden-brown eyes sparkled with happiness as he gazed into mine.

"We're having a baby." Damiano whispered, his voice filled with wonder and love. His thumbs brushed away the tears that had gathered in the corners of my eyes.

He pressed his lips to mine, pouring all the emotions we had been holding back; relief, happiness, and the assurance that our future was bright with the promise of a new life.

"I love you, piccola. I love you so much." Damiano murmured between kisses, making me smile against his lips.

"Is this really happening?" I asked, sitting up and holding him as tightly as I could without hurting him.

"I know. It feels surreal." Damiano replied, kissing the top of my head as we both turned our attention back to the screen, just to confirm one more time.

Suddenly, a wave of fear crashed over me.

"What if it happens again?" I whispered, my voice trembling with the weight of my fear. "I can't - I can't handle it again."

Damiano's expression darkened as he cupped my cheeks again.

"It won't happen again. It's going to be different this time. Not once are you going to leave my sight. No one's ever going to hurt you again. Over my fucking dead body, do you understand?" His words resonated with such fierce protection that it sent a shiver down my spine.

"What if some of them got away and are waiting to finish the job?" I whispered, the fear of reliving the heartbreak of losing another child threatening to overwhelm me. I could feel a panic attack creeping in.

Damiano's grip on me tightened, and he leaned in, pressing his forehead against mine.

"I won't let them, Althaia. I promise you because I've caught every single one of them. Those involved, and those who knew about it, their friends, their families—I'll tear them apart, limb from limb. Nothing will stand in my way."

I twiddled my hands nervously, and Damiano gently took hold of them and pressed a soft kiss on each.

"Tonight, the world will burn for you, my Althaia." Damiano declared, his eyes ablaze with a fierce determination, burning like a scorching sun.

It was a gaze that exuded intimidation and danger, yet at the same time, a haunting beauty as he vowed that every single one responsible for our suffering would pay. He would go to any lengths to guarantee my safety.

Our safety.

I smiled as his hand gently caressed my stomach, his touch filled with pride and admiration for the life growing inside me.

"I'll do whatever it takes to protect our baby." Damiano whispered, his eyes still fixed on my stomach with an enchantment in his gaze as a beautiful smile graced his lips.

A slow exhale escaped me when I noticed the absence of worry in his expression. Instead, there was an aura of absolute invincibility and an unmistakable air of danger that would strike fear into the hearts of anyone who dared to cross our paths.

"My Devil." I whispered with a soft smile and a playful gleam danced in his eyes.

"And you, my love, are The Devil's Fire." He replied, sealing his words with a kiss filled with promises, protectiveness, and an overwhelming love that left me melting in his embrace.

Just as we opened the door to step out into the hallway, Antonio and Giovanni snapped their heads in our direction. Giovanni, who had been pacing, quickly moved to stand in front of me alongside Antonio.

"What took so long? What's going on? Are you okay?" Giovanni's questions came out quickly one after the other.

"And you say you don't care about me." I teased him lightly. His reaction made it too easy for me to let it slide.

"This is not the time, Althaia! Tell me!" Giovanni almost yelled in frustration.

I glanced at Damiano and then back at them.

"You're going to be uncles." I announced with a big smile, still finding it hard to believe my own words.

But then, something unexpected happened that left me completely shocked; Giovanni hugged me.

I was stunned to the point where my eyes went wide, and my jaw dropped. I quickly snapped out of it and wrapped my arms around him as well.

"You really do care about me." I sniffed, my eyes tearing up, touched by his concern.

"Yes, just shut up about it." He said, but still hugged me tightly, and I felt his body ease.

Giovanni stepped away and glanced at Damiano, who was giving him a deadly glare.

"Sorry, Boss, I just had to. She's our Donna." Giovanni said, giving Damiano a few pats on the shoulder as he looked relieved.

"I knew you would be all right. You're one hell of a fighter, and your baby will be nothing less than that." Antonio said, as he pulled me into his arms. I felt his relief as he held me, and a few tears escaped my eyes at how much they all cared.

Then it was Antonio's turn to receive the deadly look from Damiano when he kissed the top of my head. It had us all chuckling at his reaction, but it was one of the few times where Damiano would allow it because of their worry.

"Let's get you home." Damiano held my hand as we made our way out.

"Actually, there's something I need to do before we go home." I told them.

I walked down the underground tunnel with Damiano close beside me, and the others followed closely behind. I had been here before, but this time, it was different.

The place was heavily secured with armed men stationed everywhere to ensure no outsiders could get in or out. They were on high alert, ready for any threat.

They nodded in respect as we passed them before we reached the familiar door that had borne witness to the unimaginable.

The Chamber of Torture.

Taking a deep breath to prepare myself before Damiano opened the door.

Gaetano was chained to the wall, suspended from his wrists, slumped forward. Blood dripped from his face onto the ground. He had been brutally beaten, and if it wasn't because I could hear his breathing, I might have thought he was dead.

Damiano stood by the door with his arms crossed, leaning against it. This was something I had to do, something that would give me closure.

I dragged a chair and positioned it in front of Gaetano, making sure to keep some distance even though his arms and legs were chained.

He lifted his head to look at me, and a wicked smile crept onto his lips, revealing his blood-stained teeth before he let out a low, mocking laugh. I watched him calmly, allowing him to laugh because he knew his life was over after this, and there was no escape.

"So, you win again, Althaia." His voice dripped with venom as he spat out my name. I remained unfazed, maintaining a straight face as I felt nothing for him. He didn't deserve any sympathy.

"I just want to know why." I told him. I needed to understand why he had pretended to be a loving father who wanted to protect me when he was the one I needed protection from.

"You took someone in who wasn't yours and treated him like your own. But as for me? You didn't even try. You were all I knew, and I loved you as my father more than anything." I couldn't shove the hurt away from my voice. The way he treated his stepson Carlos hurt me deeply, more than I wanted to admit.

Gaetano stared at me, trying to adjust his position to find some comfort, but the way he was hanging made me doubt he could.

"When I received the news that I was going to be a father, I was ecstatic. I was so thrilled that I didn't even care that it was going to be a girl." He chuckled, and I rolled my eyes.

My mother was right. It was such a male-chauvinist world.

"At some point during her pregnancy, I received an anonymous tip that she had been unfaithful. I dismissed it, knowing that people play dirty games to tear you apart. She barely left the house; how was she supposed to? When you were born, and I held you in my arms for the first time, something didn't feel right, but I ignored it. They say you feel different when you have a newborn in your life." He continued to chuckle as if reminiscing about the good old days.

"As you grew older, I still didn't feel anything towards you. I tried, but it just didn't feel right. It was as if you weren't mine. I thought maybe that note was playing tricks on me. I even had a hard time calling you by your name." Gaetano confessed.

It now dawned on me why he always insisted on calling me 'figlia,' and rarely used my name.

"I kept dismissing it until I received news from my doctor. I am incapable of having children." Gaetano locked eyes with me as he spoke.

"It wasn't something that happened out of the blue. I was informed about my issues when I was a young boy, but I didn't think much of it, and it slipped my mind over the years until my doctor reminded me and had it confirmed once again. That note had been lingering in the back of my mind, and that's when I finally had a DNA test. Even with the results in my hand, I couldn't believe it. Then I received another envelope containing pictures of *her* with *him*!" He hissed with his eyes filled with rage.

I remained unfazed by his fury as I listened to everything. It made me wonder if it was Alexei's mother who sent him those tips.

"I was going to kill you both on the spot. But I couldn't. A wife is a man's honor. She made a joke out of me, and I couldn't risk word getting out that my wife was being a slut and spreading her legs for the Russians."

This time, it was me boiling with rage at him insulting my mother.

"Althaia, stand up for a second." Damiano gently took my hand.

Damiano snatched the chair and brought it crashing down with brutal force onto Gaetano's head. The wooden chair shattered into splinters as he relentlessly smashed it against Gaetano's head, over and over again.

"Be careful. Don't overexert yourself." I said with concern, afraid he could hurt himself if he continued to bash Gaetano with the chair.

The chair, once whole, was now reduced to a mere stick in Damiano's hand. He was breathing heavily, and I pulled him away from Gaetano to make sure his wound was still closed.

Gaetano groaned out in pain, his head dangling from side to side before he composed himself and let out a laugh.

"Why did you pretend to be my father when I came for the engagement?" I asked, getting straight to the point.

Gaetano let out a snarl.

"You fucking almost ruined everything I had been working for!" He shouted in resentment.

"I had everything planned out, the perfect plan! But people knew I had a daughter, so I faked your death as Althaia Volante because no one asks questions about the dead. You ruined it by showing up! I had to pretend you were my daughter, and I was doing it to protect my plan. I couldn't risk anyone finding out you're Russian. It would ruin everything for me if they thought I was cuckold by one of them." His breathing came out loud and harsh in fury.

"So, I tried to get rid of you before it was too late. I always kept my eyes on you and hired people to do the job. I sent human traffickers, and I even cut that worthless piece of shit's tongue to send a message that it was my doing." He started to laugh hysterically.

My heart dropped. He almost succeeded in getting rid of me. He had pretended to care for me to my face, only to try to repeatedly stab me in the back the moment I turned away.

"Unfortunately for me, you already had protection. I had to focus on creating my army, and I was becoming bigger and more powerful. I was about to show it to the world by successfully taking down that Russian scum. Once I had his head in my hand, I was going to find you and your mother, and kill you all." Gaetano's eyes widened with joy.

"You ruined everything for me!" He suddenly shouted. "But at least, I got rid of the Devil's spawn that was growing in your belly." He laughed loudly.

I moved faster than ever before, grabbing Damiano's gun before he could react.

I shot him.

Gaetano howled in pain as I shot him in the shoulder. I would not grant him the satisfaction of a quick death. No, I wanted him to suffer as much as he had made me suffer.

He had tried to take everything from me, making my life miserable. The sympathy that once clung to my heart was gone, replaced by anger and resentment. I wanted them all to pay for the pain they had inflicted on me and my loved ones.

I tilted my head at the way Gaetano was screaming, having the corners of my mouth turn upwards in contentment.

"I understand now." I whispered to Damiano.

The satisfaction of hearing them scream in pain for all the suffering they had caused me felt euphoric at this moment. They had watched me bleed and laughed as I suffered.

Why shouldn't I?

I glanced at Damiano, and he was already looking at me, his eyes darkened with that devilish smirk on his lips. He leaned in closer, speaking in a low voice meant only for me to hear.

"I never thought seeing you like this would make me hard as fuck."

I gave him a sheepish grin, noticing the hint of lust in his eyes. I gave him a quick kiss before returning my attention to Gaetano, who was still screaming and panting in agony.

I grabbed him by the hair, forcing him to look into my eyes.

"What's wrong? Why are you screaming? Take it like the big, powerful man you so generously talked about yourself as." I taunted him, a smirk playing on my lips. "You failed, Gaetano, because I am carrying his child."

I showed him the sonogram, watching his face turn red with anger. I leaned in to whisper to him.

"I will give him something you were never able to have—a biological child. I will give him an heir, a legacy that you so desperately sought, and I will even build a whole damn army of heirs so you can never rest in peace."

"I wish they stabbed your womb to prevent you from having a child." He spat out.

I gave him a chilling smile as I laughed.

"Damiano, where is Morella?" I asked, watching the panic flicker in Gaetano's eyes.

"We've got her." Damiano's voice was laced with a sinister satisfaction.

"No! Leave her out of this!" Gaetano shouted at us, but I had no compassion left.

"Bring her here." My words came out cold and sharp.

"Don't you dare!" Gaetano screamed.

"Who's going to stop me? You killed my baby, and for that, I will take away everything from you." My voice remained calm as I addressed him. "My dear *father*, you were playing with the Devil's fire, and you're about to get *burned*." I added, giving him a vicious smile.

"I want him outside, tied to a pole." I told Damiano.

"Your wish is my command, Donna mia." Damiano replied.

For once, I think Damiano was curious to see what I had in mind.

Every one of Damiano's men had gathered outside, their eyes fixed on Gaetano, who was tied to a pole. They were filled with curiosity, eager to witness what fate had in store for him.

I smiled when I saw my mother make an appearance with Alexei. I wanted her here for this as well.

Gaetano looked like he had seen a ghost. It left him speechless to see my mother alive and well, which made me grin with delight.

"You! How are you still alive?!" He shouted, thrashing around in an attempt to break free and get to her, but it was of no use. He kept screaming, furious at the sight of my mother and Alexei. Especially when Alexei wrapped an arm around my mother and placed a kiss on her lips.

Gaetano stopped when Morella was dragged in front of him, watching in horror as she cried and begged for mercy.

I refused to show anyone an ounce of kindness, only for them to retaliate someday. I had to get rid of everyone for the safety of the life growing inside me.

I grabbed Damiano's gun.

"Althaia, no!" Gaetano shouted at me.

"Don't say my name as if I owe you any loyalty." I spat out, coming to a halt in front of my mother. I offered her the gun. "She's far from innocent. She was well aware of everything, and not only that, she encouraged Cara's father to abuse her."

My mother's emerald eyes burned with fury as she accepted the gun from my hand.

"I'll gladly make the life drain from her eyes." She declared, stopping in front of Morella. She stared at Gaetano as a slow smirk formed on her lips before shifting her focus to Morella.

For Cara.

The sound of gunshots pierced the air, one after another piercing Morella's stomach, all the while Gaetano struggled frantically to break free.

With a final act, she took a knife from her ankle strap and stood behind Morella. She lifted her head to get better access to her throat as they both stared right into the eyes of Gaetano. She slowly dragged the blade across Morella's throat, a gurgling sound ended her annoying voice pleading for mercy.

"Ah, that's my Solnishko." Alexei said with a tone of pride, bringing out a faint smile from me.

"My turn." I announced.

Everyone watched me as I grabbed the gas can.

I poured gasoline over his head, making sure every inch of him was drenched as I listed out the names of every single one he hurt and every single life he took of Damiano's men. I wanted him to remember their names before I ended his life.

I stepped away to a safe distance and Damiano stood next to me as I lit a matchstick and stared at Gaetano.

"Goodbye, Gaetano." I whispered, and I lit him on fire.

The flames consumed him in a matter of seconds, while his screams of agony pierced the night. But they fell on deaf ears, drowned out by the inferno we had unleashed.

The night air was thick with the acrid scent of burning flesh as we stood there, unflinching, watching the flames dance with an insatiable hunger, and reducing Gaetano to nothing more than ashes.

It was a symbol of our determination to protect what was ours, and a brutal reminder to anyone who dared to cross our path.

I looked at Damiano.

"He can't hurt us again." I said, tears visible in my eyes but because of relief.

Damiano held me tightly, his hand resting protectively on my stomach.

"It's over, my love."

Together, we watched the flames burning him alive.

Epilogue
Five Months Later

The sun hung high in the clear sky, casting a radiant glow over the crystal-blue waters, making Calilo Island's natural beauty even more enchanting on this particular day.

The beach was elegantly decorated, and rows of chairs lined up endlessly on the bright green grass. A mirrored aisle stretched down the middle, adorned with Angel's and Devil's trumpet flowers, creating a stunning pathway. At the end of the aisle stood a majestic gazebo, its pillars graced with vibrant, colorful flowers.

A crowd of people had gathered, mingling and taking their seats. By the gazebo, Damiano watched over their friends and family, all of whom had flown in to witness this special day.

Damiano had a small crease between his brows, shuffling around on his feet for the first time in his life as he kept fixing his tie, double-checking to make sure he at least looked decent enough on such a meaningful day.

"Nervous, brother?" Lorenzo approached Damiano, amusement clear in his eyes as he witnessed his older brother's rare display of nerves.

"If this is what being nervous looks like, then yes, I am. How the fuck weren't you nervous on your wedding?" Damiano asked as he tried to keep his hands busy.

Lorenzo grinned smugly as he halted in front of his brother, adjusting Damiano's tie.

"I lied."

"Bastard."

They both shared a laugh, and Damiano felt slightly relaxed as his brother tidied up his tie and nodded in approval.

Damiano had chosen to wear a white wedding tuxedo with exquisite white details that stood out elegantly. His tie featured white with delicate gold patterns, chosen to match his bride's white dress, and incorporated her favorite color.

"Did you remember the rings?" Damiano asked.

"Got them. It's my only job as the best man. You really think I would forget them?"

"Just making sure."

"Your woman is making a mess out of you today." Lorenzo couldn't help but smile big.

If there was one thing he was relieved about, was the fact his big brother finally found happiness in his life. It made him different, but in a good way, and he liked the person he had become because of her.

"I know." Damiano chuckled, trying to feel more at ease.

"I told you, you can't separate two souls meant to be together." Lorenzo reminded him, and Damiano nodded with a small smile.

When Damiano thought he was falling apart one more time in his life, Lorenzo kept him in check, saying she would be back.

And back she came because, just like him, she couldn't live without him by her side.

"And she's got you so fucking whipped." Lorenzo kept teasing him to give him a distraction. Damiano scoffed.

"You're telling me your wife doesn't have you wrapped around her finger? Because I've seen the way she handles you." Damiano smirked.

Lorenzo had an impressive build, and he was lethal in the most sinister way. One wouldn't have thought he would be such a softie when it came to his wife.

"Ah, what can I say? I am a pleaser." It was Lorenzo's turn to smirk when Damiano gave him a blank look.

"I don't want to hear about your bedroom activities."

"Why not? I can give you some advice."

"Do you really think I would need advice?" Damiano raised a brow, entertained by this conversation.

"Maybe. What have you done? I could give you a few tips to spice it up." Lorenzo asked with a playful smirk.

"More like what haven't I done." Damiano said smugly.

There wasn't anything Althaia didn't allow him to do. And now, with her hormones going crazy, she had become a wild freak, needing him to please her all the time, and he fucking loved it.

"Fucked her in the ass yet?" Lorenzo looked at him playfully.

"Of course. Have you fucked your wife in the ass yet?"

"I always do."

They both stared at each other before laughing out loud, amused by how their conversation took a completely different turn.

"Hey! Are you having fun without me?!" Raffaele hurried up to the brothers with a wide grin on his lips. "So, what are we talking about?" He rested his hands on his hips, looking back and forth between them.

"Get a wife and you can join the conversation." Damiano retorted, hoping he would finally settle with Ava so he could leave him the fuck alone.

Raffaele pouted at his reply.

"Oh, well, I've got other things to focus on." Raffaele looked back into the book he was holding.

For months, day and night, he had begged Althaia and Damiano to officiate their wedding. They shut him down immediately, but as persistent as he was, he annoyed the shit out of them until they were fed up with him. So much that Althaia yelled at him and then gave in to get peace.

Raffaele admitted Althaia was becoming scarier every day, and her hormones were making her a walking menace to everyone. Damiano always looked at her with nothing more than pride when everyone would steer clear of her in fear.

Raffaele mentally scoffed. Psychos really do attract psychos.

The sound of music filled the air, and everyone fell silent as they rose from their seats with their gaze fixated on the doors and awaited the bride's entrance.

Damiano exhaled slowly and waited for his bride.

Inside the master suite, Althaia took a final look in the mirror, a serene smile gracing her lips.

"Such a beautiful bride." Eleonora held her hands close to her heart as she looked at her daughter-in-law.

"I know. My baby is getting married." Jacinta sniffed, wiping away her tears with a tissue. She was looking at her daughter, barely believing this was her wedding day.

"Mamá, don't cry! You know I will cry too, and I can't help it." Althaia already felt the tears coming. Lately, she had been very emotional, and she didn't want to cry, knowing it would ruin her makeup.

"Sorry, honey." Jacinta laughed and managed to keep herself in check.

"Well, it's time to go. Everyone's waiting." Cara came back to tell them. She was the Matron of Honor, and she took that title very seriously and made sure everything was absolutely amazing.

Her sister was getting married.

"Okay." Althaia took a deep breath. She found it funny how she was feeling nervous even though they were already married, but still, it felt so different.

Before she could take a step, Giovanni and Luca made an appearance, looking at her with big smiles on their faces.

"Do you mind if we take a walk with you down the aisle?" Luca asked.

Althaia's face lit up with a grin as she turned her gaze towards her mother.

"It's okay with me. I will see you there." She smiled as they left.

Giovanni stopped in front of her, and his expression softened.

"You look beautiful." He told her, and her eyes glistened, trying her best to hold the tears back as he pulled the veil over her face.

He would never admit it directly to her, but she had won him over a long time ago, and even though he said he wouldn't, he would die for her.

Luca handed her the bridal flowers, looking at her with a warm smile. He liked her from the very first time they hung out on the day of the auction. He saw her as his precious little sister since he had none, and he loved that she was in his life with such a bright personality.

"Ready?" He asked her.

"Yes." She gave a nod and let out another breath before she would finally see her groom.

Luca and Giovanni went on either side of her and held out their arms for her to take. Together, they made their way out to everyone who was waiting.

The live orchestra was playing soft melodies as Cara, the Matron of Honor, walked down the aisle, leading the bridesmaids, Ava, Arianna, and Cecilia.

A collective smile and gentle laughter rippled through the crowd as the flower girl made her appearance. It was Antonio, cradling his adorable baby girl, dressed in a tiny white dress with a delicate bow atop her head. As he walked, he scattered flower petals, captivating the hearts of everyone present.

Everyone turned their attention back to the doors when the music changed, waiting for the bride to make an appearance.

Damiano had his hands clasped in front of him, so he wouldn't be trying to fix his tie like he had done at least a hundred times already as he waited in anticipation.

The doors finally opened, and a smile immediately found its way onto his lips, his shoulders relaxing in relief as well. Damiano's eyes never once left hers as she slowly walked down the aisle to him. He could swear to God right at this moment that he stopped breathing at the sight of his breathtaking bride.

Althaia only had eyes on Damiano with a smile so radiant on her lips. Her heart was beating faster, her entire body fluttering and tingling at the sight of him. She could see how much the sun was making his golden-brown eyes shine so brightly. Never before had he looked so breathtakingly handsome as he did on this day.

Althaia proceeded slowly down the aisle, capturing everyone's attention with the exquisite dress she was wearing. Her mother had poured her heart into designing the perfect wedding gown, and the look of sheer joy on her mother's face as she watched her daughter wear it was beyond words.

The dress was an off-shoulder design with delicate, transparent sleeves with intricate floral patterns. Its top was elegantly adorned with layered flowers, flowing into a slightly puffy skirt that cascaded into a long train behind her. It was not only stunning but also comfortable for her growing, pregnant belly.

As Althaia reached the end of the aisle, Damiano descended a few steps to take her into his arms. She stood before him, flanked by her favorite bodyguards, Giovanni and Luca, who were proudly giving her away.

Before Damiano could take her, Luca clasped a hand on his shoulder, leaning into him.

"I'm risking my life by saying this; but with all due respect, Boss, if you hurt her, we're coming after you." Luca said firmly, meaning every word.

"You've got us to deal with if you do, Boss." Giovanni backed up Luca. They knew the severe consequences of threatening their Don, and Damiano glanced at them, cocking a brow.

"Any other circumstances, you would be dead. But, since it's her we're talking about, I hope you keep your word." Damiano responded, amused with them.

He knew it was impossible not to care about her, because she was a pure soul, and in his eyes, she would always be his innocent woman, no matter what.

With Althaia's hand in his, Damiano led her up the gazebo steps, where Raffaele stood ready to officiate their marriage.

As he lifted her veil, Damiano couldn't help but feel starstruck and completely captivated by her beauty, especially her striking green eyes. His heart raced as he wondered how it was possible for her to be this enchanting. With each passing day, she only seemed to grow more and more beautiful.

Today, she radiated as brightly as the diamonds adorning her. The Tiffany Yellow Diamond hung elegantly around her neck, complemented by matching earrings. Her long hair cascaded in beautiful curls, adorned with a matching hairpiece to complete the jewelry ensemble.

"Absolutely breathtaking." He whispered to her, watching as her cheeks flushed with that reddish hue he found so damn endearing.

Althaia smiled shyly, her heart fluttering at their closeness. Nonna had separated them a week before the wedding to uphold the tradition of not seeing the bride before the wedding day.

It had been torturous for both of them.

"Welcome, loved ones!" Raffaele spoke loudly with a smile. "We are gathered here today to join Althaia and Damiano in holy matrimony." He announced as he continued with the invocation.

"May their marriage be filled with the sweet embrace of love, the joyful echoes of laughter, and the never-ending warmth of happiness. You may exchange your vows."

Damiano smiled softly as he looked into the beautiful green eyes that never ceased to captivate him.

"Althaia, I promise to cherish you always, to honor and sustain you. I promise to always have you with me, in my thoughts, my dreams, and my heart. I promise to dream with you, celebrate with you, and walk beside you through whatever life brings. I promise to always protect you, to always fight for you with my unconditional love. You are my love and my life. I will always love you, even after I've run out of breath. Because death can't do us part. You're my forever and always."

Althaia had tears in her eyes as Damiano spoke from his heart, letting her know how endless his love for her was. With a smile, Damiano wiped away a tear that escaped down her cheek.

"Damiano, I promise to cherish you always, to honor and respect you, to support and encourage you. I promise to dream with you, celebrate with you, and walk beside you through whatever life brings, because in your arms, I've found home. In your eyes, I've found compassion, and in your heart, I've found love. I accept you and love you exactly as you are because you're perfect. I promise to always pursue you, to fight for you, and to love you unconditionally and wholeheartedly. Forever and always because death can't do us part."

Damiano's heart pounded rapidly, spreading endless warmth within him at her words. He felt like he was about to explode with the emotions she drew out of him. His heart wasn't his anymore; it belonged to her.

Althaia felt the same as she gazed into those beautiful golden-brown eyes. Her heart belonged to him. They were two hearts and two souls that were now one and couldn't be separated.

They were destined to be together.

Raffaele had to clear his throat lightly. He got emotional listening to their vows, but what nearly brought tears to his eyes was the way they looked at each other, as if they were each other's entire world.

Their love was something to be envied.

Lorenzo wore a continuous smile as he handed the rings to Damiano. He kept stealing glances at his own wife, causing her to radiate with happiness each time he looked her way. Despite their wedding day having turned into a disaster, he had promised her the world and more.

Cara never thought she would have the chance to live a happy life, but now she could, with a man who had killed her past demons, allowing her to sleep soundly at night. She knew he would give her everything. All she had to do was say the word. That was why her father was still being kept alive, receiving days of torture for the years of abuse she had suffered, while Lorenzo made him long for death every day.

"Do you, Damiano, take this woman to be your lawfully wedded wife, to live together in holy matrimony, to love her, cherish her, comfort her, honor and keep her, in sickness and in health, for richer or for poorer, in sorrow and in joy, to have and to hold from this day forward, as long as you both shall live?"

"I do." Damiano replied immediately, wanting to proclaim to the world that she belonged to him.

Raffaele then turned to Althaia, repeating the same question. Althaia's smile widened, her enthusiasm matching Damiano's as she prepared to declare that this man also belonged to her.

She opened her mouth to speak but suddenly gasped and clutched her stomach, feeling an unfamiliar sensation.

"What's wrong? What's happening?" Damiano's face filled with worry as he frowned deeply. Althaia looked at him, a soft chuckle escaping her lips as she grabbed his hand and placed it gently on her stomach. That was when he felt it.

A tiny kick.

His eyes went wide at the incredible feeling. Small yet so strong. It was the first time they felt their baby kick.

"Our baby is eager for your response, my love." Damiano chuckled, feeling another kick, completely mesmerized by the sensation.

"I was getting there, my baby. So impatient like your father." Althaia smiled as she patted her round belly before looking at Damiano.

"I do!" She said with a bright smile.

Althaia and Damiano exchanged rings, keeping their hands interlocked as they gazed lovingly at each other.

"By the authority vested in me by the power of the Internet, I now pronounce you husband and wife!" Raffaele shouted with glee.

Damiano cupped Althaia's cheeks and pressed his strong lips against her soft ones. It was a kiss that ignited a fire within their bones and brought their souls to life. A kiss that bonded and sealed their hearts and souls together, forever.

Their lips never separated, even when everyone erupted cheerfully, chanting their names and firing their guns in celebration.

"Se agapó, agápi mou. Eísai dikós mou gia panta." *I love you, my love. You are mine forever.* Damiano whispered against her lips.

Althaia looked at him in surprise as he spoke in her native language.

"E ti amo, amore mio. La mia vita è completa con te al mio fianco." *And I love you, my love. My life is complete with you by my side.* Althaia responded in his native language before their lips were sealed together again in a heavenly kiss.

The sun had dipped below the horizon, and the reception was in full swing. Laughter, drinks, and the music filled the air as everyone enjoyed themselves.

Damiano stood by the bar, a smile on his lips as he watched his bride mingle with the crowd and sharing a laugh with Nonna.

"Ah, Bellavia! It seems I'm your father-in-law now." Alexei chuckled, joining Damiano.

Now that he knew Althaia was his daughter, he had no intention of staying away, especially on her wedding day. He had missed out on twenty-five years of her life, and he was determined to be a part of her future for as long as he lived.

"In your dreams, Vasiliev." Damiano sipped his whiskey.

He couldn't do anything about having Alexei at their wedding, since his bride wanted him to be here. However, Alexei was doing a good job of keeping to himself to not cause tension between him and everyone else. Good thing he only brought Nestor with him.

"That is my daughter, isn't it? That means I am your father-in-law." Alexei continued. He loved rubbing it in his face.

Damiano let out a genuine chuckle, slapping Alexei's back a few times as he leaned into him, both looking at Althaia.

"Correct. That is your daughter. And later, I'm going to slip that dress off her and fuck her all night." Alexei's smirk fell and Damiano clinked his glass against Alexei's. "Drinks are on me. Motherfucker." Damiano smirked while making his way to his bride.

Alexei scoffed and sipped his drink but smiled when Jacinta walked up to him.

"Solnishko."

"Lunnyy svet." She smiled when he pulled her into him.

He looked at her, his gaze softened as he spoke.

"Enough time has passed. When we're done here, you and I are getting married. It's time for you to bear my name, as you should have from the beginning. Your father isn't here to stop us, and neither is my mother. Let us finally live the life we were meant to."

Alexei meant every single word. He never took a partner, knowing his heart couldn't belong to anyone but her.

Jacinta watched his expression, seeing that he was being serious.

"Then let's get married." Jacinta smiled. After so many years, she finally wanted to live her life with the only man she ever loved.

She had gotten a new identity since she was supposed to be dead, but now she can finally have a name that meant something.

That was the reason she stabbed him close to his heart in the first place. If she couldn't have him, no one else could.

"As if you have a choice." Alexei teased, and Jacinta jokingly jabbed her elbow into his side as they watched their daughter being the happiest she had ever been.

Alexei was a bit disappointed that she had given up her birthright, but he understood. The agreement was to have the conversation one more time when her kids were old enough to decide what they wanted to do, and he hoped a grandchild of his would take over.

Althaia continued to laugh as Nonna had practically gathered all the young ones, lecturing them about how they should get married as soon as possible and give her great-grandbabies. Even Michael was getting the speech, as he was now part of la Famiglia Bellavia.

Damiano found him too valuable to dispose of, but he would have to work his way up. He accepted because he wanted to be close to the only people he saw as family.

Michael was happy for Althaia; his feelings for her had long faded, and he knew he would never be able to make her happy. Also, he might have just found someone he was falling for.

He looked at his date with a smile. No one knew she was the legendary Ghost, and if Raffaele knew, they would never get a quiet night.

"Don't keep me waiting too long! I'm not getting any younger! And don't wait until you're fifty like Damiano!" Nonna gave stern looks to all of them, except for Althaia.

"Nonna, I'm thirty-one." Damiano sighed, stepping right up at the time to be insulted. But Nonna ignored him.

"Arianna! Get married to Dom by the end of the year and give me babies! Cara! I expect you to be pregnant by the end of the year!"

Cara choked on her drink and laughed nervously.

"Maybe one day, Nonna."

"Ay, ay, these young people have no respect for their elders anymore..." Nonna complained, and Eleonora laughed.

"Let's get you some wine, madre." She led her away while Nonna continued to complain. Even Riccardo found it amusing. He did not miss the days when she was after him.

Riccardo congratulated his oldest son once again and kissed his new daughter-in-law on her head before he followed his wife. He had mixed feelings about her in the beginning, but now he was just glad she was making his son happy.

Cara sighed in relief and looked at Lorenzo, who was carrying Antonio's baby girl. She had always said she didn't want kids, and he knew that, but seeing Lorenzo with one in his arms made her feel something inside.

Lorenzo glanced at Cara, a warm smile on his face.

"Okay, maybe one kid?" Cara offered, and his eyes brightened.

Lorenzo wouldn't mind having kids, but if she didn't want them, then it was fine with him. He just wanted to please her and give her a comfortable life.

"Hold that thought. Hey, Damiano? How many kids are you planning to have?"

"Ten kids."

"Wait, we agreed to six!" Althaia exclaimed.

"I changed my mind. It's going to be ten."

Althaia was left stunned, and Lorenzo turned to exchange a glance with Cara.

"We're having twenty." Lorenzo said in all seriousness.

"Ha! It's one or nothing." Cara retorted.

"Cara mia, I can't let him win. It has to be twenty." Lorenzo argued, but Cara was already walking away from him.

"I told you, brother, I always win." Damiano laughed and wrapped his arm around his bride. "Come, take a walk with me." He said and led her outside.

They walked along the water on the beach, breathing in the fresh night air and watching the stars sparkle brightly above their heads.

"What do you think of having a beach house here?" Damiano stopped walking and gestured to the place.

"That would be lovely, but this is a private beach, so we can't." Althaia sighed sadly.

Calilo was her favorite place in Greece, and of course, she would love it if they could have some kind of property here. Especially this beach, as it was breathtaking with its crystal-clear turquoise waters and powdery white sand.

"I know. It's our private beach." Damiano smiled as Althaia looked at him in shock.

"You bought the beach?"

"*We* bought the beach. I wasn't about to let this place go to someone else. We got married here, and I want us to keep it. How about you take the lead in designing and building our dream beach house here? Then we can bring our children to this special place and show them where our wedding took place."

"Oh my God, yes! I love it! Thank you!" Althaia wrapped her arms around him and kissed him in gratitude. Damiano chuckled at her excitement, knowing she would adore a beach house.

He crouched down to converse with her beautiful, round belly.

"What do you think? Should we build a beach house here for you?" Damiano asked, feeling strong kicks against the palm of his hands.

"I think that's a yes." Althaia laughed.

"It's settled then." He smiled and kissed her pregnant belly.

"Hey, come on, guys! It's your wedding, you can't just leave! It's time for your dance!" Cara shouted after them.

Damiano sighed, just wanting to be alone with his bride already.

"Let's go, my husband." Althaia laughed at his expression and took his hand.

"We can always sneak away." Damiano suggested, but followed nonetheless. The temptation to kidnap his bride was strong.

"We can sneak out after the cake. And then, I want you to fuck me nice and hard all night." She winked, and he let out a small grunt at her words.

"Baby, you have no idea how long I've been dreaming about this day. I will give you a night you will never forget." Damiano gave her the devilish smirk she loved so much as his eyes darkened.

"Better keep your word." Althaia grinned.

"I always do, my love." He replied and kissed the back of her hand, making her blush.

Everyone had cleared the dance floor, making way for the bride and the groom. Althaia wrapped her arms around Damiano's neck while his arms gilded around her waist. The orchestra was playing some of the most beautiful melodies as they had their first dance.

They couldn't take their eyes off each other as they moved around like a fairytale. Damiano swept Althaia off her feet and up in his arms, making her let out a squeal in surprise as she laughed. As they twirled gracefully, the sparklers scattered across the floor erupted into a mesmerizing display, enveloping them in a magical, enchanting moment.

Their heads rested against each other, lost in their own world.

He was the master of the night, and she, the harbinger of dawn.

When he was drowning, she became his air. In the cold, she became his warmth. In the dark, she became his light.

Two different worlds were brought together and created a love with a burning desire. And if they were to live their life again, they would have found each other sooner.

The End

Bonus

ALTHAIA

I huffed and looked at the time. It was a quarter to four in the morning, and I was wide awake.

Feeling horny.

I turned to look at Damiano, who was sleeping peacefully next to me. I wanted him, but I didn't want to wake him up just to tend to my needs. He has a long day ahead of him, flying out to a meeting with Mr. Roberts and other high-end restaurant owners.

The idea of custom-designed wine bottles for Mr. Roberts was a hit, and they attracted so many customers. Many liked the concept of taking a unique wine bottle home as a souvenir, and some even began to collect them.

The sales skyrocketed and landed us a few more deals. I suggested that each restaurant had its distinct design as a trademark, but with Damiano's wine business name engraved. He was going to meet with them all and show them my sketch ideas. I would have gone with him and presented them myself, but since I was heavily pregnant, I couldn't fly.

Now, Damiano was going to be away for a couple of days, and the thought of that alone made me anxious. Not only that, but I was incredibly horny, and I needed him to take care of me since I couldn't do anything because of my huge belly.

It was funny how I always teased Damiano how I couldn't keep up with his horny ass. Well, now it was he who was doing his best to keep up with me. Sometimes I would make him come home from work to fuck me, and other times I surprised him by showing up at his office for a quickie.

Nevertheless, he loved that I was so ravenous for him.

It was a good thing we managed to get our home finished before it got too bad. If not, Raffaele would have been up in my ass about not getting any sleep. As if he and Ava had absolutely no shame and fucked everywhere in the manor.

One time I even caught them fucking in the kitchen, and he had the audacity to complain about me when I at least would keep it in the bedroom when I was sharing a roof with them all.

Also, the manor was never empty. Damiano's men were constantly around, some even crash there, yet they loved to fuck where people could see them.

Sighing, I tried to fall asleep again, but it was becoming too unbearable. I was painfully throbbing and had to do something about it.

"Damiano?" I called him softly.

He stirred in his sleep, and I heard the change in his breathing.

"Yes, baby." He grunted, almost in pleasure, with his eyes still closed.

"I'm sorry to wake you, but... I'm horny."

He snapped his eyes open, and a smirk immediately appeared on his lips. Then his eyes narrowed.

"Don't joke like last time."

"I'm not. I really need you." My hands trailed down his naked body, wrapping my hand around his length. I raised a brow, and his smirk widened when I felt he was already hard.

"I was already dreaming about you riding my dick."

I chuckled.

Damiano helped me up to straddle him. He positioned his cock at the entrance of my pussy, and with a slow, breathy moan, I slid down on his cock.

That alone felt so good I almost orgasmed.

"Shit, piccola, you're fucking dripping." Damiano grunted as his thumb played with my clit.

I moved to feel more of him, rocking my hips back and forth, hitting all the right places. It had my eyes rolling to the back of my head, and I let out an uncontrollable moan.

"Fuck, so perfect." Damiano groaned, thrusting his hips upwards, making me feel all of his cock as he circled my clit faster.

"You feel so good..." I moaned, clenching around his cock. I was so close already.

"Come for me, piccola." Damiano panted, driving in and out of me as I closed my eyes, my body tensing as an overwhelming orgasm washed over me. "Good girl." He praised, pumping inside of me a few times before I felt his release.

I stilled as I caught my breath while he caressed my hips.

"Happy?" Damiano smiled beautifully at me, and I grinned.

"Yes. Thank you, my love." I blew him a kiss, and I was ready to sleep now in satisfaction.

"Anytime, baby." He chuckled.

"Look at you, you're incredibly cute!" I sniffled, wiping away my tears as Kiara nuzzled my belly. Her irresistible charm had me tearing up as I continued to gaze at her and shower her with affectionate strokes.

Footsteps hurried down the staircase, and Damiano appeared with a concerned expression.

"Baby, what's the matter?" He kneeled in front of me.

"She's just too adorable! I can't help it." I said as another tear rolled down my cheek. He chuckled softly and turned his attention to Kiara.

"She's a cute one." Damiano stroked her, and she responded with a joyful purring. "Are you ready, my love? The others have arrived." He gently wiped away my tears.

I nodded and took a deep breath.

As I managed to keep my emotions in check, Cara, Lorenzo, Antonio, Giovanni, Luca, Renzo, and Michael joined us. Since Damiano was going on a business trip, I would be staying at the manor with everyone. Damiano had made sure that I would have additional security, even though it was just a stay at the manor.

Just as the men greeted me by calling me Donna out of respect, Cara greeted me by calling me a fat-ass.

"Fat-ass, really? I'm carrying your niece or nephew." I shot her a blank look.

We didn't know the gender as we wanted it to be a surprise.

"Yeah, but you're still huge. How do you get around? Do you roll or something?" Cara snickered. She loved making fun of me, especially when I had trouble getting up on my own.

"I can't wait till you get pregnant to give you a taste of your own medicine." I grumbled as Damiano helped me up on my feet.

"Hmm, not sure if it's going to happen. I will have to see if your butthole explodes before I decide."

Everyone stopped and looked at Cara.

"Wait, that really happens?" Luca's eyes widened. Even Giovanni looked startled, and Michael dropped his jaw.

"Yes! I saw it myself! Here, I will show you the video." Cara pulled out her phone and went to show them.

"Cara!" Damiano snapped when he saw my eyes get welled up in tears again. Cara jumped and dropped her phone in startlement and then gave an innocent laugh.

"It's not going to happen to you!" She tried to comfort me, and Lorenzo just sighed at her lousy attempt to comfort me.

"I really hate you." I choked out a sob. Damiano comforted me while sending a deathly glare to Cara. "Can I kill her?" I asked Damiano.

"If it will make you happy." He replied, and Lorenzo's eyes slowly narrowed as he looked at us.

"Which one of you will do the job for me?" I asked the rest, and Giovanni scoffed.

"Are you crazy? Lorenzo will make us all drop like fucking flies before we can even take our next breath."

"Sorry, but no one in their right mind would try a fight with Lorenzo." Luca added.

Michael's brows raised when I looked at him.

"I... I'm going to wait outside to, you know, make sure everything is safe out here." He said and went out.

I pouted, directing my attention to Renzo.

"Renzo, you're a cage fighter. I heard you ripped someone's jugular vein out with your teeth." I said, and he smiled proudly.

"With all due respect, Donna. I think I will pass on this one."

"Antonio?" I looked at him.

"I have a wife and a baby girl." He said, amused that I was asking them all.

"So much for being my bodyguards." I scowled.

"Leave us out of it and ask your man." Giovanni mirrored my scowl.

"Damiano?" I asked him, and his devilish smirk appeared.

"Anything for you, my love." He stared at Lorenzo.

"It's too soon for your wife to become a widow." Lorenzo stated.

"I don't lose, brother." Damiano let out a taunting smile.

"There is a first for everything." Lorenzo mirrored his expression.

"Oh, no..." I sighed. "I accidentally started another one of their pissing contests."

Cara ignored them as they continued with their threats and looked at me with an apologetic smile.

"Sorry, babe. I will buy you a chocolate cake on the way, okay?" She offered.

I stopped sniffing.

"Make it two."

"I will buy you five huge ones!"

"Okay. I love you again."

"I will have Cecilia bake you one." Damiano said. I was about to tell him not to trouble her when I remembered why.

Damiano had been very careful about the source of our food and even watched our personal chef closely when preparing my meals. However, in the end, he didn't trust any of them and snatched one of the family chefs from Italy to handle the job.

I felt guilty about it because often I would have cravings in the middle of the night, and Damiano would summon our chef to prepare whatever my heart desired.

I made sure to give her a generous tip every time she came over during the night, and even more when the food brought tears of happiness to my eyes because it was exceptionally delicious.

"Cara, you will have to buy me something else." I told her.

"Whatever you want, babes! You know what, I will even buy you a few diamond necklaces, and some for your baby. Get some cute pink diamonds if it's a girl, and blue if it's a boy. I'm a rich bitch thanks to Tank Man's blood money." Cara laughed, waving the black card in her hand.

Lorenzo looked at her, amused, chuckling slightly as he shook his head. He often had that soft expression whenever he looked at her, and I always felt like crying that they were so happy together.

"Gold digger." I joked.

"And a proud one!" She winked as we laughed.

"Okay, let's go, Kiara." I called after her. Kiara already knew the routine when everyone was here and followed right after us and into the car.

When we arrived at the manor, Damiano was so hesitant to leave me.

"Are you sure? I can always stay." Damiano looked at me with a serious expression.

"Yes, Damiano. I'll be fine. Besides, I won't be going anywhere and will probably just rest." I reassured him.

He didn't want to leave me, but I reminded him I was at the manor, heavily secured by his armed men and even snipers on the roof. Despite the extra security, he was still reluctant to leave.

"It won't be like last time." I told him softly and placed my hands on his cheek. He kissed my forehead and held me close.

"Keep your rings and earrings on at all times."

"I will. I love you." I smiled.

"And I love you." He replied, giving me a long, tender kiss that filled me with warmth.

"I will bet you ten grand that they are two seconds away from fucking in the driveway!" Raffaele shouted.

Damiano rested his head against mine, closed his eyes, and sighed.

"Remind me again why I shouldn't kill him?"

"He's your cousin." I chuckled.

"So?"

"Nonna will be mad at you." I said.

Surprisingly, Nonna loved Raffaele, and she fully admitted he was her favorite grandchild. Even though he was incredibly inappropriate, she loved him to death.

"He's lucky he's got Nonna on his side." Damiano frowned, looking at Raffaele, who continued to make jokes. "When are you going to get a place of your own? Fucking freeloader." Damiano asked him, wiping away the smile on Raffaele's lips.

"Don't act like me staying here is making you broke! I've seen what kind of money you spend on your wife." He grinned. "If you got it tight, just sell that big yellow diamond you got her. I heard you spent fifty mils on that one after you fucked. I mean, that pussy must be magical." Raffaele laughed so hard.

I gasped in mortification as everyone heard him.

"Run." Damiano told him quietly as he grabbed his gun, but Raffaele didn't listen, knowing he wouldn't shoot.

But he did.

"Damiano!" I yelled at him when he shot right above his head. Even Raffaele stood still in shock, not expecting him to shoot. But Damiano just tilted his head.

"I miscalculated. Let me try again."

"Wait! Okay, okay! I'm sorry! Have mercy and I will move out tomorrow!" Raffaele shouted for his life.

"Good." Damiano smiled and faced me. Before I could tell him how wrong he was for that, he crouched down and placed a kiss on my stomach.

"Keep your mom safe for me." He said softly, making me forget about everything and smile.

It was in the middle of the night, and I ripped the blanket away from me, having trouble sleeping. Not only was I struggling to sleep because Damiano wasn't here, but also because my back was killing me. No matter how I lay, it wouldn't go away.

I made my way down to the kitchen, groaning slightly in discomfort.

"Are you all having a party or something?" I asked, since everyone was in the kitchen.

"Did we wake you?" Cecilia asked.

"No, couldn't sleep. Baby is partying right on my bladder." I sighed and leaned against the counter to ease the back pain.

"Honestly, so far pregnancy doesn't -" Cara started.

"Cara mia." Lorenzo warned her not to finish her sentence.

"I don't know about you guys, but this is giving me baby fever." Ava smiled.

Raffaele looked at her in surprise.

"You want babies?" He asked.

"You don't?"

"Not really. They poop."

"It's okay if you don't. I can always have someone else impregnate me." She said in a smug tone.

"Hell no. Let's get to it."

"Oh my God, Raffaele! What is wrong with you?" Everyone shouted at him when he pulled down his pants. Luckily, his boxers were still on.

"Too much, dude." Michael grimaced.

"You are disgusting." Giovanni scowled.

"I'm ashamed to be related to you." Lorenzo commented and Cecilia agreed.

"You're all a bunch of sensitive pussies." Raffaele sulked and pulled up his pants.

"Well, don't stop on my account. I want to see how you all get down." Cara shrugged and Raffaele wiggled his brows.

"I knew you were a freaky one. I bet you like it in the ass."

"I do." Cara replied with a wink.

"God!" I threw my head back and groaned.

"Well, if you let Damiano fuck you in the ass, you wouldn't be in this situation." Cara shot at me.

"Gross! I came in at the wrong time." Arianna said as she made an appearance with Dom.

"It wasn't because of that. I'm just uncomfortable." I groaned to Cara.

"Do you need a doctor?" Cecilia asked in worry.

"No, no... I just need - Tank Man, can you help me? Damiano does this thing where he stands behind me and gently lifts my belly to relieve some of the weight." I explained to him, and I sighed in relief when he helped me as my back already felt better.

"Wow, you can see the relief that just gave you!" Cara said in awe.

"It's quite heavy. I'm amazed you haven't broken in half when you're so tiny." Lorenzo said, making me chuckle.

"Trust me, it feels like I will at any minute now." I closed my eyes, enjoying being light for a moment.

The conversation continued while I remained in my blissful bubble.

"Hi, Dami!" Cara erupted, making me open my eyes.

"Where's Lorenzo?" His voice rang out from the speakers of Lorenzo's phone.

"Would it kill you to say hi back?"

"Yes. Where's Lorenzo?"

"He's currently... uh, holding your wife's belly?" Cara looked at us, trying to explain what he was doing.

Damiano went silent, and I quietly chuckled as I knew he was displeased about that information.

"Get him on the phone right now."

"You're on speakerphone, Damiano. We can hear you." I laughed.

"He's your brother, Damiano! Don't be disgusting!" Arianna shouted to him from the other end of the kitchen, knowing what he was going to say.

"Is something wrong? Anything with the sketches?" I asked him.

"No, I just wanted to check in on you. Is it the back again?" I could hear the concern in his voice.

"Yeah, it's somehow worse today -" I stopped abruptly, and my eyes widened.

"Did you just pee?" Giovanni asked and looked at the splash around our feet.

"And all over Lorenzo's feet!" Raffaele laughed.

"Her water broke." Lorenzo stated calmly, while still holding my belly.

"What?!" Damiano yelled out. My nerves started kicking in, and I tried taking a deep breath to calm down.

"Damiano... my water broke. My water broke, and you're not here!" My voice trembled, tears welling up at the thought of him missing the birth of our first baby.

"It's okay, baby, it's okay. Take slow, deep breaths. I'm on my way." Damiano's reassuring words tried to calm me, and I nodded, even though he couldn't see me.

"Don't be scared. We've got you. Let's head to the hospital." Lorenzo said calmly, which eased my anxiety, knowing he was composed about it.

"Okay, can someone please call my mom?"

"On it!" Cara reassured me.

"It's almost time to push!" My midwife exclaimed, and the nurses began preparations.

"No! I can't! My husband isn't here yet!" I panted in pain. It was the most excruciating experience I had ever been through.

"Honey, you can't hold it in. You have to do it." My mother urged, and I vigorously shook my head.

"I won't do it without him! Where is my husband?!" I shouted in frustration, tears streaming down my face, just as the door burst open.

"I'm here!" Damiano rushed to me, out of breath and with disheveled hair.

"What took you so long?!" I sobbed to him but was relieved that he had arrived.

"I'm sorry, baby." He smiled, brushing away the hair stuck to my forehead. Then he noticed the crowded room and my exposed state. "Everyone out!" Damiano ordered, and they all hurriedly left, except for my mother.

"I can see the head. It's time to push!"

I clung to Damiano's hand tightly while he gently stroked my head, guiding me on when to breathe and push, all the while trying to keep me calm.

"One more. You've got this, baby." I focused on his voice, took a deep breath, and pushed with the little strength I had left.

Soft cries filled the room, and I gasped at the tiny voice. Damiano looked awestruck, holding his breath as our baby was laid on my chest.

"It's a girl!" The midwife announced, and I started to cry even more at the sight of the tiny baby on my chest.

Damiano let out a relieved breath as he stared at our baby girl. He was completely in awe. He leaned down to me, resting his head against mine.

"You're amazing. Absolutely amazing." He whispered, a tear escaping his eyes and landing on my cheek.

"Are you crying, my love?" I looked at him in shock.

Damiano responded with his beautiful smile and kissed me softly.

"Hi, guys." I smiled tiredly. I was exhausted, but I didn't want to sleep just yet. I couldn't as I was still overwhelmed with feelings of pure love.

My mother went out to help Alexei, who apparently had loaded an entire car with gifts.

They all gathered around me, asking how I was feeling, and gifted us flowers, teddy bears, and massive balloons.

"Where's the baby?" Cara asked.

"And Damiano?" Arianna followed right after. I chuckled and pointed at the other end of the room where Damiano was doing skin-on-skin contact.

Everyone went silent at the sight.

"Wait, did you steal a baby?" Raffaele asked, dumbfounded.

"Meet our babies, Anastasha and Angelo." Damiano introduced them proudly.

Anastasha, a name that means a new life, and Angelo, a name that means an Angel. We didn't hesitate with the names as soon as we found out we were having twins, hoping we would have one of each.

And now, we have a baby girl and a baby boy with names that were part of me and part of him, and they were the most perfect babies.

I chuckled when they all were still looking at our babies with a mixture of awe and shock. I took Angelo in my arms, smiling widely at how cute they were as they slept peacefully.

"Our beautiful new life."

BONUS
DAMIANO

"Everything is under control. Shipments are continuing smoothly and are currently being counted and repacked." Gabriele informed me.

I was in my weekly meeting to get updated on what was currently happening with my businesses, and Gabriele was the one in charge of the shipments and making sure everything was as it should be.

One of our smaller locations was found by street rats, and they thought they could blackmail me by stealing my cocaine, thinking I was desperate to get it back. What they didn't know was that the warehouse barely contained five percent of my products.

When I heard of it, I fucking laughed. It was cute that they thought they could blackmail my men to give in to their demands. What made them think they would get away with it in the first place fucking beats me.

Just to prove a point, I sent one of the low-ranking soldiers to end them.

"Good. Get rid of anyone who tries to be an annoying piece of shit." I told him, getting a nod in return.

I turned my attention to Emiliano.

"What's the status of the Genovese family?"

"They want six crates of grenades for fifty thousand."

"Tell that cocksucker he can get a single one for free, because I will be using it to shove it up his ass." I scoffed. "Make it clear that if he ever disrespects me with a price like that again, I will personally show up and end his useless life." I sneered.

They were eager for weapons yet didn't want to pay the price for them. I might just use the weapons they wanted to kill them all to spare me from any more nuisances. My patience was becoming thinner as I got older, and right now, it was barely as thick as a strand of hair.

The meeting continued, and I was getting report after report, as I mindlessly listened. Nothing urgent needed my attention since I had made sure more of my trusted men were given additional responsibility so I could spend time with my family.

Now that I was a father, it gave me a new perspective on how I approached things. I wasn't being as reckless and went on killing sprees unless it was necessary. I had men do that for me.

Before, I had nothing to lose, but now, I possessed more than I had ever dared to dream of. I had a beautiful wife and two precious children, and I had no intention of leaving them.

"I want those properties on Long Beach. I wanna flip the whole damn place and turn it into the biggest nightclub this city's ever seen. The Romanians fucked up with their drug trafficking, and we're gonna capitalize on that. Prepare to-" I halted mid-sentence and abruptly rose from my seat, swinging the door open when I heard crying.

"Who hurt you?" My brows furrowed, seeing Anastasha on the floor, crying.

"Daddy!" She held her arms up when she saw me. I crouched down, pulled her into my arms, and she cried into my neck.

"Tell me, my Diamond, what happened?" I spoke to her softly and rubbed her back.

"Are you okay, Ana?" Angelo came running to her. She lifted her head, and I wiped away her tears.

"I fell." Anastasha sniffed.

"It's okay." Angelo gave her a comforting smile and continued to rub her back. I smiled at the two of them. They were so full of life and cared for each other like no other, even at the tender age of two.

"Here's your gun, and we can play again!" He handed her the toy gun cheerfully. They both picked up their toy guns to play, finding it amusing to shoot foam darts at each other.

Althaia found it hilarious and commented that they were too much like their daddy, and it was true. They were both complete replicas of me but had their mother's striking green eyes, which I loved so much.

"It's all right, my Diamond. Just be careful and don't run too fast." I said as I kissed the top of her head. She nodded and put on a big smile when she set her feet on the ground.

"I want to shoot Uncle Raffaele!" Anastasha shouted with glee when Raffaele appeared with the rest of my men.

She aimed and shot him in the stomach with a foam dart.

"Ow, you got me, kiddo." Raffaele smiled widely and pretended to be hurt.

"You have to die!" Angelo shouted with just as much excitement as his sister.

"That's a bit aggressive. But then again, I didn't expect anything less since your parents are psychos." He snickered.

"No, I shot you, you have to die!" Anastasha ordered him firmly.

"... I'm not getting on the dirty floor." Raffaele shook his head. A sad pout started to appear on her lips, and her eyes welled with tears.

I got up and went to Raffaele, placing a firm hand on his shoulder as I leaned in to speak quietly for my men to hear.

"If my daughter wants you to play dead, then you better fucking play dead before I make it your actual funeral." I shot them a warning look and hurried back to my daughter.

"Don't cry, my Diamond. Uncle Raffaele has a hard time understanding. Here, shoot him again, and he will die." I told her, and she shot him again. This time, Raffaele did a great job of dramatizing his death.

"Oh no, I'm dying! I'm dying!" He crashed into the wall and slowly slumped to the floor.

"Yay! My turn!" Angelo laughed. It made me smile as they both continued to shoot the rest of my men, and each one fell to the floor, playing dead.

"Good job." I praised them with a chuckle. "But you forgot one." I pointed to Antonio with a smirk, and he raised an eyebrow at me.

"No, I like Uncle Nino!" Angelo giggled and ran to Antonio, who caught him in his arms.

"Thank you for saving me, buddy. Should I get you an extra big birthday present for saving me?" Antonio smiled.

"Yes, yes!"

"Me too, Uncle Nino! It's also my birthday!" Anastasha eagerly told him as I carried her in my arms.

"And you too, Ana. I will get you both extra big presents today."

"Come, let's get you some birthday presents and then go home." I kissed her cheek as she wrapped her arms around me while grinning happily.

I dismissed my men, who were still on the floor playing dead as we made our way out.

With Anastasha and Angelo in my arms, I walked through our estate and straight out to the backyard where their birthday party was being held.

Althaia had planned a grand party, inviting all the children to have a blast in Candy Land. The backyard had transformed into every kid's dream with slides, trampolines, and enough sugar to keep them awake for weeks.

As I looked around, I spotted everyone was already present, meaning I was late. My family flew in to celebrate our children's birthday, and even Alexei Vasiliev was present.

We had a special agreement, only allowing him and Nestor to enter my territory if they informed me beforehand. If not, my men were given strict orders to kill whoever tried to enter, and I didn't care who it was if it meant my family would be safe.

The agreement also allowed Althaia, our children, and Cara to enter his territory since he and Jacinta got married. This also meant I was spending more time with Alexei than I ever wanted to, but I kept that to myself since he was my wife's father and my children's grandfather.

He had been doing a better job than expected in being a part of Althaia's life, and their relationship had grown a lot over the past two years. Now, she is almost fluent in Russian.

A smile immediately graced my lips when I saw my gorgeous wife laughing at something Cara was saying.

"Mamá, mamá!" Angelo wiggled his way down and sprinted toward his mother.

"There's my Angel!" Althaia's eyes lit up as she caught him in her arms, showering him with endless kisses and eliciting joyful giggles from him.

She repeated the same when I approached with Anastasha, and just the sight and sound of them made me feel so complete.

"Hi, beautiful." I greeted my wife, placing a quick, soft kiss on her lips while the kids were distracted by the decorations in the backyard.

Angelo was fiercely possessive of his mother, never allowing me to kiss her, and throwing tantrums every time he caught me trying. Anastasha was no different and didn't like anyone coming too close to me.

"Hi, handsome." She grinned, getting that slight blush on her cheeks. "You went out early today."

"I wanted you to sleep in and took the kids with me." I always made an effort to make sure she got enough sleep, often taking the kids out in the morning to give her some peace.

"Thank you, my love." Althaia smiled brightly, warming my chest with her expression.

"Mamá, look what I have." Angelo proudly showed the chunky gold chain around his neck with an Angel pendant covered in diamonds.

"Oh, wow, look at that." She beamed, and I pretended not to notice the look she gave me.

"Me too, mamá! Daddy got me a diamond ring." Anastasha eagerly showed the ring on her finger.

"Beautiful! So bright, just like you, my Diamond." Althaia smiled warmly.

"Go play. Your cousins are here." I told them, and they didn't waste a single second before running toward the others.

"Really, Damiano?" Althaia gave me a knowing look. I wrapped my arms around her waist, pulling her closer to me.

"What?" I asked with a smile.

"Diamonds?" She raised a brow.

"That's what they wanted." I shrugged.

"My love, we cannot be the type of parents who give their two-year-olds diamonds."

"Why not? We can afford it." I argued, fighting back a smile because this wasn't the first time I have done something similar, and she wasn't too happy about it that time either.

"Obviously, but you're spoiling them too much already." Althaia sighed.

I leaned down to her, speaking in a low voice.

"Let me spoil them. And you. I haven't forgotten about you. I have something special waiting in the bedroom for you to wear for me." I smirked, and she looked at me amused.

"Lingerie?"

"No. Something red and shiny that belongs around your neck." Her brows furrowed as she thought about it.

"Don't tell me you got me a red diamond necklace."

"I did." I smiled. "I told you from the very beginning that I would be showering you and our children with diamonds." I reminded her before she could protest about the gift.

"Well, I didn't think you actually meant it." Althaia chuckled and shook her head.

"Of course, I did. Besides, remember that show you gave me with the Tiffany Yellow Diamond? I want you to give me a similar show with the red ones." I said with a devilish smirk. The thought of seeing her like that already made me so fucking excited.

"Hmm, I think I can do that for you." She winked.

"Good girl." I replied, hearing her breath catch before her cheeks flushed. She quickly cleared her throat and looked away shyly, causing me to chuckle at her reaction.

"Since we're exchanging gifts, I have something for you as well."

"For me?" I asked, surprised.

"Yes, it's already on the table. Come." She took my hand and led me to the table, and I greeted everyone as I passed by.

I raised an eyebrow at Althaia when I stopped in front of the wrapped gift, but she just smiled and gestured for me to open it. I removed the top lid, peering inside before turning to her immediately.

"Are you serious? Do you mean it?" I cupped her face, looking into her bright green eyes to confirm if it was a joke.

"Yes." She laughed and my heart started to pump faster.

I rested my head against hers, letting out a breath.

"Are you really giving me another one?" I asked, barely believing it even though I saw it.

"It's time to grow our family." She whispered softly, and I gently pressed my lips against hers, savoring the sweetness of our tender kiss.

"You are one incredible woman." I told her as I kissed her again.

"What is it?" Arianna asked, as they all wondered what was happening.

I pulled out the onesie that read 'Baby #3 Loading' along with a sonogram on it and proudly showing it to everyone.

"No way! I'm going to be an aunt again?" Arianna asked in shock.

"She's blessing me with one more baby." I smiled and placed a kiss on top of my wife's head.

"Amazing, congratulations!" Everyone congratulated us, surprised that baby number three was on the way so soon after having twins.

I pulled Althaia close, enveloping her in my embrace, and gazed at her with a depth of affection that words could never capture. She was a stunning, radiant presence who consistently filled my life with love and happiness.

Althaia smiled so lovingly and pressed her soft lips to mine before she nestled her head against my chest.

I caressed her hair as we watched our twins running around and playing happily at their birthday party.

Coming Next...
CARA

My life changed for the worse when I was fourteen. It was the time when my aunt, Jacinta, and cousin, Althaia, suddenly moved out of the mansion we all lived in. It shockingly happened overnight. Althaia and I couldn't comprehend why, barely having time to say goodbye. And the next thing I know, I was left alone in the mansion with a monster of a father and an uncle who couldn't give two fucks about me.

I was homeschooled, so no one could ever ask why my body kept getting bruises, and my face kept getting discolored. I wasn't allowed to go out much, and if I were to go out, I needed an escort everywhere, because privacy didn't mean shit to my father. God forbid if I met a boy and lost my virginity to him. I needed to stay pure for whoever he chooses to be my future husband to gain alliances and strengthen ties between families. Because that was how the underworld works, and my virginity was the only thing valued about me.

When I was sixteen, I met many creeps, *pedophiles,* also known as my father's and uncle's business partners. Dusty old men would look at me with lust swirling in their eyes as they skated over my body, licking their lips at the sight of me. After that, I made sure to never roam around the halls of the mansion whenever 'guests' were over.

Though, one day I was cornered in the kitchen by a creep, who spotted me going to the kitchen after a bottle of water and painkillers to relieve my period cramps.

"You are a pretty little thing."

I looked at him in disgust when his eyes slid down my body first, before even meeting my eyes.

"What's your name, sweetheart?" He let out that kind of smile that let people know he was a predator from a mile away.

"I'm sixteen." I spat out. He looked to be *at least* in his late thirties. I clutched the water bottle to me. I just wanted the damn painkillers.

"Oh? Sixteen is such a good age." He stepped closer to me, his hand touching my shoulder, and slid down my arm. I gritted my teeth, my eyes landing on the knife block, looking at the biggest knife as I imagined cutting his hand off.

I turned my head away when he leaned closer to me with his hands touching my body where they didn't belong in the first place, and his disgusting breath fanning the side of my face.

"Tell me, sweetheart, have you been touched before?" His hand squeezed my hip, and it took everything in me not to throw up on the spot.

"Yes. I've had countless cocks inside of me and been taken in every single way possible. Haven't you heard? I'm a proud whore." I told him and sidestepped away from him. At least that was what my father loved to call me, despite having zero experience with boys. I was sure he even forgot what my name was and decided *whore* was my new name.

The water bottle and painkillers flew out of my hands and scattered away from me when the creep had me almost bending over the kitchen counter. He had his hands on either side of me as he pressed his disgusting pelvis against my ass.

"So, you wouldn't mind if I had a taste since everyone got to?" He whispered in my ear. Fear flashed inside of me, and one of his hands started to move away from the counter. My heart started to beat frantically, and my vision darkened around the edges.

"You bitch!" He screamed at me when I stumbled away from him. My breathing was loud, and my chest heaved. I blinked once. Then twice, watching his bloodied hand with a knife pierced through. Only now did I realize I stabbed the creep with the knife I had eyed ever since he cornered me.

Hurrying footsteps coming in our direction reached my ears, and I snapped out of it. I started to run as fast as possible through the mansion to hide, knowing what would await me for what I had done. Fear gripped my heart as I dashed upstairs to my room, breaking through the doors to my bathroom, and locking the door. My father had removed the bedroom lock, and this was the only place with some sort of security.

I crept away from the door, my hands turning into fists as I swallowed hard. I clenched my jaw, avoiding any noise escaping me when I heard my bedroom door crashing into the wall, and footsteps inching closer to the bathroom.

"You fucking whore!" My father roared out and the bathroom door got knocked down. His face was red with rage, and I wondered how long I would stay in the hospital this time.

"No! Stop! He touched me! He was touching me!" I screamed at the top of my lungs when he painfully grabbed my hair to the point where some of it pulled out. But no matter how much I screamed, it fell on deaf ears.

My head whipped to the side and fire erupted on the entire right side of my face. I fell to the floor and felt the blood trickle down my cheek. He loved to backhand me whenever he wore rings. And he made sure to wear them often.

My mouth opened in a silent scream as I felt my ribs crack under the weight of his foot. A burst of pain lanced over my entire body while I fought to fill my lungs with air. But I never could as my father continued to kick me.

Over and over again, bruising and breaking my body in black and blue, and there was nothing I could do. No one cared just enough to ever stop him from beating me. No one dared to stop my father, saying it was his right to discipline his kid.

Another kick to my ribs sent me crashing into the wall, blurring my vision until darkness took over, numbing the pain as he continued to ruin me.

Why would my father ever do something like this to his own flesh and blood? His daughter he was supposed to love and protect with everything in his might. How could he?

Because I killed the love of his life, and he swore he would destroy me for it.

I was alone in an ocean of darkness. I fought hard to swim to the surface. Fought for air and light. Fought to hold onto *something* that would get me out of here.

But no matter how much I fought to get to the surface, no matter how desperately I swam with my legs and arms moving like never before, it was still a no match for the anchor tied to my feet, plunging me deeper and deeper into the dark ocean where there was no air or light.

I was doomed from the second I was born.

And to be honest, I was hoping he would kill me this time so I could finally be *free*.

Unfortunately, I lived.

Acknowledgements

I can barely comprehend that I now finally have published my very first book. I started writing this story in August, 2021 while I was doing my masters degree. It took me a year to complete the story, and while it may not be the best story out in the world, it's perfect to me because this book became my comfort when I went through the darkest time of my life. This is proof to myself that no matter what, I still pulled through and dreams do come true!

Writing a book is a journey that doesn't happen alone. I am deeply grateful to everyone who has supported and encouraged me along the way.

To my readers, who embraced this story when it was just a flicker of an idea called "Playing With Fire," your belief in me lit the path when darkness threatened to consume me. Your support, especially during the toughest moments of this journey, have meant more to me than words can express. Thank you for being my guiding light.

My husband, family and friends, I thank you for supporting me, despite me trying to hide this book from you haha! A special thank you to my husband for inspiring scenes and assisting in creating the discreet cover.

Melissa McCarthy, my editor, you breathed life into this manuscript with your insightful feedback and meticulous attention to detail. Your dedication to this project transformed it into something I am truly proud of.

To my helpers—Julie, Madeline, Jennifer, Silvia, Yousra, and Narjiss—your feedback, translations and encouragement were invaluable. Each word of advice propelled me forward, shaping this story into its best possible form.

Julie, your steadfast support has been my anchor in turbulent seas. Your belief in me, even when I doubted myself, gave me the strength to persevere. Thank you for being my rock.

And to the readers who have picked up this book, thank you for giving my words a chance to resonate with you.

MARIAM EL-HAFI

Thank you all from the bottom of my heart.
Mariam El-Hafi

About the Author

Mariam El-Hafi, a Danish-Palestinian, discovered her passion for writing in 2021, but her journey with storytelling began much earlier. As a child, she crafted short stories for herself, too scared to share them with others. It wasn't until recently that she found the courage to bring her imagination to life on the page.

Mariam's love for literature has been a constant throughout her life, and she has devoted countless hours to reading and falling in love with fictional worlds and characters. Inspired by her favorite authors and the captivating stories she's encountered, she finally took the leap to write her own tales.

When she's not lost in the world of words, Mariam can often be found indulging her other passions. She spends far too much time online shopping. In her free time, she enjoys capturing the beauty of the world through photography and gazing at the northern lights in beautiful Greenland, where she moved in late 2022 with her husband.

Printed in Great Britain
by Amazon